The Ring of Naar Chronicles

Patrick D. Catlett

Contents

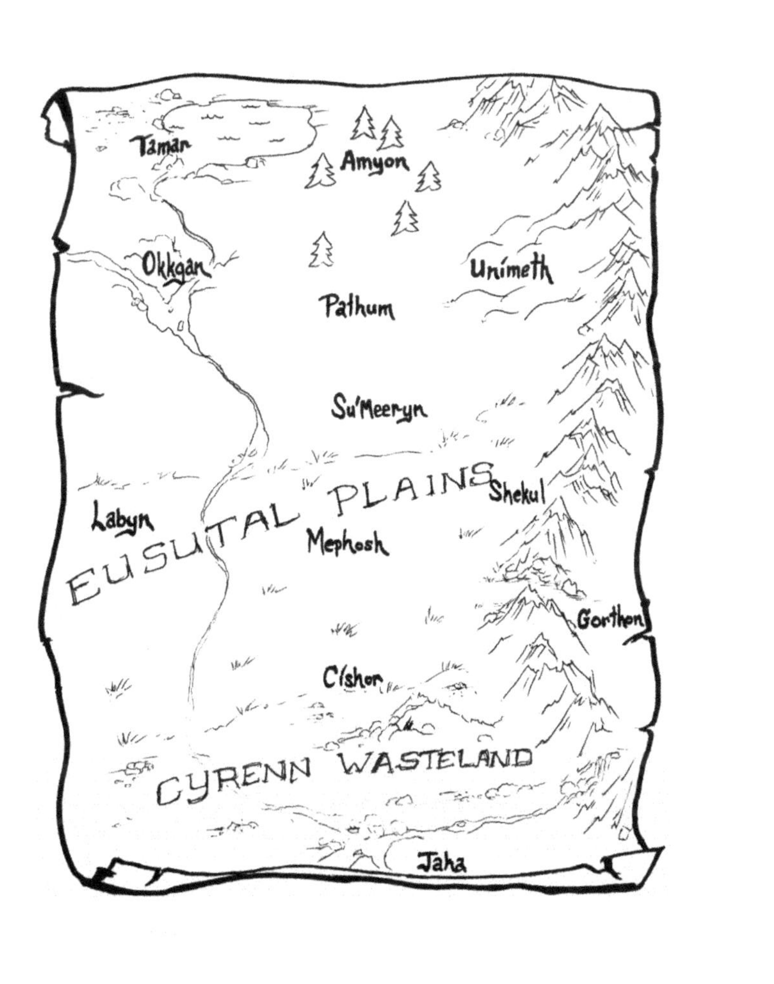

Tamar
Amyon
Okkgan
Unimeth
Pathum
Su'Meeryn
EUSUTAL PLAINS
Shekul
Labyn
Mephosh
Gorthon
C'shon
CYRENN WASTELAND
Jaha

The Ring of Naar

Patrick D. Catlett

Prologue

It was a forgotten time, in a forgotten land. The world was small then, at least the known world. History went back for countless generations, but those scholars who studied the past only knew of the land as it currently existed. The tides of war caused constant flux in the boundaries of kingdoms and nations. At times, large empires covered vast areas, leaving room for only a few monarchs to wield their power. Other cycles saw a multitude of small kingdoms dotting the land.

Technology still hovered slightly above primitive times. The peoples of this land managed to forge steel into swords and armor. They succeeded in building impressive stone castles; they had learned to craft leather into harnesses for their beasts to pull carts or tillers for soil. Knowledge of medicine barely existed; an infection, or a deep wound in battle, often meant death.

The men and women of this age knew of little or no religion. Learning reached a child's ears by word-of-mouth from parents. Only a few of the privileged managed to attend schools. Language had not evolved into differing dialects. The only variances to identify foreign regions came from geography or, possibly, skin tone.

From this age, a saga emerged.

Chapter 1

Night held the city in its claws, as a lion grasping captured prey. Dawn approached, attempting to loosen the beast's grip. The sun clasped the powerful limbs as if slowly pulling them free from the carcass. Light seeped into the city like blood gradually pouring from the wounds.

Jaleph lay in his bed as the red rays of the sunrise poured through the windows to form a pool across his face. Sleep became restless as consciousness fought to break into his mind. His eyes cracked open, and he turned his head to gaze out a nearby window. Drowsily pulling himself to a sitting position, he allowed his vision to wander across his view of the landscape. He slowly stood and staggered to the glass. Flipping a latch, he pushed it open and breathed deeply. The aroma of morning air brought memories of childhood walks with his brother through spring-time groves. A slight chill raised bumps about Jaleph's arms, and he pulled his robe tighter around his body.

The room looked out towards a castle wall. Though called a castle, Jaleph's home was actually more of a city. Within the walls, the area lay open to the sky. A maze of streets and alleys darted from the outskirts past small homes and businesses. As these passages wound towards the castle's center, the size of the homes steadily grew. At the city's core rose a relatively unimpressive palace. From his window, high in the palace, Jaleph stared past the castle wall where green, fertile ground rolled away from the stone structure. He watched as farmers already scurried about the land. Summer had recently arrived making their chores hectic. Farm homes, barns and stables dotted the area as randomly as a light drizzle left raindrops in a puddle. A few soldiers patrolled about the scene. Jaleph smiled watching the pleasant tranquility.

The land that the brown eyes surveyed was his. He was king.

His was a new kingdom: Su'Meeryn, which was once part of the powerful nation of Xavsyn. Its power had grown quickly, and two generations after the great king Nefalel, it was unable to govern itself. A number of dukes split from the kingdom to form their own monarchies. Halet, Jaleph's father, was one of them. Unfortunately, Nefalel's grandson Tubyan mustered an army attempting to keep Su'Meeryn from leaving his kingdom. Under Halet, Su'Meeryn raised an army to fight for its independence. With assistance from nearby dukes, Halet achieved victory. However, during the war, Tubyan's forces had laid siege to Halet's castle; amidst the bombardment of the assaulting army, a round of hot coal had catapulted towards the royal tower and struck Halet's wife. She died later that night. Those who attended to the duchess in her final hours wished the enemy missile had accomplished its task more swiftly.

Halet spent the rest of his life unifying Su'Meeryn's power. The next twenty years were used forging alliances with a number of the other new monarchs. The king, however, suffered a shocking demise. At his death, Halet left Jaleph a strong realm with many allies.

Nobody was quite sure of the cause of Halet's death. He was killed during one of his customary morning horseback rides around the outskirts of the castle. After an hour, an unexpected downpour had erupted. Halet's body was found next to a tree, a few paces off the trail, with a broken neck. The horse was sprawled on the muddy trail with a fractured leg. Jaleph doubted the death was an accident. His father was an accomplished horseman who had ridden often in the rain. Jaleph had ordered an investigation, but uncovered no assassination plot.

The new king spent much of the first year of his reign dealing with internal politics. He was only twenty-two, and he felt many of the older nobles were jealous of his rule. He developed friendships where he could with a few kingly favors. Those who could not be won over, Jaleph maneuvered into less essential positions, with less influence; thus, the danger from them could be controlled and monitored. He had reached the point now were he felt his reign at home was secure. During his short rule, however, the politics of neighboring kingdoms brought changes in leadership that dissolved Halet's alliances. Jaleph worried little as he saw no enemies within Su'Meeryn's vicinity.

The king walked to his wardrobe, and slipped into an orange tunic. Grasping a leather headband—with an emerald star in the middle—he pulled it over his forehead. His father never had a crown made for himself; he always felt it pretentious. Jaleph had decided to continue that tradition. This headband was the only garment he wore to signify his sovereignty.

The king's appearance was a bit of a disappointment in comparison to his title. He stood under six feet and was slightly overweight. Bright blonde hair shot out in clumps from his scalp, and two trails of skin heading from his forehead showed the first signs of a relentless trek towards the back his head. Rectangular eyes burrowed deeply into his plain face which was bordered by a heavy yellow beard. His large, round head rested atop the thin neck like a dandelion stuck in a clump of mud.

The room in which Jaleph walked was sparse. Two chairs, a reading table, a wash basin and his wardrobe surrounded his modest bed. A fine, dark fur rug covered the stone floor. Emerald curtains hung beside the windows, matching the color of the insignia of his headband. A few tapestries dangled about the room, but the dominant feature was the large portrait of his father hanging across from his bed. The picture showed Halet from the chest up with a look of determination etched on his face. Long, dark hair was held back by the leather which now rested on his son's forehead. The background was a swirl of shades of blue, and a stunning gold frame highlighted the portrait. Jaleph did not physically resemble his father, as his younger brother Fenik did, and he often wondered if their leadership abilities were also dissimilar. Halet had been a strong man and a shrewd leader. Jaleph hoped that this daily reminder of his father would encourage him to strive to match Halet's abilities.

The king had not yet married. His time had been too occupied with the obligations of his position to allow him seek after a queen. Fenik often reminded him of the importance of his marriage so that the kingdom would be given its rightful heir. Many of Su'Meeryn's nobles had introduced Jaleph to their daughters, but he had never found much of interest in any of them. Besides, he felt his reign was secure enough at home. He wanted to foster an alliance with a nearby kingdom, and a wife from one of his neighbors seemed the perfect solution. He only needed to decide on which one. Moreover, he did not want to marry a daughter of one of the nobles who might come looking for special favors at in inopportune time.

Two royal guards, waiting outside his door, met the king as he exited his bedchamber. They wore polished breast plates and leather breeches. A small helmet covered the top of each head, shining as brightly as the armor. Thin grated visors covered their eyes. An emerald scarf, covering the back of each head, signified their assignment to the royal palace and from each waist hung a jeweled scabbard.

The three men walked down a dark hallway that was lit only by small candles in gold sconces fastened to the stone walls. A maroon carpet led Jaleph to the ornate staircase also lined in maroon. The foyer at the bottom was decorated in similar fashion to the hallway; however the candle light burned brighter, and portraits of Jaleph's ancestors were highlighted by silver frames reflecting the small flames.

Jaleph began the short journey from the palace to the town's commercial nucleus. A light rain started to fall as they walked through his courtyard. Small trees and shrubs, trimmed in intricate designs, bordered a stone path. Two additional guards joined the group when they exited the gate of the palace and entered the street. "A dreary day, sire," one of the guards murmured, as they passed the extravagant houses of the nobles. The adornments, as well as the size, of the homes dwindled as they moved away from the palace. One's proximity to the palace defined the prestige of that individual, at least in theory. Jaleph always considered this tradition as pretentious as the wearing of a crown. He nodded to the guard who had commented, while the drizzle lightly struck his hair.

The group quickly reached their destination: a bustling auditorium. The building was one large room that had been used as a town hall before the monarchy. Halet had decided to turn it into his audience chamber. Within the huge opening, Jaleph's lapis lazuli throne sat opposite the immense, front portal. Three rows of benches lined the side walls. A vast oak table appeared to grow from the floor, ten feet from the throne, like the roots of the ancient tree from which it was born. Chairs surrounded the table, where the nobles would sit engaging in discussions and arguments before the king. Jaleph thought about adding decorations to the plain building, but he could never quite decide on a motif.

He sat heavily in his blue chair. Being the first day of the week, he opened the audience to the general public. Whoever wished could discuss various problems and concerns with their king. Jaleph did not happily anticipate hearing how a farmer's cow was killed by a neighbor, or how a blacksmith had lost a tooth in a scuffle with a bar keep over a tab. However, his father had taught him the importance of being accessible to his subjects. As he waited to begin, his hand absently stroked the arm of the oak chair as if it was his pet, and his fingers danced over the emeralds which decorated all its edges. The day was still young, and Jaleph did not expect the first audience for several minutes. He rested his head on the back of the chair and enjoyed the short-lived quiet.

Chapter 2

The rolling ground flowed like a sea of deep green. Purples of wild flowers crested the waves with flickers of color, emitting their sweet scent to any passerby. Trees sprouted about like groups of brown islands. The sun, which had just reached the horizon, signaled the end of another day. The dwindling light caused a golden aura to shimmer over all the different colors. Across this tranquil scene, hooves from a galloping horse pounded through the ocean of grass; the blades collapsed under the weight of the beast. Some sprang back after each hoof rose; others remained crushed, releasing the life-giving fluid from within as a treat for scores of hard-working insects.

Atop the horse, a young man rode. His sparkling eyes surveyed this luscious display of nature and searched every direction. He searched for anything to enter his vision, but nothing else moved. He was alone with his steed in this peaceful land. That was a good sign though, as he was a scout. His present mission was to patrol the land north of Su'Meeryn.

He yawned at the relative inactivity of the day. Part of him desired some action, since all his previous missions in this area never had revealed even a vagabond.

The man checked the position of the sun and reined in his horse. He looked about again, but this time he searched with more purpose. His eyes stopped at a large tree jutting from the top of the highest knoll. Long branches hung from its base providing ample cover beneath.

With a soft kick, the scout guided his stallion up the grassy hill. When they reached the tree, the man dismounted and began removing a number of supplies from the bags on the back of his mount. He pulled out a small package of breads and a wine skin, and then he threw a bedroll onto the ground.

Crunching on a hunk of somewhat stale bread, the man curled into his bedding. Looking to the darkening sky, he took a deep breath and felt he could taste the essence of summer filling his chest. Deciding the night would be dry, he left his rain cover wrapped up behind his saddle. After finishing his bland dinner, he took a few gulps of water from the container resting next to his leg. He sealed the wine skin and watched as the light continued to recede down the western horizon. The man's horse stood as a silhouette against the dusk backdrop while it found nourishment from the tall thick grass.

The eyes watching the animal quickly filled with sleep. Heavy lids shrouded the glistening orbs. Unconsciousness was graciously accepted after the long day of lonely riding around this quiet country.

***

A gentle breeze met the scout as he awoke just before dawn; the sky above showed the first traces of a purple glow. He wrapped up his bedding and tucked it behind the saddle then pulled out a few apples from a small pouch and offered one to his horse. The sun showed its first rays as the man ate the other two. He felt the need to bathe but knew of no water in the area. With the light starting to grow, the scout ran his fingers through his hair then mounted his horse to continue on with his duties.

The new morning revealed nothing of consequence. The reconnoiterer continued his solitary journey looking for any unexpected sights, but he only spotted a few animals. Feeling tired of his unappealing food supplies, he grabbed the small crossbow dangling from his saddle. He took aim at a couple of rabbits darting across the countryside, but both shots missed their targets.

Following an uninspired lunch, the scout stood next to his horse and absently stroked the beast's neck. His mind contemplated the next stage of his journey, as there was no specific route which he was required to travel. He decided to loop east then circle back to Su'Meeryn. While climbing onto the horse, another idea suddenly came to him. He felt a strong desire to continue on northward instead and head to the small village of Pathum. His thoughts wavered for a few moments between the two directions, and then it was settled. Spurs kicked into the horse's flanks as the pair galloped northward.

***

Pathum was a village of only a few dozen families. It sat almost a day's ride north of Su'Meeryn. Halet had offered to annex the town for a moderate tax; however, the leaders of Pathum saw little need for protection and had decided to remain independent. Homes sprawled through a rich valley bisected by the Tamar River. A few fishing boats cruised the river, and a number of crops circled around the entire site. It was a utopia of sorts, for those who desired that quiet type of life.

The scout neared Pathum—not for the first time. He had been this way often on similar assignments. The sun began its downward trek as the horse approached the outskirts of the crops. They had just pushed through the first line of plants when strange sounds started to reach the scout's ears. He failed to discern their source, as the noise was distorted by the crops brushing past his steed.

He thought he heard a scream. But as he pushed his horse faster, the noise of the plants giving way grew louder. Another shout, and this time he felt sure it was a scream. After a number of agonizing seconds, the scout burst through the final line of crops. He knew for certain, this was no longer an ordinary mission.

Pathum was being attacked.

The stallion shot forward. Behind a house at the back of the village, the rider saw a young girl being molested by a grimy looking soldier. The scout's sword sprung from its scabbard as he bore down on the attacker. The soldier looked up just in time to see the blade hack across his face. The girl glanced at her rescuer with an expression of gratitude, and then a man burst from the side of one of the houses. He grasped the girl and looked warily at the scout. Realizing the rider had just saved her, the man's look softened. The scout attempted to offer them a quick smile while spinning his steed about, trying to survey the scene.

Suddenly, the scout realized this was not just a band of brigands. A swarm of soldiers filled every inch of Pathum. His mind worked quickly. As he was still sitting on the outskirts of the village, it did not appear that he had been spotted yet. There was nothing he could do to help save Pathum. He spurred his horse back the way he had come. After entering the safety of this camouflage, he turned and dismounted. The scout crept back to the edge of the crops and peered out.

A number of fires began to burn, sending billows of smoke flying towards the setting sun. He saw the girl he had just saved being dragged back towards the center of town by a handful of attackers; the other man—perhaps her father—still grasping a rusty sword, lay dead across the body of the invader that the scout had slain.

Tears welled up in the scout's eyes; he felt like a coward for deserting the girl, but what else could he have done? He had a different allegiance he still needed to serve: he must warn Su'Meeryn. He was fortunate that the attackers likely thought the other man had killed their comrade, as they did not come searching for him. The last thing he saw before turning away was a dog running past the burning homes on only three legs; a trail of blood followed from the stump like an extra tail.

After he mounted and had moved a little farther from the village, the scout charged his horse forward. He needed to find out exactly what was happening. How large was this force invading the village? Why were they attacking? And most of all, who were they?

After he again cleared the line of crops, the rider turned to the east. He headed to a small hill which overlooked the valley and the river. The light continued to fade as he climbed to the top. The sight before him caused trembling in his soul. He was not looking at a mercenary expedition or a regiment from a single kingdom; instead he saw a huge army. What had seemed to be a large battalion from within the village was actually only a small percentage of this enormous force. The troops spread out before him from the apex of the village to form what appeared like the fan of a god. If only a divine hand would reach from the sky to pluck it off the planet's surface.

As the sun continued to set, Pathum became more difficult to see, but the scout needed to identify the origin of this army. He decided on a risky move and headed down the hill. Gradually the blaze erupting from the town began to compensate for the dwindling sunlight. Fire now engulfed nearly half of the village. Where ever he looked, he saw the soldiers slaughtering townspeople. The enemy spared no one. Gender or age was not a defense against this vicious horde. As he neared the hill's base, the scout began to distinguish traits on a number of faces and recognized some markings.

Horror filled the man as realization took hold within him. This was not a single army he was spying upon. And he knew in what direction they would be heading.

He needed to get back home. He must return to Su'Meeryn with all haste. Neither he nor his steed would find rest this night.

The horse ran faster than the scout thought possible. Every step was crucial, but he knew the beast could not sustain the pace. He needed to put himself a good distance from Pathum before slowing; however, before he decreased the gait, the scout nearly ran into another rider. The two stared at each other for a brief moment until the scout's eyes narrowed. Swords rang as they were pulled from scabbards. He knew that he faced a member of the attacking army.

Blades clashed. The scout tried to quickly dispatch his adversary, but the man was well trained with his sword. Unfortunately for him though, he was not comfortable fighting on horseback. With the need to return home pressing on the scout's mind, he used his steed to bump against the other horse. The unexpected move threw his enemy off balance, and the scout's blade shot through the man's throat.

Taking a moment to look about, the scout spotted a small grove of trees off to his left. He kicked the free horse and sent it galloping south, then he hoisted the dead man up and across his lap. Quickly heading to the trees, the scout tried to hide the body. Finding a small bush, he pulled it from the ground and attempted to cover the corpse. Hoping the body was sufficiently hid—unless the man was missed and searched for by other scouts—he continued back to Su'Meeryn.

While he rode, he felt lucky to have run into only the one man, who must have been from the army's vanguard. Pathum was clearly the meeting point of that force, so scouts had probably just been sent out when he had first arrived at the village. Regardless of the reason why, there was no point to worry over it now. The army would continue their journey whether he had been spotted or not. His only task now was to immediately return home and report to the king. He felt guilty for his thoughts the previous day about the tedium of his mission. This night he would settle for boring, but that luxury did not exist.

Chapter 3

A hand nudged Jaleph's shoulder, bringing him to consciousness. I must have dozed off, the king thought. "The audience will begin shortly," a guard whispered. Jaleph nodded and straightened himself on the throne.

The meeting began as usual. It opened with a shopkeeper complaining that his neighbor's children, who decided to amuse themselves by starting a fire, had damaged his door. The shopkeeper brought a reputable witness to confirm the incident, so Jaleph awarded him the price of a new door. Next, a carpenter claimed a customer refused to pay the agreed upon price for a wheel built for a cart. The customer stated the wheel was poorly made, and he brought it to the hearing as proof. Jaleph examined the wheel and observed numerous cracks in the wood. He ordered the carpenter to refund the down payment for return of the wheel.

Though Jaleph dreaded the tediousness of the disputes, he always found himself enjoying these audiences. He often wished he could simply be a judge rather than king. Jaleph felt gifted in his ability to administer justice. Sometimes he believed this was his only gift.

Jaleph pulled himself from his musings as a sailor was stating how his captain had abused him during a recent voyage when a commotion rose at the door to the chamber. The king watched a man burst through the throng of commoners and guards at the entrance. Jaleph recognized him; he believed the man's name was Iridan. He was a soldier assigned as a scout along Su'Meeryn's northern border. Iridan was a lick of fire shooting from a flame as he dashed towards the throne. He panted while attempting to regain his breath.

The guards rushed forth to deny the man access to the throne. He stopped a few feet from the king and collapsed to his knees.

Iridan looked up at Jaleph while trying to catch his breath. "Trouble, my lord," he managed to stammer.

"What is it?" the king asked.

The young scout hesitated while composing himself. "I was patrolling at the border of Amyon," Iridan continued. "They're preparing for war. I saw men from Tamar and Unimeth with them. They destroyed

Pathum." He paused to take a deep breath. "My lord, all indications showed that they're moving south."

A gasp rose from the crowd. Jaleph considered Iridan's words for a brief moment then said, "Follow me." He grabbed Iridan's arm while rising from the chair and headed out of the chamber. "Have my brother and Teraken meet me at the palace," he barked to one of his guards, "and try to keep some order in here!"

***

Four men sat at a table in the king's private chamber. A lush maroon rug circled the stone floor. The table at which they sat was carved from a dark maple, and eight plain chairs surrounded it. Oil lamps hung in each corner of the room supplying the only light. The gaze of past kings of Xavsyn, whose images covered the gray walls, surveyed the meeting.

An air of despair hung over the group as foul as spoiled pudding. Jaleph knew the situation was desperate. The land of Su'Meeryn was situated in the center of the former nation of Xavsyn. Amyon lay due north of Jaleph's kingdom. West of Amyon was the kingdom of Tamar, and Unimeth was situated northeast of Su'Meeryn. If an army from all three lands had mustered on the Amyon-Su'Meeryn border, Su'Meeryn could be their only objective to the south.

The king stared bleakly at the portraits looking down at him as Iridan finished telling his tale. "These are grave tidings brother," said Fenik. The prince was a man of average build. He stood slightly over six feet and weighed nearly two hundred pounds. His auburn hair hung straight to his shoulders. He kept a clean shaven face, and his hazel eyes darted between Iridan and the king.

"Ill tidings, yes, but tidings none-the-less," the fourth man stated. He was enormous in size and height. His head was completely bald, and a gray beard jutted from his chin. The skin of his leathery face was lined with age and a lifetime of experience conducting war. Numerous scars streaked down from his cheeks and neck to hide under his black shirt. Teraken was his name. He had been a long-time friend of Halet and, during his reign, Su'Meeryn's military commander—which he remained under Jaleph. The king thought of the immense man like an uncle. His father had had no siblings, and Teraken had always been close to the royal family. Teraken's blue eyes contracted as he contemplated the situation. "We must act," he continued.

"You're right, of course," said Jaleph. "That's why we're here, but the question is: What's our best alternative? We certainly can't win a war against such a force."

"Why do you suppose they are moving against us?" Fenik asked. "And why destroy Pathum?"

"Who knows?" said Teraken gravely. "How much time do you think we have until they march?" he asked turning towards Iridan.

"I'd guess about ten days or so," the scout answered. "The force was huge, but I think they're still gathering."

The four men sat quietly for a moment. Jaleph turned to his brother and said, "Call a general audience at dawn tomorrow. We'll explain the situation. The people deserve to know what's going on. Perhaps somebody will have a useful suggestion." The doubt on his face, however, betrayed the optimism of his words.

"Begging your pardon, sire," Teraken interjected, "but do you think that's wise?"

Fenik looked at his old friend with obvious displeasure, but his face quickly softened. He turned to his brother and said, "He has a point. We could face a riot."

Jaleph took a breath and responded softly. "That's possible, but word is already spreading. Iridan announced his news in open council. If we show the people we're not hiding anything, perhaps we can settle some nerves. I hope by doing this we'll avoid a panic. Besides, we might get some good ideas." Jaleph felt pleased with this decision. For once, he believed he had made a wise choice regarding the governance of his subjects.

Teraken stood and shook his massive head. "As you will, majesty."

The two other men rose, waiting to follow the king out of the room. As Jaleph passed, he placed a reassuring hand on his brother's shoulder. He felt that he should say more. His leadership was now facing its first crisis. He could think of no other test that could match the severity of this one. Jaleph searched his mind for something inspirational to say; sadly, no thought came to him, and he walked by in silence.

When he neared the door, he stopped and let the three men pass. Jaleph turned and stared at the table where they had just sat. As he exited the room, dread descended about him like a heavy cloth falling to cover the maple table; its edges wrapping around each corner, leaving no speck of wood uncovered.

Chapter 4

Iridan awoke the following morning with a start. Images from a nightmare quickly drained from his ethereal vision. The last perception disappeared when he sat up; the horrific scenes and disjointed story would never be remembered.

He rose from the bed within the humble shack of his home—furnished by the king in exchange for his service in the military. He pulled on a pair of brown leather breeches and a soft black shirt. Iridan was young, barely twenty years. He stood a couple inches over six feet with a medium build. Dark curly hair hung to his shoulders around a handsome chiseled face; blue eyes sparkled from within.

As he left his home, the heavens shone with a mixture of azure and orange. He gazed at the dazzling beauty of the dawn sky as he walked to the audience chamber. The splendor of the morning seemed out of place on a morning such as this. Iridan crossed his arms over his chest and shivered slightly in the crisp chill of daybreak.

Teraken marched up along side him as he approached the auditorium. "This is a bad idea," the older man said. "Everybody is nervous as it is. This will only make it worse."

"Yes sir," Iridan mumbled. A very bad idea, he thought. What does the king expect to achieve?

When they reached the chamber, the crowd was already beginning to enter. Word had spread fast from those in attendance at the audience the previous morning. Iridan sensed the nervousness and anticipation of the congregation. He noticed Jaleph sitting on the throne, and Fenik was just walking up beside the king. Jaleph said something to the prince who then turned and motioned for Teraken and Iridan to approach.

"Good," said the king as they drew near, "I want both of you at my side while we discuss this. If a panic begins, Teraken, try to keep some control." The clamor of the throng began to drown out his words. He looked at his brother and nodded his head towards the crowd.

Fenik turned to the gathering and raised his arm until the noise lowered to a level where his voice could be heard. "I'm sure most of you know by now, but let me clarify any exaggerations which may have already started. First, let's make sure we keep order in here." He paused to allow his words to register then continued. "We have received news that Tamar, Amyon and Unimeth are marshaling an army; the indications show that it will be heading south. We—"

A tumult rose from the sea of people standing before the prince like a volcanic eruption. Each of Jaleph's citizens tried to express their opinions and offer advice at the same time. Before anarchy prevailed, Teraken stood. "Quiet!" boomed forth from his massive bulk. The noise barely dwindled from the first few rows as he yelled for quiet again. A third call finally brought silence. The crowd could do nothing but obey the man who had fought to save all their lives dozens of times. As order slowly restored, he turned to Fenik, "Proceed, sir."

I knew this would happen, Iridan thought; now we're going to have to deal with a mob too.

Jaleph stood and placed his hand on his brother's forearm. Fenik nodded and took a step back. "At the moment," Jaleph began, "we believe we know their intentions. Su'Meeryn is the only destination to the south of the army—"

"What're you going to do?" someone yelled.

Annoyance crossed the king's face as he continued. Iridan knew Jaleph to be mild mannered, but he was the monarch and was obviously upset at being interrupted. "That is what we're here to discuss," the king continued. "We want to consider any reasonable suggestion before proceeding. First, although they appear to be heading south, we don't have verification that Su'Meeryn is their target."

The restlessness of the gathering began to grow. "You don't have any ideas?" "We must retreat!" "Who else would they attack?" "Let's march on them!" were some of the comments Iridan managed to pick out.

As the crowd threatened to riot, a crisp crack of steel pierced through the commotion from the back of the room. All heads turned towards the source of the noise; they quieted at what they saw: a battered figure holding a ragged staff. The multitude of lines which crossed the man's face attested to his considerable age. The top of his head was an antithesis to his chin; he kept shortly shaved gray hair, but a long untamed beard hung over a gray cloak that at one time was black. His left hand clutched a wooden staff with a steel base which equaled his height. Atop the scepter perched a steel bird. The species of the bird was unrecognizable, as the texture of the metal had worn down over the ages. Gray eyes locked upon the king as the venerable figure stepped forward and spoke:

"The king wants verification that Su'Meeryn is the target of this horde, and I shall give it. I've had a vision, a vision of three armies. They come to make war against us. We cannot defeat them in combat; however, we need not fight. In my vision, I saw a great bird soaring above Su'Meeryn, the bird Chaw Den." He held the staff out before him. "It is said if the ring of Naar is again united with the staff, the ring shall resurrect the bird Chaw Den, and Chaw Den will save Su'Meeryn." He lowered the staff, and the crack of steel again echoed through the chamber.

Iridan listened to the ridiculous words in disbelief. The man's name was Korath, the lone holy man of Su'Meeryn. Iridan had known of the old cleric all his life, but with the passing of each successive year, Korath had become more reclusive. Sometimes he went months without being seen. Now he came forward with this strange account of a vision and holy relics. Iridan shook his head. Tales had been told of Naar and this ring, but he had always considered them only fables. And Chaw Den—he had never even heard of that name before.

"Korath!" Teraken shouted as a murmuring began amongst the people throughout the audience, "you've been silent for years. Now you expect us to heed you?"

Anger splattered over the old man's face. "I had the vision. I fasted for two days, and the vision returned. I didn't understand its meaning until now." His glare bore into Teraken. "I have spoken. It's now your decision. Bring back Naar's ring," he paused and looked back at Jaleph, "or face destruction."

Once again bedlam exploded in the room. "Listen to him!" "What should we do?" "Let's fight."

Above all the other cries, Teraken's voice roared, "Quiet! Quiet!"

Jaleph stood from his throne and addressed the crowd. "I'll consider these words," he called over the pandemonium and exited the room.

Iridan stood in disbelief as he watched Fenik, Teraken and the guards attempt to calm the crowd. They began to regain control as the guards escorted out the more unruly people first. Eventually the hall emptied. Iridan gazed at Teraken across the now deserted chamber. The seasoned warrior looked back for a moment then left from a concealed rear door leaving Iridan alone.

What's the use, he thought while gazing at the vacant throne; we don't stand a chance. I should get out of this place now. To stay simply means death. There's nobody here for me anyway. If I head south, I certainly could get hired on as a mercenary somewhere.

At that moment, orange rays from the morning sun pierced the eastern windows. The light reflected off the jewels on the throne. A myriad of miniature prisms sparkled across his vision. Iridan immediately knew he would not be able to desert his king, even if staying would bring his death. He then departed the building and headed home.

As Iridan walked along, the chaos around him simmered. Crowds began to gather on street corners. The anxiety amongst the people was rising. Conversations which he overheard were heated, and he witnessed several fights that sentries quickly broke up. Passers by often recognized him as being the man who had brought the news. Many approached and questioned him about the size of the army and what he thought they should do. He said nothing and continued on his way. The throngs became sparse as he distanced himself from the audience chamber. When he reached his home, he noticed a large, dark-skinned man approaching.

Ruy was one year older than Iridan. They had trained together in the military and had been close friends ever since. Ruy's height and bulk rivaled Teraken, and he excelled in weaponry. He had short cropped blonde hair, and hazel eyes sparkled under a strong forehead. High cheek bones tapered to his cleft chin, leaving his face with an eldritch appearance. His strength and skill allowed him to surpass all the other trainees, and he was already a commander reporting directly to Teraken, while Iridan was simply a scout.

They entered the tiny home and sat at a battered table. "What do you make of all this?" asked Iridan as he poured two cups of ale.

After a pause and a gulp, Ruy responded simply: "It looks bleak."

Iridan waited a moment for Ruy to elaborate; however, through years of friendship, he had learned that Ruy did not expound much on his thoughts. "Well," he continued, "what do you think?" Besides his many skills in combat, Ruy also possessed a quick strategic mind.

"To be honest, I don't know," Ruy answered after a long time spent considering the question.

"Have you seen Dirwyn?" Iridan asked, deciding to change the subject. Dirwyn was Iridan's cousin. The two had always been very close as neither had any siblings; most people thought of them as brother and sister. She was generally considered the most beautiful maiden in Su'Meeryn, and, not surprisingly, she was in love with the handsome Ruy— who returned the affection. Their wedding was planned for the beginning of autumn, and most of the castle waited eagerly for the coming event. Iridan had not seen her since his return and assumed she had been with Ruy, who had also recently returned— after completing a mission escorting a royal caravan.

"No," responded Ruy.

Iridan took a breath and sipped his mug. Ruy, at times, was greatly annoying. "I haven't seen her in awhile," Iridan said somewhat sharply. "I hope she's doing all right."

"When're you going to get yourself a girl?" Ruy questioned, ignoring Iridan's last comment. Ruy often posed this question to his friend, especially since the announcement of his engagement.

"Still looking," Iridan responded with his usual answer. "Lucky for you I'm related to the prettiest girl around."

Ruy chuckled at the jest. Iridan knew he was too unassuming to protest his own appeal with the young ladies. Everyone, including Ruy, knew he was the most popular man in all Su'Meeryn, and he felt no need to dwell on that fact. "Perhaps I can round you up an old widow," was his dry retort.

Iridan laughed and replied, "Yeah, well, I might just have to take you up on that some time."

The two friends sat silently for a short while, and Iridan's thoughts drifted back to the gathering army. When his distress grew unbearable, he finally broke the silence. "Really Ruy, what do you think we should do?"

"Like I said, I don't know. If we are their target, how can we defeat them? We can't evacuate. Where would we go?" Ruy hesitated then continued, "We could send an emissary to try to reach terms, but I doubt that would help. They must have some other agenda. Su'Meeryn is not that great a prize."

While Iridan considered his friend's statement, a knock sounded at his door. He stood and found Dirwyn waiting outside. "I thought you two might be here," she said as she entered the room. She came to the table, kissed Ruy on the cheek and sat down.

Dirwyn's beauty immediately brightened the room. Her red hair flowed halfway down her back in luscious curls. Her body was slim with perfect curves, and a glowing smile highlighted her exquisite face. She always reminded Iridan of a goddess from ancient mythology.

"I'm glad to see you. I guess you've been too busy to come over for a visit." Iridan said with a smirk.

She turned to him and cocked her head towards her shoulder. Her grin widened and jade eyes shimmered. "I'm sorry," she replied. Nobody could resist that smile, and any irritation he might have felt quickly dissolved. He frequently wondered if she knew her power to manipulate him, and everyone else, with her expressions. "As you said, I've been busy," she added while turning back towards Ruy.

The three continued to talk lightly for some time. Dirwyn commanded the conversation, and Iridan eventually realized she was purposely trying to keep their minds off the coming events. Sometime later an embarrassing story about Iridan as a child was interrupted by another knock on the door. With a grunt of annoyance, Iridan opened the entryway and found two royal guards standing outside his home. "You're wanted by the king," one said; he then saw Ruy sitting within and added, "You too."

Iridan smiled wryly as he observed the expressions on the men's faces upon noticing his cousin. "We'll see you later," he said to her as they rose and followed the guards to the palace.

***

"Good," Jaleph said as the pair entered his private chamber. "Have a seat. I was told you two would likely be found together." Jaleph motioned for them to sit at a large, ornate table. Across from Iridan, Fenik and Teraken surrounded the king's empty chair.

Iridan sat, and his gaze shifted between the three men, trying to read their emotions. He saw determination, nervousness and anger. "How may we serve you, my lord?"

"We've discussed Korath's message and agreed that we have little alternative," responded Jaleph. "The Ring of Naar must be found. An expedition will seek it; however, we will only send two men. If the search is unsuccessful, we'll need every available man here for our defense."

Iridan was stunned. The king's words sounded absurd. Find some fabled ring to save us, he thought. But he had committed himself to serve Jaleph, and would do so despite his own misgivings. "Very good, sire. We'll leave as soon as you wish. I assume you'll have us receive some instruction from Korath," Iridan replied.

"You misunderstand," Jaleph said over a growl from Teraken. He looked directly at Iridan. "You served us well bringing the news of this army, and Teraken informs me you've been a fine soldier. I've chosen you to lead this journey. But you," he continued turning to Ruy, "we need you here."

"Who will accompany me than, sire?" asked Iridan, attempting to disguise his shock.

"We've agreed that Teracuss, Teraken's son, will join you. He has studied under Korath and is the logical choice to deal with the ring, if it's found. Teraken's expressed his displeasure over this decision. His son is young and has never studied combat, but I believe we have no other option. Please go see Korath immediately; you'll leave in the morning. Do you have any questions?"

Iridan sat dumbfounded by Jaleph's comments. He had been surprised when the king told him of the mission, but he was equally shocked at the selection of his companion. "No, sire," he stammered. "I'm honored by your faith in me. I'll do all that is possible to return with the ring."

"You just signed their death warrants," Teraken mumbled.

Noticing that all had heard Teraken's words, Fenik said, "You're exaggerating." Turning to Iridan he continued. "He's afraid you'll run into bandits on the road. As you know, it's dangerous for two men to travel south of the castle. However, the danger from that army will greatly overshadow any trouble you'll run into." The prince scowled back at Teraken; obviously before summoning Ruy and Iridan, the three had discussed this scenario many times.

Iridan stood and bowed to the king. As he was escorted from the room, he heard Jaleph continue. "Now, Ruy, we want your input in planning the defense."

I should've left earlier, Iridan thought as he exited the palace. Maybe I still should. But he had gone through this all before and knew he could not forsake Jaleph and Dirwyn, especially now that he had been selected by the king for this vital charge. Regardless of his thoughts about this ring, he would do as Jaleph commanded.

Chapter 5

Korath was seated behind a cluttered table when Iridan entered his chamber. Teracuss—who was of average height—stood over the old man. His arms were crossed over a plain brown cloak that engulfed his thin build. Iridan could not decide if the look on Teracuss' face revealed determination or nervousness. His future companion was slightly younger than himself. Bright eyes shone from Teracuss' face like two patches of sky through dark storm clouds and contrasted his brown hair which he cut short. His face was cleanly shaved, and a few red nicks were visible on his neck. The eyes studied Iridan as he entered, and Iridan thought he perceived a trace of malice behind the radiant spheres.

The home of Korath enclosed the trio with tight stained walls. The front door entered directly into his study; books, manuscripts and scrolls cluttered the entire area. Iridan wondered how the old cleric studied amidst this mess. He was amazed that the rest of the small home was immaculately clean and virtually barren. At the opposite corner from the doorway sat a small table and an even smaller stove. Behind Korath a dreary dark cloth hung from ceiling to floor; swirling shades of dirt and stains hid the drape's original color. Iridan assumed that behind the cloth was Korath's sleeping area. He doubted that there was enough space to actually call it a bedroom.

"Quite a home you got here, old man," Iridan chuckled.

"That is not your concern," Korath retorted sharply. "You best not trouble over my house. You need only concern yourself about staying alive on your venture. You can't return with the ring if you're dead."

Korath grunted and looked away from Iridan back amidst the chaos on his desk. He fumbled through the papers as if looking for an important document which had eluded him for decades. He then stopped his search and placed his withered hands on the table to help raise himself out of the chair. The wood groaned as if in agony from the weight of the old man and the library stored atop it. Iridan thought the rickety table would certainly collapse, hurling Korath headfirst into the confusion of paper and ink before him.

"This is a mistake," sneered Teracuss as Korath approached Iridan. "We both know that he—"

"Enough," Korath commanded, "It has been decided. He will accompany you."

Accompany him? Confusion etched Iridan's face. What the hell is he talking about? That weakling's going to get his head torn off before we're ten leagues from here, and I'll probably get a sword in my gut for being with him. Then his confusion transformed to anger. "I'm the mistake?" snapped Iridan. "He's going to get killed once he leaves this castle. I'm the one going on a hopeless mission looking for some magic ring, and my *partner* here has never even picked up a sword before. And I'm the mistake?" The acid tone dripped from his tongue as his vision shifted from Korath to Teracuss. Iridan's eyelids narrowed as if focusing his ire directly into Teracuss' soul.

"Calm yourself my boy. I know the area you'll be traveling in can be dangerous, but let us refrain from hyperbole." Korath attempted to smooth the tension between the two. "Teracuss also has his doubts about your ability to help him. Let's respect each other's opinions." He placed his hand on Iridan's shoulder, but Iridan could tell the smile across the old face was a mask to try to soothe their hostility.

A twist of his body threw the hand off. Iridan turned directly towards Teracuss, and his glare drilled into the blue eyes. His finger pointed at the younger man. "You're questioning my skills? You'll be the one who's going to get us both killed, wasting all your time in here, never learning to fight. I'm the one who should be concerned," Iridan barked, while his right hand pounded against his chest. The wrath in his voice was real, but from somewhere within, he hoped Teracuss would stand up to him, prove him wrong.

Teracuss' face turned red, and his body began to tremble. But the expression of hatred slowly transformed into resignation. It figures, Iridan thought as Teracuss turned away. Iridan's body relaxed, and he turned to face Korath when a fist struck his left cheek. Iridan stumbled. He regained his senses and pounced at Teracuss. Korath attempted to separate the pair but was knocked to the ground for his effort. The melee scattered books and papers across the room.

The two rolled about the floor throwing punches until they heard the unmistakable crack of Korath's staff on the ground. "That is sufficient," the old man roared.

For an unknown reason, the sound of that staff caused the two to obey the ancient cleric. Iridan rose and wiped a trickle of blood from his nose with the back of his hand. He glared over Teracuss. As the younger man slowly stood, his body clearly trembled with rage. Blood covered his face and welts started to form, showing he had taken the worst of the fight.

"This is what we're relying on to save Su'Meeryn?" Iridan sneered; he could tell the question struck Teracuss harder than his fist ever could.

Korath's staff jumped between the two as Teracuss again began to advance. "I said that is sufficient!" Korath repeated. Then the staff fell to the ground, and Korath's head dropped into his hands; wrinkled thumbs began to rub his tired eyes. "I'm too old for this," he mumbled to himself. After pausing to regain his composure, he continued. "Look, you both have your abilities vital to the success of your mission, and we don't have time for any more of this. The next one of you who makes an insult will feel my staff across his head! Do you understand?" Korath snatched the scepter from the floor and waved it back and forth between the two, as if daring a contradiction.

He received a murmur of assent from both men.

"Good!" he continued. "Do you two know you are acting like a couple of school children? This isn't a contest. You're both trying to save your families and friends, your neighbors. I know neither of you are stupid, and I'm sure you understand the seriousness of our situation; if not, then you should leave right now." He challenged both men with a long stare, but neither moved. "So, let's take the gravity of our predicament to heart. I don't care what grievances you have between yourselves. Put them aside, at least for now, and concentrate on what lies ahead."

Iridan knew Korath to be correct. What puzzled Iridan was that there was no grievance between Teracuss and him, at least none that he was aware of. "You're right of course, sir." Iridan's tone showed he had resigned himself to heed the old man. He looked at Teracuss; the scowl remained, but it had softened.

Korath turned to Teracuss. "And you?"

"I'll obey your counsel," he stated. His voice was flat, indicating he was reconciled only out of need and respect for his teacher.

Iridan shook his head. He could not understand his future partner. He felt no affection for Teracuss but wondered at the other's apparent hatred towards him. Iridan had known of Teracuss for many years, but he could not remember if there had ever been one conversation between them. While Iridan had been engaged in his military training, he had often seen Teracuss carrying his books and walking to this very home. Perhaps Iridan had offered a few jests in the other's direction, but they had never amounted to more than the jokes from anybody else. Anyway, being Su'Meeryn's lone religious student, as far as Iridan knew,

Teracuss had brought it upon himself. But what caused this strong reaction? Iridan could not recall a single incident which would have separated himself from any of the other boys in Teracuss' mind. Perhaps it was the pressure of the coming days. He then felt the same tension as that at the audience chamber returning, but to a greater degree. The mission seemed pointless and impossible, and he would probably die in the attempt. Now that he faced the contempt of Teracuss as well, the staggering weight felt like it was pulling him to the ground. How could he save his people if his only companion would apparently be happy to see him dead? Self doubt burrowed into his head like a hoard of termites tunneling into the central beam of Korath's already unsteady house.

Korath's voice pulled him out of his thoughts. "...I said let's sit down and discuss your task."

The trio walked to the table and sat on the ancient chairs. Teracuss avoided Iridan's eyes as they turned from him to Korath. "You know that you are to bring Naar's ring back," the sage began; his intuitive gaze concentrated on Iridan. "Teracuss knows the story, but I believe that you don't. If you've heard anything, it has most certainly been only rumors. You must know the truth before you embark.

"Naar was a prophet of the Creator; His greatest prophet. He lived a thousand years ago in the land of Xavsyn. During this time, the people had turned from the Creator to worship the Evil One. The Evil One misled the people and thus earned his other name: the Deceiver." Korath's words began to trail off. Iridan guessed that doubt and annoyance showed on his face.

"How can he seek for the ring if he doesn't even believe?" Teracuss demanded.

Korath turned sharply to Teracuss and glared with frustration. His expression softened as he answered, "He believes in his own way. He does his best with his limited knowledge, but he pays little heed of what is to follow. That is an issue we can address upon your return; now is not the time for such discussion. But, he does believe that the tales of the ring and the staff are simply fable. That is unfortunate. He sees my staff before him but would state we have no proof that Naar actually held it and performed miracles with it. I'm certain, however, that he'll attempt his utmost to achieve the goal of this mission."

"You're right," Iridan responded, "my king has ordered me to search for this ring, and I will. What I personally believe is of no consequence. Continue."

"There you're wrong. What you believe is of utmost importance, but you don't understand that fact at this point. As I said, we'll address it later. For now, I'll continue. The Creator revealed himself to Naar and instructed him in the construction of the staff and the ring. Upon their completion, they were a mighty duo. With the ring on Naar's finger, power emanated from it to Chaw Den: the bird of the staff. With this power, he was able to open the eyes of the people and turn them away from the Deceiver. For the remainder of his life, the people worshipped the Creator. At his death, Naar's ring and staff were passed to his most devout follower.

"This process continued for generations, the ring and staff being passed down to what came to be known as Naar's Line. However the Deceiver was not idle during this time. He was preparing his own disciple whom he maneuvered into their ranks. This man succeeded in becoming a successor in Naar's Line and managed to disrupt the following of the Creator. The people did not turn to worship the Evil One, instead he was content in subtly destroying the Creator's following. As you can see, the staff was kept in the hands of the few remaining true prophets, and eventually it came into my possession. The ring, however, was lost. Without the power of the ring, the bird has decayed into an unrecognizable mass. People still know of the Creator, but few worship him. With such a small following, those who sought for the ring were even fewer. Their quests were unsuccessful. There was a time when Su'Meeryn used to have one of the stronger followings, before Halet formed the kingdom. But that has slowly dwindled away. Now there is just the two of us." Korath pointed to himself and Teracuss. "So you can see, this issue regarding the coming army is of secondary importance. When the ring is reunited with Chaw Den, we can again bring the people back to the Creator."

"I don't give a damn about that. All I want is to save our land," Iridan spat. His mission was sounding crazier by the minute.

"It is unfortunate that you don't see the full picture," Korath calmly replied.

"And how do you expect us to find this ring when all the others failed and all this time has passed?" Displeasure flowed through Iridan's tone as he spoke.

"I had my vision, and it came from the Creator. I expect you to succeed. I was given a name in that vision, and I now believe this man can tell you where to discover the ring. Once we possess it, we will reunite it with Chaw Den. Our people can be led to victory and usher in a new era.

"Now, I'll tell you where to begin your quest, but first," Korath reached into a tattered pocket and pulled forth a small circular object, "you'll need this."

Iridan glanced at the item. It seemed to be merely an old coin. "What are we supposed to do with it?"

Teracuss stepped forward and gingerly took the coin from his mentor. A smile crossed the young man's face. "This," Teracuss said, "is a coin of the Creator."

"Yes," continued Korath, "you'll take it with you to signify you're on a quest for Him. Any of His disciples you encounter will grant any assistance they can, when they see this coin. The coin's markings indicate Xavsyn. Anyone who knows me personally will immediately recognize you as being sent by me. Do not lose this. You will not be trusted by anyone without it."

Korath then continued by describing the directions the two men would follow to start their quest.

Chapter 6

Fenik stood before his brother as Teracuss and Iridan approached. He was dressed in a burgundy jerkin, and a royal blue cloak fluttered in the brisk dawn breeze like a flag. Half-a-dozen guards wearing shining plate armor that reflected sparkling crimson from the morning sky circled behind their king. Jaleph wanted to send off the pair with an impressive reminder of Su'Meeryn. He wore his finest leather shirt; a blood red cape flowed behind him, and a sapphire medallion glowed against his chest. The emerald star on his forehead flickered while he glanced between the two young men. No crowd was present; Jaleph did not want to make a spectacle of the two's mission and Su'Meeryn's impending doom.

The small congregation gathered at the castle's front gate. Jaleph had decided against adorning the area prior to this small ceremony; he did not want to convey an air of celebration. He glanced about for a sign of Teraken. Teraken's attitude had been bordering on sedition, but he had been a friend for too long to contemplate punishment. Besides, Teraken's value for the coming days could not be jeopardized by reprimanding him now. "Where is he?" Jaleph whispered to the prince.

"He'll be here," Fenik answered, though he too scanned the street.

Jaleph tried to wipe the frown from his face while turning to Iridan and Teracuss; he was uncertain of his success. As he began to speak, Jaleph spotted Teraken's bulk approaching. The frown fully returned when he noticed Teraken wore only an olive tunic. He had made it clear to Teraken that a stately appearance was required.

"I know Korath has instructed you as best he could." Jaleph had returned his gaze to the two young men before him. "I don't have to reinforce the importance of your mission; everyone is fully aware of it. I wish I could impart some additional wisdom for your journey, but I have nothing to add. Many bandits abide south of Su'Meeryn. Under any other circumstances we would not send two men alone on an expedition through that region; however, I have a great amount of faith in your skills to survive." Jaleph wondered if those words sounded as hollow to the small crowd as they did to him.

"Be strong and be brave," he continued. "If you are able to locate Naar's ring, return with all possible haste. Two of my best horses await you at the stables. Our hopes will ride with you." He then stepped forward to embrace each.

When Jaleph finished, Fenik advanced. "Is there anything else we can give you?" he asked. When both shook their heads, he also embraced each in turn.

After Fenik concluded, all four men turned towards Teraken. A scowl blazed across his countenance as he hugged his son. As he faced Iridan, Jaleph thought the scowl softened. Teraken grabbed Iridan's wrist—which would have been appropriate for a formal greeting—and pulled him close. He whispered something then quickly strode away.

"Well then," the king continued, struggling to control his disapproval, "since there is nothing else to say, let us see you two off." And he led the small group towards the stable.

Ruy sat waiting at the royal stable when they arrived—which appeared somewhat rundown. Straw and hay lay scattered across the ground. Wood from the stalls and fences hung in disrepair. Jaleph had been planning to invest some resources into renovations, but finding time to set aside for the project always seemed allusive.

"Where's Veake?" asked Iridan, referring to Jaleph's eccentric stableman.

"I have him working nights now," Fenik replied. "It keeps him away from sane people, and I'm glad. The last thing I want to see is that disgusting man."

Disregarding his brother's comments, Jaleph turned his attention to Ruy who appeared frustrated by the sight of the quartet. Jaleph knew Ruy wanted to lead this mission, and he wondered if he had made the correct choice. If the quest failed, he doubted Ruy would make any difference to their survival by remaining behind, while he could drastically increase the odds of the ring—if it existed—reaching Su'Meeryn. But he trusted Teraken's faith in Iridan. Ruy waved to the group and walked up to Iridan. He gently grasped his friend's shoulder. Jaleph noticed Ruy disapprovingly eyeing Teracuss, who stood alone a good ten feet behind everyone else, as the two talked low amongst themselves.

Anger swelled up in Jaleph. The morning was not proceeding as he wanted. He had planned for an encouraging ceremony to send Iridan and Teracuss out. Instead, Teraken had come late, acted disruptively then left. And now his son stood excluded by his partner and Ruy. Jaleph wondered at the apparent disconnect between Teracuss and the two, but there was nothing he could do about it now. He waved Teracuss over to join them. As the young man approached, a stablewoman came out with two horses. Iridan and Teracuss mounted the steeds that already bore their supplies.

"May fortune travel with you," the king said as the two rode away.

***

After Teracuss and Iridan had left, Jaleph and his guards strolled briskly to Teraken's home. The fiery orb of the rising sun broke over the castle wall blinding his vision. The light burrowed into his eyes causing him to squint. He raised his hand to shield his brow as he approached Teraken's door.

Jaleph was not relishing this confrontation. He wondered at the prospect of chastising Teraken for what seemed as only slight disobedience. But he was the king, and he had ordered Teraken to precede him to the meeting site. He had also ordered Teraken to muster up a positive attitude.

The king stood before the door, but prior to knocking, Teraken's wife suddenly came to his mind—she had died shortly after Teracuss' birth. Teraken had never remarried, and Jaleph knew the prospect of losing his only son weighed heavily on the otherwise mighty man. He raised his hand to knock but felt frozen, as if he lay helplessly in a grave as dirt was shoveled over his prone body. He knew he must respond to Teraken's behavior, but nothing he considered seemed appropriate. He finally forced his fist to strike the wood.

When the door opened, all the marshaled anger bled out from him. He gazed at the tower of a man who had rivers of tears flowing down his cheeks. After a long uncomfortable pause, the only thing Jaleph could think to say was: "What did you whisper to Iridan?"

Teraken gathered control of his composure, straightened his tunic and answered. "Just some last minute advice."

"Look, I came here to reprimand you for your recent behavior," the king said calmly. "You know as well as I that I need your full support during this crisis; especially in front of others. I can only imagine what you're going through, so we'll just forget it for now. Just as long as you agree not to disobey me—in actions or spirit—in public."

Teraken stood still for a moment and wiped dry his face. "Agreed, and I do apologize."

"Good, let's now both get a little rest. Please be at my conference room after lunch. We'll meet to discuss our next step." Jaleph reached out, squeezed Teraken's forearm and left.

Chapter 7

The colors of the dawn sky resembled an autumn landscape of freshly fallen leaves gently flowing across the ground. A light breeze—carrying the sweet scent of flowers opening to greet the sun—followed Iridan and Teracuss. They rode under the clouds which seemed to be watching them from afar, slowly tracing their horses' movements. The pair traversed through the farmland south of the castle. Rows of grain glimmered a golden hue as they swayed in the wind.

"Wind's at our back," Iridan said. "That's a good sign. Horses should remain strong." His steed was a mighty two-year-old; it was midnight black with a white mane shining like the moon. Teracuss just grunted in acknowledgment. His mount nearly equaled Iridan's in height; it boasted a patchwork of different browns and white which gave it the appearance of an intricate map.

Korath's directions rang through Iridan's mind like a prelude to his doom:

You must travel south, east of Labyn. You will head through the Eushtul Plains to the crossing of the rivers. Turn directly west and continue for a short time. You will then pick up the southern road and proceed through Cyrenn. After fifteen leagues, you'll reach the city of Jaha. There ask for a man named Naemon. He's one of the prophets of that land. Tell him that you're searching for the ring. He'll direct you further.

Iridan glanced at Teracuss; the younger man absently spun Korath's coin around the fingers of his right hand. The coin twisted in directions seeming impossible based on the position of Teracuss' fingers. A snort issued from Iridan's throat; nice trick, he thought, too bad it won't do us any good.

Teracuss heard the sound and scowled at Iridan. Iridan turned away, and they continued to ride in silence until midday when they broke for lunch.

As they opened a packet of dried meat, Iridan stared at his companion. He still had no idea why Teracuss held such a negative opinion of him. He felt frustrated as he pictured this long quest continuing in absolute silence. The irritation eventually exploded. "Look, I'll pound your skull right here if that's what it takes to settle this."

"What did my father say to you?" Teracuss responded calmly.

Attempting to match the tone, Iridan answered. "Just some advice for the journey." He watched Teracuss' face cringe at the words. He knew Teracuss was annoyed that his father would not share the last words with him. His mouth, which opened to form a reply—or another question—quivered for a moment then closed.

"Now what?" continued Iridan.

"I've made it no secret that I don't like you," Teracuss responded, "But I suppose that taking you along is better than going alone. However, don't expect us to become friends. I don't want to talk to you. Let's just concentrate on reaching Jaha as fast as possible."

"I hate to correct you," Iridan sneered, "but I don't want to be your friend. I was just hoping to pass some time. That's all."

"Fine. But as I said, I don't want to talk to you. It'd be easier if you just dropped it." Teracuss finished his meal and walked over to mount his horse. Without looking back, he continued south down the path.

Great, Iridan thought, that bastard really plans on ignoring me the entire trip. Well, maybe it's better than trying to talk to him. He quickly climbed atop his horse and followed Teracuss.

While they rode, Iridan turned his attention to the passing scenery. They had just reached the outskirts of the Eushtul Plains. The lemon light of the noon sun bleached out the lustrous greens of the rolling knolls bisected by the trail. Iridan never understood how the plains had received their name. The ground was anything but flat. It was entirely uneven and was circled by these knolls. In the center, low hills and deep valleys dotted the land. Small sections of forest grew in a few secluded spots. Iridan assumed that the name had come from the relative lack of trees, as the vast majority of soil was covered only by grass and a few wildflowers.

The afternoon wandered slowly by like a barge adrift on a lazy river. Iridan inwardly rejoiced when evening finally arrived. They turned off the path and set up camp. In the remaining light, Iridan searched the area and trapped a couple of rabbits while Teracuss started a fire. After the rabbits were cooked, Iridan sat on the ground next to his horse and ate the meat. He noticed that Teracuss sat facing the opposite direction, with the two horses between them.

Iridan turned his gaze to the sky and the last of the visible clouds. He shrugged at Teracuss' resilience for ignoring him, as he was not used to being alone in the wilderness. Following a few more minutes of chewing on the meat, he stood to take a drink of water from one of his wineskins. "We'd better get some sleep," he said while retrieving his bedroll.

Teracuss likewise reached for a drink of water, pulled out his bedding then stretched out on the ground to sleep with his back to Iridan. He still refused to speak.

Iridan also lay down for the night. The Eushtul Plains did not boast much traffic, so he was confident a sentry would not be necessary.

***

Their second day together flowed by as uneventfully as the first. They awoke at dawn, quickly ate a small meal and continued on their way. Iridan remained ten paces behind Teracuss as they trotted down the rough path—finding that delicate balance between riding quickly while not exhausting the animals.

Being a soldier, trained in reconnaissance, solitary missions bothered Iridan little; however, he wondered at Teracuss' ability to continue this isolated trek. Iridan used the quiet time to concentrate on his mission. He created various potential scenarios and devised strategies for each. Unfortunately, he needed to admit to himself that he possessed little idea of what awaited them. Equally distressing, by the time dusk approached, he had forgotten most of the well-designed victories he had created. They dismounted and Iridan built another small fire. He pulled out some breads and dried fruits. Iridan ate his meal in silence and did not bother to see how Teracuss occupied his time. While falling asleep, he watched the sun set below the horizon like a fireball. The remaining flames of light reminded Iridan of the fires which would likely soon engulf Su'Meeryn.

Iridan awoke just prior to dawn before the smoldering ashes. He had conditioned himself to do so. As a scout, Iridan always wanted to be awake and moving before any potential enemy. He kicked dirt over the remnants of the flames and nudged Teracuss awake. He quickly ate some bread, and was packing the supplies, when he noticed Teracuss was already on his horse heading down the path. He stared at Teracuss for a couple moments in astonishment at the other's need to lead the way. He hopped onto his steed and followed after.

The day was a collage of brain-numbing dullness as he trailed Teracuss southward. Iridan's mind drifted into a daze of thoughts concerning his antagonistic companion and the rolling greens of the landscape.

The sun approached its peak and Iridan's daze grew into a hypnosis centered on the canting of Teracuss' mount. His stomach began to growl in hunger, however his mind was too dulled by the monotony of the morning to allow his appetite to register in his perception. His unfocused eyes gazed forward toward the flanks of the leading horse, and he did not realize it had stopped until he nearly rode up its back. A quick jerk on the reins, and the abrupt halt of his horse, snapped Iridan back into full consciousness.

He gazed at Teracuss in annoyed wonder. "Why did you stop?"

"Didn't you hear that?"

Iridan glanced around, "What?" He cursed himself for allowing his senses to be dulled so; not very professional for a trained scout. For the first time he noticed they sat in the middle of one of the small forests in the plains.

Teracuss pointed a quivering finger off to his left at an area where the trees wandered closest to the path. "I heard something over there," he answered in a hushed tone. "It sounded like a scream."

Neither man moved as they concentrated on the spot Teracuss indicated. Then their heads shot around to gape at each other as a cry leapt out from the trees, climbing through the air to reach the noon sun. The shrieks continued. They moved their mounts gingerly toward the noise. A clatter followed the screams as they grew louder. Iridan spurred his horse off the path towards the commotion. He did not notice if Teracuss followed.

When he neared the trees, Iridan jumped from his mount. He drew his sword and ran into the grove. His foot caught in a root causing him to stumble and nearly fall. As he wrenched himself free, he noticed Teracuss quickly approaching.

They burst through the trees into a small clearing and saw a young woman who had been thrown to the ground by two men. Her tunic had been torn, and scrapes and cuts covered her exposed flesh. The two men started to climb on top of her, and four others darted out of the trees. None of the brigands wore any armor, and their weapons appeared to consist of knives, shovels and axes. Their leering faces were unshaved above filthy clothing; greasy hair flapped in the breeze as they ran.

The men stopped when they noticed Iridan and Teracuss. Iridan took several steps forward, brandishing his sword. He glanced at Teracuss, who also stood with sword ready. Both wore armor that had been presented by the king, Iridan had a steel breast plate and Teracuss ring mail. Iridan almost laughed; he had just noticed how foolish Teracuss looked dressed for battle.

Iridan saw the indecision on the men's faces. They had obviously expected no opposition to their rape. All six were young. None appeared older than Teracuss. They nervously drew their weapons and looked behind the two, peering into the trees. When they realized nobody else was coming, their courage grew, and they charged.

Knowing Teracuss' inexperience, Iridan stepped forward to absorb the brunt of the assault. It was obvious from their unorganized rush that the vagabonds were untrained in warfare. The importance of the quest quickly shot through his mind, but he had reacted to the screams without thinking. He could not allow this girl to be raped—and probably killed—without assisting. The quest might face its death in this clearing, but there was nothing he could do now except fight.

The first man approached; Iridan feigned to his right and slashed across the exposed stomach. His opponent collapsed. The second one rushed by and tackled Teracuss. Iridan spun and engaged the next. This man carried an ax and displayed a rudimentary knowledge of combat. As Iridan deflected the first few blows, he heard a hissing followed by a number of dull thuds. He managed a glimpse forward and saw the last three brigands falling to the ground with arrows protruding from their bodies. He quickly cut through his opponent's ax handle as it swung down, seeking his head. Splinters soared into the air, and Iridan plunged his sword into the man's chest.

He turned and saw Teracuss lying pinned on the ground; he bled from a small cut on his right forearm. The knife of his opponent raised then plunged towards his face. Iridan dashed forward and chopped at the man's neck. His sword caught flesh, and the blow caused the knife to miss its target; however, it buried into Teracuss' left shoulder.

With the last adversary dead on the ground, Iridan ran for the path, attempting to see who shot the arrows. He heard horses galloping south. He saw some shapes, but they were too far away to identify. To his relief, their horses remained next to the trees.

Iridan returned to the clearing and found Teracuss sitting up holding his shoulder. Blood seeped between his fingers. Iridan quickly inspected the cut. It appeared the knife had deflected off bone and did not cause any serious damage.

Iridan then turned his attention to the woman. She lay face down, and her body shook with each of her sobs. Her tunic was so torn; he wondered how it remained on her body. He walked over to her—stepping over the three arrow pierced corpses— and gently turned her over. She was barely more than a girl, no older than eighteen years. Even through the scrapes and blood across her face, he could see she was beautiful.

She continued to cry as he coaxed her to her feet. He looked over and saw Teracuss had stood, holding a cloth to his shoulder. Iridan gently placed his arm around the girl and guided her towards the path.

When they neared Teracuss, Iridan saw, by the look on the other man's face, he had also noticed her beauty. They reached the horses, and Iridan pulled a cloak out of one of the saddle bags. He handed it to the girl. She reached out a shaking hand then wrapped it around her body. He watched Teracuss stare as her exposed flesh disappeared under the cloak. His elbow nudged Teracuss' stomach, and he motioned angrily towards the girl. Teracuss nodded apologetically.

The girl continued to sob as Iridan led her to sit next to the horses. He glanced at his companion to make sure he did not continue to gape, but Teracuss' attention now centered on his shoulder. After all three sat, Iridan asked as gently as possible: "What's your name?"

After a few attempts, she managed to stammer, "Myrin."

"Look Myrin, is there a town south of here? The two of you need some attention." The girl nodded. "If you can lead us there," Iridan continued, "you can tell us what happened, and let us know if there's anything else we can do for you."

Myrin nodded again.

Teracuss and Iridan climbed on their horses. When Myrin approached Iridan's mount, he heard Teracuss squawk in disapproval. Teracuss then spurred his horse and took off down the trail. Iridan pulled Myrin up behind him and followed the leading horse.

***

While they rode, Iridan resisted his urges to question Myrin regarding her ordeal. How did she come to this area? Where did those men find her? He wanted to reach the town and get comfortable at an inn before addressing her hardships. He asked her only about the directions to their destination. She told him that after about a half a day's journey on the trail, a branch would lead east; the town of Mephosh was only one league down. Her village was a north of Mephosh.

"Can't we just take you home?" he asked.

"No," was her reply, and she would not elaborate any further.

They traveled through the afternoon in silence. Teracuss had ceded the lead, and Iridan felt the younger man's gaze permeate his head like a flame igniting the center of a piece of paper, burning outward, heading to the edges and engulfing the entire sheet. Whatever hatred plagued Teracuss' mind regarding Iridan had clearly increased. Perhaps it would devour him to the point where Iridan would not awaken one of the coming mornings. He quickly dispelled that notion. Surely the plight of Su'Meeryn would outweigh any such conception.

True to Myrin's statement, they reached the east fork in late afternoon. Iridan felt relieved when they neared the town. He wanted to know what had happened to Myrin, but he was hesitant. He did not have the time to get involved in her plight. Hopefully she knew some people in Mephosh willing to take care of her. He planned for them to have dinner together then part company in the morning.

Iridan was anxious to rest after the battle, but between the thoughts of Myrin and the fight, the importance of their mission and Naar's Ring, broke its way back into his mind. He began to feel overwhelmed by all the responsibility and need which had been thrust upon him.

He turned to Myrin, "Let's find someplace to eat. Then we can talk." She nodded in agreement, and they headed down the main avenue.

Chapter 8

Jaleph had finished his lunch and was waiting for Teraken within his conference room. Fenik entered and sat next to him. "I don't know Jaleph," he said, "the people are becoming very nervous. We need to give them something else to focus their attention on, or I'm afraid we'll have a complete panic." The lines of anguish on his face took on the appearance of a sword engraved by a master craftsman, tempered by conflict, but ready for use. "Even if we recover Naar's ring," he muttered, "I don't see how we can save ourselves."

"We'll have to rely on Korath for that," Jaleph responded gravely.

Fenik sighed heavily. He obviously did not relish the idea of trusting their salvation on the old recluse. "How can we trust him? He resurfaces after how many years ranting about birds and rings? This is crazy. We need a substantial plan."

The king raised his hand to quiet his brother. "Let's wait for Teraken," he said softly. He grabbed a wineskin that sat nearby. After Jaleph had poured each of them a cup, Teraken entered the room and joined them at the table.

He dropped down on the chair across from the king. Jaleph immediately saw that Teraken's attitude had changed. He appeared brighter and more resolute. Jaleph wondered if he had accepted Teracuss' mission or simply put it out of his mind. Nevertheless, he was relieved. A mentally sound Teraken was critical to survival.

"Fenik was saying how restless the people appear," Jaleph said. "We're afraid there'll be hysteria if we don't provide something positive soon."

"I agree," Teraken replied. "I've noticed the same thing. We're making preparations, but we need something else." Jaleph heard determination in his friend's voice. He was happy Teraken had finally accepted his son's charge.

"What do you think we should do?" asked Fenik.

Teraken considered for a moment. "Perhaps we should send out a reconnaissance force and strike their forward positions. A skirmish or two might slow them down a little. If we captured some, and brought back a few prisoners, the spirits would definitely improve around here."

Jaleph considered the plan then responded. "Seems a smart idea." His brown eyes glanced at the goblet resting in his hand. He felt fatigued as he placed it back on the table. Self doubt swept over him; he did not believe he could lead Su'Meeryn to victory.

During this crisis, he felt fortunate to have his brother and Teraken around. He had stumbled into his role as ruler by the sudden death of Halet, and he had never felt ready to be king. At least a few more years of study as prince would have helped prepare him for this eventual outcome, but the task had been thrust upon him. Before this, his largest challenges had been dealing with squabbling nobles. Now he needed to save his people from this onslaught, and their chance for victory rested on two young men finding and returning with a mystical relic.

"You're both crazy!" Fenik interjected. "We don't have enough men to defend ourselves as it is, and you want to deplete our forces on a suicide mission?"

"I didn't say we should attack the main army," explained Teraken. "We'll scout out their forces and engage only their vanguard. We probably can take a few prisoners and return in time to help with the defense."

Fenik was not convinced. "What do you think that'll accomplish? For all we know, it might cause them to advance faster. We need to bide our time and give Iridan and Teracuss the longest possible opportunity to return."

"Some skirmishes should slow them. Besides, I thought you were worried about a panic erupting."

"That's true, but getting a number of our men killed, and weakening our defenses, isn't what I had in mind!"

"Well, what do you suggest?" Teraken asked.

Fenik paused briefly to deliberate. "I think we should try a herald. If we parley, we might reach an arrangement."

"Right, they're probably already marching. They just might decide to turn around."

"Why are you such an expert? How do you know they won't?"

"They certainly know our numbers. Assuming they have already decided to attack, what could we possibly offer them to stop?"

Jaleph watched as the two continued to argue. He realized both men had made valid points. But he also knew they could not just sit back while fear and anxiety simmered in his people until it boiled over. That condition was about to be illustrated in front of him. He felt certain Fenik and Teraken would soon come to blows.

The king made his decision but allowed the argument to continue. He thought it important that the two burn off some frustration. When

Teraken stood and grabbed Fenik by the collar, Jaleph also rose and concluded the debate. "That's enough. Unless we have any other suggestions, I've made my decision."

Teraken snatched his chair and sat back down. When the two simply glared at each other, Jaleph continued. "Very well, we'll proceed with Teraken's plan."

Fenik shook his head. "But..."

"That is final," his brother interjected. He turned to Teraken and said, "I want you to prepare the expedition. It embarks at sunrise. Make sure they get a full night sleep. I want you two back here before dawn to see them off."

He dismissed them both and retook his seat. Fenik stormed away, his face glowed an angry red; Teraken followed a few paces after. Jaleph wondered if his father would be proud of him. The strategy seemed sound, but he held no illusions regarding its risk. At least he had made a decision.

Chapter 9

Mephosh was a dingy town with no wall to offer protection. Small run-down buildings were scattered haphazardly about twisted streets. Iridan failed to spot a solitary drop of paint on any wall. He saw homes and a few small shops but nothing which signified a militia. Garbage swirled into the air from the momentum of their two horses. The entire scene reminded Iridan of a dead tree too stubborn to fall, with its bark ripped outward to disclose the decayed and infested interior.

The companions looked until they found what appeared to be the most reasonably clean inn. Using some of the funds Jaleph had given them, Teracuss ordered dinner. They took a corner table, and Iridan cleaned and properly bandaged Teracuss' gash. The cut was not too deep, so Iridan doubted it was anything serious. Myrin's wounds appeared to be only scrapes. Evidently her attackers had desired her to be relatively undamaged. Iridan asked the innkeeper if he could provide her with a new garment. When one arrived, she went off to change and clean her wounds.

By the time the food came, Iridan realized they were too tired to do anything else but eat before getting a room for the night. He only asked for a single room to conserve their money. Though the king did give the pair a substantial amount, it had been meant to provide for two. They finished their meal in silence then headed up a rickety flight of stairs to their room. Iridan insisted that Myrin take the bed while he and Teracuss proceeded to stretch out on the floor. With their camping gear, they managed to make the floor quite comfortable.

Despite his exhaustion, sleep alluded Iridan for some time. As he finally drifted off, his thoughts centered around the people of Su'Meeryn. He hoped Teracuss and he were not on a suicide mission and could find a way to help their friends back home. *I wonder if he even has any friends,* Iridan speculated. He had never seen Teracuss with anyone other than the old man.

***

Dawn came with the sounds of Teracuss preparing their supplies for travel. Iridan felt surprised Teracuss had woken before him and wondered how long he had lain sleepless the previous night. He stood and noticed Myrin was still motionless in the bed. She needs some extra sleep after all she's been through, he thought. As he turned to gather up his bedding, he noticed Teracuss was watching him look at Myrin. The pain on Teracuss' face reminded Iridan of the look on the corpses from portraits of battle scenes in Jaleph's art gallery back in Su'Meeryn.

"I'll go down and get us some warm food," Iridan offered, hoping to dispel the melancholy mood.

"No," retorted Teracuss, "I'll go." He quickly grabbed a pouch and exited the room.

After Teracuss slammed the door, Myrin stirred and sat up. She glanced at Iridan and mumbled, "What's going on?"

"He's going to get us some food." He paused knowing the remainder of their conversation was going to be awkward. "Do you feel up to telling me what happened?"

She stared into the corner of the room, and Iridan noticed water starting to pool under her eyes. The first tear formed and slid down her cheek; it glistened in the shimmering morning light which broke through the room's one window. He watched as she raised her hands to cover her face; her shoulders trembled while the sobs came quickly. She finally collapsed forward as the anguish of her recent horror burst forth.

Iridan just remained on the floor and watched. He wanted to go to her and offer comfort, but he did not know how she would react. He continued to gaze at her while she wept. He remained transfixed by the event: caught between wanting to console and fear she would recoil from his effort.

He sat paralyzed before her until Teracuss finally returned carrying a large bowl of steaming stew. Teracuss studied the scene and appeared equally perplexed. He stood for a few seconds and finally muttered, "I've got some food."

Myrin looked up and tried to offer a smile of gratitude. Teracuss pulled out some smaller bowls from his pack and gave a portion to each. As he handed Myrin hers, she began to tell them her story.

"My village is north of here. It's only a small farming community. Was. I had gone out for the morning to collect the fish caught in our overnight nets at a stream west of our town. I was pulling one out when I heard some noise coming towards me. It was my father. He was badly beaten. He told me a gang of thieves had raided our village. We call it a village, but only four families live there. Well, not anymore. They slaughtered everyone. He managed to kill the man who'd attacked him then ran off to warn me. After he finished telling me, we heard the pursuit. He convinced me to run away while he tried to delay them. He sacrificed himself to save me. As I ran, I turned and saw him lying on the ground. They were beating him with shovels. I headed towards that forest where you found me. They had just caught me when you came into the clearing."

Iridan felt certain Myrin would weep after she finished the tale, but it soon appeared clear that she would not. A look of determination replaced the despair on her face, and Iridan knew she would not cry over her loss again. She had been hardened by her ordeal like the forging of a spearhead. Her weeping was the steam after the glowing metal is thrust into water to cool. When it emerges, a new weapon is born. It no longer resembles the raw materials it was formed from when the process began.

"I don't know what I'm going to do," she continued. "There can't be anyone left back in my village."

"Do you have any idea who they were or why they attacked?" Iridan asked.

Myrin shook her head.

"Do you know anyone here in Mephosh?"

"No." She paused looking between them. "Where are you going? I'd like to stay with you, at least for a while. You two saved me… And I have nowhere else to go."

Iridan started to answer when Teracuss interrupted. "We're heading south for a town called Jaha. We're on a quest for our king."

"Why're you going there?" she asked.

Again Iridan began to respond, but Teracuss replied first. "We're looking for Naar's ring." Iridan saw the satisfaction imprinted on Teracuss' face. He was obviously trying to draw her attention away from Iridan to himself. However, Iridan could not believe that Teracuss had revealed the specifics of their mission.

Myrin appeared perplexed. "The ring of Naar?" She hesitated as she tried to remember why that phrase sounded familiar. When it occurred to her, she continued in a startled tone. "I've heard of that! An old man in our village used to tell us children's fables about Naar. Why're you looking for it? I thought that ring was only a myth."

"Some people say it is," Teracuss replied, "but my master tells us it's real. He has studied the Creator's lore all his life. In Jaha lives the prophet Naemon. We're to seek his help in locating the ring."

"But why're you looking for it?"

Iridan quickly shot Teracuss a stern look. He sympathized with Myrin's predicament, but he felt she had already been told more than was needed. He did not want to take any unnecessary risk of their quest becoming common knowledge. You never know who you're going to meet out on the road, he thought, and she might tell too much to the wrong person. Unfortunately Teracuss had already begun to tell her the rest of the story, and Iridan saw no reason to stop him now.

"We've been told that a vast army is mustering along our northern border. Our forces can't stand against it. Korath, my master, had a vision that we should seek Naar's ring. If we return with the ring, we'll use its power to defeat the army and save our land."

"Well," said Myrin, "I don't believe in all that, but I have nowhere else to go." She turned back to Iridan with a strange look he could not identify. "I can't go back to my village, and the friends we had in this area moved off last season. There's nobody around here that I know. I'd like to accompany you."

Iridan sighed and wondered if she had embellished somewhat regarding her lack of acquaintances in the area. They had just saved her, and he thought she might be developing an infatuation for him.

"We have no choice now," he said. "You must come with us since you know our mission. We can't allow anyone else to find out where we're going and for what reason." He turned to Teracuss to insure his words were fully absorbed. "Enemies of Su'Meeryn might be found anywhere. Let's not forget about those archers. If not for them, we'd all probably be dead now. Why didn't they approach? Why did they leave like that? It doesn't make sense. Even though they saved us, I've got a strange feeling about it.

"So, from now on, only the three of us need know the truth. Am I understood?"

Teracuss scowled at him, visibly angry that Iridan had given him a direct order, but the ire faded away with the realization that Iridan was obviously correct. He nodded in consent and returned his attention to the stew.

Trying to soften his expression, Iridan looked at Myrin; she likewise nodded in agreement.

They ate the rest of their meal quietly, each engrossed with their own thoughts.

***

Teracuss and Myrin sat in the common area of the inn after the meal in their room, while Iridan finished paying the inn-keeper. He came back to the table and took a seat. A filthy woman came with three cups of juice that Iridan had ordered, as he wanted a pleasant refreshment prior to another hard day's ride. He accepted them grudgingly when he noticed her grime covered hands.

After situating himself at the table, Iridan was pleasantly surprised at the conversation occurring between Myrin and Teracuss. For the first time since their departure, Teracuss appeared in a light-hearted mood. Teracuss was gushing to Myrin that her goddess-like beauty had so transfixed him that he had been hardly able to move to save her. Iridan thought Teracuss was bordering on offending Myrin, but she seemed to need a brief laugh and enjoyed the jesting. Iridan found the conversation somewhat morbid after their ordeal and believed Teracuss did also, but Teracuss was obviously attempting his utmost to win her over.

No wonder I've never saw him with any girls, Iridan thought. He almost broke in to mention that Teracuss' efforts were uninspired, to say the least, but he knew that would simply cause more problems.

Myrin looked pleased with the attention from Teracuss as the conversation drifted to a brief description of Su'Meeryn, but Iridan noticed that Myrin's eyes continued to glance towards him, even though he sat silently. As Teracuss picked up his mug and took a long drink, Myrin turned her now somber face to Iridan and smiled. Iridan smiled back uncomfortably and took a gulp of his own juice.

"We've lingered here too long," Iridan said as his empty cup hit the table. "We'll have to push hard today to make up some time." As he stood, Iridan noticed some movement at the inn's entrance. He glanced over as four figures entered.

The appearance of the men was remarkable. The first man to enter stood an immense height, approximately seven feet tall. Broad shoulders and a barrel chest tapered to a lean waist where a huge broad sword hung. He wore a suit of full plate armor covering every inch of his body. It was polished to the point of glowing, but the foremost feature was the fact that the armor glistened a radiant crimson. A red helmet covered his face which completely hid his features.

Following the red warrior, the next man appeared rather short, though he would tower over most men. He wore a padded black leather jacket, black wool pants and dull black boots. Black gloves covered his hands. He was extremely thin, to the point of emaciation. Every curve of every bone stood out through the skin of his famished-stricken face. Long thin black hair hung from this living skull. A black scabbard dangled from a black belt around the diminutive abdomen. Iridan imagined that the sheathed sword within must also be black.

The third individual stood in sharp contrast to the first two. His height would be considered of normal size. His physique was trim with a slightly athletic appearance. He wore neatly kept blonde hair which touched slightly under his collar. His handsome, smoothed-skin face was dominated by bright blue searching eyes. He bore a white tunic which apparently repelled dirt; it opened to display a fairly muscular chest. A sparkling silver belt fastened around the tunic. His pants were white, and he wore polished brown leather boots.

The last man entered wearing only a thin pale shirt and pants which hung from his withered skin in tatters. He walked barefoot. Dark hair grew from his head in patches of varying lengths. It seemed to form an intricate design of alien origin. His sinister face was as pale as his clothes and had a bluish tint. Taut skin surrounded hollow eye sockets leading to black orbs. Iridan saw no white coming from those menacing cavities. The remains of a beard and mustache mirrored the pattern on his head. Long claws grew from each finger. Despite his appearance, a youthful demeanor attempted to break through those wicked features. Iridan thought he was watching a resurrected corpse, a corpse dripping with evil.

After all four men entered, the man in white shocked Iridan when he approached their table and asked: "May we join you?"

Chapter 10

"What can we do for you?" Iridan asked suspiciously. He glanced at Myrin and Teracuss and perceived that their apprehension equaled his. While the other three men stood behind, the man in white took a chair facing Iridan and responded. "It is not what you can do for us but what we can do for you."

Iridan turned back to Teracuss seeking assistance. Teracuss was intently studying the four men. After a few heartbeats, Iridan was sure Teracuss would remain silent, and he asked, "Who are you?"

"We are travelers such as yourselves."

"I doubt that," Iridan stated after examining the man's mute companions. "That wasn't a very specific answer." He wondered why these men had singled out his small group and was feeling increasingly anxious.

The man's handsome face appeared disappointed at Iridan's suspicion. "Perhaps not, but like you, I do not want my objectives becoming *common knowledge*."

Iridan considered the comment; it seemed this man had eavesdropped on their conversation earlier that morning. "What do you mean by that?" he asked.

"It seems obvious."

This obtuse dialogue began to annoy Iridan. "What do you want?" he asked sharply.

The man seemed taken aback by Iridan's tone, but he answered calmly. "I wondered if your party will be heading south, and if so, if we might join you." He paused, for what Iridan believed to be strictly for dramatic effect. "There is safety in numbers."

Iridan had no intention of allowing this bizarre company to join them, but he turned to Teracuss for confirmation. Teracuss shook his head, and Iridan again addressed the man in white. "I think we'll continue on our own, thank you."

"Very well," the man responded, "perhaps we shall see you again." He motioned for the other three to follow. As they were exiting the inn, he glanced back at Iridan. "Many journeys lead south," he stated. With that, the four disappeared.

After a few moments of silence, Myrin said, "That was strange."

"Yeah, I've never seen anything like it," replied Iridan. "What do you think Teracuss?"

"They remind me of something," Teracuss answered quietly, "but I can't quite place it."

"I hope we don't meet up with them again," said Myrin.

"That's for sure," Iridan responded. He stood and pushed his chair back under the table. "We better get started. It's getting late."

Chapter 11

The sun crested the horizon with an amber aura presenting a cloudless sky. Jaleph stood in his courtyard and watched as the image signaled the start of a new day much like a town crier proclaiming his announcement. A yawn crossed his lips while he awaited his brother, Teraken and the expeditionary force. He had given Teraken full authority to assemble the company and assumed he would see Ruy leading the group. This type of mission—skirting a huge army, striking at its flank and melting back into the trees—better suited the young leader's skills than seeking after a legendary ring.

While he waited, he began to feel tension for the men whom he began to believe were heading out on a hopeless mission; his doubts mirrored those of when he has sent off Iridan and Teracuss. Perhaps Fenik was correct; perhaps this was not a wise plan.

As Jaleph struggled with his conflicting emotions, he twisted where he stood and acknowledged his two personal bodyguards positioned about eight feet behind him. He looked about, anxiously searching for the approach of the group. He hated waiting.

The features of the courtyard came alive in the glow of the morning light. An ornate brick path flowed past sculptured bushes and short trimmed grass. It ultimately reached a pond in the center in which swam a large assortment of fish. A variety of flowers exploded in a rainbow of colors around the base of the two foot high wall which enclosed the area.

The weight of his situation threatened to engulf Jaleph. He did not know where to turn for insight. After hearing the counsel of Fenik, Teraken and Korath, he still felt skeptical. But what alternative remained? He had not been ready to become king after his father's death; now an even greater burden sat positioned on his back. He felt that he must certainly crumble soon, which made the goal of the forthcoming mission all the more important. If the strain was wearing on him to such a degree, it must certainly be engulfing his people.

If this group doesn't succeed, he thought, we'll be emotionally crushed before the army even gets here, before Iridan and Teracuss can return.

His mind turned to the two young men who had recently departed on their quest. He wondered how they fared. Their task could not have been as dangerous as Teraken had made it sound. Not for the first time, Jaleph wondered how a ring could help even if they did return, but if Korath was to be believed, Naar's ring was their only hope.

"I guess it really doesn't matter how successful this mission is," he mumbled to himself. "The army is bound to overrun us." But if it failed, Jaleph knew Su'Meeryn likely would implode within itself. "Whatever power this ring might possess is our only hope."

Jaleph was pulled out of his musing when he heard the sounds of the approaching group. Teraken led a company of some twenty men. Fenik, who strode next to Teraken, walked up to stand beside his brother. To his surprise, the king saw no sign of Ruy.

"Welcome Teraken. This seems a fine group you have chosen," Jaleph said as he inspected the men, attempting to sound positive. "Tell me, who'll lead them?"

Teraken looked uncomfortable as he answered. "Myself, sire."

Jaleph paused for a moment. "Walk with me Teraken." He tried to stay calm and was unsure of his success.

When Jaleph felt they reached a sufficient distance so as not to be overheard, he stopped and faced Teraken. "What in the hell are you talking about?" he questioned angrily.

"You don't need me here. Ruy can do as good a job as me preparing the castle. Besides, you need someone who'll keep his wits out there."

"Yes, I agree, and I'm sure Ruy can do that just as well. I won't allow this. I want..." the king paused, "I need you here."

"Jaleph, I need to do this," Teraken responded quietly. He stopped to gather his thoughts before continuing. "Teracuss is gone and might never return... my wife... I want to do this. It's a risk, and it was my idea. Please allow me. I've got nothing to lose."

The look on Teraken's face was all Jaleph needed to see. His friend had lost his wife and was afraid he was going to lose his son. If Teracuss was risking his life to save Su'Meeryn, Teraken wanted to do the same. He wanted to make certain that the possible demise of his entire family had some measure of meaning.

The king took a deep breath. "I hate this," he muttered, glancing over his shoulder at the assembled men. He placed his hand on Teraken's shoulder and said, "Very well." He guided his friend back to the formation.

With Teraken and Fenik flanking the king, he addressed the company. The men before him fidgeted as he spoke. "You all know the importance of your mission and the risk. Don't be deceived, some of you will likely not return to see your family and countrymen, but you depart with the hope of saving them. I commend all of you. Those of you who do return, and if we survive this coming crisis, will be greatly rewarded.

"Obviously your task is not to directly engage the enemy. Your mission is reconnaissance. Maybe a few can be captured and brought back. Act like a mosquito. Attract their attention; draw a few drops of blood. If you pester them enough, perhaps you'll slow them down. We need time; time for Teracuss and Iridan to return with the ring.

"Our hopes will follow you all. Any information you return with could be indispensable, and any amount of time the army can be delayed could mean our survival. I know this speech might sound bleak, but take heart. We believe we can endure as long as everyone succeeds in their tasks.

"Now I must send you off. Make haste! Go with the thoughts of those you leave behind to protect, and be determined to prevail." He turned to Teraken and motioned for them to begin.

Teraken looked at the king for a moment then at Fenik. He turned to the men and barked, "You heard the king; let's move!" Without looking back, he led them out from the courtyard and towards the advancing force.

Jaleph turned to his brother. "I wish I could've thought of something more encouraging to say. I fear my skill at motivation is somewhat lacking."

"You can worry over that at a later time. Right now we must plan further for our defense."

"You're right. Send for Ruy. We'll meet right after breakfast."

As they exited the courtyard, Jaleph hoped his brother was correct, and that he would have the opportunity to fret over his speeches after this crisis. In his heart though, he feared the last thing he would ever be worrying about was speeches.

Chapter 12

As Iridan and Myrin exited the inn, Teracuss approached with the two horses. Teracuss appeared relieved that the animals had not been stolen. They had no idea how safe the horses would be within the stable.
"How do you feel about getting another horse?" Iridan asked Teracuss as he approached. "With Myrin sharing one of ours, we'll be moving slower."

"I don't think we should," Teracuss answered. "I'm not sure how much money we'll need at later stops. She'll have to ride with one of us." He looked towards Myrin, the longing on his face plain to see. He desperately wanted Myrin to choose his horse.

Iridan was not surprised when Myrin climbed onto his steed after Teracuss handed him the reins. Teracuss glared at him for a short moment before looking away. Iridan quickly turned and mounted the horse in front of Myrin, trying not to kick her from his awkward motion.

As they rode out of Mephosh, Iridan found himself glancing about for signs of the four strange men. He was intrigued by them, especially the man in white. To his surprise, part of him was hoping to meet them again; the other part was glad when they did not.

Back on the trail, Teracuss placed his horse in the lead. They pushed the horses harder than usually as the miles passed by without incident. Their route was now veering towards the southeast and the crossing of the rivers. Occasionally, as his mind drifted, Iridan thought he saw movement along the horizon. He was not sure, but it appeared to be shapes of red, white and black. Iridan rubbed his eyes and the shapes disappeared.

Dismissing the visions as a mirage played upon him by his anxiety, Iridan turned his attention to Myrin. He focused on the feel of her arms grasping about his body for support. He gazed at Teracuss in the now familiar lead position. Teracuss definitely felt a strong attraction toward Myrin. Perhaps he felt he loved her; however, Iridan figured the short amount of time they had known her precluded that emotion. But she had gravitated to him instead. Iridan wondered over that fact. Though he did find her beautiful, his emotions clearly did not equal Teracuss.' Iridan had done nothing to try to attract her, but still, her preference was clear. He felt her hands readjust to change their grip. For the first time, the thought of a relationship with this girl crossed his mind, but he quickly put that consideration aside. He had a mission to complete and needed to remain focused. A distraction at an inopportune time could mean failure.

They reached the river crossing at midday and found a ferryman living in a small hut. He took them across for a small fee, and they entered the land of Cyrenn. They pushed hard through some inhospitable land to pick up the main southern road.

Iridan examined the land they rode across, and it put him in a dreary mood. The ground was fairly rolling, but everywhere he looked, Iridan saw only brown. No grass grew. Occasionally Iridan spotted some mottled weeds or a few rocks. He became concerned for the horses who would have no vegetation to graze on. They shared small portions of their food with the beasts during their brief rest stops. No game moved about the barren landscape to hunt, and their food supplies dwindled.

"I wonder what happened around here," Iridan commented at one point when the horses rode fairly close together.

"Don't know," mumbled Teracuss as he kept riding.

Iridan glanced back at Myrin. "Are you familiar with this land? Do you have any idea what caused this?"

Myrin shook her head. "I've only been this way a couple times, and that was some time ago. I don't remember it looking this barren."

Following that brief dialogue, conversation remained at a minimum between the three for the remainder of the day. Iridan wanted to talk to Myrin as they traveled; however the solemn image of Teracuss plodding through the desolation somehow stopped him. What minimal discussion they did have centered on the timetables for the various stages of their mission or their need to search for game to supplement their food supply. Twice they spotted a hare darting across the destitute ground, but they were never fast enough to pull out a bow and aim a shot.

As evening bled into night, they finally stopped to make camp. While unloading the supplies, Iridan realized they only had two bed rolls. "I guess we'll have to switch for whoever takes watch," he said.

"I guess," Teracuss snarled. He snatched his bedding and spread it on the dirt. "I'll take second watch," he said then promptly went to sleep.

Iridan stood dumbfounded still holding the other bed roll. Teracuss' attitude continued to astound him. He handed the bedding to Myrin and said, "I'll take the first."

Myrin smiled at him and gently took the furs. He built a small fire from some twigs he managed to scavenge and listened intently for any sign of their four self-appointed friends.

Near the end of his vigil, Iridan heard the sound of a small party moving somewhere near their campsite. He was not surprised when he saw the man in white walking towards them with his three strange companions following. Iridan wondered why he did not see any horses as he quickly shook the others awake.

"Well met again, friends," hailed the man in white with a friendly wave. He then stopped in front of Iridan. His three followers formed a semi-circle a few paces behind him.

"What're you doing here?" Teracuss asked sharply.

"I just thought we could, perhaps, share your fire."

"Where're your horses?" Iridan questioned, glancing about.

The man in white just laughed. His eyes glistened, reflecting the small flames. "Have you reconsidered my offer to accompany you?"

"No," replied Teracuss.

"I only wish to assist you in your endeavors," the man said looking down sheepishly.

Iridan found himself wanting to believe the man, but he resisted the urge and continued to question him. "What if we refuse your help?"

The strange man sighed dejectedly then continued. "You do not understand, I am not offering my help. I am giving it."

Aggravation now grew in Iridan. The man seemed to be prodding them with his vague statements. He glanced at the other three and wondered why they never spoke. He turned to Teracuss to see if the younger man had any input. Teracuss was scrutinizing the four men and did not notice his obvious plea for aid. "You haven't answered my question," Iridan continued. "What if we refuse?"

"We don't want your help," Teracuss suddenly interjected.

"Are you sure? You certainly needed us back in the clearing when we helped you save this lovely girl."

"That was you!" exclaimed Iridan. "You were the archers!"

"Yes," the man continued, practically beaming. "You see, we have already aided you in your journey. Why not accept additional assistance?"

Iridan began to feel drawn to this man but some suspicion remained. "Why didn't you approach us then?"

"It was not the right time to introduce myself. I was waiting for a proper setting, a more relaxed atmosphere. Unfortunately, you showed little interest in conversation at the inn; therefore a more private meeting seemed appropriate." He gestured at their camp.

"Who are you?" Iridan asked. His suspicion was beginning to shift into curiosity.

The man turned a smiling face to Teracuss. "Why, I am a prophet of the Creator."

Teracuss did not appear convinced. "What's your name?"

"My name is of no importance; doubtless you would not have heard of me anyway." The man's voice turned from its friendly tone to one more serious. "We are on a mission ourselves, and it happens to be the same quest you are on."

Myrin started to say something, but Iridan quickly grabbed her hand to stop her. "And what would that be?"

"The same as you," he answered. "We are here to help you." He looked between Iridan and Teracuss with pleading eyes.

"Who are your companions?" asked Teracuss.

"They are inconsequential. They are simply that: companions. They help me with some of my more unfortunate tasks in this troubling world. Please do not concern yourselves with them."

Teracuss was obviously unsatisfied with the response. "Do they ever speak?"

The man in white sighed. "Please sir, do not trouble yourselves over them," he repeated. "They are companions, henchman of a sort."

Still not convinced by his statements, Iridan further pressed the man. "I'm afraid I must insist."

"Very well," the man in white looked displeased, "I lead them in the true path of the Creator, and they obey me."

"Sounds more like servants to me," Teracuss interjected. Iridan sensed that his partner had discerned something about the strange man which he had missed, and he decided to allow Teracuss to guide the questioning further. Iridan turned and looked at Myrin; she gazed back with inquisitive concern. The expression on her face told him she would resign herself to their decision. He felt powerless. He was unable to make a decision regarding the intentions of these men.

"Please do not be troubled. That is an argument over semantics." The man was virtually to the point of begging now. "We did save your lives in that clearing after all," he reminded them.

"Not necessarily a selfless act," Teracuss pointed out.

"True, it was not selfless, nor was it selfish. It was for the cause of the Creator."

Teracuss hesitated and appeared to be considering his next statement carefully. "You say you're on the same mission as we are, and you say that you'll help us. However, you don't say why you don't undertake the mission yourselves."

"You misunderstand," the man replied. "I am on the mission and would gladly complete it myself, but you have a more immediate need. My quest is simply a pilgrimage; you have your people to save. That is certainly more pressing, you must agree."

Displeasure spread over Iridan's face. "How do you know about that?" he snapped.

"I am a prophet."

Teracuss was not convinced. "What would you do with it if you're successful?"

"What any prophet would do—seek to learn and improve my knowledge of the Creator." The man paused and took a deep breath. "This banter has been entertaining, but it grows tiresome. We are here to help you, nothing more. You have your suspicions, and I appreciate that. I understand that my company does look sinister, to some; however, please do not make your judgments based on their appearance. We have saved all three of your lives once and just might save them again. If I wanted you dead, I could have simply allowed those brigands to kill you." He paused and rubbed his hands together over the fire. "Besides, what harm can our assistance cause?"

Iridan turned to Teracuss. The man in white was convincing. If these four posed a threat, they would all be dead by now. Anyway, he thought, if this man wants to help, why should we refuse? Their mission was to save Su'Meeryn, and any aid should not be turned down. True, he did have questions, but the man had answered them to his satisfaction, and his displeasure had dripped away during the dialogue. He had decided to accept this strange man's aid when Teracuss interrupted his thoughts:

"I thank you for saving our lives, but we can take care of ourselves from here. We won't be needing any more of your help. Now be gone."

The man in white softly smiled at Teracuss and lowered his head. He then motioned to his entourage and they left the campsite.

"What was that all about?" Iridan asked angrily after the four men had left his view.

Teracuss answered as he sat down on his bed roll. "I'm not sure, but I was reminded of someone Korath taught me about. The man in white reminded me of The Prophet of the Deceiver."

"What?" Myrin snapped, showing her apathy towards the situation had evaporated. "He just wanted to help us. It was obvious." She too had been swayed by the words of the charismatic man.

"Of course it seemed that way. That's how he operates, if that was indeed him."

Iridan did not agree. "I'd like to know what makes you think that he is this prophet."

Teracuss rummaged about the ground and threw a small twig into the dwindling fire. "While he was talking, I thought of his belt, his silver belt. I recalled what Korath said of the Deceiver's prophet: *He will deceive you with his silver tongue.* His companions also concerned me. They reminded me of something, but I couldn't quite remember it, until he mentioned helping us in the clearing. Then it struck me: death. The Prophet is said to have fire, night and death at his command. Maybe that refers to the outfits those three wore; I don't know, but I don't like it. I think we should stay away from them."

With his frustration building, Iridan felt another confrontation looming. "If they are our enemies," he asked, "why didn't they let those barbarians kill us?"

"It's obvious; they want something from us." Teracuss paused. "Look, I'd wager that almost everything he told us is true. He probably is after Naar's ring. The Deceiver can't take the ring on his own; however, if it's given to him—or one of his servants—it is said that he can use the power of the ring to wage war against the Creator. That must be what he's after. Don't you see? It all makes perfect sense."

"I don't know." Iridan was not persuaded. "We could definitely use some help." He had never believed in all this mythology. Since before they had embarked, he had wondered what good one ring could do. Now they rejected assistance based on a faith he did not even possess, but a faith they were hoping would save Su'Meeryn. For the first time Iridan truly understood what a strange situation he was in.

"He said he was going to help us regardless," Teracuss continued, "so if I'm wrong, we won't be losing anything anyway. But, if I'm right, it's important we don't accept his help. If we accept the aid of the Deceiver, we're bound to be corrupted."

Iridan turned to Myrin and asked, "What do you think?"

"I've heard none of these stories," she replied. "I can't even begin to guess. I owe you two my life and will accept your decision, but I was impressed by that man. He seemed sincere to me."

"I agree with Myrin," Iridan said. He noticed that she had moved a little closer to him. He felt uncomfortable by the gesture. He already stood at odds with Teracuss. Reminding the younger man of her affection would not help the situation.

"We're not taking their help, and that's final!" Teracuss exclaimed, seeming to not even have noticed Myrin's movement. "I was assigned to this mission because of my studies under Korath. Therefore, you will accept my decision on this matter. Now let's get some sleep." He fell to the ground, pulled his bedding about him and turned his back to the other two.

"Excuse me," Iridan barked, whipping the blanket off Teracuss, "it's your watch now. Besides, do you think it's safe to stay here with those four in the area? Assuming they are who you say they are."

Teracuss sighed in disgust. "Did you listen to anything I said? They're not going to kill us now if they want the ring. We should be safe from them while on our journey." He threw the rest of his bedding in Iridan's face and walked a short distance from the fire.

The wind started to pick up slightly and was the only sound other than the crackling of their diminutive blaze. Teracuss stood motionless, looking out in the direction from which the man in white had disappeared before returning to his companions.

Iridan gathered himself in the bedding for the remainder of the night while Teracuss stirred the fire to add a little extra heat. Maybe he'll be of some help after all, Iridan thought as he fell asleep.

***

Morning arrived and they quickly packed their equipment. "We're going to need to buy some food," Teracuss said surveying their stock.

"If I remember the maps, I think there might be a city about a day's ride from this area: Cishor," stated Iridan. "Do you know it?" he asked Myrin.

"I've heard of it," she replied. "It's south of here, but I'm not sure how far. I don't know exactly where we are."

"I hope we reach it before dark," said Teracuss. "Even though I don't think those four will try anything, I'd still feel more comfortable in a town for the night."

Iridan noticed something slightly different about Teracuss' attitude. He seemed a little more confident after their recent encounter. "I agree," Iridan said and wondered if this was the first time they had agreed on anything. "I just hope we can find some decent lodging."

Chapter 13

The light of dawn seared over the horizon as Iridan, Teracuss and Myrin prepared to leave their campsite. After loading up all the supplies, they continued the southward trek down the barren trail. Teracuss again placed himself in the lead. Iridan noticed that the change in the other man's bearing remained; Teracuss definitely appeared surer of himself. It seemed that now, for the first time, the two men had become somewhat synchronized in their mission. Unfortunately though, the obvious conflict regarding Myrin remained.

As they rode, Iridan's eyes scanned the terrain looking for a sign of their self-appointed friends. His thoughts drifted to consider Teracuss' new-found attitude. Teracuss had become more confident during their conversation with the man in white. No, Iridan consider, not more confident, more focused. He was now more focused on their task than his conflict with Iridan. Teracuss had been confronted by what he saw as an enemy, and he had placed their strife aside to deal with the situation. His disappointment over Myrin still existed, but the volatility between the two had seemed to be somewhat dissipated.

The fight in the woods must have really made him feel inferior, thought Iridan. Now he feels that I need him as much as he needs me.

As the trio continued south, the desolation of the land they traversed actually worsened. Iridan glanced around and could find no signs of life. There was no movement other than the two horses. Iridan began to feel as if they were traveling through Hell. For a time it seemed that they would never meet another soul. He was greatly relieved when they finally approached Cishor towards evening.

All three felt tired and hungry as they reached their destination, and they often grumbled under their breath. The city of Cishor boasted a large stone wall that encircled the boundaries. When they arrived at the large wooden gate, Iridan asked a guard to direct them to the nearest inn. The man offered some instructions, and they headed off. Iridan noticed that their mood improved as their thoughts turned to purchasing some fresh food and getting a good night sleep.

Along the way to the inn, they stopped at a grocer and bought some bread and vegetables. Cishor's streets possessed a clean appearance, quite the opposite of Mephosh, but many of the buildings hung in disrepair. Iridan saw a number of sentinels patrolling about, which made him feel much safer. The entire picture gave Iridan the impression of the genesis of fatal disease growing from deep within Cishor's bowels.

"How does our money supply look?" Iridan asked as they walked their horses towards the inn's stable.

Teracuss rummaged through his pouch. "We're doing all right," he replied. "We can afford a few more nights lodging and a couple more stops at a grocer, but that's about it."

After checking their horses into the stable, they headed towards the entrance to the inn. Teracuss opened the door, and a foul smell emanated from within. A pungent odor chased after the dim light which rolled from oil burning lamps in the corners of the room. Iridan wondered what type of fuel the owner used to illuminate his business. "Well, I suppose we'll get used to the smell," he mumbled to the other two.

The patrons within the establishment resembled the shabby, splintered tables and chairs they sat around. Strange curtains hung loosely over filthy windows about the room. The tailor of the draperies must certainly have been mad; a collage of haphazard colors swirled throughout the cloth in no particular order to the sane eye. Dirt stirred at the footfalls of the three as they carefully pushed past the inhabitants towards an empty table. They were disappointed by this new assault on their senses, but they felt more secure within the city walls than they had in some time.

Their mood began to improve. Iridan had just made a small joke about flipping a coin for the rights to the bed when their spirits plummeted. Seated directly across from the table, the man in white—with his three colleagues—became visible through the smoky haze.

"I am glad to see that you made it here," the man said cheerfully as he stood to greet them.

"We don't want your help," Teracuss quickly stated and searched for a table further away. He spotted one in a far corner and dragged Myrin and Iridan towards it.

Soon after they sat down, the man in white approached. "May I purchase a hot meal and some good drink for you?"

Before Iridan could even think to respond, Teracuss replied, "We want nothing from you. Now leave us alone!"

"So impolite," the man smiled, "regardless of your ill-founded suspicions, I will be of assistance to you." He gave a slight bow and walked back to his own table.

After the man returned to his followers and sat down, the innkeeper approached with a heaping tray of roasted meats and three flasks. He was a grimy man with an unkempt beard. Grease and dirt covered his white shirt and pants.

"What's this?" Iridan asked.

"A gift from your strange friends," the man replied with a puzzled look on his face.

Teracuss angrily shook his head. "Get it away!" he commanded. "We'll take nothing from them. Don't honor any gifts or offerings they make on our behalf. Do you understand?"

The innkeeper nodded his head in confusion and shambled away, promptly dropping a hunk of meat to the floor. He stooped down, and his soiled hand grabbed the roast. Before replacing it on the tray, he wiped it across a foul pant leg, then retreated back to the kitchen.

"Would it really hurt to accept some food?" Myrin asked. "Was that really necessary?"

"I'm not sure, but I think it was," Teracuss answered. "You need to understand, if I'm right, we must not willingly accept his help. If we do, we could be drawn into his spell. We could become *his* servant."

"What do you mean: 'his servant'?" continued Myrin, and Iridan noticed that she was beginning to sound angry.

"Just what I said, anyone who accepts assistance from the Evil One can become his pawn."

Based on their past meeting, Iridan was inclined to agree with Teracuss. "Well then, let's order something. I could use a good meal," he said, trying to sound diplomatic.

"Yes, maybe we can split one of those roasts," Myrin proposed. Iridan noticed that any trace of anger had quickly disappeared.

Teracuss nodded and walked towards the kitchen.

"Make sure it's not the one he dropped," Iridan called after. Teracuss turned back to him and sneered. Iridan just shrugged his shoulders; he had meant the comment as a joke, but Teracuss obviously chose to take it as an attack against his intelligence.

Teracuss soon returned with a large roast of adequate aroma and a flask of wine. While they ate in silence, Iridan began to overhear the conversation of the other patrons.

"I'll tell ya, it was a demon, a white demon," one of the squalid men bellowed.

"Y're crazy," another retorted. "A demon. And I got a gremlin in me pants."

A couple of the other men chuckled at that statement. "He ain't crazy," a woman cried angrily. "It came down one night and made off with one a your cows."

"What about your dog?" the first man asked. "I heard he disappeared, and that the only thing left was a pool of blood in a field. Right where you were a huntin.'"

"That don't prove a thing," the skeptical man answered. "I didn't see no white demon, was probably just a wolf."

"Yeah, except no one's seen a wild animal in weeks. You said yourself; you didn't see nothen on that hunt. I tell ya, there is a something strange out there."

Iridan listened more intently as the conversation continued. Despite how bizarre their words sounded, he figured this might mean trouble for his mission. The townspeople continued to talk about the disappearance of animals and even a few people. A couple claimed to have heard rumors of a white demon terrorizing some travelers several days ago. There was even talk of a house on the outskirts of town burning down for no apparent reason. While he listened, Iridan kept eyeing the white figure who sat across the room. The man contentedly stared at his table, oblivious of the surrounding discussion. Iridan motioned for the innkeeper. When the dirty little man approached, Iridan ordered a mug of ale. He asked his companions if they wanted something else; they both said no, and Iridan waved him away.

"You know," Teracuss said, "we really shouldn't splurge like that."

"What do you mean?" responded Iridan.

"An ale? We need to conserve all the money we can. Besides, you already had wine. I don't think you need any more."

"Come on Teracuss," Myrin quipped, "one ale isn't very expensive."

"I know it's not, but we need to get used to buying only what we need. We should start now." He glared at Iridan.

"What the hell is your problem now?" Iridan barked.

"Wasn't the wine enough?"

Myrin folded her arms across her chest and laughed. "Okay, mother."

Two of the townspeople had overhead the discussion during a lull in their own argument and approached. They were carrying huge mugs of ale, much of which spilled as they walked, and each grabbed the back of Teracuss' chair. "Does the old maid here dis'pprove of a ale?" the leading man slurred. He smiled and displayed a toothless mouth surrounded by an unshaven face. They both laughed then took long draughts from their mugs. Much of the liquid streamed down their chins.

Iridan stood slowly and tried not to seem confrontational. "All right, all right, that was a very good joke. Now why don't you guys go back to your friends?" He tried to mimic a good-natured chuckle.

The toothless man stumbled over to Myrin. He grabbed a strand of her hair and rolled it between his thumb and forefinger. "Very pretty," he said, "why don't ya leave these here two? Try a real man." He laughed and turned back to his partner to confirm the quality of his witticism.

Iridan attempted to gently push himself between the man and Myrin while Teracuss also stood. "Please leave her alone." Iridan struggled to stay calm. He did not want to incite the obviously drunk man into a fight, and he noticed that the remainder of the bar's inhabitants had interrupted their occultic debate to concentrate on this display. The man in white's party sat like statues.

"Are you okay?" Iridan asked Myrin.

"I'm fine," she said while wiping some grime from her hair.

"We're not done here." The man poked Iridan in the chest causing him to stumble backwards. Before Iridan could do anything, Teracuss struck the man across his toothless jaw. Then the thing Iridan dreaded most occurred. The entire room erupted in a fight. A half-full mug struck Iridan on the side of his head, and toothless' companion was upon him. He punched the man in the stomach, causing him to double over. Iridan spun around as four or five men surrounded him. He flailed about for a few moments before he felt a blow to his chest. Air rushed from his lungs. Another strike hit his face. He collapsed to the floor. As the men grabbed for him, a hand abruptly flew across Iridan's vision trailing a stream of blood.

The fighting abruptly ceased and Iridan pulled himself up. He looked about and saw the man in white. Next to the man stood the red warrior; his sword was drawn and dripped crimson. The townspeople slowly backed away, and Iridan noticed that the severed hand belonged to the toothless man. He held the stump of his wrist as his blood pooled about him. Iridan knew that without assistance, the man would soon die.

"You see," the man in white said, "we help you again." He laughed and then motioned to his followers. They abruptly exited the inn.

Iridan looked about and found Teracuss sprawled across the floor. His left eye began to swell as blood soaked through the bandage on his shoulder. Iridan helped him into his chair and tried to gather his thoughts. Next, four armed sentries burst into the inn. The first thing they saw was the injured man on the floor.

The sentries began to question everyone regarding what had happened. They quickly realized a simple bar fight had started everything. They quizzed Iridan regarding his relationship to the man in white. The guards were hesitant to believe that they were not traveling with the four; however, the innkeeper confirmed his story when he related their refusal to accept the offer of dinner. The sentries were eventually satisfied and left, carrying out the bleeding man. Iridan was surprised at the relative nonchalance displayed over the man's injury and wondered if he would survive the encounter.

Iridan approached the innkeeper to ask if they could still have a room for the night. The man was reluctant but agreed when Iridan turned to leave, threatening to find a different inn. Apparently the thought of a lost sale was too much for the dirty little man to bear. The three companions gingerly climbed the stairs and reached their sparse room. After Teracuss closed the door, Myrin insisted that the men sleep on the bed for the night. "You two have been so good to me; it's the least I can do." She quickly spread some blankets on the floor to make herself comfortable. They locked the door and scattered some of their smaller possessions across the windowsill. Iridan wanted to make sure they all got a good night sleep. He felt they would be sufficiently warned if anybody attempted to break in.

Sleep came ferociously to Iridan that night. He dreamt of a white demon snatching him from bed and dragging him to Hell. He then saw Su'Meeryn burning as the advancing army destroyed all in its path. He awoke at dawn to shouts from the street below. Through the cries, Iridan was able to piece together that three more houses had burned down that night. While they packed their supplies, he wondered if the man in white had anything to do with these mysterious incidents.

Downstairs, the inn was empty. Apparently all the patrons were comatose or giving assistance to the owners of the burned homes. Teracuss called for the innkeeper and paid their bill. They unstabled the horses and left town as quickly as they were able.

After half-an-hour of riding, they noticed tremendous storm clouds advancing from the East, like a great army preparing to attack Cishor. As the dark clouds continued to approach, Iridan felt the town had no hope of withstanding such a charge. Their own chances seemed very bleak.

Iridan glanced about for a sign of shelter, but the entire landscape was barren. They could not waste time by heading back to Cishor. All they could do was hope the imminent rain would not be too heavy. Teracuss looked back at him for advice. Iridan simply waved at him to continue riding.

The first crash of thunder startled the horses. Lightning signaled the start of what appeared to be lethal combat in the sky. The bolts of lightning struck so close, Iridan felt as if the white flashes seared his retinas. Rolls of thunder continued to crash louder and louder. Iridan did not believe he would be able to control his nervous horse much longer. He felt Myrin cling closer to him with each crescendo of the storm. Then the rain came like the charge of cavalry. Wave after wave struck the three travelers. The torrent was so thick Iridan felt like he was swimming up a river. Through the water, he saw a white discharge burst directly in their path. The explosion of thunder was so intense, Iridan felt he had gone deaf. He needed to pull on his reins with all his strength to keep his horse under control. Myrin lost her grasp on him as the horse reared, and she fell to the drenched ground. He peered through the gloom looking for a sight of Teracuss. The blurred image in front of him was undoubtedly his companion, still mounted on his steed; luckily he also was able to keep his horse restrained. Iridan then turned his attention to the ground to spot Myrin. She stood, and he was able to pull her back up.

"We need to get out of this!" he heard Teracuss yell.

"Where?" Iridan responded.

Myrin pulled on his shoulder. "There should be a hill somewhere ahead! Maybe we can find shelter!"

"Are you sure?" he asked. "I thought you weren't that familiar with this area!"

"I'm not, but I remember seeing a map once which showed a hill south of Cishor; I don't know if it's along the trail though!"

Failing to see any alternative, Iridan called out, "Let's try it!" He spurred his horse forward and continued on through the tumult.

Chapter 14

Three days had passed since Jaleph sent Teraken and his men out to what he hoped would not be their deaths. With the army heading south—and his men moving quickly north—Teraken should have spotted the army in about one day. Nothing had been heard from the men yet. The king fretted over whether that was a good sign.

Jaleph had spent most of this time with Fenik and Ruy. They sat in his chamber, pouring over maps of the castle and the surrounding area, planning their defense. While Ruy went out to implement their decisions, Fenik and he marched about the city. The mood of the people they encountered was bleak, and they saw many fights which needed to be broken up during their walks. Jaleph yearned for word from Teraken—a positive word.

Small scouting missions seemed to be constantly leaving or returning to the castle. The groups generally consisted of a pair, never more than three. They all reported directly to Ruy; he would, in turn, report back to the king if any new information came in. So far, there had been no need.

They had also heard nothing regarding Iridan and Teracuss—not that Jaleph expected to receive any word. It had been a dangerous decision sending the two men out on their own, and he wondered if they still lived. With all the bandits about, and the possibility of a branch of the approaching army circling south about Su'Meeryn, the pair stood a good chance of getting killed before finishing the mission. Jaleph and Ruy had talked much about the possibility that the invaders had sent forces to loop behind the city, but they figured that to be unlikely. None of their scouts had spotted anything, and they presumed the army saw Su'Meeryn as such a small threat that it was unnecessary. Besides, they did not have enough forces to plan for all possibilities. They needed to prepare based on their best theory.

"We've dug the trenches around the wall," Fenik was saying. "We've appropriated all the oil we could find. We'll fill the trenches when the army is nearing the castle. All the planks to cover them are done too."

"Why not fill them now and be done with it?" Jaleph asked.

"The oil will soak into the ground if we fill them now," the prince responded patiently.

The brothers continued their walk about the castle. They climbed to the top of the wall and inspected the rows of arrows wrapped in straw which would be used to ignite the oil trenches and any siege machines. Jaleph tried to encourage the soldiers they met. "We'll need you these next few days," he would say, or, "I'm glad you're at this post." He grew weary as the day wore on. All the walking and empty words took their toll.

Still, Jaleph was pleased to see that all his subjects seemed engaged in preparations. Men and women hurried about the walls delivering arrows and sharpening javelins, but only occasionally did he spot any soldiers drilling. Ruy had advised him that drills were not necessary for this type of combat. The king ordered some new banners to be made bearing bright colors and insignias of his family and Su'Meeryn. He wanted a measure of dignity to be displayed at their last moments. The king desperately wanted to swell with pride due to the efforts of his people, but it did not manage to find a foothold. He was too burdened by their circumstances to feel anything positive. Let us at least look good at our deaths, he thought.

His musings were interrupted as a messenger stumbled upon the royal siblings. He bent at his waist and gulped mouthfuls of air before he could speak. "I finally found you," he stammered, still trying to replenish the oxygen in his lungs. He then appeared shocked as he realized the casualness of his words to his monarch. "I'm sorry, sire," he continued.

"What is it?" Jaleph snapped, feeling somewhat annoyed at the man. His temper was fairly short these days.

"Word from Teraken, sir; a runner has returned from the scouting party. He is awaiting you in your meeting room with Ruy."

"Very good, we'll join them immediately," the king responded, and Fenik and he hurried back to the palace.

***

The king and prince approached the table where Jaleph had so recently decided to send Teracuss and Iridan on their mission; though not so long ago, the days felt like years. Ruy and the runner were seated, awaiting the royal brothers. They looked like contrasting bookends to their current circumstance. Ruy sat composed and still. His physique and beautiful eldritch face looked out of place, an antithesis to their plight, as if he could not be corrupted by their situation. Conversely, the messenger looked weather-beaten and worn. He was a youthful man with a skinny physique and disheveled pale hair. He nervously wrung his hands atop the table. This man definitely manifested the plight of the kingdom.

"What word do you bring?" Fenik questioned.

"Not so hasty, brother," Jaleph said, trying to muster some regal sympathy. He wanted to make the young man feel important. His task would not be completed after giving his report. He would still be needed for the castle's defense, and Jaleph wanted to offer some encouragement. "What's your name, son?" he asked softly.

"Hakath, majesty."

"Now Hakath, what can you tell us?"

The man paused for a moment to take a drink from the cup before him. "I'm sorry majesty, I've had little to eat or drink for two days." Jaleph nodded his head, and Hakath continued. "Teraken sent me back to advise that we had reached the army. It's very large. Teraken was unable to estimate its total size. We needed to keep cover to not be spotted, so we couldn't get a good vantage point to make a guess. Teraken figured they'd be moving slowly. Most of the men were on foot, and Teraken estimated they were still about five days away. They definitely are heading south. They must be four days away now. Teraken said he'd do what he could to slow them down. If we guessed wrong on their speed, and if Teraken does slow their progress, they'll be here in a maximum of six days, but no less than four."

Hakath hesitated, clearly distraught by his own words. "Majesty, the army's huge. I don't know how we can survive."

"Don't repeat that anywhere!" Jaleph commanded. His forehead dropped into his left hand, and he rubbed his face in anguish. He calmed himself then thanked Hakath. "Go home and get some rest and a good meal. Report to Ruy tomorrow for your new assignment."

After Hakath left, Jaleph turned to Ruy, "Well, what do you think?"

"Same as before."

Jaleph waited for Ruy to elaborate. When it was clear he was not going to continue, Jaleph asked, "Can you be more specific?"

"I don't know what you want me to say. We can certainly give them a good fight, but we're a small castle. We can't withstand an army from those three lands."

Fenik jumped from his chair. "That's your advice?" he interjected.

"What more do you expect?"

"With Teraken gone, we're counting on you, Ruy," Fenik exclaimed, pointing his finger directly at Ruy's face. "Teraken might not return. If he doesn't, you'll be head of the army, under Jaleph. We're relying on you to coordinate this."

"I'll do what I can. If this ring has the power it's supposed to…" Ruy paused and continued quietly. "That's our only hope."

Jaleph just shook his head with disgust. "You're quite the enthusiast," he remarked.

Ruy did not respond. The man was an enigma to Jaleph. He never had much to say, and when he did speak, he was extremely blunt. There was no doubt, however, that he garnered respect. He knew Ruy was their best hope to protect the castle as long as possible.

Chapter 15

As they rode through the storm, the heavy raindrops, flung by the wind, began to sting Iridan's eyes. The pelting water seemed to be purposefully attacking the trio. Iridan tried to peer forward for a sign of the hill he hoped lay ahead. At the same time he struggled to keep sight of the path while his horse skidded in the thick mud. Somehow, Teracuss and he kept their steeds from drifting apart. Finally the lightning began to subside, until one tremendous crash seemed to signal the end of the electric fury, leaving behind only endless waves of rain. Fortunately, the light from the last blast illuminated their goal through the ocean of water which hung in the air.

The hill appeared to be about one hundred yards ahead on the right side of the path. With their aim in sight, Iridan's mood improved, and he drove his horse towards their goal. The rain continued to envelop them, but it was now more of a steady downpour than a ferocious assault. The thunder had stopped completely, leaving only the ominous sound of the falling water bombarding the ground.

Before them, the hill stood like a foreboding watchtower over the barren land. It seemed out of place, this lone tower of rock. It appeared to have been grabbed from the bowels of the earth by the hand of the Creator himself and pulled through the turf to reign over the miles of flat land. Iridan quickly circled about the hill searching for a sign of shelter. On the far side, he spotted a large opening overlooking the southward route of the trail. The cave mouth reached about fifty feet in height, and he noticed an ancient path leading up to it. Aged stones formed treacherous steps. Streams of water flowed through the grooves in the rocks which would make the climb treacherous. Carvings appeared to be etched into the face of the hill above the steps, but they had been worn through the ages leaving them indecipherable.

Iridan returned to where Teracuss waited and led him to the path.

"Can we get the horses up there?" asked Myrin.

"Do we have another alternative? Who knows how long this rain'll continue. They need the shelter as much as we do," Teracuss replied.

Iridan agreed. He dismounted, and nearly slipped to the ground as he helped Myrin off. The path was narrow, and the edges of the stones had been smoothed and rounded by the weather over the years. In the heavy rain, footing was slippery, but they managed to reach the cave without incident.

They stood before the entrance, and Iridan looked about. He could not see much as the storm had robbed the sky of most of its light. Based on the echoes from their movements, Iridan guessed the cave to be immense. He heard no other sound from within and figured the cave to be safe. With their shelter secured, Iridan turned his attention to his clothes; he was completely drenched. He knew none of their supplies could have fared much better. "We're going to need a fire," he said exhaustedly, "and to get out of these clothes. Let's see if we can find anything flammable. Teracuss, can you get out the flint?"

They started searching through the darkness. Where Iridan guessed the middle of the cave ought to be, he found what seemed like a huge pile of straw and dead plants. That seemed odd, but he was too excited by his good fortune to consider why it might be there. He happily announced his discovery to his companions.

"I got the flint, but I can't see you," Teracuss announced. Iridan called out to him until they stood together beside the straw.

Myrin came up as well, and they separated enough of the debris to start an ample-sized fire. "You better hold the horses so they don't get frightened," he said to Teracuss. "They must be very agitated. The last thing we need is for one of them to break a leg. Try to see if you can find something to tie them to."

Teracuss handed Iridan the stones, and walked back to the cave mouth. After a few moments with the flint, Iridan shot a couple sparks into the straw; one soon began to smolder. As the fire grew, Iridan searched the cave. It was enormous, approximately three hundred feet deep, seventy-five feet high and seventy-five feet wide. He guessed that the cavern covered most of the diameter of the hill at this point. Iridan thought it strange that this cave appeared to be such a perfect room, but then he figured there must be stranger things in nature. Turning his attention to the walls, he noticed that they appeared to be black, as if from soot. There must have been many a fire in here, he guessed. It was an unbelievable stroke of luck to find this shelter during their great need.

He walked over to Teracuss and helped him strap the horses to a large rock which jutted out from the cave wall. He stroked both of their necks as Teracuss gave each an apple. They returned to the fire, and he threw some more straw onto the blaze.

"We need to get out of these clothes," Teracuss said and looked uncomfortably at Myrin who was spreading their supplies out around the fire.

Myrin turned to Teracuss, about to protest any special treatment. Before she could say anything, Iridan interrupted, "Hold on." He walked back to the horses and removed their saddles. The blankets underneath were not nearly as drenched as their clothes. "You can cover yourself with this," he said handing it to Myrin. She appeared about to reply then changed her mind. She grabbed it from him with a slight smile and walked to the other side of the fire. Iridan saw her mixed reaction to the treatment. She did not want to be dealt with differently, but she obviously still felt vulnerable after her recent encounter.

They all stripped down, and Myrin covered herself as best she could. Iridan could hardly see her through the large fire. He placed their clothes as near the flames as possible and was irritated when Teracuss placed the second blanket across their laps—mostly due to its unpleasant smell. He knew Teracuss to be more pious than himself and decided to humor Korath's student by not complaining.

"How much longer do you think we have before the army begins to march?" Teracuss asked quietly.

"They were probably fully mustered a day or two ago, and it's likely they're already moving," Iridan replied.

"When do you think they will reach Su'Meeryn?"

Iridan thought for a moment. "Well, they won't be familiar with the land, so they'll move slowly. Besides, an army that size is usually slow, from what I've heard: a week at the longest."

"You'll never get back in time," Myrin interjected.

"Not by horses," said Teracuss. "Our only hope is the ring."

"Do you really think this ring will take you back to your home and save your people?"

"Yes," Teracuss snapped, annoyed at the implication of the query. Myrin was questioning his faith. How else could he answer? Where would his faith be if he said no? He then lay back across the rocky ground, trying to make himself comfortable.

"That's a good idea," said Iridan. "Why don't we all try to get some rest? That will give our clothes a chance to dry and hopefully allow the storm to blow over. But we'll have to get moving even if it doesn't. We're running out of time."

As he put his head down, he saw Myrin's face through a momentary gap in the flames. Her expression seemed to show a longing to be in Teracuss' position—next to him. He felt uncomfortable by the attention she seemed to constantly show him. He offered her a slight grin before he rested his head against the stone surface.

The sound of the rain continued steadily and echoed through the cave. The noise was only interrupted by the crackling of the fire. Iridan tried to consider this situation with Myrin, but he could not keep his mind focused. Despite his wet body, uncomfortable bed and smelly blanket, he quickly fell asleep.

***

Iridan awoke suddenly from the snorting of the horses. He did not know how long he had slept. The rain had stopped, and light streamed into the cave. They're probably still nervous after the storm, he thought turning his attention away from the animals. Myrin and Teracuss were already up—assuming they had slept at all. The clothes were dry, and Iridan grabbed his. After he was fully dressed, they started to pack the supplies.

"How long was I asleep?" he asked.

"A couple of hours, I think," answered Myrin.

He nodded and picked up the bags Teracuss had packed. The horses nervously tugged on their reins as he approached. Iridan reached out to try to calm them when the reins pulled loose from the rock they were tied around, and the horses immediately bolted from the cave opening. He turned and watched them run past the fire—to the back of the cave. He then noticed some movement from the outside through the corner of his eye. Turning around, he saw a large white shape fly past the mouth of the cave. A moment later, it shot forward and entered.

The creature swooped to the center of the cave and landed comfortably in the middle of the fire. Iridan backed away. He knew immediately that the apparition before him was what the townspeople had called the *white demon.* It had an immense body, at least the size of an elephant. Two bat-like wings flapped and crossed over its huge back. Two relatively short legs stuck from under the bulging belly; however, they appeared to be as thick as an aged tree trunk. Three sword-like claws protruded from the end of each stump. A long pointed tail curled up towards a reptilian head. An elongated snout sported rows of razor sharp teeth. Every inch of the creature's scaled hide was an anemic white. Two pale red eyes glared at the small company which—Iridan finally realized—had invaded its lair.

Iridan had never seen one before, but he had heard stories. He had never believed the tales, until now. He knew he was staring at a dragon.

Chapter 16

Dreams invaded Jaleph's sleep that night like the advancing horde which would soon invade his land. He saw visions of red, myriad shades of red: the reds of fire and of blood. He watched as the bodies of his brother and Teraken were trampled under the mass of marching boots. Everyone he knew and loved collapsed under the relentless weight of the army. Ruy appeared. He fought bravely. He was surrounded. A score of warriors fell under his sword until clutching arms pulled him to the ground. The bodies intertwined in a fury of death which sickened Jaleph. Then the scene dissipated into a quagmire of scarlet, and he saw his father's face surveying the horror. The eyes sought out Jaleph. His father then asked, demanded, *What are you going to do?* "I don't know," Jaleph responded. "I don't know. I don't know!"

His body shook awake, and he wiped sweat from his brow with a trembling hand. He slowly stood and walked to his window. The moon had set, so dawn would soon approach. He saw fires along the castle wall and watched as people hurried about. The preparations for defense continued, even at this hour. The king turned and climbed back into bed. "I don't know," he mumbled as he tried to fall back asleep.

***

Morning finally came. Jaleph had slept little after awaking from his nightmare. He had been haunted by the questioning face of his father. As the first rays of dawn pierced through gaps in his curtains, an idea came to him. It was a desperate plan, but it seemed better than watching all of his subjects murdered. He dressed quickly and left his room. "Send for Ruy," he ordered one of the two guards standing outside his door. "Have him meet me in my private chamber. Don't let anyone else know, especially my brother." He turned and headed down the hall with the other guard trailing after.

The king entered his private room. The chamber was small, about twelve feet square. A few padded chairs sat atop a bizarre yellow rug with dirty orange swirls. Jaleph never understood why his father admired that ugly carpet. He remembered Halet seeking asylum in this room; his father would strike secret bargains within the four indigo walls or, sometimes, simply read. During their rare visits to this secluded portion of the palace, the young brothers would always be amazed by the strange color scheme. In tribute to his father, he had decided to keep the room just as Halet had left it.

After a quick look around, Jaleph dropped into one of the chairs and propped his feet on top of a small table in the center of the room. His foot knocked a book onto the floor sending dust flying from its cover. He grunted to himself and picked it up. With the tome in his hands, he read its title and smiled. It was a history of ancient warlord kings: one of Halet's favorites. His father often praised it, telling his sons how it had taught him much about ruling a kingdom. Jaleph started reading it a couple weeks after his father's death. He had only gotten through about ten pages and had not entered the room since.

While Jaleph sat, he flipped through some pages and read a few sentences but found he could not concentrate. He considered how his discussion with Ruy would proceed. He felt as if he was betraying his brother. However, he was the king, and he could choose the people with whom he shared his plans and thoughts. Fenik was a good man for working on daily tasks, but Jaleph sometimes questioned his ability to see larger themes. Ruy always seemed to have the ability to crystallize ideas and plans and foresee likely outcomes.

Ruy finally arrived and sat next to his king. "Can I help you sire?" he asked.

"Yes. We need to discuss an idea I had. I'm not sure we can prevail against the coming crisis. We need to do something." Jaleph paused, carefully considering his next words. "I think we should consider evacuating the castle."

Ruy stared at the king; his face unmoved by the statement. Jaleph could read no emotional response. No response to the possiblity of fleeing from their homes. Ruy said nothing, but Jaleph waited. He would force a response. The king glanced from the book to the stoic countenance before him. "What do you think that'll accomplish?" Ruy finally replied.

"I think that's pretty obvious," Jaleph snipped. "I'm trying to save our people's lives."

"And you think leaving'll do that?"

"Well, it doesn't appear that staying will."

"Perhaps not," Ruy agreed.

Jaleph wanted to scream: talk to me. Ruy was a talented individual in many areas, communication not being one of them. Jaleph often grew annoyed speaking to him, but he needed Ruy now. "I could use your insight," he prompted.

Ruy glanced down at his hands, which had been rubbing his knees, and stopped the movement. He looked at the king and said, "I don't think fleeing will give us any more of a chance of survival. Do you think they'd just let us leave? We'd have to take supplies to feed and shelter the people. The children, old men and women would need to be watched over. We wouldn't be able to move fast enough. Even if they just took the castle and let us evacuate, they'd worry we'd try to take it back; regardless if that's true or not. Do you think our castle is that important to them? They're probably more concerned over our numbers than our walls. They'd hunt us down and slaughter everyone. Whatever their long range plan is, they don't want us around. No, they're going to attack us, whether we're in the castle or fleeing down the road." He gazed back down to his knees and started to rub them again.

The king was amazed at the soliloquy. He had never heard so many words leave Ruy's mouth at one time. He stared at the handsome face. Jaleph felt belittled. How was it that Ruy saw so clearly what he had missed? Of course the logic was correct. The army would never allow them to escape. Why had he been unable to see that? His spirit was crushed. He felt completely inadequate to be king. It probably did not matter. He doubted his kingdom would survive beyond the next few days anyway.

The door suddenly opened, stirring Jaleph from his musing. His guards stood beside a messenger whose face appeared extremely distraught. "What is it?" Jaleph asked.

"It's Korath, sire" the man said then took a deep breath.

Jaleph quickly grew impatient. Their impending doom was weight enough; he did not need to coach this man through his information. "Get on with it!" he commanded.

"Korath, sire. He's dead."

"Dead!" exclaimed the king.

"Yes," the messenger replied, "he was found on his floor in his home. He was an old man. I was told it appeared to be nothing more than that. No wounds were found on his body." He paused for a moment. When Jaleph said nothing, he continued. "Do you need me further, majesty?"

"No, that's quite enough," said Jaleph. "You can go."

Relief showed on the man's face as he quickly turned and exited the room.

"This is great," the king continued. "Even if Iridan and Teracuss manage to return with the ring, who'll know how to use it?" He turned his hopeless eyes to Ruy, and discovered that even he appeared shocked by the news.

Jaleph just stood where he was, clasped his fingers through his hair and shook his head. He felt so dejected that he needed to restrain himself from laughing. Not laughter from humor, but the laughter of a man who believes he has nowhere to turn for comfort or support. Not laughter from joy, but laughter rather than tears. "What else can happen?" He was surprised when his guards turned to him. He had not intended to say that out loud.

"Everyone out," the king said. "Everyone except Ruy." The men left, and Jaleph sat quietly. Ruy looked at him, waiting, but Jaleph had nothing to say. He wanted to talk, wanted to tell Ruy about his despair. Jaleph needed some assurance, but he knew Ruy was not the person to provide that.

"Do you need me further, sire?" asked Ruy.

"Yes, stay with me and have a meal. I just need…" Jaleph stopped. He did not know how to finish. He wondered what it was that he needed. "Just share a meal with me."

Ruy and the king ate quietly; neither had anything to say. When they finished, Ruy stood to leave. "Thank you for the meal," he said. "I'll be going now, by your leave."

"That's fine," said the king. "Go ahead."

At that moment the door again burst open. Teraken stood before him supported by Fenik. His right shoulder had a huge gash across it, and his arm hung in a sling. Various scrapes and cuts latticed his body. He limped forward a couple steps from Fenik's grasp. Jaleph noticed a puzzled look on his brother's face as he saw the empty plates.

"Dead, sire! They're all dead!" Teraken cried. "I'm the only one who survived." He crashed to one knee and grabbed the table to pull himself back up. "We failed."

Chapter 17

The dragon stood directly over the fire seeming like a volcano erupting in their midst, with lava flowing down its sides, threatening to engulf everything in its path. Iridan felt the heat of molten rock reaching his shoes, climbing his legs, rolling up his torso and covering his head. He felt the weight of flowing magma pushing him towards the ground as it burned his skin. They had survived the brigands, the man in white and even the storm. Now it all seemed for naught. How could they overcome this current tribulation?

The creature gazed about the cave. The short hind legs bent as the beast settled down over the fire. The blaze turned the white underbelly a sparkling pink as the beast smothered the flames. A few wisps of smoke escaped the crushing blow, danced up the lengthy neck to be sucked through the nostrils in a deep breath. The crimson eyes stared at each of the intruders in turn for a few frightful moments then regarded the horses. It seemed to consider its response to this unlikely encounter, then spoke. "Who has intruded into my dwelling?" The words, uttered in their language, sounded unnatural leaving that vile mouth. A sinister laugh followed bellowing, out from somewhere within its bulk.

His jaw quivered as Iridan tried to reply. In the end, he just stood dumbfounded, engulfed in the shadow of the beast. How does a simple soldier respond to this? After the shock of confronting an actual dragon, Iridan had to face the bewildering task of speaking to one. He forced his vision to focus on his companions and found no support in their equally astonished stares. His arms inadvertently wrapped around his stomach. The fingers clutched to his bottom ribs—fingernails burying into flesh—trying to find support or comfort in any way possible.

"Speak!" the creature roared, "or I shall roast your pitiful company where it stands, quivering before my majesty!" The spiked neck dropped the head directly in front of Iridan, red pupils burning—awaiting a response.

"Forgive us," he managed to stammer. "We meant no offense. We were only seeking refuge from the storm. We'll gladly exit your home immediately."

The dragon chuckled. "No doubt you chatter truthfully, were I to chose to grant the opportunity. But, I have yet to arrive at that determination. Tell me, what circumstance found you three out amongst the downpour? Tell me, and perhaps I shall allow you further existence."

Since the albino beast continued to stare at him, Iridan knew he must be the one to reply. He also knew he would need to consider his words carefully. For an unknown reason, the dragon appeared somewhat intrigued by them. The last thing he needed to do was to offend the creature. "We're heading south, towards Jaha." He decided there was no need to lie, at least not at this point. Perhaps the dragon could sense a lie. He had no way to know. Besides, he saw no reason the truth would make any difference. If they were to survive this encounter, their destination likely would not contribute to the beast's decision.

"Jaha, a land of weaklings," laughed the dragon. Iridan gulped in terror. Maybe their destination would be a concern. "Names, quickly, advise me of your designations," the creature continued.

Iridan was startled when Teracuss answered firmly. "I am Teracuss, this is Myrin, and he is Iridan." As with their dealings with the man in white, Iridan sensed Teracuss realized something about handling the dragon he had not perceived.

Iridan thought he noticed a look of satisfaction as the huge head turned towards Teracuss. "Jokk-al Ystren," it, replied, after regarding Teracuss for a moment. "The White Inferno in your language. A fitting name in my estimation," it cackled. "Now tell me the goal of three weak humans' journey to Jaha amidst the tempest. Tell me your complete tale, or I shall unleash my breath—perhaps I shall regardless. Speak. I grow rapidly irritated articulating questions to inferior intellects."

Teracuss answered quickly. "We're looking for a man called Naemon. He's supposed to help us find an artifact that'll save our people."

Jokk-al Ystren brought its snout directly before Teracuss, practically bumping it against the young man's face. Its dark breath blew through his hair like the wind on a sweltering summer day. The dragon whispered, "I have warned you, I grow weary of these questions: What artifact?"

Terror crossed Teracuss' face, but he tried to look defiantly back at the creature. "You're a servant of the Deceiver, and we won't answer you further."

Iridan felt a coldness shoot throughout his body, in anticipation of his pending death. When Jokk-al laughed, Iridan thought he recognized genuine amusement. "I serve no one little human." Iridan flinched as one of the albescent wings extended forward, stretching out its claws.

The wing came up to the dragon's jaw and one talon began to scratch its neck. "Conceivably I exaggerated your weakness. This has been almost a pleasurable diversion. I find my mood to be affable this day. Fortunate for a trio of wayward humans: perhaps only the aftereffects of a large meal. Generosity has always been my supreme weakness," Jokk-al chuckled sarcastically.

"I shall allow you departure," the dragon continued. "I see little meat on you anyway. However, your steeds shall remain. An hors d'oeuvre shall prove pleasant shortly.

"No!" Iridan heard himself yell, "we need our horses. If we lose them, our quest is doomed, and our people will die!"

"I care nothing of your people. Your horses shall stay, or all of you shall stay." Jokk-all sneered then laughed again.

"Please," Teracuss interjected, "I am a servant of the Creator. I wouldn't break an oath. We promise to return the horses to you at the end of our journey." He looked pleadingly at the monster. "You must believe me."

"I must believe nothing. I no longer find your gibberish diverting. It has evolved from merely tiresome to offensive. You have nearly extinguished my generosity. Leave immediately or you shall never leave." The dragon raised its head, and a flicker of flame escaped the snout to tickle the roof of the cave.

Iridan began to grab their supplies when he saw Myrin approach Jokk-al. "You may keep me as a hostage," she said. "They won't trade my life for two horses. Keep me until they come back. You'll lose nothing. As you said, we'd give you little meat, and the horses will be returned."

Jokk-al looked at Myrin with a sign of frustration. Its harsh countenance dissolved, while Iridan and Teracuss stood dumbfounded by Myrin's words. "Another strong human, indeed a rare encounter." The beast considered further, then continued. "I shall allow this."

The two men began to protest the arrangement until the dragon let out a second warning flash of fire. "I shall grant no further debate. The two males and horses: depart immediately, or I will kill you all. I anticipate hunger to grow within me in three days. If your steeds are not returned by my first hunger pang, I shall kill the female. Devouring her petite body shall only remind my stomach of its emptiness, and hunger sparks my anger. I shall then hunt you both down and consume you along with your horses."

With their supplies packed, Iridan and Teracuss approached Myrin. She stood bravely before them then hugged each. "Thank you," Iridan said quietly. Teracuss started to weep as Iridan pulled him away.

They hurried out the cave mouth, much to the relief of their mounts. As they entered daylight, Iridan heard Jokk-al say, "Now female, I pray you prove a better conversationalist than your males."

"I'll try," she replied.

Iridan's stomach felt sick at leaving Myrin in the dragon's lair, but what other choice was available? Ironically, the day which greeted the pair promised to be beautiful. Iridan looked up at a bright blue sky speckled with a few shining clouds. The pure white of the clouds appeared holy after being confronted by Jokk-al Ystren. He regarded Teracuss who appeared equally ill. Without a word, both men mounted their horses and kicked them into a quick trot to continue the journey.

Chapter 18

Teraken collapsed to the floor in a heap as prey falls from a hunter's arrow. Ruy sprung from his seat and followed his king to the wounded man's side. They pulled Teraken off the floor and slumped him into a chair. Jaleph noticed his brother continued to eye him suspiciously; he waved his guards out of the room and returned his attention to Teraken.

When the door rattled closed, Fenik whispered to Jaleph, "I'd like a word with you later."

"We don't have time for that," retorted the king sharply. "Teraken, do you need any bandages or something? Have you seen a healer yet?"

"The wounds I suffer can't be healed by fabric or herbs, majesty. What I witnessed," Teraken paused as his body convulsed in pain—the king wondered how much of the trembling was caused by physical ailments—"I'll never be able to forget it. They're a vile people; we need to slaughter every last one of 'em."

"Get him a drink," Jaleph barked. When he realized only Fenik and Ruy stood in the room with him—looking dumbfounded—he angrily stamped over to the table, snatched his mug and banged it in front of Teraken. Drops of the liquid within splattered into the air then fell upon his wrist. He wanted to command fresh drinks to be brought in to them, but no servants remained. Jaleph felt his nerves about to snap. He needed to refocus his attention. "Tell us what happened," he said, trying to calm his words as best he could.

Instead of obeying, Teraken asked, "Teracuss—any word from them? Have they returned?"

Jaleph refused to respond. He could not. If he had, he knew he only would have started screaming. So he just stood quietly.

"No, nothing," Fenik replied.

Another blow appeared to have struck Teraken's battered body. He attempted to straighten himself then took a long quaff from the cup before him. He clasped his hands together over his lap, and his head dropped; his eyes intently examined his interlocked thumbs. He then began his tale.

"After we left the castle, we marched north for about a day-and-a-half. We ran into a scouting party of three. I figured it was too early to take any prisoners, so we killed them all. We disposed of the bodies then continued on. A few hours later I started to become nervous. I thought we should've heard or seen signs of another group. We flanked west of where I guessed the main army to be, since I had no idea of what we might run into if we continued on our route.

"After awhile we started to hear a humming sound. As it grew louder, we realized we were hearing the noise from a camp. We had found the main army. That wasn't what we wanted to happen. I never really wanted to find it. It'd be hard to fight any skirmishes this close to the main force. I ordered a full stop and had everyone lay quietly. I sent Hakath back and went to investigate. I crept through the trees and brush and after a few minutes reached the tree line. Ahead of me I saw a plain in which camped the entire army.

"The sun had just set, and the area was lit by fires. About a hundred yards from me, I saw a number of figures scurrying about a large dark mass. It looked like they were throwing something on it. I wasn't sure what was happening until it burst in flames. The men backed away as the mound continued to burn.

"Then half-a-dozen robed figures walked up to it. They took positions in a circle about the bonfire. They just stared at it for a number of minutes. I'm not sure how long. Just about when I planned on heading back, they began moving side-to-side. Their swaying slowly increased in speed until their whole bodies were shaking violently. They shook so much it looked like they were making themselves dizzy. A couple even fell to the ground and stood back up—fairly wobbly—to return to their ritual. I then noticed a strange rhythm to their movements, and I realized they were dancing. They danced to the fire.

"Two more cloaked figures approached—one held something like a large stick—and they both started to circle around the dancers. The dancers then began to circle in the opposite direction. The other two stopped, and I thought they were staring at the fire. Suddenly the stick shot forward and struck one of the dancers on the head. He fell to the ground, but it didn't look like he was in pain. A large crowd began to gather, and the other five dancers melted into it. The lone dancer slowly stood up, trembling. He didn't grab at his head where he was struck; the blow seemed of no consequence to him. He turned and faced the two men. Again the pole struck out. It hit him in the stomach, and this time he cried out in pain. The two men pounced on him and started to rip at his skin with their bare hands. The man continued to scream but didn't fight back. Pieces of flesh were hurled into the fire. It was hard to see, but I could tell a pool of blood formed about the three. The crowd stood still. After awhile, I hardly heard his whimpers over the crackling of the fire, and I started to smell his burnt flesh. Finally the two men lifted the mutilated body and tossed it into the flames. Then everyone started screaming.

"They were carrying out some twisted celebration. I couldn't tell exactly what they were doing, and I really didn't want to know. Some danced like the original six. Some were knocked to the ground, others thrown into the air. Of those tossed into the air, some were caught, some hit the ground. Those that couldn't get back up were trampled. A few that had been smothered by the horde were tossed into the fire. Containers of drink were passed all around. A good number apparently had drank previously, and they quickly fell. It was a shameless spectacle. If I had more men, or if more of them were incoherent, I'd have slaughtered the lot.

"I quietly retreated to my men and described the scene. We moved back a few hundred yards further. With this *celebration* happening, I thought the army would've sent out some extra scouting parties. This seemed like a good chance to attack a few. A couple skirmishes could've done a lot to slow them down. The drunken force couldn't possibly send out reinforcements; that orgy of wicked behavior would certainly leave side effects. But, we didn't encounter any soldiers that night, so I ordered my men to get as much rest as possible. They wanted to attack right then, but even if we killed a good number of them and escaped, it really wouldn't't've done much. So, we just waited.

"The next morning was quiet. The camp was obviously recovering from the previous night. We kept our position, so we could see what might develop. So far we had done nothing but kill the three scouts we'd found. After noon, we started to hear some commotion and figured they were beginning to march, and we parallelled their movement. I decided it would be a good chance to encounter a few more scouts. If the army was suffering as much from the aftermath of their party as I thought, we could've done a lot of damage.

"I didn't move too close as we obviously didn't want to attract the bulk of the force. Towards late afternoon though, we hadn't met any of the enemy. We closed in a little, and still nothing happened. I ordered the men to start to make a little noise trying to draw out some reconnaissance. We finally spotted two men searching quietly through some brush. We pursued the pair as they also moved south.

"I don't know how I could've been so stupid, but it was a trap. We stumbled right into it. We had evidently been discovered quite some time before. They acted like they didn't know we were following them and led us into a clearing. When we were right in the middle of it, they turned and faced us. Then we were surrounded. They came from the trees. There must have been a hundred of 'em. I knew we didn't stand a chance in hell of winning this battle, and I called for a retreat. We'd have to fight through a point in their line to break out. They were ready for that tactic though. As we turned to flee, they were on us from all sides. I was the only one who made it through. A couple of the soldiers came after me, but they must've been sick from the night before. I managed to kill them quickly. I knew it was no use to return; I couldn't help my men. So, I made it back here as fast as I could."

Teraken dropped his head into both his mangled hands; his body heaved in huge sobs. Jaleph knew his old friend was tortured by this failure. He could not even die in service of Su'Meeryn.

Jaleph opened the door and called for the guards to take Teraken to the healers. After they departed, he turned and gazed at Fenik. He found no words to say. He wanted to clasp his brother and cry. He wanted to cry for the deaths of the men he had sent out with Teraken. He wanted to cry over the futility of their situation, but no tears came. All he could do was turn to Ruy and ask him to leave.

"Continue with the preparations," Jaleph instructed as Ruy exited the room. "And don't let news of this get out." The two brothers were left staring into each other's eyes. The king wanted to tell Fenik how he felt; he needed some comfort, but he found he could not speak.

"What was going on in here?" Fenik asked.

After a long pause, Jaleph finally managed to respond. "Didn't you just hear what happened? I've got no time to worry about your jealousy. I needed to discuss some things with Ruy, that's all." Jaleph knew his brother was angered for being excluded from the meeting; however, he could find no sympathy for Fenik at this time. Sympathy was one of the few emotions not currently within him.

"I see. And you saw no reason for me to participate."

"Look, I decide who I meet with." Jaleph said sharply, as patience also did not exist for him.

"All right, you just tell me what you want me to do, sire," the prince said sarcastically.

"Get out of here," spat Jaleph. "Get out of here now!"

Fenik whirled and sped out of the room slamming the door behind him. Jaleph dropped back into the chair and stared hopelessly at his father's favorite book.

Chapter 19

The bright sun overhead bore down upon Iridan and Teracuss as they rode away from the hill. The torrent of rain had left the landscape one immense vision of mud. Each hoof the horses raised pulled out from the ooze with the sound of a wine bottle popping open. Teracuss had finally relinquished the lead and rode beside Iridan. Neither spoke, but Iridan knew his companion's thoughts mirrored his own. He felt like a coward leaving Myrin in that cave, but what else could they have done? Fighting the dragon would have equaled suicide. Continuing to argue with the beast would also have brought certain death. And they knew that Myrin's solution allowed their quest to continue, regardless of their chances of success.

They traveled down the path to Jaha through the wasteland of Jokk-al Ystren's domain. The road—if it could still be called that—was now nothing more than a depression in the endless sea of mud and flowed past desolate country ruined by the dragon. Iridan assumed that Jokk-al had destroyed this area in his hunting, with the additional benefit of keeping away unwanted travelers. The beast could easily hunt great distances from its home, so this level of destruction had to be for its defense. There was no cover for miles, so a large group of potential attackers would not be able to sneak up upon it. Although he had no way to know for certain, Iridan imagined the land as once being lavish and fertile before the coming of Jokk-al Ystren.

The dragon must've recently migrated here, Iridan thought, since Su'Meeryn hasn't heard any rumors of it yet. Perhaps the beast—or one of its relatives—had lived there some time in the past. That cave couldn't have been naturally formed.

The one advantage to this vast barrenness was that any movement across the horizon would easily be noticed by the two men. That was indeed the case. As Iridan looked about, he observed a small group of riders shadowing them off to the northwest.

"Iridan?" Teracuss asked.

"Yeah, I see them," answered Iridan. They both knew the man in white and his party continued to follow. "What do you think we should do?"

Teracuss shrugged his shoulders. "Continue to Jaha."

Iridan was not satisfied with that response. "But what if they catch up? What do we do then?"

"I'm sure they can catch up any time they choose. There's nothing we can do about it. We'll just have to proceed with our mission."

Still frustrated, Iridan continued, "Would we have any chance fighting them?" but he figured he knew what Teracuss' response would be.

"No. Let's just keep moving."

Trusting in Teracuss' judgment, Iridan kicked his horse into a gallop.

***

They made camp for the night then traveled the next day without talking. Iridan road as fast as was safe through the mud. Their pace began to quicken as vegetation started to reappear, and they occasionally lost sight of the trailing party. But he always felt aware of their presence.

As the two approached Jaha, they finally lost sight of their pursuers for good. After an hour's time, Iridan had no idea if they were still being followed. When they reached the town's front gate, he began to feel more secure. Of course, they had been confronted by problems within a town before, but Iridan had felt extremely vulnerable out on the open land. Walls have a way of making one feel safe, even if that safety is only imagined.

That security quickly evaporated into despair when he realized that Jaha was not the end of their journey. This was just the beginning of their search. It better not take too long, or we'll never return to Su'Meeryn in time, he thought. Of course, he still did not think one ring could help them, but that issue could be addressed later. The thought of abandoning this hopeless quest and returning to Myrin, seeped again into his thoughts. Nothing wrong with doubt, he told himself, as long as I don't act on it. I need to see this through.

At Jaha's gate, the two men were questioned as to their business within the city. The guards looked upon their haggard appearance with suspicion, and the mention of Naemon did not help. But following a passionate plea by Teracuss, the sentries accepted their request and allowed the pair to enter.

They had trotted a few paces within the city when Iridan noticed a look of agitation on the younger man's face. "I wonder if they're still following us?" Iridan asked.

Teracuss just nodded his head. "Please tell me where I can find Naemon," he asked the first person they saw.

They received vague directions, and after finding a hitch at a guarded stable, they traversed the city streets in the dwindling light. Jaha was a large town that seemed to have suffered from Jokk-al's attacks. Despite its size, only a few people walked the streets. A number of shops they passed had been boarded up; however, the taverns appeared plentifully patroned. They managed to clarify some of the more obscure directions with a couple of the townspeople who were entering one of the bars.

Leaving the business district, they passed many small, but well kept, houses until they came upon the tiny home they hoped was Naemon's. Iridan knocked on the door which had been withered practically into cardboard over years of exposure. After a long uncertain pause, the door slowly opened. As it shook, it appeared that any abrupt movement would cause a collapse of all its fibers.

The man who appeared in the doorway was the antithesis to the antique wood. While he was also ancient, he had aged in sharp contrast to the door. His deep brown skin showed the lines of abundant years, but, unlike the portal, his lines appeared crisp and taut rather than long and gaping. Miraculously, his short curly hair remained jet black. Certainly, he'd had a full head of hair most of his life; however, the hair was dying faster than the man. The man's body was lean and strong. A forest brown tunic hung tightly about his limbs, unlike the door which clung to its hinges by spider webs. His black eyes regarded the two men and followed Teracuss' arm as his hand reached into a pouch. The hand reemerged; within his dirt encrusted fingers the token Korath had given them flickered in the remaining sunlight.

The dark face smiled revealing a row of straight teeth which still sparkled, and he motioned for the pair to enter. The door closed behind them with a shudder, and Iridan gazed about the old man's dwelling. He felt surprised by the appearance of the room. Having only been in one cleric's home previously, Iridan expected to be greeted by the same chaos as within Korath's house. But here, all he saw was a small clean bed, two soft chairs and a wooden stand holding three books. Nowhere did he see the jumble of papers and scrolls like Korath kept.

"Please sit down," Naemon said pulling the chairs out for the two. "What can I do for you?" He sat on the bed and eagerly leaned forward waiting to hear their story.

While Teracuss recited the tale, along with the purpose of their visit, Iridan found himself standing up and walking about the room. He had experienced all of which Teracuss described and found no reason to pay attention.

When Teracuss finally finished, Iridan gasped at Naemon's response: "I can't help you."

Iridan spun around to face the old man. "What do you mean?" he cried. "You... you and the ring are our only hope!"

"I've heard of Korath before," Naemon said softly, "but I never knew of his teachings. I am dismayed." A warm innocent smile crossed his wizened face. "Do you know anything?" he continued while turning to Teracuss. "You're a student. What've you been taught? Have you been taught to trust in objects?"

Naemon walked to his bookstand and grabbed an object sitting next to the texts. "If you really want Naar's ring, I can give it to you." Naemon tossed a small item, and Iridan caught a plain worn ring. He could not identify the metal from which it was composed. No jewels adorned the surface, and no design was visible. "Although I would prefer if you left it with me. I keep it as a memento. I can be quite a nostalgic person. It holds no power, of course; objects have no power."

"Then why did we come here?" blurted Iridan. "We came all this way for nothing? We could've stayed and fought, instead we wasted all this time to find you! Now what? Do we just stay here as our families and friends are butchered? And what of Myrin? We've lost everything!"

"I said that I can't help you. But you are not without hope. Do you truly have no faith?"

"Faith? Faith in what? What good can it do now?" Iridan asked. "I never thought this *mission* was worth our time." His voice turned to a desperate tone. "It appears I was right."

"Perhaps that is why you did come here," said Naemon.

"What do you mean?" Teracuss questioned.

"It's simple. You need to be reeducated. You, my son, do have faith," the old man said looking at Teracuss perceptively, "although it's a little skewed. You must stop looking at things." He snatched the ring from Iridan's grasp and shook it in Teracuss' face. "Look beyond this artifact. Look past *things*, and then you can find your way."

Teracuss and Iridan stood in stunned silence. Iridan could think of nothing to say. All they had gone through appeared for naught. He felt a need to strike out at Naemon, but Teracuss interrupted his violent thoughts.

"I don't see it," Teracuss whispered.

Naemon sighed. "It's all in front of you, yet you're still blind." He then began to explain the most ridiculous idea—even more ridiculous than the search for a magic ring—Iridan believed he had ever heard.

Chapter 20

Jaleph sat down for lunch that afternoon. He ate alone. Fenik was still brooding about for being excluded from the morning's meeting and refused the king's offer to join him. Teraken was having his wounds tended to, and Ruy was out overseeing the preparations. The king was not close to anyone else in his kingdom; he found that to be fairly depressing. It was difficult to eat, but Jaleph knew he would need his strength for the coming days. His knife absently cut at the roasted meat on his plate. After he finally managed to finish all the food before him, he decided to order an additional helping. Would a bit of gluttony make any difference now?

Instead of more food, his servant returned with a message. "Majesty, I have been told that a scouting party has returned with news."

His food dropped to the table and Jaleph stood up. "Excellent. Have them meet me in the audience chamber in half an hour. And no spectators!" The servant turned to leave. "Oh, and you better ask the prince to attend," Jaleph called after him.

The king went to his rooms to wash up while he had a few minutes. He could not recall the last time he had cleaned himself. A basin of water sat on a shelf for who knew how long; it should have been changed daily, but with all the recent upheaval, that task had likely been forgotten. Jaleph reached his hands in and splashed some of the stale liquid on his face. He ran his dripping fingers through his hair and straightened his tunic. Feeling adequately presentable, the king started to head for his door. Instead, the bed groaned as Jaleph fell upon it. He tried to consider how the next hour or so would play out, but nothing came to mind. Without another thought, he pushed himself up from the bed and headed out of the palace towards the meeting hall.

Reaching the base of the building, Jaleph looked up the stairs and watched as the doors swung open. He saw the back of his brother enter into the chamber. Jaleph followed up the steps and walked through the entryway towards his chair. Fenik stood next to the seat looking straight ahead, trying to avoid eye contact. The king turned to acknowledge the handful of men situated before him. Only—to Jaleph's surprise—the group did not consist solely of men. A young woman stood amidst the soldiers. All four appeared soiled and tired. Ripped clothing hung from their thin bodies. They obviously had not found the time to clean themselves after their return. Likely they had quickly grabbed some food and reported as ordered.

The woman bowed to her monarch. "Sire," she addressed.

Jaleph felt perplexed. "I didn't know any women served in our military," he said.

"I'm the only one, sire," she replied. "I was recruited by Ruy about a year ago. He noticed my quickness and strength during some of the games we play. I have bested a number of the men in wrestling matches." Jaleph could tell the memorized response had been used many times in the past by this girl to justify her position.

"I'll have to have a talk with Ruy for keeping this from me. Did you know of this?" Jaleph asked turning to his brother.

"No."

"I assure you, sire," she continued, "I am every bit as able to handle my orders as any man."

"Calm yourself," said Jaleph. "I'm not questioning your abilities. It's only that I should know of these things, so I don't appear the fool when I'm confronted by them." He turned back to Fenik. "Remind me to discuss this with Ruy."

Fenik nodded.

"Now, what's your name?" asked Jaleph.

"Dobrah, sire" she replied, appearing nervous with this casual conversation.

Jaleph found himself intrigued by Dobrah. This was the first surprise he had had in quite some time that did not deal with the impending doom of Su'Meeryn. Dobrah was perhaps twenty years old. Short yellow hair circled her round pleasant face. Hazel eyes darted anxiously between the floor and Jaleph. Her body was thin, appearing boyish. Jaleph was certain that excessive activity and a poor diet contributed to her lack of womanly features; being a scout, she would have been required to move quickly through the wilderness for a number of days.

The king smiled—for the first time in what seemed an eternity—and said, "Please continue, Dobrah."

Her words darkened his almost playful mood. "By the end of today, the army will be one day away," she said. "When they reach here, they likely will rest one day. We don't expect them to attack with tired forces. But within two days, they will strike."

The king practically felt relieved after hearing her words. The uncertainty of when the assault would come had done much to magnify his anxiety. Knowing the day of the attack removed a small weight from Jaleph's shoulders.

"Well there we have it," stated the king. "Make sure Ruy and Teraken are informed. Now that we have a definite time table, perhaps we can use it to our advantage. I want a meeting after tomorrow's breakfast for an update on our status." When nobody moved, he ordered, "Fenik, see to it. You're all dismissed."

As the entire congregation exited the hall, Jaleph's gaze trailed after Dobrah. He realized she was the first woman that he had found interesting since taking the throne. It seemed shameful to entertain such thoughts now, but he could not help himself. Sitting by himself on his throne, he contemplated the possibilities if a miracle would occur and save them. He was about to stand when he realized he had nothing to do. That fact also made him feel guilty. Being the king, he should be engaged in his castle's defense.

He lingered on his throne for about a quarter hour. We're in capable hands, he tried to tell himself as he finally stood. Besides, it's probably better if I stay out of everybody's way.

So, Jaleph, the king, with nothing better to do, exited the chamber and walked back to the palace. He watched his subjects rushing about the streets carrying bundles of arrows, swords or torches. They hardly acknowledged him as he and his guards passed by. The doors of the palace opened as he neared. He walked in with his brain full of thoughts about Dobrah.

✳✳✳

After a couple hours of trying to keep himself busy in his room, one of his guards knocked at the door. The man entered and informed Jaleph that a group of Su'Meeryn's nobility had requested an audience with the king. Normally, this news would have made Jaleph cringe, but today he was actually pleased. He needed some activity to keep himself busy while the others continued with their tasks.

Jaleph left the palace and headed back to the audience chamber. When he entered, he was greeted by a rainbow of bright colors and the glittering of fine jewelry. About twenty of Su'Meeryn's nobles fidgeted about as Jaleph mounted his throne.

When the king was situated, four kaleidoscopic figures advanced from the group. The first was Huffeny, an extraordinarily fat man whose swirls of cosmetics gave him the appearance of a jigsaw puzzle. Huffeny's wealth had been passed down for generations. The genesis of the fortune was no longer remembered—a fact which mattered little—

95

as rumors of multiplying debts grew. Jaleph knew the man was lazy, and most people figured Huffeny would die bankrupt.

Next came Enni; the only man who rivaled Ruy for attention from the ladies of the court. He wore an elegant tailored silver shirt with metallic green pants. Fine golden hair flowed down his back. Dark eyes seemed to invite one's trust. Gossip from his friends said he shaved four times a day to keep any hint of stubble from his beautiful young face. Enni's family possessed royal blood from before the formation of Su'Meeryn. Luckily his father—who was confined to their home due to perpetual sickness—still lived and managed their funds, for Enni was quite stupid.

The third was Gentine, one of the few women in the group. She was old and short with thin gray hair. With each movement, jewels sparkled from a different location on her body. Though occasionally Jaleph found her pleasant, he usually tried to avoid her. Gentine displayed a condescending demeanor whenever she discussed business; everyone who lived in or around the palace knew her as the most ruthless person within the kingdom. Her desire for increased wealth and influence spurred her every scheme and deed.

Yonath trailed the other three. He was one of the few nobles Jaleph actually liked. He was a middle-aged man who had made his wealth by long days of work—through both manual labor and wise investments. A self made noble was scarce within Su'Meeryn's walls. He often called on Jaleph seeking favors to further his enterprises. Despite Yonath's relative pestering, Jaleph appreciated his efforts and enjoyed seeing one of his subjects working hard. Yonath's yellow cloak tussled as he bowed to the king. "Thank you for seeing us, majesty," he greeted.

"It's always a pleasure to meet with Su'Meeryn's leading citizens," Jaleph responded.

"Look, Jaleph," Gentine stated, "we want to know what you're doing about this crisis. The despair on the streets is great."

Enni gasped at the frankness of Gentine's words.

"Please," interjected Yonath, "let's show some respect for our monarch."

"We don't want to just sit back and watch ourselves get slaughtered," Huffeny wheezed.

"Nobody does," said Yonath. He turned to address the king. "We are, the nobles that is, wondering if we can be of assistance with our defense."

"Oh, quit your pandering," snipped Gentine, while examining an exquisite diamond which flickered from her right hand. "Why don't we just be honest with him?"

"Aren't we?" Enni asked.

Gentine slapped the back of Enni's head causing a ruffle in his blonde hair. A hand mirror quickly emerged from his breast pocket, and Enni spent the next few seconds engrossed with recreating his proper appearance.

"What are we going to do?" Huffeny whined. His trembling hands began to stroke the bulging sides of his body.

"We already decided!" Gentine spat.

"You might have decided," Yonath quipped. "But we agreed we needed the king's approval."

"Yeah!" retorted Enni after replacing his mirror.

The group of nobles behind the four began to murmur as the bickering continued.

"Fine, but I don't see what difference it'll produce. This is a decision we can make on our own," said Gentine.

"Yes, but we want to avoid any potential conflicts with the king's plans," retorted Yonath. "Right Enni?"

The young noble stood with his mouth agape.

"What're we waiting for?" Huffeny said, practically stamping his feet. "We have to do something."

Jaleph sat stoically, watching the scene develop before him.

Gentine's hand flicked out. She struck Huffeny's stomach causing a ripple of waves through his rolls of flesh.

"Will you stop that?" Yonath said.

"Yeah!" Enni interjected.

Gentine straightened her garments and addressed Jaleph. "Sire, I meant no disrespect. These days have been awfully trying." Her words camouflaged her malicious tone from just moments before. "We have all decided," she motioned to the group behind, "to send an envoy to the army and try to reach terms. That is, if we are not jeopardizing any of your plans."

Yonath smiled at Gentine.

"I personally have no problems with that," Jaleph replied. "But, you must be aware that we don't believe the army will accept any terms."

"'Terms' is probably the wrong word," Yonath said.

"Correct," Huffeny giggled.

Enni looked between his companions with a bewildered expression, and Jaleph wondered why he had been included in this group.

"Well then, what do you mean?" asked the king.

"To be honest, we're going to try to buy them off," Yonath replied.

"Buy them off?" Jaleph exclaimed.

"We do have a substantial amount of wealth amongst our assembly," said Gentine.

"I'm aware of that," the king replied sarcastically.

"It did seem like a sound idea," Yonath said. "What good is our wealth if we're all dead?"

"Yes," Huffeny snickered.

"I understand, but as I said, we think the army has a different objective," Jaleph offered. "Besides, they can take all of our wealth if the castle falls."

"But they could leave with a substantial amount of wealth without losing one man," Gentine pointed out.

"I don't think it'll work."

"Are you ordering us not to attempt our plan?" Yonath asked.

"No. I just want you to be aware of what you're walking into."

"Fine, but we will try," Gentine responded.

"And how do you plan to make this offer?" questioned Jaleph.

"Since we know you can't spare anyone, we're going to send one representative from our group," Yonath said.

"Who'll that be?" Jaleph looked between the four.

Six eyes turned, and Jaleph immediately knew why Enni stood before him. The handsome noble arched his back in an attempt to give himself a stately appearance. Jaleph turned a disapproving glare towards Yonath, who lowered guilty eyes to the floor.

***

Later that evening, Jaleph stood at the window in his room and watched the sun set. He wondered if he would see another. If so, he likely would not enjoy it as a free man. Perhaps the approaching army would not kill him right away. He might be kept alive to quench the enemy's thirst for perverse sport, before having his mutilated body burned in a sacrificial fire. Light flowed through the window like a stream of blood, the blood of his people.

He imagined the coming battle:

The troops stand on the hill surrounding the plateau of his kingdom. The soldiers hesitate for a moment as if in anticipation of the coming slaughter. The pause is as the calm preceding the strike of a violent thunderstorm. Horses stammer and swords rattle in scabbards signaling the gathering of the clouds. The vanguard of the army descends like the first few drops of rain; the start of the rainfall seems innocent enough until that first strike of lightning. The full force of the storm is holding back, waiting for the optimum moment to erupt. Horns blow; a crash of thunder. The tempest explodes as the troops plunge down the hill. Vegetation is swept away by the hooves of the downpour.

Jaleph shook himself out of his musings and spun from the window. He walked to the bed, flopped down and breathed a heavy sigh. He was a failure. He had not prepared Su'Meeryn for a war; he had never imagined that this could happen. He had been wrong, and all his people would die because of his mistake. He considered the decisions he made after Iridan had first brought the word. It seemed all those decisions had been wrong too. In retrospect, he still saw no other alternatives. That, perhaps, was the most depressing thought. That compounded his feelings of incompetence.

And now, what of Dobrah? His brother had been after him for some time to marry. He finally had met someone who intrigued him, but it was too late. He wondered why he found himself attracted to the scout. She would not be considered beautiful, especially in comparison to many of the noble's daughters to whom he had been introduced. Maybe the fact that she had not been offered to him increased his infatuation. A strength emanated from her. He stopped wondering why these feelings had emerged and considered the thought that he had finally discovered his queen. But the possibilities of that future, of a wife and a family, only added to all that he stood to lose.

Jaleph considered surrender, but that would likely accomplish nothing. As Ruy had pointed out, fleeing would not save anyone, so why should surrender? The inhabitants of Su'Meeryn were the threat to the army, not the castle. If they surrendered, the army would just slaughter all his people anyway. Jaleph saw no alternative but to continue with the preparations to defend his land. He did not know what good it would do. He tried to cling to the last feeble hope of Iridan and Teracuss returning with the ring and somehow figuring out how to unlock its power. If it held any power at all.

Chapter 21

"You're crazy!" objected Iridan. "That'll just get us killed." He turned to Teracuss, "Let's go."

"Wait," Teracuss replied, "I know it sounds like suicide, but do you have a better idea?"

"Any idea is better than that."

"Even if that were so," interjected Naemon, "what else can accomplish your people's deliverance? It seems you have two choices: you can take the safe route and walk away. If you do, you turn your people over to death. Choose the other route, and one of you will certainly die. But it's not suicide; it's a sacrifice, the ultimate sacrifice. You had a mission to try to save your home. You came to me for an answer, and I have given you one. It's not the one you expected, but it can accomplish the same end.

"It is your decision, not mine. I've done what I can for you. This isn't magic. You must grasp the opportunity which the Creator has given you."

Iridan had had enough with this gibberish about faith and the Creator. He had never once seen any sign of supernatural existence. Besides, what did that have to do with this ridiculous plan anyway? Jaleph had wanted him to seek the ring. Only his obedience to his king had brought him this far; he saw no reason to follow the foolish ravings of another senile prophet.

"I'm sick of this," Iridan spat at the other two. "You're a religious fanatic asking us to kill ourselves with your insane plan," he pointed a stiff finger at Naemon. "What do you care? We'll be slaughtered, and by tomorrow, you'll probably have forgotten that we were ever here.

"And you," he spun at Teracuss, "you're so pathetic you believe anything these idiots tell you. The Creator, the Creator," he mocked in a whining voice, "I'm sick of it." He wanted to continue, but his enraged brain could not form his racing thoughts into additional cohesive words. Instead, he stood before them, his red face panting, turning between the two.

Teracuss stared back. His fingers pulsed like a cobra rocking to-and-fro, preparing to strike at any moment, as his fists opened and closed.

Naemon, on the other hand, softened his gaze and let out a quiet laugh. "I see," he said. "You can't be more than you are. You're not ready for that step right now. A pity. But, I have nothing to add."

"We have to try," Teracuss stated bluntly. "I'll go through with it."

"No we won't," Iridan ordered. He had made his decision. Su'Meeryn was destroyed; there was nothing he could do about that now. A leader needs to decide when the mission is hopeless. His responsibility had changed to saving the lives of those under him. "We go back and get Myrin—then we leave. I will not allow you to risk her life."

"You don't command me," Teracuss hissed.

"We've had this conversation before. I lead this mission. You will do as I say!"

"If you're giving up on the mission, you no longer lead. I'll not listen to you anymore." Teracuss paused, and then added under his breath, "Coward."

Before Iridan was able to leap at Teracuss, Naemon pushed his way between them. He managed to deflect Iridan's fist and it struck Teracuss' wounded shoulder. Teracuss winced in pain then lashed back.

After they traded a few punches, Naemon managed to separate the combatants. "Due to the considerable pressure you two are under, I understand this outburst," the old man said calmly. "Unfortunately, this doesn't accomplish anything."

Just then the door swung open. They all turned, and before them—in the middle of the venerable portal frame—stood the man in white. A cruel, almost ridiculous smile, crossed his face. His henchman took their usual position at his back.

The strange man walked in and laughed. "The culmination of your journey: what a pity. All this way and nothing to show for it." He laughed again and turned to Naemon. "Now, give me the ring old man."

Naemon took his turn in laughter. "So, you've finally tracked me down. Found these two and followed them to me. How clever. I bow before your genius." The old prophet, with a sarcastic grin, bent slightly at his waist in front of the handsome man.

"How I came here matters little," the other retorted, and he took a few steps into the room. For the first time Iridan sensed some uncertainty in his voice. "I am here, and I will leave with the ring."

"You're still seeking it," Naemon chuckled. "Your master holds to a false hope. As I explained to these two, there is no power in a circle of metal. I would think you and your master were smart enough to understand that!"

"Enough! Give me the ring, or you all die!" With that, his three followers also entered the room.

Iridan's head spun at the confrontation. All he wanted to do was get out and try to save Myrin from Jokk-al, but he would not allow the man in white to harass Naemon. For the first time he was able to clearly see sinister motives from the man and wondered now how he had missed them before. Since the man in white had just threatened his life, he really found he had no alternative. He drew his sword, and Teracuss moved up beside Naemon.

"No violence," the old man said. "If he wants a powerless object, he's welcome to it."

"Never!" interjected Teracuss. "It may be powerless, but that doesn't mean it's valueless. It's an artifact, a remembrance of a forgotten age. It will not sit on his corrupted finger."

The smile on the man in white's face grew as his left arm rose. A bright aura grew from about his body. It threatened to dazzle the room with its brilliance, but then it started to transform. At first the change was almost imperceptible, but slowly Iridan began to see that the light was withering into darkness. Then the man's features began to alter. His clothes became tattered, and his face mirrored that of his pale follower. This new appearance was so plain to see that Iridan wondered how he had kept it masked. The hand on the raised arm began to tremble, and a bolt of black light leapt forth and struck Teracuss full in the chest. Teracuss' body flew backwards across the room. His back struck the rear wall, and he fell to the floor in a heap.

Iridan sprung at the transformed man, but the red warrior blocked his path. Their swords met with a crack which echoed through the hushed room. Iridan was an excellent swordsman, but after a few seconds of engagement, he knew he would be beaten by the huge man, if indeed a man occupied that crimson armor. There were no eyes to look into, no face to try to read; only the red helmet met his gaze. He eventually discerned that his opponent was not trying to kill him; he was just being kept occupied. The real confrontation was between Naemon and the red warrior's leader. Iridan tried to concentrate on their conversation.

"Killing me accomplishes nothing," Naemon was saying.

"That might be so, but it will be extremely enjoyable."

"You'll never win. No matter what happens here, your ultimate goal will never be accomplished. Your master's finality will be without victory," retorted Naemon.

Eventually Iridan disengaged from the red warrior. His opponent did not advance but moved back beside the other two. Iridan rushed to Teracuss' side and saw that he still lived. He helped Teracuss up and turned back to watch Naemon.

"You are a fool," the man in white sneered; he had regained the appearance of when Iridan had first seen him. "You will be destroyed along with all the other little minions."

Teracuss stirred and regained his composure. His quivering hands searched across his body. Then he surprised Iridan when he drew his sword and advanced towards the party.

The red warrior moved forward but paused when Teracuss did not confront the man in white, who continued to debate Naemon over some sort of apocalyptic conclusion to humanity. They both seemed oblivious to any other activity in the room. Teracuss stopped before the scarlet form. He stood staring at the motionless figure then slowly pushed his sword through the midsection of the mail. The blade passed through the metal as if it was slicing through a hunk of butter. The armor collapsed to the ground with a hollow ring.

All eyes immediately turned to Teracuss. The black garbed henchman pulled out his sword—revealing it too was indeed black—and advanced. Teracuss turned and lunged forward; his sword pierced the leather clad torso. His adversary turned limp and flowed to the ground.

The man in white again transformed into the appearance of his remaining follower and advanced on Teracuss. "Now you die," he sneered through clenched teeth.

Faster than Iridan thought possible, Naemon darted between the two. The obsidian light continued to expand about the man in white until it virtually enveloped his entire face, then the darkness blasted forth from his eyes and mouth. The trio of beams struck Naemon's body; however, he did not move. The cleric just stood still, glaring at his enemy. Naemon's face was barely visible through the ebony rays that continued to pour towards him, but Iridan managed to see a smile forming. Though he was not sure, Iridan thought he saw the black shafts reflecting off Naemon, back towards their source. It appeared the man in white was striving to disengage his attack; his body jerked backwards in violent convulsions, but the aura continued to flow between the two.

Iridan noticed Teracuss move behind the man in white. His sword rose, and the vile light reflected off the steel; it cast a shadow about the room wherever the reflection landed. With both hands Teracuss plunged his weapon deep into the back of their opponent.

Black light exploded in all directions as the body seemed to be energized by the now unfocused rays. The man in white rose in the air and shook in rhythm with the bolts of blackness spurting from his face and the wound. The body lowered as the power of the rays diminished, and then it dropped to the ground and lay still. An evil howl rose from the corpse and seemed to circle the room, searching for an exit. It stopped at the closed door and hovered for a few agonizing seconds. Iridan covered his ears trying to shut out the corrupt bellow. He thought the sound would explode in his head, but the noise ultimately trailed off as it passed through the door's porous fibers and left the building. Iridan turned and gaped at the body; several last flickers of energy escaped from the man in white until he lay completely still. Strangely, no blood had been spilled.

Iridan's attention shifted to the pale follower who had been forgotten during the conflict. The bizarre man gazed at the forms of his three comrades, lifeless across the floor. A grotesque smirk emerged on his face. He seemed to have enjoyed the spectacle, relishing the deaths of his associates, as if death and he were close friends. His slight body moved towards the man in white. He knelt down and brought his face close to his leader's. His head turned and looked at Iridan; the same twisted grin still remained. Iridan thought he was going to kiss the corpse, but what occurred caused bile to rise in Iridan's throat. The man bit into a cheek and ripped off a piece of flesh. He stood up with the hunk of skin still in his mouth. The hollow eyes continued staring at Iridan; the mouth still smiled as it chewed and swallowed. Then the man, who appeared to be as equally dead as the bodies on the ground, left the building.

The room was still now except for a quiet wheezing coming from Naemon who had collapsed to the floor. Iridan joined Teracuss at the old man's side and watched as Naemon gasped for his last few breaths. "There's nothing left in me," Naemon whispered. "I've used the last of my strength. My time is done." His eyes moved between the two like an ancient pendulum. "Don't give up your quest. It can still be accomplished."

Then Naemon died.

When Iridan looked up, Teracuss met his gaze. "We must continue," the younger man said.

Iridan gaped at Naemon. The events of the battle whirled about his head. He could not make sense out of what had just occurred. It all seemed surreal. If he had not been there, he never could have believed what had happened. Had Naemon sacrificed himself for them? He wondered whether he would ever know the answer to that question.

No argument remained in Iridan. How could it? He consented and they prepared to leave.

Chapter 22

The sun used the multiple number of clouds like a step ladder as it climbed to its zenith. The pinnacle of its existence was shrouded in mystery by cumulus layers. A few beams broke through the cover like the reflection of divinity further above. The sun's rays shot down to the top of the ridge circling a couple hundred yards from Su'Meeryn's castle. The light bathed the forefront of the army which had just reached that spot. Their horses stamped about as if they realized that they had finally reached their destination. The riders waved swords above their heads. The cries of the men trickled down, barely audible, to the castle walls below. Within minutes, the bulk of the horde swarmed up to the ridge top; the beams of light from the concealed sun flickered about the mass. The rays traveled to different spots like a roving spotlight as the clouds moved in the wind, revealing different openings for the sun to penetrate.

Atop the castle wall, Jaleph, Su'Meeryn's king, looked out at the forming army. Alongside Jaleph stood his brother, the Prince Fenik; Teraken, the long time leader of Su'Meeryn's army; the warrior Ruy and Ruy's future wife Dirwyn.

"Well, this is it," breathed Fenik. "They're finally here, and no sign of Iridan and Teracuss."

Jaleph turned to Teraken and saw the large man flinch at those words. It appeared he would never see his son again.

The five onlookers watched as the castle gate opened and a small group exited. All but one walked. Riding a magnificently adorned stallion, Jaleph recognized the long, golden hair of Enni. One of the other nobles checked the straps of a small case resting atop the horse. Though Jaleph could not see the imbecilic man's expression, he knew Enni did not understand the fate that awaited him. The group waved as the handsome man rode off. Jaleph shook his head in disgust; disgust at those who had convinced a simple mind to embark on this fruitless endeavor.

"What a shame," Dirwyn said as she turned away from the wall.

"They'll engage tomorrow," Ruy stated emotionlessly, completely ignoring the scene below them. It seemed he cared little for Enni, or what the morrow would bring. But Jaleph knew better.

"Is everything ready?" the king asked to no one in particular.

"We're as prepared as possible," Fenik responded, "but you know, of course, it won't be enough."

Teraken spat over the wall. "We all know that Fenik. We don't need you to remind us."

"I'm just trying to be honest about the situation," Fenik retorted harshly.

"Thanks for your candor," Teraken snapped back, "but I think we can do without it!"

"Yeah, well, there's no point disillusioning ourselves. We might as well be prepared for the outcome."

"That's enough. If we are going to die tomorrow, I don't want us at each other's throats today," Jaleph ordered.

"How are the people managing?" the king continued as he looked about at his friends. Dirwyn held herself close to Ruy. Jaleph ached to have someone to comfort during this crisis, someone to comfort him. He thought of Dobrah, and wished for that possibility.

"Better than expected," Ruy replied. "We sent some of the women and children off during the night. The battle should distract the army from pursuit. At least some should survive. That's given many of those who remain reason enough to fight."

"Why us?" Dirwyn asked. "I wonder, why do they want to attack us?" Her eyes peered out at the army on the ridge. Jaleph saw hate building up within her. The only thing to stop her from marrying the man she loved was that army.

When Ruy did not respond, Teraken finally answered. "We're just in their way. They have some other goal, and it would seem that they just need to eliminate us. They really don't give a damn about Su'Meeryn. They probably wish that we're not even here."

"Well, that's a big help," Fenik said derisively, wanting to return the favor to Teraken.

Before Teraken could respond back, Jaleph yelled, "I said that's enough! We're all on edge, but I'm not going to allow us to start killing each other before that army even gets here. From now on, we're all encouraging. If our people are discouraged, they'll fight poorly. Do you all understand?"

His four companions nodded their heads quietly. "Good! Now I want you all to get out of here and raise the morale of our troops."

They all started to leave. "Ruy, wait." Jaleph called. "I want to talk to you." Ruy turned and walked back to the king. Fenik also turned with an angry look. Jaleph started to get mad, but it quickly died away.

"Wait for me at the stairs," he said to his brother. "I want to talk to you too."

Ruy stood silently before his king as Fenik left. He rarely started a conversation.

Jaleph awkwardly considered his next few words. He felt he was acting selfishly, but he needed to do this. "Do you know Dobrah?" he asked after a short silence.

Ruy nodded.

Jaleph's head turned to his left, and he winced as he tried to control his anger. He wanted to slap Ruy. "Why don't you talk?" He finally asked the question which had troubled him for so long.

"I say what I need to say," Ruy replied completely unmoved by Jaleph's perplexity.

The handsome face stared back at Jaleph, impossible to read. He must be a great gambler, Jaleph thought. He considered Ruy's words. If Ruy did not want to talk, or felt uncomfortable when he did talk, Jaleph could not allow that to bother him. "Very well. Look, tell me what you know about her."

"She's a good fighter."

"Yes, I imagine so, but that's not what I meant, and I'm sure you know that." He sighed. "I met her, and, well... is she married?"

"Not that I know of."

"Good," Jaleph said. That was the first pleasant news he had heard in a long time. Not that it would likely matter. He felt a smile reach his face. That seemed out of place with all that was happening, but he could not help himself. "Let's go." He placed his arm about Ruy's shoulder and led him towards the stairs and Fenik. "You know what you need to do. Get the men ready for tomorrow." After a pause he continued, "And the women." He had never considered women in his army. It was a new thought, which he found hard to get used to.

When they reached the stairs, Ruy headed down. Jaleph stopped and looked at his brother. Fenik still seemed hurt, like he had been neglected, and Jaleph did not want to die with anger between them. "Look Fenik," he said, "there are just some things I need to talk about with different people. I sometimes need a different perspective. I am the king and need to consider the good of Su'Meeryn before I can worry about anything else."

Fenik's look slowly softened. "I'm sorry," he said. "It's just that—"

"I know," the king interrupted, aware that their circumstances were weighing on everyone in Su'Meeryn, not just him. They started down the stairs, and Jaleph playfully tussled his brother's hair.

About halfway down, Jaleph stopped. "There's one more thing."

"What?"

Jaleph again felt uncomfortable, but he resolved himself to speak the words. He might never have the opportunity again. "I love you brother," he said in a quivering voice.

Fenik's head bowed then looked back up with a tear trickling down his cheek. "I love you too Jaleph."

They looked awkwardly at each other. "My king," Fenik continued lightheartedly, and he softly punched Jaleph on the shoulder.

When they reached the bottom of the stairs, Jaleph put his arm about his brother's shoulder. "Meet me for dinner tonight."

Fenik nodded and continued on his way. Jaleph sighed and climbed back up to the top of the castle wall. He leaned across the edge and peered out at the opposing army. The troops milled about, setting up camp for the night. Despite Teraken's story of their vile ceremony, they appeared to be ordinary men. He wondered if the enemy's army also contained women. He had prepared himself for fighting and killing men, but what would he do if he faced a woman attacking him?

He thought of Dobrah. How would she do in the combat? Ruy had said she was a good fighter. An ache blossomed in Jaleph's head, and he cursed himself. He could not worry about these things.

In the sky, dark clouds now formed under the hidden sun. Unfortunately they were not storm clouds. Perhaps the morning will reveal darker, more ominous ones. Jaleph longed for a storm to slow or perhaps delay the attack, but that was not likely. I guess that would ruin some of our defenses though, he thought. Through the ashen haze a hole of deep blue opened in the sky. It traveled towards where the sun remained shrouded. When it reached that spot, a single ray of light shot forth. It struck the bottom of the ridge. Jaleph wondered if an omen could be discerned from that vision. Then the crack in the wall of clouds closed. He could spot no opening in that covering of whites and grays. It seemed that the sun wanted to hide itself, obscure its vision of the plain below—where Su'Meeryn's castle stood—as if the sun itself could not bear to watch the coming slaughter.

Chapter 23

Iridan and Teracuss stood about the strewn corpses and surveyed the scene. The four bodies lay at various angles upon the ground. The man in white and his two followers seemed to almost form an arrow pointing at Naemon.

Whether they had participated in an actual combat, Iridan could not decide. Despite the sword blows and the ripped-off cheek, no blood carpeted the floor; no moans sounded from dying throats. He glanced down at his sword dangling from his right hand; it hung uselessly, scratching the ground. He felt like they had just won a battle in which he had done nothing to help.

His pondering was interrupted by Teracuss. "What do you think we should do?" the younger man asked.

Without hesitation, Iridan responded, "I think we should get out of here before anybody comes by. This would be rather hard to explain."

Teracuss' head dropped and looked sadly at Naemon. This loss affected him more than Iridan had expected. While it was unfortunate the old man had died, they hardly knew him. After all, they had only just met Naemon a few minutes prior. Iridan figured something more than just Naemon's death was troubling Teracuss.

"He should get a decent burial," Teracuss murmured.

"We don't have time. We don't know if somebody heard any of this. I can imagine what would happen if sentries found us here."

Teracuss nodded in agreement. Besides, with the decision made to continue with their mission, no tarrying could be tolerated, for any reason. Su'Meeryn's time was running out.

Before leaving, Teracuss stopped and began searching about the floor. "What now?" Iridan asked feeling annoyed at the delay, wondering what had distracted Teracuss.

After a few additional moments, Teracuss stooped down and grabbed something off the ground. He stood back up and with a slight smile displayed the ring of Naar to Iridan. During the confusion Iridan had unknowingly dropped it. No light reflected off the dull metal as it twisted in Teracuss' hand. He slipped it on a finger, looked back again at Naemon then opened the door.

"We came all this way," Teracuss said. "We should at least leave with the ring." With slumped shoulders he followed Iridan out of the now uninhabited home.

Once on the street, Iridan realized that the sounds of the struggle had, surprisingly, not escaped the house. A number of people moved about the area, carrying merchandise for a shop or running an errand for a wealthy merchant, oblivious to the pair. Rather than tempting their good fortune by making a stop to pick up additional food, it seemed best to leave Jaha immediately. The two flowed behind a larger party moving past Naemon's home and headed down the dirty street. They found their horses still tied to the post where they had been left. They mounted quickly and sped out of the city as inconspicuously as possible.

After a few wrong turns, they made it to the town gate. The guards let them pass without incident, and they headed north. Iridan found himself continuing to look about for signs of the man in white and his companions. He supposed it was still possible that the pale follower might be pursuing them, but he decided that they had seen the last of that bizarre quartet.

Chapter 24

Jaleph sat in his room with his sword across his lap. Sparks fell to the floor as he distractedly sharpened the blade while staring out a nearby window. Clouds hid the stars and moon leaving only a black sky. His hands ran down the blade he had inherited—along with the kingdom—after his father's death.

Undoubtedly the army would begin moving prior to dawn, hoping to gain significant ground towards the castle before becoming easy targets for Su'Meeryn's archers. Jaleph knew he needed to be well-rested for the morning's conflict, but sleep would not be easily achieved this night.

The sword clattered to the floor as Jaleph dropped to his bed, but his mind was too consumed to allow for relaxation. He tried to divert himself by thinking of his childhood. He thought of Halet and a young Fenik. His mother, who had died shortly after Fenik's birth, was only a blurry image. Occasionally Jaleph thought he could recall a brief vision of her, but he did not know if it was a true memory or just imagining. He remembered his father putting kingly duties aside to play with his two small boys. They would run about the palace grounds, throwing balls between themselves, oblivious to the concerns of the forming kingdom.

Now with the likely outcome of the impending battle, Jaleph found himself yearning to forge similar memories with a family of his own. He had always known the importance of having children for the continuation of Su'Meeryn's royal line, but it never seemed like an immediate concern. How short-sighted he had been. He began to wonder what was worse: his mother's fate of not being able to see her children grow, or to never even have children. While his mother had been able to hold Fenik only briefly, she had at least raised Jaleph for a few short years and experienced the joy of cradling him to her chest and holding his small hand.

With death pinpointed for Jaleph in just a matter of hours, he would never experience that joy for himself. It is a terrible encumbrance to know the time of one's death. The future is decided. Dreams and plans have no bearing. The only thing to grasp hold of is memories. But memories are riddled with failures and shortcomings. The unknown future is not burdened by such frailty. The future can be shaped in an attempt to formulate one's dreams into reality. While success is not guaranteed, failure is not either. The possibilities of Jaleph's future had been ripped away from him, leaving behind only a short lifetime of memories. And those memories did not leave Jaleph with much he felt proud of. He pondered over his accomplishments, but he could not recall many. He wondered if that was the saddest epitaph to his life.

A tear began to crawl down his cheek. What a pity that the life of Su'Meeryn would be terminated shortly. He felt sorrow for his brother whose predicament mirrored his own. A few more tears began to run from his eyes. Slowly, however, Fenik left his mind and the only thought that remained was of the family he never had. He never would be able to hold his own children and watch them grow, never be able to cling to his wife late at night. Teraken had had that opportunity, and it had cost him much. After coming to terms with the loss of his wife, Jaleph knew Teraken would never trade the memories of his son to replace the pain of his probable death. He wondered over those who chose to have no family, like Korath, and had never regretted it.

Dobrah's face came again to his mind. The real reason he had not yet started a family was that he had never met a woman who sparked interest within him, though he must admit, he never had spent much time looking for his queen. But then he met Dobrah: a skinny girl in tattered clothes with ripped and dirty flesh. What a strange time to fall in love. It seemed to be a nasty trick played on him by fate. When the potential for his future looked its brightest, it was about to be cut short.

The tears flowed more steadily now. His body heaved with sobs. He cried uncontrollably for quite some time until he finally— unknowingly—fell asleep.

Chapter 25

The pair rode back through the wastelands kicking up the dust of the now dried soil. Neither spoke. Above their heads, a mass of gray clouds began to move down from the north slowly engulfing the blue sky. The clouds peered down at the two horsemen who—upon their exhausted horses—looked like a couple of lost mutant insects; an easy target for any flying predator. The heat of the day continued to rise, and the pair stopped a few times to pour some water down their steed's throats from their wineskins.

Iridan's thoughts remained filled with the events which had occurred in Naemon's home. His exhausted mind tried to make sense of what had happened. But no matter how hard he tried, he just could not reach an adequate conclusion to explain it to himself. In a grudging voice, he finally asked his companion, "Do you want to tell me what happened back there? How did you kill those two so easily?"

Teracuss took a deep breath. "I didn't actually kill anybody," he replied. "The bodies our adversaries occupied were already dead."

At this new, mystic revelation regarding the man in white and his party, Iridan again felt exasperated. "What the hell are you talking about? How could they have been dead? They followed us all the way to Jaha."

"You still don't understand," Teracuss responded calmly. "You saw what happened." He raised one of the wineskins and took a gulp, then wiped some sweat from his forehead with his wrist. "I'd be interested if you could enlighten me."

And, of course, Iridan could not. The thought of spirits inhabiting dead bodies could not be formulated into his view of the world. "What I saw is that red warrior could have killed me anytime. Yet you just walked up and stabbed him. No fight."

"The difference was that you engaged him. You offered him the opportunity to fight. I didn't."

Iridan's head still swirled trying to understand what had happened; since he could not explain it himself, he decided to further investigate Teracuss' perspective. "So why didn't he kill me?"

"I suppose his leader wanted us alive. He probably hoped that if Naemon was dead, one of us still might hand the ring over to him. I guess it wouldn't have mattered anyway, with what I now know of Naar's ring. But in the end, he would have tried to kill us."

"But how did you kill them so easily?" Iridan asked, still confused.

"I just dispatched them, struck them down. Their spirits were vanquished from those bodies. They're not dead, at least not in the sense you're thinking."

Iridan decided he really did not want to know how that could be possible. But, with all he had witnessed, he could not doubt it was feasible. "Well, if they're not *dead*, are we done with them? Or will they return? Will they still come looking for the ring?"

His companion glanced down at the artifact sitting about his finger. "Yes, I believe they will. But not right away. They'll need to answer to their master first. I guess he'll supply them some new bodies, and they'll be back. But I think we'll be safe, for a while."

Teracuss' replies, however, still left Iridan with doubts. "If you know all this, why didn't you do something while we were traveling to Jaha? Now, all of a sudden you're an expert on spirits inhabiting dead bodies."

"I didn't understand the situation fully until they entered the house," Teracuss explained. "Like Naemon said, my knowledge was skewed when we found him, but now I think I truly understand."

"Understand what?"

"Everything. The ring, the man in white, the threat to our home. What seemed as a task to save Su'Meeryn from the army, I now see as much more than just that. We need—"

"I really don't give a damn about whatever else you think we need!" Iridan interrupted. "Saving Su'Meeryn is the only reason we left on this trip!"

They continued to ride silently as Iridan considered his companion's words. He could not help but think that perhaps Teracuss was correct. Teracuss had proved him wrong before, and Iridan felt as if all his conceptions of the world were crumbling around him. Then another thought struck Iridan. "What about that fourth man? Why didn't he fight us?"

Teracuss considered for a moment. "It took me a while to figure that one out." He answered more calmly than Iridan expected after being interrupted. "If I am correct, he doesn't fight. He is Death. His task is to deal with the aftermath; that is when his service to the Deceiver is needed. I don't know what that service entails, but I suppose you can imagine if you want to. I have no desire to ponder that."

Still not fully satisfied with this information, Iridan continued, "What about those brigands in the clearing and that man in the bar? Even though they didn't attack the man in white, his grouped killed all of them. How can that be if what you're telling me is true?"

After a heavy sigh, Teracuss answered. "Look, I don't have all the answers. I studied under Korath a long time, but his teachings appear to have been faulty. He and I will need to have a talk when we get back." Teracuss stopped at that moment, and Iridan knew what he was thinking. If their plan was carried out, one of them would soon be dead. Teracuss might not have the opportunity to talk to his old teacher.

"Anyway," Teracuss continued, "I guess it could have something to do with those men's actions. The brigands were trying to kill Myrin and us. And the man in the bar, well, maybe his goal was to kill us too." Teracuss paused; apparently he felt he might be rambling. "What I'm trying to say is that I think it involved a combination of their motivations and their actions."

Iridan thought he was following Teracuss' reasoning, but another question remained. "What about Naemon? That man killed him fairly easily."

"What you think you saw is probably not what actually happened. The man was not really interested in us. What he wanted was the ring. Naemon was his real threat and kept him occupied until I could strike him down. If the man hadn't been battling Naemon, he might have been able to kill me.

"I don't know why Naemon died. It looked like he was able to withstand the assault easily enough. But he was an old man. Maybe his life was completed at the end of the confrontation. Anyway, that is still somewhat of a mystery to me."

Iridan felt uncomfortable with the discussion of Naemon. The thought of the old man sacrificing himself to save two strangers laid a large amount of guilt on him. His head dropped, and he watched as his horse's hooves continued to kick up the dirt from the wrecked trail.

Their pace had slowed during the conversation. Since the horses were getting some rest he figured they could now make up some time. But before he spurred his steed, more troubling thoughts came to him. Soon they would reach Jokk-al's lair, and their plan left open every possibility that both men, and Myrin, would be dead shortly. To take his mind off those two unpleasant thoughts, he asked the final question, the one which had gnawed at him since they left Su'Meeryn:

"Why do you hate me?"

Chapter 26

One of the servants woke the king an hour before sunrise. Jaleph had no idea of how much sleep he had been able to manage. He figured it did not matter. Come the evening, his torn body would likely feed one of the enemy's fires.

After quickly shaving, he stood before his wardrobe looking for his most regal outfit. Might as well die looking important, he thought. He chose a deep blue tunic with bright yellow edges, donned a shining silver breast plate, and a polished helmet with maroon fringes to cover his head. Over the rest of his adornments, Jaleph wrapped an indigo cape, and tied it about his neck. He then grabbed his headband and polished the emerald stone against his sleeve. Jaleph stared at it for a few moments before tying it around his neck. If his life was to end shortly, he wanted to look the part of a king, even if he lacked a good king's abilities. He refused to dress as a common soldier, despite the fact that, in this garb, he would be an easy target.

A breakfast platter came to his door, but Jaleph could find no appetite. He tried to force a biscuit and a few grapes down his throat, but his stomach was in too many knots. The king quickly decided to end his meal and left the plate atop a small table—figuring a group of fortunate bugs would indulge in the feast. His hands trembled slightly as they grasped his scabbard and fastened it about his waist. He sighed deeply while looking about. His eyes took in every inch of the room, hoping this would not be the last time they would do so. Slowly his feet turned and carried him away.

He tramped out to the courtyard which was still shrouded in the darkness of night. The absence of light allowed him anonymity as he walked back towards the castle wall. Many of his troops already were moving about. He wondered if any of them had managed much sleep. They rushed to their positions or finished some last second preparations.

He reached the steps which he had descended just a few hours before; Jaleph felt that it had only been minutes. The stairway was empty. The king climbed the stones and stood atop the wall, alone.

The sky began to show the first glimmers of light as Jaleph leaned against the battlements. The top of the plateau remained invisible to his eyes. Time seemed to flow faster than possible as the radiance of the rising sun grew. Jaleph continued to stare out where he knew the army had begun to stir—if they were not already moving. He looked up and saw a number of clouds with a pink glow beginning to expand.

Finally, Jaleph managed to peer through the morning gloom and observe the host. At that moment, a call sounded from about him. Lookouts on the wall had spotted the same vision. The crimson prelude to the still hidden sun revealed streams of troops flowing down the plateau into the valley. The swords and armor of the advancing horde reflected the scarlet light like a premonition of the blood shortly to be spilled. Down below, Jaleph could see the front line already racing through the valley, like a horde of ants rushing from their hill to engulf their helpless prey.

The trumpets continued to sound from both sides of the king. An answer blared from behind him. The entire castle echoed with the call. The enemy was moving.

It had begun.

Chapter 27

Teracuss grinned sarcastically. "I was wondering when we were going to come to this," he muttered.

"Yeah, well, now we have, and I'd like to know what I ever did to you," demanded Iridan. The question had confused him since before they left Su'Meeryn. Through all they had suffered, Iridan figured their relationship had softened somewhat. Perhaps Teracuss could now discuss his loathing more openly with him. Whatever the case, Iridan wanted to discover the truth before they faced Jokk-al.

Teracuss was silent, and Iridan saw that a deep hurt sat within the other's soul. Teracuss' right hand let go of the reins and absently stroked his steed's neck. "Peliny," he stated simply.

Memories quickly flooded back to Iridan. He had known Peliny when he was sixteen. She was pretty, but she had not been sought after by most of the boys. Peliny was slightly younger than Iridan, and at that age, most of the boys pursued older girls. He had never really noticed her until one day when Teracuss had cut himself badly on a jagged fence post. Iridan, and some of the other soldier trainees, came by. He had been impressed with how deftly she bandaged the wound. Her soft hands flowed through the job as if by a second nature. She had showed a deep compassion which had attracted Iridan—and apparently Teracuss as well.

Military training had always been fairly prestigious in Su'Meeryn, and many of the girls were infatuated with the recruits. He had easily won her over, but they had stayed together only a short time. After the initial attraction wore off, they discovered they did not get along very well. In retrospect, Iridan felt that he had acted quite immaturely. He had not expected that the relationship would last, but he'd pursued it anyway. He was proud of his training and had been very conceited. He treated her more like an accomplishment than a person, and he figured that she still harbored a strong dislike for him.

But he never knew that Teracuss had had feelings for her, and after all this time, he was amazed that Teracuss still carried a grudge. "But that was so long ago," Iridan replied.

"She was the only girl I ever loved, and you ruined it. Afterwards, she was so bitter. She wouldn't talk to me. Then her family moved off. I never had a chance, and it's all your fault. You just used her... The only girl until..."

Now, Iridan thought, finishing the statement. Teracuss' pause could not hide the truth. He had not tried to hide his longing for Myrin. However, her affections were obviously turned in the opposite direction.

"There's nothing I can do about Peliny," Iridan stated. "I was young and immature. Since I was training as a soldier, and you were a scholar, I guess I appeared more dashing to many of the girls then.

Teracuss' tone was cold and slow, "You stole her from me."

"I did pursue Peliny, but I didn't do the same thing with Myrin."

"You know the truth," Teracuss sneered. "It's just a game to you: Take away whatever you can from lowly Teracuss."

Iridan was now growing angry as well. "First of all," he spat, "I never knew you were in love with Peliny. And even if I had, I would have done the same thing. I owed you no favors. We were never friends. I loved her too; at least I thought I did."

"You knew I loved her!" Teracuss shouted, "and the only reason you pursued her was to toy with me: a weak religious student. It was just a big joke to you. Then after you won your *prize*, you couldn't get rid of her fast enough."

The harsh words caused Iridan to reflect back on his younger days. Had he noticed an affection Teracuss had for Peliny and pursued her as a cruel prank? His mind was clouded regarding those events. It did seem strange that a young man of his exposure would become so enamored with a younger girl over something so trivial. He had known of Teracuss for some time and never liked him. Iridan always viewed the scholarly minded as weak, wasting their time when they could be learning more valuable skills, such as fighting.

There might be some truth in his words, thought Iridan. "Maybe you're right," he said quietly. He regained the poise he thought he was going to lose shortly before. "Maybe not, but like I said, I was immature, and that was so long ago."

"Yeah, well, now you're doing it again."

Iridan's composure started to slip once more. "I did nothing this time. I didn't ask her to like me or try to charm her. She made her decision without any help from me." After a hesitation, Iridan continued. "Perhaps you're the one acting childish this time. You can't get over what happened so long ago, and it's clouding your judgment now." He turned to Teracuss, but the other man did not respond.

"Well?" Iridan asked after a few seconds.

Teracuss still refused to reply and kicked his horse into a gallop.

The race back towards Jokk-al Ystren and Myrin continued in silence. Iridan surveyed the desolation in the dwindling light and thought about Peliny. The more he considered, the more he figured Teracuss might be right. Had he recognized Teracuss' feelings for her and then stole her away? And maybe he had convinced himself afterwards that he had been in love with her.

As his internal argument progressed, Iridan noticed that he now suffered from a considerable headache which was compounded by the day's heat. Though the sun was fading, the air remained hot. He used one of his hands to try to fan himself, but he received no relief. After whisking some sweat from his brow, he pushed his horse a little harder and tried to turn his brain away from that dilemma. As they broke for camp, his next thought was even less pleasant: tomorrow they would reach Jokk-al Ystren's lair.

Chapter 28

The sky resembled a mural which formed a backdrop for the impending battle. The sun sought to fight through the painted clouds which screened it in a collage of reds, orange and purples. Each peak and valley in the clouds reflected a different combination of colors, and that colorful canvas hid the castle from the sun's view.

Suddenly catapults within the castle walls launched flaming coals which mingled with the colors in the sky and crashed down amongst the approaching army. Boulders and stones quickly trailed after the coal. The rocks rained down on the assaulting force, crushing helmets and skulls. The coals seared flesh; cloaks started to blaze, and war engines caught fire. Arrows shot forth from archers atop the battlements. Cries of anguish rose as they pierced skin and bored through eye sockets. But with all the soldiers that fell from the barrage, scores more continued on, dodging the missiles cascading from above.

Cavalry and infantry charged ahead. Flaming arrows from the castle landed on the planks of the trenches which had been previously dug around the walls and filled with oil. The trenches ignited, burning man and beast. The death toll continued to rise on the ground, but the first wave to reach the castle walls managed to raise siege ladders. Stones, barrels, tables and any other available objects were hurled down at the climbing men. Amidst the chaos of the defenders scurrying about to fend off this opening wave, the initial volley of arrows fell about the battlements. Jaleph's people suffered their first casualties of the attack, but they fought on.

Then there was an unexpected break in the assault. A perplexed king looked about as a lone shape catapulted from the midst of the army. Jaleph followed its path as the missile headed towards the walls. As it flew overhead, the king realized he was looking at a body. The broken and mangled corpse of Enni landed in the courtyard. Jeers of derision rose from the army as it renewed the attack.

A number of new siege ladders rose, but the defenders managed to push most of them away. As ladder after ladder fell to the ground, they carried many of the attackers to a crushing death. However, a few soldiers managed to breach the battlements. They were quickly cut down.

With the initial attack thwarted, the army withdrew out of missile range. Bodies lay strewn across the ground. They were burnt, pierced, broken and trampled, but Jaleph knew he had only one surprise left for the next onslaught.

The king stood silently atop the wall for a good number of minutes feeling only the presence of his personal guards around him. Footfalls from the stone staircase interrupted his solitude. He turned and saw his brother approaching.

"The first charge is over," Fenik sighed.

Jaleph slowly turned his head to reply, "Yes, but can we stop the next one?"

The prince came alongside and looked across the field. It had once been finely manicured with paths of lovely flowers winding their way through artistically cut shrubs. Now only death met the eye: the twisted bodies of man and horse, burnt ground, lost and forgotten weapons, trampled landscape and blood, everywhere blood.

"How many casualties?" asked Jaleph.

"I'm not sure yet, maybe two dozen." Fenik hesitated. "Teraken and Ruy believe they won't wait long for the second assault, not allowing us time to regroup."

Air exhaled loudly from Jaleph's lungs along with any hope that might have remained. Teraken and Ruy—and his brother to a certain extent—were far better strategists than he. He felt helpless. He had become a fair politician, but not a soldier. When the army penetrated the castle, he would draw sword and fight, but by then the battle would already be decided. He would die defending his land; however it would be an empty death, as Su'Meeryn would be defeated. Useless flesh: that was how he viewed himself, flesh waiting for death.

"Do what needs to be done," he said and dismissed his brother.

Again trumpets blared. The second assault had begun. This time the army moved more warily. He thought back to what Teraken had previously told him: "They'll try to overwhelm us first. If there is a second attack, they'll move cautiously attempting to see if we have any more traps for them."

When the advancing army came into range, a call rose from the castle towers. Again arrows streamed forth. They fell among the enemy taking many with them to the ground. The catapults repeated their shower of crushing death, but this time the defense was not as fierce. Jaleph watched as banners from the army signaled a change in strategy, and the advance stopped. After a brief pause, they rushed forward at a full charge.

The king managed a smile. They've taken the bait, he thought.

As the force neared the walls, missile fire shot forth in full earnest; however their targets were not the forward forces. The arrows and rocks were aimed at the middle and rear of the army. A few flaming arrows fell through the sky, and the last remaining oil trap ignited. Flesh and bone scorched as high pitched screams rang from burning throats.

Enemy archers again launched their own assault as the next round of siege ladders flew against the walls. Jaleph's forces allowed the first handful of initial climbers to advance while the bulk of the troops approached the base of the wall. Arrows fell among the defenders and sporadically found targets while the enemy began to reach the top of the battlement. Jaleph saw Ruy lead a small band to engage the assailants. Soldiers met with a clash of steel. Sword and mace fell amidst the fray; blood leapt forth from bodies like punctured wineskins. Ruy towered over the mass; his sword danced through the melee, striking death at each impact.

The invaders were quickly dispatched as the bulk of the army reached the base of the castle.

At that moment a call rang forth, and from the battlements, huge nets were cast over the walls. Some of the nets reached thirty feet in length, and the ends were anchored with stones and small logs. They fell about the enemy, ensnaring hundreds. Next boiling oil poured down the walls like a polluted waterfall. Shouts of agony rose all around. Rocks and chairs were hurled from above onto the trapped masses. As the rest of the army broke into retreat, the catapults and archers launched volleys of missiles, from their dwindling supplies, at the fleeing horde.

The second assault concluded, and the plans of Ruy and Teraken had inflicted heavy casualties. But no tricks remained. The king surveyed the scene trying to estimate the dead. He spotted a few of his subjects amongst the corpses piled on the ground.

A messenger ran forward and addressed the king. "Majesty?"

"Yes?"

"Prince Fenik reports that our estimated dead from the second charge is fifty."

Jaleph turned from the man. "Dismissed!"

He knew the third charge would be the last. He looked out at the army and saw a huge battering ram moving forward. They would take their time bringing it up, conserving energy until it came within missile range. Then, the full and final rush would begin. The castle had only a few moments to rest before the last act of the battle.

The king looked about and called for a page. He ordered that Teraken, Ruy and his brother be summoned to him.

***

The three men approached with the page following behind. Jaleph saw the exhaustion imbedded in their faces; Teraken appeared especially weary. He had engaged in hand-to-hand combat. Ruy had too, but his youthful stamina gave him some extra energy. A bandage, now solidly crimson, wrapped around Teraken's right biceps; Ruy, however, exhibited no injury.

"Your impressions?" asked Jaleph.

"We'll be hard-pressed to stop the next attack," Fenik answered.

"Yes," Teraken agreed, "the third assault will be final, for good or ill."

"Do we have any options left?" questioned the king, fearing he already knew the answer.

Teraken sighed. "We've uncovered all of our traps. We can only continue as we have, and our supplies are running low."

"Some rope broke on one of the catapults," added Ruy. "It's inoperative, and I'm not sure it'll be fixed in time."

Jaleph pondered his predicament for a moment. This would be the end. Nothing remained but to fight to the last man. And woman, he corrected himself remembering Dobrah.

"It appears Iridan and Teracuss have failed," he muttered. He then turned to Fenik. "It's time for us to fight, brother, and I want you at my side." He thought about ordering Ruy to have Dobrah assigned to his guard, but Ruy knew his soldiers much better than he. Jaleph did not want to interfere with his plans.

Teraken placed his large scarred hand on the king's shoulder. His eyes looked deep into Jaleph's as his fingers squeezed. No words were spoken, but Jaleph knew his friend's thoughts. Those thoughts mirrored his own, but a greater pain hid behind Teraken's eyes. His son had failed. Even if they somehow managed to win the battle, he would be alone. Teraken turned and embraced Fenik and Ruy then walked away; he would lead their defense with sword in hand at their final hour.

Ruy stood uncomfortably looking at the brothers. "Why don't you go spend a few minutes with your fiancée," Fenik suggested. "I'm sure you would rather be with her than with us." After a slight bow, Ruy darted off.

Now that they stood alone, Jaleph could not find the words to say good-bye to his brother. They gazed at each other for an awkward moment until Fenik approached and hugged him. Jaleph knew Fenik wanted to protest his desire to fight in the battle, but how could he? How could he deny the king his right to die with dignity, a death while fighting for his people? Could the king be expected to merely sit by in a tower and watch the slaughter of his subjects, only to be dragged out afterwards to his torture and mutilation?

"I won't leave your side, Jaleph," was all Fenik said.

***

The third call of trumpets rang. The notes echoed through the crisp air as archers shot from all angles. Catapults launched the few remaining boulders. As it sought the castle gate, the battering ram attracted arrows like a magnet draws needles.

Ladders again mounted the walls. The enemy was using them as a distraction while the bulk of the force waited to pour through the gate once the battering ram finished its job. As no other traps were sprung, the enemy did not need to worry over any hidden dangers to the ram.

Jaleph climbed down from the wall and stood in the common area, surrounded by his troops. He waited behind the huge wooden portal, anticipating the onslaught. His silver breastplate glittered upon his chest, and the deep blue cape flapped behind him in the light breeze. Around his neck, the emerald stone flickered against the leather band. The polished sword in his right hand twisted and turned nervously.

The first crash of the ram thundered in Jaleph's ears. He watched as the archers launched their last remaining arrows over the gate.

A second crash and the splintering of the gate could clearly be heard. He watched a group run towards the doors. The large wooden braces buttressing the portal had fallen. They raised the braces before the next blow landed.

Jaleph felt an arm brush against his side. He turned and saw Fenik trembling slightly. Jaleph could not tell if it was from fear or anticipation. Those two emotions currently surged equally through his veins. His pulse quickened: then the third strike of the ram sent splinters flying towards the waiting defenders.

Suddenly cries rang out from above. A force had breached the defense atop the battlements. He watched a number of his troops rush to meet that attack. Then his attention was diverted by another blow against the gate. The point of the ram pierced the wood.

Teraken's voice called out. The huge warrior stood first in the line soldiers waiting behind the huge door. The large man waved his sword in a circle above his head; he hollered and screamed, trying to ignite their ferocious spirits for the impending fight. Jaleph knew the people's love for Teraken; he was the only person who could rally the troops now. Teraken inspired them, unlike their king.

The fifth crash shattered the remains of the gate. The enemy rushed in around the ram. The first few were cut down in the furious whirlwind of Teraken's blade, but the sheer mass overwhelmed the defending line. The entire courtyard became a raging sea of blood. The scarlet liquid flew in all directions. Screams and curses issued forth like the crashing of a hurricane against a rocky beach.

Confusion raged around Jaleph. Weapons slashed and stabbed everywhere. It became difficult to discern ally from enemy. The amount of combatants in so small an area negated any advantage of swordsmanship. This benefited the king, who had never been very skillful with the blade. All Jaleph could do was raise and lower his sword. Even that became troublesome as the mass of soldiers crushed in about him.

Somehow Fenik remained at his side. At one point, Jaleph found himself surrounded by his own troops and managed to take a breath. He looked about and caught a glimpse of Dobrah. She was backed up against a wall but still defending herself. Blood covered her body. But whether it came from her or the enemy, the king could not tell. She parried a strike by her foe then slashed him across the stomach. Jaleph lost sight of her as the human shield about him gave away to the continued onslaught.

It appeared that Fenik and he had been identified. The assault became furiously focused towards the brothers. Just when they were about to be overrun, Ruy flew against the enemy. He struck down three before they could reorganize their attack. Ruy's axe swept about pulling flesh and blood along with it. The corpses piled around him making any movement difficult. When it seemed that he had killed all of the adversaries in the area, he managed a slight grin at the king. At that moment, he was forced to engage another opponent. Just when his axe chopped through the man's shoulder, cleaving the arm, a sword point pierced through his chest. He fell dead atop the bodies whose lives he had just vanquished.

As the killer drew his weapon from Ruy's body, Jaleph's sword swept down and buried into the man's gut. The attacker collapsed as a mace smashed into Jaleph's left shoulder. The king fell to his knees and watched while the mace spun around and headed towards his face.

A sword shot from Jaleph's right side and deflected the blow. The mace struck the ground leaving the attacker off balance. Fenik stood over his brother and ran his sword through the man's heart. After kicking the corpse off his weapon, Fenik stooped down to help his brother up, but his body suddenly quivered violently, and his face went cold. Blood streamed from his throat as steel emerged from the flesh. The blood showered Jaleph, and the prince's body fell across his midsection, pinning him to the ground.

The man regriped his sword, preparing to slay the king, when a screech split the air. It was so loud, pain shot through Jaleph's head making him think a spear had pierced his brain. The battle quieted as everyone looked about attempting to identify the unknown sound.

The king was still on his back with his eyes pointed upward. He thought he saw a small white cloud breaking forth from the mass of its neighbors. It raced through the sky shooting a bolt of lightening. The white streak came closer, and Jaleph knew it could not be a cloud. It headed straight for the castle. Cries leapt from every throat as the shape finally became distinguishable.

It was a dragon.

The creature flew over the castle directly towards the gate. As it did, the king managed to free himself from Fenik's body. He stood and saw two figures seated on the beast's back.

When it reached the gate, fire streamed from its mouth scorching the soldiers who had not yet entered the castle. The ram caught ablaze, preventing the troops still outside from squeezing in through the broken door. All who remained inside were trapped.

The dragon rose into the air and circled about. Fire poured from its snout towards the walls. Jaleph assumed its target was the siege ladders still vaulted against the castle.

The king did not know what to expect as it soared through the air and dove down again, but he thought he recognized one of the figures seated on its back. It looked like Iridan. Then the dragon continued its fiery assault against the army outside the castle walls.

Hope leapt into Jaleph's soul. He cried out and slashed his sword across the face of his brother's killer.

The battle renewed, but now no reinforcements could enter through the shattered gate. The enemy became terrified and disheartened by the dragon's attack, while Jaleph's force battled more ferociously than ever. They realized that, miraculously, the dragon was fighting for them. They smelled victory.

As more and more attackers fell, those who remained began to threw down their weapons and beg for mercy. They found little.

Finally the battle ended. The king spared only a few lives, so the men could return to their homes to tell of their defeat at the hands of the men and women of Su'Meeryn.

Jaleph turned and looked up at the dragon. He saw it heading towards the courtyard, just beyond where he stood. It landed, then he watched as Iridan and a woman struggled to dismount off its back. Dumbfounded, Jaleph stood, gazing at the beast.

Chapter 29

The king slowly walked towards Iridan while watching the albino creature warily. As he approached, Iridan turned back to face the dragon. "You may finish the rest," he said. Jaleph thought he saw a smile cross the beast's snout. The massive wings beat twice and the dragon rose into the air. It flew over the flaming gate towards the army remaining outside the walls. Jaleph heard the roaring of fire and the renewed screams of the dying men. He stared in wonder at Iridan then ran up the battlements to view the slaughter.

By the time he reached the top of the wall, however, little remained to watch. Small bonfires scattered the landscape like piles of red and yellow leaves which fall to the ground during autumn. Slowly, the scent of burnt flesh reached the castle causing Jaleph to gag. The army was routed, but the dragon allowed none to escape. It flew after whatever movement it spotted. Jaleph was astonished at the speed of the beast despite its immense bulk. Flames streaked at the fleeing troops. Finally the only movement left was that of the dragon and the flickering of small fires. The creature landed and evaluated the scene. It raised its head to the sky and let out a shriek. The king was sickened by the next sight; the dragon began to gorge itself on the charred corpses.

Jaleph turned away nauseated and found Iridan and the beautiful girl a respectful distance behind him. "Well, do you want to explain this to me?" the king asked.

"Of course sire," responded Iridan, "but may we leave the wall first? The smell is making me sick."

The trio walked down the steps towards the carnage of the courtyard. The people of Su'Meeryn were milling about, bewildered by their victory. A couple of cheers rang forth as Iridan walked by. A few more joined in until the entire courtyard was filled with the exaltations of the people.

Jaleph listened proudly to the cheers for a moment then steered the pair towards the palace. He was anxious for answers and saddened by the all the death around him. Time enough for celebration later, he thought. He wanted to hear their story without distraction.

Just then, Teraken dashed over. The king was thrilled to see his old friend had somehow managed to live through the conflict, though he appeared as battered as when he had returned from his reconnaissance mission. Jaleph quickly raised his hand to avert any questions. Teraken's face revealed a combination of wonder by the appearance of the dragon and horror at not spotting his son, but he too followed after his king in silence.

As they walked, Jaleph thought of Fenik. He wanted to run to the body, carry it to the palace and clean it up for a proper burial. But now was not the time. He needed to act as king, not as a brother. Guilt flowed through him. Grabbing the first soldier they saw, he ordered the man to find the prince's body and bring it to the palace.

Jaleph then saw Dobrah and his heart leapt. She was standing amidst several other soldiers. She had survived and he wanted to run to her. He would approach her soon, but not yet. Then he stood dumbfounded as he watched a young man rush towards her. Their arms wrapped about each other, and she was lifted into the air. They spun around, and then the man brought her back down. Their faces met. Jaleph quickly turned away as they kissed.

First he lost Fenik, now Dobrah. He looked about the castle. The battle had been won, but at what price? How hollow would the space between the castle walls now feel?

They finally reached the palace, and Jaleph led the other three into his private library. Before closing the door, he found one of his guards and instructed him not to allow any disturbances. Jaleph sat down and spotted his father's history book. He knocked it off the table.

"Now I'll hear your story," he said, "but first, where is Teracuss?"

Iridan turned to Teraken then back to Jaleph. "Dead my king," he answered.

Teraken fell heavily into a chair. "How?" he whispered.

"I'm sorry sir, but it's a long story," Iridan answered heavily. Jaleph heard pain in Iridan's voice. He was somewhat surprised, because he had noticed the tension between the two when they had left.

Jaleph looked at his longtime friend. He understood the agony Teraken felt, after just watching his brother die; Fenik's blood, in fact, still covered his body. They had also lost Ruy. Many of his subjects had experienced similar losses. But they could not grieve yet. The dead would be honored soon enough. Now he needed to hear from Iridan.

"I'm sure that it is," Jaleph said; "however, we shall hear it now. And I'm certain that this girl will be mentioned somewhere within your tale."

"Of course, majesty," replied Iridan. He motioned to a chair, and the king nodded. He took Myrin by the arm, and they both sat. Iridan took a deep breath then began to tell the story of all that had happened after Teracuss and he had left Su'Meeryn. He paused following the description of the battle in Naemon's house. He took a drink from a flask that had been brought in, at his request, a few minutes before.

"We had ridden all of the second night and were approaching Jokk-al Ystren's cave," Iridan continued.

Jaleph turned to Teraken who was nervously tapping the table, anxious to hear the facts regarding his son's death. The king gently placed his hand over Teraken's to silence the noise. "Please continue," he said looking back at Iridan.

"Well, we were arguing about what would happen once we entered the lair." Iridan's eyes glazed over as he continued the story:

***

The two men gingerly approached the hill that housed Jokk-al's den. Iridan trotted his steed up alongside Teracuss.' He grabbed its reins and stopped both horses. "We must decide," he said.

"Yes, we must," responded Teracuss softly.

Iridan thought back to what Naemon had told them prior to the conflict with the man in white:

When you enter Jokk-al Ystren's cave, you will have one chance to save your people. It shall require the ultimate sacrifice of one of you. It is said that a dragon can be coerced into submitting to a human, but it requires the death of a human. When a dragon draws blood from a man, if at the same time another human draws its blood, the dragon will obey that person. But remember, you must only ask of it that which does not contradict its nature. And I am certain that slaughtering an army does not conflict with Jokk-al's personality. Once the task is complete, the dragon will leave. I would suggest that you not be found in its lair once its assignment is finished. For your purpose, that will not be a concern. One of you will need to distract Jokk-al while the other prepares for the strike. The best place to draw its blood is the underbelly. Get to the base of the tail, and when the dragon attacks, make certain you don't miss.

The whole thing had sounded ridiculous, but what choice did they have?

Teracuss interrupted Iridan's thoughts. "I'll do it," he stated.

"I can't let you be the one. Your father would never forgive me if I didn't bring you home."

"I don't need you to bring me anywhere," Teracuss snapped. "You have Myrin." He hesitated; "I don't have anybody. It might as well be me."

Iridan had no idea how to respond. How do you argue with a man over which one of you will die? Of course, they could both die within the cave. Myrin could die as well. In fact, there was no guarantee that she still lived. He wondered over the comment: *you have Myrin.* Was that true? Did he truly want a relationship with her? He had no clear answers. Despite all this, a decision still needed to be made.

All he could think to say was, "I don't know."

"Look, we both know you're better with a sword than me," Teracuss said in a somber tone. "You're the logical choice to try to cut the dragon."

"Possibly," replied Iridan after a long pause, but he was still not committed. Iridan contemplated the situation. He tried to determine the scenario most likely to achieve their end. It was the hardest decision he would ever need to make, but decide he must. After another uncomfortable pause, Iridan finally made his resolution.

"Can we agree on one thing?" asked Iridan. "Can we agree that I'm the leader here?"

Teracuss glared at him but ultimately nodded his head.

"Good," Iridan continued, "then I've decided. It'll be me."

***

They reached the base of the hill as the sun began to rise, and Iridan wanted to set the horses free. However the next few minutes played out, they would have no use for their steeds. But their bargain called for the horses to be traded for Myrin. It was essential that Jokk-al suspect nothing once they enter the cave. They tried to haul the horses up the ancient pathway; however, no amount of coaxing or pulling could get the beasts to climb those stairs.

"We'll have to secure them out here," Teracuss said sympathetically.

They fastened the horse's reins around a few small rocks jutting out from the hill, and Iridan tugged hard on the leather to test them. The animals would not be able to pull free. Iridan stroked his horse's snout. "If we get out of this," he murmured to his steed, "Teracuss will let you go." The horses had shouldered their burdens admirably throughout the quest; there was no reason for them to die needlessly.

Iridan turned to Teracuss. "I'll start to talk with the dragon and try to provoke it a little. While it's focused on me, sneak around back. Stay in my sight. When you believe you've positioned yourself at a vulnerable spot, give me a signal. Make sure you strike at the right time, otherwise we'll both be dead."

Teracuss considered for a moment. "Are you sure this is the best strategy? I still think you're better suited for this."

Iridan's ire grew. It was hard enough to face death without arguing further. But Teracuss' tone had not been harsh. In fact, he was surprised by how gentle his companion sounded. It was simply a question, not an attack on his decision. But, he had a reason for his decision, and that reason could not be shared.

"Yes I do," Iridan answered. "You must trust me on this."

They slowly climbed the ancient path and entered Jokk-al Ystren's lair.

***

"Ah, I see my two humans return!" Jokk-al chuckled. "But my meal appears absent. Your eyes reveal that I have satisfied my pledge." Iridan followed the dragon's glance and saw Myrin huddled on the ground. She appeared uninjured.

"We couldn't drag them up the stairs," answered Iridan. "They're tied up at the base of your hill."

"Wise beast," replied the dragon.

"Is she all right?" Teracuss asked.

"You are fortunate. The female remains unblemished; however, I could not foresee the time period this condition would last. You departed quite a while ago, and the inception of my hunger emerged today." Jokk-al said. "She does appear tasty, does she not? but hardly suited even for an appetizer.

"Although inane, the female's conversation surpasses that of you males. It bordered on a pleasing discussion concerning metaphysics. Am I not precise, dear?"

Myrin just sat shaking on the ground; she had not moved since they entered. Iridan wondered at what tortures she had been exposed to during their absence. If they succeeded here today, her courage would be remembered in Su'Meeryn for ages.

Iridan noticed that Teracuss had started to slowly circle around Jokk-al.

"Well, we've kept our end of the bargain," began Iridan. "Will you continue to keep yours?"

"My actions conform to my own desires. If it pleased me, I would consume the three of you and your steeds. Now gather your female and depart. I grow weary of your babbling. And if your horses do not await me, I shall track you down and roast your pitiful trio!"

Iridan knew he must keep Jokk-al occupied a few moments more, but the diversion had quickly become a dangerous game. "How do we know you won't do that anyway?" he asked the dragon, hoping he sounded calm.

"You do not. And refrain from pleading for any guarantee of my good faith. I assure you, that is one area of personality in which I am deficient," the dragon laughed, obviously pleased with his own humor.

Iridan lowered his head in mock deference, but as he did, he saw Teracuss lift his hand. He was in place. Iridan quickly looked up and drew his sword, but as he did, Jokk-al spun about and faced Teracuss.

"Fools!" the dragon bellowed, "do you think me ignorant? Do you think I fail to perceive through your simple plot?" Jokk-al's snout hovered inches from Teracuss' face.

This, however, was the reason Iridan had selected himself to confront Jokk-al. He knew the dragon was extremely intelligent and would likely discern their scheme. He could only hope that his planning would be enough to outwit the beast.

The next few seconds seemed an eternity to Iridan. Teracuss' destiny was sealed. Iridan need only wait for the fateful moment to strike. He was poised and deathly still, with his sword out before him, ready to attack. The dragon must not notice him and divert its attention. Iridan stood beside Jokk-al's rear leg; he saw a patch of loose skin at the joint where the hip met torso.

Then Jokk-al struck. The snout shot forward and crushed through Teracuss. Iridan heard Teracuss' brief scream then the sound of crunching bones. Blood erupted from the body which hung limp, a few feet off the ground, pierced by Jokk-al's fangs.

Iridan lunged forward. The sword hit flesh, but it was thicker than he had anticipated. He came to a jolting halt as Jokk-al's head began to shake Teracuss' body about. Iridan lost the grip on his sword and fell to the ground. He looked up, pleading to whomever might be listening, to see a puncture wound. Jokk-al's neck swung around, and Teracuss' corpse flew across the cave. The dragon's eyes gazed into his own, but the beast did not move. Iridan looked back at the joint he had struck; he noticed a trickle of blood seeping down the leg from a small laceration.

***

Jaleph sighed heavily, lowered his flask to the table and turned to Teraken.

"Your son sacrificed himself, sir," Iridan continued looking sadly at Teraken. "We couldn't have defeated the army without him."

Teraken rose slowly from his chair. "You did well," he said, in a voice barely above a whisper. He turned to look at the king; Jaleph noted the tears streaming down from the large man's eyes and hoped part of them came from pride in Teracuss' accomplishment. Teraken stood like a large sapling swaying in a summer breeze. He stared absently at the ceiling for a long moment then exited the room.

He's truly alone now, Jaleph thought; if only he had something—someone—to comfort him.

"Well," Jaleph directed his attention back to Iridan, "you've done splendidly. I'll reward you handsomely for your deeds, of course, as well as this young lady."

"I appreciate your gratitude, sire," Iridan stammered, "but I don't know if I'd feel right accepting anything for this. I made it back alive. Teracuss is the one who deserves any honor that might be awarded."

"Your humility is inspiring."

"It has nothing to do with humility. It would almost seem that I was being rewarded for saving myself."

"Don't deny our people the chance to thank their hero," Jaleph replied. "As for Teracuss, don't worry. He'll be properly honored."

"I'm no hero," Iridan insisted. "I doubted everything Teracuss told me, and I sacrificed him. I could've prepared him to be the one to face the dragon. I feel like a coward, and I don't want to be honored for that."

"Of course you're not a coward," said Myrin tenderly, placing a hand lightly upon his arm. "You did the bravest thing I ever saw. Both of you."

Iridan stood. He walked to one of the windows facing the courtyard and gazed out. The king knew what sight met his vision: the mass of corpses carpeting the ground; Iridan saw the carnage and the rivers of blood.

Jaleph walked over and joined Iridan. In the courtyard below, bodies were beginning to be carried away, bodies of his soldiers and of the enemy. Mass graves would be dug to bury them. Only his brother, and a few others, would be able to receive their own plots.

So much death, he thought, and for what?

"What brought us to this point?" Jaleph asked.

Myrin walked over and put her arm about Iridan. She rested her head on his shoulder. Iridan stared blankly in the king's eyes.

"Come on," Iridan finally said to the girl, "we could both use some fresh clothes."

Chapter 30

Iridan sat with Myrin, alone in his home. They had both bathed and discarded their ragged, foul smelling clothes for new garb. Iridan was visibly shaken at the news of Ruy's death; he knew he needed to seek Dirwyn out to console her. But now was not the time. He needed to sit back and collect himself. He needed to reflect on all that had happened, before he could reach out to someone else.

Was this the only path to victory? Could they have found another way which would not have caused the death of so many friends? Could they have reached Jokk-al's lair quicker? Could he have pushed the horses more?

He poured some wine for Myrin and himself. The two drank quietly for a few uncomfortable minutes. They had not talked while flying upon Jokk-al's back—who thankfully had left the area after finishing his repugnant gorge. They had been too terrified and needed to concentrate on not falling off.

"What do you plan to do now?" Iridan asked, finally breaking the stillness.

"I'm not sure," she answered. But the look on her face betrayed her vague answer. She knew exactly what she wanted.

Myrin again grew silent while intently examining the base of her mug. Her fingers twirled it in every direction so she could view all its sides. Actually, Iridan knew what her decision was: she wanted to stay with him. That had been obvious since they first met. The only question which remained was whether he wanted her to stay.

He had always recognized Myrin's physical beauty. But Iridan never had the time to really decide if he had an actual affection for her, despite the long hours on his horse's back. He had used that time to prepare himself for the upcoming stages of their quest. Or was that a justification? Actually he just had not wanted to make a decision then. He had felt guilty considering that during the mission.

Too tired to be diplomatic and figure out an appropriate response, Iridan decided to say exactly what was on his mind. After all the death and turmoil, he had no strength left to worry about the tone of his words. "Look, we've been through a lot. I need time. We both need time, but I hope you'll stay here, at least for a little while. I don't want any decisions we make to be in haste."

Myrin seemed somewhat hurt by his words, but he could tell she agreed with them. "I suppose you're right," she said. Then she stood and walked over to him. She gave him a soft kiss on his forehead before sitting back down.

Iridan smiled a little looking into her eyes. He then remembered seeing her lying in a ball in Jokk-al's cave when Teracuss and he had returned. He wondered what had caused her such anguish and wanted to ask her about it, but he decided that conversation was better suited for a later time.

"Tell me about Teracuss," she suddenly said.

"What do you want to know? You knew him about as well as I did."

"You two didn't like each other very much. Why not?"

"That's another long story," Iridan began, "and I'm still not quite sure on all the facts." He paused to reflect on his discussion with Teracuss regarding Peliny. Iridan then began describing to Myrin his attitude towards Teracuss in his younger days; next he told her about Peliny. He still was unable to discern his true motivation, but he told her all he could.

"He never forgave me for that," Iridan continued. "He held that bitterness inside himself a long time. And I never matured past my smugness, my arrogance. I thought that I was so strong, and that I didn't need him. I never would have survived without him; my people would now be destroyed if not for him. He wanted to sacrifice himself back in the dragon's lair, but he finally put aside his bitterness and allowed me to make the decision. Bravery was never an attribute I would have expected from him. I was wrong.

"There was so much hostility between us when we first left here. I thought there was a lot he should learn from me, but instead, I learned a lot from him. Perhaps he did learn something from me too. I don't know, and I guess it really doesn't matter now.

"We were never friends, not even at the end. But even though it might have just been from despair, he was still willing to die in my place. He wanted to be the one because he felt he had nothing to lose." Iridan was quiet for a moment then continued. "If there had been a love between us, he would have done the same thing, but for a different reason. He would have done it *for* me, not in spite of me. I wonder what it would be like if we could just put aside bitterness and anger."

"I don't know," Myrin said, "but what I do know is that you're a good man. You realize you have short-comings. Most people would never admit they had acted so selfishly." She stood and walked to the door. "It's getting dark. Where can I sleep?"

"The king said you can stay in the palace until you find a permanent place in Su'Meeryn, if that's your decision." Might that ultimately mean his home? He knew they needed to spend some time together, apart from the quest and all their suffering, before he could consider marriage. "Come on, I'll walk you over."

Iridan placed his arm about her waist, and they started through the dusk. He realized this was the first time that he had shown her any physical affection. She nestled against him and turned her eyes to the sky. It was becoming a combination of deep orange and glorious purple.

For the first time in a long time, Iridan managed to just look and appreciate beauty.

After escorting Myrin to the palace, Iridan sought out his cousin Dirwyn. He found her alone in her parent's small home. She sat in the dark, staring blankly out a small window. She did not respond to the knocks at the door and did not stir when he entered. Iridan wondered anxiously as to the whereabouts of his aunt and uncle but decided not to ask. He sat beside Dirwyn; she still refused to move. Iridan wanted to express his sorrow over her loss, but the proper words never came. He placed an arm over her shoulder and gazed with her out the window. Dirwyn slid closer to him and started to cry. He pulled her further within his grasp, and they spent the rest of the night in that same position. Neither spoke. At dawn, Iridan guided Dirwyn to her bed, and she finally slept.

Iridan stumbled out of the house and walked back to his own. There he found a number of people waiting outside. They wanted to ask him questions about his mission and thank him for saving them. He brushed past them rather rudely and slammed his door. He reached his bed and collapsed.

***

Two days later Jaleph threw a huge celebration for the entire castle. Trumpets blared throughout the day. Brightly colored flags flapped in a light breeze, under silvery clouds, atop the castle walls like a dancing rainbow. An unsteady podium had been hastily erected in the center of the town square, and Jaleph pulled Myrin and Iridan upon the dais to the cheers from the crowd. When the shouts subsided, Teraken walked up in front of Iridan. Stillness filled the air where moments before windows had rattled. The king spoke of Teracuss' sacrifice and how it had brought their salvation. Jaleph announced that a monument would be built to Teracuss at the spot where the podium now stood. It would be a square pole pointing to the sky, and on each side Teracuss' name was to be carved.

The king handed Teraken a shining plate. Some words were engraved in it, but Iridan could not read them. "I know this will never replace your son," Jaleph said, "but accept it in honor of his deeds and his memory." The huge man grasped it with a shaking hand then strode down from the platform.

A feast followed the ceremony. All were invited. Whole pigs roasted over open fires. Fruits and vegetables lined long tables.

Iridan tried to eat but had no appetite. He left Myrin with the king and attempted to find some solitude. That was an improbable task as he strolled about the castle. He was immediately recognized by everyone he passed. Finally, finding a dark corner on the side of the entrance to the palace, Iridan sat down behind a pillar.

As the crowd streamed along, Iridan gazed at the people who had been saved by his quest. Relief and exaltation marked each face, until he saw Teraken. The aged soldier stumbled by clutching his plate, still overcome by his grief. Iridan wanted to approach him but knew that gesture would accomplish nothing. Perhaps, given time, Teraken would be able to accept his son's death, but not yet.

In the distance, he saw Myrin laugh at something Jaleph said. He marveled at her strength after losing her entire family and village. He looked back at the king and wondered at his ease in accepting Fenik's death, at least on the outside. Likely Jaleph was just trying to portray a strong, kingly image.

Iridan then thought of Korath. The old man had died and been buried before he had returned. With both Korath and Teracuss gone, he wondered if the religious studies would disappear. As far as he knew, Teracuss had been Korath's only apprentice.

His finger moved to his right hand where the Ring of Naar sat. He had pulled it off Teracuss' finger before leaving Jokk-al Ystren's lair. He spun the ring around and considered its worth. According to Naemon, the ring was composed of a valueless metal. But, in a way, the ring had saved Su'Meeryn. If they had not left in search of it, they never would have found Jokk-al nor met Naemon. Iridan thought of the apparent coincidences and wondered if they had truly been by chance.

The festival continued around him. Some cried over their loss or cried because of their deliverance. However, the mixed emotions tended to side towards jubilation. But Iridan still did not feel like celebrating. Something was wrong, and he needed answers.

Iridan stood and started to walk through the streets. The brief solitude he had found was now continually interrupted by the crowds he passed. Trying to be as polite as possible, Iridan shook numerous hands. But he continued on at a quick pace. He had a destination, and he did not want to be distracted.

Finally, Iridan reached his objective. He walked up to Korath's quiet home.

The house was empty of life but not of artifacts. It seemed to be unchanged since Iridan last stood within the walls. With the impending battle, and the celebration thereafter, nobody had found time to come and clear out the cleric's belongings. He remembered the fight he had had with Teracuss in this room, and the thought caused him to smile. What had occurred only a number of days before seemed like years ago.

He rummaged about Korath's possessions searching for something, but he knew not what. While looking around, Iridan thought of the man in white. If Teracuss had been correct, the man could return with his strange followers. He wondered why they had sought after the ring if it was, indeed, powerless. And Iridan now possessed the artifact. Would he be their next target? That was a sobering thought. He never imagined that supernatural forces could target him in their evil goals.

What could he do about it? He would have to deal with it sometime, but there were other answers he needed first. He stood and continued searching through the home. Korath's papers seemed like a labyrinth to his brain. There was something else he needed to find. But what? He ultimately came to the old man's staff leaning in a dark corner of the house. It felt unexpectedly light when he grasped it. He examined the metal which composed Chaw Den, then compared it to the ring. They both appeared forged from the same unidentifiable material.

Iridan thought of the instructions Korath had given Teracuss and him. The cleric had said the power of the ring would awaken Chaw Den, who would bring their salvation. Perhaps Jokk-al Ystren was, in fact, Chaw Den. Or was there power locked within the depths of the bird? Had there ever been? It did not seem so, based on what Naemon had explained.

But what had caused Korath to be so misguided? It seemed that Teracuss' teacher knew nothing but myth regarding Naar's ring, while Naemon apparently not only knew the truth, he had possessed the ring. The only explanation he came to was that, somewhere, somehow, the teachings in Su'Meeryn had been corrupted.

Had they lost their way? Could so much destruction have been avoided if they had not turned away from their original beliefs? Could they have found a means to their deliverance sooner? If so, what could be done now?

Those, Iridan thought, are questions for scholars and philosophers. Or are they? Perhaps that was just a rationalization to ease his mind. If others were left responsible for analyzing the recent history, he could continue in ignorant bliss. Maybe the apathy of leaving truth and decisions in other's hands was what had caused their near destruction.

Iridan knew he needed to make a decision regarding all these matters. He must find some answers, and he needed to find them quickly. He needed to find out what had gone wrong.

***

Three months later Iridan and Myrin married. It came as no surprise to any who knew them; his affection for her had grown strong during that time. At Iridan's request, the ceremony took place next to Teracuss' monument. To Iridan it was a symbol. It was a reminder of the part of him that never was and the part of him which would need to be.

143

The Wolf and the Worm

Patrick D. Catlett

Prologue

Ile-Born reigned in his horse with a shout of joy. His arrow had flown true, and the buck was dead before hitting the ground. "A beautiful shot, my prince," Gurmen remarked, slapping Ile-Born's back. "The queen will be pleased to hear of your first kill."

"Yes, I can't wait to return and tell her," Ile-Born replied.

Gurmen jumped down from his saddle. "Fourteen summers and already a master hunter, I can see that my training has not gone to waste." He motioned for Ile-Born to follow as he went to inspect the animal. "An excellent rack; it will make a fine trophy for your hall."

Ile-Born and Gurmen grabbed the antlers of the buck and began to drag it back towards their horses. "Thanks for taking me out with you," said Ile-Born. "I know my mother doesn't think that I'm ready."

"Illiyna is just being overly protective after the death of your father. I can't blame her."

"Of course, but I needed to get out of that city. So, I just want you to know, I appreciate you speaking up for me."

"And you are welcome, my prince," Gurmen said, with his wide smile displaying both his love for and pride in the young man. When the pair returned to their horses, two of the twelve royal guards took the buck and began to prepare the carcass. "It's getting late," continued Gurmen. "We should head to the creek for water then return. Perhaps we'll spot some additional game along the way."

"You are a wise man, Gurmen, despite what the others might say," Ile-Born said with a laugh as he climbed back into his saddle.

Gurmen snorted disapprovingly. "I see that your sense of humor could still use some work."

Ile-Born laughed again but stopped short when he thought he spotted movement off to the west. The setting sun obscured his vision, so he could not be certain. "Do you see something out there?" he asked his companion.

Gurmen squinted in the direction that the prince pointed. "Yes, some men on horseback are heading this way, but I can't tell how many." He called back to his soldiers to ready their weapons. Since they were still close to Labyn, he did not expect any trouble, but it was always prudent to be safe, especially when traveling with the prince.

As the horses approached, Ile-Born managed to count two dozen. At the head of the group rode a handsome man. He was dressed completely in white, and, despite the dusty conditions, there was no trace of dirt on any of his garments. The man stopped his horse just short of the prince and raised his hand above his blond hair to signal greeting. "Please do not be startled," the man in white said. "We are soldiers from Su'Meeryn out hunting some bandits. May I assume you are not them?"

"Of course not," Gurmen answered suspiciously. "Now I would ask that you be on your way. You are trespassing in Queen Illiyna's lands."

"Not a very hospitable greeting for fellow soldiers," responded the man in white. "However, we will be moving on shortly." He turned back towards his men, and his silver belt glistened in the setting sun. "Might I inquire if there is water nearby? We are quite thirsty."

"No, there is not," responded Gurmen. "Now, again, I ask you to be on your way."

"Of course, of course," the man in white replied. "Come along," he called, and with that, the soldiers charged.

The men of Labyn quickly circled their horses to protect Ile-Born, and they readied themselves as the attackers stormed forward. The soldiers met in a cacophony of cries and crashing steel. Bodies fell from horses as blades pierced flesh. Knowing that his warriors were too outnumbered, Ile-Born grabbed his own weapon and entered the fray. Gurmen would never forgive him for this, but Ile-Born knew he would need to help if they stood any chance of surviving. The prince swung about, managing to wound one man. He tried to swing again, but he lost the grip on his sword, and it fell to the ground. Without a weapon, he sat confused, unsure what to do. Looking about, he glimpsed the man in white sitting on his horse—unmoving—with a smile of satisfaction.

It was not long until Gurmen and Ile-Born were the only two from Labyn who remained. Many of the attackers had also fallen but not nearly enough for the prince to escape. Gurmen fought on, despite being surrounded by ten men; he would never surrender while the prince was at risk.

Ile-Born looked on in horror as the blades managed to break through the defenses of his friend. First, the skin of his thigh was sliced open, and then an axe collapsed his shoulder causing his arm to dangle uselessly from its socket. Gurmen cried out in pain as he struggled to continue the fight. A sword pierced his stomach with an explosion of blood. Gurmen slumped forward. A soldier's blade came crashing down, and Gurmen's head fell to the ground, rolling beside the hooves of his horse.

The man in white clapped his hands with glee then moved his horse back up to Ile-Born. "What a shame that your men were not more hospitable, prince."

"Why're you doing this? Didn't your messenger just propose a treaty with my mother?" Ile-Borne managed to stammer. "Labyn has always been friendly to Su'Meeryn."

"So young and so foolish, you certainly do not understand the ways of the world. Unfortunately you never will as you are about to join your friend." The man signaled and two soldiers advanced. Ile-Born sat transfixed with fear. He wanted to flee, but his body would not move. Two swords hovered above his head for a brief moment and then came crashing down.

The man in white hopped down from his steed and stared at the still form of Ile-Born lying on the ground. Another smile spread across his face as his handsome features dissolved. His skin became taut and translucent, giving him a skeletal appearance. He reached down and pulled a ring from Ile-Born's finger. As he straightened back up, he gave a call. His remaining soldiers stood still as a company of wolves came rushing out of the brush. They proceeded to devour the corpses as the man in white road off towards the east.

Chapter 1

A light breeze blew from the northern sky. Soft white seeds traveled along the wind, heading towards the stone walls of the castle at the bottom of the lush valley. The seeds sought for any opening within the meadow to plant themselves, with the hope of sprouting purple wildflowers. A lone man stood atop the castle wall, inhaling the sweet-scented air. White tufts circled about the man's head while a seemingly endless flow followed. He watched the seeds streaming towards him, assaulting the stronghold, and he was reminded of the army that had attacked the castle just one year earlier.

The man's head turned back to the courtyard below. A smile etched his face at the memory of the victory against that awesome horde. At the brink of defeat, salvation had literally flown from the sky. But the castle's extraordinary victory had been purchased at a tremendous cost.

Jaleph had relived the final moments of that battle often during the past year. For a time, he had visualized the death of his brother Fenik daily, while the loss of Ruy haunted him nearly as much. Then there were the countless empty faces; Jaleph had never had a chance to know most of his soldiers, but he felt all of their deaths as well.

It is a huge burden for any man to hold the responsibility for so many lives, but the kingdom had survived. While Jaleph mourned for the dead, he also celebrated their victory. He knew Su'Meeryn needed to remember those dark days and learn from their mistakes: to make sure they would never be subjected to such an attack again. Now, with the victory won, and the castle repaired, the king needed to concentrate on building alliances, as his father had done before him.

Jaleph strolled down from the wall. He acknowledged the slight bows of those he passed while making his way to the palace. A page had advised the king of the return of one of the emissaries he had recently dispatched west, to the land of Labyn, to meet with their queen: Illiyna. Despite the strenuous work that had already been completed, Jaleph knew difficult tasks still remained, and diplomacy was not one of his strengths.

After reaching the palace, he entered the new room he had designed following the battle. He called it his strategy room. It was here that the rebuilding plans had been made, and it was here where he waited for his delegate to arrive.

The room looked harsh; gray walls flowed like dirty waterfalls forming a lake of stone across which Jaleph marched. Several blue chairs circled a spacious wood table, which the king had ordered painted white. The wall across from the door displayed a painting of the albino dragon spewing fireballs at the attacking horde, while, within the courtyard, Jaleph could be seen butchering his brother's killer. He had spent many hours here—with Teraken—discussing the restoration of the castle, but this new room still seemed empty with the absence of Ruy and Fenik. He had desired to call for Dobrah to join them, but thought better of that idea. She had wed shortly after the battle, and the king saw no reason to torture himself with her presence. In an attempt to ease his loneliness, Jaleph had summoned Iridan on a few occasions. But while he enjoyed Myrin's company, he did not feel particularly comfortable around the young scout.

The arrival of the emissary interrupted the king from his musings. "Majesty," the man said, acknowledging his liege. The man was of large build. He closely matched Jaleph's age, somewhere near his third decade. He pulled forth one of the chairs and sat across from Jaleph. Teraken had mentioned that the man had distinguished himself during the combat, so Jaleph had elevated his duties. With Ruy and Fenik gone, the kingdom needed to start grooming future leaders.

"Well Pothar, tell me what you've learned." Jaleph said as he turned his eyes away from Pothar's face. The king, for some reason, always found his companion's thin red hair and pinkish skin unsettling.

"I was allowed to meet with the queen shortly after my arrival. Illiyna has yet to remarry after the death of the king," Pothar began as his fingers combed the long mustache that trailed down to outline his pointed chin. "She told me she was pleased with our victory in the battle. Clearly, that army would have been a threat to Labyn if they had conquered Su'Meeryn, but she is hesitant to make any treaty with us. She is closer to Tamar than we are and is afraid that they might march against her if she allies herself with us. Despite Tamar's defeat, Illiyna believes they are still quite powerful. She asked me to relay her sympathy to you for the death of your brother, along with her pledge that Labyn has no ill feelings towards Su'Meeryn. However, she refused any formal relationship."

Jaleph remained silent for a moment. This news was most unfortunate. He had considered Labyn to be the land most likely to ally with Su'Meeryn. Now, if the other missions also failed, they would still stand alone. "I'm sure you did your best," he stated.

"Majesty," Pothar continued, "we shouldn't give up all hope on Labyn. I sensed that the queen strongly desired the treaty. If another land agrees to your proposal, I believe she will as well. She just doesn't want to be the only one. She seemed very clever. With some additional forces, this treaty would be a wise strategic move for her. I think I should return if any of the other diplomats succeed."

The king's mood perked up at those words. Of course, he thought, she is biding her time; a wise move from a wise queen. "Very good Pothar, we'll discuss this further when the others arrive. Go home, rest yourself, then get a nice meal."

"Thank you sir," Pothar replied as he left.

Jaleph sat alone for a time. He rubbed his hands together trying to push out his frustration with his fingertips. Why is this so hard, he thought; why is everything always so difficult for me? He sorely missed the counsel he had always received from Ruy and his brother. While Teraken's combat strategies were unmatched, his prowess in battle would not help the king now. Jaleph felt completely alone.

Chapter 2

Myrin stood stoically, watching her husband rummage through their home. He flung parchments about, and they floated to the ground like oversized snowflakes. The normally bare floor had begun to take on the appearance of a spotted-white carpet.

"Where is it?" mumbled Iridan. "Where is it?"

"Do you mind?" Myrin asked sharply. "I really don't appreciate this mess." Iridan shot her a look of disappointment then continued with his searching. Myrin's tone softened quickly as she approached her husband and wrapped her arms around his back. "How about staying home for awhile?"

Iridan turned to his wife. More pages dropped to the floor as his arms circled about her. "I'm sorry, but I need to find this passage." He kissed her lightly on the forehead then gathered up all the fallen scrolls. I knew it was a mistake to bring these home, he thought; I'll never be able to study here. "As soon as I find it, I'll come right back."

"But what if you don't find it?"

"I won't be able to concentrate on anything until I do." Iridan paused, knowing that his wife made a good point. "I'll make sure I cut it short; I promise."

Myrin shrugged. He could tell that she knew he was right. He would not be good company as preoccupied as he was. "Thanks," he said as he spun out of the house with all the scrolls he had brought home the day before tucked under his arm.

***

Walking down the castle streets brought Iridan continuous discomfort. His dramatic return to Su'Meeryn on Jokk-al Ystren's back had brought gratified attention from all who recognized him. A few of the people would even bow as he passed by. All this interest—aimed at an ordinary scout—made him uncomfortable, but he could do little about it.

He moved quickly and headed for the alleys, trying to avoid the thankful passers-by. Finally reaching his destination, he gratefully entered Korath's abandoned home. Following Su'Meeryn's victory cele-bration, Iridan had asked the king to keep the house as the old cleric had left it. Iridan now spent much of his spare time in this home search-ing through the documents—searching for answers.

Many questions still remained. What of Korath's visions? Iridan glanced at the staff that rested in the corner of the room. What of Chaw Den? Nothing had happened to the bird, which still sat atop the staff. Iridan felt certain that Korath could not have been totally misled by his visions. After all, the castle had been saved. His irritation grew with each day that brought him no answers.

The task of attempting to decipher all these passages and prophe-cies, however, proved arduous, especially for one untrained in religious studies. But his months of searching had finally produced its first glimmer of hope. The previous night, he had found a fragment of a passage attributed directly to Naar. It read: *...then, Chaw Den shall soar, and the masses are saved.* The excerpt had come from a more recent prophet who quoted the great Naar; unfortunately, the writer had assumed that the reader would be familiar with Naar's teachings. This was not the case with Iridan. He needed to find the source of the pas-sage.

If, in fact, the prophecy referred to the attack on Su'Meeryn, it ap-peared to be in error. The ancient bird remained unchanged. To what could the passage be referring? Might it be Jokk-all Ystren? Although possible, it did not seem right. He had found a couple of other passages referring to Chaw Den, and they did not seem to apply to the dragon. What could it all mean?

"Did that old man organize anything?" Iridan mumbled. He contin-ued to search and read. His mind swam; he felt confounded by the ob-scure words. Parchments flew from his hands in frustration. After months of study, he still could not grasp any meaning.

Finally, after rereading one paragraph for the fifth time—still not comprehending even one word—Iridan decided to head home. He exit-ed the house and saw the first rays of the morning sun shooting over the horizon. His head shook in regret at another broken promise to his wife.

Despite his anger towards himself—for his failure to uncover any-thing of value in the scrolls, along with his failure to leave early—he enjoyed the walk through the crisp morning air. Not many people were about, so he avoided the thankful gestures that typically followed him to his door. Myrin still slept as Iridan entered their home. He dropped into a chair, and exhaustion overwhelmed him.

It seemed like only minutes before Iridan awoke. Myrin was far from quiet as she performed her morning routine. She slammed down a plate and rattled a chair to a different side of the table, for no practical purpose.

Iridan stood drowsily and approached her. "I'm sorry," he said contritely.

"Do you think that makes up for everything? That's all you ever do: apologize. But where does it leave me? I end up sitting around here all night, alone. I'm tired of it."

"I know; but it's hard on me too. I've got my scouting duties, and I still need to make sense out of Korath's scrolls."

"Why?"

"We've been over this before," Iridan sighed. "I need answers; I need to understand why it all happened."

Before Myrin could reply, a knock sounded at their door. Iridan walked over, hoping he would not find a stranger wanting to get a glimpse of Su'Meeryn's *savior*; these well-wishers regularly paid them visits, and it was becoming quite tiresome. So, he was somewhat relieved, and surprised, when he saw a herald from Jaleph.

"The king requests you both join him for lunch."

"Thank you," Iridan replied. "Please advise him we would be honored." Although the couple had been invited to the palace on a number of occasions since their return, Iridan still did not feel accustomed to dining with the king.

"Well, at least we'll get to do something today," Iridan pointed out.

Myrin refused to respond. She stood with her arms folded across her chest, glaring at her husband.

***

Following a silent morning, Myrin and Iridan headed off towards the palace. "Look, what do you want me to do?" he finally exclaimed.

Myrin stopped suddenly and swung to face him. "You were so different back then." She strode a few paces further then spun back around. "If things don't change soon, I'll leave you."

"That's it? You'll just leave?" Iridan stopped when he noticed a crowd starting to form around them. He pulled Myrin close and whispered, "Can we please just have a nice lunch? I won't go over to Korath's tonight, and we can talk." He received only a look of suspicion in response, and they continued on to meet the king.

When they reached the palace, they found Teraken waiting for them. "Good," the huge man said, "Jaleph said you were coming. I'm going to need you tomorrow. I want you to patrol to the east." Before Iridan could protest, Teraken had already disappeared around a corner.

155

He turned to his wife, displaying a nervous expression on his face.

Myrin glared at her husband. "It figures. How long will you be gone this time?"

"I'm sorry, but it is my job. I'll need to be asleep early, but we'll still have the evening. And I'll talk to Dirwyn; she can probably spend tomorrow with you."

"Great, just what I wanted, a day with your cousin." Myrin stormed past the palace guards as they opened the door.

Iridan followed meekly behind. He understood her frustration, but what could he do? He would try to give her a nice evening, but, obviously, changes would need to be made when he returned.

Chapter 3

A dark mood hung over the lunch table so thick, Iridan felt he might need to swim out of it. He glanced at the king, who sat uncomfortably silent. Myrin cut through the meat before her like it was his own flesh. The fine aroma of his meal drifted to his nostrils as Iridan dejectedly pushed the food about on his plate.

"Well," Jaleph finally said, trying to lighten the atmosphere, "is there anything new you two might be able to tell me?"

"Yes, your highness. I'm supposed to spend the next day or so with Dirwyn," Myrin answered. Only Iridan could sense her sarcasm.

"Really? Why is that?" asked the king.

"Because my husband is leaving me for another one of his missions."

Jaleph looked between Myrin and Iridan in obvious discomfort. "Yes, well..." He paused before continuing more confidently, "perhaps I can find some activity for you while our good scout here is busy."

Myrin's face brightened somewhat at those words. "What do you have in mind?"

"Oh, I don't know. What interests you? You need something to do other than just sitting around your home all day."

"That's for sure, but I've never really thought about it," she said hesitantly. "All I'm really familiar with is farming."

"Well, we certainly can't have you working out in the fields. I'll tell you what, you come by tomorrow after Iridan leaves. We'll talk it over and see what you might enjoy."

For the first time in a long while, Myrin looked at her husband with a bright smile on her face. "Choose well," he said, feeling relieved that she would finally have something to occupy her time. The remainder of the meal passed by much more pleasantly. Light conversation felt like music to Iridan's ears, and he enjoyed finally hearing Myrin's laughter again. After finishing, they walked home hand-in-hand. The lunch had turned out to be more productive then he could have ever imagined.

***

Iridan had always enjoyed the solitude of the open wilderness. Perhaps that explained his desire to continue as a scout after the dragon battle. As a reward for his deeds during Su'Meeryn's crisis, he could have chosen any new profession in the kingdom, but he had decided to remain in the position for which he had been trained. Given the tension between himself and Myrin, along with the constant attention from the people of the castle, he often found himself eager to begin his forthcoming missions. And, despite the fact that Myrin and he had finally spent a pleasurable night together, he still welcomed this break. It was unfortunate that their life so often came to this: either bickering or separated. Hopefully the tension would be lessened between them once she decided on her new vocation.

He also knew that the fact that Myrin had not yet conceived weighed heavily on her. They both were eager for children, and he knew she was becoming increasing anxious over the past year that she might be barren. Iridan tried to comfort her as best he could, but it never seemed to help.

A stiff wind greeted Iridan as he passed under the gate; he found that strange at such an early hour. With a shrug, he pulled his cloak a little tighter about him then exited the castle. Turning his horse to face the rising sun, he headed out to survey the east land as Teraken had ordered.

With his horse trotting away from the gate, and his attention focused towards the east, Iridan failed to see a figure approaching the castle from the west. A handsome man rode on horseback, dressed in a simple white shirt and trousers. A silver belt clung snugly across his waist. The man raised his head to the portal guards as his flaxen hair swept about his shoulders. He lifted a banner and was welcomed into the castle.

Chapter 4

The king was roused from sleep by a persistent knocking at his door. Jaleph slowly sat up in bed and rubbed his eyes. The light flooding in from the east window still showed the hazy glow of early morning. "Yes! Come in! What is it?" he barked.

The door opened, and one of Jaleph's guards poked his head through. "I'm sorry, Sire, but I was just brought urgent news. A herald from Labyn has arrived. He brings word from Queen Illiyna."

The words took a moment to register in Jaleph's groggy mind. Once they did, he sprang out of bed and rushed towards his wardrobe. "Have him meet me in my private chamber. I'll come down momentarily, and..." Jaleph thought of sending for Teraken to join him but decided against it. He was the king, and he needed to start making decisions on his own. "Never mind," he continued, "just tell him to wait for me there."

***

Jaleph entered his strategy room and was greeted by a large smile from the herald. The man wore a bright white shirt and sat in one of the blue chairs directly under the mural of the dragon battle. A silver belt supporting white pants glistened as he stood. "A fine likeness, your highness," the man in white commented. He gave the slightest trace of motion with his head, indicating the portrait above.

"Thank you," Jaleph responded awkwardly, taken aback by the man's words. He had not expected such a casual greeting. The man sounded like an old friend whom he had not seen in a long time. The king reached up to his headband and scratched the skin under his emerald. No words came to mind.

The visitor turned and gazed at the painting. His eyes seemed to swim over every inch, as if he saw each individual stroke of the brush. "Quite a remarkable scene. I only wish I might have been present to witness it. A glorious battle and a glorious victory." He breathed a heavy sigh of satisfaction as he returned to his chair and pulled it close to the table. "Please join me, your highness," he spoke, motioning to the space across from him.

"Thank you," Jaleph repeated—as if he was the guest—while he reached for the chair that the man offered. "What can I do for you?"

No response came for a long moment. The herald sat motionless, gazing at the king. Just before Jaleph broke the awkward silence, the man spoke: "I am here with word from Queen Illiyna," and the man pulled forth a ring displaying the royal symbol of Labyn. "She hopes you understand. Her highness desires to discuss the possibilities of a treaty; however, she first wishes to hear the results from your other emissaries prior to formalizing an alliance. You must realize, Majesty, our queen fears spies abound in her court. That is why she was rather abrupt with your man Pothar. She worried that encouraging words towards your offer might have resulted in an attack on Labyn or an attempt on her life. However, if Illiyna was to be approached by an already strong alliance, the benefits would outweigh the potential risks."

Silence again filled the room. This time the emissary was obviously waiting for the king's response. "Very wise," Jaleph finally said. He should have felt encouraged, but, instead, he just felt numb.

"Have your other envoys returned?" asked the man.

"No, not yet," Jaleph replied, wondering how the man knew of the other missions. But, before he could ask, the man continued:

"When are they expected?"

"Perhaps today, I'm told," Jaleph answered, "barring any delays."

"Ah, good. I shall return to my queen once I have news. She then asks that you personally visit her. Despite her protestations, I expect that she will still agree to your treaty, even if no other lands join you. Labyn should not remain isolated.

"My queen is anxious for the meeting. She eagerly anticipates hearing stories of Su'Meeryn's miraculous victory." The herald's eyes glistened as he continued. "As you may have been told, our Queen is quite striking. You will find her an extremely hospitable host.

"Please send a messenger to me when your envoys return." He stood and walked to the door. "Oh, by the way," he continued, "Illiyna also wants to meet the man who flew on the dragon's back. I believe his name is Iridan. Please have him accompany you, your highness."

Before the man could turn down the hallway, Jaleph managed to blurt out one question. "What's your name?"

The handsome emissary turned back to look through the open entranceway. "You may call me Ut," he replied, then disappeared.

The king sat mesmerized by the strange man, with the equally strange name: Ut; he had never heard of one like it. After further reflecting on his peculiar meeting, Jaleph pulled himself out of the chair and left the room. As soon as he entered the hallway, the king was informed that another of his emissaries had just returned. Jaleph quickly turned around and reentered his room, ordering that the man be brought to him immediately.

***

Kedin stood dejected at the doorway. He was a small man, about the size of a preadolescent boy. No one in the castle was too fond of him. He seemed to care little for anyone else and was only concerned with advancing his own position. Due to his slender build and diminutive stature, he certainly was never going to be a soldier. With no other prospects, an uncle of his had managed to get him duties as a royal page. Jaleph had allowed his advancement, not because he liked Kedin, but because Kedin was always very efficient and extremely eager to serve the king. Jaleph waved for him to enter, and Kedin's tight black clothes displayed unnatural curves as he entered.

Kedin's long face slumped to his slim neck as he faced the king. "I'm sorry Majesty, but we'll receive no assistance from Gorthon. They refused to even meet with me." He looked back up as a finely manicured finger brushed a curly blond lock of hair away from his eyes. Jaleph had known Kedin stood little chance of succeeding with his overture. The land of Gorthon sat east of the town of Cishor, and a line of hills served as a natural boundary between Gorthon and the Cyrenn Wastelands. Any attack on Gorthon from the west seemed unlikely; therefore, they would gain little from allying themselves with Su'Meeryn.

"Well, that's what we expected," replied the king. "I'm glad you returned safely, though. Much will now depend on what we hear from Toresh."

"Majesty, I heard that Labyn refused our offer too, but that a herald arrived this morning. May I inquire what occurred?" Kedin asked.

"He is not your concern," the king answered sharply, annoyed that one of his subjects would be questioning him. "Report back to the nobles. See if they have a new assignment for you," Jaleph ordered. After waving Kedin away, he sat sulking in his room, gazing up at the painting on the wall.

***

A crash sounded as wood splintered, flying like arrows in all directions. The gate burst open and scores of soldiers streamed through.

Weapons clashed as defenders ran to meet the attack. Cries of agony reached his ears while blood splashed and bodies fell to the ground.

Blades struck in every direction. Confusion reigned. Who was the enemy? It became difficult to tell. Soldiers crushed in all around him, and his sword raised and fell as often as his weary arm could manage.

His brother somehow remained at his side. Dobrah was nearby too, her body stained crimson. She was engaged with one of the assailants. The man's strike missed, as her blade ripped open his stomach.

The battle then shifted. The attack became focused on Jaleph and Fenik. They had been identified. Sword points searched for the royal brothers. Just as they were about to be overrun, Ruy flew amidst the melee. His axe struck like lightening. Every impact left carnage. Severed flesh flew in all directions. Bones shattered. The air was thick with blood as victims fell at his feet. Ruy paused for a moment to grin at the king. But the smile quickly disappeared, and his body went limp. As an enemy soldier yanked his weapon from Ruy's back, Jaleph quickly drove his own blade into the man.

Pain erupted from the king's shoulder, and he dropped to his knees. He looked up and saw his attacker re-gripping his mace, preparing to strike again. Jaleph sat helpless—waiting for death. But before the weapon fell to crush his skull, Fenik leapt forth. He buried his sword into the man's chest, piercing his heart.

As Fenik reached down to help the king up, steel suddenly burst out from his neck. Jaleph was showered with his brother's blood. Fenik fell. His body pinned the king to the ground…

***

"Here he is," a voice called from the open door of Jaleph's strategy room. The king raised a drowsy head from the table, still shaken from the horrifying images. It had been weeks since his last dream of the battle. He had enjoyed the respite, and was troubled by its return. He hoped that the dream would not become a daily occurrence again. "We didn't know you were still here, Sire," the man continued. "Toresh has returned, and he brings good news."

Jaleph's eyes brightened at those words. "Where is he?"

"He's was getting some food in the dining hall while we looked for you."

"Well, send him here." Jaleph paused for a moment. "No, never mind, we'll go there." The king followed after the guard as they raced through the hallways, while the last vestiges of his dream faded away.

They found Toresh sitting in the dining area finishing a plate of food. He set down his knife and stood as the king approached.

"Well, I heard you brought good news. Tell me what you've learned," Jaleph requested.

Toresh looked around somewhat sheepishly. "Certainly, sir. Here?"

"Yes, yes. Get on with it." Jaleph took a chair and motioned for Toresh to return to his seat.

"Of course, Sire. I met with Josu, Shekul's king." Shekul lay southeast of Su'Meeryn and was an even smaller kingdom. "To be honest, Josu seems like a weak man. It appeared obvious that he was manipulated by those in his court. When I explained your offer, he seemed unsure of what to do. Some of the nobles met together and convinced him to agree. Considering the size of the armies from the three northern lands that attacked us, they were eager to bolster their defenses. Josu offered to come to Su'Meeryn, at your convenience, to formalize the treaty. I'm not sure how much assistance he will be, but I guess anything will help."

"Fine," Jaleph replied, somewhat irritably. He was growing weary of all his subordinates and their freely offered opinions. "You did well. Now we have something to build on. You may return to your duties." He turned back to the guard who had accompanied him. Jaleph was about to summon Ut then remembered the meeting he had planned with Myrin. He smiled in anticipation as he made his way to his study.

***

Myrin's simple green dress flowed gracefully about her as she entered the room. The royal escort closed the dark stained door behind Myrin, leaving the pair alone. "Good afternoon, your majesty," Myrin greeted the king as she sat in a chair opposite him.

"Please, we don't need to be so formal in here. Call me Jaleph; after all, I do owe my life to you." Myrin's face glowed with obvious pleasure at the king's words. "I'm sorry that we couldn't meet earlier. I had a number of matters to deal with," Jaleph continued as he admired her long hair and lovely face. Iridan is a lucky man, he thought. "Have you decided on any areas you might wish to pursue?"

"It's all I've thought about, but nothing has come to mind. As I said, all I really know is farming."

"That just won't do. We can't have one of Su'Meeryn's heroes farming." The words sparkled off Jaleph's tongue. "Maybe we can think of something new."

"Yes sir, I mean Jaleph. I do know something of foods. I used to prepare most of my family's meals. I kind of enjoyed that, I guess."

Jaleph consider for a moment. "How would you feel about being a chef?"

"I suppose that'd be all right," answered Myrin, somewhat skeptically.

The king smiled. "I'm not sure you understand what I mean. The palace has many cooks but only one chef. You would be in charge in the kitchen. The chef is responsible for the preparation of the meals, but you wouldn't be doing all the work, the cooks would. It's a demanding position with a lot of responsibility. But it is a position of some stature."

Myrin's eyes brightened as the king spoke. "That sounds wonderful, Jaleph. You know, I think I'd do a good job. When can I start?"

"You won't be able to just walk into it. You'll need to train for a while under Markis. He is our current chef. He always complains about how busy he is, so I'm sure he'll be happy to get some help. You can report to him whenever you'd like."

"Can I go see him now?" She appeared to be practically bubbling out of her chair.

"Hold on. You'll need to dress like a chef first. Why don't you go to the market and get some new clothes? Actually, I think I'll go with to help you find what you'll need. If you don't mind."

"Of course not," Myrin exclaimed.

"Good, then let's get going."

Myrin stood and moved towards the door, but then she turned back and asked, "Can we stop and see Dirwyn first? She's expecting me to come by today."

"Certainly," Jaleph replied. He watched her leave the room and felt an ache of loneliness as he was reminded of Dobrah. He still felt some desire for the lanky soldier—despite her marriage. His eyes briefly surveyed Myrin's figure as he again thought: Iridan is indeed a lucky man.

***

Jaleph reached Dirwyn's home with Myrin at his side. After a knock on the door, a haggard looking man appeared. He smiled at Myrin until he saw the king, then a startled look jolted his face. "Sire, how can I help you?"

"Hello, Uncle Festin," Myrin said. "We came by to see Dirwyn."

Iridan's uncle rubbed his wide hips and uncomfortably peered backwards. He turned around nervously and seemed at a loss. Guessing the man's concern, Jaleph said, "Don't worry Mr. Festin, we'll wait here." Jaleph often found that his un-expecting hosts felt their homes to be unsuitable for their monarch to enter.

The old man slammed the door, and the pair heard him scurrying about. A few moments later, Dirwyn greeted them. Her stunning face beamed at her cousin's wife before turning towards Jaleph. "Hello, your majesty. It's been awhile." Her smile broadened as her head tilted slightly towards her shoulder.

"Yes," replied the king, "an unfortunate circumstance that we must find a way to remedy." Since Ruy's death, Jaleph had seen little of Su'Meeryn's loveliest subject.

"That would be charming." She glanced back to Myrin and her bright smile turned to a puzzled expression.

"We stopped by so I could tell you that we'd have to change our plans. Jaleph said he's going to make me one of his chefs and I need to get some new clothes," Myrin declared proudly.

"Oh?"

"Yes, isn't that wonderful?"

For some reason, Dirwyn did not appear to agree with Myrin's evaluation of the situation. "Well, have fun," she answered flatly. She turned back to Jaleph. "I hope to see you again soon, your majesty."

Jaleph smiled. He took Myrin's elbow and led her away from the small home.

Chapter 5

Iridan stood next to his horse, as it contentedly drank from a small stream, and his vision searched the eastern horizon. Throughout the day, he had seen no movement other than some small animals. He stroked his mount's neck until he noticed a brown shape rustling in the brush to his right. He quietly pulled out his bow and strung an arrow. The hare flinched upon hearing the snap of the bowstring, but the shot flew true and impaled the creature before it could bolt. Iridan happily retrieved his kill, and shortly thereafter, he had the rabbit skinned and spinning over a small fire. The aroma of the roasting meat nearly overwhelmed his senses until it finally appeared thoroughly cooked. When he had finished his meal, he leaned back, gazing into the sky. The sun had set, and the first stars were just starting to flicker.

He stretched out on the ground and continued to stare upward as more stars began to reveal themselves in the deepening gloom. Iridan enjoyed sitting for long stretches and viewing the night sky. A number of shooting stars passed overhead, and his thoughts returned to the castle. The words of Naar echoed in his mind: *then Chaw Den shall soar, and the masses are saved.* What did it mean? He felt the past year had been wasted. He was no closer to finding the answers than when he first started searching through Korath's materials.

I'll circle around south tomorrow then head back to Su'Meeryn, Iridan thought. He planned to reach the gates by nightfall, which would allow him to spend the following day studying. Iridan hoped that Jaleph would have found a job for Myrin by the time of his return, so he could continue his readings in peace.

***

A heavy wind blew against his back causing a chill, while Iridan stood atop a jagged boulder. His clothes rippled, and his hair whipped about his eyes. He glanced down through an abyss of haze, which led to the base of the mountain. Then he cautiously tilted his face upward, searching for the peak, but it eluded his vision.

He carefully slid down from his perch; the cracks and hard texture of the skin of the mountain felt as if it had been sunburned from constant exposure. Small pieces of rock flaked off as Iridan reached out, and his hands began to pull himself higher. He climbed for what seemed like hours, constantly struggling to keep moving. His muscles ached; they felt as if they would burst through his flesh at any moment. Still he climbed. Blood began to seep from nicks and cuts all across his fingers and hands. Despite his agony, the unexplained compulsion continued to draw him towards the summit.

A sharp stone snagged a corner of his shirt; it tore loose. It seemed that the mountain had grown probing fingers. Up and down his legs, rocks and pebbles pinched into his trousers, grabbing hold of the fabric. Piece by piece the remainder of his clothes ripped from his aching body. Now nothing protected him from the biting wind that continued to blow. Still he climbed.

His skin grew tight. Even in the cold, the sun burned a layer of pain to blanket his throbbing muscles. As his ascent continued, sections of his dead flesh peeled from his body until his ragged skin matched the surface of the mountain. More hours passed, but the sun showed no signs of setting; its rays continued to bore into his skin. He felt that his muscles would soon be exposed directly to the rays of the sun.

Finally, mercifully, his bloody hands reached a ledge. As he dragged his tortured body onto the peak, the sun abruptly disappeared. He stood in a void—all around him blackness—while the wind continued to rage. Blindly he began to walk. But instead of toppling back down the side of the mountain, his feet continued to find solid ground. Miles passed. Hours passed. Still he found only blackness. Finally, the brutal wind slowed to a breeze, then stopped. Iridan sensed that his journey had reached its culmination. He tentatively advanced a few more paces; however, his last step found no ground. He tumbled forward and felt the air rushing through his tattered flesh. After a few terrifying moments, he landed hard. Slowly he pulled his aching body up.

Iridan tried to look about, but still no light reached his eyes. A rumbling began all around him, which grew in intensity. The noise then began to form itself into a strange pattern. It continued to take shape until Iridan realized it was a voice.

Who are you?

Iridan wondered at the question. After his tortured journey, he could not form a coherent thought. He found no answer.

Who are you?

Who am I? He could not respond. Why could he not answer? It was, after all, a simple enough question.

Who are you?

He slowly gained control of his mind. Who am I? A name began to form, but he did not recognize it. It was a strange name.

Who are you?

Finally he managed to form a sound. "Iridan," he blurted out.

Incorrect! Who are you?

Incorrect? How could that be? That was his name, after all, and he should know.

Who are you?

Who am I?

Who are you?

Who are you?

Iridan awoke with a start. He sat up and looked around. The sun shone brightly, which was troubling. He had trained himself to wake before dawn, but he had overslept by a number of hours. Shaking his head, Iridan stood and packed his supplies. He mounted his horse and rode off. With such a late departure, he decided to cut his planned route in half then head back to the castle. As he surveyed the land, his dream remained fresh in his mind. It was a strange dream, a dream unlike any he ever had before.

Chapter 6

The king approached his private strategy room. He dreaded opening the door and facing the strange man again, but he had no alternative. Jaleph entered and found Ut sitting in the exact position he had occupied when they first met.

"Ah, your highness," Ut said, "a pleasure meeting with you again. You left me waiting for a long time. I happened to hear that your emissaries arrived several days ago."

"Yes, well, I have to apologize. It's been busy around here. I've neglected my audiences with the townspeople. There were many disputes I needed to mediate. I hope that you've been comfortable."

Ut looked at him knowingly. "What news do you bring me?"

"We've received a commitment from Shekul; they agreed to an alliance. With our three lands together, we'll make a formidable force."

Ut sat, unmoving. He stared at Jaleph. "Yes," he finally replied, "a strong alliance." But he seemed completely apathetic to the king's words. "Great deeds shall be accomplished." He rose from his chair and headed to the door. "I leave immediately to bring word to my queen. Labyn shall make ready for your arrival to celebrate this new age.

"Prepare to leave tomorrow at dawn. And do not forget, Queen Illiyna desires to meet Iridan as well," Ut said, smiling at Jaleph.

"Of course," responded the king. Once again he felt mesmerized by this man. How was it that Ut's words affected him so deeply? He knew not why.

"Good, good," Ut said. "I shall see you in Labyn." Then he was gone.

Jaleph remained alone, feeling more like a servant than a monarch.

***

The room in which the king now sat was huge. Golden candleholders hung on bright white walls that reached to the high ceiling. The noon sun shone luxuriously through arched windows, so all the candles remained cold. A long table rested in the middle of the room; the light reflected in its dark, polished surface. A score of high wooden chairs circled it. Sparkling silverware rested atop golden place mats. The decor had been passed down to Jaleph's father from a time before the splintering of Xavsyn: the last empire. Halet had always appreciated the beauty of this room, and the scene continually left quite an impression on first time visitors.

Teraken approached the table and sat next to Jaleph. The king had invited the large warrior to join him for lunch and to update him on the preparations for his departure the next day. Teraken grabbed a hunk of meat and ripped off a portion. As his companion chewed, Jaleph thought about the past year his old friend had endured. Everyone had lost much during the attack from the armies of the north, but the death of his son at the teeth of the dragon had devastated Teraken deeply. Rarely was he seen around the castle other than when he was about his duties, but over the past few months he was starting to return to his old self. While he had not forgotten Teracuss, the state of mourning could not continue forever. Teraken needed to move on, and, finally, he had begun.

"Well," Teraken said, still chewing his meal, "everything will be ready by tomorrow morning. Your best horses are being rested today. I assigned twenty soldiers to accompany you. Iridan should return later today. We'll be ready at dawn."

"That's fine," said Jaleph. "Look, I have a question for you. I've been noticing the attention that Iridan has still been receiving. What do you make of it? I wonder if it's a good idea to bring him along."

Teraken started to reply but decided to finish chewing first. He swallowed, took a drink of wine, then answered. "I've noticed it too. He seems to be handling it pretty well. He's been quick to accept any mission I send him on. He's probably just anxious to get away. That does worry me somewhat; after all, he is running out on his lovely wife. I guess he still needs to adjust to everything. His life took a big change when they returned. Anyway, I expect he'll be fine. This attention is bound to wear off eventually. I'm surprised that it hasn't already.

"As far as bringing him along, you really don't have a choice. Queen Illiyna requested his presence. We can't afford to offend her. Besides, I'll feel better having him accompany you. He's proven his ability under conflict before." Teraken took another quick bite. "I have to make sure you're safe. This whole thing bothers me. I would prefer to be going along."

"You'll be needed here while I'm away. You're the only one I trust to remain in case anything happens."

"It's not just that. It's this Ut. I've got a strange feeling about him. I'm not sure that sending you out is the best idea right now. I don't trust him."

"This is my decision to make!" Jaleph snapped. "We're finally about to have the alliance we've been working for, and we don't need you or anyone else ruining it!"

Teraken look dumbfounded at his friend. He was obviously not used to this tone coming from the king. That realization made Jaleph feel powerful. He enjoyed it.

They ate the rest of their meal in silence. When he finished, Teraken quickly excused himself and left. Jaleph sat alone. The great table spread out before him like the ancient oak trees from which it had been cut. His lone form in that huge hall looked like a small squirrel ready to bolt into the high branches seeking refuge. His fork echoed throughout the hall after it fell to his plate.

***

Dusk approached, and Jaleph was anxious for the coming day. He felt anxious to leave his mark on Su'Meeryn's future. If the attack one year ago had been due to his shortcomings as king, he wanted to make amends. Now, perhaps, Su'Meeryn could take a primary role on events in this region. And maybe, just maybe, he might lead an army north to further avenge himself on those who had killed Fenik, but such a decision would come later. Right now, he needed to concentrate on forming this alliance. Despite Ut's promise, a treaty had not yet been signed with Labyn. He must make certain of nothing occurring to interfere with the pledge he had received from Ut, and after that, he would finalize the treaty with Shekul. Yes, everything was starting to take shape.

Prior to retiring for the evening, Jaleph decided to take a stroll through the castle, alone. Fenik and he had often walked the grounds at night by themselves, despite the protests of his guards. The brothers enjoyed the brief feeling of anonymity, but they always remained close to the palace: a king and prince must make certain of their safety after all.

A warm evening greeted him as his thoughts again turned to Dobrah. She still served in the military, and he occasionally found ways to accidentally run into her. After her marriage, Jaleph thought she might retire her position, but she never did: most likely because she had remained childless. Dobrah seemed content to continue as a soldier for the time being.

The thought of one appealing woman who had not become pregnant brought to his mind another. He remembered Myrin's arrival in the castle courtyard atop Jokk-al Ystren. Despite her tattered appearance, her beauty had been immediately evident. And that loveliness had multiplied with some minimal attention. With her treated and styled hair, some flattering clothes and a few cosmetics, only Dirwyn's beauty surpassed hers. Too bad, he thought, too bad; and Iridan doesn't even appreciate her.

Sweat began to form on his brow; he pulled the leather strap from his head and wiped off the perspiration. He had not realized how humid the night had become. Some of the guards who patrolled the area noticed him and moved closer. Realizing he had been spotted, the pleasure of his walk evaporated. He turned and started back as a gentle wind rose, ruffling his cloak. The breeze tried to dissipate the humidity, but it fought a losing battle. He thankfully entered the palace and closed the doors on the guards who had trailed after him.

Jaleph reached his room and collapsed into a chair. He felt like bathing but knew he would need to in the morning anyway. So, despite the clammy feeling of drying sweat, he climbed into his bed.

Chapter 7

The horse skidded to a stop before the castle gate. Its nostrils flared while its rider signaled to the guards stationed on top of the wall. Iridan enjoyed the quick burst of speed from his mount as they approached Su'Meeryn. Other than his unusual dream, the trip had been rather uneventful. The only excitement he had managed to muster was this short sprint. Fortunately, the more mundane his missions were, the better the news for his king. So, all-in-all, his trip had been successful.

Iridan passed through the gate and hopped off his steed while the sky above continued to darken. The warm breeze tussled his hair as he walked the horse through the castle. When he opened the stables, Veake, the old stable keeper, shambled forwarded.

"Ah, hullo sur," the short man said when he recognized Iridan. He bowed stiffly as he pulled a bug out from his uneven beard that did not cover his upper lip. A mossy glow seemed to emanate from his skin, which was covered by a filthy yellow tunic that hung to his ankles. A layer of dirt—along with other substances from the stable, which Iridan preferred not to consider—covered his bare feet like a pair of cracked leather shoes.

"T's 'n honor t' see ya ugain," Veake continued as he rubbed his scraggly mane of long ashen hair.

"A pleasure seeing you too, Veake." Iridan apprehensively squeezed the man's shoulder and immediately regretted that decision when he felt the grime on Veake's tunic. He reached around to scratch his back and quickly wiped off his hand.

Despite Veake's rather disturbing appearance, Iridan had always liked the man. They had first met when Iridan was beginning his training in the military. In their youth, Iridan and his friends enjoyed taunting the unusual stableman. Veake, however, never seemed to notice; he always showed unexplainable kindness to the boys. Eventually Iridan grew to enjoy his riding drills under the watchful eyes of Veake and quickly learned that Veake's accent and strange appearance were not indicative of a slow mind. Iridan had always thought that the stableman never comprehended the cruel pranks of the boys. How wrong he had been. Veake understood everything happening around him, but instead of lashing out in anger, he responded with kindness. That character had led more than just Iridan to eventually call Veake a friend.

"Ya, ya," Veake smilcd, then his face twisted into a knot. His head bent back, and he spat out a substance of unknown color. "Jaleph's savior back fr'm 'is mission."

"Don't say that Veake. I just did what I could." Iridan paused for a moment. "Wait a minute, what are you doing here now? I thought that you were tending the stables during the day."

"Ah, ya know. Da big heads git some crazy toughts 'n next ting I know, 'm worken nights agin!"

Iridan shook his head in mock disgust.

"It'll be diffrunt soon." A huge smile revealed Veake's disintegrating teeth. "Beeg chunges 'r comin. Evryting diffrunt soon!"

"What're you saying?"

"Diffrunt soon, diffrunt soon," Veake cackled as he grabbed the horse's reins and led it back into the stable.

Iridan just shook his head at the disappearing figure. Crazy old man, he thought. He then left to report to Teraken regarding his mission. Teraken briefly advised him about the treaty overture from Labyn and told him to return first thing in the morning. As Iridan strolled towards his house, a white figure with a silver belt shadowed his movements.

***

Before Iridan reached the safety of his home, a trio of grateful inhabitants surrounded him. "I knew it was him," the man exclaimed to his wife; his young skinny daughter stared wide-eyed at Iridan with her mouth agape. The man exhibited a nervous smile and reached out to grab Iridan's hand.

"We just want to thank you for what you did," the woman said.

Iridan took a deep breath to gather his patience before responding, "You're welcome." He patted the girl's head and spun away from the family.

When is this all going to end? he thought, as he finally reached his door. A year later and people were still acting like it had been yesterday. True, the outpouring of adoration had diminished somewhat, but when would it cease completely?

Myrin greeted him with a warm hug. Iridan was somewhat surprised; it had been a while since he had seen her looking so happy. "How'd it go?" she asked after kissing him on the cheek.

"Just fine," he answered. "I didn't run into anything." He went to a cupboard and grabbed a flask before collapsing into a chair. "Do you ever think that it's weird that people are still thanking us about the battle?"

"It happened again, huh?" Myrin asked. As Iridan nodded she continued, "I think you're making too much out of it. Maybe they just moved into the castle, and this is the first chance they had to see you. You know, it is a big deal. Everyone could be dead."

"I guess you're right," Iridan replied. "Now tell me, what happened with the king? Did he find something for you?"

Her face brightened even more. "Yes, I'm going to be trained as one of the royal chefs." She told him about the job and her responsibilities; she also detailed her day in the market with the king. "Let me show you some of the clothes Jaleph bought for me." She darted back to snatch some of the garments.

"Jaleph huh, kind of personal isn't it?" he asked and flashed her a wry grin.

"Oh, he just wanted me to call him that when we were alone. I guess it made him feel a little more comfortable."

"I hope not *too* comfortable."

Myrin appeared perplexed until she saw a smile emerge on his face. "Now you just wait there a moment," she said as she pulled out a beautiful amber dress that sparkled as she turned it. "What do you think?"

Iridan considered for a moment. "The color's too similar to your hair."

Myrin playfully threw the dress at him and pulled out another. "What about this one?"

It was another beautiful gown, which caused Iridan to have a thought. "I thought that you were going to be a chef. What's with the dresses?"

"Well, there will be other functions, not just cooking. I have some more practical clothes here too." She plopped down on the bed looking extremely disappointed.

Iridan stood and laughed. "I was just teasing. They all look lovely. And they'll look even better with you in them."

He then watched dutifully as Myrin systematically displayed the remaining articles of her new wardrobe, while giving the appropriate reactions to each. After she concluded, he stood and walked to bed. She joined him, and they enjoyed a peaceful night together.

***

Morning arrived much too quickly as Iridan rose to prepare to meet

175

with Teraken. Myrin also stood from the bed and readied herself for her first day of training.

The couple walked through the castle streets enjoying a brisk breeze. When they reached the palace, two guards escorted them into the building and to Jaleph's library. Iridan looked around the small room—in amazement at the offensive appearance—while they waited for the king. He pulled one of the burgundy chairs towards himself, and its legs burrowed into one of the orange swirls of the yellow rug. He sat on the cushioned seat and gazed at the shelves of books against the indigo walls. Dust hung from every corner of the small library. Iridan wondered why he was to meet with the king and why Jaleph had chosen this room; obviously nobody had entered it for some time.

"I think the king could have used a decorator rather than another chef," Myrin quipped quietly as she sat.

Iridan chuckled but silenced himself when the door swung open. He stood up as Jaleph and Teraken entered. The king nodded to the pair and the three men sat down.

Jaleph regarded the couple for a moment and then spoke. "I'm glad to see you both. Let's begin. First, we should deal with our lovely lady. Markis will arrive shortly; he has been informed of your new duties and will begin your training immediately. As for you, Iridan," and Jaleph gestured towards Teraken to continue.

"Yes, your highness," Teraken responded. "As I mentioned to you last night, Labyn has agreed to a treaty with Su'Meeryn. Their queen, Illiyna, has requested that the king travel to their land to finalize the arrangement, and that you accompany him. Ut, her messenger, says she is anxious to meet the man who flew on the dragon's back. So, tomorrow morning, you will leave Su'Meeryn with a company of twenty soldiers. Jaleph has ordered me to remain here while you are gone; therefore, I'm assigning you the responsibility of protecting the king. You'll be in charge, and I expect both of you to return safely."

Before Iridan had time to consider this news, a soft tap sounded from the door. "Markis, is that you?" Teraken bellowed. The muted response sounded affirmative. "Well, get in here!"

Having never met Su'Meeryn's chef before, the man's appearance shocked Iridan. Based on his meek reply from behind the door, Iridan had expected to see a slight man, but Markis was anything but small. The chef stood close to seven feet tall. As he walked in, his huge, rolling belly reminded Iridan of the tide from a large lake; it seemed Markis consumed much of what he created. His stained white shirt could have been a tent for a small family, and black trousers clung far too tightly to his legs. A few wisps of dirt brown hair poked from his bald head. Pink splotches covered his face, which culminated at his gargantuan nose. Long fingernails hesitantly scratched at the back of his neck.

An odd aroma drifted off the large chef to Iridan's nostrils. It smelled like a combination of baking materials and sweet perfume. Iridan tried not to think of what additional odor the huge man might be trying to camouflage.

Markis peered about the room until his narrow eyes rested upon Myrin. He tried to soften the gaze before turning to Jaleph, but Iridan immediately knew the chef did not appreciate the king appointing him a partner. A wheezing sound emanated from the lungs buried under layers of fat as Markis took a few steps forward. "I'm here as requested, Majesty," Markis said, sounding much like a small boy.

"Yes, I can see that Markis," Jaleph said in a sharp tone. "Everybody can see that." The king stood and Markis flinched at the motion. "Now, will you come here!"

Markis lumbered over; his wheezing increasing with each step. "How may I help you, Sire?" he asked, though he certainly knew the answer. The chef's high-pitched voice pierced Iridan's brain, and he felt an immediate dislike for this man.

Jaleph shook his head in exasperation. "Myrin is here, as you can plainly see. Will you escort her to the kitchen and begin her training?"

Following a long pause, Markis replied. "Of course, Sire." His look hardened as he turned to Myrin. A plump hand raised and pointed to the door.

Myrin glanced at her husband with a look of trepidation. She had been anticipating this moment; however, she clearly felt uneasy with her new teacher. But she would not back down. Mustering her resolve, she stood and followed the chef out of the room.

Iridan regarded his two companions. He tried to fight back a laugh, but it blurted forth. "He's obviously not happy with this situation." His head dropped into his hands, and he laughed again at the man who appeared more like a caricature than an actual person.

"That fat man is never happy," Teraken spat. "I'm over-worked. I don't need help," he mimicked Markis in the highest pitch his booming voice could manage. "I don't want a woman getting in my way; when do I have time to train someone? You should just get rid of him, Jaleph."

"He is an annoyance, but he's a marvelous chef," the king pointed out. "Besides, if I removed him, where would he go? He'll give Myrin a hard time, but she's strong. She can handle herself against him."

Iridan chuckled again. "He better not be too hard on her, or he might find an unwelcome ingredient in his dinner. Myrin doesn't exactly have a long temper."

"She'll do fine," said Jaleph. "Now let's get back to our business. Iridan, we decided to postpone our departure by a day. Since you returned so late yesterday, we thought, perhaps, you might need a little time to rest and prepare yourself."

"Yes," Teraken added, "one day shouldn't make too much of a difference. Now, let's have a look." He called out and, moments later, an aide brought in a few maps and spread them on the table. The three men studied the route to Labyn, and Teraken pointed to some areas of difficult terrain. With the king traveling to another land, they needed to consider every precaution. Knowing the area well from years of scouting, Iridan contributed his own suggestions regarding their course.

After settling on the route, the trio discussed the meeting with Queen Illiyna. There was not much to say, as they all knew the objective of the mission. The conversation slowed and Iridan asked to be excused. Teraken gave him directions to the kitchen and Iridan left to see how Myrin was managing.

While on his way through the palace, Iridan turned a corner and bumped into Pothar. He immediately smiled at the site of his fellow soldier. The two men had known each other most of their lives, but they had not spent much time together. Since Pothar was several years older, his circle of friends never seemed to intersect with Iridan and Ruy. After the dragon battle, a bond grew between the two, as Pothar had also lost his closest friends. Now Iridan sought Pothar out on the rare occasions when he was not on patrol, with Myrin or studying in Korath's home.

"What're you doing here?" Iridan asked.

"Oh, there was some trouble out at the farms. A few of the men caught a couple bandits, and I was looking for Teraken to give him the report."

"He's still with Jaleph. Why don't you come with me to the kitchen? I'm going to see how Myrin's doing." Pothar nodded and the pair continued down a hallway. "So, I understand you're a diplomat now," Iridan continued.

"You heard about that," Pothar laughed. "I guess the king just doesn't trust any of the nobles, and he figured I couldn't do too much damage. But what about you? Leading the expedition, huh?"

"News travels fast around here."

"Well, I'll be joining you. Teraken assigned me with the king's guard."

"It'll be good to have you along," said Iridan.

"Yeah, I just don't know what it'll be like taking orders from you."

"You'll just have to remember to keep your place," Iridan quipped.

"So how do you think Myrin will do?" Pothar asked after a pause.

"What do you mean by that?"

"That fat man is mighty tough."

Iridan stopped and faced Pothar. "Is he that bad?"

"You obviously don't know Markis very well. He's a dictator in that kitchen. I'm sure he's not happy having someone, someone..." Pothar paused to consider his next words, "...usurping his autonomy."

"Well, I thought you knew Myrin better than that. I'd wager on her over that chef anytime. Besides, how is it that you know Markis so well? I had never met him before today."

"I guess I'm just a more important person than you. Well, at least I was before you became our savior."

"Yeah, whatever," responded Iridan. "But like I said, Myrin can deal with him."

Pothar chuckled and wrapped his arm around his friend's shoulder. "Fine. I guess we'll find out soon enough."

The two approached the staircase, which led to the kitchen. As they started down, they became aware of a commotion from below. It grew in intensity, and Iridan rushed to confront whatever was causing the noise. He burst in and saw the huge chef holding a kettle to ward off a barrage of utensils and pans being launched from Myrin's hands.

"Don't you ever do that again," Myrin screamed as she flung a large spoon that clattered against the kettle before rattling to the floor.

The onslaught of cutlery continued. Markis' wheezing grew with each deflected shot. "Stop it!" he squealed.

Iridan darted over to his wife and seized her arms. "What's going on?" he bellowed. Pothar reached Markis and stopped the chef from flinging the kettle at Myrin.

"That disgusting pig!" Myrin blurted. Her breath heaved in anger. She wanted to continue her verbal attack, but she just stood, fuming at Markis. Soon her rage converted to tears, and she dashed up the stairs.

Iridan stood before the chef, and his own wrath emerged when he saw a sick, satisfied smile emerge across the fat face. He just pointed a stiff finger at Markis then followed after his wife. At the top of the stairs, Iridan caught up to Myrin. He grasped her shoulder, and she spun about on him, ready for battle. After seeing his face, she collapsed into his arms.

Iridan allowed Myrin a moment to compose herself then whispered, "Come on, we'll go home and you can tell me what happened." Her head nodded against his chest, and they searched for the exit from the palace.

When they finally located the door leading outside, Jaleph approached the pair. "Pothar told me that there was an incident. What happened?"

"I'm not sure yet," answered Iridan. "I'll let you know after she calms down."

"Well, I'm sure Markis was behind it," Jaleph replied. "Send word to me later and I'll deal with our chef."

"Thank you, Sire," Iridan said.

"I'll walk you out a bit." Jaleph briefly rubbed Myrin's trembling shoulder, and he led them out the door.

The trio started down the path from the palace to the street. After a few paces, the king stopped and said, "Don't forget, I want to hear what happened."

"Thanks, Jaleph," Myrin managed to say, appearing to have calmed down somewhat.

The king smiled softly, but before he could head back, two young men approached. "Iridan!" one of the men said, and then glanced over at his companion. "I told you it was him. We've wanted to meet you for a long time but never had the chance before today."

"Yes," the other man interjected, "thanks for saving us."

The two bowed slightly to Iridan then hastened away. Iridan noticed a disapproving look on Jaleph's face, but before he could apologize—for what, he did not really know—the king turned and strode back to the palace. He pulled his wife closer, and they hurried home.

***

Myrin was on the bed trying to compose herself, with Iridan sitting beside her. He gently took her hand and said, "Whenever you're ready, tell me what happened."

"We were heading towards the kitchen," she began, with all traces of distress having left her voice. She sounded like she was retelling a story from many years past. "He'd started making snide comments towards me as soon as we left you. I ignored them all, and that seemed to just make him angrier. When we got to the kitchens, he began to reluctantly show me how he makes his pastries. I couldn't see what he was doing, so I was bending over to get a better look. I'm not sure what happened, but, the next thing I knew, there was cream running down my chest. My blouse was open a little, and he might have used his hand." She shuddered at the thought. "I yelled at him, but he said it squirted out from one of his tubes. He apologized, but I could tell he was lying. He then said that I shouldn't be working there if I can't take getting a little dirty. I told him it had nothing to do with getting dirty and that he knew it, but he just smiled back at me. So, I hit him on that big belly with a ladle, but he just laughed. Then I started throwing things at him, and that's when you walked in."

She stood and ripped off her soiled dress. Grabbing a pitcher of water, she scrubbed herself clean over the washbasin.

Iridan watched his wife in amazement. Her turn in emotions marveled him. She was sobbing one moment then talking calmly the next. She's a strong woman, he thought, no, a strong person; she's stronger then anybody I've ever known. He approached Myrin from behind and kissed her shoulder. "You're something," he said. "And I'm sure Jaleph will take care of Markis."

She turned and smiled before falling into his arms.

Chapter 8

"What am I going to do with him?" the king asked his old friend Teraken. "I can't let Markis get away with this." They sat together in Jaleph's strategy room, each with a mug of ale before him. The king's hand hovered over the goblet, while his left forefinger absently circled its top.

"I think you should let me run my sword through that huge belly," Teraken spat.

Jaleph felt confounded by the incident. He had never liked Markis, but his father had made him promise to keep the chef working. For some reason Halet had always considered Markis a friend. In fairness, Jaleph had to admit that the chef had not always been so irritating. While his size had remained static, his personality had darkened over time. Jaleph remembered the chef visiting his father many times when Fenik and he were boys. Markis had never been what one would call a nice person; he was always one to throw an insult at someone when possible. However, Jaleph could not recall Markis ever being vicious. But lately the chef seemed happiest when he managed to belittle someone, and if he saw tears, Markis was in ecstasy. The king had no idea what had brought about this change. More complaints were coming in every day about the chef. Jaleph had hoped that easing Markis' workload might have resulted in a softening of his personality. It still could, but the king knew that he would no longer be able to ignore the situation. Action needed to be taken after this incident with Myrin. But he could not forget his promise to his father.

"You know, I still don't understand why my father liked that man," said the king.

Teraken sighed heavily. "I never did either. Halet always knew that the two of us hated each other, so he tried to keep us apart. I can only imagine that Markis was different when he was alone with your father."

"Well, we have to think of something," said Jaleph.

"You should just get rid of him," Teraken stated.

"You know I can't do that."

Teraken considered for a moment. "You promised to keep him working, right?" Jaleph nodded in agreement. "So, how about assigning him to Veake for a few days?"

Jaleph shook his head in disagreement. "No. That's just semantics. We both know what my father meant. He knew that Markis was not very popular, and he wanted to make sure Markis continued being the royal chef."

"I suppose," Teraken grunted in assent.

"Yes, but that still leaves us with our problem."

Teraken's face brightened. "How about letting Iridan take care of him? I'm sure that'd be quite a sight."

Iridan, Jaleph thought, I'm getting tired of that name, and I don't like the way things are going with him. It's been a year and townspeople are still bowing to him, like he's the king. They don't seem to care about me. It was I, after all, who sent him out on that mission. And what of Myrin? She deserves better than him. He's never there for her. I don't remember seeing her happier than when I took her to the market. Yes, she'd be better off without him.

"Well, I guess you don't like that idea," interrupted Teraken.

"I'm sorry," the king replied, "I was thinking about something else." He was growing tired of the discussion. Jaleph had no idea how to handle the problem without breaking his promise to his father. "I'll leave the punishment in your hands," he eventually decided. "Just make sure it doesn't jeopardize his job."

Teraken sat with a puzzled expression. "Fine... fine, I'll take care of it, I guess."

After dismissing Teraken, Jaleph sat despondently. He had never felt such intense solitude before. The weight of the loss of his brother hung more heavily on him than any other time over the past year. How could he run this kingdom alone? Where would he find guidance? His hand reached over and snatched the mug before him. He took a deep draught from the flask before smashing it on the table. He stormed out of the room and slammed the door. His guards hurried after and followed him out of the palace.

A stiff wind greeted his face when he reached the street. The king took a deep breath and smelled the vanguard of the forming storm. Not caring, he started to walk. With his guards following, and with no destination in mind, he just walked. Rain began to fall, but he continued his aimless trek. Water streamed down his head; hair clung to his skin as if he had just passed through a tightly woven spider web. The rain came down heavier. Nobody else moved about the street; no one but Jaleph and his two guards. The wind blew strong, forcing the rain sideways. Jaleph's clothes stuck heavily against his body, but he did not care. He did not care about his guards either. He leaned into the wind and pressed on. Finally, the torrent began to abate. Peering back from where he had come, he saw the palace, tiny in distance, shrouded by the remaining drizzle. After a few more minutes, when the rain had completely stopped, Jaleph turned and walked back to his palace.

When they reached the door, Jaleph stood still for a moment. He glanced at his two soaked guards. Though they tried to hide it, he could see traces of bewilderment on their faces. Jaleph wanted to say something. He wanted to explain himself, but what could he say? A few additional guards looked about uncertainly as he passed through the doorway and headed quietly to his room. A trail of water followed him up staircases and through hallways. After passing through his door, Jaleph quickly tore off his drenched clothes and collapsed naked on his bed.

The king slept for many hours, but it was a fitful sleep. His dreams were invaded by a myriad of horrifying visions. When he finally awoke, he had forgotten them all, and he felt anything but refreshed.

Chapter 9

Blue water lapped rhythmically over a rocky beach. The waves rushed forward against large gray and white stones that absorbed the unending torment. Farther inland, the boulders increased in size, culminating in a lone mountain which overlooked the ocean.

A solitary figure, wearing only a white robe, stood atop the peak. Iridan walked to the edge of the cliff and peered towards the water. He stood still, as if in a trance. A breeze blew his hair about his face, while his body remained frozen like a statue. But then his arms rose slowly from his sides to form a rigid line. With his fingertips outstretched to their full length, his body arched, and he dove from his perch.

Iridan fell through the sky. He plummeted towards the sea and impacted the water surface with a crack. His body spasmed with pain. He felt like a spear had pierced his skull. Despite the pain, he brought his arms forward and started to swim. In unison, hands and feet propelled his body further down.

The light from above faded as Iridan continued his descent. The pain in his head began to overtake his senses as an aching formed in his lungs. He needed to breathe, but still he swam. Darkness eventually engulfed him. He saw nothing. His chest burned for air. The pressure of the water grew and increased the pain in his head. The increasing cold caused his limbs to shudder. His lungs felt brittle. Soon they must crumble at this depth.

Still he swam.

Air, he needed air. He needed to exhale and pull oxygen in. The agony within his chest felt like it would burst out and rupture his skin. The pain from his skull ripped down to meet his lungs. His fingers ached from the frigid temperature; his toes no longer moved. Still he swam. The bones in his left arm began to tremble; he heard a crack reach his frozen ears. Another crack followed as the bones shattered in a new explosion of agony. The arm hung dead before him, but he continued downward. His mouth opened, pleading for air.

Finally he surrendered. He expelled his remaining breath and sucked in the icy water. He immediately gagged on the liquid. Just as consciousness began to desert him, he collided against the ocean floor.

A current lifted his limp body and pushed him forward. He dropped again on the hard surface and vomited all the liquid from his lungs. Now he could breathe. As he drew in air, he no longer felt the frigid water. His battered body slowly rose and shambled forward in the blackness, with his ruined arm dangling helplessly against his side. With each stride, the pain he endured slowly dissolved away. Iridan continued to walk until he stepped into a large hole. He fell about six feet and landed in pool of water that reached to his waist. Lifting his good arm, he tried to grab the side and climb out. His fingers found no hold, and he remained trapped.

As he continued to search for an egress, a soft rumbling slowly began to reach his ears. It increased in volume until Iridan realized he did not actually hear it; he felt it. The thunderous vibrations surrounded him. His head swiveled in all directions, but still he saw only blackness.

Who are you?

He considered the question. Where had he heard it before? He could not remember.

Who are you?

Why could he not answer? Had the agony of his journey to this location dulled his brain so that he could not remember his identity? No. He needed to answer. He must answer.

Who are you?

"I am Iridan," he finally responded.

No longer. Who are you?

No longer? What did that mean? A name began to form in his mind. It was familiar, but where had he heard it before? He could not remember. He could not recall the name.

Who are you?

"I am Iridan," he asserted. He knew who he was. He needed his identity. He would not give it up.

No. You are not. Who are you?

"I am... I am..." he could not continue.

Iridan jumped from his bed. His eyes blinked as the reality of his environment crystallized in his mind. A few rays of early-morning light seeped in from his windows. He glanced at his left arm and hesitantly flexed his fingers. He mopped the sweat from his brow, as Myrin stirred beside him. She turned and reached for him in her sleep. The feel of his wife's arm against his body comforted Iridan. His head dropped down onto a pillow. Thoughts of the dream ran through his brain until sleep returned.

The sun was already up when Iridan finally awoke. He quickly dressed, kissed Myrin and rushed from their house. When he reached the royal courtyard, he found the entire company awaiting him anxiously.

"Where have you been?" Teraken barked.

"I'm sorry sir," Iridan replied apologetically. "I had a bad night." He turned his attention to Jaleph. "I'm ready to leave as soon as you are, Majesty."

"Hey!" one of the soldiers called from the crowd, "where's his dragon?" A few chuckles followed until the company saw the displeased look on their king's face.

Pothar came forward, leading two horses. He handed one set of reins to Iridan. After the pair had mounted, Iridan looked back and saw Dobrah standing next to Karus, her husband. The couple kissed, and then Karus pulled his steed over to Iridan and Pothar. "Gentlemen," Karus said to the two before climbing into his own saddle.

"How are you Karus?" asked Iridan.

"I'm fine; except I don't know what it'll be like taking orders from you." Karus' hazel eyes surveyed the scene, and then he turned to scrutinize Iridan with a small scowl that morphed into a grin. Iridan was pleased that Teraken had assigned him to the company. "Some gathering," Karus continued as he brushed his sandy brown hair, which was tied back in a long tail. "It'll be nice to see Labyn. I'm getting tired of this place."

Iridan smiled at the jest. He had known of Karus for years, but it was not until after the dragon battle that they had become friends. They had gone on a number of missions together, and Iridan had been drawn to Karus' sense of humor. "When are you going to bring your Dobrah over for dinner?" Iridan asked. "It would be nice if our wives could get to know each other."

"Oh, but I don't want to ruin your marriage. Once Myrin saw a proper husband, she'd drop you before your inept intellect saw what was happening."

Pothar chuckled as Karus waited for a reply. When none came, he laughed too, before trotting his horse away.

"Uh, Karus," Iridan called after. "Where are you going? You can ride in the back and clean up the dung." Karus laughed again and continued forward.

"He's a good man," Pothar said. "I'm glad he's coming. I'll like having him by my side if we run into any trouble."

"Excuse me ladies, but, if you don't mind, I believe that the king would like to get this expedition started," Teraken barked as he approached Iridan.

"Sir, are you sure you want this guy as our leader?" Pothar asked.

"You forget your place," Teraken snapped. "This is no time for jests. Though you may think that you're on an ordinary mission, don't forget that you're leading our king away from his stronghold." The large man seemed in a foul mood. Obviously something more than the playful banter was bothering him.

"Yes, sir," Pothar responded.

Teraken dismissed Pothar and waved the remainder of the nearby men away. Iridan had not seen the giant man looking so distressed since the death of his son. "What's wrong?" he asked.

Teraken looked back at the king amidst his soldiers. "I ought to be leading this group, not staying back here. I need to be at Jaleph's side."

"There shouldn't be any problems," Iridan tried to sound reassuring. "After all, we're not riding through hostile territory. I've traveled that area many times and have never seen any trouble."

A strange look came over Teraken's face. "Make sure he gets back here safe, or I'll take it out on you! Do you hear me?" Teraken stormed away, and Iridan was reminded of when he and Teracuss had left on their mission. It was not until this moment that he realized Teraken viewed the king like his own son.

"If you don't mind," Iridan heard Jaleph call from behind. "Haven't I waited long enough? Let's get going."

With a signal to the company, Iridan's heels struck the flanks of his horse and he guided his steed through the castle gate. As the company sped away through the surrounding farmland, no one noticed the lone figure watching from the rooftop of a fragile house. He was a handsome man wearing only a bleached white robe and a silver belt. The man's lips curled into a knowing smile as he made his way down.

Chapter 10

The pounding hooves of horses trampled long grasses and brush as the company pressed forward past low rolling hills covered with sturdy trees. Having made only one brief stop for lunch, the group had ridden throughout the day without any incident. Iridan wanted to cover as much territory as possible so that they would reach Labyn early the following day. As the afternoon progressed, Iridan led the company alongside a slow running stream. With the light beginning to fade, he slowed his horse and moved next to Jaleph.

"Sire, I think we should stop soon."

"How far are we from Labyn?" asked the king.

"I'd say about half-a-day."

"Very good," Jaleph said, "I'll leave it to your discretion."

Iridan nodded and spurred his horse back up beside Pothar. "Signal the stop, please," he said to his friend.

"Sounds good to me," responded Pothar. "I'm pretty hungry."

The company walked along the stream that dropped down into a small ravine a short distance away. A path wound down the ravine wall into a good-sized clearing, which was bisected by the creek, so Iridan figured they might as well take advantage of the fresh water. Additionally, tall green grass—which would provide ample sustenance for their mounts—flapped in the wind that howled down into the clearing.

After the group had eaten dinner, Iridan assigned sentries then joined Pothar and Karus beside their fire. He had invited Jaleph over, but the king had declined. Jaleph instead sat beside the creek, talking with a few men Iridan did not recognize.

The three men remained quiet for a few moments as Iridan gazed at the dancing flames. "Ya know," Pothar said, interrupting the silence, "you really need to spend more time at home with Myrin."

"What business is it of yours?" Iridan snapped at the abruptness of the comment, but his mood immediately softened as he realized that Pothar was just trying to be helpful. "I know," he continued. "I promised her that I would. But things shouldn't be as bad now that she'll be working in the palace."

"Pothar told me about that little incident in the kitchen. I'd have loved to see some wooden spoons bouncing off that fat belly," Karus joked before biting into a piece of bread he had saved from dinner.

Iridan turned a disapproving glare at Karus. He still did not find the scene between Markis and his wife amusing. "Am I the only person in the castle who hadn't met Markis before?" he lamented.

"I wouldn't say that meeting Markis is anything to be proud of," Karus pointed out.

"She'll be fine," Iridan continued, ignoring the comment. He remembered how Teracuss and he had found Myrin in a state of shock after her ordeal with Jokk-al Ystren. She still refused to discuss her time alone with the beast, even with him. "If she managed to survive the dragon, she'll be able to deal with our chef." He paused to take a bite from his own hunk of bread and absently twisted the gray ring on his finger as he chewed. "It's been hard on her that we haven't conceived a child, so it'll be nice that she can get out of our home and do something. She's not used to having so much free time, and she hasn't made any friends yet."

"Why are you gone so much anyway?" Pothar asked. "I still don't know what you do at Korath's home all the time."

"It's his scrolls," Iridan said after a long pause—considering his response. Despite his desire to discuss the subject with his friends, he felt uncomfortable talking about it. "After the battle, I felt the need to get some answers. They seemed to be the only place to do that."

"You're studying Korath's scrolls?" Karus laughed. "Next thing we know you'll be taking sewing lessons." Pothar slapped Karus across the back, causing bread to spew from his mouth, but that only made Karus laugh harder.

Iridan sighed, knowing it was difficult for Karus to identify with the suffering so many had endured following the battle. He had lost none of his family, and Dobrah and he were actually married shortly after. "It's just something I need to do," he said. "If you had seen what I did, perhaps you'd understand."

"All I know is that you have a good position and a beautiful wife. Everyone in Su'Meeryn loves you, and you're still looking for more?" Karus shook his head in disbelief.

"That doesn't surprise me," Iridan retorted sharply.

"Don't be so hard on him, Iridan," said Pothar. "A lot of people don't understand what you've been doing. I really don't either."

"Maybe that's one reason why I am doing it," Iridan stated.

"What do you mean?"

Before Iridan could respond, Karus broke in. "If you keep talking like this, people will begin to think that you are Korath, and you'll lose the adoration of all your fans."

"Let's just drop this," Iridan pleaded. "I'll go check with Jaleph, then we can get some sleep."

***

Some hours later a commotion roused Iridan. Next to him, Pothar and Karus also sat up. One of the soldiers stumbled by, and Iridan grabbed the man's leg. "What's going on?" he asked.

"Oh, there you are," the man said. "I was looking for you. One of the sentries heard some noise over the ravine wall. He didn't spot anything, but he said it sounded like troops passing by. I don't know why anybody would be on the move at this late hour."

"I agree," Iridan said, reaching for his sword. "Wake the camp. Make sure everybody has weapons ready." He turned his attention to Karus and Pothar. "We better get to Jaleph."

"Well," the king said when the three approached. "What's happening?"

"We're not sure yet, Sire. One of the sentries heard what he thought was soldiers moving above the ravine," said Pothar.

"Yeah, it seems strange that anybody would be about now, unless they have ill-designs," Karus added.

At that moment, a flaming arrow fell through the air and landed between Jaleph and Iridan. "Take cover," Iridan yelled. He grabbed Jaleph and dove into the creek. Beside him, Karus and Pothar also plunged in. Iridan surfaced and peered about, but he saw nothing but their dying campfire and the one flaming projectile. He then saw a flickering from the top of the ravine, and two more bolts flew into the clearing. They heard a scream of pain as one of their men fell with a shaft protruding from his chest.

"Flaming arrows?" Pothar questioned. "Why would they use flaming arrows?"

"What do you mean? They seem to be doing the job," said the king, pointing at the corpse that was burning a few paces in front of them.

"They're no more effective in a battle like this. They already know where we are, and it gives us a better opportunity to see," Iridan answered.

A few more arrows shot down into the makeshift camp, but, by this time, all of Iridan's men had managed to find cover. One of the missiles did strike a horse, and it squealed in agony as it tried to pull free from its reins.

"Get ready," Iridan called out, "they should be coming soon. Make sure to protect the king."

A few moments later, a single note sounded, and their adversaries charged down into the ravine. "Out of the water," Iridan commanded. He pulled his dripping body from the creek, and held his sword ready. He glanced over and noticed that Jaleph was equally prepared with his weapon.

They saw the first sign of their attackers through the dim glow of the small fires. The crack of steel rang as swords met. Suddenly Iridan was surrounded. He had no idea of the size of their foe, whether or not they were outnumbered. Iridan ducked under the swipe of a large axe. He spun and sliced his sword out. The blade caught his opponent's knee. The man collapsed, and Iridan stabbed forward, piercing the soft abdomen. Iridan kicked the body from his sword and took a moment to examine his opponent. He immediately knew that their enemies were not soldiers. The man wore a tattered black shirt and dirty trousers. Long, unkempt hair blew across his now lifeless eyes. The axe, however, was a soldier's axe, double-sided with a fine carved handle. Something about this attack seemed terribly wrong.

He turned back to Jaleph and saw Karus hack down, nearly severing a man's arm from his shoulder. But two more men quickly took the place of their fallen comrade.

"There're a lot of them," Pothar said, stepping next to Iridan, keeping Jaleph in the rear.

"Yes, but they don't know how to fight."

Three more men rushed wild-eyed. Pothar's sword sliced down, splitting a spear aimed at Iridan's face. The attacker fell off balance, and Iridan parried a blow then smashed his skull. The two others approached more warily. One swung a mace and lunged forward. Iridan easily sidestepped the strike. As the man flew by, Iridan's sword hacked across his back, leaving a gaping wound. His blade struck a bone causing his foe to collapse to one knee. Iridan slashed again, finishing the job. Turning back, he saw Pothar still stood—his sword dripping blood over another motionless body.

The light from the fires began to fade. "How are you, Sire?" Iridan managed to call out, before the next wave of attackers struck.

"Still here," Jaleph answered, as another half dozen adversaries stepped before them.

Iridan pulled Karus over. The three men stood beside the creek. Dripping sweat and water from their drenched clothes, they attempted to form a shield between their foes and their king.

The six attackers charged, trying to collapse the shield. Iridan parried one sword-thrust but then felt a sharp pain from his left thigh. He punched the face of the man who had stabbed him and swiped his sword at the other. His blade took off two fingers from his foe, causing the sword to fall. Iridan sprung at his now defenseless enemy and drove his weapon into the man's chest. He bounced back just in time to see another sword plunging at his face. There was no time to react; he would not be able to stop the blow. But right before the blade struck, the man's momentum stopped, and he stood erect. Iridan backed up and readied his weapon. His enemy slowly fell forward, and although Iridan saw black smoke smoldering from the man's back, no arrow was visible. He looked about in an effort to spot who had saved him, but he saw nobody.

Next to Iridan, Karus desperately fought off three adversaries. He saw Jaleph step forward and slash the wrist of one. Karus thrust his sword, slicing the jugular of another while Jaleph finished off the first. The third man swung his morning star; the spiked ball crashed into Karus' unprotected left shoulder causing blood to spew forth. Karus grasped his shoulder in agony; his adversary swung again, but he lost his footing on one of the corpses. His blow struck Karus' hip rather than his head. Iridan leapt over and hacked at the man's neck, sending him in a death sprawl, which knocked Karus to the ground.

Before Iridan could check on Karus, he heard the ring of clashing swords from his other side. Pothar stood engaged with two men. Iridan spun and deflected one of the men's swords before slashing down and splitting his stomach wide open. The man fell and Iridan's blade cut his throat. Pothar quickly disarmed the other. The defenseless opponent fell to his knees seeking mercy; he found only a steel blade piercing his heart.

"It's getting harder to see," Pothar managed to point out.

"Yeah, the fires are dwindling," Iridan panted, grasping his injured leg. He felt the blood escaping from the wound. "I need to bandage this before I'm too weak to fight."

Pothar peered out into the gloom. "I don't hear anyone nearby. Do it quickly."

Iridan looked around trying to decide what to use for a dressing. Unable to think of anything, he hurriedly ripped the sleeve of his shirt off and tied it around his thigh. "Keep an eye out, Pothar," he ordered and knelt down to check on Karus.

"How is he?" Iridan asked Jaleph, who was already tending to the wounded man.

"I've been better," Karus mumbled.

"He's hurt pretty bad," Jaleph said. "We've got to get him out of here."

"We all need to get out of here," Iridan replied, as the sounds of battle rang about them. He grasped Karus' hand and asked, "Can you stand?"

"I think so," came the reply, and Iridan pulled his friend up. Karus still held his sword and balanced his weight against it.

"There's more coming!" Pothar yelled.

Iridan readied his blade in anticipation of the next onslaught. He heard the footsteps approaching through the darkness around them. He tried to gauge the distance, but before he could strike, a spear tip scratched his neck. With the fires now all extinguished, he barely managed to make out his new enemy before him. The man could not swing again due to the close quarters, and Iridan quickly cut him down. But he could not see clear enough to then help his friends. He heard the sounds of combat and the cries of pain. When the noise subsided for a minute, he called for Pothar.

"I'm here," Pothar answered.

"Jaleph?"

"Aye," the king answered, "and Karus too."

"Good," Iridan said. "We've got to get to some cover. If we stay here and fight, we're liable to kill each other."

"Right, but where?" Pothar asked.

Iridan thought for a moment. He did not want to go into the creek again. The noise of splashing water might give away their position. He thought of only one alternative. "Back to the ravine wall. Maybe we can find some large rocks to hide behind. If not, at least the rocky terrain will give us a better warning of any attacks. It'll be hard for anybody to move silently." He regretted retreating from the rest of his troops, but he knew that his primary objective was to protect the king. Grabbing what he thought was Karus' arm, he headed backwards. "Come on!"

The four stumbled their way to the wall. As they reached it, a few more flaming arrows shot down into the clearing, and they managed to get a view of the rocks. Iridan saw a small, natural rock shelf a few feet above. "Let's climb up there," he said. "That should be easily defensible. Can you make it Karus?"

"I think so."

"Good. You three go up." He turned back to face the dark clearing. A few arrows still flew, ablaze, in a random fashion. This allowed him to discern a little of the scene. He saw bodies laying everywhere, horses and men. Sounds of battle still reached his ears, yet the logic of it continued to baffle him. Why the flaming arrows? How did these men know where to find them? Who are they? They seemed more like beggars than robbers; why the attack? How could such poorly clothed men acquire those well-crafted weapons? And what of the man who nearly killed him? Before he could strike at Iridan, he had fallen dead. What had killed the man and caused his back to smolder? No, it did not make sense, but Iridan could not concern himself with these questions now.

Once the other three had reached their destination, Iridan climbed up as well. He saw that there was barely enough room for him on the rock, and he pushed himself as far against the back wall as possible.

"Now what?" Jaleph asked in an agitated tone.

That was a good question, and Iridan was not sure he had an answer. His plan had taken the four out of immediate danger, but if the rest of his troops lost the battle, they would eventually be found and killed. He felt like a coward for leaving his men and thought that he and Pothar should climb back down to help with the defense. However, before he could decide, an arrow struck the rock just above their heads; sparks fell among them. As the missile fell away, Iridan knew they had been illuminated to those still on the ground.

"We've got to get out of here," Iridan barked.

"Where?" Pothar questioned.

"I don't know, but we can't stay here. They'll slaughter us with those arrows."

"We'll have to climb to the top," said Karus. Iridan could tell by his tone that Karus was growing weaker by the moment.

"We don't know what's up there. There might be a legion of troops waiting for us," Pothar responded.

Two more arrows hurled up to the bank. One landed beside Iridan scorching his right hand. "We have no choice. Climb!" he commanded, as he pushed Pothar up the ravine wall. Iridan sent Jaleph up next. "Now you, Karus. Let's move!" He wanted to keep Karus near him and not jeopardize the king's safety if the other man fell.

As Karus struggled to begin his ascent, a few more arrows landed—seeking a target with their flaming eyes. One struck Karus just above his right ankle. It bore through his skin causing Karus to cry in pain. Iridan quickly pulled it out, and burned his hand again in the process. Karus began to slip, but Iridan held him up.

"You've got to keep moving," ordered Iridan. "Don't think about the pain!"

Air sucked through Karus' teeth as he tried to reply. "I'll…" was all he managed to say. His body trembled as he fought to continue.

Iridan labored to climb a few more feet while pulling Karus up by his shirt. The rocks he found were of good enough size for handholds, but the darkness still prevented him from seeing anything but a black wall. He had to search for each grip with his fingertips. After securing his position, he yanked his wounded companion up behind him and kept climbing. And so it continued: Iridan climbing a few feet then pulling Karus' struggling body up with one hand.

The ravine wall sloped forward as Iridan and Karus neared the summit. With more of an angle, Iridan had an easier time pulling Karus, but his muscles had fatigued; he nearly slipped down a few times. Once he struck his injured hip against a sharp rock, and the searing pain almost caused him to drop his friend. When they finally reached the top, Jaleph and Pothar pulled the two up. Iridan lay panting on the ground; Karus did not move.

"Is he alive?" whispered Iridan.

He saw the silhouette of Pothar bend over Karus' body. "He's still breathing."

"His leg needs to be bandaged. He took an arrow just above the ankle." Iridan said then listened for sounds of any lurking foes. He heard nothing. "I guess we're safe, at least for now," he continued in a hushed tone. "We better try to wait for dawn. We need some light to survey the scene and settle on our next move."

After a few long hours of nervous waiting, the sky finally began to glisten with an azure hue. Karus forced himself to sit up, and the four peered over the ledge. They saw a number of figures, unidentifiable through the miniscule light, milling about the camp.

"We need to get some horses," said Pothar.

Iridan agreed. "If we can't find any up here, we'll have to go back down."

"But we don't know who's down there," Jaleph exclaimed.

"Look, if these men came out here to kill you, they'll soon know that you're still alive. They're obviously not normal thieves," Iridan said sharply. "We won't be able to get away on foot, and Karus won't be able to walk very far. Somehow we will have to get horses, and besides, those could be our men down there."

"Well, we'll need some more light before deciding," Pothar interjected. "There's nothing we can do until then."

The retreat of the night sky was agonizingly slow. When enough light had finally emerged, Iridan peered back down into the ravine and counted a dozen figures searching through the camp. He was unable to make out their clothes, but despite the poor combat skills of their opponents, he knew that twelve of his men could not have survived the attack. Iridan's small group would be forced to fight for their steeds, but they needed a plan.

"I wonder what they're doing," asked Pothar as he stood beside Iridan.

"They're probably looking for Jaleph's body," Iridan replied. "But why wait till dawn? Why not light a fire? They don't need to hide themselves."

"None of this makes any sense. Didn't they know that we were up here?" Pothar replied as they could now plainly distinguish the faces of their enemy.

While their foes continued to search about, Iridan noticed another problem. Only two horses appeared to have survived. Why would all the others have been killed?

Iridan turned his attention to their immediate surroundings, and he desperately searched for anything helpful. "Does anybody see any supplies we can use?" All four looked around, but the attackers had brought everything down with them.

A call then sounded from below. "I guess we won't need to worry about going down there now," Karus quipped.

"What's going on?" asked Pothar as Iridan and he rushed to Karus' side.

"They've seen us," Karus answered, "and they're climbing up."

"Climbing, why would they do that?" Iridan was surprised. Their attackers could have easily used the path that had brought Iridan's company into the ravine and tracked the four down. Plus, calling out only alerted their quarry. But Iridan had to put those thoughts aside; their first foe had already reached the top of the ravine wall.

Iridan sprung and his sword cracked the man's skull open. Next to Iridan, Pothar sent a headless body rolling down the rock wall. Jaleph also easily dispatched another as Iridan turned his attention to his new target. He swung his weapon, but the blade did not bite. It glanced off the man's head and hit a shoulder. The man howled in pain but managed to keep his grip. Iridan pounded his foot on the fingers clutching the edge beside him. The man lost his hold and fell tumbling to the ground below.

By now, six of the attackers had vaulted over the side. Iridan saw Karus stab one in the chest before he could find any footing. A straight fight'll decide this now, Iridan thought as their enemy's advantage had evaporated.

Two of the men rushed at Iridan. The first to reach him swung a mace at his head. Iridan ducked, and the weapon clipped his left forearm on the down-swing. The next man sliced his axe at Iridan's stomach. Iridan somersaulted backwards. The curved blade only struck air while Iridan quickly hopped back to his feet. He swiped at the axe wielder before the man could regain his balance. Iridan's now dull blade struck ribs but would not pierce the skin. His opponent fell back in pain, clutching at his chest.

Iridan spun around. He dropped his nearly useless weapon and caught his other adversary's arm before the mace could land. The two turned about as if in some bizarre dance as each tried to gain control of the weapon. Iridan knew he needed to act fast before the other man could return and cut him down from behind. He let go of his foe's arm with one hand. The man lurched to one side as his own force disorientated his balance. Iridan swung behind and wrapped his free arm around the man's neck, pinning his windpipe closed. The man pulled his weapon free and sought for an opportunity to strike at Iridan. As Iridan's other hand fell to the side, it felt a handle above the man's belt. He pulled out a dagger and drove it into his enemy's stomach. As the man fell, Iridan yanked the knife out and slit his throat.

Iridan's other opponent had now recovered and was rushing towards him. Before the axe swung, Iridan hurled his dagger. The attacker growled in pain and rage as blood burst out from his left forearm. Iridan jumped forward. He ripped the axe from the man's faltering grip, who then fell while trying to pull the weapon free. Iridan stood over his adversary and buried the axe deep into the back of his neck.

As he struggled to pull the axe out from amongst the crushed vertebrae, Iridan glanced about and saw that each of his companions was engaged with an opponent. At Pothar's feet lay a bloodied corpse, and he was pressing his other foe. Iridan figured that Pothar would have easily killed this man by now if his sword had held its edge, and he silently cursed himself for being lackadaisical with the upkeep on their blades. Jaleph was barely managing to keep his own attacker at bay, but Karus was taking the worst of it. He had suffered additional wounds and could not mount any offense against his adversary.

Momentarily forgetting about the king, Iridan rushed forward just as Karus was disarmed. The man drove his sword through Karus' stomach and the blade emerged from his back. When the man turned, the last thing he saw was Iridan's axe cleaving his skull.

Iridan spun and saw that Pothar still had not finished off his man. Both were covered in blood and looked exhausted. Pothar's right arm quivered as he tried to swing. Blades clashed and Pothar's sword fell from his grip. His momentum carried him forward, and Pothar fell to his knees, looking up helplessly at his enemy. Before another of Iridan's friends was killed, an axe severed the attacker's arm from his shoulder. Iridan stood over the mortally wounded man panting ferociously. Cursing himself again, this time for forgetting about the king, he pulled Pothar to his feet and they rushed to Jaleph, who was still engaged in battle.

The sight of Jaleph and the man fighting was almost comical. Both were inept with a sword. If this man had had any skill with a weapon at all, he would have killed the king some time ago. When he saw Iridan and Pothar approaching, however, the man fell to the ground and begged for mercy.

Before Jaleph could crash his sword down, Iridan stopped his arm. "Hold on," he said. He grabbed the pleading man's collar and pulled him up. "Who are you?"

The man blubbered for a few moments then was quiet. Iridan shook him and yelled, "Answer me!" But the only response was a sick grin as the man leapt at Iridan. They collapsed to the ground and rolled about throwing punches. Iridan saw the man pull a knife from within his shirt, but then Jaleph and Pothar pounced. They yanked him up, and as the man flailed about, he somehow managed to plunge the blade into Pothar's left hip. Before he could think clearly, Iridan grabbed Jaleph's sword from the ground and buried it in the man's throat.

Pothar moaned in agony as he clutched at the dagger. Iridan rushed over, "Don't pull it out yet," he ordered. He turned to Jaleph, "Get some clean clothes."

"Where?" the king asked.

"Anywhere! Move!"

In addition to the wound to Pothar's hip, Iridan saw a deep gash in his right arm. After a few moments, Jaleph returned with some shirts he had obviously pulled off their dead foes. Iridan tied one around Pothar's arm and wrapped another around the dagger.

"Okay, I'm going to pull it out, get ready," said Iridan. Pothar braced himself, and Iridan yanked the blade out. Pothar whimpered for a moment then passed out as Iridan pressed the grimy shirt against the wound.

The king handed Iridan another shirt. Iridan ripped it and managed to tie it around Pothar's leg and waist, holding the makeshift bandage in place. With a sigh, Iridan turned his attention to Karus. The sword still stuck out from each side of his body amidst a pool of his own blood. While Iridan looked down at his dead friend, he heard a cry from behind. He turned and discovered that one man had survived the battle.

Although injured, the brigand had managed to sneak up behind Jaleph. An arrow now protruded from Jaleph's back as the king writhed on the ground, next to the wounded foe who had also fallen. The man grabbed a rock and slowly pushed himself up on his knees. As the rock wavered for a moment—seeking its target—Iridan sprung. His fist smashed into the attacker's face. The man's nose exploded from the impact, and he fell backwards. Blood poured from a number of additional wounds about his body, and before he could do anything else, Iridan watched the man lose consciousness and stop breathing.

"Jaleph!" Iridan called as he knelt before the king. There was no response. Iridan examined the injury, and saw that the arrow had pierced the fleshy part of the back just above the hip. He had no idea whether the shaft had damaged any organs.

Finding unsoiled clothes to serve as more bandages proved a difficult task. Following a few disgusting minutes of plundering the corpses, Iridan came away with two shirts. He pulled the bolt from Jaleph's back and bound the gash as he also managed to stop the bleeding from a few other cuts.

Iridan stood amidst the carnage. He looked at the unconscious forms of Pothar and Jaleph; their survival depended on him getting them back to Su'Meeryn. Karus' body also met his gaze. Dobrah would never see her husband again. Iridan sat down and covered his face with his hands. As his fingers closed about his eyes, the last light he saw was a flicker of silver and white against the horizon.

Chapter 11

The scene within the ravine was even more appalling than the one up top. Bodies lay everywhere. The floor of the ravine reflected a scarlet hue from the rising sun. Iridan checked all of his soldiers, but none had survived. He wanted to drop to his knees and weep, but the thought of Pothar and the king forced him to focus on recovering the two remaining horses.

After quite a bit of coaxing, the horses nervously followed Iridan up the path, and out of the ravine. The aura of death clung heavily in the air, and Iridan was surprised that the beasts were not anxious to escape the horror. He finally reached the top of the trail and hurried over to his injured companions. His next challenge was to find a way to secure Jaleph and Pothar for the trip home; the wounded pair still remained unconscious from their blood loss. Unfortunately, necessity dictated that all the corpses must remain where they lay.

Iridan pulled Jaleph's limp body off the ground and struggled to push him onto the back of one of the steeds. The animal—still skittish from the recent battle—jerked and neighed while nearly bolting away. Iridan pulled the horse back and stroked its snout. He circled to the other side and pulled Jaleph's left leg over. Carefully guiding the king, Iridan rested Jaleph against the animal's neck.

When Jaleph appeared reasonably secure, Iridan turned his attention to Pothar. He knelt down next to his friend, and gathered Pothar in his arms. Before he stood, however, he glanced up and saw the king beginning to slip. Iridan dashed over but Jaleph spun down the horse's side and fell on his head. He examined the king, but despite a new scrape, Jaleph appeared to be not any worse off—as far as Iridan could tell.

Prior to starting again, Iridan realized he would need some rope so that the incident would not be repeated. He looked about the area but promptly decided he would have to go back down to the ravine. He ran down the path and quickly hunted through the carnage. When he found a few long strands, he dashed back up to Jaleph and Pothar.

Iridan managed to get the king back on the horse. This time he tied Jaleph's arms around the neck of the animal. He pushed Pothar up behind Jaleph and tied his arms around the king. The last of the rope was strapped around the abdomen of the animal and tied to Pothar. Not sure if it would hold, Iridan decided he could do nothing more. After finding a sword with a sharper blade, he mounted up and led his wounded companions back towards Su'Meeryn.

***

The journey home proved itself quite a challenge. Being exhausted and injured himself, Iridan struggled to ride while leading the other horse. The animal likely had never carried two people before, especially when it was not being guided by its burden. Iridan decided he must reach Su'Meeryn without stopping. He felt certain that someone had sent the raiders to assassinate Jaleph, and he did not want to risk running into additional attackers.

With each step of his horse, Iridan felt the aching in his left thigh increase. He grew weaker as the day progressed. A hot sun burned overhead, and a stiff wind out of the east did not help with his trek. Iridan continually found himself pulling the other animal back up alongside him. Deciding that he would not be able to manage without a few stops, he stretched out his leg and checked on the two men during his brief rests. The knots needed tightening several times to keep the pair secured to their mount, and neither seemed close to regaining consciousness.

Knowing he was traveling at a greatly reduced speed, Iridan tried to quicken their pace. Unfortunately, the increased gait also increased his pain, but he needed to ignore that. His priority was to deliver the king, and Pothar, safely back to Su'Meeryn.

Iridan continually scanned the horizon as he rode. Occasionally he thought he saw movement to the south, but nothing approached. As the setting sun trailed behind, the path before him grew dimmer. But Iridan could not risk stopping for the night, as another ambush seemed possible; also, the condition of Jaleph and Pothar worried him. They both remained unconscious despite the fact that he saw no vital wounds. They must have each lost a lot of blood, he thought. He needed to get them medical attention quickly.

When night finally overwhelmed him, Iridan figured he was still about seven hours from the castle. The pain in his thigh throbbed so much that he could barely move his leg. His stomach ached from hunger, and sleep constantly attacked his eyes. He rubbed his face with the back of his right hand. Naar's ring gently scratched his nose, while the light from the stars above reflected dimly in the dull metal. He took a deep breath and slapped his cheek trying to force the sleep back into the depths of his brain.

The heads of the horses hung heavily, and he could hear fatigue in their labored breaths. Iridan stopped the beasts and jumped to the ground. As he landed, his leg gave way, and he fell with a cry. After remaining on the ground for a moment, he gingerly stood and stretched out his suffering limb. Checking his companions again, Iridan placed his hand against their vile bandages. He felt no fresh blood, but he needed to get them some clean ones. He let the horses graze as he pulled a wineskin out from a saddle bag. He took several gulps of the warm water and forced some drops down the throats of his companions. Why aren't either of them awake? he thought. But then, worried that he might have heard some rustling in the area, he mounted up and continued on.

The hours crept by at a snail-like pace. By the time he finally neared the out-skirting settlements of Su'Meeryn, the first traces of dawn had begun to appear. At the castle gate, he called to the guards for assistance. The portals were opened, and when the guards spotted Jaleph, they hurriedly cut the ropes. As the king and Pothar were rushed away, exhaustion finally overwhelmed Iridan. He collapsed. The faces peering down at him turned black as Iridan passed out.

Chapter 12

The familiar surroundings of his home greeted Iridan's eyes when he awoke. His filthy clothes had been stripped off in favor of a loose, soft robe. He reached down and felt a bandage strapped to his left leg. When Iridan sat up, he ignited the agony in his thigh. He issued a soft whimper and fell on his back.

Myrin heard the stirrings of her husband and came to his side. "You're finally awake," she said. "You've been asleep a long time."

Iridan smiled when he saw her lovely face. "How long?" he asked in hoarse tone.

"About half the day. It's nearing dinner time."

Ignoring his pain, Iridan forced himself back into a sitting position. "Pothar and Jaleph, how are they?"

"Someone came by to check on you a few hours ago. He said that they still hadn't come to. Nobody knows what happened out there. Are the others all right?" She stroked his forehead and snuggled a blanket against him. "There's a messenger waiting to bring word to Teraken when you're ready."

Iridan tried to speak, but his memories overwhelmed him. How could he tell Teraken that his soldiers had all been killed? His first assignment as a leader had been a failure; he was lucky to have gotten the king away alive, if just barely.

"Dead," he finally said, "they're all dead. Karus, everyone else. I had to leave their bodies at the ravine. Somehow we were the only ones who survived. It was all I could do to get the king and Pothar back here." He again fell back on the bed. "Tell the courier to summon Teraken. I'll tell him everything." He draped his right arm over his eyes, trying to shield out the light. He wanted to shield out the entire ordeal: the past twenty-four hours as well as the future he would be forced to meet.

***

Teraken sat in front of Iridan's bed with a blank expression on his face; Myrin stood behind him, her left arm wrapped around her chest and her right hand covered her mouth. When Iridan finally finished his tale—neglecting the part when Jaleph fell off the horse—Teraken shook his head in disgust. "That bitch," he said, "that treacherous bitch!"

"What do you mean?" he asked.

"Illiyna! She must've planned this whole thing. I didn't trust that Ut since he first got here. She wanted to get Jaleph away from the castle to ambush him."

"Are you sure?" Iridan quizzed. "Those vagabonds didn't look like they were sent out by a queen. Wouldn't she have sent trained soldiers?"

"Not necessarily. If she had, it would've looked even more obvious to any potential survivors."

Iridan shook his head in disagreement. "Yeah, but with better soldiers, there'd have been no survivors."

Teraken grunted angrily at Iridan's logic. "Who else could it have been? Remember what you said, they were all well armed, better weapons than they could've afforded." He rose from his chair and stepped over to Myrin. His heavy hand rested on her shoulder, then the large man turned back to face Iridan. "We'll have to wait for Jaleph to recover before we can do anything about it anyway."

"Is he doing better?" Myrin asked.

"The healers say that he should be fine. He had many wounds, but nothing that looked too severe. Pothar is their main concern."

"I hope he's all right," Iridan whispered, and then he turned to Teraken. "What do you want me to do now?"

"Nothing. Just take the next few days to rest. You've been through enough for a while." Teraken walked to the door then looked back at Iridan. "You did good work out there, Iridan. I'm proud of you."

Iridan frowned. Good work, he thought; I don't think so. How can it have been good work if everyone else is gone? "Don't think that way," Teraken continued, reading the expression on Iridan's face. "If it wasn't for you, Jaleph would be dead now too." The large man paused then said to Myrin, "If you want to spend some time with him, I'm sure Markis won't miss you in the kitchens."

Myrin managed a smile at Teraken as he left. When the door closed, she joined her husband on the bed. She held him close and they sat quietly for a long time.

***

Myrin and Iridan emerged from their home the following morning.

A messenger had informed them that, although Pothar's condition remained unchanged, Jaleph had been released to his chambers. Iridan limped alongside his wife, as they headed towards the palace to visit the king. Cheers followed the couple down the street. Everyone they passed seemed to have heard about Iridan's newest heroics. He saw the same questions on all the peering faces: what next? First, the valiant return on Jokk-al Ystren, now this. Myrin smiled back at the onlookers, while Iridan tried to hide his embarrassment.

"This is all I need," he said to his wife, "just when I thought the attention might start dying down, it's actually going to increase."

Myrin pulled him close. "You deserve it," she replied. "You saved the king—again. I'm sure he'll be very grateful."

"As you know, it wasn't just me last time. I couldn't have done anything without you and Teracuss, not to mention Korath and Naemon, and even that dragon. No, I don't need this. If anything, I failed. I lost everyone under my command—except two, and we don't even know if Pothar will survive."

"Don't be so hard on yourself. You did save Jaleph. You should accept the appreciation."

"I don't know. The whole thing makes me uncomfortable. Something just doesn't feel right."

"Relax," said Myrin. "Let's just get to the palace."

Iridan quickened his pace as much as his leg would allow, but a crowd was beginning to form behind them, so Iridan pulled Myrin into a small alley. After turning another corner, they neared the royal stables, where they saw Veake shambling forward to greet them.

"Oh great," Myrin mumbled as the filthy man approached.

"Ah, tere 'e is," the stableman slobbered at Iridan. Veake stopped before the couple; crooked fingernails scratched at his arm as dark flakes fell to the ground.

"How are you doing, Veake?" Iridan asked, looking over his shoulder. Apparently the trailing group had decided to leave them alone. Nobody was coming from around the corner.

Myrin pulled anxiously at her husband's sleeve. "We better not keep Jaleph waiting."

"Yah, yah, king wunts to see 'is saviour. Bet 'e gunna give ya rewurd." Veake giggled as hair fell over his face, and when he tried to comb it back, his fingers stuck in a tangle of knots and grime.

"I'm sure Jaleph'll be very grateful for Iridan's courage," Myrin responded sharply.

Veake's eyes flashed at Myrin. "Watch yurself," he said seriously, with his thick accent almost disappearing. "Changes 're coming. Not evrybody's 'appy t' see changes." He turned and shambled back to the stable. "Ah, yu'll all gitch yur 'ay soon," he barked towards the waiting horses.

"Come on," Myrin pleaded, "let's get out of here."

They left the stables and a new crowd began to form behind them as they continued towards the palace. Iridan ignored the calls of adoration, while Myrin smiled and waved. Grabbing her arm, Iridan pulled her faster, and they darted like two skittish flies into the palace. Iridan closed the door and stroked his aching leg.

"We came to check on the king," Myrin said to the pair of sentries that they faced.

The two men looked at each other. "There's been no word you're expected, sir," one of them replied.

Myrin turned an annoyed eye towards the man. "What do you mean? Iridan just saved the king's life. I'm sure Jaleph is anxious to see him."

"Wait here," the guard said, and he hurried off.

Iridan stood next to Myrin. He looked at the remaining sentry, but the man refused to meet his gaze. While turning back to his wife, another stab of pain shot from his thigh. He grasped his leg and leaned against the wall.

"Are you alright?" asked Myrin.

"The leg's still sore," he answered, "and that dash into the palace didn't help, but I think it's okay." Iridan was not sure whether that statement was actually true, but he saw no reason to worry her.

Myrin softly stroked his arm as they waited. After a number of silent moments, the first guard finally returned. "Follow me," he ordered and led the couple through the palace to Jaleph's private quarters.

Chapter 13

Weary lids cracked open revealing blurry pupils. Eyes squinted against the daylight, which streamed through the uncovered windows. The skin, wrapped across the turning head, felt like it was peeling from the skull. A decade of time seemed to have passed during just one year. Focus gradually returned, and the first sight to reach Jaleph's haggard eyes was Myrin's beautiful hair cascading past her shoulders like glistening lava flowing down the side of a volcano. He concentrated on her face and smiled weakly, until Iridan appeared beside her. The king tried to murmur a greeting, but enough strength to produce sound had yet to return.

"Our king still recovers from his wounds," said a soft voice. Jaleph had forgotten that Kedin had been keeping watch over him. He wondered how long the other man had waited in the room while he slept.

"We just came by to see how you were doing, Sire," Iridan remarked.

"Yes, when they arrived at the palace, I thought that you would like to see the heroic Iridan and his lovely wife, Majesty," Kedin purred as he removed a wet rag from the king's forehead.

"It looks like you should be up and around any time now, Jaleph." Myrin said as she sat on the corner of the bed and gingerly patted his knee with the tips of her fingers.

Jaleph enjoyed seeing Myrin, but he was annoyed that Iridan had decided of his own accord to come to the palace. Subjects should not arrive unsolicited to visit their king.

"I'm sure his majesty wishes to express his gratitude to you for saving his life," commented Kedin, "but as you can see, he is not quite up to entertaining guests."

"Of course," Iridan responded, "we'll let him rest. Good-bye your majesty; I'm glad to see that you're recovering. Come on Myrin."

Jaleph tried to wheeze a farewell as they left his room, but the effort only increased his pain. His vision drifted after Myrin as she passed through the door, and his consciousness again evaporated under the fresh cloth Kedin placed on his forehead.

***

Pain ripped through Jaleph's back and flung him awake. As he became aware of his surroundings, he noticed that his body lay in an awkward position. After straightening himself out, the suffering gradually subsided. He felt somewhat stronger and sat up. Kedin sat in a chair with his head resting on an arm. "Kedin," Jaleph said, testing his voice. The name pulled reluctantly from his throat, barely audible to his own ears. "Kedin," he called again, this time a little louder.

Kedin stirred and rose from the chair. "Yes, Majesty? I'm glad to see you awake. It looks like you're doing better."

"How long have I been in here?" the king asked. His voice grew stronger with each word.

"A couple days." Kedin flowed over to the bed and lifted Jaleph's hand. He examined the color and texture of the fingers and checked the pulse. "Yes, yes," he said, "doing much better."

Jaleph tugged his hand away from Kedin's tender fingers. The king glared at the other man and tried to raise himself from the bed. The walls about him began to spin, and he fell back against his pillows. He caressed his forehead with both palms, trying to drive away this newly discovered pain.

"Well, perhaps not that well," the slight man commented. "I think you might just need some food."

"Why are you here anyway?" Jaleph questioned angrily. He never enjoyed being in Kedin's presence. Although exemplary in his duties, the slender man's self-interested demeanor was always quite taxing. "Where are my healers?"

"One left not too long ago. She said that you were fine and just needed to rest. I volunteered to keep an eye on you. Once you appeared strong enough, they said to bring you some food." Kedin twirled towards the door. "I'll be back momentarily."

The ache from Jaleph's head had subsided but threatened to return with every movement he made. As he looked blankly at the ceiling trying to remain still, memories of the battle began to return. He had been told a number of times—during his brief moments of wakefulness—of the last attacker stumbling over and driving the arrow into his back. But this was his first chance to truly dwell on those events. He recalled the sword piercing Karus' body and his still form lying on the blood-soaked ground. Teraken had told him that Pothar was the only other man to have survived the battle, but that he still might die. The king thought of Dobrah and knew she must be heartbroken. His mind drifted to different ways to call her to the palace. As one plan formed in his thoughts, it was quickly chased away by another. But no, he thought, not yet. She needed time to grieve over her husband's death. Slowly his thoughts shifted from Dobrah, and he was left with one image—the face of Myrin. He could not get her out of his mind.

A knock at the door pulled him from his musings. "Come in, Kedin," he called out.

The door swung open, but it was not Kedin who stood there, holding his food. Ut walked in with Jaleph's meal resting on a long wooden case. "Your faithful servant allowed me to bring this tasty meal to you. He was quite tired you know, waiting at your bedside for all those hours. A good man, you should not lose track of him."

The king glared at Ut. "You! What're you doing here?" he spat.

"Of course," Ut replied in a soothing voice as he strolled up to the king. "You have not heard anything substantial regarding the incident. I rushed back to Su'Meeryn when you did not arrive in Labyn as planned and then heard of the attack. I must commend you regarding your soldiers. They nearly killed me after my own return here. Your fine man Kedin needed to convince Teraken that I certainly had nothing to do with the unfortunate incident that befell your party. After all, why would I return here if I did? Following some heated—from what I was told—deliberations, I was allowed to enter." Ut smiled softly as he placed his offering on Jaleph's bed. "Quite a pity. Be assured, I will use all of my resources to find out who was behind it. Now, please, eat."

He has to be right, Jaleph thought. Why would Labyn attack me? And why would Ut return if they had? Slowly, the king turned, trying to keep the waves of agony from rolling through his head while he reached for a piece of bread. As he pulled it to his mouth, Ut lifted the plate of food from the case, and Jaleph noted that its surface was checkered by light and dark squares. When Ut opened the wooden container, white and black pieces tumbled from its interior. Ut turned the case over, and Jaleph realized that it formed a board.

"After you finish your meal, I suggest a game of chess. I assume that you are familiar with chess." Jaleph managed a nod in spite of the pain. "I find it most relaxing. We shall play a game. And we shall talk."

Ut pulled a chair close to the bed. He sat back and smiled while Jaleph struggled through his meal.

Chapter 14

Myrin and Iridan walked down the castle streets trying to avoid attention as much as possible. Iridan felt uncomfortable after leaving Jaleph's chambers; he thought he had sensed some animosity towards himself from the king. He tried to shake the feeling away as just a result of Jaleph's condition, but he was not sure. Unfortunately, their next destination did not ease his mood. The couple was heading to Dobrah's home. Iridan hardly knew the woman, but he felt obligated to see her. His friendship with Karus had just begun to grow before the battle at the ravine, and he needed to tell Dobrah of her husband's deeds. Without Karus, the entire company most certainly would have died.

They approached the door, and Iridan stopped. He rubbed his aching thigh, then turned to his wife. "I don't know if I can do this."

Myrin's left arm rose and patted his back. "You'll be fine. Hearing from you how Karus fought should help."

"You're right, but that doesn't make this any easier." Iridan replied, gingerly knocking on the door.

Following a brief wait, the door swung open, and Iridan stared into an unfamiliar face. An older man stood in the entryway. When he recognized Iridan, he turned back into the home and motioned for someone to approach. "We'll come back later," he said as he and another woman left.

Iridan and Myrin had only been to Karus' home once before. A few weeks prior, Karus had invited them to dinner. The four had spent a pleasant evening together, but the occasion had not been repeated. The house appeared more cluttered than Iridan remembered; clothes lay scattered about. Dobrah signaled for the two to enter as she sat on a corner of the bed.

Iridan stuttered for a moment before he could form any words. "I'm sorry," he managed to say. "It was a tragedy." Dobrah nodded. Iridan pulled a chair from the small table, while Myrin sat beside Dobrah on the bed.

"I just wanted you to know how bravely Karus fought," Iridan continued. "Without his help, I don't think we could've saved Jaleph. You should be very proud of him."

Dobrah slowly stood and walked to the nearest window. "You know, being a soldier myself, I always thought I would be ready for this situation if it ever occurred," she said and then took a deep, shaky breath. "But, I'm not. I keep thinking that if I had come along, maybe I could've saved him. I don't know. It's just so hard."

"Karus and I didn't know each other very long, but I could tell he was a special man. I wish we could have had more time together."

"So do I," said Myrin. "Believe me, I've been through a lot myself—losing my whole family. It was hard. If you need someone to talk to, you can come see either of us any time." Iridan nodded his agreement.

"Thank you," Dobrah replied. "I appreciate your offer. But right now I just need to get out of this house. I told Teraken not to take me off any of my duties. He is sending out a party this afternoon to search for any other bands of mercenaries, or whatever those men were, and I volunteered." She dug through a pile of clothing on the floor and pulled up her scabbard. As she wrapped it around her waist, she said, "I'd better get going."

***

Iridan sat across from his wife that evening as they ate their dinner. He was finishing a large piece of meat that he picked up from a market. It was a cooked a little more thoroughly than he preferred, but it was not too bad. Following the battle the previous year, Jaleph had increased his pay, and Iridan was certain that he was the highest-paid scout in the kingdom.

"So," he said to Myrin, "you're going back to the kitchens tomorrow. I'm sure Markis is thrilled."

Myrin smiled. "He'll just have to get over it." She stood and walked over to the bed. Her arms stretched over her head, and she collapsed onto the mattress. A small yawn escaped from her mouth.

Iridan cleared off the table and headed to the door. "Well," he said casually, "I'm going over to Korath's home; there are a few passages I want to look up. I shouldn't be long."

It took a moment for the words to register in her brain, and then Myrin jumped from the bed. "What do you mean?" she demanded.

"It seems pretty obvious."

Myrin scowled at the sarcasm. "I thought you decided to spend more time with me."

"I did," Iridan answered, trying to remain calm, "and I have, but I need to get over there. It's been too long since I had a chance to study. You know that this is important to me."

"And I'm not?" Myrin demanded, but Iridan just scowled at her. "Why can't you bring that stuff here?"

"We don't have anywhere near enough room. Look, I said that it'll just be for a short time."

"I've heard that before!"

Iridan grimaced at the return of this same argument, which they had fought so many times. He had hoped that, with her new profession, this problem would have been alleviated. "This probably wouldn't be such a big deal if you had some friends to spend time with," he added.

"So, you're going to blame me? Well, I'm sorry that the pampered women in this damn castle haven't taken the time to get to know an orphaned field worker!"

"When was the last time that you worked in a field?"

"That's not the point," Myrin yelled, but she regained her composure before continuing. "I'm different than the people around here. I had to work hard just to stay alive. Nobody here can understand that."

"You're wrong. Everybody in the castle needs to work. Sure, the king takes care of his subjects, but not if they don't work."

"It's not the same, and you know it! I have nothing in common with these people. I've done what I can. Maybe if we lived with the farmers outside *you'd* understand."

"I understand perfectly," Iridan replied. "But what about me? I grew up in this castle. If you dislike all of us so much, why did you marry me?"

"That's different."

"Why?" Iridan knew what his wife was getting at, but he decided to continue the argument. He was angry for being made to feel guilty about wanting to study, so he decided the only way to get back at her was to prolong the fight.

Myrin paused, stammering for words. "I don't know," she finally said, "and I don't care. I don't think I need to define the difference. We're married, and there's no way I can change that fact. At least not right now."

"Oh really," Iridan spat as his anger started to take over his reasoning. "Well, maybe we can find a way." He spun to their door and threw it open. "Maybe then you'd be happy, huh? You could move out with those farmers you cherish so much. Perhaps a few weeks living in squalor would make you realize what you have here!" He stomped outside their house and turned back to face Myrin. He hoped to see tears streaming down her face. She deserves it, he thought.

"That'd be better than staying with you!" she shouted.

Iridan slammed the door shut and stormed away. I'd be better off without her, he thought; I don't need to put up with this. He headed down a dark street to Korath's deserted home, relishing the solitude he would find.

***

The dust-engulfed room of the dead cleric's home was a welcoming respite. Iridan sat at the old table and stared at the parchments. As had become his habit, he spent most of his time in the house rummaging through documents he had already seen. He knew he should spend some time just organizing the parchments, but he had not yet found the patience for such an undertaking.

After what must have been two solid hours of searching, Iridan came across a scroll he had never read before. The writing was attributed directly to Naar himself. This was the first direct quote he had found from the original prophet. All the other writings with words from Naar were paraphrases from later authors.

The passage began as a diary entry. In it, Naar related—at length—a temptation with which he had struggled. He discussed how arrogance always seemed on the brink of overwhelming him, as he felt his intellect rivaled that of any person who had ever lived. But, at those times, he reminded himself that his supreme intelligence was a gift of the Creator, as were his marvelous prophetic visions. Iridan wondered whether Naar's rationalization actually displayed that humility, when he came to the part of the writing, which he found very interesting. Naar went on to describe one of those visions:

As I thanked my master for His most generous gift of wisdom, He caused me to fall into a sound sleep and blessed me with yet another vision. While my body rested, my consciousness stirred from deep within my soul. The eyes of my mind opened despite the fact that my lids remained sealed. I took flight from my resting place. I flew through the sky, into and over the clouds.

From my vantage point, I peered down at the land and viewed the final days. I saw the return of Chaw Den. The armies of the Deceiver poured forth as Chaw Den flew to my side. We watched as the battle ensued. Then Chaw Den returned to the land to lead the great fight against the Apprentice.

Although excited about his discovery, these words did little to answer any of Iridan's questions. Korath had obviously thought this passage referred to the northern lands attacking Su'Meeryn; hence the quest Teracuss and he were sent on. Iridan glanced at the staff resting in the corner but still saw no evidence of the bird—Chaw Den—coming to life, and what of this apprentice? He had never heard of that designation before. Then there were the terms of the final days and this great war. No, this did not fit, and it did not sound very appealing either. It seemed that the more he came to Korath's home, the more questions with which he left.

Iridan stood from the dusty chair, and walked over to the farthest corner of the room. He cleared all the paper and unused cooking instruments from the area and placed the scroll, alone, in that corner. This would be the area to place all the important writings he came across. Perhaps he would need to establish a better sorting system later, but for the time being, it would have to suffice.

After exiting his personal library, Iridan emerged into the night air. The sky above him was black. He saw no moon or stars, so he could not estimate the time. Having little desire to return home, Iridan turned towards the infirmary to check on Pothar's condition.

***

Pothar's body lay motionless on the bed. Iridan stood in the doorway and watched as a thin woman emerged from a shrouded corner and approached her patient. She wore the loose dark blue blouse customary to all the healers, and pants of matching color, which flowed over her sinewy legs. She bent over Pothar's body and rubbed a pair of leaves across his forehead. As the leaves crumbled, she gathered up the pieces. Her hand reached into a pocket of her shirt, and she pulled out a small tube. She carefully placed each bit of the leaf in the tube, sealed it and hid it back within the pocket. The woman turned, and her gray hair shook with surprise when she saw Iridan.

"Sorry to startle you," Iridan said. "I just came by to check on my friend. How's he doing?"

"He still hasn't regained consciousness," replied the healer in a hushed tone. She continued back to the corner and rummaged through a large box sitting on a high table.

"It's kind of late," mentioned Iridan. "I didn't expect to see anyone here."

The woman continued with her work and was slow to look up. "What? Oh right, it is late." She turned around and moved back to Pothar carrying the tube with the leaves. She pulled the blanket away from Pothar's naked body. She shook the tube vigorously and emptied its contents onto Pothar's hip. From within another pocket, she produced a small white cloth. She placed it on the wound then pulled the blanket back up.

"You're Iridan, aren't you?" she asked as she headed towards the door.

Iridan felt apprehension swelling within him. He was not in a mood for more adoration. "Yes," he mumbled.

"I thought so." She stopped before him and continued. "The wound is healing. He's expected to survive. He must have lost a lot of blood, but I expect him to regain consciousness soon. You shouldn't worry." She brushed past Iridan and disappeared down the hallway. Iridan peered after the healer. Strange woman, he thought.

He approached the bedside and gently stroked Pothar's hair before quietly leaving the building. He knew he would need to face Myrin soon; however, by turning down several different streets, he managed to lengthen his trek, but, inevitably, he reached their house. His leg ached from the extended walk, as he paused at the door. He took a deep breath—trying to shake away his dread—then entered.

Chapter 15

"Chess," said Ut, "is the ultimate contest." He set the board between Jaleph and himself. "The game is simple, only sixteen pieces each." He slowly placed each piece on its proper position. "And only sixty-four spaces upon which to move. Yet, chess is extremely complex to master. Luck plays no role. There are no dice. The only asset a player brings to the table is his skill.

"The game does exhibit one flaw, however. The white player holds an inherent advantage." Jaleph noticed that Ut had kept white for himself. The strange man pushed his queen pawn forward and continued his soliloquy. "If two equally matched players face off, white should always prevail, barring any mistakes." Jaleph moved his own queen pawn out. "You see, white's advantage is the attack. Properly played, white will force black to defend. But white cannot waste even one move. Each move must be designed for the ultimate goal: checkmate. The opening concentrates on the center squares. Control those squares and leave lanes of attack open." After a few more moves, Jaleph found that Ut completely controlled the board's center. Jaleph pondered a way to break through, but he saw no options. "A superior player, however, will win with black." Ut seemed to move his pieces without even looking at the board. His unwavering stare remained locked on Jaleph. "The trick is to find that one defensive move which also serves as an attack. If that move can be made, black will force white to defend. Then black can mount his own attack."

Sweat began to form on Jaleph's forehead. Ut forced him to take a defended pawn with a bishop. The bishop quickly fell, leaving an uncovered check on the black king. Jaleph surveyed the board. Half of his pawns had been captured along with the bishop. Ut had lost only one pawn. "Most games will conclude with few pieces left on the board, unless the players are unevenly matched." Jaleph concentrated on the board, barely hearing Ut's words. He took minutes of thought before each move. Ut, however, moved and captured pieces within seconds.

"You see," continued Ut, "you must prepare your attack from the opening moves. Each play must be made to increase your tactical advantage, preparing for the eventual attack on your enemy's king."

Jaleph sat mesmerized. He was down to his king, queen and a couple of pawns. Ut had lost one additional pawn and a knight.

Another black pawn fell. Ut lovingly twirled the figure in his fingers and watched light reflect off the finely carved wood. "While each piece holds it own level of importance," Ut placed the captured soldier next to its comrades, "the most vital is the only woman on the board: the queen. The queen's power is supreme. An early loss of her can be devastating, even to a superior player. The queen must be protected and cherished. A king without a queen is quickly defeated." Ut placed Jaleph in check. When Jaleph moved his king, it left his queen exposed to an attack by Ut's rook. Jaleph's king sat in the middle of the board. The only other piece to survive was a pawn. He pondered the board, searching for a stalemate. Finally, he tipped his king over. It fell on top of the pawn, and they both rolled off the board. Ut sat motionless and smiled.

Chapter 16

Pushing his way through the door, Iridan braced himself for a continuation of the previous fight. Instead, he found only silence. Although the home was still dark, he immediately realized Myrin was gone. A wave of relief washed over Iridan, until he started to wonder if she had actually left him. He quickly lit a nearby lamp and surveyed the room. He noticed that Myrin's clothes—most significantly, her new outfits for the kitchen—remained. Despite the many harsh words that had escaped their mouths, Iridan was relieved. The thought of losing Myrin devastated him.

He collapsed on the bed and wondered where she had gone. Perhaps she had just needed to find a different environment as well, but where could she go? Before Iridan could begin to worry further, he succumbed to the call of sleep.

***

Iridan awoke to a room bathed in light. His leg was still sore, and he could barely move it. He did not know how long he had slept, but he still felt considerably tired and wondered what had roused him. He turned and saw Myrin, motionless in a chair, staring angrily at him.

He managed to sit up and waited for her to say something, but she remained silent. Feeling very ill-at-ease, Iridan finally spoke. "Where were you?" He tried to keep his tone calm.

Considering her countenance, Iridan expected an explosion from Myrin. "I went for a walk," she said softly. Iridan was again amazed at how Myrin handled conflict. Rage could burst from her in an instant, but when he most expected it, she controlled herself.

"Must've been a long walk. Where'd you go?"

"I went out to the farms. After our argument, I needed to leave the castle. I needed to see people that reminded me of my family, of myself."

"And how was it?"

Myrin stood and walked to their window. She looked out and sighed. "I tried to sleep after you left, but I couldn't. I fidgeted around here for a while. I was waiting for you to come home, and I planned on really giving you hell. When I got tired of waiting, I finally just left." She returned to her chair, and gently sat back down. "I went to the palace and walked around the kitchen, but I could only sort the cutlery for so long. Jaleph was sleeping, so I couldn't see him. Finally, I left the palace and the castle. You should have seen the looks on the guards' faces when I told them that I wanted to leave, but neither of them were willing to argue." Myrin smiled, and Iridan sympathized with the sentries' plight of facing an angry Myrin.

"I reached the farms just before daybreak as the workers were starting to enter the fields. They were clearly surprised at seeing this strange woman walking amongst them, but most waved and tried to appear friendly. It was odd, watching the men and women working: laboring over the soil, tending the livestock or fixing a broken fence. Part of me missed that simple life. I wanted to go talk to them, but I didn't know what to say. So, after walking about a little longer, I headed home. The walk soothed me; I don't know why. I don't want to fight anymore."

"Me either," Iridan responded. "So, what's next? Do you want to leave me?"

Tears pooled in Myrin's eyes. "No," she said, appearing hurt by the question.

"Well, you're the one who brought it up."

"I was mad." She paused. "Why? Do you want me to leave?"

Iridan stretched out his leg and slowly stood. He reached behind Myrin and wrapped his arms around her shoulders. "There's no one else I'd rather be with. Besides, I'm related to the only girl in the kingdom as pretty as you."

Myrin managed a slight giggle. "What are we going to do?"

"I thought your job was going to help."

"It probably will. At least I'll have something to occupy my time, but that's not going to change anything between us. And something has to change."

"What?"

Myrin stroked her husband's wounded forearm. "Time. We need time. And I know what you're going to say. You have your job, and you need to study. Whether I understand it all or not doesn't change anything. We need to be together."

Iridan kissed Myrin's forehead. He knew she was correct, but, unfortunately, he did not know how to improve their situation.

"I have to get to the kitchen," said Myrin as she opened her wardrobe.

While she changed, all Iridan managed to say was, "I'll try."

Chapter 17

The immense frame of Teraken approached Jaleph and Kedin, acknowledging the king with a grunt and nod of his bald head. As he sat, Teraken turned a wary eye to Kedin. A server placed a plate of steaming meats and potatoes in front of Teraken. "Thank you," Teraken mumbled as his teeth greedily ripped into a slightly scorched turkey leg. "I'm happy to see that you seem to be doing better, Jaleph."

"The king is recovering nicely from his wounds," purred Kedin. "The healers say he will be himself in no time at all."

"The back still hurts, but I fell okay. Thank you," Jaleph said while trying to swallow a second spoonful of his bitter onion soup. "Well, it appears Markis has been replaced as chef." He banged a hard roll against the table to emphasize his point.

"You did ask me to handle the situation," Teraken pointed out.

"And this is what you decided?" The king pushed the bowl of soup away before the aroma overpowered him. "I see the two of us will finally lose some fat, but poor Kedin here will dwindle to nothing soon without a decent meal."

Kedin giggled and daintily wiped the corners of his mouth. He continued in his efforts to digest the meal without complaints.

"Myrin is new to the kitchen. She's probably just not used to cooking such large portions. I'm sure she'll improve," said Teraken.

"Will you mind telling me what you did with Markis?" Jaleph asked flatly.

"I didn't know what to do. Since I couldn't just replace him—which is what he deserves—I figured I'd temporarily reassign him. He's to clean the kitchen for the next month—every inch of dirt and grease. I told Myrin that he's not to be dismissed until each corner of that kitchen sparkles. And every time he mouths off, or doesn't follow an order she gives him, his punishment will be extended one day."

"A worthy penalty I agree, but do you have to punish the rest of the palace as well?" Jaleph responded, trying to force back his irritation with some semblance of humor.

"I've eaten worse plenty of times in the wilderness," Teraken replied. "Maybe a little adversity will be good for us."

"We know all about adversity around here," Jaleph stated. "I wouldn't think that I need to point that out to you."

"Well, maybe we just need a reminder sometimes!"

"You're not the one to make those decisions," the king snapped.

"Pardon me, Sire," Teraken responded sarcastically, "but I think I am. You did tell me to deal with Markis, and I have. It seemed appropriate." He angrily took another bite from the turkey leg, relishing the meat far more than possible.

"I did, but I never anticipated having to eat slop due to your poor judgment."

Teraken hurled the leg at the far wall. Jaleph and Kedin both flinched as it smacked loudly against the stone. "Well maybe you should've handled the situation yourself then," Teraken said as he stood. He glared at Jaleph and stormed from the dining hall.

"Quite a belligerent man," Kedin said.

Jaleph turned sharply to his companion. "Shut up!"

***

After forcing down a bit more of his unpleasant lunch, Jaleph headed towards the castle's audience chamber. A number of Su'Meeryn's nobles had requested a conference to discuss the logistics regarding his plans for the new alliances.

As the king traveled the streets, the heat of the day caused an uncomfortable sweat to escape his pores. Jaleph pulled the leather band from his head and wiped his scalp. Before replacing it, he gazed at the emerald which signified his reign. "Such a pretty stone," he mumbled.

"Pardon me, Majesty?" one of his guards asked from behind him.

"Nothing," responded the king, as he entered the large building.

Six of Su'Meeryn's nobles milled about the throne room, awaiting his arrival. Jaleph immediately recognized Yonath. He was one of the four nobles who had come to the king the previous year, prior to the battle, with the plan that had ultimately sent Enni to his death. Jaleph's affection for the man had dwindled as a result of the manipulation of the simple-minded Enni. But, despite the cool reception he now always received, the man still came to the king with false flattery and hopeful requests for favors.

Beside Yonath stood I'a'uju'uh—a dark-skinned man who had come to Su'Meeryn early in the reign of Jaleph's father. The man wore his long, black hair braided in a tail that swayed down to his hips. As usual, I'a'uju'uh wore only a black tunic tied about his waist. He never spoke much, and nobody knew from where he had originated. Jaleph had never heard of a name even similar to his before. Many people suspected I'a'uju'uh was a thief, as he had immigrated to Su'Meeryn with a large amount of wealth. Halet had allowed him to buy a home within the castle, but nobody knew of any business in which I'a'uju'uh was engaged. Despite the suspicions that surrounded the man, he never bothered anybody and typically kept to himself. So, Jaleph left him alone as well. The king was very surprised to see I'a'uju'uh taking part in this group.

The only other member who had been present at the fateful meeting with Enni was Gentine. The past year seemed to have aged her more than most. She looked frail in comparison to her previous appearance, and her substantial array of jewelry had decreased significantly. Jaleph felt certain that guilt for her role in Enni's death accounted for her rapid demise. But suffering from guilt was the last thing that Gentine would admit. Despite these signs of mellowing, Gentine remained the most adversarial of all the nobles.

Next stood Zorine. The young woman fidgeted before the king. Her cheeks blushed, and her head dropped when he looked at her. She was the daughter of Goranon—a respected noble who had died several months prior. Jaleph knew little of her personality, as she had never been included in any of these meetings in the past. She wore a simple cobalt blouse and lemon trousers. Short ivory hair covered her small ears. Nervous eyes gazed at the floor. Goranon had negotiated many times, trying to marry her to the king, but Jaleph had never considered the option as Zorine was quite hideous. Despite a few promising features, all the lines of her face pointed towards a large, misshapen nose. And under that nose, a crooked mouth displayed twisted, decaying teeth. Jaleph always wondered whether Goranon had actually thought that the king had taken his requests regarding marriage seriously.

The other two nobles were men Jaleph had never seen before. They stood behind Gentine and I'a'uju'uh, barely visible.

"Well," Jaleph began as he sat down, "what can I do for you today?"

Yonath stepped forward. "My king, first of all, we wanted to express our concern over your condition. I don't believe any of us have seen you since your ordeal. How are you faring?"

"I'm fine. Now what do you want?"

Gentine pushed Yonath away. "We understand a truce is to be signed shortly with Labyn," she stated in an authoritative but quiet voice.

"Not if Teraken has his way," replied Jaleph.

"When 'ts signed, we wunt to be represented," I'a'uju'uh said, ignoring the king's statement.

"Trading terms," Zorine added meekly.

"We would like a representative present to bargain with Illiyna," Yonath added.

"I think he figured that out," Gentine sneered.

"Diplomacy is an admirable quality to which one should aspire," Zorine commented, barely above a whisper.

"What are you trying to say?" barked Gentine.

"It's quite plain, I think," laughed Yonath.

"Wull you quit your bickering?" I'a'uju'uh requested.

"We're never going to get anything accomplished this way," one of the two remaining nobles added.

"But we don't need to waste time with pointless insults either," Gentine snapped.

"All of your quibbling is such a waste of time," Zorine whimpered.

"Can we continue?" the other nameless noble asked.

"I'm sick o' th's," I'a'uju'uh spat, and the strange man abruptly turned and stormed from the audience chamber.

"Who needs you anyway?" Gentine shouted at the retreating figure.

"May I please proceed? Yonath inquired.

"By all means," Jaleph responded.

"Will you be sending another emissary to Labyn?"

"That has yet to be decided. I'm still investigating whether Illiyna was behind the ambush."

"Very wise, of course, but may we assume you'll notify us if an emissary does goes out, Highness?" asked Gentine. "Will it be an inconvenience for one of us to join?"

"I'm sure that can be arranged. I will notify you," the king replied. "Is there anything else?"

"No," answered Yonath.

"Then please leave. My headache has returned."

Zorine smiled shyly and thanked the king as the remaining four turned and left. Jaleph rubbed his eyes, grateful for the silence. When he looked back up, though, he felt perplexed. He realized he did not know what to do with the rest of his day. Normally he would meet with Teraken to discuss some type of royal business, but his anger refused to allow him to seek out his old friend. And no petitioners had requested an audience. After a few minutes of pondering, he decided to track down Ut. He always enjoyed talking to Labyn's ambassador.

Chapter 18

After Myrin had left for the kitchens, Iridan returned to visit Pothar. No word had come from Teraken regarding a new mission, so it seemed Iridan had the entire day to himself. As he moved through the streets, the throbbing in his leg returned, but it was not as bad. The wound was healing.

He reached the building after being stopped only a few times by grateful passersby. As he entered Pothar's room, one of the healers was just leaving. She was a different woman than the one Iridan had seen the previous night.

"How's he doing?" Iridan asked.

"He is improving," she replied as she placed a small flask within a pocket in her blue outfit. "He is beginning to regain consciousness, but he's only awake for short periods of time."

Iridan glanced at his friend's body and noticed how thin Pothar looked. "Is he starving?"

"We've managed to drain some juices, along with some healing herbs, down his throat. It's been a difficult task, but he should be able to start consuming more now." Her hand rested against Iridan's forearm, and she turned it to quickly examine his healing scar. "If he fully awakens, he should be fine; otherwise, there's nothing else we can do."

"Thank you," Iridan said. He was grateful for the candor of the woman.

"I'll be back in a while. You can sit with him till then."

After the healer left, Iridan looked around and realized that there was no chair in the room. So, he sat on the corner of the bed, staring at his friend. Pothar's leg was uncovered, leaving the unbandaged wound on his hip visible. The edges of the wound were beginning to scab, and the color seemed to be a more healthy shade of pink. It does look better, Iridan thought, but still, he turned his head away, feeling sick: so many of his friends had died within such a short time. Iridan took Pothar's hand and held it tightly. The hand was cold, but he could tell that blood continued to flow—though weakly.

"Oh," Iridan heard from behind him. He turned and saw Dobrah peering in from the doorway.

Iridan looked at the woman. He wanted to say something, but nothing came to mind. The guilt of Pothar laying comatose in the bed, and the death of Dobrah's husband, hung like a boulder adorned amulet around his neck. His fingers let go of Pothar's hand, and his chin dropped down to his chest.

"I don't blame you," Dobrah said as she came beside him. She placed a reassuring hand on his shoulder. "Karus was a soldier, like myself; your responsibility was to the king, not to him. I'm sure you did what you could to save everybody."

"Thank you," Iridan managed to reply, "but it's still hard to live with."

"I imagine." Dobrah sighed and motioned towards Pothar. "How is he?"

"I guess he's doing better. They say that he's starting to regain consciousness,."

"Pothar's a good man," Dobrah said, and she began to leave. "We certainly don't need to lose any more."

"Wait," Iridan began. Dobrah turned back, and Iridan realized he had nothing else to say. He just did not want her to go. She had said that she did not blame him for Karus' death, but he needed something more. What that might be, though, he did not know. "How was your mission? Did you find anything?"

"No. It was pretty quiet. No tracks, nothing."

"Where are you going now?"

"Sentry duties at the castle gate," she answered and tried to smile. "What else can I do?" When Iridan did not respond further, she exited the room.

After sitting quietly with Pothar for a few more minutes, Iridan also left to return to Korath's home.

Chapter 19

Ut entered Jaleph's strategy room and sat in one of the blue chairs. A golden goblet studded with a rainbow of jewels rested on the table before him. A thin, exquisitely-manicured finger gently circled the top of the chalice. He took a delicate sip of the fine wine as his eyes studied Jaleph's face. Uncomfortable under the gaze, the king found that he had to force himself to look back at his companion. The handsome man's outfit had never changed from the day they had first met. Ut still wore the same sparkling white shirt and trousers with the silver belt.

"I am pleased to see you are feeling better. How may I assist you, Sire?" It seemed as though Ut had to force the last word from his throat.

"I just felt the need to talk," the king responded.

"I have not seen you since our chess match. I was beginning to worry," Ut continued.

That seemed a strange comment to Jaleph. What would Ut have to fear? What could happen to Jaleph within the castle walls? "I've been busy. Running this kingdom takes much of my time."

"Yes, I am sure," Ut replied, a bit too knowingly.

"It's just..." Jaleph paused. Apprehension about sharing his next comment swelled within him, but somehow the appeal of Ut overcame his wariness. "I don't feel like there is anyone I can talk to around here anymore—since my brother died."

"Yes. His death was certainly a tremendous loss for you—for all of Su'Meeryn."

"It's not just that." Jaleph felt the trepidation of revealing any more of his inner desires crumbling away. "It's..."

When Jaleph failed to complete his thought, Ut leaned forward. His eyes glistened invitingly. "Majesty, please feel free to continue. My only desire is to be of service to you."

"Sometimes I feel that I'm not receiving the thanks that I deserve."

"Oh," Ut smiled, "I see. I have noticed the attention directed towards Iridan. It does not seem appropriate that a simple soldier should receive more accolades than his king."

"Yes, exactly!" Jaleph replied, and any remaining discomfort about revealing his hidden thoughts disappeared as he eagerly awaited Ut's next words.

"This is a situation which should be remedied, I believe," Ut remarked.

"I agree, but what should I do?"

"Well, let us see." Ut stroked his chin, emphasizing his deep thought. "If I understand you, the problem is the on-going attention this Iridan is receiving. I believe it has increased since he saved you from that unfortunate ambush. And you would like some of that adoration turned back to its rightful target—back to you."

"That would only be proper."

"What could we do?" Ut stood and paced behind his chair. "Perhaps the best scenario would be to have him disappear from your citizens' eyes for a while."

Ut returned to his chair, and the pair sat quietly for a few moments. As Jaleph sorted through his companion's words, trying to think of a way to remove Iridan, Ut exclaimed, "I know! With the new treaty between Su'Meeryn and Shekul, you will need to send an ambassador there. Due to your abbreviated journey to Labyn, and your subsequent injuries, you have neglected to summon Josu to your court. Send Iridan to Shekul to formalize the treaty. He would be the perfect choice—a fitting promotion for him after all his heroic deeds."

Jaleph smiled at the idea until a thought came to him. As if reading his mind, Ut continued: "Unfortunately, until Markis' punishment is completed, I am sure you cannot spare your new royal chef to leave."

The grin on Jaleph's face returned, and to an even greater extent. "I'm glad I summoned you."

"So am I. I only hope that next time you do not wait so long."

"Now, with that settled, what about the ambush? I'm still not convinced that your queen was not behind it."

"You may be right, but I do not believe so," responded Ut. "She would gain nothing from killing you, and, as I have said, there is much intrigue within her court. If you had been killed by her hands, her enemies would gain much if Su'Meeryn would attack in response."

"Yes, I see."

"I have already advised my operatives to investigate what happed. They will report to me as soon as they have found something, and I will, of course, advise you immediately regarding what I hear."

Jaleph took a drink from his own wine goblet, and the two talked for several more hours about Jaleph's father and brother, and the king's dealings with the nobles. As the afternoon passed, Jaleph grew even more comfortable and found himself revealing the secrets of his flaws and shortcomings. He told Ut about the days before the dragon battle. He spoke of his insecurities concerning his leadership skills, and how he had relied on Fenik, Ruy and Teraken for all the planning. He confided to Ut how he wanted to become more self-reliant and make his own decisions, how he wanted to become a strong king.

"Do not worry, we shall take care of that," Ut reassured his companion.

Chapter 20

Iridan sat at the desk in Korath's cluttered home. The parchment before him was intriguing, as it contained the first passage that he had found to have been written by a woman. Her name was Oniu'la, and she spoke of the age before the final day. What initially struck Iridan as simply an oddity became much more interesting as he read.

I saw before me the hideous head of a great creature. From that head, long legs grew, then arms. As they grew, the appendages tried to pull away from the head, but sharp teeth bit down and kept them in place. Blood seeped from the wounds. The creature's tongue licked at its injuries, trying to stop the crimson flow. It failed. Blood poured forth at an even greater rate. One arm ultimately broke away and then a leg. The severed limbs fought against the creature, which howled in a rage. The creature's snarling mouth reached for the arm. As it bit down, I heard the crunching of bones. But blood was now pouring forth from the beast where it had lost its extremities. Sharp teeth lashed out, trying to recapture the detached appendage, but it was too late. The creature flailed about in a fury, and its sharp teeth shredded all of the limbs. The creature roared one last time then died.

I continued to watch as the beast disappeared, but where it had stood, new limbs grew in its place. Some lived, and some died. Some grew to immense size while others dwindled. Those of you who read my words, remember them with much fear, but also with wonder.

Iridan's head was spinning by the time he had finished the passage. This creature falling apart and its severed appendages growing: he wondered if he would ever make any sense of these bewildering texts. He felt extremely inadequate in his self-appointed task. If only I had a teacher, he thought.

He dejectedly dropped the parchment on the table and decided to return home—further studying was the last thing he wanted to do now. When he opened the door, he noticed that dusk had not yet arrived, and Iridan was glad that he had not stayed at Korath's house too long.

When he reached his home, he found Myrin lying on their bed. "What are you doing back so early?" he asked.

"I felt kind of sick. I was hoping that getting away from the kitchen, and the smell of all the food, would help settle my stomach." She draped her arm over her eyes as Iridan approached her. He had just begun to stroke her hair when she sprang from the bed, raced to the eating area, grabbed a bucket and proceeded to vomit into it.

Iridan came up to her as she finished. "Are you all right?"

"I think I feel better now," she said as she straightened up and wiped her mouth.

"How long have you been feeling this way?"

Before Myrin could respond, a knock sounded. Iridan sighed angrily at the intrusion. He stumbled over to the door while glancing back at his wife.

"The king requests the presence of you both, immediately," Kedin announced while staring with a concerned expression towards Myrin who was still cleaning herself up.

"May we have a few minutes?" requested Iridan.

"A short few," Kedin responded. "I'll be waiting outside."

"I'm fine," Myrin said to Iridan as she smoothed her wrinkled clothes, "we can leave now."

"Are you sure?" Myrin nodded as Iridan pulled a strand of hair away from her cheek and twirled it in his fingers. "Maybe you should wash your face first," he said as he plucked away a piece of filth.

***

Myrin walked slowly beside Iridan while Kedin looked back anxiously. "Are you sure you're all right?" Iridan asked again.

"I'm just a little weak, but I don't feel nauseous anymore."

Iridan grasped Myrin's arm to support her, and they continued after an increasingly aggravated Kedin. "Can't we see the king later?" Iridan asked. "Myrin isn't well."

"He asked to see both of you immediately," Kedin whined, "and I shall deliver you to him."

Iridan muttered a curse under his breath. He never cared for Kedin, and this experience increased that sentiment. "Let me know if you need to turn back," he said softly to his wife.

***

The king looked annoyed as the pair entered the audience chamber.

His fingers tapped sharply on the emerald stones dotting the arm of his throne. "Where's Kedin?" he snapped.

"He said that he had another errand to run," Iridan answered.

"What kind of errand?" Jaleph asked angrily.

It's not my job to keep track of your lap dog, Iridan thought. But his only response was, "He didn't say."

Jaleph grunted as he looked over his shoulder, apparently searching for someone else. "And where is Ut?" he barked.

"Not here, my lord," one of the royal guards responded.

Jaleph's mouth clenched as he waited a moment to compose himself before continuing. "Well then, I'll get right to the point. Now that we have a treaty with Shekul, I have decided we need an ambassador in Josu's court. You have shown yourself to be a very capable man, so I am appointing you to this position."

The words shocked Iridan. He was just starting to grow into his own as a soldier and leader, and now he was to become a diplomat? And what of Korath's documents? How could he continue his studies from Shekul? His mouth opened to protest, but, unfortunately, the king's words left little room for debate. "When do we leave?" he asked.

"*You* leave tomorrow. Your wife has duties here. She may join you after Markis is restored to his position."

As Jaleph's head nodded in satisfaction over his decree, Myrin promptly collapsed to the floor.

***

Myrin awoke a few minutes later in a soft bed in one of the empty rooms of the palace. Her eyes glanced between the faces of Iridan and Jaleph, before she managed a soft smile.

"I'm glad to see you're doing better," said the king.

"She's been sick all day," Iridan explained as Myrin tried to push herself out of the bed. He gently eased her back down and continued, "Jaleph said we can stay here tonight. His personal healers will be close by."

"Really, I feel fine."

"That's what you said earlier."

"You will stay here, and that's final," Jaleph ordered. "After Iridan leaves tomorrow, I'll come back to check on you."

Myrin's expression quickly turned to disbelief. Her eyes shot toward Iridan. "You're still going?"

Iridan glanced apprehensively at Jaleph then back to Myrin. "I'm not sure," he stammered. "I…"

"I'm sorry," Jaleph said to Myrin, "but it is his assignment. We need him in Shekul immediately." He patted her lightly on her shoulder. "You can join him when you're well. Now, I'll leave you two alone."

The king offered a smile—which to Iridan appeared manufactured—and left the room.

Chapter 21

The clouds overhead rolled in increasingly darker shades of gray as the lone horse trotted southeast. The man kept a close eye towards the threatening sky. He figured there was a good chance of being caught in a downpour soon, so he spurred his horse to a gallop. With a stiff wind blowing directly at his back, as if chasing him away from Su'Meeryn, the rider made remarkable speed.

Iridan wanted to cover as much ground as possible before the rain started, but, after an hour of hard riding, he slowed to rest his steed. The animal continued to breathe hard, so Iridan stopped and pulled an apple from his bag. The horse gratefully took the fruit from his hand while Iridan stretched his back and gazed up at the clouds. The afternoon continued to darken prematurely, but rain seemed no closer than it had an hour before. He took in a deep breath and distinctly smelled the scent of a storm brewing. Guessing one-and-a-half days remained of riding, Iridan wanted to make sure that he reached Shekul by the following night. He ate a second apple before getting a drink for himself and his steed. He then mounted back up and continued his trek.

He rode for two more hours before the fading light made continuing on seem unwise. After eating a quick dinner consisting of some hard bread and nuts, he set up a rain cover. I wish I could see the stars, he thought as he stretched his tired body out on the ground. He finally fell asleep despite the worries regarding Myrin's condition.

Dawn arrived to reveal dry ground. Iridan was shocked that the rain had missed him. He pulled the remaining two apples from his pack, and handed one to his horse as he ate the other. After relieving himself, he loaded up his supplies and resumed his journey.

The morning grew brighter, but although Iridan noticed that the sky remained overcast, it was not nearly as dark as the previous day. It had to have rained yesterday, he thought; how did it miss me? No answer came, and he spurred his horse to maintain a quick pace, trying to make up for the time he had lost due to the premature darkness of the previous day. Fortunately, the strong wind remained at his back, and he reached Shekul by late afternoon.

Josu's kingdom reminded Iridan of Su'Meeryn. He rode through outlining farms and a few small villages. He spotted a couple of patrols, but they paid no heed to a lone rider. He traveled down a wide, dirt road that led directly to the castle; however, unlike Su'Meeryn, this castle was completely self-contained. It showed no semblance of being a city. Iridan guessed that the villages he had passed handled much of the commerce.

He approached the castle gate, which was open, and two guards stopped him to ask his business.

"I am Iridan of Su'Meeryn," he announced. "I am Jaleph's ambassador to King Josu. Please advise him that I have arrived." The guards cast a confused expression at each other and ordered Iridan to wait while one of them left. "What's the problem?"

"We were not informed to expect you," answered the remaining man.

Iridan was puzzled at the statement. Why would a dignitary from a new ally not be expected? Perhaps Jaleph had failed to send word ahead of his departure. That seemed a likely explanation. Regardless, Iridan would have to wait. He dismounted his steed and stretched his arms.

"How are you?" he said to the guard, hoping a conversation might soothe his growing anxiety.

"Fine," came the abrupt reply.

Iridan looked back over his shoulder. "It was a long ride. I thought I'd get caught in the rain."

"Oh?"

"Yes. It looked pretty threatening out there, but it missed me somehow. Did you get any rain at the castle?"

"No."

"Well, I hope I can be of some assistance to your king, but between the two of us, I'm just a soldier like yourself." Iridan said, trying to play on the guard's sympathies. "I was pretty shocked when my king appointed me to this mission."

The man failed to respond.

"I hope I'll be able to succeed as a diplomat."

"Yeah."

"But remember, this is just between us two soldiers."

"Yeah."

After the fifth one syllable response, Iridan decided to give up on the conversation. The guard obviously had little desire to speak to him. *I guess I have a lot to learn about diplomacy,* he thought.

After a few more tortured minutes, the other guard returned with two additional companions. He looked sternly at Iridan. "Follow these two," he commanded.

"Is there a problem?" asked Iridan.

"Follow these two," repeated the guard.

The man led Iridan's horse away as the other two took him down a long hallway. At regular intervals, flickering torches of varying heights illuminated the stark walls. Iridan spotted no tapestries, and no rugs to soften the floor. After a few turns and three flights of stairs, the guards brought him to a large, wooden double door. One of the men knocked, and a moment later, the doors swung inward. He had expected to see a throne room, but Shekul's monarchy obviously gravitated to a different tradition. He peered into a thirty-foot square area. A soft, yellow rug reached to each corner. Against the far left wall sat four large wooden chairs. A number of smaller seats circled a round table to his right, along with a pair of purple sofas. Across from him, a huge chest rested by the back wall. A large open area remained in the middle of the room, which Iridan figured the king used to mingle about with various nobles. A few abstract paintings of swirling colors hung on the walls alongside some polished weapons, and streams from the afternoon sun poured in from large windows above his shoulders.

A trio of men and one woman rose from the couches as Iridan entered. The first man to approach towered a full head taller than anyone else in the room. He wore a narrow gold crown over wispy white hair that trailed below his shoulders. His thin face tapered to an elongated chin, which, with his sallow skin, gave him the appearance of a concave moon. Gray eyes sunk into his skull like lunar caverns. Jade and orange robes jutted at anomalous angles from his bony body.

The woman came alongside the king; her right hand pressed against Josu's left elbow—causing Iridan to wonder if she was guiding his. As she moved out from behind the king's shadow, her exquisite face, which was surrounded by long curls of almond hair, came into view. Every curve of her luscious figure was displayed by her scanty white dress. She surveyed Iridan's body, and he sensed desire flowing from her dark eyes.

The other men, fixed with harsh expressions, remained by the couches. Iridan also noticed, deep in the shadows, a guard standing motionless in each corner of the room.

"You are Iridan?" Josu asked in a cracking voice.

"Yes, Sire." Iridan bowed slightly.

"Tell me why you are here."

"My... my king sent me," Iridan stuttered as his tension returned. He wondered why he would be sent to Shekul if his presence was not expected.

"Why should we admit you?" the woman questioned in a husky whisper.

"I'm sorry Sire, I'm a bit confused. I thought Shekul agreed to a treaty with my land. If you are concerned with my presence here, please tell me."

Josu looked back at the woman, and she gazed into his eyes while stroking his arm. She turned back to Iridan and smiled.

"His majesty agreed to your messenger's proposal," one of the other men said, "but your presence was not requested."

"If we have a treaty, what is your concern?" asked Iridan.

"The treaty has not been formalized yet," the woman explained.

"We have no proof of who you are," added the other man from the back, "and that will be necessary if we are to allow you access to our king and his castle."

"I understand," Iridan said, restraining his anger at Jaleph for sending him out without a royal seal. And he restrained his anger at himself for not realizing the mistake prior to leaving Su'Meeryn.

Josu again looked at the woman and she nodded her head. "Take him to the cells!" Josu ordered triumphantly to the guards. "You'll have to wait in the prison until we receive word back from Jaleph. If you're identity is not verified, you'll be killed," and with that, despite his protests, two of the guards dragged Iridan away from the room.

Chapter 22

A light mist saturated the air as Jaleph trotted down the streets of Su'Meeryn, amidst the growing illumination of dawn. He followed two of the royal guards while another pair trailed behind. Ut had pointed out that the size of his stomach was becoming far too large to display a proper royal image to his subjects. As this was only his second day of engaging in formal exercise, Jaleph grew tired quickly. After only covering about half of his planned route, the king ordered the guards to slow down and turn back. When they reached the palace, Jaleph headed to his room. He pulled off his shirt and wiped the moisture from his face before collapsing on the bed.

A knock at his door aroused the king from a brief nap. He gratefully rose from his damp bedding and ordered his visitor to enter. Ut passed through the door and smiled. "The running not going well, Jaleph?"

"It's hard to get started, and I'm exhausted. I'm not sure I'm ready from this. Maybe I should just get out on my horses more, like my father."

Ut ignored Jaleph's suggestion and said, "I was told you stopped your run early. That will not do."

Jaleph felt annoyed by Ut's comment, but he could not make himself chastise the man. "It's going to take some time. I'm not accustomed to physical exertion," he pointed out.

"I have news," Ut said, once again ignoring the king. "A rider is approaching from Shekul and will be here today. Apparently Iridan is in some trouble."

"What happened?"

"You neglected to send Iridan with your seal. Josu has him in prison until he can confirm his position with you."

Jaleph wondered how Ut knew all this if the rider had not yet arrived, but all he said was, "So?"

"Think carefully, Jaleph."

"About what? We'll just give the information to the messenger and clear up the misunderstanding."

"Yes, we could do that. But, I should tell you, if his identity is not confirmed, Josu will kill him."

"So," Jaleph repeated, failing to grasp Ut's meaning, "we'll confirm it."

"Or, if we say nothing," Ut replied patiently, "Josu will take care of him for you."

Jaleph looked hard at his companion. "You want me to kill Iridan?"

"You would not be killing him. Josu would."

The king disliked the implication. Though he did wish to be permanently rid of Iridan, he refused to orchestrate the murder of one his subjects. "No," Jaleph snapped. "We'll confirm my order. Let me know when the rider gets here."

"He is expected this afternoon. Perhaps you should check on Myrin's condition before then."

Jaleph's tone softened as he responded. "A sensible idea, I hear she's still not doing well."

"I am certain that a visit from her liege will do much to improve her condition."

"Of course."

"May I be of any further service to you, Majesty?" asked Ut.

"Actually yes," Jaleph answered as he began to wash the sweat from his body. "Is there any word regarding your investigation into my ambush?"

"Nothing definitive yet Majesty, which does trouble me somewhat. I should have heard something by now. I will certainly let you know the moment that I do."

"Good, good," responded the king. "That is very good."

***

The combined smells of soap and vomit reached Jaleph's nostrils as he entered the infirmary. His guards waited outside while one of the healers led him to Myrin's room. "How's Pothar?" the king asked the old woman as they walked.

"He's doing better. He finally regained full consciousness a couple days ago, but he's still very weak. Would you like to see him as well?"

"Maybe later."

The woman opened a door and they entered Myrin's small room. Jaleph saw another woman cleaning vomit off the floor, but Myrin's appearance was what startled him. Her skin looked like polished ivory, and she barely turned to see who had entered. She tried to smile, but she only managed a grimace before grabbing her stomach in pain.

"What's wrong with her?" Jaleph asked sharply.

239

"We don't know, Sire. No signs of illness have been found. She throws up anything we give her. It makes no sense."

Jaleph walked next to the bed. "I'm here for you," he whispered.

"Thank you," Myrin murmured, and her body contracted in a spasm of agony. After her misery subsided, she turned towards Jaleph. "I appreciate you visiting, but please go. I don't want to be seen this way." Her hand reached out and tried to pat his arm. Jaleph squeezed the fingers lightly and turned to the healer.

"We should leave, your Majesty," the woman said.

"Make sure she receives whatever she needs. Do you understand me?"

"Yes, Sire." As the king turned towards the door, the healer asked, "Would you like to see Pothar now?"

"Oh, yes, of course. Pothar. Let's go."

The pair entered Pothar's room to a far more pleasant scene. Pothar sat up in bed and smiled as he greeted the king. Jaleph immediately noticed how pale and thin he looked, but at least he was improving.

Pothar said, "Thanks for visiting, Jaleph."

The king turned away and looked at the healer. He hoped that Pothar noted his displeasure at being addressed so informally. Jaleph did not like the thought of having to rebuke Pothar in front of this woman, after they had so recently fought side-by-side.

"I see you're doing better," said the king.

"That's what they tell me, but I feel like hell." Pothar's voice sounded weak.

Jaleph looked back at the woman and asked, "When can he return to his duties? I hate paying a man to stay in bed all day."

"A week, maybe two," she said, smiling at the jest. "It depends on how long it takes him to regain his strength."

"Good, good," Jaleph said, and returned his gaze to Pothar. "It'll be good having you back."

"Sire," Pothar said, making Jaleph happy that he had recognized his previous mistake, "where's Iridan? I figured he'd have been the first person to come by."

"Yes, of course, you wouldn't have been informed. I sent him to Shekul as our ambassador to Josu. I don't expect he'll be back for some time."

"Oh, I'm sorry to hear that. But I'm happy for him, I guess."

"Yes, well, stop and see Myrin when you get a chance. She needs our support."

"What do you mean?" Pothar asked.

"She's taken ill. She's in a room down the hall."

"That's too bad," replied Pothar as he lay back down. "I'll go see her as soon as I'm allowed. What's wrong with her?"

Jaleph began to grow weary of the conversation. He liked Pothar well enough, but how much of his time must he give to cheer up one wounded subject? "You'll have to ask our friend here," he said, indicating the silent woman next to him. "I need to get going. I'm glad you're feeling better, and I'll try to come by again soon." And with that Jaleph turned and left. He did not wait to hear Pothar's farewell.

Chapter 23

Thick air and a foul stench greeted Iridan as Josu's guards led him into the dungeon. A number of torches covering the hallways kept the area illuminated brightly; Iridan assumed the sentries wanted to maintain a close eye on any movement. As they walked, the wide hallway narrowed before splitting into two separate corridors. One of the guards grabbed his arm and steered him down the left branch. As Iridan stumbled forward, he struggled to see in the increasing gloom. Looking about, he noticed that the torches were now spaced farther apart.

At regular intervals, they passed large doors with small openings covered by thick steel bars. The hallway eventually stopped at a dead end, and Iridan realized that was the reason why the light had been allowed to dim to such a degree. "I guess the king expects to have a lot of prisoners," Iridan quipped as one of the guards opened the cell door.

"If your story is verified, you'll be released immediately," was the guard's only response. Since he expected that release to come within a few days, Iridan passed into the cell without resistance. He figured he would only have to deal with the discomfort for a short time.

The lock clicked into place, and Iridan listened as the guards strolled away from his new home. He turned to view his temporary dwelling, but the last remaining streams of light from the setting sun, which passed through a tiny window, revealed little. As he waited for his eyes to adjust, Iridan realized he was not alone. He heard a light breathing which turned into a chuckle.

"You've noticed me," a voice said from his right.

Iridan glanced down, but he failed to spot his companion. "Yes."

He heard a rustling then saw the outline of a head as the man stood from a bunk and spoke. "Don't worry, I won't hurt you."

"I figured as much," responded Iridan, "otherwise they wouldn't have put me here. They can't risk me being injured once my story checks out."

"Your story? What do you mean?"

Iridan realized that the man would have no idea who he was, and he saw little reason to educate his cellmate. No sense to take any chances, he thought; after all, this man is in prison. "Never mind." Iridan sat down on the stone floor and continued, "What's your name?"

"Worm."

"What?"

"Worm," the man repeated. "At least, that's what everyone calls me."

"Worm?"

"Yes."

"And why does everybody call you that?"

"Oh, it started with a few friends, and then it just stuck."

"Friends, huh? It doesn't sound very complimentary," Iridan pointed out.

"Do you have a problem with it?"

"No. I really don't care."

"Good."

Iridan shook his head, reminded of the maddening conversations he used to have with Ruy. Ruy had been his closest friend, but they had never had to share a room together. Iridan surely would have killed Ruy if they had. He hoped that this annoying conversation would not continue throughout their incarceration together.

Worm broke the silence a short while later. "What's your name?" he asked pleasantly.

"Iridan."

As his eyes had adjusted to the dim light, Iridan could see that Worm was pondering over his name. "Iridan?" Worm repeated. "I know that name. Iridan."

"What're you talking about?"

"I know somebody named Iridan."

"What?"

"Yes, I certainly know somebody with that name. Have you ever..." Worm paused to peruse his memory further. "No," he continued, "I didn't know anybody with your name, but I've heard of it though."

"It's a common name," Iridan lied, in an attempt to appease his companion.

"No, I'm serious." Worm said, sensing Iridan's patronizing tone. "Wait a minute. Are you from Su'Meeryn?"

"Yes," Iridan replied hesitantly.

Worm's hand shot forward with his finger pointing at Iridan's face. "You flew on that dragon, didn't you?"

Iridan's anxiety grew; he wondered how a criminal of Shekul would be familiar with him. "How do you know about that?"

"It's pretty common knowledge."

"No it's not. Not for..." Iridan paused to carefully consider his next words.

"A criminal," Worm finished his statement.

Iridan wondered how to respond appropriately, and then he decided to abandon tact and said, "Yes. That's right."

"I'm not really a criminal."

Iridan sighed as he stood and walked to the cell door. "Then why are you here?"

Worm chuckled. "Are you a criminal?"

"No."

"Yet you're here."

"Good point. There are exceptions, but I'd still like to know why you're here?"

"Stealing."

"Well, there you have it. How can you say you're not a criminal?"

"I said I'm not *really* a criminal, but I was caught stealing."

"Would you mind explaining that?" Iridan requested.

"I stole some of the king's livestock: actually just a chicken. But, I'm not a thief, usually."

Iridan felt that his companion was playing with him, but since he had nothing else to do, he figured that he'd continue the conversation. "Why did you steal it then?"

"I was hungry."

"Oh, I see; you stole to stay alive. Are you poor?"

Worm laughed again. "No. Actually, my family is quite wealthy."

"How come you stole it then?"

"I already told you; I was hungry."

"So, you're saying you took it for no particular good reason," Iridan concluded.

"I think hunger is an excellent reason!" Worm retorted.

"But if you're wealthy, you had no reason to steal a chicken, and you risked getting caught."

"Exactly!"

Iridan thought he was finally starting to understand Worm. "So, you stole it just for the excitement, for the risk. And I assume you'll be let out of here in some short amount of time."

"The king hasn't decided the length of my stay yet, but you're probably right."

"And here you sit," Iridan pointed out. "Was it worthwhile?"

"All of our actions result in consequences, some positive—the others negative," Worm replied philosophically. "I suppose your question really is: Is this a positive consequence? That is a more difficult question than you might think. Do I like sitting in this dank prison? No, of course not; however, will the long-term effect result in a positive outcome? I do not know."

Iridan walked back to the wall and sank to the ground as he clapped his hands. "A marvelous display of intellect, but you didn't answer my question."

"But I did. Apparently you failed to comprehend."

"Well, please enlighten me, if you don't mind."

"At the moment, I would prefer to be sitting in my cozy room, curled in my soft chair and reading the works of Naar; however, the future might show that the time I spend in this cell will be more valuable than my entire fortune. We'll have to see." Worm stretched his arms above his head before dropping down onto his bed.

"Yes we will," Iridan said as he climbed into the bunk above Worm, hardly able to believe his good fortune. Iridan desperately wanted to question his cellmate further regarding those readings of Naar, but it appeared that Worm was no longer interested in conversation. Too excited to fall asleep, Iridan instead lay staring at the dark ceiling. He knew that he would need to find a way to tolerate this man.

Chapter 24

The herald from Shekul had recently departed and Jaleph sat, a solitary figure, on his throne. His right elbow rested on the arm of the chair and he cupped his chin in his raised hand. He pondered the fact that, despite the recent removal of Iridan from his kingdom, he still found little pleasure in his life. He had hoped to be spending more time with Myrin, but her illness thwarted that plan. And now Teraken, his old friend and advisor, avoided him whenever possible. His only companion was Ut.

Despite repeated warnings from Teraken, Jaleph had granted Ut residence within the palace, and he did enjoy the strange man's presence. But he still felt empty. He knew he needed a queen. Unfortunately, both times he found himself attracted to a woman, she was already with another man.

A few of the nobles entered into the audience chamber to begin one of their meetings. Yonath approached the throne and looked quizzically at Jaleph. "Will you be staying for our meeting, Sire?" he said, stirring the king from his musings. "We would be greatly honored."

"I don't know. What will you be talking about?"

"Nothing out of the ordinary: trading rights with Labyn and Shekul."

Jaleph stirred from his throne and stood. "I don't think so, but report your decisions to Kedin."

"Sire?" Yonath asked in confusion; Jaleph had never requested the nobles advise him on their dealings before.

"You heard me. I want the full details before you take any action," Jaleph ordered as he strode from the chamber.

As his guards rushed to follow, Jaleph stopped and stood indecisively on the street. He had nothing to do and nowhere to go. He scratched the back of his neck then made a decision. He turned back towards the palace. As he reached the entrance, he ordered the guards to bring Ut to his private chamber.

Chapter 25

Sleep had not arrived. It was still evening when Iridan hopped down from his bed. He glanced over and was happy to see that Worm was also awake. "You mentioned that you're familiar with Naar?" he asked hopefully. "Do you possess many of his writings?"

"Why do you ask?"

"I'm trying to study him too, but I've been experiencing some difficulties."

"Study? I said nothing about studying."

"I don't understand. You said you'd rather be reading Naar than sitting in the cell."

"Reading and studying are two different tasks. I enjoy reading Naar's works. I find them pleasurable. But I see no value in studying them."

Iridan absently twisted the plain ring that still rested about his finger. "Why not?"

A quiet sigh emanated from Worm's throat. "Would you study the poetry of Myshella or Opolusky's dramas? Of course not! Nobody would, but they are valuable for entertainment purposes."

"I find it strange that you'd compare Naar's writings to that pair, not that I've read them much. What I've read of Naar provides me nothing close to entertainment."

"Perhaps you've not found the proper volume."

"You're probably right. I've been searching for a compilation of his works, but, I still don't understand how you can compare Naar to those other two."

"Do you find anything of substance in Naar?" Worm asked.

"Don't you? Naar is considered to be a great prophet who—"

"I know that," interrupted Worm. "I'm not ignorant. But just because people say that he is doesn't make it true."

"If you think that way, why did you mention Naar in the first place?"

"I might just as easily have said Myshella; it was just an example. Now if you don't mind, I'd like to get some sleep."

"Before you do, can I ask a favor?"

"We hardly know each other. Why should I do you a favor?"

"Because it's very simple."

"And what might this favor be?" asked Worm.

"When we're both out of here, can I see the writings of Naar that you have?"

"I suppose so, but only if you stop talking." Worm then turned his back to Iridan and pulled a blanket up to his chin.

Maybe this imprisonment will be beneficial after all, Iridan thought while climbing back up to his bunk. As he tried to make himself comfortable on the old, worn-out mattress, he could not keep his mind off what he might eventually discover within the writings Worm possessed.

***

A dull pain in his lower back awoke Iridan. He tried to stretch it out, but that only helped a little. Damn mattress, he thought as he looked down and saw Worm's back rising and falling with the deep rhythm of sleep. Iridan quietly climbed from his bed and called for the guard.

"What is it?" the man said gruffly as he approached.

"I need to relieve myself," Iridan answered.

The guard pointed to a jug in the cell's corner and walked away.

"What should I do with it when I'm finished?" Iridan called after.

"It'll be collected when your breakfast is brought," the guard called back exasperatedly.

"Sorry," Iridan mumbled to himself, "I've never been in prison before."

After Iridan had finished with the jug, Worm stirred and turned over. With the added light, Iridan managed a better look at his companion. He seemed to be about the same age, maybe a year or two older. His black hair hung in thin waves to his shoulder. A small, sharp nose angled from his close-set bronze eyes; the stubble of an infant beard grew about his lean face. Worm sat up and stretched. With his arms raised above his head, Worm looked like a sapling in the middle of winter.

"Good morning," Worm said cheerfully as he reached around, trying to scratch his back. "They're not much for bedding here are they?"

"No," Iridan agreed as his stomach started to grumble. "When will they bring breakfast?"

"They should be by soon," Worm said as he grabbed the jug. "And they better not be late. This thing is not going to be smelling too good."

True to Worm's estimation, two guards arrived shortly. The door was opened and plates of fried eggs and toast were handed to Worm as a guard motioned for Iridan to bring the jug—which was traded for a clean one. "I guess they don't want to upset you too much," Worm said. "Eggs are a rare treat."

"So you've been here before?" asked Iridan.

"Once or twice," Worm answered, but Iridan did not believe him. He was certain that Worm had seen these walls many times.

They ate their breakfast in silence, but once they finished, Iridan decided he needed to know more about his companion. He placed his plate on the floor, leaned back against the wall and asked, "So who are you?"

"You know my name."

"Yes I do; well, not your real name. But anyway, what I meant was, what do you do when you're not stealing or sitting in prison?"

Worm laughed then looked intently at Iridan. It seemed as if he was debating with himself whether to respond truthfully. "My father owns a good deal of land outside the castle. Our family has accumulated a large amount of wealth exporting produce for the past couple of generations, but as for me, I don't do much. I do whatever I feel like."

"Don't you find that to be a waste? Don't you want to accomplish something?"

Worm's face twisted into an ugly scowl, and Iridan actually thought for a moment that his companion was going to pounce at him. "Guard!" Worm shouted, and when an immediate response failed to come, he continued to shout until the same man who had brought in their breakfast arrived.

"Is there another cell you can put me in? I need to get out of this one."

"You stay where you were put."

"If you move me, I'll make it worth your while when I'm released." The man looked reluctantly at Worm. "Oh, it's not really a bribe. It's not like you'd be letting me out."

The guard looked at a cell on the other side of the hall and then he unlocked the door and led Worm out. "Now, I don't want to hear anything from either of you again," he ordered. "Do you understand?"

"Yes, and thank you sir," Worm answered contritely.

The guard looked at Iridan who just sat—unmoving—in the back of his cell, wondering what he had said that so angered Worm.

The remainder of the day passed in silence. Lunch and dinner of decent—yet unappetizing—food came at regular intervals. Iridan was used to eating bland food from his many scouting trips, so the meals did not bother him. As the light slowly dimmed, Iridan climbed up to the top bunk to sleep. He knew Josu's messenger should arrive in another day or two, at which time he would be released.

***

"All right, you can go now!" a guard called as he approached the cell.

"Who?" Iridan heard Worm ask from across the hall.

"Both of you," answered the man as he opened the cell doors, "but Josu said he doesn't want to see any more worms crawling about around here."

"So, I guess you were telling the truth," Worm said as he and Iridan followed the guard down the hallway. "Did you enjoy your stay?"

Iridan glanced over his shoulder. "What got you so mad the other day?" he asked.

"I'm sorry about that, but I'd really prefer not to talk about it," Worm replied. Iridan was eager to question Worm further, but he figured that we would not press the issue. He did not want to risk angering him again.

As the two approached a pair of royal guards, Worm winked at the guard, offered a wave to Iridan and quickly darted out of the dungeon. "Josu sends his apologies," one of the guards said to Iridan as he watched Worm scamper away. "We're to lead you to your room. After you clean up and change, he asks that you join him for breakfast."

Iridan wanted to snap angrily, but he knew his incarceration was not the man's fault. And actually, it was not Josu's either. He supposed that he would have acted similarly in Josu's situation. "Very good," he replied with forced cheer as he patted the man on the shoulder.

The trio climbed the stairs from the prison level, and when Iridan smelled clean air, he wondered how he had managed to tolerate the rank odor of his cell. They twisted and climbed until entering a fairly deserted portion of the castle. They walked down the hallway until it reached a dead end. "Take a few moments to prepare yourself," the guard said as he opened the last door. "When you're ready, Kile here will lead you to Josu." The man departed, leaving Kile in the hallway.

Iridan entered a small but comfortable room. A large bed sat in the corner above which a thin window displayed a lovely view of Shekul's farmland. A basin of fresh water and soap sat on a tray in the other corner. Next to the door, he was pleased to see a small wardrobe held his belongings. Iridan sat on the bed and removed his boots; he then collapsed backward and enjoyed the soft mattress for a few moments.

When he stood up, his feet sank into a lush rug of a dim yellows and purples. After cleaning himself, he pulled a dark blue tunic from the wardrobe and donned a pair of slippers. Deciding that he looked presentable enough, he opened the door, and Kile led him back down the hallway.

Chapter 26

"Complacency, my friend, will destroy your kingdom," Ut stated. "Complacency is what nearly destroyed you before, if I understand your recent history well enough."

Jaleph took a deep drought of wine. "What do you mean?" he asked.

"You had not prepared Su'Meeryn for an invasion, and no plans existed to defend your realm. Much death resulted."

"That's right, but we've started to take steps to strengthen ourselves," the king replied uneasily.

"Defense is important," Ut agreed, "but remember what I taught you in our chess match: while building your defense, look for your own attack. *That* is how victory is achieved."

"Fine strategy," agreed the king.

"Yes. Now, we must search out the move—whether bold or subtle—to mount your attack."

"Attack!" the king exclaimed. "Attack who? Tamar and the other lands? They are too weak to be of concern now, and we don't have any other enemies."

Ut sighed. "You do not understand. Capturing a single pawn may be the first move towards checkmate. Think back to the invading army. What did they do first? They attacked Pathum—a small village hardly worth noticing. Was Pathum their enemy? No. They captured the pawn in preparation for victory."

"But they lost," Jaleph pointed out.

"True, but the strategy of capturing Pathum was still sound."

Jaleph scratched his head in bewilderment. He thought he could sense logic within Ut's words, but he failed to grasp the meaning. Why could he not see the strategies of those around him? "Who are we supposed to attack then?"

"Open your mind to the possibilities. It is true, you do not want to create any foes yet, but Su'Meeryn must be ready when an enemy emerges—and history teaches that an enemy will always emerge. Your new warriors must be trained in combat. Always remember, complacency can destroy." Ut raised his own goblet and took a sip. "Identify an unprotected pawn and seize it. Begin to advance your pieces and solidify your king's position."

The rationale of Ut's words had begun to crystallize in Jaleph's brain, but he thought he sensed a flaw in Ut's reasoning. As he tried to pin it down, however, the feeling slowly began to dissolve and only one thought remained: his army must learn to attack. "Where were you thinking?" he asked his companion.

Chapter 27

Kile led Iridan through a dizzying number of corridors and hallways. Iridan had never actually been inside a true castle before, and he found the experience somewhat disconcerting. He considered his guide and noted that they appeared to be of like age, except Kile was far more muscular. Traces of short blonde hair barely stole past his helmet. Kile kept his face clean shaven, and though his round nose was somewhat large, it did not detract from his handsome face. "How do you keep your bearings in here?" Iridan asked.

"Doesn't Su'Meeryn have a castle?" Kile questioned back.

"Not in the strict sense. Su'Meeryn is more of a walled-in village with a palace."

"Oh. Perhaps I could see it some time," responded Kile. "I've been in the royal guard about three years, and you get used to the all the directions in here fairly quickly."

As the hallways grew larger and brighter, Iridan realized that they were not heading towards the same room where he had initially met Josu. "Where are we going?" he asked.

"I was told to take you to the dining hall. You are to meet the king for breakfast."

They continued past a number of servants and dignitaries bisecting the hallways. Iridan attempted to commit some of the castle's decor to memory in case he needed to find his way around on his own, but the bland tapestries and paintings seemed to run one into another. He could not spot any distinguishable features. Realizing that mapping the castle in his head was a hopeless cause, he decided to broach another important issue. "Do you know that man I was in the cell with?"

"Who Worm? Yeah, I know him," answered Kile.

"Can you tell me anything about him?"

Kile stopped and his bright green eyes considered Iridan for a moment. "Why?"

"I'm just curious, that's all," said Iridan.

"He's a friend of mine."

As they started to walk again, Iridan asked, "If you're friends, why didn't you say something to him at the cell?"

"That's none of your business. Now what else do you want to know? Or do you just like to pry?"

"We talked about some interesting things while we were in the cell together. I'd just like to visit him when I have a chance."

Kile seemed to regard Iridan with some suspicion now. "We're here," was all he said. He opened a large double-door and led Iridan into Josu's dining room.

The morning light shone through high windows causing a sparkling radiance to reflect from the king's table. As he entered, Josu and the two men Iridan had met earlier stood. The same woman was there as well, and she remained seated at the king's side.

"Please come in," Josu said. "I hope you are not angered with me over your unkindly treatment, but I had little choice. After all, we did not know who you were."

"It's understandable, your Majesty," Iridan replied. As he neared the long table, the woman pointed him to a chair beside her, and Iridan thought he noticed an expression of disapproval cross the king's face. Iridan sat and looked across at the two men.

"Oh, I am sorry, but I don't think you were introduced to my companions before," said Josu, as he also took his seat. "These two gentlemen are Surik and Forim; they are the son's of Hurik, the wealthiest merchant in all of Shekul. And *this*," he continued emphatically, as he indicated towards the woman, "is Flicia."

"It's a pleasure to meet you again," Flicia purred, and her long, milky fingers gently brushed Iridan's wrist.

"Our beautiful lady is the daughter of Onil, my general," Josu continued. "These three are my most trusted advisors."

"I'm pleased to meet you all, under better circumstances," said Iridan. He was glad to be out of the dungeon, but he still did not feel comfortable around Shekul's nobility.

"You may go now," Surik said to Kile and waved the guard from the dining hall.

"I'm sorry you won't be able to meet my wife. She and the children rarely visit me anymore," Josu explained, and Iridan heard a hushed giggle from Flicia.

"By the way," Forim said to Iridan, "Jaleph sent word that your wife is still ill, so she won't be able to join you. But he did ask us to advise you that you are not to leave for your home. He said that your mission to us is too important."

"And what exactly is your mission?" the king questioned.

"What's wrong with Myrin?" Iridan asked, ignoring Josu.

"Who? Oh, your wife. I don't know, but I'm sure it's not too serious or you would have been asked to return," Forim replied.

"I believe you failed to answer Josu's question," Surik interjected. "Why are you here?"

"I'm Su'Meeryn's ambassador. I thought we had this worked out."

"We know that, but why do we suddenly need an ambassador?" pressed Surik. "The treaty hasn't even been finalized."

Iridan's discomfort was ripening into annoyance. He had been subjected to constant badgering since his arrival, and now he was told that, although Myrin was still sick, he would not be permitted to leave. "Look, this wasn't my idea. Jaleph wanted an ambassador to represent Su'Meeryn's interests in your court. If you don't want me here, I'd be happy to return home."

"Will you three leave the poor man alone," Flicia pleaded. "He is obviously upset over his wife. I thought we were going to have a pleasant meal. Let's leave these discussions for tomorrow."

"That's wise counsel. Bring the food," Josu roared with a smile. Iridan noted that the king's mood had immediately turned from one of suspicion to exuberance.

At the clap of Josu's hands, a number of servants entered the room carrying trays of steaming breads and sliced fruit.

Josu buried a large piece of melon into his mouth. "The guard will show you the rest of my castle after our meal," he mumbled through his chewing. "We'll meet first thing in the morning to discuss business."

"Yes, and now, I think we'd like to hear all about your battle and the dragon," Flicia said. "You are that same Iridan, are you not?"

Iridan nodded, as he regarded the food before him. The meal appeared delicious, but his hunger had vanished. To be polite, he forced down a few mouthfuls between responding to the questions of his companions, but he found it difficult to remain focused, as all he could think about was Myrin.

Chapter 28

Teraken's hands strangled the goblet as it rose towards his lips. The displeasure blazed from his face like a bonfire as he gulped the wine. Jaleph had expected his old friend to disapprove of his plan, but acceptance was not required. Teraken need only obey his king's orders. The two men regarded each other across Jaleph's table. No words were spoken, but the meanings behind both stares were clear. Teraken did not want to proceed with Jaleph's proposal, while the king wanted him to submit.

"I don't like it Jaleph," Teraken insisted. "We shouldn't attack anyone. We're just starting to build our alliances. This plan of yours could cause all that to crumble."

Jaleph glared back at the commander of his troops. "Your concern doesn't interest me. We're here to decide on a target."

Teraken leaned forward with an accusatory finger pointing at Jaleph. "A target, for what? Malicious destruction?"

"It's my job to protect Su'Meeryn. I can't worry over anyone else. We need to get our army into shape."

Teraken slumped back in his chair and laughed. "You're not serious, Jaleph, are you?"

Jaleph's teeth clenched as his lips began to quiver. "You are not to call me that anymore," he said. His palm slapped the table as he sprung from his chair. "You will address me by my title."

Teraken slammed his goblet down, and wine splashed in a crimson shower. "What are you talking about? I've called you Jaleph since you were born!"

"Well I guess I should've corrected that mistake sooner!" Jaleph sneered. And he thought back to the time when he had confronted Teraken after they had sent Iridan and Teracuss on their mission to find Naar's ring. He knew now that he had made a mistake by not punishing Teraken then. After all, a king must discipline his subjects.

"I can't believe this! What's happened to you?"

"What are you implying?"

"You're not the man that I used to know."

Jaleph smiled. "Perhaps a little more confident, able to make decisions on my own?"

"Are you sure?"

"That's enough!" Jaleph commanded. He sat back down and tried to remove the smile from his face. Despite the animosity that had surfaced between the two long-time friends, he was actually enjoying himself. He felt that he was in control of the situation, and he liked the feeling. "Now, do I need to plan the attack without you?"

The king snapped his fingers and Kedin entered the room carrying a number of maps. As the parchments were placed before them, Jaleph noticed the disdain on Teraken's face as he eyed Kedin. The king was well aware of the ill will felt towards Kedin within the palace. Perhaps it was time for that to change too. The young man bowed deeply to Jaleph and exited.

Jaleph spread the maps across the table, and drops of spilled wine began to soak through the edge near Teraken. Jaleph ran his fingers through his yellow hair as he tried to soothe his conflicting emotions of anger and joy. "Let's get started," he ordered.

***

Scores of horses exited Su'Meeryn's gate. Lead riders carried emerald and yellow banners; however, the flags, which flapped in the morning breeze, displayed no crest or insignia. Jaleph thought that the time had come for a new symbol of Su'Meeryn, but he had yet to design his own crest.

Following the cavalry, the armor of infantry glistened in the dawn sun. Two hundred troops exited the gate. Behind the force rode Jaleph and Ut. Their destination was Okkgan, a small merchant village northwest of Su'Meeryn. Since Okkgan brought a good deal of wealth to all the nearby kingdoms as a trading center, the leaders of the town had never viewed themselves as a target for attack; therefore, their defenses were kept at a minimum—only enough to fight back an angry trader or two.

"Ah, your Majesty, I believe we have chosen a fine objective," Ut commented.

"Are you sure this is a good idea?" asked Jaleph. He still felt somewhat apprehensive regarding their plan.

Ut turned to the king and smiled. "You need to expand your kingdom. What better town to annex than Okkgan? You shall add trader wealth to your treasury, and it is close enough to defend. Yes, a fine choice."

Ut's smile broadened. "Perhaps your title will change in the future.

Perhaps it is time the world sees a new emperor."

Jaleph's face brightened. Emperor, he thought as his head nodded in agreement.

***

After three days of marching, Jaleph's force neared the river valley where Okkgan lay. Teraken broke away from the front and rode back to the king. He spun his horse around and allowed a short glare to shoot towards Ut. "We're here, Sire," he said sarcastically.

Ut's eyes considered Teraken for an uncomfortable moment before turning to the king. "I do not like his tone, Majesty."

Jaleph sighed heavily. "I can't deal with this now." He turned back to Teraken. "Have you positioned the men for the attack?"

"Of course, Sire, not that it'll be necessary. There are only a few troops in the city. It will be taken shortly after we enter." Teraken turned towards Ut. "You're sure Illiyna will not protest this attack. We're not too far from Labyn, after all."

"No need to worry yourself over politics," said Ut. "Just remember your place."

Teraken snarled and kicked his horse back to the front of the troops. Jaleph watched as the signal was given, and his force invaded the city.

The horses stormed forward. From the top of a small hill, Jaleph and Ut watched the attack. Teraken led the charge, but the king saw no weapon in his hands. As the fighting erupted, it seemed that Teraken was trying to herd the people of Okkgan into a group. The large warrior then used himself as a shield between the townspeople and his soldiers.

Elsewhere in Okkgan, the blades of Su'Meeryn whirled death in every corner. The people of Okkgan offered little resistance. From his perch, Jaleph saw only a few of his own men fall.

"Come, your Highness," Ut said, "let us take a closer look." And Ut led Jaleph into the town. The king wondered if he should enter Okkgan while the fighting still progressed, but if Ut thought it safe, why not?

As the pair's horses passed the first few buildings, they saw that most of the combat had already quieted; however, one man still flung himself in the direction of any townsperson he saw. The man was tall and slim with long-flowing white hair. But the hair only covered the right half of his head. The remainder of his scalp glistened in the morning sun. Jaleph remembered seeing the man before—he was, in fact, a hard person to forget. His name was Rynkor, and he had built an impressive reputation for his ferocious combat. During the dragon battle, it was said the he killed fifty men single handedly. Jaleph watched on as Rynkor spun a whirlwind of sword blades with each hand. Corpses fell to the ground wherever he moved. Age or sex was irrelevant to his savage assault.

Two of Okkgan's sentries confronted Rynkor as he approached an old man trying to protect a few small children. They managed to knock one of the swords from his hands before the remaining blade severed a windpipe and split the other's skull. Rynkor stared at the old man before him as he panted for oxygen to feed his lungs, but rather than strike—which is what Jaleph expected—Rynkor's back arched as a wolf-like howl burst from his lips. Standing over the old man, he sheathed his sword and laughed.

Jaleph tore his eyes away from Rynkor and surveyed the bloody scene. Bodies lay in a conglomeration of limbs and flowing blood. As the king turned away in disgust, he noticed Ut smiling happily. For the first time, Jaleph considered having Ut hauled away to a dungeon. While he was still lost in thought, Teraken stormed forward.

"I hope you're happy!" Teraken screamed. "Is this what you wanted?"

Jaleph's quickly forgot his disapproval of Ut as he confronted Teraken. "You will not yell at me again! Mind to your duties while you still have them!"

Teraken stammered for a reply, but nothing intelligible came out, and he spun away from the king. Rynkor approached and stopped next to Jaleph's horse in the place where Teraken had just stood. A blood-soaked face regarded Jaleph, and Rynkor's pink eyes glittered in ecstasy. "Marvelous day," Rynkor giggled.

"Get him away from me," Jaleph said to Ut.

"Please leave us for now," Ut said, "but I'm certain that we will want to talk to you later."

"I liked battle. I almost tripped on corpse walking here," Rynkor babbled to no one as he walked away. "Next time king has fight, he should call me again. I will always make great amount death when..." And the king was relieved when he could no longer hear Rynkor's ramblings.

***

Emerald and yellow flags hung limp within Okkgan's administration room. No monarchy had ruled over the village previously; a committee of merchants had administered by election from the various trading guilds. In the past, decisions were by a majority vote, but that had now changed.

The tables of the room had all been removed, except one, where Jaleph and Ut sat. Behind the two, Teraken and Rynkor stood. Jaleph had not wanted the strange warrior near him, but he had relented at Ut's urgings. Two women and one man were led before the king; they represented the only surviving committee members. Guards surrounded the trio, but their demeanor demonstrated that no will existed to assault the king.

"The annexation of Okkgan could have been less bloody if your people would not have fought back so hard," Jaleph said. The three heads he addressed stared at the floor, and Jaleph wondered if his words had registered.

"Okkgan is now claimed by the kingdom of Su'Meeryn," announced Ut, "where your remaining troops will return to join the army there. Troops from the castle will stay here as a defensive force. Your new king has appointed his servant Kedin to rule Okkgan. You may continue with your normal system of governance, with Kedin's approval. A twenty-five percent tax on all business and trade will be paid to King Jaleph to help fund your protection and all other activities he deems necessary. Any attempt at rebellion, or subversive plans against Su'Meeryn, shall be dealt with immediately and harshly. Are there any questions?"

No response came, and Ut continued. "Good. You may begin to prepare your new committee. Kedin should arrive in a few days to formalize and approve any of your decisions." He then motioned for the guards to remove the three.

Teraken stepped from behind the table and scowled at the king. "Congratulations!" he spat as he exited the room.

Ut turned to the king and whispered, "You need to do something about him, Majesty. You cannot allow this insolent behavior to continue."

"I know."

"And perhaps you should appoint a new leader of the army," Ut said as he motioned back to Rynkor.

"Let's not get ahead of ourselves," the king replied. Yes, he was angry with Teraken, but he did not like this Rynkor at all. "Teraken is still a fine man, and he will learn his place."

Chapter 29

Footfalls echoed through an empty audience chamber as Jaleph strode towards his throne. He sat and tried to bury himself as deeply as possible into the soft cushions; his fingers absently stroked the emerald stones decorating the arms of the chair.

The events of the past few days filled his mind. He thought of the people of Okkgan and wondered whether he had made the proper decision. So many had died from the attack, but, fortunately, few of them were his subjects. However, they were all his subjects now. Perhaps Teraken had been right. Perhaps the attack had been unnecessary.

"Ah, Majesty, I was wondering where you had disappeared to," Ut said as he entered the hall and approached the throne.

"It seemed that I needed to contemplate recent events," Jaleph stated.

"My exact feeling. Have you considered what we discussed?"

"What do you mean? Kedin is already on his way to Okkgan."

"That is not what I was referring to. I meant Teraken."

"What about him?" asked Jaleph.

"You were going to replace him with Rynkor."

Jaleph's mind seemed to snap out of a cloud as he focused on Ut's statement. He had never decided to remove Teraken from his position. True, Teraken had acted disrespectfully to his king, but he was an old friend. And now, Jaleph wondered whether Teraken had been right. He looked at Ut, and it appeared that his handsome face had somehow lost its appeal. Perhaps it was the shadows in the room, but Ut looked emaciated. His eyes appeared sunken and his skin had lost its glow. He could have been mistaken, but Jaleph had the impression of death as he looked at the man. "I made no such decision!" the king snapped.

"But his actions were completely—"

"I said I have not made a decision!"

"My apologies Sire," Ut said in a soothing voice. He lowered his head in a show of deference.

The king rose and stepped from his chair. He stood above Ut, but Labyn's ambassador refused to raise his head. Jaleph sensed that Ut was hiding something, that his appearance had truly changed. The king began to wonder why he had ever listened to the man at all.

"I was only looking out for your best interests, Majesty," Ut mumbled. "If you believe Teraken remains your best man to lead your army, I will, of course support you."

"And why, exactly, do I need your support? I am the king."

"Of course. All that I meant was that I will continue to do whatever is in my power to help you."

Jaleph's teeth clenched as his heart filled with contempt. Who was this Ut, anyway, and why should the king listen to him? "I'm beginning to think that it is time for you to return to your queen. You have been away from your home too long."

Ut's mouth quivered as he seemed to struggle for words. "I nearly forgot the reason I was looking for you, Sire," he said, looking up suddenly. "I was told that there is news about Myrin's condition."

"Why didn't you say so!" barked Jaleph, and he dashed out of the hall with his anger towards Ut nearly forgotten.

***

Despite the light breeze which drifted in from the one small window, Myrin's room smelled stale as Jaleph entered. He approached the bed and Myrin's unconscious body. Even through her unkempt appearance, Myrin's beauty still dazzled the king. She stirred as he grasped her hand but did not awaken.

Jaleph turned to the old healer who had followed him in and asked, "So, what is your news?"

"We couldn't initially identify her symptoms due to the strong effects of her illness, but some of the signs have now become evident. Myrin is pregnant."

"Pregnant!" Jaleph exclaimed.

"Yes, but her body is not adapting well. The baby and she aren't out of danger. They have to be watched closely, and she should remain here."

"For how long?"

The woman sighed. "Until the illness passes or she delivers."

"So, there is no way she can join Iridan in Shekul?"

"The travel could kill her."

Jaleph's emotions swirled through his body. Myrin's pregnancy seemed to solidify her marriage, but it also required that she remain in Su'Meeryn, apart from her husband. He knew that somewhere within this scenario an advantage existed for him. Now he only needed to find that advantage. While he gazed at Myrin, and considering the situation,

Pothar entered.

"I heard you were here Sire, and I wanted to see you," Pothar said with a smile.

Jaleph turned towards the door. "You look better."

"Yes, I should be leaving here tomorrow."

"Do you think you'll be able to ride?"

"He'll be fine for whatever you need," the healer answered for Pothar before she left the room.

"I guess that someone should go to Shekul and give Iridan the news," the king said and he proceeded to advise Pothar regarding Myrin's pregnancy.

Pothar's expression brightened. "You don't know how bad I want to get out of here." But his smile disappeared as he turned towards Myrin. "I just hope she gets through this."

"We all do."

Pothar turned to leave then looked back at Jaleph. "Is there anything else you want me to do before I return from Shekul?"

"Oh, stay a few days with your friend. If he needs you for anything longer, just send word back."

"Thank you Sire," Pothar replied as he exited the room.

Before Jaleph left, he knelt next to Myrin's bed. Her eyes opened briefly and she managed a slight grin towards the king. He returned the expression as her eyes closed again. Jaleph left with his emotions still whirling through his head like a tornado.

Chapter 30

Teraken approached Jaleph who was standing before the castle gate. They watched as the few remaining troops from Okkgan entered Su'Meeryn to take up their new positions. Teraken's expressionless face regarded the king for moment, then turned away. Jaleph watched as the men from Okkgan's militia shuffled passed. They looked dejected—beaten, which, of course, they were.

He heard a soft chuckle and saw Ut now walking up to him with Rynkor trailing behind. "It is a wonderful sight, your Highness: the beginning of the new empire," Ut remarked.

"New empire, wonderful thing," agreed Rynkor.

"What're they talking about?" Teraken asked angrily.

Jaleph ignored the question. He was tired of fighting with his old friend, and this was definitely not the time to start again. "What are you doing here, Ut?" he asked. "I didn't ask for you."

"You are correct, of course. I just came to offer a suggestion, if I am not found to be too presumptuous. It might be a good idea to appoint one of your soldiers to supervise the transition of the new forces into your army."

"I hate to admit it," said Teraken, "but that is a good idea."

"And I take it you're thinking of Rynkor?" the king sighed, looking at the bizarre warrior.

"Rynkor? Oh no," laughed Ut, "he is far too valuable for other tasks. I was thinking of that female soldier: Dobrah."

Hearing her name raised old thoughts in Jaleph's mind. With Karus dead, he was now free to pursue Dobrah for his queen; however, that idea no longer appealed to him. A warm spot still remained for her, though, and she had proven herself a capable soldier. "Yes," he agreed. "Teraken, see to it."

"Of course, Sire," Teraken said. "She'll begin today."

***

Later that afternoon, Jaleph trotted through Su'Meeryn's streets in what had become a daily ritual. As the days passed, he noticed his endurance growing. He enjoyed the exercise but found the running somewhat lonely. Yes, his guards did accompany him, but they never engaged him in any conversation. He had once mentioned this in passing to Ut, and the ambassador had offered to run with him. But Jaleph now had little desire to see his self-appointed advisor. The images of the butchery at Okkgan weighed heavily on him, along with constant doubts regarding the justification for the attack.

Perspiration dripped from the yellow hair of his dwindling mane, which bounced with each step. He wiped his hand over his head to whisk away the sweat. His breathing came with increasing difficulty, but, just a few paces ahead, his guards showed no signs of slowing. Jaleph began to feel annoyed. He knew he had only started his exercising a short time ago, but despite the gains he had seen, he wanted faster improvement. He stopped suddenly, startling the guards behind him.

"Sire? Are you finished?" one of the men asked.

"Yes," Jaleph panted. "Let's return to the palace." As he trudged home, Jaleph felt angry with himself for stopping early, but he figured he could use some rest anyway. And he wondered if his annoyance was due to his ineptitude in comparison to his guards or his solitude, which each run seemed to magnify.

The king continued in silence—brooding over his situation—until he decided it was finally time for action. It was time to put an end to his loneliness.

***

"It's nice of you to invite me to dinner, your Highness," Iridan's cousin commented as she tilted her beautiful head to one side. She lifted a silver fork and nibbled a roasted potato.

"Please, we're alone, you can call me Jaleph," the king replied. He admired her luscious fiery-red curls as they flowed with each movement she made. "I haven't seen you in a while; that was an oversight which needed to be remedied."

Dirwyn's smile brightened the already well-lit room. "Well, thank you," she replied, and she began to tell the king about an amusing misunderstanding she'd had with a merchant the day before. Jaleph's knife sliced through his tender steak as he thought, yes, she is beautiful, even more so than Myrin. But the thought of Myrin made him wonder if this dinner was a mistake. The king shook the thought from his mind and tasted the surprisingly spicy meat. And he marveled—not for the first time—at the talents of his annoying chef.

"Oh, isn't it sad about Myrin," Dirwyn continued. "I hope everything works out, and I suppose Iridan should be returning soon. It has been a long time since I've seen him."

"No, he won't," Jaleph responded flatly.

"Why?"

"He's busy with his duties in Shekul."

"I'm sure he can take a few days to visit his wife."

"Well, I'll have to see about that," and Jaleph began to grow irritated at this prodding by Dirwyn. But then in an attempt to smooth over his harsh tone, he said, "Perhaps Josu will be able to spare him for a few days."

Her smile seemed to emit the radiance of the noon sun. "Good. It's been pretty lonely lately..." and an eclipse of darkness reached her face, "especially without Ruy."

"We all miss him," Jaleph acknowledged.

The door to the dining room opened and Markis entered carrying a large tray. He waddled to the table wearing his customary white shirt and tight black pants. Even this deliberate pace seemed too strenuous for the enormous chef. He breathed heavily with each step until finally dropping the tray on the table. Jaleph eagerly admired the cream-filled pastries and powdered fruits.

"Dessert for the king and his guest," Markis panted with a self-congratulatory tone.

"They look wonderful, Markis," Jaleph said.

"Yes, very beautiful," agreed Dirwyn.

"Of course, of course," squeaked the chef. Markis' bulk seemed to dwarf both of his patrons together, as he stood motionless before them.

"Is there something else?" asked Jaleph.

"Please taste one. They're extraordinary."

"We haven't finished our meal yet," said Jaleph.

"But it would be a travesty if I'm not allowed to see your delight when you taste my masterpieces," Markis pouted.

Jaleph sighed deeply as his utensils smacked the table. "Markis, get out!"

The chef whimpered and wheezed his way from the dining room.

"I'm sorry about that," Jaleph returned his attention to Dirwyn, "but I'm sure he's right about the pastries.

Despite a still nearly full plate, Dirwyn delicately lifted a pastry from the tray. As she bit into her dessert, her expression confirmed Jaleph's comment. The king watched as she savored each bite, and he remembered his chess game with Ut. *A king without a queen is quickly defeated.*

Chapter 31

Iridan smiled as Pothar approached through the door to his room. The pair hugged and slapped each other's backs heartily. "It's good to see you moving about," Iridan said. "You looked pretty bad when I left."

"Yeah, it was rough. But somehow I got through it." Pothar smiled warmly as he again slapped his friend's back.

Iridan sat in his chair and asked, "So what're you doing here? Is this just a social visit?"

Pothar's expression quickly dissolved. "I came to bring you news about Myrin."

"What is it?"

"She's pregnant," Pothar replied, "but she's not doing well. I guess her body's not adjusting to the baby. The healers have no way of knowing how she'll handle the delivery."

Iridan quickly headed for his door. "Where are you going?" Pothar called after him.

"I need to let Josu know that I'm leaving." As he looked back, he noticed that Pothar appeared uneasy at his statement. "What's wrong?"

"I'm not sure that Jaleph wants you to come back right now."

"Why? It's not like I've done anything since I've been here."

"Still," said Pothar, "he didn't tell me to have you return."

"I don't care. You can stay here if you want, but I'm leaving."

***

Josu peered uncertainly at his companions as Iridan finished his story. Flicia approached and placed a reassuring hand on Iridan's shoulder. "Of course you should return home," she said. "Leave as soon as you can. Isn't that right Josu?"

"Of course, of course," the king agreed.

"When do you think you'll return?" Flicia asked. "We will need you back soon. We need to get moving with our business." And her smile seemed to reflect two meanings.

"Take care of your wife, Iridan," said Josu, "and send us word of her condition and when you'll be able to come back."

"Thank you, Sire," Iridan said sincerely as Surik and Forim also offered him their sympathies.

Josu grinned, displaying his pleasure at the decision that he had made. The king then looked back at Flicia, but she continued to stare at Iridan. He turned again to Iridan and responded, "You're welcome."

Chapter 32

Seated on his throne, Jaleph watched as the last of his petitioners marched from the hall. He had found himself putting off these meetings for too long. Despite the pettiness of many of the disputes, it felt good to get back to mediating for his subjects. He looked up and his face brightened as he saw Dirwyn strolling towards him. She was carrying a basket, and he noticed that she was wearing riding clothes.

"I see your meeting is finally concluded," she said.

"Very observant," replied the king.

"It's one of my best traits. May I assume that the king has no other appointments today?"

"Actually, I planned to run this afternoon."

"That can wait, I hope," said Dirwyn. "I took the liberty to have some horses prepared. They are waiting for us, along with a couple of your guards. I was thinking that we could go for a ride through the farmland then have a picnic for dinner."

The king smiled with surprise and pleasure. "Yes. That sounds wonderful." He stood and took the basket from Dirwyn. She hummed softly as they headed for the door, with her arm wrapped through the king's.

As they approached the stable, Jaleph spotted Ut trotting towards them. The handsome man displayed a look of apprehension. The king's pace did not slacken as he asked, "What is it Ut?"

"May I inquire regarding where you are going?"

"For a ride, if you must know."

"Are you certain this is a wise idea?" Ut continued.

"Guards will be present. Now, what do you want?"

For the first time, Jaleph thought he saw Ut at a loss for words. "It is just that I wanted to discuss the need of some scouting parties to the south," he finally managed to reply.

"Go find Teraken and discuss it with him. I'm busy."

"But Sire, I really think that I should confer with you. You are aware of Teraken's misguided opinion of me."

Jaleph stopped and turned to Ut. "I said no. Now go away!"

"My apologies Majesty. I will, of course, follow your instructions," and Ut quickly left.

"Sometimes I don't know about that man," Jaleph mumbled as they continued towards the stable.

"I'm sorry Jaleph, what was that?" Dirwyn asked.

"Nothing," he replied, "nothing."

***

They rode through the gates with four guards trailing behind. A soft breeze tickled their skin as the small group rode through the warmth of the sun in the cloudless sky. With a quick look back, and a laugh, Dirwyn kicked her horse into a gallop, and Jaleph chased after. He marveled at her beauty, as he watched the flaming hair flowing behind her. They traveled passed farmers going about their chores, oblivious that he was their king. Eventually they reached a small brook, and Dirwyn jumped down from her horse.

"Iridan and I used to come here sometimes when we were kids," Dirwyn said. "Isn't it pretty?"

Jaleph cringed slightly at Iridan's name. Can't I get any peace from him, even here? he thought. "Yes it is," he replied and tried to make his smile return.

Dirwyn pulled a blanket from her pack and spread it on the ground. Jaleph sat down and motioned for his guards to move back a little further. "It seems strange," she said as she retrieved her basket, "me here with the king."

"Why is that?"

"I'm not a daughter of a noble or anything."

"We've known each other for quite awhile."

"Yes, but that was only through Ruy. It wasn't because of me."

"You sell yourself short."

"I'm just a common girl, and with Ruy gone, I have little prospect for anything else."

"You are certainly not common," said the king. Dirwyn smiled. Jaleph wanted to praise her beauty, but he felt somewhat uncomfortable doing so, following the talk about Ruy.

"Thank you."

"Now, let's see what food you packed for us." He pulled out some cheese, bread and a skin of wine from the basket. They started their meal, and Jaleph asked, "How is your father's shop doing? He's a blacksmith, right?" Dirwyn nodded. "I've meant to stop by and ask for a new sword, but I've been too busy to get there."

"We're doing okay," Dirwyn replied. "He's starting to slow down

271

some, but I help out as much as I can."

"That's good," Jaleph said. They continued to discuss some of the chores Dirwyn managed around the shop, then some gossip regarding Su'Meeryn's nobility. As the shadows of the trees about them lengthened, one of the guards approached and suggested that they head back.

Jaleph nodded and began to gather the supplies. Dirwyn packed the blanket away and soon they had remounted and were trotting back to the castle. When they reached the gates they jumped from their steeds, and Dirwyn thanked him for their dinner.

"No, I should be thanking you. It was one of the most enjoyable evenings I've had in a long while," he replied, and a sudden wave a melancholy swept over him as he tried to recall the last time when he did have such a pleasurable experience. He felt pathetic. Wasn't it bad enough to be such an inept king, but must he also be so socially hopeless as well? He was trying to change that, but what of all the wasted years? He should have children by now; he should be grooming a prince. "It's getting late," he continued. Let me take the horses back. You should get home." Dirwyn happily handed him the reins and strolled away.

Jaleph tried to shake off his gloom. Self-pity would not do. It was time to move forward.

Chapter 33

Dobrah's fortunes had altered considerably throughout her young life. She had been the first woman to enter Su'Meeryn's military and endured the abuse associated with any such drastic change to an ingrained organization. She had faced the battle to save Su'Meeryn and survived. Marriage followed shortly after, but within a year, she had already found herself widowed. At one time, Jaleph had, unbeknownst to her, desired her as his queen, whereas now she was virtually forgotten. But with her new position of overseeing the integration of Okkgan's troops, it seemed that her life was again on an upswing.

She stood on the castle wall and watched her charges from Okkgan trudge towards the soldiers of Su'Meeryn. Knowing the importance of a positive beginning, her soldiers had been ordered to welcome their new comrades. She had not yet introduced herself as she wanted to see some of the interaction first.

Troops from Su'Meeryn began to mill about the new arrivals, trying to make them comfortable. They were to discuss commonalties; the decisions of state were made by kings and city rulers, not the ordinary man. What happened in Okkgan had nothing to do with them; there was no reason why they could not become friends.

As Dobrah headed towards the stairs to join the drills, she saw a slim, handsome man walking towards her along the castle wall. He wore a cloud-like shirt and glistening pants. The sun's rays sparkled off a silver belt. His soft shoes padded effortlessly across the stone walkway, and he smiled easily at her while the light breeze tussled his blonde hair.

"I see that the soldiers from Okkgan have arrived," the man said.

She looked at him with a queer expression. "Yes, they have. And who are you?"

"I am sorry. I forgot we have actually never met. I am Ut."

"Oh yes, the ambassador from Labyn."

Ut bowed slightly. "At your service."

"Well, what do you want?" Despite his attractive appearance, Dobrah felt an immediate aversion to the man.

"I just came to see how things are progressing."

"We've just begun. I was going to start some joint drills to incorporate the new soldiers with ours."

"A wise procedure," agreed Ut.

Dobrah continued on her way and noticed Ut was following her. "Is there anything else?"

"Yes, actually." Ut grasped Dobrah's arm and led her away from the stairs. "I understand you are a friend of Iridan?" Dobrah nodded. "And his family?" She nodded again.

Ut's voice lowered. "I am not certain whether you have noticed, but the king has been acting rather erratically lately. The attack on Okkgan was not wise. I think he might be going mad. Do you agree?" Dobrah stared at him blankly, stunned by his bluntness. "Your king is becoming obsessed with Iridan. He is jealous. Iridan has become too popular. That is why Jaleph sent him away."

"And what do you expect me to do?"

"I believe his family is at risk. I think you should encourage Myrin to leave. She should join Iridan in Shekul. Dirwyn should likely leave as well. There is no telling how Jaleph might react to such a close relative of his after Myrin leaves."

"From what I'm told, Myrin's in no condition to go anywhere," Dobrah pointed out.

"Perhaps not right now, but the option should be considered."

She looked skeptically at him. "I'll think about it."

"Fine," Ut said, "think about it, but do not think for too long, or I am afraid you might find your friends dead." And with that, he left.

Dobrah watched Ut as he turned towards the stairs and quickly descended. She had no idea what to make of the man. She questioned his sincerity, but he was correct about the attack on Okkgan. It made no sense. Maybe something was wrong with Jaleph, and Dobrah decided that she should watch the king closely.

Chapter 34

As Pothar and Iridan approached Su'Meeryn, a small scouting party hailed them. When the scouts recognized them, they were allowed to pass. The brief encounter seemed strange to Iridan. He had patrolled this area many times but always by himself. When they reached the gate, Iridan found it to be more heavily guarded than he could ever remember. The sentries seemed confused when they saw him. They hesitated, not allowing the men to enter.

"What's the problem?" Iridan snapped.

"We weren't told to expect your arrival, sir," one of the guards answered.

"Well here I am. Let me by!"

The guards milled about for a few seconds then parted before Iridan's horse.

"I'm going to go see my father," Pothar said as they entered the courtyard. "I'll come by your house later tonight."

"Good. I'll see you then." Iridan hopped from the back of his horse and led it to the royal stable. A few people approach and tried to engage him in conversation, but Iridan ignored the attention. He walked in silence until Veake met him and grabbed the reins.

"Ta mast'r back fr'm Shekul. I's glud t' see it," Veake slobbered.

"Don't call me that, Veake. Please," Iridan pleaded.

The stableman cackled. "Mast'r, mast'r. Sounds guud, eh?"

"No it doesn't."

"Ya bett'r git ussed t'it," Veake laughed. As he took the reins, he continued laughing so hard that he began to choke, and Iridan saw an unidentifiable item fly from his mouth.

"And why, exactly, do you think that I should get used to it?" Iridan asked angrily. His life was beginning to feel like one, long, complicated question, and he saw no answer in sight.

Veake wiped his mouth with a grubby sleeve and motioned for Iridan to wait as he left to stable the horse. When he returned, Veake continued, "Jaleph's time ees endun. A new age whiil sturt soon." But, before Iridan could respond, the stableman scurried away.

***

Sitting on the edge of the bed, Iridan gazed at his wife's pale face. She smiled weakly as her hand absently stroked her swollen stomach. "I came as soon as I heard," he said.

"I know," she whispered.

He took her hand as one of the healers came in and wiped Myrin's forehead with a damp cloth. She helped Myrin sit up and gave her a mug of a steaming, pungent liquid. The woman left after Myrin emptied the cup.

Iridan watched as Myrin's head dropped back onto her pillow, and her eyes slowly closed. He watched as her breathing softened, and he watched as her hair dropped over the edge of the pillow when her head turned with the arrival of sleep.

After gazing at his wife for a few more moments, Iridan slowly stood. He kissed her gently and quietly exited the room.

***

Iridan lay on his bed—with several scrolls resting on his stomach—staring at his dusty ceiling. He had been planning to study, but he was too concerned about Myrin to get any work done. A knock at his door roused him from his bed, causing the scrolls fall to the floor. Iridan was expecting Pothar, so he paid little attention to his appearance, and he was quite surprised—and embarrassed—when he saw Dobrah. He quickly patted at his hair and brushed at the dust that remained on his trousers before beckoning for her to enter.

"I'm sorry. I was expecting someone else. How are you?" he asked.

"I've been busy, so it's keeping my mind off things. I visit Myrin as often as I can. It seems like she's a little better."

Iridan shrugged his shoulders and sat down. Dobrah shut the door and pulled up a chair next to him. "Did you hear what happened?"

"What?"

"About Okkgan?"

"What about it?"

"We attacked it," she replied, while glancing apprehensively over her shoulder at the closed door.

"We attacked Okkgan? Why?" Iridan's surprise equaled his bewilderment.

"That's a good question. Nobody really knows. Jaleph has been acting strangely. A friend of mine—who is a guard in the palace—tells me that Teraken and he had not been talking, then this attack. It probably has something to do with Ut."

"Who?"

"Ut. You mean you never met him?"

"No. Who is he?"

"He's the ambassador from Labyn. He's been seen with Jaleph quite a bit since he arrived." She paused for a moment and again looked back at the closed door. "Well, Jaleph has declared Okkgan as part of his kingdom. He sent Kedin there to run things with some of our troops, and we're integrating what soldiers they had left here in the castle. Then Ut came up to me and questioned Jaleph's motives. He also mentioned getting Myrin and your cousin out of Su'Meeryn, but I don't trust him." She stood up and sighed. "Everything seems to be changing."

Iridan just sat and stared at Dobrah. He could think of nothing to say. Why would he need to get her out of the castle? He felt numb regarding the whole situation, and he had no room within his heart to add any concerns regarding the condition of Su'Meeryn.

Dobrah looked at him, waiting for a response, but nothing came. He saw the frustration on her face, but he did not care. "Keep your eyes open. If you notice anything strange let me know." She continued to stare at him. "Okay?"

"Yeah."

Following a few more moments of silence, Dobrah left. Shortly after, Pothar arrived and asked about Myrin.

"She's not well," Iridan replied.

Pothar tried to continue the conversation but received little response. Iridan noticed a growing level of irritation from his friend. It seemed out-of-place; Iridan could not recall ever seeing Pothar aggravated in the past. "Look, I know that you're having a hard time with all this, but we need to talk," Pothar stated.

"About what?"

"I've been thinking about our battle at the ravine. None of it makes sense. Where did those troops come from? It was like they knew we would be there. They clearly weren't trained. School boys would have used better tactics."

Thoughts of the battle temporarily pushed Myrin's condition from his mind. "I agree," responded Iridan, "and one of the men was about to strike me when he fell dead with his back smoldering. I don't know what could have caused that."

"What do you think we should do?"

"Do? I don't know if there is anything we can do."

"Maybe you should mention it to Teraken."

"And what could he do about it?" Iridan asked. "By the way, why didn't you tell me about Okkgan?"

"What about it?"

"You mean you didn't know either? Jaleph attacked it. Dobrah just told me."

"We attacked Okkgan? I was with the healers so long, I didn't hear anything. Then Jaleph sent me to see you as soon as I was released.

"Well, I'm sure I'll be sent back to Shekul soon. It seems like Jaleph is anxious to get rid of me. You better keep an eye on things around here while I'm gone. Now, if you don't mind, I'd like to try to get some sleep."

***

He stood on an open plain. All around him, tall grass rippled before a steady wind. Tiny seeds blew through the air; they swirled around and pelted his bare skin like a swarm of angry mosquitoes. Iridan glanced down and noticed he was naked. As the nearly microscopic red welts began to rise, Iridan heard a low rumbling. He glanced about the open expanse, but he found no source for the sound.

The high grass gave way as Iridan began to push forward. He walked, but no landmark was visible to disrupt that field of golden-green. He walked, but towards no destination.

The rumbling grew louder. Iridan stopped and look about. Still nothing but grass met his gaze. The sound continued to build, and Iridan realized it came from under his feet. He started to walk again, this time a little faster. Vibrations began to emanate from the earth, and he broke into a run. The vibrations increased into a steady shaking. He heard a sharp crack, then another. A small hole collapsed in the ground before him, and he stumbled over it, nearly falling.

Finally, he spotted a break in the grass. As he flung himself towards it, he twisted an ankle when he stepped on a large rock. Pain seared up his leg, but he continued to run. Each step caused his pain to increase, and he wondered if he had fractured his ankle. Upon reaching the opening, he realized that he had come across a slim path.

The intensity of the noise grew and bored through his ears. Iridan looked ahead and saw a seam forming in the dirt, bisecting the path. The line grew into a crack, and then opened even more. He tried to jump to the side, but he was too late. Before his feet could leave the ground, he fell into the chasm. With his arms outstretched, he caught the side of the earth under his armpits. His body struck against the jagged ground and tore at his naked skin.

He attempted to pull himself up, but that only opened his cuts wider. Blood flowed freely, and he began to slip. He struggled to brace himself with his feet, but his efforts merely multiplied the agony in his ankle. Suddenly the chasm opened even wider, and he lost his grip with his right hand. He dangled haphazardly, clinging to grass and dirt. He swung slightly against the tiny razors piercing his skin. Slowly the fingers on his left hand began to slip away. He reached up, desperately trying to prevent the inevitable plunge into the dark gorge.

He fell.

The light vanished. His body bounced against the side of the chasm almost in rhythm with his heartbeats. Long, agonizing moments passed until, finally, mercifully, he stopped hitting the earthen wall; however, his plummet continued. But once the battering stopped, Iridan noticed that the temperature had begun to rise. Sweat welled up, and his own salt burrowed into his cuts. He felt a multitude of stings piercing every inch of his body. The heat grew, burning with each breath he strained to force into his lungs. Still he fell. He felt his skin begin to scorch, and he smelled the pungent aroma of burnt hair. His eyes felt like hot coals buried in his skull.

As the last drops of sweat burned off, Iridan noticed a small white light below. It grew at an alarming rate as he approached. His flesh contracted and torturously cracked open. He tried to scream, but no sound escaped his parched lips. His fingers melted into a jumble of confused skin and bone.

The light grew and pierced his already agonized eyes. He tried to close his lids, but they refused to move. The white light surrounded him in a blinding fury. Suddenly his fall ended as he smacked against the ground. Somehow he stood, and as he did, all his agony melted away.

Who are you?

His head turned; at least he thought it did. The white light enveloped him; it did not allow any other sensation to pierce into his soul. The only thing that he could comprehend was the light, the light and the now familiar voice with the familiar question.

Who are you?

He knew he needed to reply. But what was the answer?

Who are you?

"I am Iridan," but he knew the voice would reject his response.

That is for the past. Who are you?

The past, he thought, am I dead? No, not dead. He knew that his life had changed drastically in less than two years. But had it changed so much? Was he now a different person?

"I am Su'Meeryn's ambassador," he said, hoping he had solved the riddle.

Insignificant. The egg must open.

Egg? What now? He puzzled over the absurd statement. What was the reason behind this questioning? He needed to uncover the truth.

Who are you?

"I am Iridan," he repeated with a tone of defeat.

No. Who are you?

As the question echoed within him, a sliver of realization sought to etch its way into his mind. He grasped for it. He tried to dig it out from a quagmire of disjointed thoughts and emotions. But, just as the answer began to surface, the bright light disappeared, and all his agony returned.

Iridan's eyes opened, and he sat up on his wet mattress. The dream remained a vivid image, and the voice continued to echo in his mind. He knew that he needed to solve the puzzle; he must find the answer to the question that plagued his dreams.

Chapter 35

Jaleph sat unhappily in his chambers. News of Iridan's return had reached him. I could punish him for this, he thought, but how would Myrin react? The last thing he wanted to do was anger her. I suppose it's understandable; how could he be expected to remain in Shekul after finding out about her pregnancy? So, he decided to let the issue pass.

The king rose to prepare himself for the day. He moved to his mirror and examined the reflection that met him. His stomach appeared to be smaller, and lines of muscle were starting to form. He ran his hands across his chest and up the side of his neck. When they reached his hair, his small smile disappeared. He pulled at the yellow locks in disgust.

I look like a fool, he thought. The hair hung farther down his back than ever before, but unfortunately, his forehead glistened in the daylight streaming through his window. Hair stuck out in unwanted directions and retreated from areas where it was needed most.

His fist struck the wall before him in anger before grabbing his razor. The blade chopped at his hair and clumps fell to the ground like a golden windstorm. When Jaleph finally stopped, the only adornment that remained on his skull was blood leaking from numerous small cuts. He grabbed a towel, and after wiping his head, he donned his leather band. The emerald seemed to sparkle brighter than ever before without the distracting globs of yellow hair.

Jaleph twisted and turned before the mirror until finally offering it a satisfied grin. "Much better," he said as he left the room.

***

The scent of roasting lamb filled the royal dining hall. Jaleph sat at the front seat of the long table with Dirwyn to his left. She picked absently at the appetizer of fresh vegetables and grated cheeses with a silver fork. Her smile seemed different to Jaleph, but he assumed she was just taken aback by his new appearance. She's not used to such a handsome man, he thought as his hand absently rubbed the back of his skull and discovered an awkward lump next to some strands of hair that he had missed.

"I see you like the new look," he said. Dirwyn nodded. "Much more sleek, I must say."

Dirwyn quickly shoveled some salad into her mouth.

"I was beginning to think that you weren't hungry, but the lamb should be here shortly," he said as a fresh trickle of blood ran down past his ear.

"Yes, Jaleph," she coughed while covering her face with a finely embroidered napkin.

"I look much more regal now, do I not? Doesn't my emerald seem to glisten more?"

Dirwyn nodded again as Markis wheezed into the room carrying a plate of glistening meat. The aroma was so intoxicating that Jaleph thought he could almost feel it. "Majesty," he said with a huge smile, as he gently placed the tray on the table.

Jaleph nodded, but Markis failed to move. "Thank you Markis, it looks wonderful."

"I know; I know. I basted the meat all night with orange butter, then I rose early to roast it over a low flame for—"

"Yes Markis," Jaleph snapped, "we don't want a cooking lesson."

Markis huffed and lumbered out of the dining hall with one long wheeze.

The king grabbed the carving knife, and it seemed to slide right through the meat. "Annoying man but a marvelous chef," he mumbled. As he handed a plate to Dirwyn, she stood from her chair. "What's wrong?" he asked.

"I'm sorry Jaleph, but I'm starting to feel a little sick. I'll see you later." And with one quick glance back at the king, she fled the room.

She must be really sick, he thought; that came on pretty fast. The king looked around at the empty hall and proceeded to eat his meal alone.

Chapter 36

Hooves trampled green moss under a high noon sun. The steeds galloped past farms as gusts of wind blew dust into their rider's faces. Jaleph kicked his horse's flanks, and the animal surged forward. He turned back to Ut, who had been next to him, and laughed. Ut rushed his own horse ahead and reached the king's side. Jaleph slowed the pace as they had almost ridden up the backs of their two leading guards.

"It is nice to get out in the open; you must agree," Ut said to his companion.

"Yes it is," Jaleph replied.

"So, I saw Dirwyn left your dinner date early last night. Was something wrong?"

Jaleph was annoyed at Ut's implication, and he was annoyed at Dirwyn for her untimely exit. "She had a headache," he replied.

"How unfortunate." Ut paused. "Have you made any future plans with her?"

"Not yet."

"That is good. I am not certain that she would be the right queen for you, as yesterday demonstrated."

The king sneered at Ut. "I don't need your advice on this."

"I am just trying to help."

"Maybe I don't want your help."

"You must do as you see fit, Majesty."

Jaleph thought he noticed a condescending tone within Ut's words, and he made a sudden decision about his self-appointed advisor. It was a decision he now felt he should have done a long time past. "Why don't you leave?"

"Majesty?"

"You heard me. Go back to Labyn. Your investigation into the ambush doesn't seem to be getting very far. Perhaps you could accomplish more if you return."

Ut sighed, and his head dropped. He looked back at Jaleph. "I will leave tomorrow if that is what you desire."

Jaleph smiled to himself and kept riding, but then another thought came to him: Why should Ut decide when he would leave? And his displeasure bloomed into anger. "How about leaving right now?"

"Now?" Ut asked, and the appearance of his face seemed to distort for a moment. His beautiful features melted into a hideous shadow, and Jaleph thought he saw a semblance of rage threatening to boil over. The king was taken aback, but, as quickly as his features had transformed, his exquisite countenance returned. Jaleph wondered if he had only imagined the change. "But Majesty, I am completely unprepared. Certainly you would not force a man to embark on such a long journey when he had only planned for a recreational ride."

"It seems that you enjoy making decisions for me." Jaleph halted his horse and called his guards to approach. "It's time for me to make some of my own decisions. Return to the castle to gather your belongings, then be gone! If I ever feel the need for your presence again, I'll send for you."

Ut kept his horse still for a long moment, regarding the king. The king sensed an air of superiority coming from the man. Ut's stare revealed no anger or distress; rather, it was the look of a rancher viewing his livestock. "As you wish Jaleph," Ut said. "I hope to see you again soon. If I learn anything about the ambush, I will send word." With that, he spun his horse around and rode back towards the castle.

The king gazed at the disappearing form of Ut, then turned back to his guards. "Let's continue with our ride," he said cheerfully.

Chapter 37

Heavy brush to the north came to an abrupt end at a rocky valley. A dirt road acted as a boundary between them and the entrance into Okkgan. The path narrowed as Dobrah and Pothar approached. She signaled for the trailing riders to halt. "Wait out here," she called to the soldiers while Pothar followed her into the city.

Most of the townspeople they passed refused to meet her gaze. The few who did look up scowled and quickly walked away. "They're not very happy, are they?" Pothar pointed out.

"Would you be?"

"Are you questioning Jaleph's orders?" Pothar asked.

Dobrah's laugh revealed no humor. "I don't think these people are our enemies. At least they weren't." She searched Pothar's face for a reaction to her statement. She wondered if he shared the same perplexing thoughts regarding their king, but he just kept riding.

"Please lead us to Kedin," Pothar said to the first Su'Meeryn soldier they spotted. The man nodded. The two dismounted and walked their horses behind their guide.

They entered a dark room where Kedin sat behind a small table, his thin fingers dancing through a pile of documents. When he recognized his guests, he quickly stood and smoothed out the wrinkles from his lace shirt. "I'm sorry," he whimpered, "but I wasn't expecting any visitors. What do you want?"

Pothar handed Kedin a parchment sealed with Jaleph's insignia. "Word has reached Su'Meeryn of bandits in this area," he said. "Jaleph sent us out to track them down. You are to supply us with some additional troops for our task."

Kedin opened and scanned the scroll to confirm the order. "Very well," he responded, sounding somewhat exasperated. "Would you like to rest and leave in the morning?" Kedin stood and flowed towards the pair.

"We are supposed to leave immediately," Pothar replied.

"Our company is waiting just outside the city. Have a score of your troops and horses meet us immediately," Dobrah ordered.

After returning to their mounts, Dobrah and Pothar headed back out of Okkgan. Dobrah glanced about at the people walking down the streets. She saw many of the merchants haggling with customers until spotting the pair. Most stopped and turned away until the two went by. They passed a number of troops, and Dobrah offered a slight nod to the few she recognized.

"What do you think of Kedin?" Pothar suddenly asked.

"How do you mean?" she answered, and she wondered whether Pothar was testing her.

"Do you think he makes a good leader for an outlining province?"

"I don't know him well enough to judge," replied Dobrah. She then decided to take a risk. Knowing Pothar was a friend of Iridan—and her dead husband—she thought he might make a good ally in the future, if she ever needed one. "But what I've seen of him, I don't really like." When Pothar failed to reply, she pushed a little further. "I know Karus never liked him."

"Who does?"

"Jaleph," she answered and stopped walking, staring directly at her companion.

Pothar looked back then mounted his horse. "We should return to the men," he said.

Dobrah also climbed into her saddle. She wished Pothar had continued the conversation, but she thought she saw a look of agreement on his face. It seemed that he might be coming to some conclusions about their king, but he was not quite ready to acknowledge them, at least not to her.

The horses trotted towards the outskirts of the small city. Dobrah saw the troops milling about in the field before them. But before Pothar and she could get any closer, they saw a horde of attackers pounce from the light brush which surrounded the field. Cries of distress reached her ears as swords and axes rose and fell. Blood erupted in all directions, bathing the lush field with a crimson hue.

"Back to the town," Pothar yelled.

"But we have to help them," Dobrah replied as she saw more assailants swarm towards the doomed soldiers.

"We can't!" Pothar grabbed her reins and kicked his horse around and back into Okkgan.

Chapter 38

The stone of the gray walls reflected flickering rays from the candelabrum held by Teraken. He stood in the doorway of the forgotten room while the flames threatened to illuminate every hidden corner. Dust swirled from footsteps and trailed after the light—seeking to protect the now exposed crevices. Cobwebs glistened and twirled from every movement of the two intruders.

"When was the last time somebody was in here?" Teraken asked as he rested the candles on a table that creaked under the minuscule weight.

"I don't know," responded the king, as his gaze continued to survey the room.

"What did you want to do?"

Jaleph took a deep breath and coughed out the musty aroma. "It struck me that there are rooms in the palace which I've never entered. I thought I might as well see what was in them."

"Well, I don't find this old table or pounds of dust very interesting. Can we leave?"

After satisfying himself with the sparseness of the room, Jaleph turned towards the exit. Teraken lifted the candelabrum and followed his king from the room, leaving it to its desolate blackness.

Jaleph walked to the next door, and it opened with a loud creak. They entered and found this room to be even more barren than the previous one. The pair continued on, and after a few more rooms revealed much of the same, Teraken finally asked, "Are you looking for something in particular?"

The king's hand stopped, poised above the next door handle. He was looking for something, but how could he tell his old friend? How could the king tell a subordinate he did not know what he was looking for? Was his life so empty that he was left to search through forgotten hallways and rooms for the remote chance that he might uncover some undiscovered treasure? Was there nothing more to his life? He suddenly found himself extremely pathetic. He pulled his hand away and led Teraken back towards the stairs.

"I'm sorry. We can keep looking if you want," Teraken said in a sympathetic tone.

Jaleph sighed. "Don't worry about it. It was just a stupid idea."

Teraken followed Jaleph out from the palace and into the street. Four guards scurried after the pair as they left the building. "Where are you heading to now?" Teraken questioned.

"To the audience chamber," replied the king without looking back. "I think I'll check in on the nobles' council. Why don't you come with?"

"All right Jaleph."

The king quickly spun around in anger. "I told you before that you need to address me by my title. Please remember that, especially when we're in public."

The abrupt outburst caused the large man to halt in mid-stride. "Yes... Sire," was all Teraken managed to say.

The king and his group mounted the steps then entered the large room. Jaleph saw about a dozen men, and a few women, circled around the huge oak table. As usual, Yonath was leading the discussion:

"But we haven't brought in any new merchants! We can't continue..." Yonath stopped immediately after spotting Jaleph. "I'm happy to see you joining us Majesty," he continued with a huge smile. "Shall I update you on what you've missed?"

"No Yonath. I just came to observe. Please continue." Jaleph walked to his throne and motioned for Teraken to accompany him.

"Whut d' you purpose?" I'a'uju'uh asked, apparently oblivious to Jaleph's entrance.

Yonath appeared perplexed, as if he wanted to patronize the king further and was not ready to enter back into the debate.

"Have you all forgotten about Iridan?" Gentine jeered at the seeming stupidity of her colleagues. "He should ask Josu to steer some of their merchants our way."

"A military treaty does not necessitate an economic one, Gentine," replied one of the men.

"But it gives us a starting point," she retorted briskly.

"Maybe one of us should go with Iridan when he leaves again," Zorine offered shyly. "I—"

"That's a wonderful idea," Yonath interrupted. He then quickly turned to address Jaleph. "Might we know when Iridan will return to Shekul, Majesty?"

"It hasn't been determined," Jaleph replied. "Myrin is still very ill." He turned away from the group and muttered to himself, "He shouldn't even be here anyway."

"Whu'll go?" asked I'a'uju'uh.

The group looked amongst themselves apprehensively, but no one responded.

"Sire, might we indulge you in this matter?" queried Yonath.

"Regarding what?" the king asked.

Yonath rose from the table and approached the throne. "When Iridan does leave, whom would you suggest accompany him? We would like to negotiate with Josu."

Can I never get any peace from that man? Must I hear of him where ever I go? Jaleph thought. "Who said that any of you should be negotiating with a foreign king?" he asked angrily.

"I'm sorry, Sire. We thought that with the new treaty, we ought to find ways to bring in some more trade."

"Well think again. *I* will let you know when *I* think you can begin these negotiations." Jaleph stood and the group, with bewilderment, watched him storm from the chamber.

Chapter 39

Dobrah galloped into Okkgan with Pothar close behind. Pothar dismounted and, grabbing the first guard they saw, he called for a defense to be mounted. The man just stared back until Dobrah nearly pushed him to the ground. "We're under attack," she shouted. "Marshall the troops!"

As soldiers began to form around Dobrah and Pothar, some of the men who had survived the assault were riding towards the city. Dobrah was surprised that they were not being chased since it had appeared that they had been overwhelmed when she last saw them.

"What's going on?" she asked the first man who approached.

"I'm not sure," the soldier panted, "but we were being routed, then, all of a sudden, some troops emerged from the brush. They were fighting by our side. As soon as we had an opening, I ordered the men around me to retreat to the city to report to you."

Before Dobrah could reply, Kedin came up next to her. "What happened?" he whimpered nervously.

"We have some hostiles just outside the city," replied Pothar.

Dobrah noticed that what appeared to be the bulk of Okkgan's troops had arrived. "It looks like we can go back and help them out now. Let's move," she ordered.

They approached on foot as there had not been time to gather horses for all the troops, and when they neared the melee, Dobrah saw that, despite the assistance of the unidentified soldiers, they were still outnumbered. She could not count the number of attackers, but they had left Su'Meeryn with fifty warriors, and their opponents appeared to double that. Perhaps they could still prevail with their unidentified allies.

Once they reached the combat, Pothar broke from her side and was the first to engage. Dobrah noticed that their enemy was pretty well armed, but they did not seem very skilled with their weapons.

Dobrah's sword whistled before her. The blade fell and pierced her foe's stomach. She quickly kicked the corpse away, whirled about and cut deep into another man's arm. As the man collapsed in agony, she struck down one more and bought herself a moment to survey the forces who had come to their aid. They, too, seemed well armed; however, only a few remained standing. She wondered who they were and why they had come, and she was shocked when she saw that Ut was leading them.

Suddenly Pothar approached her, holding his right arm as blood seeped between his fingers. "We're going to have to retreat," he panted. "There's just too many of them."

She thought for a brief moment. "I guess we have no choice but to leave Okkgan and Kedin to them. Sound the withdrawal."

Pothar seized a horn that dangled from his waist. He blew three short notes. The remaining Su'Meeryn troops began their retreat, away from Okkgan. To her surprise, Dobrah noticed that Ut's remaining men covered their escape. "I can't believe that I'm actually glad to see him," she muttered.

Pothar took a quick count. "There's just twelve of us left. We better hurry back to Su'Meeryn to let the king know what's happened."

"If only we knew what did happen here," Dobrah replied. "Who attacked us and why? How did Ut know to be here? And why did he defend us?"

"Yeah, this all seems just a little too familiar."

Dobrah nodded. "I'm surprised they're not following us," she said as they rushed away.

"Maybe they think that they can't risk losing any more men," Pothar replied as they turned back and saw their enemy streaming through Okkgan's gate. "The few soldiers Kedin has left won't be able to stop them, and they'll need all their troops to hold the city."

"You could be right, but why let us get away to report this?" she pointed out.

"They didn't seem like very good soldiers," answered Pothar as he tied a cloth around the cut on his arm. "But does it really matter? Let's just get home as soon as we can."

***

After about an hour into their march, the group entered a small forest. They were traveling along a path that ran beside a tiny creek when they heard sounds of pursuit. Pothar unsheathed his sword and turned to confront the noise. Dobrah came up beside him and crouched down next to a tree while the other men also readied their weapons.

"It doesn't sound like too many," Pothar whispered. They waited breathlessly until one bloodied man suddenly crashed into view through some thick brush. He appeared startled when he saw Pothar, and he stumbled, falling face first onto the ground. Pothar cautiously turned the man over onto his back, and Dobrah scowled when she recognized Ut.

"Why am I not at all surprised?" she asked.

"I am glad that I was able to find you," Ut panted, ignoring her comment. Dobrah noticed a number of wounds across his body, but none appeared to be very serious.

"What were you doing at Okkgan, and with those troops? Who attacked us?" Pothar demanded. "You obviously know something about all this."

"Those were troops from Labyn," replied Ut. "Jaleph had requested that I return there. When I did, I discovered there was evil at work within the Queen's court. It seems that someone in Labyn was behind the king's ambush. It might have been Illiyna, but I'm not sure. Then I heard of the plan to attack Okkgan. I was able to rally some of my supporters, and we came to try to stop it."

"Why?"

"What do you mean?"

"It's a pretty straightforward question. Why help us after Jaleph sent you away?" Pothar asked with a scowl.

Ut's face contorted with pain, and he took a few deep breaths prior to answering. "Okkgan is important to the strength of Su'Meeryn." He grimaced again and looked deep into Pothar's then Dobrah's eyes. "My loyalty is to Jaleph."

Dobrah had to suppress a laugh. After her conversation with Ut on the castle wall, she felt certain he had some motivation other than the well-being of Su'Meeryn or Jaleph. What that motivation was, she did not know. What she did know was that she could not trust this man.

Chapter 40

"It's time for you return to Shekul," Jaleph informed Iridan after taking a large gulp of wine.

"What?" Iridan responded in a bewildered tone. When Jaleph had summoned him, he had assumed that the king would want to be briefed regarding any information he had learned while in Shekul. How can he expect me to leave now—with Myrin still so sick? he thought.

"Your job. You need to return to your job."

Iridan sat dumbfounded for a few painful moments. He could not believe Jaleph would send him away now. "But Myrin…"

"Don't worry. I'll take care of her."

"Sire?"

"I'll make sure she's attended to." Jaleph absently stroked his bald head and Iridan thought he sensed some deception from the king. But what would Jaleph be hiding?

"I'd really like to remain here. After the child is born, we could all move to Shekul, once Myrin recovers," Iridan said timidly.

Jaleph did not even pause to consider his response. "That will not do. You will leave tomorrow."

"But Sire—"

"Tomorrow!" the king commanded. "Now you are dismissed." Jaleph signaled to his guards, and Iridan knew that the issue could not be discussed further. And he came to the conclusion that Jaleph had changed. He felt animosity directed at him from the king, and he realized now why he had been the one made ambassador. The king did not want him in Su'Meeryn any longer, but Jaleph obviously wanted Myrin to remain. Iridan needed to start making plans. What they would be, he did not know. He would need to talk to Pothar, and maybe Dobrah—and soon.

***

Iridan sat in the dark corner of a small pub with Teraken. He grasped the mug before him and took a drink of the bitter ale. "It just doesn't seem right. Why would he send me away now?" Iridan asked.

He was uncomfortable speaking to Jaleph's old friend so bluntly, but with Pothar and Dobrah away from Su'Meeryn, he felt he had no choice. Besides, he had heard from a number of people that the two had been at odds lately.

The door to the pub swung open and a few soldiers entered. They walked to the bar and did not seem concerned with the pair in the corner. "Jaleph has been acting strange lately," Teraken whispered. "It all started when Ut arrived. I don't trust that man. I was glad when Jaleph sent him away, but I have a feeling we'll be seeing him again."

Iridan eyed the soldiers suspiciously. He was concerned that Jaleph might be spying on him, but it would not be out of the ordinary for Teraken and him to have a drink together. Besides, the soldiers were not looking back in his direction. "Dobrah told me about Ut, but I've never met him."

"It was his idea to attack Okkgan, and I'm sure he's done something to Jaleph. I don't know what, but I don't like it."

"What do you think we should do?"

Teraken glanced up at the soldiers at the bar then returned his gaze to his companion. "I'm not sure what you mean," he breathed. "Jaleph is our king, and I am satisfied with that, regardless of how he's currently acting. Do you understand?" Iridan nodded. "But I will never forget what you did for Su'Meeryn—you and my son—so I'll tell you this: it probably would be best if you left for awhile."

"Leaving isn't the problem. Jaleph has already ordered me back to Shekul, but what about Myrin?"

"There's nothing you can do for her right now." He took a long gulp from his mug and wiped the remaining traces of ale from his mouth. "Look, I'm not in the king's confidence the way I used to be, so I don't know what he's planning; however, I'm certain she'll be safe here. He's been visiting Myrin often, and he seems very fond of her."

"I'm not sure that I like the sound of that," Iridan said as the soldiers at the bar rose and turned towards the door. They spotted Teraken and him, and one of the men waved. Iridan nervously waved back.

"We're all fond of her," Teraken continued after the men left.

"Yes, but Jaleph has seemed pretty uncomfortable when I've been around him."

"I can say this," Teraken responded, "I think you're in danger. I have no evidence; it's just a feeling. Return to Shekul. With you gone, I think Jaleph will be more at ease. After the baby is born, come back quietly and take them with you. But remember, Jaleph is my king. I will help with you this—and only this—if I can."

"That's all I ask. Now, to hold you to your promise, it would be a great help if you could find a way to send Pothar to me when he re-turns. I'll need to begin making arrangements, and I trust him."

Teraken sighed. "I'll find a way, but remember, I will only help in making you and your family safe."

Following the comment about his family, Iridan's thoughts turned to his cousin. "And what about Dirwyn? Do you think she's in any danger?"

"I don't think so. She has been spending a lot of time with Jaleph lately."

Iridan took another drink and shook his head. "I wonder what brought all this on. What did I do to anger him so much?"

"Jealousy?" the large man replied. "I don't know, but as I said, he's not been acting like himself."

Iridan dejectedly placed a few coins on the table. It seemed unfair; after Su'Meeryn's victory, his marriage and Myrin's pregnancy, his life should be heading in a different direction than it was. He grabbed Tera-ken's arm and thanked him. As they stood, Iridan felt some pangs of guilt. He felt that he was deceiving his friend. There really was not much to plan with Pothar, but he was not satisfied with just ignoring the problems brewing in Su'Meeryn. He needed to receive credible information, and Pothar was his best resource. Iridan had no idea what he would do with that information, but he figured it would come with time.

After they exited the pub, Teraken quickly turned from Iridan and strode away. Iridan could not help but wonder if Teraken guessed why he wanted Pothar sent to Shekul. Teraken would never openly oppose Jaleph, but he might be more of an ally than he was letting on.

***

His wife looked even more frail when he entered her room. Her white sheets appeared soaked through with perspiration. Hair clung to her face and pillow like wet weeds.

"She finally fell asleep," Dirwyn whispered as she stood from a chair and approached him.

Iridan nodded. He motioned to Dirwyn, and they stepped into the hall. He checked about for an empty room into which they entered. The room had obviously gone unoccupied for some time based on the amount of dust present.

"What is it?" Dirwyn asked.

"Jaleph is sending me back to Shekul tomorrow. He doesn't seem to want me around." He walked to the wall and looked out the lone window. The people milling about below were barely visible through the dirt; it was as if the glass was returning to its original form. "I'm concerned," he continued, while attempting to remove some of the grime with his elbow. "After the baby is born, I'm going to try to get them to Shekul without Jaleph knowing." He turned back to her. "And I believe that you should come too."

"Leave? Why? Jaleph seems to have been courting me lately."

"Don't you think it's strange that he's sending me away while Myrin is pregnant and ill?"

"He has been acting a little differently, but who isn't after all we've been through?" She paused and looked at her cousin. "Is this really necessary?"

"I know the thought of becoming queen has to be tempting."

"Do you think that's all I want, to be queen?" Dirwyn asked sharply.

"Look, there's nothing wrong with wanting to be queen." Iridan glanced out the door and surveyed the empty hallway before turning back to Dirwyn. "Jaleph was a good man, but I'm not so sure anymore. I can't think of anyone else I'd rather see as queen, but Jaleph might have somebody else in mind."

"You believe he wants Myrin, don't you?"

"Yes, I think so." Iridan leaned against the wall and sighed heavily. He could hardly believe the words coming from his mouth. He had to force himself to not ponder them and simply react. If he dwelled on all that was happening, he felt that he would just collapse. "You don't have to decide right now. Stay close to Pothar, and watch Jaleph closely, but you will have to make up your mind by the time the child comes."

"Alright," she agreed. They left the room and Iridan went to be with his wife while Dirwyn returned home.

***

How many hours passed, Iridan did not know, but when he awoke in the chair, Myrin was smiling weakly at him. "How do you feel?" he asked as he straightened himself up.

"A little better."

Iridan stood and looked out the door. After making sure nobody was nearby, he told her about what had been happening and his plan. A frail hand reached for his neck and pulled him towards her. She leaned up and kissed his forehead.

"Do what you need to. It'll take me some time to recover after the delivery; probably more than usual because of, well, all this. So keep that in mind," she said.

"Of course. I'll make sure somebody, Pothar most likely, sends word when the baby comes. I probably won't be back until then." He paused. "That is not my choice. I'd stay here with you, if I could."

"I know, but I'm asleep most of the time; so, I wouldn't even know if you were here." With an effort, she pulled herself up a little higher and her voice grew in strength. "We've had our problems, but they seem so long ago. I have a hard time even remembering what we were fighting about." She collapsed back down with a heavy sigh. "If Su'Meeryn is not the place for us, that's fine. I've only been here a short time, so I'll be happy to go with you to Shekul."

Iridan sat on the bed and held his wife close. He felt the sweat soak into his clothes and again marveled at her strength. "I need to get my things together. I'll come back in a little while and stay the night with you."

Myrin smiled as her eyes closed.

***

At dawn, he awoke on the floor next to her bed. Myrin still slept. Iridan grabbed his pack and kissed his wife. As he was leaving, one of the healers entered the room. "Say good-bye to her for me, would you?" The woman nodded and Iridan set off for the stables.

Veake was waiting for him, and Iridan knew this would likely be his only send-off. "I thought you were working nights," he remarked.

Veake just laughed then cackled, "Mastur es leaven, eh?"

"I told you not to call me that," Iridan replied sharply.

Veake laughed again and drops of a green liquid spewed from his mouth. "Ah, mastur dusn't like t' ear it, but tings 'r changun, Irudun, tings 'r changun. Watch yur sulf." Veake finished tightening the saddle, and gave the horse a friendly slap on its rump. "I've a questun fir ya. Would 'r crops grow wuthout worms?"

"What the hell are you talking about?" Iridan snapped. He always prided himself on his patience enduring Veake's incoherent ramblings, but with the growing pressures of everything that was crumbling around him, that patience had vanished.

"Worms. We'd ull be 'n trubble without 'm, eh?"

Iridan wanted to snap again, but the change in Veake's accent gave him pause. Worms, what do we care about worms, he thought, but then he considered Worm back in Shekul. Was that what Veake was talking about? What else could it be? But how would he know? "What do you know about worms?" Iridan asked.

"Just thur value. Worms, gotta huv worms…" and Veake's voice trailed off as he shambled away.

Iridan stared motionless at the retreating figure before securing his packs to the back of the saddle. He hopped onto his horse, but as he started to trot towards the gate, a small group began to gather and follow him. He heard people calling, "Where are you going?" "Why are you leaving again?" "We need you!" Iridan acknowledged the people with a slight wave, and a burst of applause erupted. One ran up and patted his thigh; then a few others also tried to reach up to him. Iridan spurred his mount slightly to increase its pace. As he neared the gate, he noticed Jaleph standing atop the wall. The king looked down with his arms crossed over his chest and a scowl on his face.

Chapter 41

Dobrah stood before the king with Pothar and Ut on either side of her. When she finished her tale, Jaleph rose from the throne and began to pace as he rubbed his head. He felt stubble beginning to form and knew that he would need to shave soon. The king stopped and his gaze rested on Ut.

Teraken stepped forward to whisper in Jaleph's ear, but the king signaled for him to stop. "It appears I owe you an apology, Ut," Jaleph said.

"I'm just happy to be of service."

"Why?" Teraken asked the strange man.

"I believe there is some madness at work in the Queen's court, and I believe that your king is the man to lead this land to greatness. I offer my loyalty to him alone." Ut turned to Jaleph, and the king perceived a longing in Ut's eyes.

"Well, I must say that you did prove yourself to me," Jaleph remarked, and he found himself pleased to have Ut back in Su'Meeryn. He began to wonder why he had ever sent the man away.

"Thank you, Sire."

Teraken grunted and sat on the floor next to Jaleph's chair. The king cringed but refrained from chastising his friend. "Well, what do you think we should do now?" he asked.

"Sire, perhaps I should return to Labyn. Maybe the queen would grant me an audience," Pothar interjected.

Jaleph turned to Pothar with a look of surprise on his face. He had virtually forgotten that Dobrah and he were still in the chamber. "I'm sorry," he replied, "you two are dismissed. Have the healers look at that wound. I thank you for your service in this matter."

"Of course," Pothar said, somewhat stunned at the hasty dismissal, and he followed Dobrah to the door.

"May I offer a suggestion, Sire?" Ut asked.

"Of course."

"I am certain the attack in the ravine was ordered from Labyn. I am not sure if it was Illiyna, but, from what I uncovered, it did come from her court. I believe we need to undertake an extreme measure. We should attack Labyn."

"What!" Teraken stood and confronted Ut. "What are you talking about? You're not going to listen to any more of this, are you Jaleph?"

The king turned slowly to Teraken. "Sit back down, now," he breathed.

"But Jaleph, this is crazy. Attack Labyn. We don't have nearly enough soldiers, and—"

"Shut up!" Jaleph screamed. "Now!" He turned back to Ut and resumed calmly, "Please continue."

Ut walked slowly to Jaleph with a soft smile. "Well Sire, if we attack Okkgan and retake it, we will just be back in the same position in which we currently find ourselves."

"Yes, you're right."

Ut's smile broadened. "You see, I still have friends in Labyn, and they are not happy with Illiyna. They could marshal perhaps half of her troops to your cause."

"Jaleph, I beg you, don't listen to this," Teraken pleaded.

The king did not break his gaze from Ut's face as he replied. "Please do not force me to have you removed. Now, Ut, please continue."

"You see, with the soldiers that I can provide, you would be able to secure Labyn and then Okkgan. With the extra troops from Labyn, and the funds from the trade routes of Okkgan, you will be the most powerful king in the land. You could be Emperor."

"Please Sire, don't," Teraken pleaded.

"Ut, would you do me a favor?" Jaleph asked.

"It would be my pleasure."

"Ask my guards to come in."

"What are you doing?" asked Teraken.

Jaleph disregarded the question and remained silent until Ut returned with four guards. "I would like Teraken removed from the chamber. If he gives you any trouble, put him in a cell."

"That will not be necessary," Teraken spat, and he stormed away.

When they were alone, Jaleph turned to Ut. "Now, tell me more about how we can accomplish your plan."

***

The long breakfast table seemed like a desert horizon, with the king the sole cactus to break the lifeless visage. Jaleph had thought of inviting Dirwyn, but he was still annoyed with her for her early departure from their last meeting. He slowly ate the warm biscuits that sat before him while thoughts of his discussion with Ut raced through his mind. Once Su'Meeryn acquired Labyn, they would quickly retake Okkgan. Afterwards, who knew? Emperor of the Known Lands: he liked how that sounded. With the troops Ut would provide, the ease of the venture seemed almost shocking. He smiled as he grabbed a piece of sliced melon. Yes, this was most fitting. It was time for Jaleph to obtain his due.

His musings were interrupted when a page entered the chamber. "Majesty, Teraken requests an audience."

The king frowned. He had no desire to see Teraken, but out of reverence to the memory of his father, he advised the page to allow the old soldier to enter.

The man stepped out and soon returned with Teraken. "Jaleph," he began, "I'm sorry. Sire, I'd like to talk to you about these plans you have been making with Ut." Jaleph felt satisfied as he noted a dejected tone in his friend's voice. When he did not reply, Teraken continued. "I think this might be a mistake. I don't trust Ut and—"

"Your trust does not determine policy."

"Yes, but I have misgivings, and I'd like to discuss them with you."

"Go on," said Jaleph.

"Like I said, I don't trust Ut. We know nothing about him, and this could be trap."

"Why do you think so?"

"Sire, I'm not sure how to say this, but you've seemed different since he first arrived. I think he might be manipulating you for his own purposes."

Despite his irritation, Jaleph was able to keep his voice calm. "What evidence do you have regarding that?"

"I don't have any," Teraken replied as he took a seat across from Jaleph. "It's just... everything that's happened of late seems, well, orchestrated. He could be leading us into a trap. Rather than Labyn becoming part of your kingdom, Su'Meeryn could become part of Labyn."

"But you know what happened at Okkgan. His troops have fought for me before, and there is no reason to think that they will not again. His strategy is sound."

"Yes it is, if he's being truthful, and if this is what you really want," Teraken said.

"What do you mean?"

"Emperor? Why do we need this? Why send more of your men to die? Su'Meeryn is a fine kingdom. Isn't that enough? Rather than fighting wars, why not take a wife and secure your legacy?"

The emotion and frustration of the past year began to overwhelm Jaleph. "I've had enough of your criticisms," the king said, his voice rising. "By undertaking Ut's plan, I will finally get that which I deserve. No longer will Su'Meeryn be a joke."

Teraken sat speechless for a moment. "What do you mean, joke? Su'Meeryn is an honorable kingdom, and agriculture is a noble profession. We are an honest and hardworking people. We have all we need now. Why put everything at risk?"

Jaleph rose from his chair and glared at the large man he had known all his life. He wondered why he had never noticed the cowardice and lack of ambition in Teraken before. "Your opinion is no longer appreciated. You may leave."

"But Jaleph, I'm not questioning you. I thought we were friends, and that I could bring my concerns to you. You used to listen to me."

"And look what that got us," the king replied.

"What do you mean?" Teraken asked, his tone a mixture of anger and disappointment.

"I think it's pretty obvious. The kingdom was almost destroyed. If I had listened to you back then, I never would have sent Iridan and your son on their mission. Where would we be now?"

"That's not fair," Teraken retorted, with increasing hostility.

"I think it is quite fair. Your *guidance* is not worth much."

"Your father didn't think so." Jaleph began to tremble with rage and called for the guards. "Don't do this," said Teraken.

When the guards arrived, Jaleph pointed a shaking finger at Teraken. "Put him in a cell." When the guards did not immediately move, he screamed, "Now!"

Teraken remained silent as he was taken from the room. Jaleph was still trembling when he returned to his seat. After a moment, he had calmed down enough to continue his meal. He was just finishing when Ut arrived. The king smiled and motioned for Ut to join him.

Chapter 42

Iridan sat on his bed and ran his fingers through his hair. His return to Shekul the previous day had brought little activity. The majority of his time had been spent alone, and not by choice.

It seemed that his life had completely unraveled. Myrin was pregnant and ill, and he could not be with her. He was concerned about Jaleph's demeanor, and how that might change the complexion of Su'Meeryn. And, in the midst of all that, he found himself stuck in Shekul, with nothing to do. "This is just great," he muttered as he began to pace the room. Veake's farewell words came to mind, and he decided it was time to seek out Worm. It was time to assert himself into the atmosphere of Shekul. Since the king's court did not trust him, perhaps Worm had some knowledge about Shekul that could be of assistance. Besides, he still needed to find out what Worm knew about Naar.

He left his room and wandered through the maze of corridors within the castle until he reached the dining hall. He took a deep breath and strode across the stone floor to the polished table where Kile sat. Iridan felt some uneasiness as he remembered the less-than-friendly attitude he had received from the guard upon his release from prison. Unsure of the reception he would receive today, Iridan apprehensively stepped behind the table as a few soldiers stood to leave. He took a seat under a large window through which the morning breeze carried in the scent of flowers from Josu's garden.

Kile acknowledge Iridan with a nod, but the conversation he had been having with the man who sat next to him ceased. "Please don't let me interrupt," said Iridan.

"We were just finished," the other man stated, as he left.

"Is there something you want?" Kile asked, and Iridan noted suspicion in his tone.

A servant placed a plate of eggs in front of Iridan. "Just some food," he replied, taking a bite.

"I hope you enjoy it," Kile said and stood to leave.

"Wait. I was hoping that you could direct me to Worm. I would like to visit him."

"Why?"

"He just seemed interesting when we were in our cell together. And, well, until the king gives me some specific work, I really have nothing to do."

Kile gazed at Iridan for a few moments. Seeming to not have heard his answer, Kile said, "I was told that your wife is ill—and pregnant."

"That's right."

"It must have been hard for you to leave Su'Meeryn."

"Yes."

Kile's head tiled a little to his side as he asked, "Why didn't you stay with her?"

"I had no choice. My king ordered me to return here."

Kile considered Iridan for another moment. "I can lead you to Worm, but I'm not sure he'll want to see you."

"How come?"

"You don't know him very well, do you? That's fine, but I guess you'll learn. Come on."

"May I eat first?"

"Look, I have to get going. I have duties to attend. If you want me to take you, we'll have to leave right now."

Iridan gobbled down a few bites of egg as the pair left the hall. They exited the castle and walked silently through the lush farmland. It was not long before they came to a large estate, and Kile led Iridan to the front door. "Here you are," he said, turning to leave.

"Wait," Iridan said. "Can you stay awhile?"

"You asked me to show you to Worm, and I have. Now I must return to the castle. Goodbye," and Kile walked off without another look.

Iridan knocked on the door, and after a short wait, an attractive young woman let him in. He stood in a large foyer, while the woman took his name and retreated into the home. He glanced about the room and noticed a beautiful tapestry of three horses, each of a different color. Numerous candles sat on ornate holders of shining gold. On a shelf to his right, Iridan noticed a silver plate engraved with a horse. As he examined the plate, Worm entered the room. "What are you doing here?"

"I came to see you."

"Why?"

"To be honest, I don't have much to do." Iridan paused and rubbed his hands over his thighs. "I enjoyed our conversation in the cell, and I was hoping to talk to you some more."

"About what?" Worm asked.

Iridan paused before answering. "I really don't know. It seems like a lot of people in Shekul don't want me here. The king and his advisors, Surik and Forim, will have nothing to do with me. Neither will the guards. And Jaleph doesn't want me in Su'Meeryn. My wife's sick, and I can't be with her." Iridan paused as he absently twisted Naar's ring. "I just need someone to talk to."

Worm motioned Iridan to follow as he led him into the den.

Chapter 43

Dobrah glanced about her home, taking note of Karus' remaining belongings. She felt a sense of emptiness, but it was more than just missing her husband. Being told that Su'Meeryn was going to war against Labyn was enough to intensify her despair. Illiyna had attacked them at Okkgan after all, and she was possibly behind the attack that had killed Karus as well. But now, Dobrah had learned she would be the one to lead Su'Meeryn's troops in the assault. Why her, and why had Teraken been thrown into jail? Many other warriors possessed more experience, why had Jaleph singled her out?

None of it made sense. She felt no love for Labyn, but had Illiyna behaved any different from Jaleph? Both rulers had invaded Okkgan. If the queen had been the one behind Karus' death, she would gladly lead the assault and drive a blade through Illiyna's heart herself. But if not… No, there was something more happening here than what appeared on the surface. She remembered Ut's disparaging words about Jaleph when they were alone on the castle wall, then he pledges his loyalty to Su'Meeryn? Ut clearly could not be trusted, but, somehow, he was in the king's confidence. With no answers forthcoming, she would, for now, need to just follow her orders.

Dobrah gazed out her window towards the setting sun. Pothar won't be here for awhile yet, she thought. She tried to busy herself by organizing Karus' things, again. She had told herself that she would only keep a few, but there were too many memories.

When Pothar finally arrived, they sat together at her small table. His furrowed brow told her he was having misgivings as well. "What do you make of all that's happening?" she began.

"Is that why you asked me here?" Pothar replied as he leaned back and folded his arms.

The words immediately aggravated her. She had no desire to banter with Pothar and decided to take the risk of confiding in him. She needed someone with whom she could openly talk. "I'm not in the mood for this," she began, "so I'll be straight with you. I think there is something wrong with our king. I do not trust him anymore, and I don't trust Ut. You're a friend of Iridan, so I think that I can trust you. If not, tell me now."

She saw him looking at her, not considering her words so much as gauging her intent. "Go on," he said.

"First you have to answer me. Can I trust you?"

"For what?"

Her hand slapped the table and a cup rattled off, smashing to the floor. "Look, I know what you're doing. I had to do the same. I needed to determine if you were the person to ally myself with, but now it's time to make some decisions. We are soldiers and we have pledged to serve Jaleph and Su'Meeryn. But I'm starting to think we can no longer do both. We might have to oppose Jaleph. I'm not sure, but I do know that something must be done. Now, can I trust you?"

Pothar studied Dobrah for a moment before replying. "Yes," was all that he said.

"Good," she stated, feeling a wave of relief sweep over her. Of course, Pothar could be lying to her, but she doubted it. She believed he was a man of his word. "Now that that's been established, I'm not really sure where to begin. Do you have any thoughts?"

Pothar leaned forward, and she saw a different look in his eyes. His jovial manner had disappeared. He was going to open up to her, and she knew he was not going to leave anything back. "I need to start with Iridan. Jaleph has clearly developed some hostility towards him. I told him I'd help protect his family. We should get Myrin out of the castle after she delivers, possibly Dirwyn too."

"Are you sure that's wise? If Jaleph isn't pleased with Iridan, we might end up causing even more problems. Besides, Ut suggested the same thing to me. If it's something he wants, I'm not sure it's a good idea."

"Possibly, but we'll have to risk it. If Jaleph is unhappy with Iridan, and if he is becoming so unpredictable, who knows what might happen to them? If you want my help, then that's our first objective."

Dobrah sighed and hesitantly agreed. "Okay, but what would our next step be? I'm sure Iridan will have to be a part of this. He's in She-kul; perhaps he can find some support for us there."

"We'll have to see," Pothar replied. He stood and walked to the window. "So, you're leading the attack against Labyn. Do you know when it's going to be?"

"I haven't been told yet, but winter is approaching. We might have to wait until spring."

"Good, good. The more time the better," Pothar said as he sat back down. "Listen, after Illiyna betrayed us, and considering what happened to Karus and me, I really have no problem with attacking that witch, so that's not my main concern—"

"It should be if it's a trap," Dobrah interrupted.

"Why would you think that? Labyn did attack us, after all."

"According to Ut. I don't trust him. He came to me a while ago, questioning Jaleph's actions. Now he's pledged his loyalty to Su'Meeryn?"

"Well, I don't think there's anything we can do regarding the attack," Pothar stated, "but a delay would give us some more time to observe Jaleph's actions. Perhaps we'll find an opportunity somewhere, for something."

"I agree."

"We should try to get me to visit Iridan, at least a couple times before the attack. I'm not sure we can make any other plans right now."

"Fine," Dobrah said. "One last thing: if the attack does have to wait until spring, Myrin will have delivered by then. I'll assign you to the castle, and you can get her out while we're gone."

"Good, but first see if you can get me sent to Shekul. We can talk further after I return."

Pothar left, and Dobrah sat at her table pondering her future. Intrigue and scheming against her king, she never could have predicted this development in her life. However, before she could contemplate these thoughts any further, she was summoned to meet with Jaleph.

***

The freshly shaved head of her king met Dobrah's gaze as she entered the empty audience chamber. "Majesty," she said as Jaleph shuffled through some parchments on his lap. He looked up, and the bump on his head glistened in the candlelight, and she saw some trickles of dried blood by his ear.

"Ah, there you are," he said. "I just got done arbitrating for some of my subjects. I really should be doing more of that. But now, we need to make our plans. The attack must commence soon. I want to capture the city before winter." She nodded. "You see," he explained with a large smile, "with Labyn secure, we will be able to retake Okkgan at the start of spring. What better way to symbolize rebirth than my coronation as emperor? Now, Ut and Rynkor will meet you at your home after dinner to work out the arrangements."

She stood speechless. She had no idea how to reply. Emperor? So that was his plan.

"You're dismissed," Jaleph barked.

As Dobrah turned to leave, a thought came to her. She looked back at the king and said, "Majesty, if I may, perhaps it would be a good idea to find out what our new ally thinks of our plan. We could send someone to Shekul to have Iridan inquire."

"No," he bellowed. "We don't need to confer with anyone else. Who knows where Labyn's spies might be hidden?"

"Perhaps then we should get some information on how they might react. We don't have to give any specific details, just see what Josu's response might be. I could send Pothar. He can have Iridan report regarding his thoughts on the strength of Josu's will: what he might do. I don't think it would hurt. It won't cost us anything if we get no information."

The king thought for a moment. "No we'll send him after you leave for the attack. Then we can learn of Josu's reaction to my plan. Yes, that would be perfect."

"But Majesty," Dobrah interjected, "that will not be of any help to us. Once the attack is underway, we wouldn't be able to stop it. We should get word from Iridan first."

"No!" shouted Jaleph. "Pothar will be sent after you leave. Understood?" And the king's tone was clear; he would accept no further discussion.

"Of course, Majesty."

Chapter 44

Jaleph took in a deep breath of satisfaction as he walked into his court-yard and surveyed the scene. Dobrah and Rynkor stood before the host of Su'Meeryn's military. It was strange to see the army preparing to march to war without Teraken there to lead them. But he had revealed his cowardice, and a cell was where he now belonged. The notion of a woman leading the attack was also strange, but Dobrah had proved herself. Besides, there was nobody else he could trust in that position, certainly not Iridan. Rynkor would be invaluable in the fighting, but he was not a leader, at least not yet.

"Wonderful," Ut remarked as he approached the king. "A magnifi-cent sight, is it not?"

"Yes, the attack will be a marvelous event," agreed Jaleph. "Are you're sure I shouldn't accompany them? I really don't want to miss this."

"Majesty, as we discussed, you will be safer here. Once Labyn is secured, you can attend the retaking of Okkgan. You will want to be there when you are crowned emperor."

"But it doesn't seem too dangerous. With the troops you are sup-plying, I should be safe."

"Majesty please, we have been over this all before. There is no need to take unreasonable chances now. We are so close to our goals."

"Careful Ut, if I didn't know better, I might think that you just in-sulted me. Let's remember, these are *my* goals, not ours."

"Of course," Ut responded with appropriate contrition. "Now, if I may, I would suggest that you address your troops."

Jaleph scowled at Ut before turning to Dobrah. He never felt com-fortable making speeches. "You all know what you need to do," he barked. "Now get moving."

The troops stood stunned for a moment as Jaleph walked away. "You heard the king. Let's go!" Dobrah called and they marched out of the castle.

Ut nudged Jaleph and pointed to the top of the castle wall. Jaleph nodded and the two men climbed the steps. When they reached their destination, Jaleph looked out and saw Dobrah meeting with more of

Su'Meeryn's soldiers, who awaited them outside the castle. The size of the force was impressive, and with the additional troops from Labyn, which Ut had promised, the city would not stand long. The return of Empire, he thought; the return to order, and I shall rule.

"It is glorious," Ut remarked.

"Quite, but what will it be once Labyn falls and Okkgan is retaken? Imagine the army I will command then."

"Soon your army will rival that which attacked Su'Meeryn."

Jaleph turned his eyes away from the advancing troops towards his companion. "You know Ut, it's strange. Without that attack, none of this probably would be happening; I would have not started down this path. In a way, I think that my brother would approve. I think he would have been willing to sacrifice himself for this return to glory. Su'Meeryn will be stronger than ever."

"Yes Majesty," Ut smiled. "You *are* learning."

***

After completing his now customary daily run, Jaleph sat in his room. He felt tired, but not nearly as much as he had when he'd started the endeavor. He looked at himself in the mirror and grinned. He was getting stronger and leaner with each passing week. Good, he thought. A king should be an impressive figure. Not the silly-looking king of days passed.

His fingers passed over the yellow stubble on his head and noticed that the bald patches were increasing in size, but he did not care about that anymore. He would never permit his strange looking hair to grow out again.

He bathed then shaved his head. Once done he cursed himself for still not being able to complete the task without causing at least one cut. As he wiped at the blood, he turned his attention to his beard. He had taken to keeping it trimmed closer to his face, but the yellow hair still annoyed him. So, his blade went back to work and shaved that off too. More blood had puddled around him by the time he was finished, but he was pleased with the outcome. Younger, I definitely look younger now, he thought.

Searching through his wardrobe, he pulled out a turquoise tunic and black pants. "Yes, they are fitting looser these days." Next he pulled out his headband and polished the emerald jewel on his shirt. He tied it around his head and surveyed his appearance one last time. "Yes, much better."

***

Markis lumbered into the dining area with perspiration glistening on his forehead. His enormous arms jiggled under the weight of the tray that he carried. The glaze on the small pig sparkled as he approached. "It smells wonderful, Markis," commented Jaleph.

The tray hit the table with a bang, and Markis had to take a moment to suck in some air. "Thank you Sire, the young ones are very tender." He had to pause again to take another deep breath.

"Very good, you can go now," Jaleph responded and turned his attention to his guest. Dirwyn smiled at him and reached for her mug. "So, how are your parents doing?"

"Things are okay, for now. My father is still having a difficult time at his shop," she answered.

"I'm sorry," said Jaleph. "Remind me again what he does."

"He's a blacksmith. He's been sick, and he's been having a hard time with his hands. I'm not sure how much longer he'll be able to continue. It will be very hard on us if we have to close the shop."

"Well, shall we examine this fine meal that Markis has provided?" Jaleph began slicing the pig, and when he looked up at Dirwyn, he noticed a strange expression on her face. "Is there something wrong?"

"No," she said, though Jaleph thought he could see that her appearance had darkened somewhat.

The couple began to eat in silence. Jaleph continued to glance over at Dirwyn. She is quite beautiful, he thought, but she seems to be very moody. He had been annoyed at how she had abandoned him at their last meal, and he was starting to think he had made a mistake with this brief courtship. Her beauty would not cover up her shortcomings. He desired a woman with more personality: a strong personality, as well as beauty. Maybe I'm making too much of this, he thought. "That was such a nice dinner we had at that creek," he said, breaking the silence.

"Yes, it was," was Dirwyn's only reply.

"I haven't had such a day since I was a boy." This time Dirwyn did not reply at all. She continued to eat, and Jaleph realized she was trying to avoid looking at him. Yes, a mistake, thought the king; one which will need to be corrected. She will not be my queen.

Thoughts of Myrin filled the king's head as they finished their meal in silence.

Chapter 45

Worm sat in a large chair and offered a seat to Iridan. "Care for some wine?" Worm asked as he poured himself a glass.

"No thanks."

Pointing to Iridan's hand, Worm asked, "Is that the famous ring?"

Iridan glanced down. He rarely remembered that he still wore it. How sad that we can so quickly forget, he thought. "Yes it is."

"Not very impressive looking is it? Now, what should we talk about?"

"I'd like for you to tell me what you know about Naar."

Worm laughed. "That again? I told you, it's just a myth. Sometimes I enjoy reading mythology, but I don't think it's worth discussing." Worm paused to take a drink of his wine. "I can tell you're struggling here: in a strange city, apart from your sick wife. If you're looking for a diversion, I'm happy to provide you an afternoon of conversation, as long as we are talking of something of value. If not, don't waste my time." He took another large swallow then refilled his glass.

Iridan wanted to press the matter further, but he recalled Kile's words when asked about Worm. Iridan was concerned over angering Worm and losing his potential resource, so he decided to change the subject. "What can you tell me of Josu?" he asked.

Again Worm laughed. "Josu. You've talked with him, huh?" Iridan nodded. "He's a good man but a bit ineffectual." Worm took another deep swallow then his expression turned more serious. "I think people underestimate him, and I think he underestimates himself. He has potential. And, I think you can trust him."

"What do you mean by that?

A smile was visible from around the edges of the glass as Worm took another drink. "It's obvious. You feel your world crumbling around you, and you're wondering who you can turn to. Perhaps Josu? He might be a good ally." Iridan heard a sharp bark as a small brown and black dog ran in and jumped on Worm's lap. Worm's face softened as he stroked the animal's back. "You can trust him," Worm repeated.

"But can I trust you?" asked Iridan.

"Very good," Worm replied. "Very good. No, you can't. You don't know me, so you shouldn't trust me. But I have no reason to lie about this. Josu is an honest man—by-and-large—and he means well. Unless you have some vile intentions, you don't have to worry about him."

"And what about you?"

"You seem to have some infatuation with me. I'm just an unruly son of a rich noble. Why do you care?"

"Because I think there is more to you than you let on."

Worm smirked with what appeared to be agreement to the comment, but Iridan could not be certain. "Most people believe there is actually less to me, and most people don't trust me. They know I'm only concerned about myself. But since your questions don't impact me at all—as I said, I have no reason to lie." Worm continued to pet the dog as he watched Iridan.

"Well, I thank you for the conversation," Iridan said as he rose to leave. "I hope we can meet again sometime." Worm was obviously an abrasive man—and a little annoying—but Iridan figured he might be helpful in the future. And he hoped that he still might be able to gain some information regarding Naar.

"Certainly," Worm replied as he poured himself another drink. "After all, it's not like I have much else to do."

"Thanks again," Iridan said as he showed himself out.

***

The long days seemed endless. Iridan's many requests for a meeting with Josu had gone unanswered, so he instead inquired regarding Josu's library. He had been granted access and visited it often. After searching through numerous scrolls and parchments, he had found nothing of value regarding Naar. He had also tried to meet with Worm again, but those requests had been ignored as well. So, with little else to do, he decided to visit the stables. He was provided a horse and he took to riding about Shekul. After one extended ride he returned to his room to clean up when a messenger arrived to advise Iridan that the king requested his presence.

After pulling on a fresh shirt, Iridan followed the man to the king's chamber. They entered the room to find Josu and Flicia waiting for him. "You're dismissed," the king said to the messenger and angrily motioned for Iridan to sit. "Do you care to explain what's happening?"

"I'm sorry. What do you mean?"

"Aren't you the ambassador to Shekul from Su'Meeryn?" Flicia questioned, with no trance of her mischievous demeanor.

"Of course," answered Iridan with increasing agitation. He glanced

314

between the two, and Josu's face glowed red from his rage. "But I still don't know what you're talking about."

"Is that so?" the king bellowed as he sprang from his chair. Two guards appeared—with swords drawn—from behind tapestries, but Josu waved them away. "I have offered you my courtesies, and I do not appreciate being deceived."

Iridan was starting to feel angry himself. "Listen, unless you tell me what's going on, I can't help you. And I don't appreciate being accused of something I know nothing about. I never even wanted to come here. My wife is sick, and all I've been doing is wasting my time. I have no friends here and nothing to do. So why don't you just enlighten me?"

Josu's mouth quivered as he struggled for words, but before he could speak, Flicia calmly stood up between them. "I can see it was wise for us to kept Surik and Forim from of this meeting." She placed her hand of Josu's arm and guided him back to his chair. "They are far less… restrained. Iridan, are you aware that Su'Meeryn has marshaled an army? They are heading west, and it appears they plan to attack Labyn."

Iridan was stunned. "I had no idea," he responded after a long pause. "I don't know what to say."

"What do you think?" Josu asked Flicia.

Flicia gazed at Iridan for a few moments. "I think he's telling the truth."

Josu's appearance began to soften. "Please understand. I was concerned, obviously." The king then turned back to Flicia.

"Yes," Flicia continued. "You see, you come to us as an ambassador, then we have to hear from our scouts that Su'Meeryn is going to war. You must admit, that appears suspicious. We had to determine if you were here to deceive and distract us."

As Iridan pondered the situation, Worm's words regarding his ability to trust Josu came to his mind. But he did not want to say too much with Flicia around; he still had no idea what to make of her. He wanted to tell Josu about the attack on Okkgan—of which they were obviously unaware—and Jaleph's recent unusual behavior. He wanted to tell Josu that he was concerned himself about his king; however, Iridan was not yet ready to take that step. He did not know what the implications would be for his homeland.

Flicia motioned for Iridan to sit, and the three remained silent for several awkward moments until a guard entered the room. "I'm sorry Sire, but I have word that a friend of Iridan has arrived. His name is Pothar."

Relief swept over Iridan. He felt certain that he would get some information now. "If I may be excused, this might provide us some answers."

"Of course," Flicia said. "Please let us know what you learn."

Iridan left the chamber and asked the guard to have Pothar meet him in his room.

***

The two friends sat in Iridan's sparse room. A servant had just departed after leaving some fresh bread and a flask of wine. "How's Myrin?" Iridan asked as Pothar broke off a piece of the bread and stuffed it eagerly into his mouth.

"Not good," he mumbled. "The healers don't think she'll recover until after the birth. But we also have other problems." He took a drink of the wine then continued. "Look, I've had a talk with Dobrah—who's leading the march on Labyn, by-the-way. There's something definitely wrong with Jaleph. We don't believe you'd be safe in Su'Meeryn any more, and I'm starting to think the same thing about Dirwyn and your wife."

Pothar's words threatened to crush Iridan. He was not expecting Myrin to have healed, but he had thought she would have at least improved. And now there were concerns for her safety? "Why do you say that?" he asked, his voice just above a whisper.

"It's just… I was thinking. If Jaleph is so displeased with you, might he take it out on your family?"

Unsteady fingers ran through his hair as Iridan said, "I guess it's possible, but I always thought that Jaleph liked Myrin. He has also been courting Dirwyn."

"Well, I used to think Jaleph liked you, but he isn't the same man he used to be. I wouldn't rely on how he acted in the past, if I were you." Iridan nodded as Pothar continued. "And what about Myrin's illness?"

"I thought it was just that her body wasn't reacting well to the pregnancy."

"Maybe it is, or maybe it's something else."

"What do you mean?"

Pothar finished chewing another bite of bread then answered, "It all seems kind of suspicious, don't you think?"

"Poison?" Iridan asked, and he was now becoming very agitated. "Is that what you're getting at?"

"Perhaps. You shouldn't rule anything out. Didn't she get sick around the time these problems with Jaleph started?"

"I guess so," Iridan replied, "but what are you proposing we do about it?"

"I'm not proposing anything. I'm just telling you what's been happening. We're attacking Labyn, but I'm not so sure that Illiyna was behind our ambush. I'm leery of this advisor of Jaleph's. Something isn't right. Su'Meeryn is a peaceful land; how can we be heading to war again?"

As Pothar paused, Iridan gazed at his friend. He knew he had to do something, and then he thought again of Worm's words regarding Josu. He still wondered how much he could trust Shekul's king, but it appeared he had no choice, and a plan began to form in his mind.

"Jaleph knows you're here, right?"

Pothar nodded. "Dobrah convinced him to send me, to get Josu's reaction to the attack. I still don't know what he hoped to accomplish by sending me *after* the march began."

"When we're done here, it'll be risky for you to stay in Su'Meeryn. Jaleph will suspect that it was you who sparked any move we make."

"What do you have in mind?"

"I'm going to return to Su'Meeryn and sneak in at night. With the army marching, I should be able to enter easily enough and get Myrin and Dirwyn out. I think we'll be able to return here safely, assuming the other part of the plan works out."

"And what's that?"

"I'm going to talk to Josu," Iridan continued, "and tell him everything. Shekul isn't the strongest kingdom around, but we will need some allies if we're going to try to go up against Jaleph."

"Who said anything about going against Jaleph? Look, I don't want to see something happen to you or your family, but you're talking about going to war against our home. And besides, what makes you think you can trust Josu? He is an ally of Su'Meeryn, isn't he?"

Iridan sat back and took a drink. "First of all, I didn't say anything about going to war. It might come to that, but we'll have to see. If Jaleph is becoming so erratic, I don't think we can just sit back and let him destroy everything we fought for. I sacrificed Teracuss; I watched him die, and for what? for Jaleph to go insane and jeopardize our home? How long will Su'Meeryn last if the lands to the north march against us again? We can't stop the attack on Labyn, but we will have to decide what to do next.

"As for Josu, he's not too happy about what's going on. He's been pretty suspicious of me since I arrived, and they already have word about our army. We've got to go to him, because I don't think we have any other choice."

"Alright Iridan," Pothar replied softly. "We'll try it your way, but I'm not going to leave my home."

Iridan eyed his companion skeptically. "Are you sure?"

"Yes. I will stay in Su'Meeryn. It may be dangerous for me, but I'll deal with it."

"Okay, if that's your decision. Let's go see Josu," Iridan responded. He was not happy with the thought of his friend remaining in Su'Meeryn, but that was Pothar's choice. "If everything goes as I expect, we'll have to leave right away." Pothar nodded and they departed.

***

Josu and his three advisors gazed at Iridan as he completed his story. He told them about the attack on Okkgan, his concerns regarding Jaleph and his fears for his family. "You see," Flicia purred, "I knew we could trust him. You go get your wife and cousin, and we will discuss what to do from there. We will have a place for all of you when you return."

"Yes, yes, go," Josu added, allowing Iridan to sigh with obvious relief.

"This is quite a concern," remarked Surik. "We are not a large kingdom, but if Jaleph's plan is to expand his borders, Shekul would be the next logical target. I just wonder though: where is he getting this strength from to attack Labyn? Pardon me, but Su'Meeryn isn't too powerful."

"It's not just Su'Meeryn's troops," Pothar replied. "Ut, Jaleph's advisor from Labyn, is supplying soldiers from Labyn that are loyal to him."

"Why didn't you mention this before?" growled Forim.

"I'm not used to this sort of thing," Pothar answered sharply as the pinkish tone of his face grew a little darker. "I'm not used to committing treason. So, you'll have to forgive me if I'm somewhat distracted."

Josu stood from his chair and looked about, appearing bewildered, and Flicia motioned for the king to return to his seat. "Gentlemen," she said, "let's not lose focus on our situation and the threat which could be coming our way."

"I agree," Iridan responded, "that's why we came to you. I see no reason for Jaleph to be making the enemies he is. He certainly can't survive a major war. There's something more going on here, and we need to stop it."

"Is that so?" Forim asked angrily. "And why should we believe you two anyway? How do we know this isn't just some part of the plan?"

"You can believe what you want," Iridan replied with equal ire. He then softened his tone as he turned to face Josu. "I'm just trying to help. You already know that Su'Meeryn is marching, and we're not asking you to do anything. All I want is a place to stay once I get Myrin out of there. In the meantime, you might want to negotiate with some of your other neighbors while we're gone." He then looked directly at Forim. "Does that sound like we're trying to manipulate you?"

Forim scowled but did not respond, as Josu again stood and looked at his five companions. "You're right; we can't just sit back and do nothing while Su'Meeryn conquers Labyn. Go, and you will be welcomed back upon your return, unless I uncover some deception in your absence. If I do, you'll be dead." He looked at Flicia and his stern expression turned into a grin once he saw her reassuring smile.

Chapter 46

The army marched in relative quiet throughout the day. Dobrah rode at the head of the column, feeling very unsure of herself. She had often been teased as the only woman serving in the military, and now she was leading the call to war. Why not Teraken? He was certainly the most seasoned of all Su'Meeryn's warriors, but Jaleph had inexplicably thrown him into jail. She glanced at Rynkor, who rode on her right. His pink eyes stared straight ahead, unmoving, and the bald half of his skull glistened in the sunlight. Although she could not dispute his prowess in combat, she shuddered at the possibility that the bizarre man might ultimately become the leader of Su'Meeryn's army. *I really wish Pothar or Iridan were here,* she thought. *Or, of course, Karus.* But none of them were, and she felt very alone. Alone amidst the host.

A horse trotted up on her left, distracting her from her musings, and she was not surprised when she saw Ut at the reins. "What are you doing here?" she asked. "I thought you were staying at the castle."

"No. That would not be wise. I will need to be here when we meet up with my troops from Labyn, which should be in about four days."

"More horse," commented Rynkor. "Move faster. Get to fight sooner."

"Your enthusiasm is commendable, Rynkor; however, we could never manage enough horses to move an entire army," replied Ut. "Patience my friend, you will get to fight soon enough."

Rynkor giggled then spurred his horse in the direction of a hare that he had spotted. "A fine man," Ut laughed. "Yes, fine indeed."

Dobrah fought to keep the revulsion she felt towards her companions hidden away, and she missed her husband even more.

***

Atop her horse—before of the army of Su'Meeryn, which rested on a small ridge—Dobrah gazed down upon Labyn under a moonless night. The city appeared very peaceful; she saw very few people milling about in the dim lights from the small buildings. She had not seen Ut lately, and that was fine with her. She often thought everyone would be better off if she just put her sword through his heart. Looking back, she noted that the soldiers from Labyn had been positioned at the front. It seemed as though Ut viewed them as expendable, as if he did not want them to survive.

Rynkor fidgeted next to her. He was obviously anxious for the fighting to commence, but he would have to wait. The strange man stood in his stirrups and looked back at the troops. Dobrah grabbed his arm as he was about to wave them forward. "Not yet," she ordered. "We wait for dawn. We will need some light so we don't start killing each other." Rynkor sat and frowned before turning his attention back to Labyn. He stared down, as if in a trance.

Dobrah just shook her head. She wished Rynkor was anywhere else, but he was too dangerous to be left unattended. He'll do fine once the fighting starts, she thought. Although a part of her hoped that he would not survive.

They waited in silence for another hour. As the sky awakened into shades of deep purple, she again wondered what had happened to Ut. "Now remember," she said to Rynkor, "we wait until after the first wave before you and I engage." Rynkor just nodded. Dobrah pointed to a herald who raised a banner, bringing the nearby troops into formation. She took a deep breath as a horn sounded. Soldiers rushed forward. Rynkor squirmed on his saddle for a moment until he too took off with the first wave. Dobrah tried to restrain him but then let him go, hoping she would never see the man again.

To Dobrah's surprise, the assault found Labyn completely unaware. No troops met the initial onslaught. She had expected that spies or scouts would have tracked their movements, which, clearly, had not occurred. Siege ladders found only a handful of defenders who quickly fell. Rynkor's peculiar head was clearly visible atop the wall, searching for victims. Dobrah imagined the sick smile on his face.

Since the first wave had already breached the city walls, Dobrah now lead the remaining troops forward. After climbing one of the ladders, she saw that a meager defense had been formed. Many of Labyn's troops had not even managed to grab any armor or a shield. They fought back valiantly with just their swords, but the troops from Su'Meeryn quickly overwhelmed them. The steel of Su'Meeryn pierced skin with increasing frequency as bodies plummeted from the parapets. Blood flowed down the castle walls like an unholy waterfall. Flesh and bone intertwined into a grotesque jumble. And, among the turmoil, Rynkor swirled about, unleashing death with each stroke. His blade dripped onto his head as he raised it high and cried out in joy. Many defenders threw down their weapons and ran. Labyn was being routed.

This isn't right, Dobrah thought as she climbed down. We shouldn't be able to take the city this easily. "The queen!" she called when she reached the ground. "Make sure Illiyna is taken alive!" She looked back and found all of her troops to be within the city. Taking a few moments to survey the dead, she noted that most of their casualties were from the troops that Ut had supplied.

She just shook her head and turned back to the battle. Rynkor ran by in what could only be classified as glee. Already prisoners were being rounded up. A few skirmishes remained but those quickly ended. After a few more minutes a soldier approached to advise her that the queen—and all her children—had been found dead in her chambers.

"That just figures," she mumbled. "No, this isn't right at all."

Chapter 47

A few patrols were about, but Iridan and Pothar managed to reach the castle unseen. Pothar approached the gate on horseback with Iridan hidden within a cloak in front of him. He told the guards that Iridan was an injured farmer he had come across on his way home. The guards had no reason to doubt Pothar, and they let him pass without any questions.

Once within the city, they headed straight to the infirmary and Myrin's room. Her taut face displayed her unquestionable weakness, and Iridan wondered how they would ever get her all the way to Shekul. He gently stroked her arm and repeated her name until her eyes barely cracked open. A slight smile crossed her lips as she recognized her husband. She tried to speak, but no sound escaped.

"I don't have time to explain," Iridan whispered, "but we need to get you out of here. It's not safe for us." As Pothar checked the halls, Iridan gingerly gathered her frail body into his arms. Due to the late hour, they managed to get her out of the building undetected. They brought her to the royal stable as Pothar went off to find Dirwyn. Iridan knew it was dangerous, but he had to take the risk. Getting a couple horses and a small carriage was their only way to reach Shekul. Once he managed to make Myrin as comfortable as possible, Iridan breathed a sigh of relief when saw the filthy stableman approach. He felt certain that Veake would help them.

"Ah, t' 'ero 'as ruturnd, t' save 'es wife 'n chuld. Quite prupur. Yes, yes, quite prupur."

"How do you know why I'm here?"

"Veake not stoopud, 'spite whut some say. Why ulse? Ya wan t' bring 'er back t' Shekul, 'n ya need Veake's 'elp, eh? But just ya two? I not 'xpect thut."

"Pothar's gone to get Dirwyn. I want to leave as soon as they return."

"Yis, yis, a course. Puthar and Dirwyn. But, no, ya can't leave rught uway. T' gurds would 'ave too muny questions, leavun in t' middle o' night. At dawn. Ya leave at dawn. No questions thun. Shroud your face, Puthar druve t' coach. No questions. Yes, no questions. Purfuct."

Iridan stared at the strange man. It was as if Veake had been expecting him and had already worked out a strategy for his family to flee the city. He could hardly believe his good fortune. "But Pothar's going to stay here. He can't come with."

"Puthar druve. Nued t' gut cha out. Thun 'e come back."

"So, you'll help me?"

Veake cackled loudly. His laughter turned into gagging as the green tint of his face began to darken, but the fit quickly passed. "O' course. 'Elp the 'ero. I must."

"Please don't call me that," Iridan pleaded, and he was once again reminded of the vision of Teracuss' mangled body flying from the dragon's mouth.

Veake just kept giggling, and as he strolled away, Pothar returned with Dirwyn. Iridan's cousin was puzzled about being summoned from her home at such a late hour, and she was not at all sure about the necessity of her having to sneak away from the kingdom. Iridan then told her about his concerns regarding Jaleph's recent actions, and his suspicion that Myrin had been poisoned. Dirwyn commented that the king had seemed more aloof and detached the last few times they had been together. She reluctantly agreed to leave when Pothar promised to watch after her parents. After Iridan explained Veake's plan, they sat in a dark corner of the stable to await the dawn. Myrin lay in his arms, too weak to stay awake. He gently stroked her hair and rubbed her swollen stomach. Just before dawn, Veake returned with a carriage he had prepared for the four. Iridan thanked the stableman as he made Myrin as comfortable as possible with the extra blankets he found in the back. They rode off, thanking Veake profusely, and, as he had predicted, they managed to leave Su'Meeryn without any questions.

***

After a couple of hours of riding, Pothar stopped the wagon. "I'll walk back from here," he said to Iridan.

"What will you tell the guards?"

"I wouldn't worry about that," he replied as he hopped out. "I doubt that they even really noticed us leaving. Besides, there'll be different guards on duty when I return."

"But Jaleph will certainly investigate when he finds out that Myrin is gone. You're risking a lot by returning."

"I know, but one of the healers is a friend of mine. If he asks, she'll say that she treated the farmer I brought into the castle, and that I was just bringing him back this morning. I should be fine."

Iridan reached his hand down to Pothar. "Thank you my friend. I'm not sure when we'll be able to talk again. I'll send word to you if I get a chance."

A tear glistened in the corner of Pothar's eye as he grasped Iridan's wrist. Iridan knew it was not only due to their parting. They both sensed changes on the horizon. Much like a tornado comes through and ravages the land; at first the air is calm. There is a building of clouds but nothing to predict the onslaught. Then the winds increase, and the coming of the storm is evident. The only question is: where will it strike? Iridan knew that Pothar was wondering where, and when, the storm would erupt.

"I hope to see you soon," Pothar said and quickly strode away.

"Take care," Iridan uttered in a whisper. He then turned his attention to the rear of the wagon. "How are things back there?"

"Not too good," Dirwyn called out. "She's still unconscious. We better get moving."

Iridan glanced back at Pothar one last time before flicking the reins.

***

They had been riding along the southeastern trail for most of the day when Iridan spotted a lone rider approaching. His stomach tightened at the sight, but it was only one person coming from the opposite direction of Su'Meeryn. Still, Iridan readied his sword, but as the rider neared, he thought the man looked familiar. Finally, Iridan recognized Worm. "I thought you might need some assistance," Worm said as he came alongside.

Chapter 48

Jaleph wiped sweat from his head and sat down heavily on his throne. With the audience chamber empty, his sigh sounded louder than normal. No petitioners stood before him, and none of the nobles milled about. Despite their constant annoyance, Jaleph rather missed them. Fenik and Ruy were gone and Teraken was in prison. He had no one to talk with. A queen, the now all-too-familiar thought returned, I need to take a wife. His mind drifted to Iridan and anger swelled like a river during a heavy rain. Perspiration returned to his bald scalp, and his hand again whipped it off as the door to the chamber swung open.

"Ah, Majesty," said Ut as he strode down the corridor towards the throne, "here you are. I have been searching everywhere for you."

"How come? Why aren't you in Labyn?"

"I rode off as soon as I could to bring you news." Ut's smile was larger than normal. "Labyn has fallen. It is in your hands now. Soon you can retaken Okkgan and proclaim yourself emperor."

Jaleph's head nodded in joyous agreement. Everything was coming together better than he could have imagined. "That's wonderful, Ut." When the other man did not leave, Jaleph continued, "Is there something else?"

"Yes, and I am sure that you will find this of equal importance. Myrin has disappeared from the infirmary, and Dirwyn is gone too." Ut paused for a moment. "Iridan must have returned."

Jaleph's irritation returned when he saw that Ut's smile had not softened. "Do you find that amusing?" he spat. The king wondered how Ut would have heard of this news before him, but he was too exasperated by the thought of losing Myrin to question the matter.

"Amusing is not the exact word I would use, but I am pleased."

"You're pleased? Why would you be pleased? Iridan has disobeyed me and taken Myrin. Explain yourself."

"Majesty, it is an opportunity. Think about it. As you have so astutely noted, Iridan disobeyed you. There is no dispute to that. They cannot be moving fast due to Myrin's condition, and I am certain they are heading back to Shekul. I suggest you send out troops to intercept them for return to Su'Meeryn: the women, but not Iridan. You can now be rid of him for good." And Jaleph's smile returned as he nodded his head.

Chapter 49

"What are you doing here?" Iridan asked.

"Not the most hospitable of greeting for an old friend," answered Worm as his gloved hands gently tugged on his reins—which were laced with exquisite stones. Iridan also could not help but note Worm's steed. He was a magnificent black stallion with a lone silver spot on his forehead. "I was bored, so I thought I'd go for a ride." Iridan waited for Worm to continue, but he said nothing more.

"Really, is that so?"

"Yes. It is a beautiful day: blue skies, just a few clouds and a pleasant breeze."

Iridan wanted to stop the wagon and confront Worm, but he knew that he could not risk even a slight delay. "Look, I'm in no mood for your banter. I have my pregnant wife back there, and she's very ill. I'm also fleeing from my king and my home. Now, you either give me a straight answer or leave."

"Fine. I came looking for you. You might not believe this, but I was impressed with you in our conversations. I'd hate to see anything bad happen to you—or your family."

Iridan was surprised at the frankness of man's words and— based on Worm's willing profession of his selfish motivations—he doubted Worm's altruistic declaration. "How did you even know I'd be out here?"

"I have friends. Well, maybe friends is too strong a word. I know people who serve the king, and I'm able to learn things."

As they were talking, Dirwyn climbed out from the back of the wagon. "Who's this?" she asked with a quizzical eye turned towards Worm.

"An acquaintance from Shekul," Iridan replied, and he smirked at Worm's stunned expression when he looked upon Dirwyn. The man from Shekul was clearly impressed by her beauty.

"What's he doing here?"

"That's what I'm trying to find out." Iridan said and turned back to Worm.

"As this striking woman is clearly neither ill nor pregnant, she is certainly not your wife," Worm responded happily. "Will you introduce us?"

"Look Worm, just give me a straight answer."

Worm sighed deeply. "It's just as I said. I was worried when I heard what you were attempting."

"You'll have to forgive me if I doubt you," Iridan replied. "I thought that you were nothing more than a selfish man with little to do and not very caring about anyone else."

"Iridan, I want to help. Just give me this opportunity… for once."

"The last time somebody offered me his assistance, it wasn't for my benefit," Iridan said. He looked back down the path, remembering, from what seemed so long ago, his travels with Teracuss and their interactions with the man in white.

"What're you talking about?" Worm asked.

"Nothing. Forget it. You want to help? Fine. By the looks of your horse, he will be of great assistance pulling the wagon. You can ride up here with Dirwyn and I'll sit in the back with my wife."

***

The wagon was moving slower than Iridan had anticipated, even with the added benefit of Worm's horse. Having never traveled in this fashion before, he'd had no basis by which to estimate the duration of the journey. Iridan sat with Myrin's head in his lap, and he wiped her brow as she stirred. Her eyes opened and a slight smile crossed her lips. "Your son is stirring," she whispered, her voice barely audible above the sounds of the wagon and horses.

"How do you know?" he replied. "It could be a girl."

"I know. It'll be a boy. He'll be strong and will make you proud."

As Iridan bent down and kissed her, the wagon shook with an acceleration. "What's going on?" he called out.

"Riders are coming from the north, and they're gaining quickly," Dirwyn answered. There was another jolt as their speed again increased.

Iridan squeezed Myrin's hand as he gently eased her head from his lap. He peered out from the back and saw a group of about a dozen riders galloping towards them. The wagon would certainly not keep its lead for long. "What do you think?" he asked as he moved to the front.

"It's not good," Worm answered. "There's no way we can out-last them. They'll be on us in a few minutes. I don't think that there's anything we can do but surrender. They must be from Su'Meeryn."

"Look," Dirwyn called out. She pointed ahead, and they saw another group of riders approaching from the opposite direction.

"What do you make of that?" asked Iridan.

"I don't know. But we're nearing Shekul. It could be a scouting party," Worm answered.

"Should we try to reach them?"

"We might as well," Worm responded. "I don't think your king will be too happy with you if you return home."

"I agree," said Dirwyn. "Iridan, I'll take care of Myrin. Worm, get these horses moving." Dirwyn crawled into the back of the wagon as Iridan climbed out.

After a few minutes, the riders approaching from the south reached the wagon. They reined in, and Iridan recognized their leader. It was Kile.

"Well, I'm glad to see you've made it back, but you seem to have brought some unwanted company," Kile said as he pulled a bow from off his back while the seven other riders did the same. "May I assume they're hostile?"

"They certainly don't look friendly to me," replied Worm.

Iridan looked back to discover that the trailing riders were nearly on them and had managed to loose a few arrows in their direction. Most of them harmlessly hit the wagon while Kile and his men returned fire. Then the soldiers of Shekul dropped their bows, unsheathed their swords and rushed forward. Iridan and Worm also grabbed their swords, jumped from the wagon and followed Kile as more arrows landed.

When they reached the battle, four of the men from Su'Meeryn had fallen from Shekul arrows, and two of Kile's men were down. Iridan and Worm were at a disadvantage as all the other warriors were on horseback. Realizing his predicament, Iridan quickly mounted the steed of one of the fallen men. While the soldiers from Su'Meeryn were engaged with Kile's group, Iridan and Worm managed to approach, unnoticed, from the side.

Iridan's sword struck the first Su'Meeryn soldier he reached. His blade crashed against the bridge of the man's nose, and blood erupted as he fell from the horse. When Iridan turned to engage his next opponent, he saw that Worm had also dispatched an adversary. Iridan deflected a sword thrust and drove his steel into the man's throat. The impact of Iridan's strike shook the man's helmet free, and Iridan realized he had just killed Toresh: a man he had known since his first days of training. Before grief could overwhelm him, Iridan realized that Toresh knew whom he was coming to kill. *Things have truly changed,* Iridan thought. With the numbers now having turned on their side, the men of Shekul brought down the other five men while losing only two more of their own.

"Thank you," Iridan panted to Kile and the three other men from Shekul as they surveyed the carnage, "but what are you doing here?"

"We were afraid something like this might happen, so Josu ordered out several scouting parties to watch for you."

Iridan thanked him again as Kile returned to his fallen comrades. Although he had anticipated a confrontation, Kile was clearly shaken by the loss of his men. The surviving scouts from Shekul secured the fallen bodies to their steeds as Iridan returned to the wagon. He climbed in then stood paralyzed. He saw Dirwyn crying so hard she did not even make a sound. Myrin lay in her blood-covered arms. An arrow protruded from her neck; lifeless eyes gazed back at her husband.

Chapter 50

Jaleph sat on his throne; the audience chamber before him was full. Ut stood at his right and Teraken was on his left—with his wrists in chains. The nobles, various merchants and prominent townspeople filled the area, completing the scene. Jaleph raised his hand—calling for quiet—then stood.

"I have wonderful news for all of Su'Meeryn," he announced. "Labyn has been conquered. Our casualties were minimal, but, unfortunately, Illiyna—the treacherous queen who betrayed us—was not so fortunate. She was killed during the assault. With Labyn secured, new troops are being raised who will be loyal to Su'Meeryn. Our next step will be to retake Okkgan. Once that is done, well, the possibilities are endless. Now, I cannot be any more specific for fear of spies from other lands learning of our plans. But let me assure you that all here will profit greatly." The crowd stirred before him, murmuring their cautious approval.

"Now, to other matters," Jaleph continued, motioning to Teraken. "All of you here know Teraken. He has served Su'Meeryn well under my father and me. He was invaluable during the siege of our castle. So, it pains me to have him before you in chains. But what am I to do with disloyalty? It cannot be tolerated, no matter whom the person is or what his past deeds may have been." Jaleph paused and smiled as he thought of Iridan. "Despite giving him every opportunity, Teraken's disloyal actions continued. Now, here he stands: a prisoner."

Jaleph turned to face Teraken. He pulled a jeweled dagger from his belt and quickly slashed both of Teraken's cheeks. "Let these marks be a reminder to Teraken and all who see him as to the price of disloyalty.

"Now, Teraken, due to your long history of service to the kings of Su'Meeryn, my benevolence is offered one last time. You may leave here a free man, but you are stripped of your rank. You will serve as a common guard at the gate. Despite your recent behavior, I am certain you still care for the safety of our kingdom. But I assure you Teraken, I will hear of any other actions of disloyalty. And if I do, you will be classified as a traitor to your king and immediately executed. Do you understand?" Teraken nodded, and the king paused to let the full effect of his words hit everyone in the chamber. "Now, I present to you all, the new leader of my army," and Rynkor strolled forward from the crowd. Jaleph motioned to Rynkor who removed the shackles from Teraken's wrists. With his hands finally free, Teraken reached up and wiped the blood, which still streamed from his cheeks.

"I would like to thank everyone for your time; you are dismissed. Teraken, you will immediately report to the gate. You are not to return to your home to tend to your wounds. Your blood will be a message to all." With that, Jaleph returned to his throne as the audience chamber emptied. Rynkor was the last, and he left giggling profusely. Jaleph, who was now alone with Ut, said, "Proceed,"

"A wonderful job, Majesty. You showed both your strength and compassion. Anyone who dares to consider crossing you will have to think about this day."

"Any word yet regarding Iridan and Myrin?"

"No Majesty, and that does concern me. We should have heard something by now."

"Well, what have you done about it?"

"Riders have been sent to investigate. I am certain Iridan could not have reached Shekul before being intercepted. We should know something soon."

"Good, we need to get this matter resolved quickly," the king stated. "I want Iridan killed. Once he is gone, Myrin will become my queen." He paused for a moment. "After she delivers his child." Finally, he thought, finally I will have my queen; the queen I always wanted.

"Jaleph, have you decided?" Ut asked.

"Decided what?"

"What you will do with the child? Everyone will know it is not yours."

"Yes, of course it can't be raised in the palace. It should be killed."

"Forgive me Jaleph, but I am not sure that is a wise idea. You will have enough problems with Myrin as it is. She will never forgive you if you kill her child."

"And she will forgive me for killing her husband?"

"That is a different situation. Iridan has brought his fate upon himself, which, given time, she can come to understand. You can force her to marry you regardless of what you do with the child, but I am trying to help you so that your future life with her will be as pleasant as possible."

"What do you suggest?"

Ut considered a moment before continuing. "The child will have to be given to someone else to raise, someone who is close—so that

Myrin will be able to visit it—but not close enough where it will be a distraction."

"Yes, yes, fine. See to it. Now, on to other matters. Are we ready for Okkgan, or do we wait until spring?"

"Everything is prepared. Rynkor has his troops ready. We leave in the morning."

"Are you certain that Rynkor is ready for this? I know he's a fine warrior, but leading the army is a different job."

"Based on his performance at Labyn, I am certain."

Jaleph was not convinced. "What about Dobrah? She has served me well, and I think her temperament and personality would be better suited for that position."

"I am certain, Sire."

"Fine," the king replied, "and you believe I should accompany the troops to Okkgan?"

"This time, yes. The battle will be short, and I have a surprise for you once it is over."

"And what might that be?"

"Please Majesty, do not make me spoil it. I have planned this for some time. You shall see soon enough."

"Very good. I'd hate to deprive you of a little joy."

***

The column marched out from the gate. Scores of soldiers held spears, which reflected the blood red light of the rising sun. A strong wind hit their faces. Banners flapped loudly. Rynkor rode at the front of the column. At the rear came Jaleph and Ut.

"This wind will slow us down a little," Jaleph said once he crossed the gates. He glanced up and saw Teraken above him. His old friend gazed down with an emotionless face.

Ut peered to the sky and snarled. "Yes. It can slow us but not stop us." Jaleph turned to Ut with some confusion at his companion's strong reaction, but he just shrugged and kept riding.

They marched on, and Jaleph noticed that Ut had Rynkor push the men harder than expected. He was concerned the company would be too tired once they reached Okkgan, but with the size of their force, a little fatigue would not matter.

At dusk of the third day, they reached Okkgan, and Ut seemed pleased with the timing. Rynkor ordered a halt at the outskirts of the town and began to form the men for the assault.

Troops from the small town came out to meet the attack. They would be no match for Jaleph's force. The king knew that, and those in Okkgan must have known it as well. But there they stood: with swords ready. Jaleph heard a cry of glee from Rynkor. His horse bucked, and Rynkor raised his sword, pointing it into the wind. In response, the defending troops dropped their swords as one man walked forward. Jaleph felt disappointed by the surrender, as he had been eagerly anticipating the battle. But then Rynkor's horse raced forward, and his sword pierced the chest of the leading man. As the body fell, the troops of Su'Meeryn rushed to attack.

The battle was short but fierce. The men of Okkgan scrambled to grab their weapons, but they were swept up like debris in a hard running river. Blood splashed in all directions as the blades of Su'Meeryn cascaded down like sheets of rain. Cries of agony reached Jaleph's ears as a sea of scarlet flooded his eyes. Then, almost as quickly as it had begun, the battled ended. No defenders remained to slay. Okkgan was secured. Rynkor returned, his flowing hair—stained by the blood of his victims—now matched his pink eyes. "Done," he said as he stood before the king and sheathed his drenched blade. He laughed as he looked about, searching for additional foes.

"Good," replied Ut, "is everything ready?" Rynkor nodded. "You may now lead the king into the town."

Rynkor nodded and brought the two into Okkgan. A tiny hill, with buildings circling it, stood in the center. Ut took Jaleph's elbow and led him to the top. The king looked about as Ut waved towards one of the buildings. Kedin emerged, flanked by two soldiers of Su'Meeryn. His time of having been held hostage in Okkgan had left Kedin looking even more fragile than ever before. As he approached, Jaleph saw that he was carrying a banner. Ut took the banner, and unfurled it. It was royal blue with black trim. In the center was a wolf of silver and black.

The crowd about the hill stood silent as Ut handed the banner to Jaleph. "Now I present to you all our new emperor, Jaleph!" Ut called, and the soldiers of Su'Meeryn cried out in accord. The emperor held the banner high as his troops raised their swords in salute.

Chaw Den

Patrick D. Catlett

Prologue

Hooves splattered sheets of mud as a heavy rain fell from swelling dark clouds. The stink of drenched fur and unwashed men followed the scores of horses that streamed forth beneath powerful burst of lightning. Cracks of thunder drowned out the sound of water pelting steel. Dark blue flags flapped against the torrent, proudly displaying wolves of ebony and silver. The nostrils of galloping steeds flared, expelling small puffs of breath into the rain-soaked air as the cavalry approached the defenders with their lance points dipped. Battered shields rose to deflect the onslaught and the attackers cried out as the wood shattered. Blood mixed with the rain to blanket the scene in a pink hue. The defending troop line quickly evaporated before the advance, while horses trampled bodies into the sludge.

Arrows launched from behind the line sought victims, but few found targets. The attackers' horses veered left to flank the main body of their quarry while foot soldiers rushed forward to engage. Morthon readied his axe as he wiped the cold rain from his brow. A bolt of lightning displayed the attackers' menacing faces through the gloom. At the head of the column, Morthon saw a strange man leading the charge. His long white hair, matted down by the rain, covered only half his head. A sick smile twisted the warrior's face as one of his twin swords claimed its first victim. The blades continued to deliver death until Morthon's attention was diverted towards his own adversary. The man lunged forward but his foot slipped in the grime. He stumbled, leaving the back of his neck fully visible, and Morthon's axe skillfully found its target.

As he pulled the axe free from his victim, Morthon saw his brother fall beside him with a gaping wound across his chest. Without allowing himself time to grieve, Morthon turned to engage his next opponent. The warrior swung and his sword struck Morthon's left arm. He stumbled from the impact as his attacker swung again, but before the blade made contact, his axe shot up and split the man's chin. He dropped to the mud with blood pouring from his face as Morthon's axe plunged down, quickly ending the man's suffering.

The battle raged on and the combatants continued to fall to the rain-soaked ground; however, the number of defenders' bodies far outnumbered those of their enemy. Despite the overwhelming odds, Morthon and his men fought on. The surge of a fresh assault overran their defenses, and Morthon found himself separated from his comrades. He limped heavily from a fresh blow to his left thigh and his blood continued to flow, intermingling with the rain. Waves of assailants pressed forward, surrounding Morthon. He could not see any surviving countrymen but still he fought on. It did not matter if he was the last warrior; surrender never entered his thoughts. His axe swung wildly about, searching for any target until it was knocked from his hand. He glanced about at the enemy as he dropped to his knees, exhausted and defeated. The strange warrior with the white hair pushed his way through and stared down at Morthon with his head tipped quizzically, his pink eyes sparkling in the rain. The corners of his mouth rose as he readied his sword. Morthon refused to look away as the blade came crashing down against his skull.

Chapter 1

The walls felt like a noose constricting around his throat. He dropped down onto the bed, but no matter how hard he tried he could not seem to get comfortable. It was a familiar routine. Seeking escape in his room which never provided comfort, but at least he was alone. Here he did not have to listen to endless words of sorrow and offers of assistance. Not that he found fault with the sentiments offered, but they could not help. Where could he find solace in this foreign land amidst virtual strangers?

After a few more restless moments on the bed, Iridan gave up and crossed the small room to his mirror. He regarded his hair which now hung far down his back and the beard which he had not shaved. Sickened by his reflection, Iridan knocked the mirror off the table.

His eyes peered around the room, searching, but he did not know for what. Looking out his window over the fields of Shekul, Iridan remembered that Josu had requested a meeting with him. So, for no other reason than he was tired of looking at walls, he pulled on the closest shirt he could find and left his room.

***

"We can't just sit back while Jaleph conquers all the northern lands!" Surik bellowed from his seat in the corner as he turned to his king.

"And what do you suggest I do about it?" Josu shot back.

"We all know that Shekul will be his next target if he succeeds," continued Surik. "He is certainly aware that Iridan is here, and he probably knows that Myrin is dead." He paused momentarily to cast a sympathetic eye towards Iridan, who sat quietly across the room virtually oblivious to the debate. When Iridan did not respond, Surik continued. "I don't mean to be indelicate, but we are all aware of Jaleph's interest in both of them."

"My question remains: why didn't he attack Shekul first?" Forim interjected.

"We've gone over this for months," Forim's brother responded irately. "He certainly didn't want to give the northern lands time to regroup, and he doesn't view Shekul as a threat. He will come after us as soon as he secures the north." The anger in his voice quickly dissolved into hopelessness. "Assuming he does secure them."

Josu stood and walked to the center of the royal hall. "We still need a plan." His moon-shaped face turned to the ceiling high above. "What is our plan?"

Flicia also rose and came alongside the king. "Gorthon. We must send envoys to Gorthon. They have to ally with us, or there is no hope."

Iridan's long fingernails scratched his coarse beard, and he observed his companions for the first time in months. Flicia's appearance remained as striking as ever, and the king and his advisors were appropriately groomed and bathed. He wondered how they managed to tolerate being in his presence.

"You keep mentioning Gorthon, but why would they help?" Forim asked.

"After we fall, Gorthon will be his only remaining target," answered Flicia. "They must join with us, or face their own destruction."

"But why would Jaleph attack Gorthon? Even if he conquers the entire realm, he couldn't get an army through those mountains."

"We didn't think he could conquer Labyn and launch a successful invasion north either."

"That's different. No matter how strong he is, no army can get through those mountains." Forim's face grew red as his agitation grew.

"I wouldn't put anything past him now," Flicia responded hotly.

Iridan listened to the familiar bickering as he twisted the dull ring on his finger. He thought of the day he had received the ring from Naemon and the battle with the man in white: the black light exploding from his bloodless corpse, and the pale follower who ate a piece of his flesh before leaving the home. Then he remembered the sight of Teracuss' body being ravaged by Jokk-al Ystren. He thought also of all his friends who had died; Ruy and Karus, and of course, Myrin. He turned his attention away from Naar's ring, back to the people in the room with him. While he did not consider any of them friends, they had taken him into their land in his time of need. Would he sit back and let the fate of his wife befall them too?

"Enough!" Surik bellowed. "I'm tired of this same argument. We need to make a decision. Spring is upon us and we can no longer wait."

Josu looked about with his cavernous mouth agape. "What? What do we do?"

He is a fool, Iridan thought, but he is a good man. Josu does not deserve the fate Jaleph will rain down on him. None of them do. Jaleph had ruined his life, and he refused to continue to sit by and allow his former king to ruin the lives of everyone else around him. He mustered his resolve and he forced himself to speak. "I will go to Gorthon."

Iridan was not surprised when all eyes turned to him in bewilderment. He had sat through many of these meetings since burying his wife and unborn child, but he had not spoken until this moment. His companions had initially tried to get him to contribute his insight regarding Jaleph. After a time, however, they had given up asking and Iridan was amazed that they still requested his presence. But he could no longer sit quietly. Winter had passed. Jaleph was taking steps, and it was time for Iridan to act. "Gorthon is our only hope. I will convince them to join us."

***

The meeting ended shortly after Iridan spoke. He returned to his room, picked up the largest pieces of the broken mirror and again gazed at his reflection. With a shake of his head, he grabbed a blade and proceeded to hack off his beard. A good amount of blood and skin joined the hair on the floor before he was done. Then, turning his attention to his head, he cut that hair to its more familiar shoulder length. With this done Iridan opened his door, but hesitated before the empty hallway. After many months of sitting alone in his room Iridan found it difficult to leave. His habit had been to depart only for meals, occasionally leaving the castle to wander around the farms. He considered seeking out Worm and demanding to be shown the writings of Naar, but he no longer cared. Nothing had been gained from his efforts in the past, so why bother now? Worm had actually asked to visit a few times, but Iridan always refused. He had wanted to see no one, especially Worm. Worm reminded him too much of that day in the wagon: the day Myrin died. Iridan only agreed to requests to visit from his cousin, Dirwyn, who remained in the castle. Even her warm personality failed to comfort him, and her visits had become brief and less frequent. He took comfort in the knowledge that she must be making new friends, and with her beauty and charm she was certainly being courted by many of the nobles. She did not need him as much as when they had first arrived, so he had felt justified by his self-imposed exile. However, after his meeting with Josu and the court that morning, he could no longer stay hidden away. When he figured that lunch had ended, he marched to his cousin's room.

"What are you doing here?" she asked sharply, with a mixture of surprise and anger.

"It's time," he answered. "Time to stop feeling sorry for myself, and time I do something."

"I'm glad to hear that," she said as her familiar smile glowed from her beautiful face, and Iridan realized how much he had missed it. "I didn't know what to do with you," she continued, closing the door behind him. "I was so worried, and so angry. You brought me here and then left me alone. I know it was hard, but…" The smile disappeared as tears formed in her eyes.

"I'm sorry. I knew how I was treating you, but I just didn't care," Iridan said as he hugged his cousin. "I didn't care about anything, but I have to get past it. Something has to be done about Jaleph; we can't allow him to continue."

"What can we do?"

"I'm going to Gorthon to ask them to join us against Su'Meeryn."

Dirwyn looked at him skeptically, but all she said was, "Good luck."

"Good luck, huh?" He wanted to laugh. He wanted to lash out at her. Luck? I have no luck. If I had any, Myrin would be alive and we would have a child. "Will you be alright?" he asked flatly, restraining his anger.

"Don't worry about me. I have some friends here now, and Surik has been courting me."

"He has? He said nothing to me."

"Does that surprise you? You haven't been one for conversation of late."

Iridan actually managed a chuckle. "Yes, you're right, of course," and he turned to leave.

"Where are you going now?"

"I need to plan my trip and advise my companions that they've just volunteered."

***

Iridan sat in the den for over an hour. A small dog ran in occasionally to check on him, but as soon as Iridan reached down to pet her, she immediately bolted away. He paced the room, looking at the various exquisitely-painted murals of horses. Unfortunately there was nothing to read or anything else in the room to occupy his time. He picked up a silver candle holder and was examining the carvings—which were also

344

of horses—when Worm finally arrived. "I'm sorry to have kept you waiting," the slight man said, "but I was not expecting you."

"That's okay. I wasn't expecting to come."

Worm sat on one of the chairs, and the barking of the dog signaled its return as she bounded into his lap. "Yet you finally left your room, and here you are."

Iridan stood quietly for a moment, debating how to respond. Worm had never been the easiest person to talk to, and he was certain his news would not be greeted with delight. But for some unknown reason, Iridan knew that he was right: he needed Worm on this mission. As he could think of no other way to detail his plan, he decided to just speak forthrightly. "I told Josu that I would travel to Gorthon to enlist their help against Jaleph, and I want you to come with me."

Worm stifled a laugh. "You want me to go to Gorthon? What do you think I can accomplish there?"

"This is a journey I should not attempt alone, and I believe you could offer much in our discussions with their king."

"You do, huh?" Worm turned a questioning eye to Iridan. "I haven't seen you for months, and now you want me to join you on this foolhardy expedition?"

"I haven't talked to anyone for a long time, and you know why," Iridan said with a sharper tone than he had planned. He took a deep breath and softened his voice before going on. "I did not ask you to come and search for me when we were returning from Su'Meeryn, but you did."

"A mistake I don't foresee making again. I could have been killed you know."

"Worm, your protests are empty words. You knew the risk, but you still came. Don't give me your mock selfish demeanor anymore. It won't work."

"So, now you think you're an expert about me? I don't have to listen to this anymore. You may show yourself out."

Worm stood and turned to exit the room, but Iridan grabbed him by the shoulder and spun him back around. "You will listen to me. Shekul is at risk. If Jaleph's northern campaign is successful, Shekul is next to fall. Your estate, all your horses and all your wealth will be gone." Worm's body began to tremble as he tried to pull away, but Iridan would not release him. "I've thought a lot about our first meeting in that cell. We were having a somewhat pleasant conversation, when all of a sudden, you were mad. You bribed that jailer to put you in a different cell. At the time I had no idea what I said to get you so angry, but now I understand. I was questioning you about what you were doing with your life: stealing food just for the risk. You became furious because you knew I was right, and you could not stand the thought. You hated the fact that despite your wealth and privilege, all you did was steal for the sake of stealing: annoying the king just because you could think of nothing else to do with yourself, being thrown in jail for a couple of days so you could think up your next pathetic scheme. You were tired of having no purpose. That is why you came after me, and that is why you will come to Gorthon."

Iridan could feel Worm's shoulder tighten under his grasp — he stood as rigid as a statue. Worm's lips rose in a sneer to match the slits of his eyelids and hatred hung in the air like mist from a lake in fall. "I will go nowhere with you," Worm breathed. But even as the words escaped his mouth, Worm's face had begun to soften.

"Of course you will. I can see it in your eyes. It's time for us both to emerge from our self-appointed exiles. Yours just happened to be a bit longer than mine."

Worm continued to stare at him; the conflict on his face still clearly visible. He abhorred the fact that someone had seen through his façade and summed up his life so succinctly, but Iridan also saw relief; relief that he would not have to play his well-rehearsed role any longer. That character which he had so carefully crafted over all his years, and Iridan also witnessed the emergence of another emotion: connection. Worm finally had someone with whom he could identify. Both men needed to cast off their malaise. It was time to show who they were made to be. "I will go," was all that Worm said.

"And when we get back, you will teach me all you know of Naar."

***

With Worm at his side, Iridan headed off to enlist his third partner, who was harder to locate as he was on duty about the castle. They finally found Kile in the armory, providing weapons to some new recruits. Kile finished with the men before he turned to acknowledge the pair. "So, I hear you are going to be our savior," he said as he hung a newly-sharpened sword onto the wall rack. "First Su'Meeryn, now Shekul. You are quite the man, aren't you?"

Iridan was taken aback by Kile's hostility. They had not seen each other since returning to Shekul with Myrin's body. Kile had never been overly friendly to him, but why this reaction? "I'm just trying to do what I can," Iridan replied angrily. "Do you have a problem with that?"

Kile glanced briefly at Worm then back to Iridan. "I know it must have been difficult losing your wife, but you hide yourself away and now want to be Shekul's emissary to Gorthon? Why don't you return to your room, and take him with you?"

Further confusion swept over Iridan as he had thought Worm and Kile were friends. He could not imagine what had sparked such strong antagonism. He might not have a positive image around the castle, but he was just trying to help in any way he could. That was all that mattered now, and after his argument with Worm, he had no wish for further banter. "Well, since you know of my plan, I don't have to tell you about it. You will be joining me… us. I plan to leave in two days, so be ready by then. And before you tell me that you don't want to, I really don't care. Josu has agreed; you are coming with us."

Kile stood still for a moment. Iridan expected further protest, but all Kile said was, "Why me?"

"You are the only soldier I know in Shekul. I want another good sword with me if we meet with any trouble."

Kile nodded, "Sensible, but why him?" he asked, pointing at Worm.

"I have my reasons. Is that a problem?"

A snort escaped from Kile's throat. "If you don't think so, I guess I won't be able to convince you otherwise."

"No, you won't. It's settled. We will meet for dinner to discuss our route," Iridan said as he moved towards the door. "Come on Worm, I have a few more matters I'd like to discuss with you."

"I'm sorry," Worm said, "but are you suddenly our commander?"

"Actually, I think I am. We can confirm with Josu if you'd like."

Worm smirked back at Iridan. "I don't suppose that is necessary."

"Good, let's go to my room." Iridan led Worm through the door, leaving Kile alone in the armory.

***

Worm sat on the chair as Iridan pulled off his boots. "Now what do you want?" Worm asked.

"It's just that I wasn't expecting such a strong reaction from Kile. I thought the two of you were friends."

"*Were* is the appropriate word," answered Worm as he began to fidget with one of his bracelets.

"Care to explain?"

"Not particularly."

"Look, I thought we had an understanding. I can't keep having these discussions with you. I need plain answers. The three of us will be leaving the castle soon, and I need to know what is going on between you two. I don't want to go through that kind of trip again."

"What do you mean?"

Iridan sighed heavily. "It's not important."

"Oh, so you want to hear everything from me but you won't reciprocate?"

After a long pause, Iridan responded. "Fine. You know about the trip I took to search for this," and he raised his hand to display the ring on his finger. "Well, I didn't get along very well with Teracuss, the man I went with. I can't deal with another such journey again. Is that sufficient for you?"

Worm smiled, but Iridan saw that a struggle still brewed within him. Following a few false starts, Worm finally began. "Kile and I were close friends as boys, despite the differences in our upbringings. While I was being schooled, he was training as a soldier but we would meet during our games times. We often fought on the same teams, and… well… that's not important. We stayed friends even after his training ended. You might think of yourself as smart for your little epiphany regarding me earlier today, but Kile figured me out years ago. We argued about it often." Worm stood and looked out the window. Iridan saw how uncomfortable he was discussing this, but Worm continued. "For a few unimportant reasons, our friendship had become strained when you first arrived here. We had our last argument about a month ago, and as a result, I got him punished for something he didn't do. I'm not proud of it, but that is what happened. So, perhaps you might like to rethink your plan."

"Actually, I don't," Iridan replied, amazed at how much personal information Worm had revealed. He understood the predicament, but he could not worry about it. "We have to leave soon, and as I said, he is the only soldier I know here. You two will have to figure a way around this."

Worm laughed. "Who knows? Perhaps we can. It's funny how one conversation can change things so much, but I doubt he'll be able to. He is very stubborn."

"We can discuss this further at dinner if necessary. For now, why don't you return home and start to prepare? I'll see you this evening."

When he was alone, Iridan spread out on his bed and stared at his finger. As usual, Naar's ring turned his thoughts to his wife. He then thought of Ruy and Karus and all the others that he had known who had died so recently. Tears streamed down his cheeks as he thought of Jaleph's brother, but when his former king came to mind the weeping stopped, and he was left with anger and determination.

Chapter 2

The smell of mildew filled the empty chamber. With the squish of mud from his footfalls, the emperor strode to his throne. Since the army had recently marched out to begin its northern campaign, things were quiet around the castle. The nobles had been advised that further meetings would not be required; there was no reason to discuss trade with the kingdom at war. He had not spoken to Teraken since administering his punishment the previous year, and Rynkor was leading the army, not that the emperor would want to spend time with that strange man anyway. Pothar was with Rynkor, and Dirwyn was gone too. Jaleph had not talked much to Ut after the unsuccessful ambush against Iridan and Myrin. Despite all his recent conquests in battle, Jaleph felt more alone than ever before.

After a few long moments of sitting in solitude, Jaleph returned to the palace. Another overcast sky dimmed the light in the dining hall as he sat down for his lunch. A servant went about lighting candles, and the small flames glistened in the polished wood of the table. While he awaited his meal, Jaleph arranged his elegant, silver utensils and looked impatiently about the room. Markis arrived, wheezing and panting as he carried a tray of roasted duck and steaming potatoes to the table. "Here you are, Majesty. I am certain you will find the meal to your liking," Markis blustered before turning to leave.

"Markis wait, where are you off to?"

"Back to the kitchens, Majesty. I can't leave those servants alone for too long, otherwise the place will never be cleaned."

The emperor took a moment to consider the large chef. He recalled the times Markis had spent with his father when Fenik and he were young. Nobody understood Halet's attraction to the annoying man, yet the two had been close friends. Was there something more to Markis? "Come back and sit with me for a moment," Jaleph said. "It has been too long since we talked."

Markis stared at the emperor wide-eyed since Jaleph normally hurried the chef away from the table. This was the first time the emperor had ever invited Markis to stay for a meal. "Are you certain Majesty? If the kitchen is not properly cleaned, I may have difficulty getting your dinner prepared timely."

"Are you questioning me?" Jaleph spat.

"Of course not, Sire," Markis replied hastily. "I just want to make certain that I will not be punished for a dinner that might not be served promptly. Certainly you will not fault me for that?"

"I understand Markis, sit down." Jaleph snatched a potato and stuffed it in his mouth. "Now tell me," he mumbled through his chewing, "where did you find this bird, and how did you prepare it?"

Markis happily grabbed a plate as he launched into an intricate tale recounting the preparation of the meal. The emperor continued to shovel food in his mouth as he forced himself to listen to every annoying word.

***

After completing his now daily run, Jaleph retired to his royal chambers to clean up before heading over to the library to find something to read. When he found nothing of interest, he returned dejectedly to his lonely room. Standing in front of the mirror he grabbed a blade and shaved his head. As he was wiping away the last traces of blood, a knock sounded. "Markis sends word that dinner will be late," Ut said as the emperor opened the door.

"I figured as much," Jaleph responded. "Is that all you have to say? Are you now my messenger boy?"

Ut chuckled at the jest, but Jaleph found no trace of humor in the laugh. "No, but there is an issue I would like to discuss."

The emperor stood quietly for a moment, waiting for Ut to continue. "Go on," he finally said, breaking the uncomfortable silence.

"I do not mean to offend, but I believe it is time for you to take a wife. Myrin will not be returning to Su'Meeryn—"

"No thanks to you!"

"Jaleph please, we had a sound strategy which should have succeeded. It is time to move on and you need an heir. We don't want any of the nobles getting devious ideas. If something were to happen to you, there is no successor."

Jaleph threw his washrag to the floor and glared at Ut. "Are you insinuating that someone is looking to kill me?"

"No, I am not saying that. But without an heir, I believe it would be prudent for you to consider the possibility."

The emperor considered this as he looked over to the window. With Myrin and Dirwyn gone he had no wish to marry, but he could not escape the feeling of solitude which engulfed him. "We have conquered lands, have we not, Ut?" Jaleph's companion nodded. "And we will soon conquer more. I have been considering this for some time. There must be an ample number of beautiful women within my domain."

Ut nodded again. "Very wise Jaleph. By taking a wife from one of those lands, you will strengthen your ties. I will see to it."

"No, you don't understand, Ut. I have no intention to marry. I have earned the right to indulge myself. Su'Meeryn will have a new custom. I will create my own harem."

"That is of course your decision, Jaleph, but I still think you should take a wife. A bastard for an heir will not make for a strong claim to your throne."

"I don't care!" Jaleph shrieked. "I am done with this conversation. You should leave, now!"

Ut stared back at the emperor; his eyes narrowed and his mouth tightened. As he struggled to maintain control, it seemed that Ut's beautiful features began to disappear. However, as a few moments passed, the emperor's advisor covered himself. His exquisite face returned and he left without speaking another word.

Jaleph returned to his mirror with a smile. He had enjoyed watching Ut squirm, and soon his palace would be filled with beautiful concubines. He felt the power growing within him, and there was no one who could stifle it.

Chapter 3

Thunder rumbled through dark clouds while the three men rode under the gate. A few cracks of lightning were the only fanfare to their departure. More thunder boomed as rain finally began to fall. "I can't recall ever seeing so much rain," muttered Iridan as he wiped his brow, but fresh precipitation immediately replaced the water that he had whisked away.

"The farmers must be happy," Worm replied motioning to the fields they were passing through.

"Yeah, I guess so," was Iridan's only response.

They did not talk much during the morning as the driving rain made it difficult to hear. By noon, the rainfall finally began to lessen and Iridan ordered a stop for lunch.

Kile dismounted and unpacked their food while searching about the countryside for any sign of movement. Iridan spotted a large tree and stepped beneath it to get shelter from the remaining drizzle. Worm approached and handed Iridan a piece of soft bread and a bag containing some mixed nuts. "Should we look for a rabbit?" Worm asked.

Iridan shook his head. "I don't want to linger too long. We need to get to Gorthon as soon as possible." He tossed a handful of nuts into his mouth as he looked over at Kile. The soldier remained near the horses peering about the countryside. "Do you think he'll act like this the whole trip?"

"Yes," Worm answered. "As I told you, he is very stubborn. You should have brought someone else along."

"I know what you think, but we'll have to make do. We can't waste time turning around."

Worm ripped off a piece of bread and uncorked his water skin. "Don't worry about him. He's angry that you forced him to come along but he will not shrink from his duties."

The unpleasant memory of Teracuss came again to Iridan's mind. "Well, I'm going to try to do something about this." He swallowed another mouthful of nuts and marched over towards their steeds.

"I haven't seen any movement. The horses are ready whenever you are," Kile said. "There will be plenty of water along the trail with all this rain."

"Good," Iridan responded. "Look, I'm sorry about forcing you to come along. I just felt you were the best person to have at my side."

"You don't need to apologize; it's my job to serve my king. If he deemed it a necessary task, I obey willingly."

"But I can see that you and Worm aren't getting along. I had a similar experience on a journey, and I know it is not pleasant."

"Don't concern yourself with that," Kile snickered. "I can deal with Worm. I just don't know why you think he will be of help."

Iridan looked back at Worm, who was sitting under the tree, munching happily on his bread, seemingly oblivious to the impending threat of Jaleph and Su'Meeryn. "I take it you've been to Worm's home?" Kile nodded. "Have you seen his library?" Kile nodded again. "Have you ever read any of his materials?"

"I don't know how to read."

"Oh," Iridan said trying to mask his surprise. "Well, anyway, he is familiar with some texts that should be of value to me."

"What does that have to do with our mission?"

"I wish I knew." He turned back to Kile with a resolute expression on his face. "I told Worm that I believe he's ready to offer more than he has in the past." Iridan took a deep breath as he continued, trying to shut out his own painful memories. "He displayed a different attitude when he came to help Myrin and me." When Kile's face remained unconvinced, Iridan knew he had not explained himself very well. "He certainly won't be of much use in combat, but he is very savvy. We might need him when negotiating with Gorthon's king."

"It's your choice," Kile shrugged, "and as I said, you need not worry about me."

"Will you be able to forgive him for what he did to you?"

"We better get going," was the only response as Kile repacked his supplies then mounted up.

Iridan was not sure if he should feel relief at his words. While he did not have to worry about Kile handling his duties, Iridan still hoped the two would be able to repair their damaged relationship.

"Didn't help, did it?" Worm asked as Iridan returned to the tree.

"No," answered Iridan as he picked up his food pack, "but I don't think he'll give us any problems."

"Of course not; Kile knows what's at stake. He won't jeopardize the mission because of me."

They strode through the mist back to their animals. "I guess that's all   I   can   ask   for,"   Iridan   said.

Chapter 4

Orange banners—soaked by the driving rain—flapped in the wind. Countless soldiers streamed down from a small hill to meet the attacking Su'Meeryn horde; battle cries issuing from their lips. The orange of the flags, reflecting off the rain-soaked armor of the troops from Tamar, danced in myriad directions. "Keep going!" Pothar yelled to his men as they struggled out of the muddy riverbank. Jaleph's troops greatly outnumbered the defenders, but Pothar knew that his warriors were in a precarious position: struggling through the thick mud while their enemy poured down from the ridge above.

He heard a scream to his right as the first casualty of the battle fell. Damn that bastard, Rynkor, Pothar thought, I told him I needed more men here. But his thoughts were cut short as the melee reached him. He struggled to defend himself from the swords swirling everywhere. The repeated clashes of steel pierced his ears as a stream of arrows flew from behind, searching for targets among the enemy. "About time," he muttered as his blade sliced the throat of a Tamarian warrior.

Thunder shook the ground as the men of Su'Meeryn began to push the defenders back. Unfortunately that meant up the ridge, so Pothar's soldiers remained at a disadvantage. He continued to push his men on, but for each Tamarian warrior who fell, two or three from Su'Meeryn joined him.

Pothar momentarily dropped back to survey the scene. The numbers of the enemy were greatly reduced, but his men were bunching up in the middle of the hill as they tried to climb. Pothar ran to his left. "To the side!" he called. "We can flank them. Move to the left!" His words went unheard, drowned out by the sounds of combat and the storm. Pothar raced back up the hill and began pulling men out from the battle. "To the left!" he ordered and finally his words began to register. As the warriors on his left started to spread out, his archers caught up and he sent them left as well.

When the soldiers of Tamar finally recognized the tactic, they tried to retreat. But now the hill worked against them— they could not turn to flee. Those who tried were quickly cut down, unable to climb quickly enough through the slippery mud. Dark blue banners rose as one last bolt of lightning blazed across the sky. The battle cry of Su'Meeryn echoed through the land as they pushed their attack further. The carnage became gruesome. When just a handful of defenders remained, the Tamarians finally threw down their weapons but to no avail. Fresh blood continued to spill until Pothar managed to force his way amidst the bedlam. "Enough!" he screamed, his pink face heaving with rage and exhaustion. "We have won. We will not butcher unarmed men." But when he turned back, he saw that only two soldiers from Tamar remained standing. He took a deep breath and ordered a count of his remaining troops. One hundred. Damn that Rynkor. They had left Okkgan with six hundred. All their battles had ended in victories, but five hundred soldiers were too many to lose. "Come along men, we have significantly weakened their defenses. We will return to camp and await new orders from our *leader*."

***

Pothar looked around at his battered and exhausted men as they trudged through the open fields southeast of Tamar. The weeks of constant marching and battle had taken their toll. He felt a strong sense of pride in them; despite all they had been through, no one complained. Everybody followed their orders without hesitation.

He sometimes wondered if the campaign would ever end. They had left Su'Meeryn at the first sight of spring, and upon reaching Okkgan, Rynkor—who had been assigned as the new military leader— took the main army towards Tamar. Dobrah had been left behind as the commander of Su'Meeryn's defenses with Teraken also remaining there as a guard. Pothar was given command of the force which had been ordered to strike from the northwest. It was a strange feeling being in charge of such a large number of soldiers. Certainly he had been in combat many times but never before as a leader. Along with his trepidation, Pothar occasionally felt conflicted about the whole operation. He felt no love for the people of Tamar, which had been one of the three countries responsible for the attack against Su'Meeryn, and he had heard the stories regarding their evil practices from Teraken. But having seen the emperor's treatment of Iridan and Myrin, he now wondered if Jaleph was any better. What would the land be like if Jaleph conquered all the neighboring kingdoms? Dobrah and he had talked much during the winter about what actions they should undertake, but what could the two of them do? Lacking any decent suggestions, they had decided to just continue as normal for now and wait to see what might develop.

355

Towards late afternoon, Pothar's drenched and muddy group finally slogged their way back into Su'Meeryn's camp. Other weary troops were also returning but Rynkor had yet to arrive. Pothar would not be able to do anything until his leader returned, so he got some fresh water to wash with and grabbed some food.

It was well after dark when he was awakened by a jolt to his shoulder, causing a lump of bread that was still on his chest to fall into the mud. He squinted up at Rynkor who said, "Here you are."

"Yeah, we returned in the afternoon," Pothar replied groggily.

"How it go?"

"We crossed the stream and defeated their force at the hill, but we lost a lot of men."

"You kill many?"

Pothar sat up and shook his head sadly. "Yes, we killed nearly all of them, and we brought back two prisoners. But we wouldn't have lost so many if you had given me the numbers I wanted."

"Good," Rynkor said, and Pothar wondered if the man had listened to all of his words. "We continue tomorrow. Attack again. Straight ahead. They all together."

"Tomorrow! Are you crazy? We need to rest, at least for a day or two."

"Tomorrow," Rynkor repeated as he turned to leave.

Pothar jumped up and spun Rynkor around. "We can't leave tomorrow. The men have been through too much. We need some rest."

"I in charge," Rynkor said, his pink eyes glowing in the light from the campfires. Pothar sensed—not for the first time—a boiling fury within Rynkor, as if he were a coiled snake ready to strike. "Tamar also tired. Tomorrow."

"Listen, I know you are in charge, but you need to be sensible." If that is even possible, he thought. "The men are tired and they can't continue in this condition. One day will not allow Tamar to prepare any better defense. If you attack tomorrow and we lose the battle, what do you think Jaleph will do to you?"

Pothar watched as Rynkor weighed the pleasure of his bloodlust against the consequences if he failed. "Next day." And with that Rynkor was gone.

Two days would be better, Pothar thought, but one day will certainly help. He returned to his bedroll with more feelings of doubt and wondered if he just should have said nothing. A defeat would certainly bring Jaleph's wrath down upon Rynkor, but Pothar could not face the idea of leading his troops into a losing battle. But then the question returned: what if we win?

Chapter 5

Mountains loomed menacingly to the left of the trio as they guided their horses silently under the ever-present overcast sky. They had only spotted one scouting group from Su'Meeryn, which they had easily avoided. After two days of riding through the non-stop rain, Iridan and his companions reached the pathway through the mountains that led into Gorthon.

"Here we are," Iridan announced, with some trepidation. He turned to Kile who was looking towards the mountains above them.

"We're being watched," commented Kile.

"We've probably been watched for several hours," Worm agreed. "There are plenty of places for sentries to hide in these mountains."

"That doesn't really matter," Iridan pointed out, "as we want to meet with them anyway." But his statement did little to quell the apprehension building within him. They had all heard stories of the dark men of Gorthon, and none were very pleasant. "Well, let's go in." Iridan turned his horse and started down the path.

It was only a matter of minutes before a dozen soldiers appeared from the rocks to confront them. Brown animal hides covered their ebony skin on which they all also wore a number of golden chains, arm bands and earrings. Superbly crafted swords and spears pointed at the trio, and they were ordered to dismount. One man stepped forward, his dark eyes examining the three. "Who are you?" he asked. "You are obviously not traders."

"We are messengers from Shekul. We have come to speak with your king," replied Iridan.

"Gorthon has no king, and we have no desire to hear from Shekul." The man turned away, displaying a long trail of black hair which was tied at his neck by a gold strand. He marched off as the remainder of the men pressed forward with their weapons raised to Iridan's eye-level.

"Wait," Iridan called. "You must let us speak. We come with urgent news."

The leader of the group paused for a moment before turning back to face Iridan. "Your news is of no consequence to us. We care not what you consider urgent."

"You don't consider war to be of concern?" asked Worm.

The man paused again as he regarded Worm. "Does the other one speak as well?" he asked motioning towards Kile.

"We all speak, my fine man," Worm continued. "In fact, that is why we're here, to speak with your people."

The man stared at Worm for a moment, obviously pondering his response. "We are aware of the war that is occurring, but it does not worry Gorthon."

"Perhaps not now, but if Su'Meeryn conquers the northern lands, Shekul will follow," Kile interjected. "Where do you think Jaleph will turn his sights after that? Besides what harm would it cause to allow us to speak?"

The man snorted at Kile's words. "Su'Meeryn attack Gorthon? You make me laugh my friend."

"You see," Worm responded with an inviting smile. "We are an entertaining group. So why not let us come and bring you more merriment?"

"Very well," the man replied with obvious amusement. "Come with me."

As Iridan and his companions were led through the mountainous terrain, none of the men of Gorthon spoke to them, and the three remained quiet as well. After about an hour of marching, they reached a large canyon and Gorthon's city, which was built into the very walls of the canyon itself. Iridan had known the people of Gorthon were miners, but he still marveled at the skill required to build such a city. "Very impressive," he murmured as they approached.

"Thank you," the leader of the group replied.

"I see nothing resembling a castle or a palace. Where does your king reside?"

Their guide huffed in displeasure. "I told you, Gorthon has no king."

"My apologies. We hear very little of Gorthon in the western lands as all requests to trade were always refused," responded Iridan. Can I at least ask your name? I'm Iridan, and this is Worm and Kile."

"I am Wox. Now, we are here. Leave your horses with Pak and follow me."

The trio handed their reins to the man Wox had indicated, and they headed down a pathway into the canyon. They passed a number of openings until they were brought into a large cave. Iridan was extremely surprised by the items of comfort present: thick animal furs covered the stone floor and large chairs circled the walls. A green light emanated from globes hanging on the walls, but Iridan could not discern the source of the light. He tried to examine the lanterns, but was interrupted by the guards at the cave entrance removing his weapons.

A large man emerged from the shadows of the cave and approached. He was very tall, with skin even darker than that of Wox and his group. He wore the same skins as Wox although his were dyed a deep red. Rather than the wide assortment of jewelry that all the other men possessed, he wore only one large necklace of shining platinum. From that chain dangled a huge gold amulet with a sparkling ruby in its center.

Next to him walked the first woman of Gorthon Iridan had ever seen. Her caramel skin shimmered in the strange light as her dark, exotic eyes examined the small group. The animal skins covering her slender body were dyed a lighter shade of red, almost pink. Thick silver bracelets covered her slim wrists, and a woven golden headband tied back her long, black hair. Her necklace and amulet mirrored that of her companion but was of half the size.

Iridan turned his eyes away from the striking woman back to the obvious leader of Gorthon. "Why are you here Wox?" the man asked angrily.

"My apologies, Vol, but these are messengers from Shekul requesting an audience."

Vol's face showed irritation as he repeated, "Why are you here?"

"I felt it important that you hear them."

With a look of exasperation, Vol motioned for the group to enter. As Iridan stepped forward, two guards followed just behind his companions. Vol motioned to the chairs and the group sat. "Now, can you tell me why Wox felt it necessary for you to interrupt my day?" Vol questioned.

Iridan began, "I'm sorry… Sir—"

"We have no titles here," Vol interrupted, "call me Vol."

"Of course. As we told Wox, Su'Meeryn is waging war in Tamar. If they prevail, which we expect they will, Amyon and Unimeth will certainly fall as well. Shekul would then be next. We have come to Gorthon seeking your aid against Su'Meeryn."

Vol laughed when Iridan had finished. "We know all about your war, and it does not concern us."

"But it should," Worm interjected. "Gorthon would certainly be Jaleph's next target after Shekul."

"You forget Mephosh," Vol pointed out.

This time Worm was the one to laugh. "Mephosh? That town and the others further south are of no consequence. Jaleph will never feel safe if Gorthon remains unconquered. You will be next."

"Perhaps," Vol responded with all traces of his irritation dissolved, "but we are safe here. Any army would have to come through the pass, and it is easily defended."

"Can you be certain of that?" Iridan asked.

"Yes."

Iridan began to respond but Worm placed a hand on his forearm. "Gorthon is certainly strong within your mountain realm, but Jaleph obviously has unseen forces at his disposal. How else can you account for the relative ease with which they conquered Labyn?"

Vol considered Worm for a moment with a smile, and Iridan's spirit rose until the leader of Gorthon spoke again. "Jaleph is a fool, and I care not what he does. We can defend ourselves against any attack from the west."

"Sire," Iridan began, "I mean Vol, you have heard about the attack against Su'Meeryn?" Vol nodded. "Well, that army had no reason to believe they would be stopped but we all know what happened there." Vol nodded again.

"And my friend Iridan here should know," Worm quickly continued, apparently figuring he had come up with a way to appeal to Vol. "He is the one after all who flew on the back of that dragon."

"Is that so?" asked Vol.

"Yes," Iridan responded apprehensively.

"Well, you must tell me all about it as we plan our joint campaign against Su'Meeryn," Vol stated.

"Really? That's wonderful news!" Iridan proclaimed.

"What do you find me to be, a fool?" Vol stated, showing pleasure with himself at his jest. "Now look my white-skinned friends, it has been a pleasant diversion meeting you, but our time is done. Wox, escort them out of our land."

"But you can't just—" Kile began, until two swords flashed in front of his face.

"Do not try my patience further," Vol ordered. "You were allowed your audience, and your plea has been rejected." Vol grasped the arm of his woman and disappeared back into the dark recesses of the cave. Clearly there would be no further discussion. Wox motioned for Iridan and his companions to follow, and once they left the cave their weapons were returned. They climbed back up the trail with Wox as he led them to the mountain path alone.

"Forgive me, I am not familiar with Gorthon's ruling structure," Worm said to their guide, "but Vol certainly appeared to be your king."

"We have no king," Wox stated.

"I know, you said that before. Might you educate me then?"

"Vol is our leader. When he dies, we will select another leader."

"Interesting," Iridan said. "So Vol's heir won't be your next leader."

"No, not if he isn't chosen."

They walked a few minutes in silence until Worm asked. "Why was it so difficult to be granted an audience with Vol? Don't you receive emissaries from other lands?"

"Not usually."

"Vol seemed angered that you brought us to him. Will you be punished?" Iridan continued questioning their guide.

Wox stopped and turned an angered eye towards his charges. "Why would I be punished? Do you think the people of Gorthon to be uncivilized?"

"Of course not," Iridan responded, stunned by Wox's strong words. "It is just that if my king were to be so angered with one of my actions, I might certainly be punished."

Wox looked into Iridan's eyes, apparently attempting to determine if he was sincere. "No, I will not be punished."

"Good, I would not have wanted to cause you any trouble."

"But why was Vol so annoyed that you allowed us the audience?" asked Worm.

Wox snorted. "Vol's temper is short and he enjoys to bluster, though just because I won't be punished doesn't mean it was a pleasurable experience."

"Wox," Worm continued. "May I ask you? What do you think of what we had to say?"

"Why?"

"You certainly found it important enough to bring us to Vol."

Wox considered for a moment. "Vol is correct. Gorthon is safe, but safety should not always be our only concern."

Iridan was somewhat shocked when Kile spoke up. "Why are you so certain that Gorthon is safe? The mountain pass gives you a strong defense, but a large enough army would certainly be able to break through."

"You need not worry about Gorthon," the dark man replied. They continued on until Wox turned to Iridan. "Are you truly the man who flew on the back of the dragon, or was that just a ploy?"

"No, it is true," Worm answered. "Can't you tell? Look at those strong arms and that determined face. Could it have been anyone else?"

Wox chuckled at Worm's jest. "I like your friend. Too bad I have to send you away. I would like to hear stories of the adventure," he said to Iridan.

"I don't consider it an adventure," Iridan retorted as they reached their horses. "Many of my friends died because of that attack, and I don't care to discuss it. Now more will die because of your decision." As they mounted up, Iridan immediately regretted his last words. It was not Wox's fault that Vol had rejected their request. Wox had allowed them to enter the land and brought them before Vol, but Iridan did not feel much like apologizing. The thought of Jokk-al Ystren killing Teracuss being called an adventure was too aggravating. Certainly Wox had not meant it that way but Iridan did not care. He just wanted to leave this land of cowards.

Chapter 6

Sweat from his scalp mingled with the rain and burned his eyes as it streamed down his face. He wiped it away, but the gauntlet on his hand opened a new cut on his face. Pothar swore to himself while studying the battle. Su'Meeryn had routed the last of the Tamarian army and the retreating troops would never reach the safety of their castle. He flinched when a boulder, launched from Tamar's castle, fell ten feet to his left. As the boulder rolled away, it left the carnage of what had only seconds ago been a man. Fools, Pothar thought, they don't even know who they are shooting at.

To his right, Rynkor swung his customary twin blades. Bodies dropped around him as blood splattered in the pouring rain. When the last victim fell, Pothar was a bit surprised to see Rynkor gasp for breath. He approached Rynkor, who was clutching at a large wound on his arm. The pair looked around as another boulder flew from the castle. But the battle on the soaked ground had ended; the last of Tamar's soldiers had been killed. Rynkor stared at him and Pothar realized that the strange man – their leader - had no idea what to do.

"We have to keep going," Pothar said. "They are still trying to organize their defenses in the castle. We can't give them that opportunity."

"Must rest," Rynkor panted.

"No, it will be worse for us if we do," continued Pothar, aware of the irony that he was the one now arguing to push their attack. "We have to take advantage while they're still disorganized."

"Yes," replied Rynkor, and Pothar saw the man's eyes change as exhaustion gave way to his returning blood lust. "How far back the ladders?"

"They should be arriving soon," Pothar replied, but Rynkor just stood silently before him. Rynkor's combat skills were certainly unmatched. Unfortunately strategy eluded him and once again Pothar marveled at the stupidity of putting such a man in charge of an army. "Archers," Pothar continued, "we need to keep their troops occupied." But Rynkor remained motionless. "Never mind," and Pothar turned away from his leader. "Archers up!" he called. "Let loose over the castle walls. Don't stop until the ladders arrive!"

As Su'Meeryn's archers took position, scores of arrows flew down from the castle. Some found targets, but most fell harmlessly to the ground. The boulders also continued to catapult towards them, but the men of Su'Meeryn were able to avoid them easily enough.

Arrows continued their assault through the rain-bathed sky until the siege ladders finally came up. "Don't stop," Pothar ordered. "Straight to the castle!" Soldiers rushed to set the ladders and began their climb. More arrows shot down from the castle and many of the attackers fell with shafts protruding from their bodies. Some of the ladders were pushed off, but despite the defenses the Su'Meeryn soldiers continued their relentless assault. The fallen ladders were hoisted up again, and the attackers finally reached the top. Once Rynkor saw combat begin on the castle wall, he rushed gleefully towards the ladders. Pothar looked back over his shoulder, noting that the archers had dropped their bows, and followed them to the castle.

Most of Su'Meeryn's soldiers were now on the castle wall. When Pothar jumped off the ladder he spotted Rynkor already down in the courtyard. Blood and flesh erupted in all directions from Rynkor's blades. The rest of their troops swarmed the castle like ants on a rampage. Nobody was providing direction to the assault, but there was no-one nearby to whom Pothar could give orders. To his left, Pothar saw a large throng of Tamarian troops burst from a door and begin to overwhelm a small group of his men. He unsheathed his sword and rushed forward.

By the time Pothar reached the group, a number of his men had already fallen. Pothar leaped over corpses and drove his sword into the stomach of one of the defenders. He spun as his weapon sliced the next man's neck and was temporarily blinded by a crimson shower. He quickly dove to the ground and tried to roll away, but was stopped by what he figured was another body. As he tried to wipe the blood from his face, he felt a blade cut his thigh. He cried in pain awaiting the next blow but it never came. Finally able to see, he noticed that another group of Su'Meeryn attackers had come to their aid and all of the defenders were now engaged. He stood, quickly checking his leg. The cut was long but it did not appear to be too deep, so he took a step back and looked for Rynkor. He easily spotted the strange white hair, stained with trails of pink from all the blood and rain. Bodies were heaped all around him, and Rynkor's head spun around looking for his next victim. As soon as he located the nearest enemy he sprung, swords poised to rip through flesh. That bastard, Pothar thought, he has no concept of leading an attack.

"To me," Pothar called to the Su'Meeryn soldiers about him who had finished off their immediate adversaries. "Stay together and follow me." Pothar ran through the increasingly slippery mud and heard the men behind. They darted through the courtyard to the palace door. Two surviving guards tried to stop them but fell quickly. They pushed through a huge foyer and were met by a large group of well-armed defenders in shining armor. "Here we go," Pothar murmured, "these must be the royal bodyguards."

A shining axe swung towards Pothar which he quickly deflected with his blade. Pain shot from his wounded leg as he spun around to engage another guard. Their swords clashed as Pothar sought for an opening in the man's defense. The melee continued until Pothar's sword sliced through and cut the man's arm. The Tamarian stumbled for a moment which was all Pothar needed, and he drove his sword through the armor, into the man's heart. Pothar looked up and saw a large man wearing a silver breast plate, purple robe, and a small crown of glistening jewels atop his head. "Take him alive!" Pothar called as he rushed forward. He pushed past a defender and engaged the king.

The king's sword shot forward quicker than Pothar expected and nearly caught him in the face. Pothar managed to turn his head and the blade glanced off his helmet. Tamar's monarch sneered as he struck again. At least he fights, Pothar thought; however, he also realized that he was quite outmatched by this man. Before he had time to worry about the king's skill, one of the guards had pushed in front of his monarch, and sliced through, cutting his stomach. Pothar stepped back as his opponent pressed his advantage, feigned to the left and caught the man's thigh. Steel clashed against steel as both men sought an opening. Pothar tried to overwhelm his man with a rapid series of blows as blood began to pool about them from their respective wounds. The Tamarian was nonplussed by the maneuver, but the onslaught unfortunately caused Pothar to slip on the blood-soaked floor. With Pothar on the ground, the king's guard lunged and caught Pothar's sword with the edge of his axe. The man twisted his weapon and Pothar lost his grip. As his sword rattled on the floor, the axe was raised above his head and Pothar instinctively raised his left arm to ward off the blow. The axe fell and sliced through his wrist. He shrieked in pain as his hand bounce off his head and hit the ground, but before the man could swing again, two swords flew above Pothar and drove through each of the defender's eyes. Pothar managed to glance up as he saw the crimson-soaked form of Rynkor leap towards the king.

"No," Pothar managed to say as he grabbed at his wrist, trying to stem the tide of streaming blood. He watched helplessly as Rynkor engaged the king. Rynkor's blades swirled around in a dizzying display of speed and coordination; however, for the first time, Rynkor's attack was held off by the expert swordsmanship of the king. But Rynkor was relentless. His twin blades eventually started to break through and find flesh as Pothar's head began to swim. His vision became cloudy as Rynkor spun around in what appeared to be a bizarre ballet. The strange warrior squealed with joy as the sword flew from his opponent's hand. The king dove to the floor, desperately grasping for his weapon, but two sword points immediately pressed against his neck.

"No," Pothar whimpered again as the agony threatened to overwhelm him. Heavy eyelids began to close as the king slowly rose, and he stood defiantly before his victor. Pothar whispered a final no, but whether Rynkor heard him, Pothar did not know. Rynkor giggled as he swung one last time. The king's head flew from his body as Pothar collapsed, his pain finally gone.

Chapter 7

Jaleph's boots splashed through puddles as he trotted down the streets of his castle. When he and his guards approached the palace, he was pleased to notice that his endurance seemed to improve with each passing day.

After finishing his run, Jaleph washed and went down to lunch. He had again asked Markis to join him since he could think of no other companion with whom he wished to spend his time. "So, what have you prepared for us today, Markis?"

The whole floor creaked when Markis dropped his incredible bulk onto the chair opposite the emperor. "I have some wonderful venison with which I prepared a marvelous stew. I experimented with some new seasoning. I am certain that you will be very pleased."

"Your creations always please me Markis."

While Jaleph and Markis indulged in the delicious meal, the door to the dining hall opened and Ut strode in. "Please excuse us Markis, but I need to speak with Jaleph."

"Ut, what is the meaning of this?" Jaleph spat through his still full mouth, "You do not send anyone away from my table."

"Markis, leave now," Ut continued. "Jaleph, we need to discuss the campaign."

The large chef's eyes danced uncertainly between the two men. "You may leave, Markis," Jaleph eventually said in a barely controlled voice. He was angered at Ut's words, but he figured the news must be important to cause this interruption.

When Markis had left the room, Ut sat at the table. "The battle with Tamar is not going as well as planned."

"Are we losing?"

"No, but we are not winning as handily as we should. Tamar will fall, but we are losing too many men. Our ability to conquer Amyon and Unimeth may be jeopardized."

"Perhaps we should pull back after taking Tamar. We would certainly have enough strength to take Shekul, and then we could rebuild our forces," Jaleph replied, pleased with himself for deciding upon such a wise strategy.

"No! That won't do. We must continue!"

"Watch yourself Ut," Jaleph whispered menacingly. "You will not talk to your emperor in such a tone."

Jaleph watched as Ut glared at him. This was the first time he could remember seeing such obvious disapproval on his advisor's face. He also noted that Ut was not trying to hide it. "Jaleph, if we stop our advance we will also be giving Amyon and Unimeth more time to prepare" Ut hissed. "And let us not forget, Iridan is still alive. That concerns me. He might be attempting to thwart our plans."

"What can one man do against us?" Jaleph asked as anger started to grow into a simmering rage.

"You of all people should know the answer to that!"

Jaleph exploded in fury at the discussion of Iridan and his haunted memories of Myrin. His fist slammed the table, but stopped short at a continued look of anger from Ut. Jaleph was beginning to feel a sense of fear towards his advisor. "Fine, what do you propose?" he replied while faltering in his attempt to muster a sense of superiority.

"We need to start conscripting soldiers," Ut stated flatly. "Our forces have to be strengthened."

"Conscription? Su'Meeryn has never undertaken such measures."

"You have no alternative. If you don't, you risk not being able to continue the campaign beyond Tamar. What would happen then? Su'Meeryn would face the possibility of another attack next year."

Jaleph did not like the idea of conscripting troops, but he also realized that another attack on his castle could be devastating. And besides, what did he really care about those people? When the campaigns came to a conclusion he would have far more subjects to replace any he might lose. "Very well. How should we go about this?"

"Summon the nobles and order each of them to raise troops. They all have many dealings with the farmers and merchants. Provide some soldiers to each in case there is any trouble. If men won't come willingly they will be taken. Provide one thousand gold pieces for every fifty men they bring."

"One thousand! Are you crazy?"

Despite Jaleph's strong words, the anger on Ut's face had dissipated to one of perverse joy. "One thousand will be nothing once our conquest is complete."

Jaleph also smiled at the thought. "As usual, you are right. We will start today."

***

The empty audience chamber echoed like a dungeon as the nobles entered, bewilderment etched on their faces. While they had met with Jaleph many times in the past, this was the first time he had actually summoned them, and they obviously had no idea of what to expect. They reached the emperor, sitting on his throne and surrounded by guards. Yonath, of course, was the first to speak. "How may we serve you, Sire?"

As Jaleph recounted Ut's plan, the looks on the nobles' faces grew from bewilderment to utter disbelief. "Forced conscription? You can't mean that," Gentine interjected.

"I meant every word. If my army isn't strong enough, we risk losing all that we have gained," Jaleph replied forcefully.

"I wunt," I'a'uju'uh stated.

The emperor slowly stood from his throne. He glared at I'a'uju'uh before turning briefly to face each of the other nobles. "You will do as I command. You all will. Am I understood?" He then motioned to his guards who each took a threatening step forward.

"Sire, you are, of course, more than generous," said Yonath. "A thousand pieces of gold is a fair compensation." All the other nobles nodded nervously in agreement, all except I'a'uju'uh. He continued to glare back at the emperor.

"Good," Jaleph responded as he kept his eyes riveted on I'a'uju'uh. "We will meet again shortly, and I expect to hear positive results of your endeavors." He then dismissed the nobles and returned to his throne. He pulled the leather band from his bald head and gazed at the emerald stone. The leather around the stone was starting to fray and multiple sweat stains were clearly visible. Despite the fact that the band had belonged to his father, it no longer held the appeal it once did. This will not do, he thought; I am now the emperor; it is time for me to have a proper crown.

Chapter 8

"It's about time," Iridan muttered as they reached Shekul's castle gates, which loomed overhead like a foreboding nightmare. The damp journey home had been one of reflective silence, as their failure with Gorthon left feelings of despair. Iridan had found little desire to speak to Worm, and Kile, as usual, had refused to say much. Iridan had hoped that this mission would be his one chance to finally move past the anguish of his lost family. Instead all he carried back was another failure.

As they passed through the gate, Kile dropped from his mount and handed his reins to a guard. Iridan was about to do the same but Worm stopped him. "No Iridan. I would like for you to come to my estate with me."

Iridan shook his wet head. "I need to report to the king, and then I just want to go to my room and dry out."

"What is there to report? Kile can handle that," he said, motioning Kile to go into the castle. "Now you'll come with me."

"I really don't want to Worm."

"And I really don't care," Worm continued. "I didn't want to go with you to Gorthon, but I did. So you can indulge me."

"Fine," Iridan replied. "If you want me to come, I'll come." And why not? Iridan thought. He did not relish the thought of recounting their mission to Josu. Kile could handle that, and he could sit in one of Worm's rooms as easily as his own.

***

When they reached Worm's family estate, they rode around to the back of the main house. Iridan's eyes were greeted by a lush, rolling plain with scores of large horses milling about. Worm and Iridan hopped down from their mounts, which a servant led away, and with an offering gesture, Worm directed Iridan inside. After changing out of their filthy and saturated clothes into warm robes, they entered the study. As they sat, the pair were each handed a large goblet of water before being left alone. Iridan took a deep drink as he sunk into a soft chair.

"A difficult trip, wasn't it?" Worm asked.

"Yes."

"What are you going to do now?"

Iridan took another drink before replying. "What do you mean?"

"Well, your plan didn't succeed, but the threat still remains."

An ironic laugh escaped from Iridan's mouth. "Why is this up to me? Haven't I done enough already?" Why does it seem that everything is always up to me?

Worm stared at his companion with a look that seemed a bit too knowing. "I don't know. You tell me."

Iridan set the goblet on the floor and slumped further down into the chair. The familiar self pity began to creep back into his spirit as he recounted all the death that had surrounded him. He thought he had finally overcome those feelings, but now, following his failure at Gorthon all the despair came crashing back. "Maybe it is someone else's time," Iridan replied quietly as he stood to leave.

Worm jumped from his chair and grabbed Iridan's wrist. Both pairs of eyes looked down and caught sight of the gray ring on Iridan's finger. "The tables have turned, have they not?" Worm noted. After a pause he continued. "Why don't you stay here for a while? You said you wanted to read about Naar. I'll give you what I have."

"Thank you, but not just now," responded Iridan, feeling some of his depression melt away due to Worm's newfound interest. But despite that, he no longer cared about reading the words of Naar. What good could it do now? "Please just show me where I can relieve myself before I return to my room. We can talk further tomorrow if you would like," he offered as a concession to Worm's thoughtfulness.

"It will take some time for your clothes to be cleaned and dried. There is no need to rush off. Kile would have reported to Josu by now, and besides, I thought you wanted to study Naar. That is what you have always badgered me about, isn't it?"

"Yes it is, but I'm no longer interested in that now." After a pause he continued, "Why this sudden concern in having me read it?"

Worm returned to his chair and sat quietly for a few moments. Iridan could tell his friend was searching for the appropriate words. "To be honest, I'm not really sure. It just seems to be something you need."

"I appreciate your kindness, but I'm too exhausted to worry about Naar right now." Iridan stared at the exquisite paintings on the walls then ran his hands across the soft robe hanging on his body. He shook his head thinking of the tiny home he had shared with Myrin in Su'Meeryn. "I'll come back tomorrow. For now, I really just want to be left alone and leave as soon as my clothes are ready."

"If that is what you want. I'll see you then."

***

Thick trees and brush engulfed him. Overhead, branches and leaves blotted out the sky while dense grass reached his knees. The sweet odor of moist foliage penetrated his nostrils as shades of green met his gaze in every direction. But despite the vegetation, no movement betrayed any sign of life and no sound reached his ears.

He raised a large knife with his right hand and began to slice a path before him. The branches and vines began to fall, and Iridan advanced with the rhythm of his blade. As he pushed his body through the jungle, the uncut foliage ripped holes in his shirt and trousers. Blood began to trickle from his flesh under the constant attack of the sharp thorns which surrounded him.

He continued on despite the pain of the unrelenting assault of vegetation. Blood poured freely from his wounds as his shirt snagged on a branch. The fabric tore from his body when he pulled himself free and a tangle of thorns caught his arm, ripping off a large hunk of skin. Iridan cried out in agony, but still he fought his way through the thick jungle.

The foliage seemed to have its own malevolent mind. Despite his efforts to cut a clear path, the organic attack continued. Vines snuck up his ankles and bore into his legs. He stumbled for a moment as he pulled free, leaving his trousers and more patches of flesh behind. The misery radiated up from his legs all the way to his brain; he had no idea how he could continue. His entire body was now bathed in blood. Thorns continued to avoid his blade, grabbing at exposed muscle. The agony threatened to overwhelm him and he crashed to his knees, vomiting. The filth ran down his crimson-stained body, seemingly finding every hole in his skin.

But he fought through the misery as he rose to his feet and continued his journey.

The exertions of his forced trek now caused sweat to teem from his pores, increasing his suffering as the salt mixed with blood and vomit, and entered his gaping wounds. Tears welled up in his eyes, but still he continued. Dense brush grasped at his shoes and pulled them from his feet as he fought to get free. With his next step, his foot found a sharp rock, its razor-like edges cutting him all the way to the bone.

He cried out from the torture, but did not alter his pace.

The fight through the jungle threatened to tear away all his skin. With each new gash, his agony multiplied. His blade hacked at a branch but it just pushed away and sprung back at him. The pain was too much to bear as it hit his face and thorns pierced his eyes. He could not continue and dropped to his knees weeping. His head hung heavy at his neck and he fell forward into the dense brush. Iridan lay there for an undetermined period of time as the pain coursed through his body and his blood drained away. He had no idea how he still lived. Mercifully, as consciousness began to seep away from his mind, the pain also vanished.

He opened his eyes and slowly rose. Instead of vegetation, a huge mountain loomed before him. A wide plain opened up to his right, and to his left he saw an ocean. He turned around and found the jungle, and at his feet a deep chasm which bore into the earth.

Iridan examined his body. All his wounds had disappeared, but he remained naked, except for Naar's ring. He stood still for a moment before taking a couple steps forward, away from the chasm. A tingling sensation then began from his finger, under the ring.

Who are you?

Not again, Iridan thought.

Who are you?

"What do you want from me?" he cried. The tingling increased, and he looked down at the ring. The metal appeared to transform as the ring glowed with a white light.

Who are you?

A name, he sensed a name. "I'm..." The glow of the ring grew brighter. His finger no longer tingled; it now began to sting.

Who are you?

The stinging sensation grew more intense as the illumination increased. He tried to ignore the pain as he fought to uncover the name which remained buried within him.

You must arrive.

His finger burned as hot flames flickered from the ring. "I'm Iridan." He knew his name, but he also knew that somehow his answer was wrong. As his mind sought for the correct response, the fire grew and engulfed his entire hand.

No more. Who are you?

The white flames crawled up his arm and he roared out in pain. The name was just in front of him, but misery kept forcing it away.

Who are you?

His body withered as the white-hot flames consumed him. He screamed, seeing nothing but white. Skin melted and dropped from his body as he continued to scream. The agony was too much. *Who are you?* Muscles and tendons fell away. *Who are you?* Bones snapped and crumbled. Organs smoldered; they billowed away like smoke. His brain fell to the ground and landed on the ring. The pain was gone. He was gone; everything was gone.

Who are you?

"Iridan!" A hand shook his shoulder. "Iridan, wake up!" Iridan's eyes opened and he looked into the beautiful face of his cousin. "Thank goodness. I didn't think that I'd ever be able to wake you. Are you alright?"

With a shaking hand he slowly wiped the sweat from his brow and forced his body up. "It was just a dream," he mumbled.

"Just a dream?" Dirwyn exclaimed, "I don't think so!"

"As a matter of fact it was," he replied sharply, as the torturous visions remained fresh in his mind. "What time is it?"

"It's morning," she answered cautiously, obviously still concerned regarding his wellbeing. "Kile informed the king of your mission. Josu asked me to bring you to his chambers. He seemed upset that you did not report to him yourself."

"I had something I needed to do."

"Yes, but you were in charge. You should have been the one who reported to him."

Iridan wanted to lash out at his cousin again. Must everything in his life seem so difficult? But, it was not her fault. She was just relaying Josu's message. "The report was brief; there is no reason why Kile couldn't handle it."

He stood from his bed, unable to push away the images from the dream. It had been a long time since the last one of those dreams, and they never had been this intense before. He hoped this was not an omen for future nights. After splashing some water on his face, he followed his cousin from the room, dreading the thought of confronting Josu with his failure.

As they started down the hallway Iridan glanced down at his ring. It remained its usual, unimpressive shade of gray. He briefly scratched at it with his finger, but still he found nothing of significance. "I'm going to need to get some food first," he mentioned as he realized how hungry he felt.

"I'm not sure that you should keep the king waiting."

Iridan looked angrily at Dirwyn's face, but he only saw an expression of worry. His irritation quickly dissolved. "Dirwyn, always so concerned about everyone around her."

"Maybe you should have a quick bite first," she replied modestly, ignoring his comment. "But please make it quick. I would hate for Josu to find any fault with my favorite cousin."

Chapter 9

"Isn't this a little premature?" Jaleph asked as Ut strode through the crowd of the audience chamber to stand before the emperor.

"No, we need to show them that you are in charge here, and that they must obey all your directives without hesitation." Ut motioned towards the merchants and various other townspeople standing silently behind the nobles.

"Of course. By the way, I was thinking, I believe it is time that I have a crown. I am emperor now. This old headband no longer seems appropriate. A crown would portray the proper image."

The corners of Ut's mouth pulled up slightly. "I like your idea, but let us discuss that at a later time. Right now you have business to attend to."

"Of course," responded Jaleph. "Is everyone here?" Ut looked out at the crowd then nodded for Jaleph to continue. "Very good." The emperor stood from the throne and raised his hand. The assembly quieted as he began. "As everyone here is aware, I ordered the nobles to go back to their lands and muster troops for my army. You have been called before me to advise regarding your progress." Jaleph turned to Yonath and said, "Proceed."

"Certainly, Majesty," Yonath responded quickly. "However, before I begin, I would like to say that this process continues. I secured twenty-five men who have reported to the castle to begin training. They were not very happy about the assignment, and as word spread, it became more difficult to find willing men."

"I do not want to hear your excuses Yonath," barked Jaleph. "This is a compulsory assignment. I expect you to enlist more than twenty-five men."

"As I mentioned, the process is ongoing. I will have more men soon and I will double my efforts."

Jaleph glared at Yonath. "There should be no need for that. Were you not giving me your maximum effort previously? I should not be getting your full cooperation only now."

"I apologize Majesty, just a poor choice of words," Yonath replied nervously. "Rest assured, you will be fully satisfied with my efforts once they are complete."

"You had better hope so. Now, Gentine, what do you have to report?"

"Like Yonath has stated, the procedure continues. As of today I have conscripted forty, and I expect for that number to increase substantially. However, may I say Majesty, this loss of men will create a significant hardship for their families. Too few will be left behind to harvest crops."

The emperor's mouth curled into a sneer. "Are you questioning my judgment, Gentine?"

"I would never do anything of the kind," she stated, and even though she bowed her head in deference, Jaleph thought he sensed a trace of sarcasm in her words. He decided to ignore her attitude, as the task of bolstering the army was too important for him to be distracted. "I'm just pointing out that we will need help in the fields. The castle inhabitants will suffer too if we don't harvest enough food.

"We will suffer more if our army is defeated. I want an update from both of you in two days, and I expect to hear good news regarding your results. Understood?" Both Gentine and Yonath nodded. Jaleph then turned his attention to the next noble. " I'a'uju'uh, I hope that you have better news." I'a'uju'uh stood motionless before him. "Well," Jaleph continued, "report. How many men do you have for me?"

"None," I'a'uju'uh replied flatly as a gasp rose from the crowd.

"Quiet," Ut bellowed.

"Now, would you care to repeat that?" Jaleph asked, feeling completely stunned by I'a'uju'uh's response.

"None."

"Explain yourself," the emperor commanded.

"I tuld ya, I wunt."

"Is that so? I know that you heard my order, so are you telling me that you decided not to obey?"

"I wunt force men t' fight," responded I'a'uju'uh.

Ut leaned down and whispered instructions in Jaleph's ear. The emperor turned a shocked expression towards his advisor, but Ut's face displayed stern resolve. Punishment was certainly called for; however, was Ut going too far? But what did he care? He had lost so much, and he would not let one disobedient noble risk his recent gain. He ordered I'a'uju'uh to the back of the chamber and had all the other nobles advise on their progress. Once they had each provided their reports, he returned his attention to I'a'uju'uh. He stammered for a moment from the weight of his next words when he ordered his guards forward. Half a dozen soldiers came up to the throne as he continued, "Take I'a'uju'uh out to the courtyard and execute him. I don't care how." When the guards failed to move Jaleph's voice boomed over the shocked audience, "Now! I will not suffer anyone in my empire who refuses to obey." He turned his attention to the crowd. "I hope this is understood. Anyone else who chooses to follow I'a'uju'uh's example will meet the same fate."

As I'a'uju'uh was dragged from the building, Jaleph dismissed the nobles with a stern warning regarding the success he expected from their additional conscriptions. Once the audience chamber was empty, he turned his attention to Ut. "Now, what kind of crown do you think I should have?"

***

With his new-found feelings of power, Jaleph returned to the palace. His personal guards followed him up the stairs to the recently renovated room which now housed his harem. He had not entered the room since work had begun, so it was with some apprehension that he opened the door. The soft scent of flowers greeted him as he entered. Large pillows sat in every corner of the dimly-lit room and a few couches rested atop a silver and blue rug. A painting hung across from the door with the face of a black wolf staring back at him. He walked in, and two young girls entered from a dark alcove. I guess Ut needs more time to find some additional girls suitable enough for me, Jaleph thought. He glanced back at his guards, not quite sure what to do with them. He then remembered Ut mentioning something about the measures he had taken with the girls to guarantee his safety. With a wave of his hand, Jaleph dismissed the guards and joined the girls on one   of   the luxurious couches.

Chapter 10

"I'm disappointed to hear that Gorthon will not be joining us against Jaleph," Josu said as Iridan stood next to him at the large table. "And I was not too happy that you did not report to me yourself upon your return." Iridan looked down apologetically at the king and tried to divert his eyes from the bits of crusty egg entrenched in the corners of Josu's mouth. Iridan was surprised to find the king sitting alone. In fact, he could not remember ever seeing Josu without his entourage before. After taking a drink of a sweet-smelling juice, Josu raised a bony arm and offered a chair to his visitor.

"I apologize for that, Sire," Iridan replied. "There was a matter that I needed to attend to with Worm, and I felt Kile was capable of delivering the unfortunate news."

Josu's eyes narrowed for a moment before his face returned to its usual bright disposition, again reminding Iridan of a convex moon. "A mistake that I am sure you will not make again. I am just sorry that the mission ended in failure."

"You need not concern yourself with me, Majesty. We have enough to worry about as it is."

"Yes, of course. I do worry for my kingdom. But I am concerned for you as well." The focus of Josu's eyes sharpened as he wiped his mouth.

"I'm gratified," Iridan said, somewhat perplexed. "Unfortunately, my well being is of little consequence right now."

"I told you he would respond this way," Flicia purred as she entered the room. She stopped at the table and sat close to the king.

"Ah, the lovely Flicia," Josu bellowed, and he reached over to kiss her on the cheek. He then turned his attention back to Iridan. "What should we do now?"

"Why are you asking me?" Iridan asked, fatigued by the fact that every major crisis over the past couple of years always revolved around him. "Shouldn't you be asking Flicia, or Surik and Forim?"

Josu glanced at Flicia before responding. "I trust you."

"Well, I thank you for that; however, I don't know what you think I can provide."

"Josu believes that you are a wise man, Iridan," Flicia interjected. "You are our best hope."

"How can you say that? I failed at Gorthon, and I don't think I can be of help to anyone again." Certainly not Myrin, he thought as his chin dropped to his chest.

"Snap out of it Iridan!" Josu barked, startling Iridan at the sudden harshness of his words. "You're depressed and I understand that. I also understand the threat facing my kingdom. We must act!" But the king's attitude quickly softened as Flicia lightly stroked his forearm.

Iridan stared at the king's strange face before turning his gaze to Flicia. He silently thanked her for the simple gesture which had dissipated the king's anger. Her beauty caused a stirring in him that he had not felt in some time. Their previous meetings suddenly came to mind, as did her obvious flirtations with him. But why now? It was not the time or place to indulge in such feelings. Besides, Flicia obviously had a special relationship with Josu. Even if she truly yearned for him, he could not act upon that; he certainly did not want to make an enemy of this king too. He felt immediate guilt at this surfacing of his lust at such a time and quickly buried it away, realizing how truly lonely he had become since losing Myrin. As reflections of loneliness swirled through his head, he considered his cousin and her new found relationship with Surik, which only deepened his despair.

"Iridan!" Josu screeched, interrupting his musings.

"Fine," Iridan replied, cursing his self pity. "Let me consider this for a while."

"Certainly," Josu replied softly, smiling again, and Iridan sat in awe of the king's sudden and intense mood swings. "We shall meet for lunch." Flicia gently squeezed his hand, and Josu corrected himself. "No, dinner. We shall meet at dinner. That will give us all some time to consider our options."

"Thank you," Iridan said as he excused himself. He left the king's chamber and walked aimlessly through the castle, wondering what the scant few hours before dinner might reveal to him. Finally reaching his room, he gazed at his reflection in the filthy mirror. The guilt over his new-found lust for Flicia returned. He missed Myrin, but he also missed the pleasures of being with a woman. "We could all be dead soon, and I'm sitting here thinking about my own personal desires" he muttered to himself as he pulled his boots from his feet. "Some hero."

He needed to leave his room. He had wasted too much time there over the winter and he refused to fall back into his old habit. "Fine!" he spat, snatching his sword from the wall and rushing out the door. He trotted to the troop barracks where he was greeted with some surprise.

At his request, he joined the other soldiers in their drills. His skills with the blade had certainly diminished over the months of inactivity, and his swordplay would certainly need to improve for the future. When the drills were completed, he was tired but also invigorated. His sword had remained sheathed for too long. As the men left, he thanked the instructor and sat on the ground, looking at the weapon knowing that more blood would need to be spilled.

Chapter 11

The mess hall was alive with soldiers eating and talking amongst friends, but Iridan sat alone trying to force some food down. He had little appetite despite all the exercises he had subjected himself to, but knew he would need the energy. The sounds of laughter reached his ears, causing Iridan's foul mood to worsen. What the hell do they have to be happy about? Don't they know what's happening out there? He angrily slammed his knife to the table when he noticed a man walking around to sit across from him. He glanced up to see Kile looking down with an expressionless face. "Oh yes, please join me," Iridan said sarcastically.

"I think I will," Kile responded as he shoved a piece of bread into his mouth.

"What do you want?"

"This is a small castle, and word spreads quickly. I know that you are to meet with Josu at dinner to discuss another plan."

"Really?" Iridan spat. "Perhaps you need to check with your sources. You're not getting accurate information."

"How so?" Kile asked, unphased by Iridan's sharp words.

"I have no plan, if you must know. Yes, the king wants to talk about what we should do next, but I have no idea."

"Well, what are you going to do? Go back and hide in your room?"

Iridan banged the table again. "What business do you have judging me?"

"Funny, but I don't recall judging you."

Iridan paused for a moment to control his emotions. "Fine. Look, what do you want?"

Kile's seemingly playful mannerisms disappeared as he answered in a serious tone, "I want to know what you're going to tell Josu."

"As I said, I have no plan." Iridan blindly took a mouthful of food. While chewing, he continued, "For some reason Josu seems to think that I have something valuable to contribute. Unfortunately, I have no dragon at my disposal this time."

"Would you mind if I make a suggestion?" Kile asked quietly.

Iridan's anger threatened to return, but he looked into Kile's eyes and saw no evidence of sarcasm or superiority. "I'll gladly accept any advice you can offer."

"Scouts report that Jaleph's army is regrouping at Pathum. They must be planning to attack Amyon next; we should send a force out and attack Jaleph from the rear. I doubt he would be expecting that. If they are defeated at Amyon, Jaleph would be stopped and Shekul would be safe."

Iridan paused for a moment to consider Kile's words. He felt little aspiration to come to the defense of Amyon after their participation in the attack on Su'Meeryn; however, he recognized Kile's logic. The only alternative he could think of was to attack Su'Meeryn directly, but Shekul was not strong enough for that. Besides, he could not bring himself to consider attacking his own home, at least not yet.

"I guess you're right," he finally said. "We will go to the king tonight and tell him of your plan."

"We? I was not invited," Kile pointed out.

"Too bad, it's your plan. You're coming with me."

***

Iridan and Kile stood before the table where Josu and Flicia sat. Forim motioned to a chair next to Dirwyn as his brother and he also took their places. "I'm sorry Iridan," the king said, "but we have only prepared food for you."

"Don't worry, Majesty, I'm not hungry. Kile and I have discussed our situation and it appears we have only one option." Iridan motioned for Kile to continue.

"Yes, Sire. Iridan and I believe that we should strike Jaleph's army from the rear when they attack Amyon. That appears to be our best chance of stopping them."

Josu's head swiveled uncertainly between Surik and Forim, but before he could speak, Flicia questioned the pair herself, "Are you sure this is a wise idea?"

"No," Iridan answered, "but do you have a better plan?"

"What about Unimeth?" Dirwyn interjected. "They must know they will be Jaleph's next target if Amyon falls."

"Very true," said Surik. "We sent a messenger to Unimeth. He was told that they do not wish to be involved."

"Fools!" Forim spat. "What do they think will happen to them?"

"Without Gorthon, we remain alone," said Iridan. "I believe Kile's plan is our best chance."

Before anyone could respond further, Josu stood. "Very good. I agree; we attack Jaleph. Iridan, I want you to lead the assault."

"Me! Why do you want me? I'm not even a member of your army. What about Brynton? He is your war leader."

Josu's face beamed like a full moon at midnight. "You are the man I want. Kile will help you with organizing the attack. See to it."

"Of course, Majesty," Iridan said somewhat dumbfounded.

"Now, if you do not want to eat with us, you are excused. Our meal is getting cold." Josu waved his long arm as he dug into the plate before him.

***

"So, you are our new war leader," Worm said with a chuckle as he sipped a glass of wine, despite the early hour. "I wonder how Brynton will respond to that." He stroked the neck of the small dog sitting in his lap as he placed his glass on the table next to him.

"I didn't ask for it," Iridan noted.

"Of course you didn't; however, that does not change the outcome."

"No, I suppose not. Do you think he will give me any trouble?"

"Brynton? Not really. He will not be happy, but he will do his utmost to continue serving Josu. Now tell me, why is it that you wanted to return today?" asked Worm. "You're not going to ask me to join in the attack are you?"

"Look, I wasted a lot of time this past year when I could have been studying Naar, but I don't have the time now as we need to get the army ready to march right away. I was hoping you could tell me something before I leave."

Worm set the dog on the floor and took another sip of wine. "Iridan," he said stoically, "I would like to help you, but I can't. As I've told you before, I never took those writings seriously."

"But you have read Naar before."

"Yes I have, but it has been a long time. I never thought of it as important, so I didn't study it. I remember some part about a bird flying to save the world from the dark forces and such. You know, apocalyptic stuff. It all sounded intriguing when I was younger. That's about it. You are welcome to search through the library whenever you like; unfortunately I don't think I can offer you anything more than that."

"I understand, but I don't have time right now," and Iridan cursed himself again for the wasted months hiding in his room.

"Hopefully you will when you get back."

Iridan smiled at Worm's reassuring words. "You are certainly a different man from the one I met in that cell."

"As are you."

Iridan paused at the comment. While he still felt the loss of Myrin and his child deeply, was he really so different from when he first met Worm? All that he was doing now—all that he ever did—was trying to cope with the extraordinary circumstances which surrounded him. Unfortunately, his recent responses had not always been the most productive. "I'm just doing what I can," he whispered.

"Do you think it is just that easy, after all you've been through? Think about all that you have accomplished so far."

"I'd rather not," Iridan said as he stood. "Thank you for the offer of your library. Let's hope that I do get the chance to use it, but I need to be off. Kile and I have much to prepare."

"Of course. I'll see you soon."

Chapter 12

Light slowly forced its way through his closed eyelids. The stench of death filled his nose causing him to wake sooner than propitious. With consciousness returning, so did pain and a cry of anguish escaped from his parched lips as nausea overwhelmed his body. His stomach heaved and he spewed vomit. With a small whimper of agony, he fainted.

***

Pothar was roused again from his fitful sleep some time later—he could not recall how many times he had awakened before then. He tried to sit up and immediately felt a searing pain from his wrist. His eyes turned to the bandaged stump, and he felt a strange sensation when he tried to move his fingers. The pain from his cauterized wound shot up his arm as his body heaved. He fell back, but this time sleep did not come to grant release from his suffering.

Following a few moments of gathering his will, the waves of nausea subsided and he managed to push himself back up. "Pothar's come to," he heard from across the room. "Go get Rynkor." While Pothar waited for his commander to arrive, he glanced around in an effort to acquaint himself with his surroundings. He found himself resting on one of many beds which filled a large room with wide windows. Tables were pushed against bare walls and piles of plates and cutlery sat heaped in one corner. He was in a dining hall, only now bodies sprawled about everywhere he looked—on beds and the floor alike.

When Rynkor entered, Pothar gingerly stood, igniting a fresh wave of agony at his stump. "Where are we?" he asked hoarsely after taking another moment to compose himself.

"Tamar still. Castle secure. Tamar ours," replied the strange warrior in his flat tone, devoid of any emotion regarding Su'Meeryn's victory or concern for Pothar's condition. Now that the bloodlust of battle had passed, he had become just an empty shell. Pothar realized at that moment he truly hated this man.

"Good, what's next?" Pothar asked with some strength returning to his voice.

"Message from Emperor. More troops arrive soon. We meet at Pathum then continue to Amyon. You go home." Rynkor stood as rigid as one of the tables lying against the wall, with no expression whatsoever on his still crimson-stained face.

Pothar wanted to argue. He felt like a coward having to leave his men, but he knew it was the only prudent arrangement due to the loss of his hand. The wound required proper treatment from the healers and rest; besides, he knew he would not be much good in fight now. "I'll need the pain to subside some before I'll be able to ride, and you will need to send a rider with me to make sure I make it back. I've never ridden one-handed before."

Rynkor nodded and left the room without another word. "What a pleasant man," Pothar mumbled. He started to walk about the room, searching for familiar faces among the soldiers, when one of the men began to gasp. A couple of the healers rushed over as the man's body heaved violently. Their fingers frantically probed his face and chest, but the gasping stopped abruptly and Pothar knew that the man had died. He walked back and dropped onto his bed, covering his eyes with his undamaged wrist. The throbbing returned to his blackened stump and he wondered whether the pain had actually stopped, or had he forgotten it due to the distraction? Doesn't matter, he thought as he uncovered his eyes. He examined the burnt flesh where his wound had been cauterized, and the searing pain erupted again.

"Hey," Pothar tried to cry out, but he could manage only a whimper. "Hey."

"What is it?" one of the healers answered as he approached.

"Give me something for the pain." The woman reached into a pocket and pulled out a small vial. Pothar raised his head as she poured the contents down his throat. After a few minutes, the effects of the drug reached Pothar's head as all his senses faded away.

***

Following a full day of riding, Pothar found a clearing and ordered a stop for the night. After hopping down from the horse, his wrist began to throb again so he pulled out a vial and swallowed some more of the elixir. He checked through his supplies and noted that—despite his rationing efforts—he was already running low on medicine. The jarring of the ride was a constant irritation to his wound, and he realized that he had not taken enough before leaving the camp. Smaller doses would be required to allow him to reach Su'Meeryn before running out. The respite from the pain would not last as long, but there was not much else he could do about it; besides, he would be home soon.

Waking the next morning, he ate a quick breakfast with his escort before continuing on their southward journey. By midday he was starting to feel comfortable enough handling the reins with one hand, so he ordered the man to return to Rynkor. Now alone he figured he could take the opportunity to ride to Shekul and speak with Iridan. The side trip would cost him a couple of extra days on his way back to Su'Meeryn, but nobody would notice that. And he should be able to acquire more of the elixir. Unfortunately though, within a few hours he ran into a patrol from Su'Meeryn. He faced no problems as he was immediately recognized; however, having been spotted he now wondered if the delay to Shekul would prove costly. But he decided to take the risk. If he was questioned when he reached home, he would blame it on difficulties due to the loss of his hand.

The rest of the afternoon remained uneventful, but the following day he was again stopped, this time by a patrol from Shekul. He had a near impossible time convincing the men that he was a friend of Iridan's, but after surrendering his sword he was escorted to Shekul. When they reached the castle, Pothar was taken to a small room where he remained under guard. After some long moments of waiting, Iridan finally walked through the doorway.

"When they told me there was a man with one hand asking for me, I had a hard time believing it was really you," Iridan said happily when he saw his friend.

Pothar took a quick look at his stump. "Yeah, it's me."

Iridan's face darkened while looking at Pothar's stump. "You've been through more than anybody I know."

"I guess I should just be happy to be alive."

"Does it hurt?"

"Yeah. They burned it, and it still bothers me. Hopefully I can get some medicine here. With this detour, I'll run out long before I reach Su'Meeryn."

"Of course," Iridan replied as he threw his arm over his friend's shoulder and lead him away from the guards. "It's been a long time hasn't it? Let's go to my room and talk."

Pothar noticed wary eyes directed towards him as they headed through the castle. He knew that he did not have anything to worry about, but he still felt relieved when they entered the privacy of Iridan's room. "Are you certain that you want to return to Jaleph?" Iridan asked. "I'm sure Josu would allow you to stay."

"With you already here, I should return home and see Dobrah."

Iridan nodded. "So what news do you bring?"

"Tamar has fallen, but we lost a lot of men. Jaleph is gathering his troops at Pathum and will then strike Amyon."

"We've heard."

"I, obviously, will not be part of any further attacks," Pothar said, raising his bandaged arm. "What's happening here?"

Iridan paused before answering. Pothar realized that—despite all they had been through—Iridan was wondering what he should say. Technically he knew they were actually enemies. "Nothing good," was the only reply.

"Really? Well that's helpful."

"I'm sorry Pothar, but you are still part of Jaleph's army."

"I don't have much choice about it, do I? Should I have refused to head off to battle? What would Jaleph have done then? I know all this has been hard on you, but this is a dangerous game I am playing." Pothar pulled out a chair and sat down. "Besides, I was the one who helped you and Myrin get out of Su'Meeryn. How is she by the way, and the baby? Did everything go okay?" Iridan fell to his bed staring blankly, and Pothar immediately regretted his words. "I'm sorry. I guess I just figured she'd get through the sickness."

"It wasn't that," Iridan said flatly. "We were attacked by troops from Su'Meeryn before reaching Shekul. Myrin was killed."

The shock of Iridan's words hit Pothar hard as tears formed in his eyes. "I'm sorry," Pothar repeated. "When the soldiers did not return, we just assumed that you made it here safely." He hesitated before speaking again. "Is Dirwyn okay?"

"Of course, you wouldn't have had any way to know." Iridan slowly raised his face and Pothar saw that his expression had hardened, the hurt buried away. "Dirwyn's fine," he added. The pair sat quietly as Iridan looked at Pothar, contemplating what to say next. Finally he told Pothar about their failed mission to Gorthon and the plan to attack the Su'Meeryn troops from the rear. "Strange isn't it? Me leading a force to defend Amyon."

"Things have sure changed," agreed Pothar. "I'm just glad that I won't be a part of any more battles. It all seems wrong, and that Rynkor. I knew that nobody liked him, but I didn't realize how vile he was until recently. When you look into his eyes… it's like he's not even human."

"You're right, he's a sick man." After a pause, Iridan continued. "I just wonder why Unimeth won't help defend Amyon. It makes no sense. Those two kingdoms have always had strong ties. If Amyon falls, Unimeth must know they'll be next."

"I don't know," Pothar agreed as he noticed the throbbing returning to his stump. "But what do you think I should do when I get back to Su'Meeryn?"

"That's a good question. I don't know. Is Dobrah still there?" Pothar nodded. "Go to her. You know what we are doing here, and we can use any help you might be able to provide."

"To stop Jaleph?"

Iridan took a deep, apprehensive breath. "That is what we're trying to do. Are you on board with that?"

Visions of the slaughter at Tamar ran through Pothar's mind as did the image of Rynkor's twisted face. He then thought of Myrin being killed by Su'Meeryn warriors, and he knew that he had only one answer. "Yes."

Iridan nodded with a sour expression. "Don't you want to rest and eat before you leave?"

"I better just grab something to eat along the way. I have a lot of riding ahead of me as I'll need to circle back to enter Su'Meeryn from the north. Since I was spotted, I can't afford to be too much later in arriving, otherwise I might arouse suspicion."

The two stood and Iridan gave his friend a warm hug. "Be safe my friend. I hope to see you again. Now let's go find you some more medicine."

Tears again formed in Pothar's eyes as he looked at Iridan. He really could not conceive of any way the two would meet again. Before leaving the castle his sword was returned to him by Dirwyn, which only caused his tears to flow even faster. When the three stood together at the gate, Pothar kissed Dirwyn on the forehead, then whispered to Iridan, "I'm sorry about Myrin." They clasped hands before Pothar mounted his steed and kicked his horse to a gallop without looking back.

Chapter 13

The new crown felt strange atop the emperor's head. The weight of gold was more than he had anticipated, and the edges did not sit quite right against his bald head. He kept turning the crown, hoping to find a more comfortable position, but no matter what he tried the edges always seemed to find one of the dents on his scalp to bore into. Jaleph wanted to just throw the thing away and return to his previous headband, but Ut had counseled against that idea. Following the ceremony of presentation, Ut said he would undermine his regal appearance if he did not wear it. When Jaleph continued to complain, Ut promised that they would have a new one made after the conclusion of their campaigns. At that time, a new crown would be an appropriate symbol of their victory. Jaleph had reluctantly agreed, so for now, the emperor had to make do as best he could.

"Jaleph, hello," Ut called out as the doorway to the empty audience chamber opened, causing light to scatter off the crown.

"Ut," was the only acknowledgement Jaleph offered as he continued to struggle with the gold against his head.

"I have news from our army, and finally a report from Shekul."

Upon hearing the name Shekul, Jaleph immediately forgot about his discomfort as his mind filled with thoughts of Myrin... and Iridan. "Tell me!"

"Tamar is secure and we are poised to strike Amyon. I believe they will fall quickly."

"Yes, yes, yes. What about Shekul?"

"Our spy had a hard time getting access to the castle. When he finally secured access, finding out news of Iridan and Myrin was equally difficult. None of the inhabitants were willing to talk, though he managed to befriend a willing servant about a week ago. Unfortunately he had to walk all the way back to Su'Meeryn. His horse was—"

"I don't care about the details!" Jaleph barked. "Get on with it!"

Ut's brow furrowed as his chin fell to his chest. "I am very sorry to report that Myrin is dead."

A rush of air exploded from Jaleph's lungs and his stomach twisted into a tight knot. With a whimper, his head fell back against the throne, catching the back of his crown which burrowed into his skin. "What happened?" he whispered.

"Her illness," continued Ut. "It never subsided and she died in childbirth. Neither she nor the baby survived." He paused to look back up at the emperor. Jaleph saw heartbreak in Ut's reddening eyes and a quivering mouth which mirrored his own. "I'm told the healers in Shekul are not as sophisticated as ours. If only Iridan had not snuck her out, she might still be alive."

"I'll butcher them!" Jaleph cried as he vaguely wiped at a trickle of blood behind his ear. "I'll butcher them all, every last one. Everyone except Iridan. Him, I'll drag home and skin alive with my own hands!"

"Of course, Majesty, we are well on our way. Our spy brought additional news. Shekul is mustering their army. Their plan could only be to attack us from the rear when we move against Amyon. It is a sound strategy, but unfortunately for them, they are not aware of our pact with Unimeth. When they hit our forces in the rear, they will be flanked by the Unimeth troops. Shekul's troops will be crushed."

Jaleph took a deep breath as he wiped at his ear again and rose from the throne. "Once Amyon falls, we will turn my forces south. Shekul will be razed."

"Let's not get ahead of ourselves. After Amyon is conquered, we take Unimeth."

Jaleph shook his head. "No. I still do not like that plan. They have allied themselves with us and are providing me with a generous tribute. We need not attack them."

"But you must have your revenge."

"I care not about that anymore. Shekul, I want Shekul."

Ut approached and placed his hand on Jaleph's shoulder. "Have I steered you wrong yet? Trust me again."

"You have been a good friend Ut, but don't test me on this. I have made my decision. We will not attack Unimeth. Amyon, then Shekul."

Ut continued to stare at the emperor as his eyes seemed to grow dark, "Jaleph, we must subdue Unimeth."

"Why? They are my allies."

What little color Ut's fair complexion displayed drained away, leaving only a pale hue. "They will always remain a possible threat unless they are directly under our control."

"*Our*? You assign yourself too much honor Ut," Jaleph hissed as he lost all patience. "I am the emperor, and we will do things *my* way. No. Enough of this. Be gone!"

Ut stood stoically before the throne, and his dark eyes turned completely black. His lips curled into his mouth leaving an evil sneer across his translucent skin. The black eyes sunk into his cavernous head, and it seemed that most of his hair had disappeared. "You will not speak to me in that tone again," he commanded. "I have endured your idiocy for long enough."

"Guards!" Jaleph cried, but a black aura flowed out from Ut's body, muffling Jaleph's call.

"They will not come," Ut laughed, and with a strength Jaleph could not have imagined, he shoved the emperor back onto the throne. He hovered over Jaleph and pointed a bony finger at his face. "Everything you have now is because of me. Everything." The black aura continued to ooze from his body and fill the hall. "I have chosen you to be emperor. You have followed my directions all this time, and for that I have given you a power not seen in this land for ages. If you turn away from me now, I will kill you and find someone else. Do you understand?"

"But..."

"I said, do you understand?" Ut screamed, and the aura grew even thicker and larger. Jaleph felt its cold emptiness approach and probe his body. Strands of blackness encircled his hand before climbing up his arm. Unable to back away, Jaleph sat paralyzed. The aura continued up to his shoulder, circled his neck and began to squeeze. "Do you understand?" Ut repeated.

"Yes," Jaleph managed to wheeze through the choking grip.

"Good. You are mine, and I will do with you as I please. Now, you will send word that once Amyon falls, the army will turn on Unimeth. Once all three of the northern lands are secure, then we will take Shekul, unless I change my mind."

Jaleph stammered as he stared at Ut. As the black grip loosened slightly he managed to say, "Of course." The aura slowly dissolved and Ut's appearance returned to normal.

The emperor's horrified body sat shaking on the throne after Ut left. The thoughts of the last few minutes remained too vivid. What could he possibly do? But the futile answer came: nothing. How could he stop a man who had that kind of control over him? His fear gradually turned to anger and he struck his fist against the armrest before storming from the chamber, trailed nervously by his guards as he marched towards the palace. When he reached his harem room, two of his concubines welcomed him with an uneasy greeting. He slammed the door and dropped onto the nearest couch. The women approached apprehensively as he ordered them to please him, but he found no satisfaction   in   their   arms.

Chapter 14

Despite the late morning hour, the sky above remained black as Iridan and Kile led their soldiers away from the castle. They could barely see a horse length before them until a large bolt of lightning erupted, momentarily illuminating the road ahead. It was followed almost immediately by deafening thunder as a drizzle began to fall, but Iridan knew it was only a precursor to the full storm.

"This will not be a pleasant ride," Kile remarked, regarding the first few drops.

"At least it is going to be a ride," commented Iridan. "Su'Meeryn never had enough horses for all our soldiers."

"I guess that is one advantage in having a smaller army," replied Kile.

"Any further orders, *Sir*?"

Iridan heard the mocking voice coming up behind him. "Don't start with my Brynton. I'm not going to continue this argument with you."

"Whatever your orders are, I will certainly obey."

Iridan turned towards the blond-haired man. "Why don't you worry about succeeding in the task before us and not who is in charge? I really could not care less, but this is what Josu ordered. Are you going to jeopardize our mission by disrupting my command?"

Brynton's thin face softened somewhat as he moved his horse alongside. Iridan had known that Shekul's military leader would have a difficult time relinquishing his command to an outsider, but he could only hope Brynton would do his job when they entered into battle. He needed all his soldiers ready to serve and obey. "I guess I'll have to apologize again," Brynton said.

Iridan's eyes rolled as he recalled the arguments which followed Josu's announcement. "Fine, but we can't continue like this," Iridan responded, and then lowered his voice. "I don't care whether you like me or not, but I need you to show me respect. If I am the leader of these men, you need to treat me as such. Otherwise how do you expect them to follow me? When we reach Su'Meeryn's army I need to know that I can trust you."

Brynton nodded. "I will serve my king and fulfill my role."

The rain started to fall harder, and more lightning erupted all around making further conversation impossible, but Iridan did not feel like talking anyway. He shook his head trying to relieve himself from the smell of wet horse hair before focusing his attention on the precarious road. Mud splattered up from hooves and Iridan hoped their supplies would not be too soiled. I guess it can't be helped, he thought; we need to get to Amyon without delay.

As the morning passed, the rain began to slacken and sometime after midday it stopped completely prompting Iridan to order a halt for lunch. The men pulled out their supplies and everyone worked at rinsing off the food and airing out their clothes. Once those tasks had been completed they sat to eat, and despite his better judgment, Iridan ordered Brynton to sit with him.

"This is not necessary," Brynton remarked before biting into an apple.

"I think it is. The men need to see us together."

"Ridiculous. I don't know about Su'Meeryn soldiers, but my men know their duty. They will all do what is expected of them when we reach the battle."

"You never know what is going to happen in combat."

Brynton took another bite, but his face soured and he spit it out. He twisted the fruit around before his eyes then hurled it away in disgust. "I have been in combat many times and seen my men fight. You have nothing to be concerned about. They do not care whether we like each other, and as I told you, despite my disagreement over the king's decision I will obey. Now, if you don't mind I'd like to return to them." But Brynton did not move, and it took a minute for Iridan to understand.

"Thank you. You are dismissed."

When Brynton left, Kile came over and took his place. "He's ill-tempered, but a fine soldier."

"Why does it seem that everything is always more difficult than it should be?"

Kile chuckled. "It's a good thing the rain stopped, otherwise I don't know what kind of shape we would be in when we reach Amyon."

When Iridan realized that he had still not eaten anything, he bit into his own apple—he should have examined it a little closer. The gritty taste of mud lingered in his mouth, but lacking anything to clean it with, he had to force the rest of it down. One apple was not a sufficient lunch, but he'd had enough. "Saddle up, there is still a lot of riding ahead of us," he ordered. Kile nodded and they gathered their muddy provisions.

As the company prepared to continue their northward trek, all heads turned back at the sound of a horse trotting through the mud. Iridan pulled out his sword as did the other soldiers. Once they noticed that it was one lone rider, the men relaxed somewhat. As the rider neared, their swords returned to their sheaths, and Iridan finally recognized the rider.

"Do you mind if I join you?" Worm called out cheerfully.

Chapter 15

To his relief, the only questions Pothar received when he reached Su'Meeryn concerned his hand. After passing his horse to one of the guards, he immediately reported to the healers to have his wound examined more closely. The constant bouncing of the ride had taken its toll. His hand throbbed more than it had since the injury, and he had run out of all his remedies. At the infirmary, the healers boiled some herbs and leaves into a thick paste which they assured him would aid in the healing. After spreading the paste on his stump, they replaced his bandage and gave him a fresh supply of the pain-numbing elixir. Pothar thanked them for their kind assistance and left quickly, grateful that they had not asked him to remain; he had spent far too much time in that building already following the battle in the ravine.

Passing the stables as he made his way home, he found Veake hard at work brushing down a horse. The pungent stableman spotted Pothar and waved a gnarled hand, urgently motioning for him. He nodded and reluctantly approached. "Hello, Veake. What can I do for you?"

"'Ere, come o'er ere," Veake whispered as he looked over his shoulder.

"Where?"

"Shh!" the stableman commanded. "Must be quiet. Come wit me."

Pothar shrugged and followed Veake into one of the rear-most stables. "You really need to do a better job of cleaning this up," he said picking his way through piles of manure. "Is this good? Now, what do you want?"

"'Ow's Iridun?"

"What do you mean?" Pothar asked suspiciously.

"Ya saw um. Ow is 'e?" When Pothar's only response was a stern glare, the stableman continued. "Ya dun't 'ave t' 'orry 'bout me. Ah 'elped ya b'fure, dudn't I?"

"How do you know I saw him?" Pothar breathed through clenched teeth.

"Veake knows," the shabby man cackled. "Now tell me. Ow's 'e?"

"If you know that I saw him, how come you don't know how he is?"

Spit suddenly flew from Veake's mouth as he cried out, "Whure's yir 'and?" His filthy hair flapped about as he looked back over each shoulder. "Shh," he whispered to himself.

"Lost on the battlefield."

"Ah dudn't see tat. No 'and, eh? Not gud. No, not gud."

"Yeah, I'm well aware of that," and at the mention of his hand, Pothar noticed the familiar ache returning.

Veake pulled his eyes away from Pothar's stump and stared him in the face. "Dobrah," he said. "Ya need to see Dobrah. The two a yah. 'R only 'ope."

Pothar sighed deeply. He wanted to escape from the foul-smelling stable and dismiss Veake as just a crazy old man, but he knew better. It had been Veake's plan to get Dirwyn, Iridan and Myrin out of Su'Meeryn. The thought of Myrin brought fresh pain, but he turned his focus back to the stableman. "I was planning on talking to her later. I need to get some rest first."

"Yah, yah, gud. Ya rest, th'n the two a ya talk. Make plans. Stop Jaleph."

"Stop Jaleph!" Pothar blurted, trying very hard to keep his voice down. "What do you mean stop Jaleph?" he continued in a hushed tone.

"Yah, stop Jaleph," Veake responded, his stern eyes belying any semblance of idiocy. "Someun must. If nut, dark days a'ead. Yep, yep, dark days," he said as he shambled away. Veake's final words echoed through Pothar's head long into the night.

Chapter 16

"What is he doing here?" Kile mumbled, sheathing his blade.

"That's a good question," agreed Iridan. "What are you doing here?"

"I thought you might need some help," Worm answered with a smile cracking through his mud encrusted face.

"Well, we certainly can," Iridan admitted, "but what do you expect to do? You have made it clear you are no warrior."

"I have helped you in the past."

Iridan nodded in sad agreement. "Fine, if you want to come you're welcome to join us." Kile spat with obvious disagreement, but Iridan did not care. Turning his attention back to the trail before them, he ordered the trek to resume.

***

The following day finally revealed a clear sky, though a strong wind from the north brought a chill to the weary riders. After a quick breakfast, the soldiers of Shekul mounted their horses. As they rode off, Kile and Brynton motioned for Iridan to join them. "I think you should send him away," Kile advised. "He will be of no use in battle and will bring nothing but trouble."

"He's right," Brynton concurred. "I've never cared for that Worm, and I can't imagine what he's doing here."

"If he wants to offer his assistance, I see no reason to refuse him," Iridan countered.

"And what help do you think he can offer?" asked Kile.

"I don't know, but if he wants to assist us, I'm not going to stop him."

Kile let out a disapproving huff. "He'll just get himself killed."

"I thought you didn't care."

"Maybe I do."

"Well, I'm glad to hear that, but it is his choice." Iridan noted that the other soldiers were starting to pull ahead, so he spurred his horse and motioned for Kile and Brynton to follow. "I'm not going to send him away."

"You know as well as I that he won't be able to help us in battle. Sure, he gave us a hand when we saved you from Jaleph's men, but that was different. It was a small fight and the two of you were able to surprise the Su'Meeryn soldiers."

"Will you two ladies please make a decision?" Brynton barked.

Iridan let out an exasperated sigh. "What exactly do you want me to do?"

"I don't *want* you to do anything. Worm is no soldier and everyone knows it. I just think you should find out why he is really here."

Why can't anything ever be easy? Iridan thought. "Fine," he spat. "I'll talk to him."

***

At midday, Iridan ordered a brief stop for lunch to allow the horses a chance to rest. He grabbed some food from his pack and looked for Worm. "I want you to tell me what you are really doing here," Iridan said after he finished chewing a piece of dried meat and dropped down to the muddy ground.

Worm smiled back at his companion. "I already told you, I'm here—"

"Don't," Iridan interrupted. "I thought that we were past this. I don't want to hear your ambiguous responses anymore."

After swallowing a gulp of what Iridan hoped was water, Worm's smile disappeared as he wiped his mouth. "Like I said, I'm here to help." Worm raised his hand to stop Iridan before he could protest further. "But you must understand, what I mean by help is not what you're thinking. When you hear 'help', you think about swords in battle. Perhaps I will be able to contribute to the fight, although we both know that's not very likely. I intend to assist in another way."

"And how might that be?"

"To be honest with you my friend, I'm not really sure; however, I just know I need to be here."

"That's all you can tell me?" Worm nodded in response. "We are heading into battle, and many of us won't return. I can't watch over you."

"I'm not asking you to, Iridan. Besides, what's your alternative? Send me back to Shekul? I'd just turn around and follow anyway."

Iridan felt his anger starting to return but decided it was not worth arguing over anymore. "Fine, I can't stop you from coming. I'd just like to understand, that's all."

"So would I." Worm finished the last bite of his bread and turned to Iridan. "It's not that I want to be here, but something is telling me to be at the battle. I don't know where it's coming from. It feels like a memory I can't seem to place. I'm sorry Iridan, but there is nothing else I can say."

Iridan considered Worm's face for a long moment. All the usual playfulness and deception had vanished, and Iridan thought of his own incomprehensible dreams. "Very well, but please, I would appreciate you telling me if you discover anything."

"You'll be the first."

***

The remainder of their journey passed uneventfully. Iridan knew that Kile was still frustrated by Worm's presence, but nothing further was said. Brynton remained relatively silent as well. When they neared the remnants of the village of Pathum, Iridan tried, unsuccessfully, to forget that horrible battle when he had discovered the plan of the northern kingdoms to attack Su'Meeryn. The haunting images only began to fade as they approached the forests on the southern border of Amyon. Iridan called for a halt just outside the first line of trees and jumped down from his horse.

"What now?" Brynton asked as he approached. "Is there a path through this forest?"

"Yes," Iridan replied, "but I don't remember exactly where it is." Iridan ordered two pairs of men to go in opposite directions along the tree line and find the trail. "Jaleph's men will be moving from the west," he continued. "The trail should give us a good chance to hit them on their flank."

"Very good, I guess you are smarter than I thought," Brynton responded with a laugh. He then looked back towards Worm. "I still don't know what he thinks he is doing here."

"Neither do I, but it's his decision."

Brynton began to respond but stopped himself; instead, he pulled out his sword and examined its edge. After returning it to the scabbard he said, "You are our leader." As he returned to the men, Iridan could not decide whether he had heard sarcasm or not.

The soldiers took the opportunity to relieve themselves and stretch their muscles while waiting for the scouts. The first pair returned about an hour later to report that the trail sat to their west. When the second pair also arrived, the group set out towards the battle they would soon join.

Chapter 17

Pothar sat on his bed examining his stump. The throbbing still lingered, and strangely enough, he even felt pain from where his fingers should have been. Despite telling himself it was not possible, he failed to lose the sensation. He had returned to the healers and they wanted him to remain in the building, but he refused. Pothar just wanted to be alone. Soon he would need to speak with Dobrah, and it would not be a good idea to risk having someone on the other side of his walls.

He eventually rose to prepare his dinner but struggled to prepare the lovely slab of meat he had purchased, spilling an entire bag of roasted seeds in the process. He knew it would take time to adjust to the loss of his hand but it did not relieve his frustration. This was the first proper meal he had eaten since his injury, and he had not realized how difficult cutting food would be. Stuffing some fruit or hard cheese into his mouth had not been a problem, but using utensils was a different matter. He quickly realized that the only way he could hold the meat down to cut it was by grasping the fork in his mouth, but the task still took a lot of effort. With increasing aggravation, he finally managed to finish his meal and set out to search for Dobrah.

Pothar found her in the courtyard leading the training for some new recruits. When she spotted him, she quickly finished the drills and ordered a break. As the new troops broke formation and headed to the water buckets, Pothar joined her.

"It's good to see you," Dobrah said. "I heard about your hand. How are you?"

"Things are hard, but I'm getting by," Pothar replied as he unconsciously rubbed his stump. "Where did all these new recruits come from?"

"Conscripts from the nobles' lands," Dobrah said flatly. Pothar tried to hide his shock, but was not sure how convincing he was. "I hear that the northern campaign is going well," she announced casually while glancing back over her shoulder.

"Yes, our men have fought hard." Pothar then leaned forward and whispered, "See if you can send us off on patrol together so we can talk freely."

Dobrah nodded as she ordered the conscripted men to reform for more drills. Pothar stood and watched the new men for another moment. Conscripts, he thought; what next? I can't believe what is happening here. As he turned away, he realized that he was still rubbing his wrist. The elixir would be losing its effect soon, and he had no more with him. He returned to his room for a fresh supply, still shaking his head in disgust.

***

Pothar jumped down awkwardly from his horse and joined Dobrah as she gazed sorrowfully into the ravine. Memories of the battle where Karus had died, and Pothar had almost lost his life, remained vivid. They had not talked much after leaving the castle, waiting to make sure that they were a good distance away first. Pothar knew that they had no need to ride so far, but when he began to guess their destination he said nothing. Perhaps she needed to stand at the spot where her husband had died in order to gather her resolve for what was to come next. He watched Dobrah wipe at her eyes before he spoke. "I saw Iridan."

"What did he have to say?"

"Iridan is leading Shekul's troops to help defend Amyon."

"Iridan is defending Amyon?" She turned away from the ravine to look into his eyes, her face flushed. "What's happened to us?"

"Jaleph."

"You know he is conscripting new troops," she said, "but that is not the worst of it. When I'a'uju'uh wouldn't comply, Jaleph had him executed. He even made the order in open chambers."

"Executed? Can this get any worse?"

"I don't know, but Jaleph needs to be stopped."

"How?" asked Pothar.

Dobrah pulled some nuts from a pouch and shoved them into her mouth as she considered Pothar's question. "We need to await word from Amyon first. Perhaps Iridan will be able to stop Rynkor, but we should see if there are other soldiers who are as concerned as us."

"I'm not so sure that's wise. What we speak of is treason."

"Don't you think I know that! It is what we are talking about! Do you have another suggestion?" The red color on her face grew brighter. "We can't just sit back and do nothing while more good men die!" She turned back towards the ravine as fresh tears started to roll from her eyes.

Pothar sat quietly for a moment, thinking of Rynkor and the northern battles, of the Tamarian king and his family being slaughtered. "No. You're right. We can't wait around any longer."

She took a deep breath and Pothar noticed a slight tremble across her body. "Certainly anything we do will be risky, but we've risked our lives many times." She turned her hardened face away from the ravine, and Pothar saw no trace of sorrow. "We should start with the men from Okkgan. There must be plenty of them who aren't happy with Jaleph and his recent orders."

"Okay, but let's keep things slow," Pothar said as he pulled himself back into his saddle. "By the way, we shouldn't say anything to Teraken. Despite what has happened, I don't think he would betray Jaleph under any circumstance."

"Agreed," Dobrah replied. "Let's get going."

Chapter 18

Horses burst out of the forest carrying Iridan and his men down the muddy path. Steel rang as clutching fingers pulled swords from their scabbards, and a stiff headwind carried the stench of blood and death. Entering the low ground of the open battlefield, the nostrils of the horses flared as they fought through deep mud which slowed their advance. To make matters worse, drops of rain struck the riders' faces as they pushed through the wind. In the field before them, the silver and blue banners of Su'Meeryn flapped. The battle for Amyon had already begun.

"Engage!" Iridan called, rushing into the melee before them. His blade crushed the skull of a Su'Meeryn soldier who had turned to confront the noise from behind.

Kile, Brynton and the men of Shekul followed Iridan through the splashing mud, striking the Su'Meeryn soldiers from the rear. As Iridan's blade pierced the back of his next adversary's neck, he felt an overwhelming sense of loss. His last battle against Su'Meeryn had been in defense of himself and his wife. Now, the combat was his choice. He had planned this attack; he had chosen to raise arms against his land and his king.

A call rang out before him, bringing Iridan's attention back to the battle. The soldiers of Su'Meeryn had turned to face their new threat and to his right, Iridan saw Kile rush forward. His sword struck out and an arm fell to the mud-soaked ground.

The Shekul soldiers followed Kile. Though outnumbered, they had the advantage of being on horseback and were causing confusion among the ranks of their foes. Iridan's men began to push a wedge into the Su'Meeryn line. "Forward!" Iridan cried as his blade swirled about while Brynton rode at his side, spilling blood with every stroke of his sword. Iridan tried to spot Worm, but he could not divert his attention away from the battle.

The soldier to his left was pulled from his horse down into the muck and soon disappeared, overwhelmed by the steel of Su'Meeryn.

Iridan continued to drive his steed forward, shocked by the ease of the advance. The enemy simply fell away, and Iridan realized it was not due to the casualties being inflicted. Iridan took a brief moment to halt his horse, and as Kile and the others pushed onward, Iridan scanned the scene around him. The men of Shekul were well beyond the Su'Meeryn line. While his plan had been to reach the Amyon forces and split the Su'Meeryn army, their thrust had been too easy. If they continued at this pace they faced the likely possibility of being surrounded. "Halt the advance!" Iridan called. "Halt!"

"What?" he heard Brynton respond. "We have them!"

"Retreat! Now!" Iridan pulled at the reins to turn his horse around. At that moment, the Su'Meeryn soldiers mounted their own attack at the cavalry, who began to fall as they tried to push their way out. But before Iridan could take a moment to reconsider his strategy, he saw another line of soldiers emerging from the forest behind them. As the new troops advanced, Iridan was able to make out the snake emblem on their banners: Unimeth had come to their aid after all. But his happiness was short-lived as the Unimeth archers unleashed their first volley against his cavalry. This was why Unimeth had not responded to Shekul's overtures. Unimeth had joined Jaleph, and Su'Meeryn has somehow learned of his plan. "It's a trap! Flee!"

But the men of Shekul could not flee; they were fully surrounded. Kile rode up next to him. "How did the bastards know?"

"It doesn't matter now. We'll have to try to punch a hole in the Unimeth line and get back into the forest." Iridan ordered. "If we stay here, we're dead."

"Let's go." Kile spurred his horse, and the remaining men of Shekul followed.

The sudden shift caught the soldiers of Unimeth unprepared. They had clearly not expected Iridan and his men to recognize the trap so soon and most of them had only just dropped their bows to grab their blades.

Kile's mount reached the line first. He swung his sword about and enemy warriors fell all around. Other horses reached the fight as the men of Unimeth skidded about in the increasing slickness of the mire-covered ground. The defending line buckled against Shekul's initial onslaught but it quickly reformed.

Iridan allowed the Shekul troops to pass as he glanced back over his shoulder. Scores of Su'Meeryn soldiers were rushing forward and would be at their backs soon. If they did not manage to punch through in time, they would be slaughtered.

He charged ahead and immediately suffered a stab to his right thigh. Spinning around he plunged his sword down on his adversary's head. Blood splashed into his eyes, and he was temporarily blinded. He tried to continue moving, but felt another strike against his opposite side. Fortunately the blade did not pierce his armor, but it caused all the air to expel from his lungs. He struggled to regain his breath as he swung his sword to the left. The blow landed but with no force behind it. Iridan's vision finally cleared, and he saw his attacker preparing to strike again when a horse pushed its way between them. Iridan did not recognize the rider, but he knew the man had saved his life.

"Push on!" Iridan managed to call out. "We've got to get free!"

They managed to slowly inch their way forward, grateful for the rain and mud which splashed in every direction. Seeing became difficult, but the more confusion the better their chance of breaking through. Brynton was now beside him. The old warrior was covered with filth and obviously wounded as he swung his blade awkwardly. Several Unimeth soldiers noticed as well and swarmed. Iridan unsuccessfully tried to fight them off and Brynton was pulled, cursing from his horse. There was no time to mourn. He must continue to fight, but due to the growing pain in his chest all Iridan could manage to do was swing at anything below waist-level. Each time his weapon found a target, his misery increased. He felt his blade strike metal once more before his horse stumbled. "Keep going," he cried, pushing his injured steed forward. The animal stumbled again, and at the same moment his right thigh suffered another blow. Screaming in pain as the steel dug deep, he tried to strike back but his sword found no targets. A few horses from behind pushed his steed on. Sweat flowed down his body, mixing with the grime and causing his wound to burn. He felt like he was about to fall from the animal.

"We're through!" a voice called from behind Iridan. He tried to keep going, despite the labored breathing of his horse which was slowing. "C'mon!" the same voice said, but despite all his coaxing, the horse stopped. Seeing how badly injured the animal was, Iridan knew it would no longer be of any use.

He dropped down from the animal and saw the soldiers of Unimeth and Su'Meeryn streaming towards him. As soon as he hit the ground, his right leg buckled from the impact and he collapsed in agony. The blood continued to escape from his body as his strength waned and his vision blurred. He felt certain his life would end in this mud, his own victim of another failed plan. Would his body even be recognized when the enemy was through with him?

As he began to lose consciousness, he felt hands clutch his arm. Weary eyes tried to focus on the person pulling him up. A slight man struggled to remount his horse, and Iridan managed to drag his body up behind him. Once they were both on, the horse bolted towards the trees.

"I bet you're glad now that I came," Worm said as Iridan passed out.

Chapter 19

The aroma of roast lamb filled the hall like fog rising off a tranquil river in the morning sun. A servant poured rich red wine into a glittering silver goblet while the emperor's fork pushed the ripe chunks of sliced melon about his plate. All the food looked delicious, but Jaleph had no appetite. In fact, he had not eaten much since his last encounter with Ut. Markis—who was the only person Jaleph sought out anymore—joined him at the table.

"Not eating again, Majesty?" Markis gurgled as he shoveled spoonfuls of soup into his mouth. "I am afraid you will wither away to nothing."

"I'm not hungry," Jaleph said, thinking a little withering would do Markis some good.

"But I went to so much trouble preparing the lunch. The sauce itself required—"

"I really don't care what was required," Jaleph barked.

"Apologies, Majesty. I'm just concerned that you no longer enjoy my meals."

Jaleph dropped his fork and reached for his goblet, guzzling down its contents. "Your meals are always fine Markis." That is all that's fine around here these days, he thought.

"Good, good," Markis replied while happily stuffing a biscuit into his huge mouth. As the emperor motioned the servant to refill his wine glass, Markis continued, "It has been nice spending this time with you, Majesty. It reminds me of my days with your father."

"He was a fine man," Jaleph agreed after emptying the contents of his chalice again. Rather then asking for the servant to refill it, he snatched the container and drank directly from it.

"Are you certain that's wise, Majesty? What, with an empty stomach and all."

"Shut up, Markis." Jaleph's surly tone echoed through the dining hall. "I don't need you telling me what to do too."

"My apologies, again. I would never consider telling you what to do. I was just trying to offer some—"

"Get out Markis," commanded the emperor. "Get out right now. I don't want to see you. I just want to be left alone."

With significant effort, Markis extradited his immense bulk from the chair and away from the table. Jaleph wondered whether he heard some muttering from under Markis' labored breaths as the chef shambled from the dining hall, but he could not be certain. Deciding to ignore the potential slight, the emperor returned his attention to the wine. When that was gone, he ordered the servant to bring him another flask.

***

Jaleph slept fitfully on the sweat-soaked sheets of his bed. When he woke, the sun still shone through the window onto his throbbing head. He slowly sat up, wondering what had roused him. A light knocking came from the door and he heard a muffled voice. "Majesty?" it called.

"Go away," Jaleph muttered back.

There was a slight pause before the knock sounded again. "I'm sorry, Majesty, but I'm afraid it's urgent."

"What is it?" he hissed, raising his aching head.

"Ut has asked for you, Majesty."

Jaleph cringed as he rose and with a shaking hand opened the door. "Where is he?"

The messenger looked back nervously at the emperor. "He is in the library, but—"

"I know where it is," Jaleph replied angrily, pushing past the messenger.

"But Majesty," the man said, "may I suggest that you change your outfit?" Jaleph looked down and saw that he was wearing nothing but a filthy shirt.

"Of course," he replied as he turned back into his room.

***

"Drunk again, huh?" Ut remarked as the emperor stumbled in.

Jaleph noticed that with just the two of them in the room, Ut again resembled death: emaciated lines in his face and only a few strands of straggly hair. "So, I suppose this is your true appearance, and you no longer have to hide it from me."

"That is none of your concern; however, your appearance should be. You need to look appropriate for your role as I still need you to lead your people."

Jaleph laughed. "I thought that you were the person in charge here."

Ut stood angrily and kicked the table away. "The people of Su'Meeryn see you as their emperor, and you need to lead them. *I* will tell you what to do, and you will tell your people. Do you understand me?" Jaleph paused as he considered the totality of Ut's words. He was nothing but a servant, and there was no way he could change that fact. He knew that if he tried, Ut would kill him. Since he had no other option, he dejectedly nodded his head. "You will *answer* me. Do you understand?"

"Yes."

"Good. Now, if you wish to drink, I don't care. But you will no longer drink during the day. Is that understood?"

"Yes," the emperor repeated as he moved the table back to its original position and sat down. "Why did you send for me?"

"The campaign goes well. The force from Shekul was slaughtered; however, Iridan managed to escape. I've turned our attention to Unimeth, which will soon fall."

"What do you want me to do?"

"The conscription of new troops goes too slowly. Our army is performing well but we are losing too many men. We require additional reinforcements. You will push the nobles even harder and if they are not successful more will suffer I'a'uju'uh's fate."

"Of course," Jaleph responded flatly.

"Muster your resolve Jaleph and see that it is done," Ut ordered, his face appearing even more hideous as his round eyes bulged from their sunken sockets. "Now you may leave."

***

The effects of the wine had dissipated by the time Jaleph sat down for dinner with his lone companion. The pair sat quietly as the food began to arrive. "I'm sure that you'll be pleased with the selection tonight, Majesty," Markis began, obviously very satisfied with himself. "I roasted a few ducks in orange sauce and—"

"Yes Markis," Jaleph angrily interrupted. "I have eyes. I don't need to be told the menu at every meal." Jaleph wondered why he had been spending so much time with the chef, but then he remembered that there was no-one else in the kingdom with whom he could. Yes, he had his growing harem, but he found no contentment with its fleshly pleasures. For the first time in a long while he missed his brother.

"Ah, here are the vegetables. We have some sweet peppers with baby carrots. Then I—"

"I said that I don't want to hear the menu. Do you listen to me?"

"Of course, Sire. I just get so excited when I see my creations."

"Well, learn to control your exhilaration. Do you understand?" The many folds on Markis' face rippled as he nodded before turning his attention to his plate. "I asked you a question!" Jaleph bellowed. "I expect you to answer me!"

"Certainly, Jaleph. Yes, I understand."

The emperor slammed his hands on the table. "You will address me by my title!" Markis flinched at the outburst and picked up his goblet which had fallen over. "Bring me more wine," Jaleph commanded as he pushed his food away.

"But Sire, you really should eat something before drinking again."

"I'm not hungry," Jaleph snapped as his head searched around for a servant. "Where is that wine?" When the flask was dropped in front of him, the emperor immediately started drinking directly from it.

"Sire, I'm really worried about you. You've eaten nothing in days, and all the wine…"

Jaleph banged the flask to the table and glared at Markis. "Your job is not to keep track of the food I eat, just prepare it." He looked from his plate back to Markis and was sickened by the huge face staring back at him. "At least that was your job, but not anymore. I am tired of you. You'll report to the healers where your job will be to clean their floors. Now get out of here." Markis sat dumbfounded, the rolls of his body quivering. "I said now!" Jaleph screamed, "or I'll have a sword driven through that fat belly!"

* * *

The dawn sun arrived like a sharp spear through Jaleph's eyes. As he sat up, his head spun as if he was in the center of a cyclone. The memories of the previous day swirled through his mind and Jaleph considered staying in his bed, but he figured that he should actually try to eat something. Besides, he wanted to see what had happened in the kitchens with Markis being banished.

By the time the emperor finally reached the dining hall, he was already regretting his decision to leave his room. His stomach began to churn as a plate of plain eggs arrived. The emperor chewed a few pieces before another servant entered. "What is it?" Jaleph asked angrily.

"One of your guards has requested an audience," the man replied.

"Now is not the time for an audience. I am dining."

"He says it is important," the servant continued anxiously.

"Well, then, by all means, send him in," Jaleph spat as he threw his plate across the room. "The emperor certainly does not want to keep a guard waiting."

"Sire… it's Teraken."

"Teraken? Why didn't you say that before?"

"My apologies, but I am aware of, well…"

"Yes, yes, yes. Certainly you must know that I do not want to see him." Jaleph's anger rose with each word.

"Of course, but he said that it is very important, and he will only speak with you."

Jaleph's body relaxed as he waved the man away. "If he wants to see me he may, but if his message is not important, I will have him killed."

The servant stared back at Jaleph, stunned by the words though obviously relieved the emperor's animosity had been directed away from him. He then left briefly to usher Teraken into the hall. The large warrior stood before the emperor, the red scars on his cheeks clearly visible as he no longer sported a beard—as if he wanted a constant reminder of his king's displeasure. But his head was no longer cleanly shaved, and hair trailed down from around his ears and the back of his neck to his shoulders. Jaleph thought he saw a slight tremble from the large man as Teraken stepped in front of him. He looked even more distressed than after the death of his son. Smiling at his former friend's unease, he felt the power of the throne flow from him — a sensation he had not enjoyed for some time. "You were informed what would happen to you if I find your message not to be urgent?"

Teraken nodded. "I'm certain that you will find my news important, Majesty."

Jaleph leaned back in his chair and took a large gulp of wine. "Very well, you may continue if you wish."

"While I no longer maintain the position in your army I used to, I still have a number of friends. I hear things."

"That's wonderful news. Now get on with it."

"Some of your soldiers are unhappy with recent developments. They are trying to raise a rebellion."

Jaleph put his wine down, interested but also suspicious. "Is that so? Why should I believe you?"

"You've never had to question my loyalty."

"Really?" Jaleph asked with a sarcastic laugh, examining Teraken's scars.

"You might have been displeased with me, but I would never betray you."

"Then I will allow you to enlighten me. What have you heard?"

"It is like I said. There is an attempt being made at a rebellion."

"And who is responsible for this?"

"Pothar and Dobrah."

The emperor leaned back in his chair with a trace of a smile crossing his unshaven face.

Chapter 20

With a feeling of trepidation, Pothar closed the door to the armory behind him. He tentatively pulled his sword from its scabbard and examined the blade. Scratches crisscrossed the steel and its dulled edge displayed a number of ragged chips. Rather than having the weapon sharpened, he placed it on a wobbly table and searched through a barrel for a new blade. With the loss of his hand, he knew that he required a lighter sword. He would never overpower an enemy opponent again, so would now have to rely on speed if he ever found himself in a battle. As he sheathed the new weapon, Dobrah entered. "What took you so long?" he asked.

"I was busy," she snapped, grabbing an axe off the wall and absently spinning it in her hand. "It's not easy you know—what we're doing."

"Sorry. I guess we're both pretty tense."

Dobrah hung the axe back up. "What have you found out?" she asked, ignoring his apology.

Pothar's eyes dropped to his new weapon, and for the first time he began to feel despair. He had always been a competent soldier, but that was when he had both his hands. Now for the first time the reality of his condition set in: he was a cripple. And if that was not enough, he was also trying to conspire against his king. Nothing seemed to bother him much in the past, but his current situation threatened to overwhelm him. "Not much," he muttered. "Nobody I talked to is willing to commit to anything. I think people agree with us, but they are too afraid."

"Yeah, that was pretty much the reaction I got." Dobrah glanced at the door then made herself busy searching through the barrel of swords.

Pothar turned his own attention to a shelf of daggers. He grabbed a few until he found one with good balance and shoved it into his belt. "I don't know what else we can do, so I guess we will have to think up a new plan."

The door to the room suddenly opened. Pothar and Dobrah spun around clutching at their swords, wondering if their treason had been discovered. "A' 'ere ya 'r." A dark-cloaked form shambled in and Pothar relaxed his hand when he heard the unmistakable voice.

"What are you doing here?" Pothar asked with relief. "You're not allowed in the armory."

"Needed t' find ya. Both ya."

"What do you want, Veake?" Dobrah hurriedly asked.

"Jaleph knows," Veake blurted. "'E knows wut ya d'ing."

Pothar eyes darted around the empty room. "What are you talking about? How could you know?"

"I know. Teraken tuld 'im," came the emphatic response. Veake grabbed each of them by an arm and tried to pull them from the room.

Dobrah shook off the stableman's hand. "Wait a moment. I want you to answer Pothar's question first. How do you know this?"

"I wus tuld. Ya must leave," Veake pleaded. "I've two 'orses ready. No mur d'lay. Ya must come, and 'urry."

Dobrah turned towards Pothar and asked, "What do you think?"

Pothar sighed in frustration and despair. "I don't know, but he's been right before. Teraken could have heard what we were doing. It was a stupid idea to begin with. Maybe we should go, to be on the safe side. We've gotten nowhere with our plan, so what else can we do here? If he is right, we will be out of harm's way. If he's wrong, we're not losing anything."

"But where would we go?" Dobrah's voice rose as her face began to turn red.

"Come, now," Veake implored. "Git t' the 'orses. Shekul. Go t' Shekul."

"That would seem to be our only choice," Dobrah agreed. "But the two of us alone won't be of much use there."

"Shekul, then Gorthon," continued Veake. "Y'll need t' go t' Gorthon."

"Why would we go to Gorthon?" asked Pothar.

"Gorthon," Veake repeated urgently.

"Let's go," Pothar said, but before leaving he took one last look about the room. He saw all the weapons and the banner of a silver and black wolf on the wall. He quickly turned his gaze away, and his eyes came to rest on his old sword which lay alone on the battered table.

Chapter 21

Iridan stirred, still on the horse in front of Worm, as they rode away from the battle. His thigh throbbed and he glanced down at a blood-soaked bandage. He lifted his eyes to see Kile and the few remaining soldiers who had survived. "How long have we been riding?" he murmured.

"A couple hours," replied Worm.

He wondered how he could have managed to remain unconscious for so long with the sharp pain in his leg, but he was grateful for the respite. "Nobody's following?"

"Not that we know."

Iridan grimaced as the horse stepped on a rock, causing a new wave of agony from his wound. "How could it happen?" he asked after a moment.

"What do you mean?"

But Iridan did not answer. Why would Unimeth ally with Jaleph? Had they fought with Amyon (as they had previously when Su'Meeryn was attacked), Jaleph's army might have been defeated. And why would Su'Meeryn go to so much trouble just to ambush Iridan and his men? They were a relatively small force. Besides, Jaleph wanted revenge against Unimeth. There was something strange going on, but Iridan had no idea what that might be. He would have to consider it later as, for now, they needed to focus on returning safely to Shekul.

Their trek was hampered by Iridan and Worm having to ride double, which would need to be rectified if they were to make a timely return. Despite his injuries, Iridan commandeered a horse from a farm they passed along the way. He felt bad stealing the mount, but speed was of the utmost importance as they needed to report to Josu. He had no idea what their course of action might be, but nothing could be done until then.

By the time they caught sight of Shekul's walls, the ache in Iridan's leg had become unbearable and his entire body was stiff from the awkward ride. He was following Kile into the castle when Worm approached. "Let's go to my home," Worm said. "It will provide a more comfortable surrounding in which to recuperate, and I will have one of the healers come by."

"Thank you, but I really must report to Josu," replied Iridan.

"Kile can handle that," Worm responded. "Come along."

"No, we've been through this before. Josu put me in charge, and I will report to him." But the torturous ride and blood loss was too much, and as Iridan dismounted he collapsed.

"Go with him" Kile said, as he helped Iridan back onto the animal. "I'll tell Josu and the others what happened to the mission and about your wound. The king won't begrudge you recuperating at Worm's estate. I'll also send a healer to you right away." Kile then took the remaining soldiers into the castle, leaving Iridan and Worm alone.

"Very well. We'll go to your home," Iridan agreed. He certainly needed some rest and to have his wound treated. He nudged his horse forward and followed Worm, pondering what Worm felt was so important to discuss.

***

The following days were a blur. Vague memories of healers giving him herbs to keep him sedated interspersed with intense throbbing while they treated his injury briefly entered his consciousness. After one night of undisturbed sleep, Iridan awoke on a soft bed to the enticing smell of hot eggs steaming from a table in the corner of his room. He slowly sat up and the warm blanket fell from his naked body. His eyes turned to his wound. A fresh bandage pulled gently against his skin as he moved. As he tentatively stood—testing his leg—he grabbed the luxurious maroon robe hanging next to the bed. The fabric seemed to massage his flesh as he pulled it on.

When he had finished eating, he sat motionless at the table wondering about Worm's whereabouts. He had not seen his friend since they arrived home the previous day. A servant had immediately taken him away to a private room to be cleaned and have his wound dressed, after which he had quickly fallen asleep.

Iridan rose from his chair and opened the door, finding a servant standing outside. "Ah, sir, I see that you are feeling better," the man said.

"Yes, surprisingly."

The man smiled. "Is there something I can get for you?"

"I'd like my clothes."

"I'm sorry, sir, but they had to be discarded. They were too filthy and tattered."

"Of course," Iridan said, quickly glancing down at his scarred hands. With relief, he saw that Naar's ring still rested on his finger. "Are there any other clothes I might borrow?"

"I am sorry, again, sir. We have nothing that would. As you are aware, the master is quite a bit smaller than you."

"Do you expect me to ride back in this?" he asked in frustration, indicating to the robe.

The man laughed. "Certainly not. I will fetch you your own clothes. I was simply waiting for you to awaken first, in case you needed something from me before I left."

"I apologize," Iridan replied feeling foolish. "Can you tell me where Worm is? I believe that he is waiting to talk to me."

"Yes, he asked that I take you to the library after your breakfast." As the servant led Iridan through the large home, Iridan was again astonished at the lavish furnishings. Silver glistened all around him, from candelabrum to vases to picture frames. And in every direction he saw horses: masterful paintings, carved figurines and intricately detailed candles.

"How come I never see anybody else here?" Iridan finally asked after he passed yet another empty room.

"The master's parents rarely return anymore," the man answered.

"Why is that?"

"One might consider that a personal question, sir."

Iridan said nothing further and let the matter drop. He was not willing to involve himself with another mystery.

As they entered the library, the servant excused himself to fetch Worm. Iridan sat down and found a large container of water waiting for him. He sipped from a silver chalice until Worm arrived. "You are looking healthier," Worm said.

"The thigh still hurts, but I do feel better. Thank you for your hospitality."

Worm sat in the chair directly across from him, turning his attention from Iridan's leg to his eyes. "It was a tragic day, wasn't it?" As the memories of the ambush flooded back, Iridan immediately felt guilt for enjoying a nice breakfast and worrying about the state of his clothes. So many fine soldiers had been left dead on the battlefield and he was sitting comfortably in this large estate.

"What did you want to talk to me about, Worm?" Iridan's sharp tone was directed at himself over his self absorption rather than Worm.

"Kile and you were wondering why I wanted to join the attack."

"I told you as much."

"Well, I think it is finally time we discuss Naar."

Chapter 22

The gates of Shekul opened slowly, allowing Dobrah and Pothar entrance. The heads of their exhausted steeds hung low as they were led away. They had ridden away from Su'Meeryn as quickly as possible, knowing that if Veake's warning had been true, a search would have been immediately undertaken. Fortunately, they managed to escape before any of the guards had been alerted to stop them, so Pothar continued to wonder if they had made the right decision. I can't keep second guessing myself, he thought. We are here, and we are safe—at least for the time being.

When Pothar was recognized, they were escorted through the castle, dejected and fatigued from their hard ride. Their guide took them through the maze-like corridors to rooms where they could wash, and after receiving a meal, they were led to Josu's hall.

Pothar followed Dobrah into the room and gazed apprehensively at the king. Josu's lanky frame rose awkwardly from his chair. "Friends of Iridan, eh?" he said as he turned to Flicia. Pothar tried without success to read the king's expression, but then Flicia gave Josu a slight nod and a smile lit up his face as he sat back down.

"Yes we are," Dobrah replied.

"Is he here?" asked Pothar.

"No," Flicia pouted.

A door to Pothar's left opened and Dirwyn came running in. She swung her arms around Pothar and began to cry. When they separated, she reached down to his stump and gently stroked the scarred skin. Her beautiful face quivered at the sight of the wound as she looked back up. "And you're Dobrah," she said, giving the skinny warrior a hug too. "It's nice to see someone from home."

"Come in," Josu bellowed and waved his bony hand to the two men still standing just outside the door. "Surik and Forim," he introduced.

They all sat as refreshments and flasks of wine were brought in. After a sip, Dobrah told the group about their failed attempt to gather support to move against Jaleph and their need to flee their home. When she had finished, Flicia recounted what had happened to Iridan and his men.

"This is not good," Josu interjected. "Soon, Jaleph will march against Shekul. We are no match against his forces."

"That's certainly true," agreed Surik despondently.

"What should we do?"

"I hate to recommend this," Forim said, "but we should consider joining the *emperor*. I don't see that we have any alternative."

"You have not seen what Jaleph has done in Su'Meeryn," Dobrah countered. "He is mad. He's conscripting soldiers and had one of the nobles executed. Countless people have died because of these conquests, and for what?"

"He is not the same man I used to know," Dirwyn added. "Jaleph was a good man, but not anymore. Besides, he would certainly have Iridan killed if we joined him."

"Where is Iridan by the—"

Josu erupted from his chair. "I will never surrender!" he shouted, interrupting Pothar and glaring at the group. "I would rather die."

"Well, that might be our only alternative," Forim remarked.

Flicia reached her hand out, guiding Josu back to his chair. "Neither option is very appealing, but we do still have one other alternative. We should send another envoy to Gorthon. With Jaleph's recent victories, perhaps now they would be more willing to send aid. They will know that Shekul cannot stand alone against Su'Meeryn; it is our only chance."

"But what if they don't?" Surik glared at his glass of wine. "They are still pretty safe in the mountains. They have little to fear from Jaleph even if Shekul falls."

"Do you have any other ideas?" Flicia asked.

Surik shook his head. "And what if we are rejected again?"

"Then we must choose—surrender or death."

Pothar recalled Veake's words to Dobrah and him before they left Su'Meeryn. If Veake had been correct, Gorthon was their only hope. "I would like to travel to Gorthon with your envoy," he said, "but can someone tell me where Iridan is?"

"He's likely still with Worm," answered Flicia.

"Is he okay?"

"Worm's servant went to his room to retrieve some clothes. He said that Iridan was fine and was recuperating from his wounds."

Josu glanced uneasily about the room. His mouth opened and closed several times before Flicia continued. "Then we are agreed; we will send one last emissary to Gorthon."

***

Kile, Dobrah and Pothar left with a small contingent of soldiers after breakfast the following day. Kile led the group south while continually giving Dobrah a quizzical look. "Do you have a problem?" she eventually barked.

"Nothing you need to be concerned about."

"Are you sure about that?"

"Forgive her," Pothar intervened. He had seen the same expression on many of the other soldiers they had served with. "Dobrah is kind of sensitive about her position."

Kile glanced at Pothar then back at Dobrah. "A one-handed warrior and a woman. This is great. I certainly hope we don't meet up with any trouble."

Dobrah's pale face flushed, and she shouted, "Get off your horse and I'll show you what I can do!"

Kile laughed and kept riding. "Very well, let's just get on with our mission", and they continued on their way to the mountainous crags of Gorthon: their last hope for survival against Jaleph's forces.

Chapter 23

Teraken stood in the audience chamber along with a host of soldiers and the nobles. The emperor leaned back on his throne with the satisfaction of having such a large group before him, but the crown scratched his bald scalp as it got caught on the chair. He managed to suppress a squeal as he readjusted himself. Jaleph looked at Teraken's long scars which stood out noticeably against his clean-shaved cheeks. Despite the punishment, Teraken still stood proudly before his king with fierce loyalty flashing in his eyes. "I'm sorry Majesty," Teraken stated as his face softened with regret, "Dobrah and Pothar are nowhere to be found. They must have known that we discovered their plan and escaped."

"I'm not pleased," Jaleph muttered at the news, "but it doesn't matter. We will have them back soon enough." He turned his attention away from Teraken to glance about the hall. He felt strong as the power of ruling over his subjects coursed through his veins, but before he could revel in the feeling any further, Ut entered and approached the throne.

"Greetings, Majesty," Ut proclaimed, while ignoring the hard stare from Teraken. "I'm happy to see you looking healthy. The last time we were together, you were not doing well." Jaleph wondered if anyone else recognized the sarcasm in Ut's words.

"Yes, it comes and goes."

Ut laughed. "Strange how that happens, is it not?"

"What do you want Ut?"

Ut's stare held Jaleph for a moment, and the emperor immediately regretted his short words. He could sense Ut's composure waning, but the slight man managed to control it. "Word from the army, *Majesty*." Jaleph knew that Ut struggled to pull the last word from his mouth. "Amyon has fallen and Unimeth has been secured. All the northern lands are now controlled by Su'Meeryn."

What once would have put a smile on Jaleph's face now brought only apathy. "That's wonderful news," he said flatly. "What's next?" he asked as he motioned to a servant.

"Shekul."

Now Jaleph smiled, not only at the one-word response from Ut but also the goblet of wine the servant presented to him.

Ut sneered at the sight of the amber liquid, but as his mouth opened for what Jaleph knew to be another rebuke, Teraken interrupted. "Pardon me, but winter will be upon us soon. I don't think it wise to move again until the spring."

The emperor ignored Teraken's words as he took a long drink. Ut shook his head at Jaleph before taking a deep breath. "Perhaps you are correct. We do not want to risk the strength of our troops marching through winter weather. We will take the time to assimilate our conquests into our army. Come spring, Shekul will be overrun with little resistance." Ut glared towards the throne as Jaleph emptied his goblet and requested a new one. "How go the conscriptions?" When Jaleph failed to answer, Ut's tone increased. "Jaleph, the conscriptions?"

"They are progressing."

"Good, we will prepare a force that has never before been seen in this land, and then…" Ut stopped abruptly. Jaleph realized that his advisor had almost given up more information than he wanted to, but the emperor did not care. Come spring, Iridan would be captured and killed as would the traitors Dobrah and Pothar. That was all that mattered to him, and he drank from the fresh wine goblet while Ut left in disgust.

***

Orange rays of sunset bathed the naked body of one of his concubines as Jaleph awoke to a rattle at the door. "What is it?" he bellowed and immediately grabbed his head, regretting the volume of his own words.

"Teraken wishes to see you, Sire," came the hesitant reply from behind the door.

The emperor had no desire to see the warrior, but what did it matter? What did anything matter? Jaleph slowly stood and pulled on his robe. "Fine, where is he?"

"Your study, Sire."

Jaleph grunted as he pulled the door open. The two guards made certain not to look into the room as they led the king down the hallway. As they walked, they passed a couple of soldiers which the emperor did not recognize, and he wondered why they were in his palace. Had they been recruited to assassinate him? Why were they there? "Who are those men? Who let them into the palace?"

"New royal guards, Sire," one of his guards answered, "assigned by Ut."

Not knowing whether he should be reassured by the comment, Jaleph was pleased when they finally reached the study. At least he knew what to expect from Teraken.

"Thank you for seeing me," Teraken said as Jaleph entered his study, his heading spinning from the walk.

"What do you want?" the emperor asked as he sat down with a wheeze.

Teraken paused for a moment. "May I have permission to discuss a sensitive subject with you?"

Jaleph guessed what Teraken would say, but he did not want to discuss anything. Will this never end? he thought, but he felt too weak to reject the request. His head nodded slightly in assent.

"Sire, I know that you wish to conquer Shekul, but we could certainly retrieve the traitors and Iridan with diplomacy. You don't need to send any more of your subjects to their death. Let's end this now."

"I can't."

"I thought as much, so I will not attempt to persuade you away from that plan. However, we do not need Ut. Shekul will fall easily before us. I must ask you again to send him away."

Jaleph just shook his head.

"You are the king here," Teraken said in an emphatic yet soft tone, "You can do whatever you want."

"I am emperor!" Jaleph shouted, but he saw only concern on Teraken's face. Concern for Su'Meeryn, but mostly the concern was for his king. Jaleph looked at the old warrior—the friend of his father—through alcohol-riddled eyes, and he wanted to ask forgiveness of the man for his flawed judgment regarding Teraken's motives. He wanted to apologize for the scars which glistened on his cheeks as well as the rejection of their life-long friendship. But he could not offer it. He could not make his mouth speak those words. "I can't," was all he said.

Teraken stared at his liege with sorrow. He looked out the window then back at Jaleph. "Then have me discharge him. I can take care of the situation for you."

"I can't. He wouldn't listen to you."

"Then I will drive my sword through his black heart." The emperor just shook his throbbing head. "But Jaleph, certainly that would be better than continuing down this path."

The thought of Teraken's plan intrigued Jaleph. The possibility of being rescued from his subjection to Ut created an aching aspiration . With Ut dead, he would truly be the emperor, not a slave. Besides,

Teraken was correct when he said that Shekul would fall easily regardless of Ut's presence. And when Jaleph considered it, he really did not care about Shekul. Surely they would hand over Iridan and the others to forgo destruction. But he knew Ut's vile magic and Teraken could not succeed. "You will not attempt it," he ordered, and despite all the two had been through recently he knew that Teraken would obey. "Now, please leave me and have some more wine brought in," the emperor ordered, as there was nothing more to say.

Chapter 24

The small band reached the passageway through the mountains and stopped. "What's wrong?" Pothar asked. "Let's keep going."

"No, we should wait," responded Kile. "I don't think we should enter Gorthon without invitation. The last time we were here, we did not receive a pleasant farewell."

After a few silent moments, Dobrah jumped down from her horse and began to pace. "How long should we wait here?" she snapped at the soldier from Shekul.

"Look, I'm the one who has been here before and met with their king, and I say that we wait."

Kile and the rest of the group also dismounted to allow the horses to graze, but within a few moments a large group of men emerged from amongst the rocks. Spear points aimed at their chests warned the messengers to remain motionless. One man strode forward and looked into Kile's face. "You are the quiet one, aren't you?"

Kile looked about at the soldiers before replying. "Wox, isn't it?"

"Yes, you remember," the dark-skinned man nodded.

"This is kind of a coincidence isn't it, meeting you here again?"

"No coincidence," Wox replied. "I am assigned to this location. We've been monitoring your movements for some time."

"We need to speak with your king, again. It is of utmost importance."

"Gorthon has no king."

"Yes of course. It is a habit, but we need to speak with Vol."

"Vol will not want to see you."

"Do you know what is happening out there?" Dobrah interrupted. "Jaleph's forces have conquered all the northern lands and Shekul will fall next. Does Gorthon intend to sit back and do nothing?"

"Why should Gorthon care?"

Pothar looked with disgust at Wox. "Innocent people are being killed, and Gorthon doesn't care?"

Wox gazed steadily at Pothar and the others in the group. Pothar watched a silent struggle battle across the dark man's countenance. "I will take you to Vol," Wox replied with resignation, "again."

***

The group stood in the hall before Vol, and Pothar examined the impressive man. An air of authority engulfed Vol but his countenance revealed none of his emotions. Gorthon's leader had not invited them to speak and he sat expressionless until he noticed Dobrah. "A woman warrior?" Vol exclaimed as his stoic face lit up with surprise.

"Yes, Sire," Dobrah replied.

"I am not Sire. I am Vol."

"I'm sorry. It is what I am accustomed to."

"Of course." Vol turned his attention to Kile. "I remember you, but not the others. Why have you been brought before me again?"

"They seek another audience to discuss Su'Meeryn, Vol," Wox replied.

Vol turned a disapproving eye to Wox. "Let them speak for themselves, but I doubt they have anything new of interest to offer."

"Vol," Pothar began hesitantly, feeling uncomfortable at not using a title to address the leader of Gorthon. "I know that you are aware of the actions of Su'Meeryn. We seek your help to stop them from destroying others."

"That is what was asked of us last time. Why should I change my mind?"

"After Shekul falls—which it undoubtedly will—Gorthon will certainly be Jaleph's next target."

Vol laughed. "Su'Meeryn is no threat to us."

"Are you certain of that?" Kile asked.

"We are more than safe in our mountain realm."

"Is that all you care about," interjected Dobrah, "your own safety?"

Gorthon's leader looked back at Dobrah, and Pothar noticed his scowl soften. Vol sighed as he ran his fingers through his long black hair. He motioned for his woman, who came and whispered in his ear. After considering for a few more moments, he turned back to the group from Shekul. "Perhaps you are right. Perhaps we have only thought of ourselves, but Gorthon will not fight Su'Meeryn for you; however, I would be willing to offer sanctuary to any who seek it."

"That's all?"

Vol's sympathetic expression quickly dissolved. "I offer you life, and I suggest that you do not anger me," he said coldly, "or I will leave you to the blades of Su'Meeryn. Sanctuary or death: what do you say?"

"We are sorry Vol," Pothar quickly responded. "Your offer is a most generous one. We will present it to Josu, and we offer you our thanks. Is there enough space in your land for all of Shekul?"

A nod of approval greeted Pothar's words. "You are a wise man and yes, we have ample room for all your people. Now, you may leave to converse with your king. I would like the woman to remain though. She intrigues me."

Dobrah took a step back at Vol's words. "I should return with the others," she replied nervously.

"No, I want you to stay." Vol continued as Pothar moved in front of Dobrah. Vol quickly stood and four of his guards jumped forward. "Do not be stupid," he breathed. "My patience is near its end, as is my offer." But Pothar refused to move and just stared back at Vol. The leader of Gorthon strode towards them and stood towering above Pothar. Vol glared down at him but then just laughed. "You are a brave man. Perhaps a little stupid, but brave; perhaps that is why you lost that hand? You need not worry about your woman. She will not be ravaged." Vol returned to his seat before continuing. "But it is now time for you to go." He gazed at Dobrah. "Will you remain with us?"

"Should I assume your offer will be rescinded if I leave?"

"What is your name?" asked Vol.

"Dobrah."

"Gorthon has no women warriors," Vol continued. "I would like to talk with you, nothing more. You will be safe here. A favor has been asked of Gorthon, now I choose to ask a favor of you."

Dobrah looked at Pothar, but there was no response he could offer her. The decision was hers. "Certainly Vol, I will stay with you."

Pothar, Kile and the other warriors left the mountain pass of Gorthon with some semblance of hope. They had not received the response they sought, but now at least, the people of Shekul had an alternative to facing Su'Meeryn alone.

***

Pothar and Kile slowly climbed the staircase, exhausted from the brisk ride back to Shekul. The thought of leaving Dobrah alone in Gorthon weighed heavily on Pothar, but then he realized that she was safer than any of the rest of them.

Pothar felt nervous as they approached the door to Josu's hall. The news they were bringing was not what they had sought, although at least the people of Shekul would have a chance of survival. The two stood still as Kile took a deep breath before opening the door. They were escorted in and offered chairs. After being handed some water, Pothar took a long drink then relayed their story to Josu, Flicia, Surik and Forim.

"I don't think we have any other choice," Kile concluded. The brothers turned red with anger as the king's elongated face remained blank.

When no response came, Pothar began to fidget nervously. "Gorthon won't come to your aid, but at least they offer refuge."

"Flee? I can't imagine it," Flicia responded softly as she began to stroke Josu's hair.

"We can't just leave our land," Forim agreed.

Pothar shook his head. "If you stay, you die."

"Is that any worse?" asked Forim.

Pothar failed to restrain an angry laugh. "Are you serious? You'd sacrifice yourselves and your people to indulge your pride?"

"We could surrender to him." Surik pointed out. "We could join Su'Meeryn's army."

This time Flicia laughed. "Haven't you been paying attention? That's what Unimeth tried, and Jaleph destroyed them."

As Flicia finished speaking, Josu finally stood and glanced about the room at each of his guests in turn. He ended on Flicia and a look of confidence crossed his face. "I will not subject my people to Jaleph's attack. We cannot stand up to his force alone so we will go to Gorthon."

Surik scowled at the king's words. "Are you sure you want—"

"I am sure," Josu said emphatically. "We don't know what will happen when we arrive there, but at least we may have a chance to reclaim our lands at a later time." Before Forim could interrupt, Josu motioned for him to stop. "I have made my decision," he stated, without displaying the usual smile he gave after making one of his rare decisions. "You will all begin the preparation."

Before everyone rose to leave, a notion came to Pothar. "Has anyone heard from Iridan?"

"He's remained with Worm, recovering from his wound," Forim answered. "From what we've been told he's doing much better."

Chapter 25

Footfalls echoed through the audience chamber as Jaleph dropped onto his throne, flinging an empty wineskin across the room. He glanced about the empty hall, then over to the crown which sat on the arm of his seat. Trembling fingers reached for the cold metal and placed it on his head. As it slid into place it tugged at the loose strands of yellow hair which had returned to his scalp. Jaleph winced, but the pain quickly dissolved under the numbing effect of the alcohol. He reached beneath his belt for a fresh wineskin, oblivious to the returning flab around his stomach, and took another long gulp of wine which left crimson trails dripping from the corners of his mouth. But the emperor did not notice or care. He cared about nothing anymore.

News of Shekul's retreat had brought a mixed reaction to the emperor. The wars were over, but Iridan had escaped as had Dobrah and Pothar. Now he would never be able to exact his revenge. Shekul was reported to be fleeing towards Gorthon. Despite the gains from all Su'Meeryn's victories, they were certainly not strong enough to fight through those formidable mountains. What did it matter? With Myrin dead, why worry about Iridan? Why worry about anything?

He raised the wineskin again but paused before it reached his lips. Through his muddled brain, he considered the wars, reminding himself that they were over. He had won, but now what? Yes, it was time to move on, but what did that mean? He resealed the wineskin. Now was the time to figure that out.

"There you are," Ut sneered as he approached the throne. Jaleph winced at the sight of the skeletal face and wisps of hair which were fully visible whenever Jaleph saw the man alone.

"What do you want now, Ut?" the emperor asked sharply.

"Watch your tone with me."

"Of course," he slurred dejectedly. "I do not mean to offend you."

"Much better, and you best remember that." Ut glared at the wineskin, and Jaleph awaited another rebuke. He was surprised when none came. "We must make preparations for our next move," Ut continued.

"What do you mean? It's all over. We've won and Shekul is fleeing to Gorthon."

Ut laughed. "We are far from over. Iridan lives, so now we must conquer Gorthon."

Jaleph felt that he should be surprised by Ut's words, but nothing surprised him anymore. "I want him dead more than anyone," he noted as his head cleared slightly at the thought of killing Iridan, "but we would be slaughtered."

Ut's already hideous face twisted into an even viler sneer. "Your opinion is irrelevant."

The weight of Ut's words struck the emperor deeper than any sword could penetrate. How had it come to this? How was it that the emperor's thoughts were of no value in his own land? But how he had come to this state really did not matter. What mattered was the fact that it was true. He remembered the game of chess the two had played so long ago. Ut had referred to Jaleph as the king on that board, but that was not true. With despair feeling like a lump in his stomach, Jaleph now knew that he had been nothing more than Ut's pawn. "What do you hope to accomplish with this?" Jaleph said, practically pleading.

"My motives are my own. You will do as you are told." Ut took one step closer to the throne and the black aura began to slowly emanate from his mouth. "Do I make myself clear?"

The emperor glanced down at the wineskin and then back at Ut. He snatched the wineskin and took a quick drink, his only remaining act of defiance. "Winter is coming," he noted with a self-congratulatory smile. "You'll have to wait 'till next year."

"No! Now!" Ut shouted. "Get started." He spun around and marched out of the hall. Jaleph gazed at the retreating figure and took another drink.

***

The look on Teraken's face was unmistakable. "We can't do this," he said. "Please Sire, I beg you to reconsider. Send Ut away."

Jaleph finished a bite of his roasted duck. "As I told you before, I can't send him away," he said softly.

"Why?"

Jaleph pushed the plate away as he remembered the thought of the black aura constricting around his neck. He grabbed his cup and said, "I just can't. Now don't ask me again. We'll have to proceed with the plan."

Teraken stared quietly at the emperor for a few moments, and Jaleph knew he was searching for an alternative. *It's no use my old* friend, the emperor thought. "So you've stopped shaving your head," was all Teraken managed to say.

"I figured I'd let it grow for a while."

"You've also stopped running, and I've seen you drinking a lot."

Jaleph put his cup on the table. "You think it's your place to criticize your emperor?"

Teraken shifted uncomfortably in his chair. "Of course not, I'm just concerned about you. You were never like this before Ut. He is taking you and Su'Meeryn down a dangerous path. This is all because of him. Please Sire, just—"

"Enough!" Jaleph screamed. "Get out! Start the plans! Now!" He brought the cup to his lips before realizing that it was empty; regardless, he feigned a long drink. "Move!" After Teraken left the room, Jaleph gazed at the empty cup before smashing it against the table.

He sat alone in the room feeling enraged at his situation. He was trapped by Ut. He had to obey the man or die, but Ut's commands would bring about the destruction of Su'Meeryn. However, he would die either way as the people of Gorthon would certainly not allow him to live after the attack failed. They would come to Su'Meeryn and execute him. Was that Ut's true plan: the destruction of Su'Meeryn? No, that could not be it; Ut certainly must have something else in mind. Ut would not have made him emperor just to watch it all crumble away. Yes, he was the emperor, but that meant nothing. He felt much like the child he was when his father was still alive. The people of the kingdom had always respected him then, but he had no power. Now he was powerless again.

"There is something different I have now," he mumbled as he strode from the room and headed to his harem. If he could not rule, he would at least indulge his physical desires.

Chapter 26

Rain fell harder than Pothar had ever seen. While holding tightly to the reins, he wiped at his brow with his stump, gazing for a moment at his wound through the sheets of water. While the ache had thankfully lessened, it had not fully disappeared. Happily he no longer suffered from the phantom throbbing that had plagued him for so long, and he no longer needed the pain-numbing elixirs.

Despite the hardship of the weather, the march had progressed uneventfully. Pothar looked back at the inhabitants of Shekul with admiration. While there had been a deal of grumbling and complaining, there had not been nearly the amount which he had expected. A number of farmers had argued that they were not soldiers and therefore would not be attacked. They had refused to desert their homes and only left when sword points had been leveled at their chests. If Shekul was to be evacuated, everyone needed to leave. Josu had been adamant that his people remain together. He would not allow anyone to fall under Jaleph's rule.

"A very sad day." Pothar turned and saw that Josu had come alongside him.

"Yes, but I must compliment your people. They have displayed considerable courage."

Josu's bony shoulders rose with pride. "They are a remarkable people. I am honored to be their king."

"If I may say, you're a fine king. Many would rather face death than give up his kingdom for the good of his people."

"Neither option is very appealing."

"Of course not," Pothar replied as he wiped his face again.

"It takes courage to do what you did as well: betraying your king and joining his enemy."

Pothar appreciated the praise, but he did not see it as deserved. He felt that Dobrah and he had made the only decision possible, but then something else struck him. "Pardon me for saying this Sire, but you seem different to me, more sure of yourself."

Josu's face brightened and he giggled slightly. "Perhaps so. I guess a time comes when a man must look at his own reflection and make some determinations."

Pothar nodded his head as Josu steered his horse back to Flicia. I guess some things don't change, Pothar thought.

***

"I don't know how our entire population will be able to set up camp in all this rain," Kile said as a new round of thunder rolled overhead.

Pothar looked back through the pouring rain at the long stretch of Shekul's inhabitants trailing behind. "I feel sorry for them. I still think we should be willing to give up our horses, at least for a time."

"You know we can't do that. The warriors must be rested in case of attack."

"I suppose," Pothar replied, not entirely convinced. The scouts had found no evidence of any soldiers moving against them, and a force strong enough to pose a threat would not be able to hide. "This certainly is not the ideal situation is it?"

Kile remained silent for a moment. "I never thought I'd see a sight like this. Shekul has seen its share of skirmishes over the years, but I never expected such a large army to attack us."

"Su'Meeryn didn't expect it either, but we survived." Pothar sighed. Who would have thought the kingdom would go down this path after they had defeated the siege? He shook his head as he continued "Your people have shown tremendous strength through all this."

"Yes, I am very proud of them."

"You know, I was talking to Josu a little while ago. Does he seem different to you?"

"Now that you mention it," Kile said after a pause, "I did notice something when we started the evacuation. He didn't turn to Flicia as much for advice, or Surik and Forim."

"It seems that the weight of our circumstance has brought out the best in him." Unlike Jaleph, he thought. "I'd still like to know where Iridan is."

"We sent word of the evacuation to Worm's estate, but we were too busy getting all the farmers off their lands to send someone back there when they didn't show."

Pothar felt considerable annoyance at Kile's words. "Why is this the first time I've heard this?"

"Oh, I am sorry, do I now report to you!" Kile responded sarcastically.

"Well, how do you know they received the message?"

"Listen, watch yourself Pothar. We are all going through a lot, but you have no right to speak to me this way. The message was delivered. I'm sure Worm and Iridan are trailing after."

"But they would be on horseback. They should have caught up by now."

Kile's aggravation was clearly growing as much as Pothar's. "They are grown men and they know what is occurring. We can't make the entire kingdom wait for those two," Kile spat before angrily steering his horse away.

He's right, Pothar thought, but there must be something wrong. It's unlike Iridan to not be present in a situation such as this, but they should be safe. Jaleph's spies certainly have word of Shekul's evacuation. There would be no reason to attack the castle or Shekul's lands, besides Jaleph will probably think Iridan is with us. I just hope I see him again; I think we will need him before all this is over.

Chapter 27

"It took quite a bribe to get them to leave," Worm said, "and I had to promise that we would be leaving shortly." He sat on a chair across from Iridan and regarded his companion's face. The silence was broken by a few short barks, and the small dog ran in and bounded onto Worm's lap. Worm smiled and scratched the animal behind the ears before taking a sip of wine. When the goblet rested again on the side table, Worm wiped his mouth then continued to pet the dog with a growing expression of sorrow. "It will be hard to leave him here, but I don't suppose a dog will be able to make the trip to Gorthon." He looked back at Iridan and offered him the goblet. When Iridan shook his head, Worm took another sip.

"All right," Iridan said, "let's talk about Naar."

"Yes, this has been a long time coming."

"Pardon me if I have a hard time believing you," Iridan began, annoyance slipping into his tone. "Why after all this time do you want to discuss him now? I thought you felt it was all fiction?"

Worm tapped the dog on the rump and it quickly jumped from the chair, and ran out of the room. Gazing into Iridan's eyes he leaned forward. "I do," he said, "at least I did." He reached for the wine goblet one more time but his hand hesitated for a moment before returning to the chair. "I'd been thinking about how important Naar's writings were to you. It always seemed like a waste of time to me, but you are not a stupid man. So, as I continued pondering it, something struck me. When you and Kile were to head to Amyon, I had a vague memory of a passage I had read in Naar. I couldn't remember it exactly. It had something to do with an individual going to the north, being ambushed then rescued. I couldn't stop thinking of you. I searched for the passage before you left but couldn't find it and when the time came for you to leave, even though I hadn't come across the passage again, I felt compelled to go with you. After we returned home and you were recovering, I finally came across it." Worm pulled a parchment from his robe and handed it Iridan.

He had searched for clues for so long but had pretty much given up hope. So with conflicting emotions, Iridan took the parchment and read the section Worm indicated:

Then he led his small band north. They prepared to meet the forces of the Apprentice, but he was ambushed. If not for the worm, he would have been left to die on that field. But after his return, he was made ready for the final conflict against the Deceiver's army.

"That's it," Worm said. "It's just a fragment, so I never gave it much thought. The whole 'worm' thing at the time just seemed like a strange coincidence but it certainly can't be the case now."

"No," Iridan agreed quietly as he stared at the parchment with a feeling of relief. It was gratifying to know that he had been correct: that there was truth to be found in Naar's words. But as quickly as it came, the relief grew to anger. While the fragment seemed to refer to him, there were still no answers to be found. What did it all mean? He reached for a glass of water while fighting back a yawn. After a drink the yawn returned and forced itself from his mouth. He tried to fight back this unexpected wave of exhaustion and re-read the words. Perhaps there was something else within the rest of the parchment, but his eyes suddenly lost focus. The sound of Worm's voice asking if he was okay barely registered in his brain. Why had he become so tired? Years of scouting had trained him to fight through sleepiness; besides, he was fully rested after his days of recuperating. He yawned again as his eyes began to close.

"Iridan, what's wrong?"

Why couldn't he stay awake? More words came from Worm, but Iridan could not make them out. Water spilled in his lap as he dropped the glass, but even the cool splash failed to awaken him and his eyes closed completely as his head dropped limp against his shoulder.

***

He stood on a field. He could make out nothing of his surroundings due to a driving rain that engulfed him. A tremendous crash of thunder struck overhead. Another burst erupted which was even louder, then a third. Thunder continued to boom, the volume increasing with each crack. He dropped to his knees in the mud, covering his ears, trying to protect himself from the deafening blasts, but to no avail. His ears rang and he felt a warm flow of liquid starting to stream from between his fingers. Still the rain and thunder continued. Now each blast brought a blinding light to join the reports. The lightning seared his eyes and he threw his face into the mud, desperate to escape the onslaught. But each blast pierced his meager defenses, driving a fresh wave of agony into his senses. When he thought he would go mad from the assault, all became quiet. He swayed back to his feet, his head throbbing with each heartbeat as waves of nausea and pain coursed through every inch of his body. The flow of blood from his ears slowed as a rumbling began from under his feet. He tried to look about, but his eyes were only greeted by a curtain of black. As he stood motionless he felt the fluttering of a breeze against the back of his neck. It began to blow harder, bringing a new onslaught of pain as it beat against his head. The rumbling increased as the wind stopped, but still he saw only black as the howling moved. It flowed from beneath his feet to in front of his face, growing in intensity until it was directly above him, and then it stopped. He looked up just in time to see one last bolt of lightning shoot down and strike him. As he fell, his scream was drowned out by the thunder. His whole body spasmed from the agony. Why he was still alive was a mystery. He begged for death to end his torment; how could an individual endure such pain? Then the darkness dissipated as a soft light came down from the sky. The light intensified and he recognized the sun. Bathed by the rays, his face grew hot and he tried to protect himself by covering it with his arms. His skin grew dry from the heat and he cried in pain as it began to crack. The light burrowed in through his arm and burned his eyes. A cry escaped his mouth as his hair withered.

Who are you?

He tried to answer, but could not form any words.

Who are you?

What was happening to him? He pulled his arms away and looked up. The rays of the sun drilled deep into his eyes but he managed to see a cloud drifting down from overhead providing a shadow from the sun. He managed to look about and saw that he was somehow still surrounded by rain on all sides. The cloud continued to descend and once it touched the top of his head, all his pain vanished.

Who are you?

The cloud completely enveloped him and he realized that he was beginning to ascend. As he continued to rise he noticed that he was standing in the cloud. He turned around and saw a white-robed man next to him. "Who are you?" Iridan managed to ask.

The man grinned. "Isn't that my question?" Iridan just gazed back, dumbfounded. "I am Naar," the man answered.

"And who am I?"

Naar stepped forward and placed a hand on Iridan's shoulder. "Why, Chaw Den, of course. Welcome."

Chapter 28

The crowd stood deathly silent in the courtyard. Blue banners flapped in the breeze, blurring the silver and black faces of the wolves. Jaleph strode unsteadily to the pillar honoring Teracuss, which had been built after Iridan and Myrin flew atop Jokk-al Ystren, saving Su'Meeryn from the attacking hordes of Tamar, Amyon and Unimeth. The rays of the sun reflected off the glistening metal causing Jaleph to squint in pain. His eyes were no longer used to the light, as he now spent most of his days drunk and hidden away in his palace or with his harem.

He stumbled again and braced himself against the pillar. His fingers felt the grooves of the letters of Teracuss' name, which were carved on every side. He turned and regarded the monument, trying to remember, unsuccessfully, the last time he had seen it. Teracuss was a good man, the emperor thought; why did he have to die? Why not Iridan? The thought of Su'Meeryn's savior caused a pang of envy to shoot through his cloudy mind. Yes, everything would be different now if Iridan had been the one who had been killed. Myrin would still be alive, and she would have become queen. No, none of this would have happened. Ut never would have been granted such access to Su'Meeryn's king, and he would not have this control over Jaleph. "It's all his fault," Jaleph mumbled. Iridan was the leader of the expedition to search for Naar's ring. He should have been the one to sacrifice himself. I wouldn't be in this position now if he had done what he should have, the emperor thought; I might not have conquered the lands that I have, but at least I would still be king. I would have my power.

Ut—his hideous features masked for the benefit of the crowd—brushed past the pillar, taking his place next to Jaleph. The emperor looked at the slight man with utter contempt. He wanted to order his guards to seize Ut, but was held in check by the memory of that vile black aura. It's all Iridan's fault, Jaleph thought again, but at least I will get my revenge.

"Now," Ut commanded and waved to his right. Soldiers entered the courtyard, dragging someone behind them.

"I don't want to do this," whispered the emperor.

"Shut up," Ut responded under his breath. "It has been decided."

"But—"

Ut spun around and his eyes darkened in warning. Jaleph's mouth closed immediately: just one more reason to hate the man standing before him.

"Please, please," the man whimpered as he was hurled before Ut and the emperor. Dust swirled from the ground as he landed with a groan. "Please."

"Stand!" ordered Ut. The battered figure rose to his feet—the face of Yonath now visible to the entire crowd.

Ut motioned to Jaleph, but the emperor did not move. Thoughts of Iridan still swirled through his thoughts: *soon he will be dead. I will order him to be taken alive so that I can drive my sword through his heart.*

"Your emperor has asked me to handle this matter," Ut began, giving up on Jaleph. "While he recognizes the importance of this task, he does find it distasteful. Of course, he wants nothing but the best for all his subjects; however, when one is disloyal, action must be taken for the good of all."

"I did nothing," Yonath pleaded. "I was only trying to serve my king. That is all I have ever done. Please Sire, you have to believe me!"

Ut turned his attention to the crowd. "Do you see the desperation of this guilty man? He will say anything to save himself. This is an example to all; Jaleph requires your loyalty. If you are loyal, you have nothing to fear from him. But those who refuse will suffer the same fate."

Jaleph snickered and received another glare from Ut. *Loyalty, if anyone here is not loyal, it is you.* Yonath had done nothing wrong except to provide the smallest number of conscriptions, and that had given Ut his motivation. With word of Pothar's and Dobrah's sedition spreading, Ut was concerned that no one had been punished. It set a bad precedent, Ut had said. An example was needed to help quench any further thoughts of rebellion, and despite Jaleph's protests, Yonath had been selected to be that individual. It all seemed unnecessary; the army would be leaving soon. Why punish an innocent man? Dobrah and Pothar would receive their due, as would Iridan.

"You may proceed," Ut announced. Two guards dragged the crying body of Yonath to his feet. He screamed in terror as they forced his body to bend at its waist. Yonath struggled to break free but the strong hands would not let go. Another guard came up carrying a large axe. He stopped at Yonath's side while raising the axe and with a mighty swing he brought it down on the back of Yonath's neck. Blood erupted, covering all three soldiers as the crowd gasped in unison. A deep cut was visible in Yonath's neck as blood continued to pour to the ground, but his head still remained attached to his body. The guard swung again and this time the head fell to the ground. The two men dropped the body next to the head and left the courtyard. Ut clapped in delight as the crowd began to disperse then turned to Jaleph who remained motionless. After a few moments Ut shrugged his shoulders and left Jaleph alone with his personal guards. The emperor again ran his fingers across the engraved letters of Teracuss' name as his thoughts returned to Iridan. *Yes, this is all because of him. I would not be the joke of a monarch that I am if not for him.*

***

Jaleph reclined on a sofa with an empty flask of wine. Two of his concubines lay asleep with him. The harem had grown to six women—all beautiful—but despite the bodily pleasures he received in that room, he found no joy. He was the king of Su'Meeryn and the emperor of many lands, but in truth, he was just a servant. He was the servant to an evil man with vile powers. One of the women stirred beside him and Jaleph glanced at her face. Yes, she was lovely, but she too was just a servant. Given the choice she would certainly flee from this room and the palace, as would they all. Jaleph lifted the blanket to display her naked body. He relished the image for a moment before covering her again, disgusted with himself. He realized that establishing the harem had been a mistake. While they all satisfied him physically, none of them quenched his true craving. *There was only one,* he thought, *and she was taken away from me. Only one.*

A knock sounded against the door causing the women to stir as Jaleph slowly stood. He opened the door and was advised that Ut had requested his presence.

***

"Very nice, drunk again," Ut noted as Jaleph entered the strategy room. "You certainly make an impressive, regal sight."

"What do you want?" the emperor slurred.

"The army is just about ready to embark," Ut said as Jaleph took the seat next to him, "and you will need to prepare yourself. You will be joining in the attack."

Jaleph turned his spinning head to regard his companion. "Me? I don't think so. What could I do? I'd prefer to stay here."

443

"I did not ask you if you wanted to go. My statement was clear!"

"Why? What possible use would I be on the battlefield?"

"That is not your concern. You will join. Am I understood?"

The emperor turned away, not wanting Ut to see the despair on his face. "Of course, Ut."

Ut stood and walked away from the table. As he approached the door he turned back. "And Jaleph, you will leave the wine here," he ordered with finality in his voice.

***

"I don't know!" Jaleph barked. "Ut said I should go, so I have to!" He rose from his throne and the anger in his eyes quickly turned to dejection as he peered about the empty audience chamber.

Teraken's attempt to soften his countenance was not completely successful. "I just wish you would tell me why you have to do what Ut says. This is madness."

Jaleph turned to his friend. Despite the lingering effects of his last serving of wine, his eyes managed to focus on the scars. His mouth opened, trying to force the words "I'm sorry" out as he had tried so many times before, but he failed. He could not force himself to express remorse. "Just follow my orders."

"That is wise counsel," Ut interjected as he approached the pair.

Teraken's lips tightened at the sight of the man he despised. "What do you want, Ut?"

Ut's eyes narrowed, and Jaleph knew he was fighting to control his appearance. "I have come to make sure that we are fully prepared to leave tomorrow."

"What difference does it make," Teraken asked. "We will be slaughtered when we reach Gorthon's mountains. How do you expect us to survive that pass?"

A small chuckle escaped Ut's lips. "We will do just fine. I have a surprise waiting. Soon Su'Meeryn will rule this whole country."

"I will truly be emperor then," Jaleph muttered. A few months ago, that statement would have pleased him immensely but now he just did not care. His only thought was the revenge he would exact from Iridan.

Ut turned to Jaleph with thinly-veiled disdain. "Of course." Ut then addressed Teraken. "Make certain everything is set. We leave at dawn."

Once Ut had departed, Teraken turned back to Jaleph. "I wish there was some way I could convince you to end this before it is too late."

I wish for that too, Jaleph thought. "I am tired of this same discussion. I don't want to have it any more."

"The nobles were not able to persuade you either, I take it," Teraken commented softly, and Jaleph's memory was immediately taken back to the sight of Yonath's headless body lying on the ground before him. "If only there was someone else in the kingdom that you would trust."

"It has nothing to do with that," Jaleph replied as he dropped back down on the throne. "Now, do not speak of this again to me. The decision has been made."

Teraken stared at the man he had known since his birth. Jaleph saw the look of frustration and sorrow and he wanted to scream. He wanted to order the guards to haul Teraken away, but his emotions mellowed as Teraken departed. Despite his insolence, Teraken was loyal to the crown. He would never disobey the king of Su'Meeryn, whether he agreed with the king's decisions or not. Before he left, Teraken turned back and said, "Goodbye Jaleph."

Chapter 29

The host from Shekul stopped at the mountain pass into Gorthon; mud splashed all around as Josu's tall frame dropped from his horse. He strode through the drizzle and stood before Vol. "It is an honor to meet the leader of Gorthon. I am Josu, King of Shekul, and I thank you for your generosity of welcoming us to your country."

Vol reached up and placed his hands on Josu's gaunt shoulders. "We are pleased to welcome Josu and his people, and to provide our hospitality."

"I was surprised at your offer." Josu looked around with the trace of a tear forming in his eyes; the emotion of leaving his home and the generosity of a foreign people threatened to overwhelm the king. "I hope my people will not be too much of a burden."

Gorthon's leader smiled widely as his waved back towards his mountainous realm. "We have plenty of space for all of you."

"But Jaleph will certainly move against Gorthon now."

"He would be a fool if he does," Vol laughed. "Now, I'm sure that you are hungry after your long journey. Come join my wife and me for dinner. The rest of your people will be cared for."

Vol steered Josu away and Pothar stared in wonder at the two rulers. He had never heard Josu speak so coherently before, and Vol's hospitality was completely unexpected. As Josu and Vol disappeared, the people of Shekul advanced through the rain-slicked pass. Pothar and Kile handed their reins to a servant, and they waited for hours while everyone entered into Gorthon. When just the two of them remained, they too made their way in.

"I wonder where everyone is going to stay," Kile remarked.

"Vol didn't seem too concerned," Pothar responded, "so I guess we shouldn't be either."

"There you are," Wox interrupted, "the one-handed warrior and the quiet one: wanted to make sure everyone made it in safely, I see. Now, please follow me." Wox guided them up the path, and it was soon clear they were heading in a different direction from where they had previously met with Vol.

The echo of the trio's footsteps rang through the rocky corridor for longer than Pothar had expected. He glanced around, trying to commit something of his surroundings to memory, but the terrain left few distinguishing features. They ran across a few intersecting trails and Pothar knew that he would never be able to find his way out of Gorthon on his own. As they continued their hike, a suspicious thought came to him. "Why haven't we met up with any of our people? They must certainly be traveling slower than us."

Wox waved for them to continue forward. "I am taking you to a different area, but do not worry. You will see your people soon enough."

Pothar scowled at the ambiguity of Wox's words. "And where exactly would that be?"

"Vol wanted me to show you something first. We are well aware that Jaleph will press his attack against Gorthon now, but as he said, we are not concerned." Wox continued on until they reached a cave entrance in a mountainside. "Here we are, please follow me in."

As he entered, Pothar stopped in amazement. The cave opened up before him to reveal an immense cavern. It seemed to encompass the entire width of the mountain and a strange green light illuminated the entire area. Pothar looked around for the source until he realized that the light emanated from a green moss which covered the walls and the floor deep below. Everywhere he turned, the room teemed with activity. "This is amazing," he whispered.

"We have many caves of similar size," Wox stated proudly.

"And that light, it comes from the moss?"

"Yes, the moss is self illuminating. As far as we know, it grows only in Gorthon."

"What are all those people doing?" Kile questioned their guide.

"We mine many precious metals in these mountains."

The thought of the scope of mining operation intrigued Pothar, but he set aside his questions. What mattered was Jaleph's inevitable attack. He continued to stare at the moss as he asked, "Are all the other caves this busy?"

"Many, but not all."

"Are most of the men trained to fight?" Wox nodded. "How do you feed everyone?"

"There are lands east of us. The world does not stop at our mountains," Wox answered sarcastically. "With the amount of gold and other metals we mine here, we have no problem trading for enough food." The guide paused for a moment before continuing. "And weapons."

"If Jaleph tries to move through the pass, he'll be slaughtered," exclaimed Kile.

Wox's teeth glowed an eerie green as he smiled.

***

Pothar and Kile sat in a cold, stone room after changing into dry clothes, trying to make themselves comfortable on the hard ground. They had been led by Wox to a different cave where many of Shekul's inhabitants were being housed. All around the interior of the cave, small alcoves had been dug into the walls, which would now serve as living quarters. As the people of Gorthon no longer mined this cave, the luminous moss had grown very thick. The entire cave glowed from the green light—and Pothar wondered how anyone would get any sleep—but that was the last of his worries at the moment.

"I guess I've slept in worse places," noted Kile.

"Yeah," Pothar agreed.

Kile pulled at his blanket as he tried to make himself comfortable. "I still wonder what happened to Iridan and Worm. They should have arrived by now."

"It's not like Iridan to disappear, especially at a time like this," Pothar grunted as a piece of stone pushed through his bedding when he turned onto his side.

"I'm worried about them."

"Them?" Pothar said with some surprise. "You had nothing good to say about this Worm the entire way here."

The softening of Kile's hard face was particularly amplified in the green light. "He can be a bastard at times. I guess I just realized now that I need to forgive him."

"Here you are," a soft voice interrupted as a lovely face with flowing red hair entered. "I've been looking for you since we left."

"Hello, Dirwyn," Pothar responded as he sat up.

She settled down next to him and placed her hand on his stump. "We haven't had any time to talk."

Pothar had to fight to withhold a gasp as he looked at Dirwyn. He had always recognized how beautiful she was, but the green aura seemed to transform her. The unworldly light darkened her hair which made her face stand out even more than normal. Surik is a lucky man, he thought. "The journey through the rain and mud did not lend itself to much conversation," he finally managed to say. "Have you heard anything about Dobrah?"

"Oh yes, she is fine. She apparently spent a good amount of time talking to Vol. She should be coming this way soon, as I was told that all of Shekul's warriors are to be housed together."

"What about Josu?" Kile asked.

"He went off with Vol and the others," Dirwyn replied. "I believe they are discussing plans to defend against Jaleph's attack."

"He couldn't be that stupid," Kile remarked.

A snort escaped from Pothar's nose. "I don't put anything past him anymore."

"But attacking Gorthon would be suicide, wouldn't it?" asked Dirwyn.

"With the width of the trail into the mountains, Jaleph's forces will be easily slaughtered," agreed Kile, "especially against forces familiar with the area."

"Is there any other way in here?"

"Not that I'm aware of," Pothar responded. "The people of Gorthon don't seem to be very concerned, so I tend to think not."

Dirwyn reached out to Pothar and Kile, giving each a quick hug. "I better head back, but I just wanted to make sure I saw you," she said as a dark cloud seemed to cross her face. "Just in case… well…"

"I understand," Pothar replied. "I'm sure you want to return to Surik. If you hear anything about Iridan, will you send word?"

"Of course," Dirwyn answered as she headed out of the small alcove with a wave.

"She is a lovely woman," Kile said, as his eyes followed after her, "in more than just appearance."

Pothar nodded in agreement as his thoughts returned to Iridan. What could have gone wrong? Had they met with some kind of accident? Perhaps they had run into a scouting party, but that was not likely. What would Su'Meeryn have to scout for? Despite the coming of winter, he was certain that Su'Meeryn would be preparing to move towards Gorthon. Jaleph would be aware that Shekul had fled, so he would be focusing all his attention on Gorthon. Then another thought crossed his mind, which he quickly dismissed. Iridan would never desert them. No, something had to have gone wrong, terribly wrong.

Chapter 30

Scores of royal blue banners adorned with the face of a silver and black wolf flapped wildly in the stiff wind and heavy rain. Behind the flags, the army of Su'Meeryn covered the ground before the gate of the castle like a pool of molten lava ready to erupt from a volcano. Jaleph sat before the army with Ut, Rynkor and Teraken at his sides. The emperor fidgeted in his saddle as he adjusted his crown—which he still could not find a comfortable angle on his head. Teraken had objected to Jaleph wearing it into battle but Ut had insisted. Jaleph's head felt heavy, and not just from the weight of the metal. In a few days, the soldiers of Su'Meeryn and all his conquered lands would assault the mountain fortress that was Gorthon. Ut remained unwavering in his confidence despite the misgivings of Teraken. He had not said how, but Ut had informed Jaleph that they would succeed in breaking through the natural defensive barrier surrounding Gorthon. He hoped Ut was correct as Iridan was certainly hiding safely within the mountains. When Jaleph mentioned he wanted to see Iridan die, Ut had revealed that Iridan's death was a top priority. Why Ut cared so much about the life of one man did it matter. His moment of vengeance was at hand.

The emperor glanced wordlessly at Ut and his hatred grew even more. He thought back to the chess game they had played so long ago, and he realized that despite Ut's words, he was just a pawn. He was Ut's pawn for some unknown purpose. Again his thoughts turned to Iridan. This never would have happened if not for him! I might be a pawn, but at least Iridan will be dead soon!

He noticed Ut speaking with Rynkor, but Jaleph could not hear the words. Besides, he really did not want to hear them. Most likely it was something regarding the forthcoming battle and he had no strategy to offer. Jaleph just hoped that once it was concluded, Ut would finally leave him in peace. But what then? Would Ut depart after the battle or return with him to Su'Meeryn? Jaleph could not fathom what Ut's next plan could be. Would he continue the campaigns to other lands? Was this just the start? Was war all Jaleph had to look forward to? I'll kill him when this battle is over, Jaleph thought. I'll drive my sword through his foul heart and I don't care if he kills me. This will be the end. But the image of Ut's ebony aura reaching out to his neck and squeezing all the air from his body dissipated Jaleph's resolve. *I'll drag Iridan's lifeless body back to Su'Meeryn to hang from the front gate, and I will butcher anyone who tries to protect him!*

"We're almost ready," Teraken announced.

"Good." Rynkor bounced in his saddle, unable to contain his excitement.

Ut's body straightened on his horse. "Soon," he breathed. "Soon, I will have my victory. Nothing can stop me now."

Teraken was clearly shocked and disgusted, but Jaleph ignored him. He didn't care how many would die. They were heading towards the man who had caused Ut to take control of his kingdom; the man who took away the one woman he had truly loved. If not for Iridan, Myrin would still be alive and be his queen. He could have children by now, a family. And with that, his thoughts unexpectedly turned to his brother and Ruy, and he reflected on how it had been a long time since those two had come to his mind. He wondered what they would think of all this. "It doesn't matter," he muttered. "They're dead."

"What is that, Sire?" asked Teraken.

"Nothing, let's begin."

Teraken looked at Rynkor then back to the army. "The last troops are still coming," he said after a heavy sigh.

"They can catch up," Jaleph said as he turned reluctantly towards Ut. The slight man nodded his head. "Move out!" Jaleph called as he nudged his horse forward. *It's time to end this.*

Chapter 31

The sight of the mountains through the rain was even more ominous than Jaleph had imagined. "How can we hope to get through that?" he cried. "And in this rain!"

"The rain?" Ut laughed. "The rain is of no consequence. Do not worry my friend. You have nothing to concern yourself with. Now come." Ut motioned and Jaleph, Teraken and he advanced. Ut had asked Rynkor to come with them as well but Jaleph refused, and to his surprise Ut had acquiesced.

The trio rode to the base of the mountains and Jaleph raised his wolf banner as instructed. "People of Gorthon," he called above the sound of the rain, "Su'Meeryn has no qualms with you. We know that Josu and the people of Shekul have taken refuge in your realm. Turn them over to me, along with Iridan, and you will all be spared. If not, I will unleash my army against you." Jaleph paused for a moment. "I await your response."

"Very presumptuous of you," came the answer as Jaleph saw a number of figures emerge from the rocks. "Your force is certainly large, but how do you expect to penetrate our defenses?"

"To whom am I speaking?" Jaleph asked, straining to see through the downpour.

"I am Vol, leader of Gorthon." He then motioned to the tall man next to him, "and this is Josu, King of Shekul. You will be destroyed if you attempt to enter my realm! Now be gone!"

A few other people were behind the two, and Jaleph recognized Dirwyn amongst them. The times they had spent together immediately came to his mind. Her startling beauty shone brightly—even amidst the rain—and a pang of desire welled up in him. The pleasures of his harem had never quenched that desire, and he wondered why he had not been able to take her as his wife. This was his last chance to break out from his downward spiral: taking Dirwyn as his empress after killing Iridan. It all seemed so clear now. With a sense of resignation he turned to the one person who could make this happen. "I want her, Ut. I want Dirwyn."

Ut's beautiful faced regarded the emperor, and Jaleph saw no trace of his former malice. "Are you making a request of me?"

"Yes."

"I can do this for you, but you will be mine completely. Do you understand," Ut said quietly, so that Teraken could not hear him.

Those words caused Jaleph to pause. He despised Ut. His life had been threatened and he had no power to make any decisions. What was left of his life? But what did it really matter? Ut already held control over him anyway. Why not make the most of this foul relationship? "Yes," he repeated.

Ut smiled. "Very well then, it shall be. Now you are mine."

"Well?" Vol called out.

"Dirwyn will come to me as well," Jaleph responded as his anger began to grow. He might just be a pawn, but he would at least be a dangerous pawn.

"I'll never go with you," Dirwyn shouted.

"I should never have given you the opportunity to leave Dirwyn. You will be my queen."

Josu drew Dirwyn close to him. "She was married yesterday, Jaleph."

"I am your emperor!" Jaleph screamed. "You will address me as such!"

"You are not my emperor."

"Soon I will be! You can bow to me now, or I will mount your severed head above my throne. And Dirwyn will be my queen!"

"Jaleph," Vol called. Despite the distance and sound of the rain his sarcasm was clear. "Nobody here will ever bow to you."

All the anger and frustration that Jaleph had been dealing with finally erupted—any semblance of the previous man disappeared. He had completely lost control and knew that he was falling into Ut's plans—whatever they might actually be—but it did not matter. Jaleph was following Ut down that path and he would not come upon a crossroad again. Now his rage would only be quenched by slaughtering the cowards who were hiding amidst the mountains. "Then you all die!" he shrieked. "All except Dirwyn! She will be my empress!" He spun his horse around and returned to his army, Ut and Teraken falling alongside.

"Very good," Ut laughed. "Very good."

***

Waves of rain continued to fall as the ever-darkening sky descended to blanket the mountains. Lightning burst in every direction with deafening crashes. Pothar peered down as Dobrah and Kile tried to hide under an outcropping of rock. The three had been positioned as reinforcements high up the path with no expectation of actually entering the battle, and he had a hard time seeing during the brief respites from the electric fury. "I think they are moving," he said. "Fools."

Orders called out from the base of the mountain to those stationed above his head, confirming he was correct. Jaleph's forces were launching their assault. The battle had commenced.

The hissing of arrows echoed everywhere as boulders of varying sizes bombarded the attacking army. The narrow entrance into the mountain passage made the attackers' advance seem impossible. "They'll be slaughtered," Kile laughed.

Dobrah shoved him angrily against the rock wall. "This is not amusing," she spat. "Pothar and I still have friends down there."

"Well, I'm sorry if I'm not sympathetic," Kile responded angrily.

Dobrah pushed him again. "You had better learn to be!"

"Both of you knock it off," interrupted Pothar. "We're doing what we have to; there is no sense fighting each other. They might have been our friends and companions before, but not any longer."

With a short grunt Dobrah turned back to survey the battle. Pothar joined her and he too peered down, though he was barely able to see the soldiers of Su'Meeryn through the rain. Gorthon's missiles continued to fall. The battle—if it could be called that—would not last long.

***

"This is insanity!" cried Teraken. "How do you expect our men to get through?"

Ut's beautiful countenance remained unmoved. "Do not worry."

"Jaleph, please!" Teraken implored. "Put a stop to this. What do you hope to accomplish?"

The emperor turned his stare from Teraken to Ut. What was he to do? Ut had promised that the army would be able to penetrate Gorthon's defenses, but he had yet to explain or demonstrate how their victory would be accomplished. He nervously began to fear that his hunger for revenge would not be satisfied. How could he kill Iridan, Vol and Josu this way? Even Rynkor—who sat next to him—appeared to be apprehensive.

"Do not worry Jaleph, everything is progressing as planned. Continue with the assault," Ut commanded.

"No, we have to retreat. This is suicide." Teraken's hand went to the hilt of his sword. "Don't you care about your men?"

"Stop," Jaleph yelled. "They laughed at me, and now they will all pay!"

"But Jaleph—"

The emperor's face turned bright red with rage. "I said stop!"

Teraken removed his hand from his sword but his fist remained clenched, and the scowl across his face only deepened. "You'd better know what you're doing Ut," Jaleph heard the large warrior whisper, "or I will kill you right here." Ut ignored the threat, and the slight man lifted his head to peer through the rain. As if in response, shrieks—louder than the thunder—exploded through the sky. Jaleph and his companions turned their heads to follow Ut's eyes and they saw large, dark shapes darting overhead towards the mountain.

***

The rain finally began to slacken as arrows continued to plummet towards the ground. The Su'Meeryn soldiers who survived the initial missile barrage had entered the pass, but the dark-skinned warriors of Gorthon met their advance. In the tight quarters, Jaleph's men experienced the difficult task of trying to unleash their assault. The soldiers of Gorthon seemed to emerge from the rock, strike down an opponent then disappear. The attackers' blood ran down the pass like a crimson river.

"How many of them do you think we know?" Dobrah asked in a quivering voice.

"Too many," replied Pothar.

"There was nothing else you could do," Kile commented softly after a pause.

"That doesn't make it any easier."

"At least it should all be over soon," said Dobrah.

The battle continued below. A few of the defenders had fallen as the men of Su'Meeryn managed to form a bastion in a small opening in the passage. The year of constant battles had hardened the warriors and they fought with such veracity Pothar began to wonder if they might actually succeed. But as a new round of thunder rolled overhead, more arrows found their marks. The attacking force began to thin and the fallen bodies of their comrades became a new obstacle to their already impossible advance. The assault was halted — they had no chance — and Pothar sighed with mixed emotions at the imminent defeat of Jaleph's army. But then a bolt of lightning exploded near him and his companions, followed by a piercing screech, then another. Pothar looked up to see a number of dark silhouettes plunging from the sky and heading towards the mountains. As they neared, Pothar thought he saw wings flapping at their sides.

***

"What did you say?" Iridan asked in amazement.

Naar's face offered a toothy smile. "You are Chaw Den. You fly from the sky to save your homes and you lead the defense against the armies of the Deceiver to dismember the serpent."

Iridan stood dumbfounded as he tried to make sense of what this man was saying. Wasn't Chaw Den the bird atop Korath's staff? He tried to recall what the prophet had said so long ago, and for the first time since Teracuss and he headed out on their quest began to sense a notion of order. "What do you mean, I *fly* from the sky? That was two years ago when Myrin and I flew on Jokk-al Ystren."

"Two years ago? Hum, is that right? It could be. Time means nothing here, so I suppose you may be correct."

"Of course I'm right," Iridan responded with a tone of irritation. "I was there."

"I know you are there. I see it, but past and future mean nothing to me now."

"How can that be?"

The man claiming to be Naar grasped Iridan by the elbow. "Follow me," he said and they walked a few steps. "Look down." Iridan peered into the clouds and watched as an opening formed. Staring down at Su'Meeryn he saw the attack. The invaders had just broken through the gate, and he saw Fenik and Ruy fall. Then Jokk-al Ystren flew in with Myrin and him on its back. "You see?" Naar continued as the clouds reformed covering the vision.

"No I don't. What does this mean?"

"Why, it means you are with the great prophet Naar, and you are outside of time. Look again." Naar turned to the left and another opening in the clouds displayed the battle in the ravine where Karus had died, and Iridan had saved Jaleph and Pothar.

"Do you ever see anything pleasant up here?" Iridan quipped.

"Not usually."

Iridan saw an eternity of sorrow deep in the man's eyes and immediately regretted his comment. "What am I doing here?" he asked trying to redirect Naar's attention.

"You stand before me to learn the answers to all your questions."

456

"Well, if it is as you say, that I am Chaw Den, then that answers a lot. I guess Korath was not wrong when Teracuss and I were sent out."

Naar laughed briefly. "Korath! He is a fool. He means well, but he is ignorant."

"Korath is dead."

"Dead. I see his death, but then I see everybody's death. I see your death. But, as I have said, as I am outside time, it is all somewhat meaningless to me."

Iridan was taken aback at the man's words. "Death is meaningless? How can you say that?"

"I see life and I see death. There is little difference from my vantage point," and Iridan again saw the sorrow which Naar's eyes were unable to hide.

"I can't understand that," Iridan conceded with frustration. He still felt annoyed at Naar's cavalier attitude towards death, but he also saw no point in pushing the matter further. "Fine then, what can you tell me about my dreams?"

"Hum, your dreams. I call you to me in your dreams."

Iridan stared at Naar as those still-vivid images rushed to his mind. "You! That was all from you? You put me through hell? Why?"

"Hum!" Naar responded angrily. "I call you to me. Your reaction is your own."

"So why have I only just come now and not before?" Iridan asked, not fully convinced by Naar's answer.

"Now? Now is always to me. It is hard for me," Naar responded with evident consternation on his face. "I was in time prior to being out of time. But is there a past when you are not in time? Perhaps, as you were in time you were just not ready and needed to be purged."

Purged? Was that what he had gone through? Were the dreams a way to prepare him? As he pondered Naar's words, he was forced to conclude that he would never fully understand. How could he make sense of being outside of time? Obviously it was still a difficult concept for Naar to process as well. "I suppose I will have to concede that one too, but I have to ask, why did this all happen? What happened to Jaleph, and how did Su'Meeryn manage all those conquests?"

"Look," Naar said, pointing to his right. Iridan looked down again and this time he saw the man in white meeting with Jaleph. He saw Okkgan falling, and once again the battle at the ravine. The man in white stood above the ravine as he directed the assault. When Iridan's foe was about to strike him down, he saw the man in white shoot a bolt of fire from his hand, killing the man. "That is Ut," Naar explained.

"The man in white is Ut? So I guess he wasn't killed, but I don't understand. Why did he attack us but then save me?"

"Hum, you understand nothing," Naar responded smugly. "Ut wants Jaleph. Jaleph is his key to conquering the world. Jaleph acquiesces to Ut and Ut controls him. But Ut needs you alive to build on Jaleph's jealousies. Jaleph wants Myrin."

Naar turned Iridan around and another opening formed, and he saw the attack when Myrin was killed. "So, once Ut was fully in control, then I was no longer of use to him. That's when he wanted me killed."

"Hum," Naar responded, and Iridan sensed the prophet was annoyed that he had at least figured that out.

"But why did he court Dirwyn if he wanted my wife?"

With a wave of his hand Naar displayed another scene below. Iridan watched Ut and Jaleph discussing Dirwyn. "Ut uses Dirwyn to show Jaleph his own loneliness," Naar answered as his haughty smile returned, "but when Jaleph begins to love her, Ut turns him away. All the plans hinge on Jaleph's longing for Myrin."

"So why did he have her killed?"

"Ut's plan is set. He no longer needs Myrin. Her death is inconsequential when Ut finally attacks Chaw Den."

Iridan paused for a moment. He did not appreciate Naar's attitude regarding the death of his wife, but he needed to continue. "What about Veake?" Iridan asked. "Why did he seem to know certain things that were happening, but not completely?"

Naar laughed again as his face regained its arrogant countenance. "Veake? Yes I know Veake. He thinks he knows me, but he too is a fool. He managed to learn some things; unfortunately, his idiotic brain does not allow him to understand all that he gleans."

Iridan knew he should have additional questions but his mind was having a hard time grasping his surroundings and everything that was happening to him. "Where does that leave me now? Why am I here? I still don't understand."

Naar huffed in disgust at Iridan's lack of knowledge. "You stand before me to learn your identity and to thwart Ut's plan. You are Chaw Den. That is why Ut wants you dead." Naar stepped forward and opened his arms wide. The clouds parted again and Iridan saw the mountain fortress of Gorthon. He saw the soldiers of Su'Meeryn being slaughtered in the pass, then Jaleph, Ut, Teraken and Rynkor sitting atop their horses. He heard shrieks from the rain-filled sky as dark shapes plunged towards Gorthon. Fire burst from the forms descending towards the mountain, setting the defenders ablaze; he heard their cries as they were burned alive. The shapes took form and he realized they were dragons.

The aerial onslaught continued, but Gorthon's defenders were not the only targets. A number of dragons turned away and concentrated their fiery attack at the base of the mountain. Iridan wondered why until he saw rocks beginning to crumble and fall away. The beasts spewed flames, blast after blast, until the protective walls of the mountain pass gave way creating a wide opening. With that accomplished they turned away and returned to search for any remaining defenders on the mountain.

"They won't be able to survive this!" Iridan cried.

"You are right Chaw Den."

***

Jaleph laughed with glee. "You are a genius Ut." The cries of the burning men of Gorthon had begun to drown out the shrieks of the dragons. He gazed up in the rain and watched in awe as the number of flying beasts increased. He had only seen a dragon once, and that had been inspiring enough. But now there must be several dozen, and they were all different colors, giving the appearance of a gruesome rainbow. Amidst the brilliance, Jaleph spotted one dragon of pale white which could only be Jokk-al Ystren.

"I don't believe this," Teraken muttered. "How did you manage it?"

"We go!" Rynkor cackled as he spurred his fidgety steed.

Ut quickly grabbed the reins. "Patience my friend, we do not want our own troops caught in the maelstrom."

The emperor glanced back at his remaining soldiers and saw looks of wonder and anticipation on all their faces. Soon Iridan will be dead, Jaleph thought, and I will have Dirwyn; I will finally have my peace.

***

Pothar stared at the new assault in amazement. Since the force of the dragons was concentrated at the passageway, his companions and he were not yet targeted, at least for the moment. "What should we do?"

Kile stood bewildered as Dobrah managed to turn herself away from the destruction. "I don't know," she whispered.

With his hand shaking, Pothar grasped the hilt of his blade. He wanted to sprint down to help in the defense, but what assistance could they offer? What use were three soldiers against the combined might of countless dragons? "We better just wait here. We can't be of aid right now, but ready yourselves."

***

The dragon barrage continued and the slaughter of Gorthon's men mounted at an astonishing rate. The soldiers of Su'Meeryn stood back with awe-filled eyes watching the destruction. Jaleph could see that their anxiousness to administer death themselves mirrored his own. The year of constant war was about to reach its climax with the conquering of Gorthon and the death of Iridan. Jaleph squirmed with delight. He was desperate to send his soldiers in, but with the dragon fire engulfing the mountains they had nowhere to attack. "This is too easy," he laughed.

"It would have been nice if this had started sooner, Ut," Teraken muttered, but the emperor sensed doubt in his words. Certainly the large warrior wanted Su'Meeryn to be successful in the battle, but it was a battle he had never wanted.

"Our losses are inconsequential," Ut answered dryly.

"Tell that to those men's families."

Ut did not bother to respond and continued to watch the assault. The passageway had been widened by the fiery bombardment, and the dragons were beginning to move their attack further up and around the mountain. "You will soon be able to start your attack, Rynkor. The entryway will be open, but a sizeable force of the enemy still remains."

Rynkor practically burst from his saddle. "Ready!"

***

"How could he have managed this?" Iridan asked in disbelief.

Naar stared down through the clouds and watched as the dragons flew about the mountains spewing fire. "Ut commands many forces," Naar replied with a flat tone, which annoyed Iridan greatly.

"What are you going to do about it?"

"Me? I do nothing. That is why I call Chaw Den."

"And what exactly do you think I can do?"

"Hum, well stop them of course." Naar's tone had changed again from emotionless to one of superiority, and Iridan was discovering that he strongly disliked this prophet.

"How?"

"You are as thick as Veake. Must I spend eternity constantly explaining everything to simpletons?" Naar turned his attention from the battle and looked at Iridan. "You stand in a cloud do you not? I assume you see the rainstorm below." Iridan nodded in agreement. "I send you back and you use the power of the storm."

"How?" Iridan repeated.

"Hum," Naar interjected angrily. "I show you."

***

"We move now," Pothar ordered as the dragons turned their attention away from the passage and towards the rest of the mountain. They sprinted from the ledge down the rocky path, past a number of fires still not doused by the continuing rain. Wet stone and gloom from the storm made each hurried step treacherous, while storm clouds thickened overhead and covered the land in darkness.

As they neared the passage, Pothar felt pangs of grief at the sight of the charred and broken corpses which had been Gorthon's defenders. I guess this is the end, he thought as he stumbled over another lifeless body. The dragons would be able to thwart any concerted defense the warriors of Shekul and Gorthon might offer. Their flames would find every hole and passageway into the mountainous domain. Some might manage to survive in the larger and hidden caves, but they would meet their fates against Jaleph's blades. He knew a dash to the ruined entrance was futile, but they could at least die fighting the enemy.

Suddenly the entire realm was illuminated by a burst of lightning. Pothar turned his head away, trying to screen his eyes from the blinding light. His knees buckled and he was knocked to the ground by a deafening blast of thunder. With his hand raised as a shield against the blasts, he raised his eyes to the sky—trying to see what was happening. This new round of lightning continued at a hectic pace. Then a hole in the storm clouds opened and he saw streams of untainted light pouring forth. He heard a shriek as one of the dragons stopped its attack, turned and flew towards the gap. The beast rose, shrieking in defiance, but climbing nonetheless. Through the radiance of the newfound sunlight, Pothar saw a figure emerge from the clouds and jump onto the back of the white creature. The man grabbed the beast's neck and pointed to the ground; it screeched again before plunging back towards Gorthon. Pothar crouched beside his equally mesmerized companions, unable to imagine what might happen next.

With the man on its back, the white dragon continued its descent while the glowing hole in the sky closed behind them. The lightning abated for a moment, but the rumbling thunder continued to build. When it returned, the bolts were no longer random. They shot out now in what seemed to be an orderly fashion. A booming crash fell, followed by an agonizing wail which pierced Pothar's ears. He watched sparks and smoke billow from the back of a purple dragon as it plummeted towards the ground. Another blast caused a second beast to fall, and Pothar realized that the electric bolts were somehow targeting the dragons.

Crying in unison, the remaining creatures turned away from the mountain to confront this unexpected foe. Their sinewy necks swirled about, searching for an opponent. Lightning struck again, and a red and black dragon fought to withstand the impact. Its wings beat erratically while burnt flesh smoldered in the rain, but the effort was useless. Finally it plunged from the sky, crashing to the ground, never to move again.

The confused dragons flew madly about trying to avoid the bolts, but the eruption of lightning continued with deadly accuracy. The beasts spewed fiery venom towards the sky; however, their blasts dissipated harmlessly in the rain-filled air. The remaining dragons' fury multiplied as their comrades plummeted to the battlefield one-by-one, and their shrieks grew in intensity as did the force of their own feeble attacks.

Pothar watched in awe as the sky became filled with the brilliance of dragon breath and lightning. He was trying to wrap his mind around what he was witnessing when he noticed one of the creatures flying in a different pattern from its kin. Rather than shooting fire towards the clouds, it seemed to be circling the aerial battle. It was the albino beast, and a man on its back seemed to be guiding it. He watched the man point at a silver and gold dragon, and almost immediately it was struck by a bolt of lightning. He pointed again and this time a dark blue dragon felt the blast.

Like a conductor, the man continued to lead this furious orchestra, lightning crashing with each point of his stiff finger. The screeches of the beasts decreased as they fell away amidst the Su'Meeryn soldiers. The creatures continued to assault the clouds, unable to find their foe. Pothar wondered why the remaining dragons did not flee the area, but they were clearly not going to retreat.

Pothar gasped as the albino dragon dove through the air and flew closer. Sitting proud and terrible on its back was Iridan, conducting the storm. Finally Jokk-al Ystren landed on the ground among several of its dead companions with a howl, and Iridan jumped off. With a gesture of his hand, one final bolt erupted from the sky slicing into the last attacking beast. Then it was over. All the lightning and thunder ceased. Jokk-al Ystren's head rose into the driving rain and let loose a shriek of anger and sorrow. The creature swung an angry head around to glare at Iridan, and Pothar's heart froze as he waited for Iridan's demise. The two stared at each other, unmoving, but the dragon eventually turned away. Beating its pale wings powerfully, Jokk-al Ystren rose into the sky and flew towards the last vestige of the gap in the clouds. But before it could disappear a concluding flash struck and engulfed the last dragon. With a cry of agony, Jokk-al Ystren tumbled to the ground, a lifeless hulk.

Pothar stopped and gazed at the scene in wonder. How could this have happened? He glanced at Dobrah and Kile beside him, seeing his own bewilderment mirrored in their faces. Then a call from below reached his ears. "Come men of Gorthon." Iridan's voice filled the air, much louder than possible. "Defend your homes!" Answering calls sounded from above as the remaining soldiers of Gorthon and Shekul rushed down to meet their attackers.

***

"That was Iridan!" Jaleph bellowed in a blinding rage before swinging around to confront Ut. "What has happened?"

Ut remained transfixed atop his horse—Jaleph had never seen the man appear so unsure of himself. His beauty had melted away leaving the emaciated features and thin strands of hair which the emperor had become all too familiar with. "I should have expected it," Ut mumbled as he struggled to marshal some semblance of resolve, but his beauty did not return. "No matter, the dragons have weakened their defense and provided an opening. Victory will still be achieved." He turned his grotesque face to Rynkor. "Full assault, now!" But Rynkor did not move. His mouth hung open as he stared back at Ut with a blank expression. The dragons, the electric assault, and now this? It was too much for his simple mind to comprehend.

"Now!" Ut screamed. "Now!" But whatever desperate threat Ut could deliver would be meaningless. Rynkor remained paralyzed.

Teraken regarded Ut with a look of both shock and disdain. After turning away from Ut's hideous appearance he called out with resigna-

463

tion, "forward men." He then tried to muster some bravado with his next order, "Attack!" Following a couple of false starts, the Su'Meeryn soldiers rushed forward.

***

Iridan rushed up the ruined passageway and snatched a sword from the first corpse he found. As he turned a corner he ran right into Pothar. Pothar clasped his shoulder, and Iridan smiled at Dobrah and Kile. "I'd like to know how you accomplished that," Pothar said, "but you can tell me later."

"Are the rest of the defenders coming?" Iridan asked.

In response, he heard the unmistakable sound of troops storming down the path. "Why did you call them down?" Dobrah asked. In response, Iridan pointed up. Rocks and boulders were falling from above. It seemed that the onslaught of the dragons had weakened the structure of the mountains.

"We need to get onto the plain or we will all be crushed," he explained as the four were engulfed by the streaming troops of Gorthon and Shekul. "Let's go," Iridan said, and they joined the surge.

***

The opposing forces met at the base of the mountain. Driving rain muted the clashing steel and cries of death as Pothar stood next to Iridan, furiously spinning his sword. Of all the battles Pothar had participated in, none had compared to the size of this, and in the confusion he hoped his blade only struck enemies. The dark-skinned men of Gorthon were evident, but he could not always tell if the man he faced was from Su'Meeryn or Shekul. Occasionally he recognized a face; unfortunately that meant he had to kill.

Mud paired with the bodies of the fallen made footing extremely treacherous. Pothar nearly slipped a number of times as he was forced to concentrate on too many things.

A blow to his shoulder nearly knocked him to the ground and pain ripped through his body. He spun his sword to where his opponent must be and the blade struck a blue shield displaying a wolf without inflicting any damage. "Traitor," the man spat as he swung his hammer again. Pothar quickly ducked, the hammer barely missing his head. He thrust his sword up, but the man side-stepped away. The two regarded each other for a brief moment; the man wore a full helmet, so Pothar could not recognize him, but what did that matter? The only thing which did matter was who would survive the encounter.

Pothar feigned a few attacks but the man was too skilled to fall for his deception. Instead, he pushed his hammer at Pothar's chest, trying to knock him off balance. Pothar managed to avoid the thrust but knew he was in trouble. The pain from his shoulder was making it difficult to raise his weapon, while his stump hung uselessly at his side. Any moment now the crushing mallet would find its opening. They kept probing each other's defense but each deflected blow caused Pothar's misery to grow. His shoulder threatened to seize up just as Pothar saw his one chance. He quickly rushed forward, startling the man so he took a step backwards, and tripped over the body which lay on the ground behind him. He fell hard. Pothar immediately sprung and plunged his sword into his foe's neck. Blood exploded in a gruesome shower, mixing with the falling rain which quickly washed the filth away. But the force of the fatal blow sent a shock wave of pain up through Pothar's arm to his shoulder and he screamed. The agony coursed through the rest of his body before he collapsed.

***

Jaleph, Ut and Rynkor watched the battle silently as their horses stamped nervously in the mud. Ut's face remained hideous and Rynkor's transfixed. The emperor's anxiety grew as he felt his opportunity at vengeance slipping away. "How can this be, Ut? You promised me victory and Iridan's death."

"Shut up," Ut hissed.

With the despair of losing everything, Jaleph glared into Ut's menacing eyes. Had this all been for nothing? Would his forces be thwarted at the brink of their greatest victory? "Were all your plans a mistake?"

"No!" Ut spun his horse to face Rynkor and slapped him across his face. "You are needed! Do not disappoint me!" The bizarre warrior did not move. "Attack!" Still Rynkor did not move; however, Jaleph thought he saw some consciousness starting to reveal itself. Ut drew his sword. "Rynkor, you will attack now, or I will kill you. Is that how you want to die, a coward?" As his skeletal hand lifted the blade, Rynkor grabbed his own weapons. Battle lust returned to his eyes and he spurred his horse forward, a sword held high in each hand.

With Rynkor gone, Jaleph and Ut sat alone. "Is this what you always wanted?" asked the emperor. "All along you just wanted us all to die?"

465

"Spare me your self pity—I made you emperor. You will still rule this entire land."

"While answering to you."

"We all answer to somebody."

Jaleph wanted to ask Ut who he answered to, but he did not care. Nothing mattered now. Victory or defeat, all that mattered was seeing Iridan's lifeless body before him. Then a troubling thought came to his mind. "You plan on killing me when this is all over, don't you?"

"No," Ut said flatly. "I've always needed you alive."

"Needed, huh? Not wanted?"

"No."

"Well, I guess that is the most honest thing you've ever said to me." Jaleph dropped his dejected head, his hair flopping down to cover his eyes. "Now I will never have a queen."

Ut's responding tone was surprisingly soft. "Perhaps you will. I can still make you great."

Jaleph brushed his yellow hair and regarded Ut. He despised the man before him, but he hated Iridan even more. Could Ut still deliver on his promises? Accepting his companion's words, the despair which had filled Jaleph's body as he watched the dragons fall dead to the ground dissipated and his rage at the obstinacy of Vol, Josu and anyone who protected Iridan returned. "What should we do?"

"Come Jaleph. Draw your sword. To the battle! We need every blade!"

***

Boulders continued to crash down from the mountain at an alarming rate. Iridan had seen a number of men crushed or knocked to the ground—only to fall victim to Su'Meeryn's warriors. The defenders continued to push forward, as they needed to distance themselves from the mountain. But having recognized the situation, the men of Su'Meeryn tried to hold their ground, in a sense giving Gorthon's soldiers adversaries before and behind them.

In the center of the battle, Iridan wielded his blade with deathly precision. With Dobrah and Kile fighting beside him, the trio managed to punch a hole in the attacking line. With a call, his companions and he advanced. The soldiers of Gorthon followed. He looked frantically for Pothar, but was engaged by two men as their blades sought to breach his defense. He was forced to give ground until one of the men fell to a thrust by Kile's sword. Iridan quickly shifted to attack, managing to knock the weapon from his foe's hand while Kile plunged his blade into the man's stomach. The soldier screamed as his entrails spilled out amongst the mud.

Turning away, Iridan saw Dobrah in a desperate struggle with a large, powerful man. She bled from a number of wounds, but was managing to keep her attacker's axe away. Iridan leapt into the melee and sliced the man's thigh. Her opponent stumbled, and Dobrah quickly finished him off.

Before engaging his next foe, Iridan stole a quick glance about. The defenders had managed to get far enough away from the mountain to avoid the rubble which continued to fall to the ground. Unfortunately their advance had come at a price. The number of defenders had dwindled considerably, but so had that of the attackers. One of the men of Gorthon joined him, and Iridan recognized Wox.

"Nice to see you," Wox said in a pained tone. "I'm not really sure what happened, but we are certainly glad for it."

"No time to discuss," Iridan replied. "Let's go." And with raised swords the two rushed back into the fray.

*****

By the time the emperor had reached them, Rynkor and Teraken were both on foot. Jaleph's horse struggled as it panted and shied away from the fallen bodies, so Jaleph decided it would be safer to dismount. As the battle swarmed about him, Jaleph mostly just tried to stay out of the way. He had parried a few sword thrusts offered in his direction, but with the blows of death being orchestrated by the other two, he was largely ignored. Rynkor spun his twin blades like a pair of tornados, his fear now dispelled. Bone and flesh flew in all directions. Beside him, Teraken's sword also dripped with the blood of countless victims.

The cadaverous form of Jaleph's advisor joined them as Rynkor cut down two men with one strike. Ut held his own blade, but did not strike with it. Instead Jaleph noticed the familiar black aura beginning to form around the slight man. With a deadly stare he pointed at a defender as an ebony streak shot from his hand. Ut had turned his attention to another soldier before his previous victim had even hit the ground.

We still might win, Jaleph thought; with these three, they can't stop us. "Keep going!" he commanded. "Force them back!"

As their murderous onslaught continued, Jaleph spotted the tall figure of Josu fighting ferociously together with the two men Jaleph had seen previously at his side. "To Josu," Jaleph ordered. "Move!"

Rynkor stopped for a moment to see where Jaleph had pointed. With a cry of joy he climbed over corpses and sprinted past defenders to reach Shekul's king, but Josu did not back down; he braced himself for the charging warrior. Two men who stepped forward to block Rynkor's path were dispatched by his blades with ease. As they fell, Josu's sword crashed down with a mighty swing, striking Rynkor's left arm. The pink-eyed warrior wailed in pain as one of his weapons clattered to the ground. With his left arm hanging uselessly at his side, he lunged at the king. Josu deflected the blow with surprising agility and swung again, catching Rynkor on the chest. The warrior let out another howl, but with speed Jaleph had never witnessed before, Rynkor sprang. His remaining blade thrust over and over. Finally piercing through Josu's defense, he buried his blade into the king's heart. Josu's long face went blank as blood poured across his body, and before the corpse fell to the ground, Rynkor stabbed it five more times.

"Josu is dead," Jaleph called in glee. "Find Vol. He will be next." The emperor turned to Ut, but he remained shrouded in his black aura, whetting out death blows at an alarming rate.

***

The cold rain continued to fall among the bodies which now far outnumbered the living. Iridan had watched in horror as Surik, Forim and Josu had all fallen to their deaths. "Over there," Iridan panted from his grime-covered mouth as he pointed towards Rynkor, who had spotted Gorthon's leader.

"We have to protect Vol," Wox cried.

"Let's go," responded Kile as the three men and Dobrah fought their way towards Jaleph and Vol.

The path they chose was costly for both sides. Men of all lands joined their companions in a deathly mingling of corpses in the mud. The foursome stumbled their way over men and blades, reaching Vol at the same time as Rynkor and Teraken. A black streak struck down one of Vol's guards as Wox quickly leapt to his leader's aid, but Teraken's bulky frame stopped him. Wox swung his weapon which Teraken parried easily. The two traded blows until Teraken stumbled. Wox lunged instantly, but it was only a ruse. With a precise thrust, Teraken slit Wox's throat wide — Rynkor now had a direct path to the leader of Gorthon. Vol tried to defend himself, but he was no match for even a one-armed Rynkor and with only a few thrusts, Rynkor sent Vol's head flying through the air.

***

Despite his injury, Rynkor continued to fell the warriors of Gorthon who had swarmed to avenge their leader. Their attempts to surround him failed as Rynkor spun with inhuman speed. Every direction he turned brought a river of blood from a defender. Teraken also pushed forth, his blade nearly matching Rynkor with its victims.

Jaleph watched as black death continued to spring from Ut's hand when he spotted Iridan and Dobrah enter the melee next to the Gorthon men. "There he is!" the emperor called out joyously to Teraken, but the large warrior did not hear him. "To Iridan!" Jaleph ordered, but his lifelong friend remained engaged with the soldiers of Gorthon. "Go!"

"No matter," Ut said. "Chaw Den will now die," and Jaleph watched as Ut gathered the deep black aura around him, taking longer than usual to build his power. The blackness threatened to spill out into the mud, and Jaleph joyfully realized that Ut was preparing for one powerful strike. He would finally be rid of Iridan.

***

Raindrops stinging his face finally caused Pothar to stir. He spit out the taste of mud and blood then looked up. Where the battle had previously raged in every direction, bodies of the dead now surrounded him. He pushed himself out of the grime and pain immediately returned to his shoulder. He wondered if the battle was over, but then he heard the unmistakable ringing of steel to his left. Staggering toward the battle he remained completely unobserved, using the large corpse of one of the charred dragons as a shield and quickly assessed the scene. He spotted Iridan and Dobrah, and then saw Jaleph and Ut. A huge black aura was forming around Ut as he directed all his attention towards Iridan. Pothar had no idea what was happening to Ut, but he figured it could not be any good for Iridan.

Pothar moved in front of the dragon, yanking a knife from his belt. When Ut began to raise his arm, Pothar—ignoring the pain from his shoulder—pulled the dagger back. The blackness flowed along Ut's arm to his hand as Pothar let the knife fly. The dagger flew true and struck Ut in the chest. With a cry of fury from his curled lips, the black light from Ut shot up harmlessly into the sky. Pothar then pulled out his sword and rejoined the fight.

***

Jaleph watched in horror as the deadly fire intended for Iridan dissipated harmlessly above their heads. Ut dropped to his knees with a blank stare emanating from his sunken eyes. "Bastards!" Jaleph bellowed. He hefted his weapon and charged, joining Teraken. Jaleph swung wildly but his blade rarely found a target. When Teraken noticed his king, he repositioned himself as a shield and increased the intensity of his attack—the ground at his feet covered with crimson mud and the remnants of the fallen.

A blade nicked Jaleph's cheek as he continued his undisciplined assault. Were it not for the presence of the large warrior, Jaleph would certainly have fallen, but he no longer cared. His empire was gone and he would never have his queen. Everything was over. Only one goal remained: to kill Iridan. Even if he had lived his life as a coward, at least he would not die that way.

***

The battle continued on the rain-slick ground. Iridan noticed that there were perhaps a couple hundred men left on the field, but nobody considered stopping the fight. That was not an alternative. The only way for this to end would be the death of the enemy.

His sword rose and fell in rhythm to what could have been the beat of a vile song. Adversaries surrounded him and he lost sight of his friends. Iridan tried to fight off his enemies, but there was no ally nearby to assist. Desperation and exhaustion filled his being and his attempts to break free failed. He would certainly die here, never knowing if they had stopped Jaleph. As sword points began to find his flesh, he heard hooves pounding towards him. A horse crashed into the melee and a rapier sliced first one man, then another. He glanced up to see Worm atop the steed, who offered him a grin as he struck again. Iridan managed to recover enough to press his own assault and kept his back to Worm's horse, using it as a defense. Opponents fell at his feet until he felt a jolt from the animal. Iridan continued to assail his foes, but they rallied as the horse collapsed behind him.

The Su'Meeryn warriors swarmed, though in their haste they left themselves vulnerable. A few quick thrusts and a well timed lunge left his immediate foes sprawled on the ground amidst the carnage. Iridan quickly turned his attention to Worm. While his surprise entrance and superior position on the horse had caused much damage, Worm's skill with a sword was limited. Iridan found his friend next to the animal, blood pouring from a gapping wound on his neck.

"When you disappeared from my house," Worm gurgled through his escaping life essence, "and I couldn't find you, I knew you had to be..."

Tears rolled down Iridan's cheeks as Worm's words trailed off. He reached out a battered hand and brushed Worm's hair away from his face. "You are a good man," Iridan managed to choke out. Worm smiled as the flow of blood slowed—his eyes finally at peace. Iridan swallowed his grief knowing that he was needed elsewhere, as the sounds of the battle continued all around. Worm's body would have to remain where it lay.

Iridan sprang up, searching for his next combatant as he dashed forward despite his fatigue and sorrow. Continuing the fight he seemed to cut down men with every stroke. As he battled his way through, he came upon Teraken and Jaleph. The large man's sword hacked all about, and Iridan saw the look of melancholy on his old friend's face. Despite his misgivings for this battle, Iridan knew Teraken would never leave his king, no matter the cost.

"There!" he heard Jaleph call as Teraken spun about. Iridan braced for the attack when Kile jumped in front of him, swinging at Teraken. Just then Iridan saw a motionless figure on his knees who could only be the man in white. Iridan darted past Teraken and Jaleph with his sword raised. He jumped, and his blade pierced Ut's chest, joining a dagger that still protruded from it. Ut's emaciated face remained expressionless as he fell. No blood came from the wounds as Iridan continued to strike, but a trail of black light dripped from Ut's body. His sword rose once more, and with a mighty blow Iridan severed Ut's head. A howl erupted from the body and black light poured out like water from a dam break on a powerful river. Ut's body convulsed with each fresh wave of the ebony aura. The rays slowly diminished—and the howl disappeared—but still Iridan did not stop his attack. He had witnessed this scene once before and he did not want it to be repeated again. Again and again his blade crashed against the severed head, each blow causing pieces of skull to fly into the air. He had left Ut for dead on Naemon's floor, and after all the agony Ut had caused, Iridan was determined to finish this task.

***

The emperor's stomach turned at the sight and stench of the carnage all around him. He tried to keep pace with Teraken—who was battling fiercely beside him—but Jaleph had only been in combat once before. As waves of nausea threatened to overwhelm Jaleph, the emperor froze when he saw Iridan sprinting towards him. Certainly he could not hope to overcome such a seasoned warrior, but then Iridan dashed by. Jaleph's vision followed his nemesis as Iridan's sword struck Ut's prone body. The emperor realized that his opportunity was before him as Iridan continued his assault. At least I will be rid of you both, he thought as he pounced. Iridan's weapon was poised for another blow against Ut's corpse when Jaleph's sword pierced his back. Iridan's body went rigid. As the point emerged from the other side, Jaleph shrieked with exhilaration. All the rage of the past several years flowed through his sword and out Iridan's body. The impossible outcome had actually come to pass. His thirst for vengeance towards the man who had caused all his grief and ruined his life was finally quenched with blood. "I killed him!" the emperor cried in disbelief.

At that moment the force of the rain increased. The lightning resumed with a deafening crash of thunder and Iridan's body turned as he dropped onto Ut. He gazed up at Jaleph while the eruptions of the storm continued to multiply. "You are a fool," Iridan stammered through his blood-filled mouth. The emperor stood above him, his sword ready to strike again. Iridan's eyes turned away from Jaleph and towards the storm clouds. "Myrin," he breathed, and then Iridan died.

***

With horror, Pothar saw Iridan collapse before Jaleph. He gathered all his remaining strength and lunged towards his former king, completely oblivious to the agony in his shoulder. But the explosion from the sky caused him to fall also. As he stumbled back to his feet, he saw debris flying towards the battlefield. Pothar turned back towards Gorthon and saw lightning battering the mountains. Rocks flew amongst the combatants; everywhere the mountains crumbled, stones and boulders crashed down. Every peak disintegrated against the onslaught and where proud spires of earth had once stood, all he saw now was dust. "Dirwyn!" he cried. Then with an ear-splitting crash, one concluding bolt struck the nearest mountain and the entire area was razed. Rubble and stone billowed out to be immediately quenched by the rain. How can this be? he thought. But then he remembered Iridan and jumped back into the fray.

He saw Kile and Teraken engaged, and Pothar marveled at Teraken's loyalty. Despite all that Jaleph had put him through, Teraken still stood by his king, which caused Pothar to briefly wonder at his own decision to betray Su'Meeryn. But his choice had been made, and he did not regret it.

The large warrior swung a mighty blow, but Kile ducked under the blade. Teraken found himself off balance and Kile sprung, his sword catching Teraken in the biceps. Teraken's weapon fell, but he swung out with his massive left fist. The blow caught Kile on the side of the head causing him to stumble in the mud. Teraken pounced as Kile fell and Pothar dashed forward while the two wrestled on the ground. The misery returned in his shoulder as he struck down an adversary who tried to block his path. When he finally reached the pair, Kile had pulled a dagger from his belt. The two continued to fight in the filth, but suddenly the melee was over. Teraken's body went limp as Kile pushed himself to his feet—the knife no longer in his hand.

Kile grabbed his sword from the ground just as Rynkor reached him. The two engaged in ferocious combat, with Rynkor quickly gaining the advantage but just as Kile was about to be overwhelmed, Dobrah rushed to his defense. They tried to fight off Rynkor, and Jaleph who had joined in. A few others had also entered the fight when Pothar finally reached the pair. Dobrah had managed to isolate Jaleph, who was clearly no match for her, and his attempts to strike her were easily deflected. On his last attempt she disarmed him. She glared at the emperor as he stood helplessly before her, unmoving. He knew what was about to happen and there was no way he could prevent it. She regripped her sword while he remained paralyzed. With a quick breath she drove the blade into his heart. Blood splashed from his chest into her face but she did not wipe it away. As Jaleph's body crumbled, she spat at him and kicked his body off her blade.

With the ache in his shoulder nearly blinding him, Pothar dispatched his last adversary before turning his attention to Kile. Rynkor and he were the only remaining combatants on the field. Surprisingly, Kile managed to deflect most of the blows, but he was dripping blood from every part of his body. Then with a flurry that was difficult to see, Rynkor's lone sword crashed down. He repeatedly struck Kile's weapon ferociously until it fell to the mud, then Rynkor's blade crushed Kile's skull. With equal speed Rynkor spun about, preparing for the next fight but he was too late. Pothar had already attacked. His sword struck the bald part of Rynkor's head and the crazed warrior fell with a look of disbelief in his pink eyes. Pothar's shoulder went limp but he needed to fight through the pain for just a few more seconds. With his stump he forced himself to lift his weapon one last time. Rynkor swayed, trying to push himself up, but his body spasmed in the puddles of water. With one concluding strike, Pothar ended Rynkor's loathsome life, and the battle.

He turned, exhausted and drained to Dobrah. The two surviving warriors looked back towards what had once been Gorthon. The mountains were gone, with nothing remaining except for rubble. "I don't understand," he managed to say as he dropped his sword.

The shock on Dobrah's face slowly melted as she fell to the ground and began to cry. Rain continued, but there was no sound of thunder and the two friends remained still for a long time until Dobrah finally rose. She gazed at the body of Rynkor, and then Jaleph. "Where is he?" she asked. Without a word, Pothar led her towards Iridan. By the time they reached him, the rain had finally stopped; overhead the sky had turned a dark burgundy. The ground remained covered with the dead, but all the blood and filth had washed away. As they stared down at Iridan and what remained of Ut, Pothar wanted to say something. He wanted to comfort Dobrah, but after all that they had experienced, what could he say?

They just stood until they saw a lone figure approaching from the distance. As they watched they realized it was a man dressed in tattered rags. Pothar stopped Dobrah as she grabbed for her sword. The strange man shambled up to them, his taut face and sunken eyes reminding Pothar of death. He smiled at the pair, displaying three or four rotten teeth, and a few wisps of grimy hair flapped from his bony head as he turned to the remnants of Ut. At that moment Pothar realized the man reminded him of a hideous version of Jaleph's advisor.

The man stooped and pushed Iridan's body away. Seeing the decapitated corpse, he gazed about. After smiling again at Pothar and Dobrah, he crawled over to what was at one time, perhaps, part of Ut's skull. The man grabbed a piece and stood up. The foul-looking face tilted to one side as he again regarded the pair, then placed the piece of Ut into his mouth. After chewing it a few times, he swallowed. He looked back up at Pothar and Dobrah one last time before walking away.

Dobrah's eyes followed the man as he disappeared into the debris of what had once been Gorthon. "I wonder, did we win?" she asked softly.

"I don't know," Pothar replied, "but Jaleph certainly didn't."

"That might be, but was this all worth it?"

Pothar paused for a long moment. "What would have happened if Ut and Jaleph had prevailed?" he commented as he lifted his head. A heavy wind kicked up while a gap formed in the red sky. The sun shone through and bathed the land in bright light. "At least now we can start over."

475

through and bathed the land in bright light. "At least now we can start over."

Rumblings of the Earth

Patrick D. Catlett

Prologue

The old storyteller let out a slight groan as he lowered his aching body onto one of the many rocks. The children had come running, and they sat eagerly on the ground around him. He lifted his frail arm and waited a moment for his audience to quiet down. When they were all silent, he began his tale:

"It was at this very spot that our story comes to end. We have all seen the rubble, but what you may not know is that this used to be a mountain realm. A mighty nation once thrived here; it was called Gorthon. However, that was many ages ago. Nobody knows quite for certain what caused the destruction of the mountains—but I'm getting ahead of myself, aren't I? Who begins a story at the end?" The storyteller shook his head as the children around him laughed.

"We need to go to the beginning, don't we?" he continued once the children settled down again. "Our tale begins in a land far away—a kingdom call Sumaran. Mighty Jolef was the king and his greatest warrior was prince Iridan. The brothers were the closest of friends. Their father died when they were young, and they spent all their time together. Hunting was their favorite endeavor. That is, when they were not off to war.

"It was during one of these hunts when the royal brothers learned of a coming attack against the kingdom—"

"I've heard this story many times before!" one of the children angrily interrupted the storyteller. "I want to hear a different one!"

"Is that so," the old storyteller replied in exasperation. He glared at the child, but realized that his angry expression instilled no fear in the boy—or any of the other children. With a sigh of mock indignation, he started again. "You may be familiar with that part of the other story, but the other children are not. So please sit quietly until I get to the second part."

The boy huffed in impatience and dropped his chin into his hands.

"Where was I? Oh yes, let me see, Jolef and Iridan were out together on one of their many hunts when they spotted a large army marching south. The brothers, who were not dressed in any of their royal regalia, decided to approach. They were carrying a few rabbits which they had shot, and used them to bribe the leader of the army. 'Where are you fine men heading to?' Jolef asked. 'Please tell us, as we certainly do not want to get in the way of such a fearsome force!' After handing over the rabbits, the man told them they were marching towards Sumaran—"

"Please get on with it," the boy interrupted again.

The storyteller offered the impatient child an annoyed glare before continuing. "So Jolef thanked the man, promised they would stay out of the way, and Iridan and he road back to their castle as quickly as their tired horses would allow. After returning home, Jolef sent his brother and Traken—Sumaran's prophet of the Creator—on a quest for a mighty artifact: the ring of Naar. Only this ring would be able to stop that army from conquering Sumaran.

"Without even a moment's rest, Iridan and Traken rode away from Sumaran. They had many adventures while searching for the ring, and it was during one of those that they saved the lovely Marin from a desperate band of brigands. As time was running out for their home, they found the ring in a small village south of Sumaran, and Traken used its power to locate a dragon. The ring allowed them to control the beast, but in so doing Traken was killed by it. Not allowing himself an opportunity to grieve, Iridan mounted the back of the dragon with Marin and ordered it to fly back to Sumaran. When Iridan finally arrived at the castle, the battle had already begun. Iridan ordered the dragon to descend, and using the breath of the beast, Iridan managed to slay many of the attackers. With the destruction of the bulk of the invaders, the hearty soldiers of Sumaran killed the rest. The castle was saved, thanks to Iridan."

"Finally, now get on with it," the boy interjected.

The storyteller took a deep breath as he offered the boy another angry gaze. "Now that you have heard about Iridan, Marin and the dragon, I will tell you the rest of Iridan's story. This tale has much intrigue, betrayal and adventure! I will tell you of Pathor, Dobrah and Josul; Kale and, of course, the evil man with the forked tongue!" The children were all leaning forward with eager anticipation for another adventure of their heroes, Jolef and Iridan.

"As I told you, Jolef and Iridan were, as brothers, the closest of friends. But what you may not know is how that began to change after Iridan saved Sumaran. Iridan and Marin married shortly following the battle, and the king became jealous of his brother. Jolef sent the newly married couple away to the land of Cekul and King Josul.

"With his brother gone, Jolef became very lonely, until one day a messenger arrived to his castle. Jolef welcomed this messenger, who almost immediately became the king's confidant. But what Jolef did not know was that this man, who has no name, was an evil emissary of the Deceiver." He paused again as his eyes surveyed the children. With pleasure he noted the expressions of trepidation staring back at him. "Yes, it's true. Our great hero Jolef fell under the influence of evil.

"Now, at the behest of his new advisor, Jolef launched many wars, and Sumaran conquered much land, but none of his conquests rid his mind of the growing jealousy for Iridan. He came to hate his brother and desired to take Marin for his own wife.

"So as the wars raged on, two new warriors emerged in Sumaran: Pathor and the beautiful Dobrah. They distrusted the man with no name and worried over what Jolef was doing to their once peaceful kingdom. They fled to Cekul to join Iridan. With the blessing of King Josul, the three soldiers of Sumaran raised an army to stop Iridan's brother. When Jolef heard this, his mighty anger grew into a blinding rage. He assembled the largest army this land had ever seen, and they marched towards Cekul.

"Fortunately, Prince Iridan was just as wise as he was skilled with the sword. He heard that his brother was coming to kill him and all of his friends. He knew that his army was not strong enough to stop the king, so he and the soldiers of Cekul fled to this very spot where we sit." A few of the children gasped as they looked around at each other with bewilderment.

"Wait a moment," the same boy spoke up once more. "Jolef tried to kill Iridan? You're making this up! Why haven't we ever heard this before?"

The storyteller stood straightened his fragile leg and walked slowly approached the child. His gray eyes peered down at the boy and then the storyteller smacked him across his head. "Be quiet! You were all too young before. Now that you've reached your sixth summer, you are old enough to hear the rest. No more interruptions. Let me finish.

"Yes, Iridan and his army fled to this spot and joined forces with the people of Gorthon, but still Jolef would not relent. When he heard that his brother was fleeing to Gorthon, the army of Sumaran issued chase. Fortunately, Iridan reached Gorthon first and they took refuge in the mountains. But when Jolef arrived, his army laid siege. While Jolef's warriors far outnumbered the defending army, they could not pierce the mountainous defenses. It was then that the man with no name called to his evil companions and five hundred dragons came flying to the battle. The beasts spewed their deadly breath at the mountains, killing many warriors, and Iridan knew his forces would not be able to withstand this new attack. Soon death would visit them all with its cold embrace."

The storyteller paused again, allowing his words form pictures in the minds of his young audience. This was much for the children to take in—the revelation that one of their greatest heroes had turned to villainy, and their other hero was about to be killed by his brother. The old man again sat on his rock, leaned back with a wry smile and waited. When the delay became too much for them, the children pleaded for him to continue.

"What was Iridan to do? The mountains which had offered such a strong defense against the Sumaran soldiers had now become their prison. The fire of the dragons found every crevice, every indentation, and the defenders were slaughtered without even being able to fight back. But then, when all seemed lost, storm clouds rolled in. Rain began to fall, quenching some of the fire—but not enough. At that moment, Iridan called to the heavens in a desperate plea for deliverance. His prayer was answered and he was lifted into the clouds, and from those clouds he called up an immense storm. Thunder roared and lightning poured from the heavens, terrifying all below, but the deadly bolts of lightning had only one target. One after another the smoldering carcasses of dragons fell from the sky amongst the Sumaran soldiers, crushing many of them. When all the dragons had been dispatched, the soldiers of Cekul and Gorthon stormed from the mountains.

"The battle was fought right here. The two armies clashed with such force that the ring of steel was heard from many leagues away. Pathor, Kale and Dobrah led the charge, and Iridan returned from the clouds to join them. The battle was fierce. Many warriors died, but Iridan's forces were being driven back. With a loud cry, Iridan rallied his soldiers and they fought even harder. Finally only Iridan, Dobrah, Pathor and Kale remained from the defenders, while Jolef still had fifty men from Sumaran. But Iridan would not surrender. The four fought on, ignoring every wound they received. They slaughtered their enemies until Kale was surrounded and killed. Now the remaining three faced twenty-five warriors. They pushed on, and Iridan cut down the man with no name, but in so doing, the king managed to strike his brother. Even as Iridan fell, he killed two more foes until slain by his brother.

"Finally, only four combatants were left on the battlefield: Dobrah, Pathor, Jolef and a mighty warrior from Sumaran. The four battled for hours until Dobrah smote the Sumaran warrior. The two turned on Jolef, and it was only with their combined force that they ultimately overpowered and killed Sumaran's king."

The children peered at the storyteller with their mouths agape. "Yes, it's true. Only two warriors survived that mighty battle. Beaten and bloody, Pathor and Dobrah turned back to Gorthon. They turned their backs to the mountains to head back to their home, past the bodies of the fallen as well as the huge carcasses of the slain dragons. But before they managed to get too far, an earthquake began to rumble. Some say the mountains were weakened by the assault of the dragons, others say it was from the storm—or perhaps it was a last gasp from the Deceiver whose plan Iridan had thwarted—but for whatever reason, the mountains began to crumble. Pathor and Dobrah watched in disbelief as the entire realm of Gorthon crumbled before their eyes. All the innocent people hidden within the mountains were crushed by this final act of devastation. And since that day, Gorthon has remained unchanged: a wasteland of destruction as a memory to that terrible day."

With his story concluded, the old man took a deep breath and watched a hawk fly overhead, searching for any movement of vermin scurrying within the rubble. He then forced his aged joints to push himself up from his rock. He offered himself a silent congratulation at the shocked looks peering back at him.

"Now, children, it's getting near lunchtime. Hurry off to your parents. I'll tell you all another story tomorrow!"

Chapter 1

A pair of horses thundered down the snow-covered path as heavy flakes continued to fall from the sky. The riders held their spears high as they pushed the animals for any small amount of additional speed. When their quarry veered to the right, the horses left the path and continued after through the barren plain. They dashed past a few bushes still displaying white remnants of the hard winter while they pushed on.

Thin layers of ice shattered under the hooves of the horses, causing muddy water to splatter into the air as they made a quick turn to the right. With their prey getting closer, the arm of one of the riders shot forward. The spear flew, but it landed harmlessly on the snowy ground.

The horses continued their sprint after another sudden turn to the right. The arm of the second man rose. The spear hovered above his head for a moment. His arm whipped forward in a blur of motion as the weapon launched from his hand. The spear tip glistened in the morning sun before piercing the skin of its target. The large buck quickly went limp while skidding across the snow.

The two men jumped down from their mounts and followed the short, bloody trail. When they reached their quarry they knelt down. "Dead?" one of the men asked.

"Yes," his companion answered after checking the throat.

"Father will be pleased."

The man stood up and stretched out his back. It had been a long chase, longer than they had anticipated. His body was stiff from the pounding of the ride. "We should get a good price; he's a big one." The brothers gathered up their game and prepared to head home.

***

A smoke-filled haze hung about the room as the brothers entered through the door. Following a quick glance about, they headed toward an empty table. After sitting down, a disheveled man brought them two mugs of ale. "How went the hunt, boys?" he asked as he dropped the goblets down on the weathered wood.

483

"We got ourselves a nice deer," one of the brothers replied after a deep drink of the bitter ale.

"Do you know how lucky you are to be able to hunt on the king's land?"

"Yes, you mention that often, Uzon," the other brother responded.

Uzon shook his huge hair-strewn head in self-disgust. "Yes, you're right, Merreck. My memory is not what it once was."

Merreck grabbed his brother's forearm before the other could speak. "Telleck and I are grateful for the opportunity the king has given us."

"Yes, yes. Well, it could not have happened to a nicer couple of boys." Uzon stood motionless above them for a moment before continuing. "Enjoy the ale, and greet your father for me." The brothers nodded and Uzon made his way back to the counter.

"How is it that you can always be so patient with him?" Telleck asked after offering his mug a sour look.

A short laugh escaped through Merreck's lips before responding to his twin. "He means well."

"I suppose." Telleck attempted another sip of the ale before dropping it in disgust. "When are they supposed to be here?"

"Just after lunch." Merreck took another drink himself, then looked at his brother's goblet. "It really isn't that bad."

Telleck's scowl only increased at those words. "You wouldn't know good ale if it dropped from the sky."

"We may have to be here a while, so I suggest that you find some way to occupy yourself."

Telleck's eyes displayed disdain as they surveyed the room. "I'm certainly not going to eat anything in this place. Why did they want to meet here anyway? It doesn't seem like an appropriate location for royalty."

Now it was Merreck's turn to scowl. "How do I know? This is where the messenger said, and I didn't question him."

Telleck's face softened until he attempted one final drink from his mug. With a shudder, he pushed it away as he looked at the other patrons, searching for any familiar faces. When that endeavor failed, he returned his attention to his brother. "I guess I need to give you some more lessons with the spear."

After a chuckle, Merreck let out a loud belch. "Yes, you got this one, but I've had my share of kills." The twins entered into a long discussion regarding their many hunting trips as patrons entered and exited the pub. Their conversation had become particularly heated regarding who had the greatest number of kills (Merreck had always been the superior gamesman, until Telleck's skills improved recently to the point of being renowned throughout the kingdom as the greatest hunter in the land) when they noticed that the room had became quiet, and they turned their attention toward the door. Within the entryway stood a man and woman, both finely clothed. They were of similar height with matching skin tone and jet-black hair. Both exhibited smooth facial features and sparkling blue eyes. The man glanced around, and upon spotting the brothers he motioned toward the woman. She nodded and they headed over to the table. Merreck and Telleck stood, then all four sat at the same time.

"Thanks for agreeing to see us," the man began. He turned his handsome face toward Uzon and signaled for two more ales. He brushed his thick hair away, then his hand dropped and began to stroke the maroon amulet which hung against his fine olive-colored tunic.

"We would certainly never refuse the prince and princess," Merreck responded as his eyes almost involuntarily drifted in the direction of the woman. Despite her resemblance to her brother, nobody in all the kingdom failed to be enthralled with her beauty. Dark, soft hair hung farther down her back than her brother's, and her eyes seemed to absorb the atmosphere around her. She raised her ring-covered fingers to her face and gently brushed a luscious strand of hair behind a delicate ear. Rosy, full lips parted as she spoke.

"It was a request, not an order." Her soft smile seemed to brighten the entire dank room.

"Of course, however, it still would have been inappropriate for us to refuse," Merreck continued.

"Quite so," the man noted.

"Yes, yes, very polite," Telleck interjected with obvious irritation. "Now what is it we can do for you?"

Despite Telleck's sharp words, the woman's beautiful smile only increased. "Poor, impatient Telleck. Never willing to engage in idle conversation. Perhaps that is why I've always liked you—never any hint of pretense. Isn't that right, Remen?"

"I suppose; however, that does not give him leave to be impolite to his royal family."

"Very true," Merreck responded before his brother could speak again. Telleck and he had known Remen and Shyan their entire lives. When Shyan and her twin brother had been born nineteen summers ago, the entire land considered the twins to be an omen of good luck. Then news had arrived to the castle that another pair of twins had been born to a merchant and his wife on the outskirts of the kingdom the following day. Two sets of twins—well, the people of the kingdom had a hard time comprehending that notion. Surely it was a sign of great things to come. So, despite their differences in social station, it had been decided that the two sets of twins should become acquainted. They were brought together at many occasions, and during their upbringings they had gotten to know each other very well. Shyan liked both of the brothers well enough, but Telleck and Remen always seemed to clash. Remen did not appreciate Telleck's abrasiveness, who in turn resented the fact that he was forced to watch his words around the young prince. "Now," Merreck continued, "may we proceed?" His eyes returned to Shyan and he tried hard to avoid gazing at her azure blouse, forcing his attention to remain on her face. It really was amazing how similar the sets of twins were. Merreck and Shyan, each the first born, were quite mild and anxious to please, while their respective brothers displayed short tempers and impulsiveness. Throughout the recent years, Merreck had tried to win Shyan's favor. While knowing that the idea was improbable because of their social differences, her beauty and temperament made the undertaking worthwhile, even when it became clear she did not return those feelings.

However, to his surprise, it seemed that she was becoming attracted to Telleck.

His brother and he were not considered handsome. Sandy hair hung low, but Telleck let his grow longer. Short, spotty beards covered their round faces, and their hazel eyes were equally unimpressive. So, he wondered to himself, if she were to be attracted to one of them, why would she pick the angrier one? Despite his initial feelings of jealousy, he resigned himself to the fact that the benefits to the possibility of joining the royal family would make up for his loss. He had encouraged Telleck to speak with Shyan but his brother continually refused the recommendation.

"Of course," Shyan said, interrupting Merreck's musings. "Our mother wants a return for the favor of allowing you hunting privileges on her land."

"What can we possibly offer Yenyn?" asked Telleck.

"Queen Yenyn!" Remen corrected.

Telleck sighed in response, deciding it was not worth antagonizing his longtime rival any further. "What does the queen want of us?"

Shyan gently placed her hand on her brother's forearm as Uzon finally arrived with two mugs of ale. She pulled out a coin and handed it to the shambling man. "This will take care of the four of us," she said. Uzon gleefully looked down at the gold coin as he scurried away. "Everyone knows that you are the two best hunters in all of Karren. She wants you to teach us."

"Both of you!" Telleck laughed as he stared at the princess.

Shyan's composure faltered for a moment. "I assure you, I am more than capable of handling myself on a hunt. I am not completely inexperienced at the task."

Before Telleck could respond again, Merreck spoke up. "We would certainly be honored to offer whatever assistance we may to the prince and princess."

"Of course you would," Remen said as he stood.

"However, we leave on a trading mission tomorrow," Merreck continued, "and will be gone for a few days."

"Fine. Five days from now should allow you time to return. You may meet us for breakfast at the palace then, before you…" Remen's pause displayed his obvious distaste at continuing his sentence, but despite his annoyance, the fact that Telleck and Merreck were the most accomplished hunters in the kingdom of Karren was indisputable.

"Before we train you?" Telleck finished the prince's statement with a laugh.

Remen's face turned red as Shyan laughed as well. "Yes, before you train us," and she led her brother out of the pub before he could speak further.

"This should be interesting," Merreck said to his brother. "Wait till Father hears."

***

"Very good, very good," Urik said to his sons as he sat his frail body down in front of the table in their small home. "It's about time we had some good news; perhaps this will be the first step to getting us into the palace." He turned his haggard, unshaven face to his boys and offered a smile.

"Let's not get ahead of ourselves, Father," Merreck responded. "Just because they want to go hunting with us doesn't mean we will be asked to move to the palace. Besides, the fact that we are allowed to hunt on the king's land might be compensation enough." Merreck hated squelching his father's hopes—the death of their mother this past year had been particularly tough on Urik, but he did not want his father to be unrealistic.

Telleck joined Urik at the table. "But if things go well when we return, who knows what may happen next?"

"Then you better keep watch over your temper!" Urik spat with more exasperation then was necessary. "Try to get along with Remen."

487

"I always try," responded Telleck with a wry grin. In actuality, he did not dislike Remen. Yes, the prince was fairly annoying at times, but Telleck viewed their mutual antagonism more as sport than anything else. Besides, he was not oblivious to Shyan's apparent interest in him He was wise enough to realize that making Remen a true enemy would be a bad idea if an opportunity ever presented itself to speak with her regarding the matter.

"How was the venison?" Merreck asked, trying to change the subject.

"Oh, it was very good," answered Urik. His face softened as he turned back to Telleck. "You are both good boys. Please don't think I question that." He paused for a moment before continuing. "It's been hard on me lately, and I guess I put too much stock into the thought of moving into the palace. I know you two will do what you can for this old man."

"Of course," Merreck said as he dropped a fresh log on the fire, shed his clothes and dropped onto his cot. He wanted to make sure he had plenty of sleep, as Telleck and he would need to rise early the following day.

Chapter 2

The gray sky overhead encased the caravan with large, wet clumps of snow as the horses headed east toward the ruined rocks of the land that had once been the realm of Gorthon. Telleck looked up and marveled at the white onslaught. He could not remember such a deluge of snow so late in the year before. After wiping more of the fresh flakes from his brow, he wrapped his cloak tighter against his body. He glanced at his brother, who was taking the last bite of an apple before tossing it away and repositioning himself in his saddle.

"When are we going to get a break?" Telleck asked. "I'm sure that I'm not the only one who needs to relieve himself."

"I'm sure Volx will order a stop soon," answered Merreck.

"Volx," Telleck muttered. "Why does Regen continue to assign that fool to lead these missions?"

"He's one of the few people in Karren that can speak the language of Cishor."

"I know that! But just because he can speak their language doesn't mean he should be our leader."

"So, who should? You?" asked Merreck.

"At least I'd know when to stop for a piss."

After a couple more leagues down the trail, Volx finally raised his dark hand to order the stop. "It's about time!" Telleck barked as he jumped down from his horse and immediately turned the snow beside a nearby bush yellow.

"Very nice," he heard from over his shoulder. "Couldn't you have found a spot a little further from the group?"

"It wouldn't be anything to worry about if we didn't have women come along on trading missions," Telleck retorted quickly.

"Who else would keep you boys out of trouble?"

"Linny, why don't you get back on your horse and head home? I'm sure there are some stalls that need cleaning."

Linny punched Telleck's arm in response and stood before him expectantly. "Well?" she finally said.

"What?"

"I would like some privacy, if you don't mind."

"By all means." Telleck laughed as he returned to the group.

"You done?" Volx asked angrily as Telleck approached his brother.

"What do you want now?" Telleck responded in a challenging tone.

Volx's blue eyes bore into Telleck's as he shook his head slightly and the un-melted snow flakes fell from his long, black hair. "Guards say movement to south."

"I guess it's a good thing we have them with us then, isn't it?" Merreck responded. While he did not share his brother's distaste for Volx, he believed that Volx was not capable of making sound decisions if they found themselves in a crisis.

"Scout say may be big group."

"Fine, a big group. What do you want us to do?" Telleck asked.

"Ready selves."

"Volx, my brother and I are not warriors, we're traders," Merreck said. "That's why the king assigned guards."

"May be too many for guards," said Volx, and Merreck could not tell if the blank look on the dark man's face was one of confidence or stupidity.

"Then what do you want us to do? I don't think anyone here wants to die over a few hides and cloaks." Volx's blank face turned into an expression of befuddlement. He looked toward the south, then back at the twins. "Well?" Merreck asked.

"What's going on?" Linny questioned as she joined the three men.

"Volx said there is some movement to the south of us, and it could be a large group," Telleck answered.

"So what? Are you *men* afraid of movement?"

"Could be enemy," said Volx.

"And it could be a hunting party or scouts or other traders."

"So, what do you think we should do?" Merreck questioned the slim woman.

Linny brushed the snow from her short blonde hair. "Mount up, boys. Let's get to Cishor." She grabbed the reins to her horse and climbed into the saddle. Without looking back, she guided the animal down a narrow trail through the boulder and rubble that had once been an immense mountain range. Merreck glanced at his brother, then with a shrug took a quick look at the carts of trading materials before he too pulled himself up onto his steed. Within a few minutes, the entire caravan was continuing its easterly trek towards the kingdom of Cishor.

The path on which the group traveled was difficult going for the two horse-drawn carts. Small stones, made slick by the snow, littered the makeshift trail, and the horses had to continue slowly to avoid damage to the wheels of the carts. It was a difficult path, but even though the large rocks and boulders provided many places for an attacker to hide, a large group would be easily spotted unless they spread themselves out. And in that case, due to the treacherous footing, a coordinated attack on travelers would be too difficult to mount. It had been many years since anybody had heard of any raiders hiding in this land. So, Regen normally assigned only four guards to the trading mission, unless the cargo was of greater value.

It was a mission the brothers had many times. Once they reached their destination, Telleck and Merreck would do the bargaining for the price of the goods coming from Karren. Volx would serve as translator, while Linny inspected the produce the group would return with. The last member of the group was Bront. He was a frail orphan of about fourteen summers. Regen had taken the boy as a servant for menial labors after his parents had taken ill and died several years prior. Bront rarely spoke through the thin strands of greasy hair that hung over his pox-scarred face, and his task was to make sure the goods were taken care of during the trip, and to handle all the supplies.

True to Linny's words, after continuing their trek, the group did not see any more from the travelers to the south, and at the end of the second day of their journey they arrived at Cishor. They passed many scouts and guards once they entered the fertile fields before finally reaching the massive castle. Volx raised his hand, and when his dark face was recognized, the portal opened before them. As the horses passed through, each member of the trading party handed their weapons to a guard, and the mounts were lead off to the stables for fresh water and much-needed fruits and grasses.

Telleck always hated the trip to Cishor. He did not care for Volx, and the fact that the people of Cishor were of the same race did not help. He did not believe all the of dark-skinned people were as annoying as Volx, but what he really despised was not be able to understand what was being said around him and having to rely on Volx for their information and safety.

Merreck, however, enjoyed coming to this castle with the possibilities of finding new experiences. Despite the difficulties in bartering through an interpreter, he appreciated the patience of their polite hosts. He always tried to pick up a new word or two during each visit, but learning the language proved difficult, even though it appeared to be structured around short, staccato sentences. There were obviously many nuances to the words which he failed to master.

Their group was brought some water while Bront took the carts over to the trading center. After Volx shared a few words with a man who was in charge of something, he took the rest of the Karren traders to Bront while the guards headed off to find the nearest pub. "We meet with Tor," Volx said. "He nobleman and friend to king. Very important."

"Why someone of that stature to trade for hides?" Merreck asked, but Volx just shrugged.

Telleck sighed deeply in exasperation. "What good are you?"

Whether he was oblivious to the insult or he just did not hear it, Volx failed to respond. So, the four gathered around Bront and helped unload the carts while awaiting the nobleman of Cishor. The hides and garments were starting to emit an odor from the snow, which had managed to seep through the coverings, but Telleck refrained from chastising Bront for his failure to properly protect the cargo. He realized it was not the boy's fault. Nobody had expected the snowfall to continue at such a steady rate, and Bront had obviously not been provided with sufficient coverings.

When the group had all the material stretched out on the ground to begin drying out, Bront built a small fire as a tall, muscular man approached. He wore a purple cloak which was opened in the front, displaying a thick chain of glittering gold with a golden amulet hanging against a maroon tunic. The man's skin was darker than Volx's or any of the other people of Cishor, and he cut his hair shorter than most of the men. He looked the hides over before turning his attention to Volx. After the two conversed in their language for a few moments, the man began to inspect the hides while Volx announced the obvious—the man before them was Tor. Tor ran his fingers along the skins and brought several of the other garments to his nose. When he was done with the inspection, he said a few more words to Volx, who pointed to the brothers in response.

"The garments are of good quality, despite the stench," he said, surprising the rest with his mastery of their language. "I'm sure the aroma will dissipate once they are allowed to dry in the fresh air. Now, your friend Volx tells me that you two, who are obviously brothers, will handle the negotiations. Is that correct?"

"Yes sir, and please forgive us, we did not know that you speak our language," replied Merreck. "And you speak very well at that."

"I thank you for the fine compliment. I spent many of my early years around your light-skinned brothers and partook in my own share of merchant trips."

"What will you give us for the hides?" Telleck asked, as Merreck winced at his brother's abrupt words.

Tor smiled despite the breach in protocol. "Patience, my friend. You have only just arrived. As I said, I have found your goods to be of fine quality. We always trade fairly with our Karren friends. We will fill your carts with a generous amount of produce."

"I would like to inspect your offerings," Linny interjected. "As you are certainly aware, Karren experienced a hard winter, and we are in need of quality staples."

"That will not be a problem. We have maintained an ample amount in storage this winter. Our quartermaster will be arriving shortly, and he will accompany you to make your selections. Now, is there anything else?"

"Yes, if I may?" Merreck responded. "Why has someone of your stature decided to meet with us over such a minimal trade?"

"A fine question indeed. There is something I would like to discuss with you privately."

Merreck nodded while wondering what a nobleman of Cishor could possibly want to discuss with common merchants.

After the quartermaster had arrived, Linny left with Volx and Bront to inspect the produce and load their carts. Telleck and Merreck trailed Tor through the streets of Cishor, both men curious as to why Tor had requested their presence.

Following their short walk, Tor led the brothers into a large hall. The oak ceiling vaulted high above their heads, and thick pillars of dark wood which rose to reach the ceiling were adorned with gold, silver and other precious materials. Rows of benches circled the hall, all facing the center dais, which was carpeted with skins. A few chairs sat near poles from which hung baskets of torches that were currently extinguished. Tor motioned toward the nearest bench and the three men sat.

Without knowing what to say, Merreck spoke the first thought that came to him. "We really need to return soon to barter for our food."

Tor chuckled at his words. "At the risk of making you feel unimportant, my friend, as I had mentioned, that will not be necessary. Your woman will be able to pick out whatever food she wants for your return to Karren."

"I guess we didn't need to come then," Telleck mumbled, feeling very annoyed by the wet and cold trip from their home.

"I would not say that. I do want to speak with you, both of you." He turned back to look at the door before continuing. "Volx seems to be a fine man, but I take it he is not too bright." Both brothers nodded. "It pains me to say this about a countryman, but I am glad he is not the one here. You both seem like smart young men. Can I trust you?"

"Regarding what?" Merreck asked sharply, and he was beginning to feel as irritated as his brother. How could this stranger request their loyalty to him?

Tor searched both of their faces, obviously realizing his mistake. "You are right, friends. It was an inappropriate comment. You two do not know me, and I belong to a different kingdom. So, let me start again. When word arrived of traders from Karren approaching, I had advised the guards that I would handle the negotiations. I understand your puzzlement as to why I chose to partake in this task."

The nobleman stood, and light from the windows reflected a prismatic glow from his amulet. "Cishor is a peaceful kingdom, as you both know, friendly to its neighbors. We have lush fields and the best storage facilities known to man. We are happy to trade with any reasonable and accommodating land; however, despite our hospitality, you light-skinned folk seem to be uncomfortable around us." As Tor sat back down, Merreck wondered what this sociological discussion had to do with anything, while Telleck's aggravation was increasing. "So, we have very few of your brothers who live in this land. But that was not always the case. Long ago—"

"Can you get on with this?" interrupted Telleck. "We are not interested in your history and have business to attend to."

To Merreck's pleasure and relief, Tor was unprovoked by Telleck's sharp words. "I am well aware of that, but please indulge me for another moment or two. Now, as I was saying, Cishor was not always a land of my kind, and as the years have passed, fewer and fewer of your people have remained. Only a handful live within the kingdom permanently now. It is in regards to one of those I want to discuss."

"If you would like for us to take this person back with us, I don't think it would be a problem," Merreck stated, feeling that he had gathered what Tor was getting at. "But we can't promise anything once we return."

"No, that is not what I meant, my friend. This person is a very special man and the people of Cishor have come to appreciate his wisdom much. He says there is an evil brewing in Karren, and all the land need worry."

"In Karren," Telleck spat. "That's nonsense. Come on Merreck, let's get out of here."

"Please hold for a moment," replied Tor. "I am not accusing you or anyone in your land of anything. We respect King Regen and consider Karren our friend. All I ask is for you to be watchful. You are both traders and have been to Cishor many times. If you notice anything out of the ordinary, you can always return here and tell me. Now, that is not unreasonable, is it?"

"Can we report this to Regen?" Merreck asked, beginning to feel suspicious at this man's words.

"I will not ask you to keep secrets from your king. But if there is truth to what I say, we do not know where from where this evil will come. The fewer who are aware of this, the better—at least for now. I would advise you two to not discuss this with anyone."

"But you have told us," Merreck pointed out.

"Yes, that is true," Tor laughed. "I do not think I need to worry over a couple of young traders. Now, that is all I ask. Keep an eye out, and let us know in Cishor if you spot anything unusual."

"Why should we not report something unusual to our own king?" asked Telleck.

"I am not asking you to keep any potentially dangerous news from Regen, but if it is just something unusual, well, your brother who lives among us is the best person to notify. Now, to show you my good faith, I am able to offer you a third wagon full of food to return with. That will make your king happy and put a few extra coins in your purses, will it not?" He offered the twins a reassuring smile. "Do we have an arrangement?"

The brothers looked at each other and sensed that they were thinking the same thing: What could it hurt? If Tor wanted to offer them an extra cart of produce to simply report any unusual sightings, why not? With teaching the prince and princess to hunt and a substantially larger than expected return on their trade, their standing within the kingdom was certainly improving.

"Very well," replied Merreck. "We have an arrangement."

***

The brothers offered no answers to Linny's many questions regarding the extra cart of produce, other than to say it was due to their fine negotiating skills. When pressed further, Telleck had simply responded that she should just leave the negotiations to the men, where they belonged. He knew that once she was aggravated enough she would drop the matter, which is exactly what happened. Volx, as expected, had nothing to say. The fact that the group was heading home from a successful trade was all that mattered to him. The guards had no notion regarding what they expected to receive in return for their hides, and all Bront cared about was the fact that he had more cargo to worry about.

Upon their return to their homeland, the brothers were rewarded with the largest amount of coins that they had ever received. They quickly excused themselves from the castle and returned home.

"Very good boys," Urik said when they showed him their reward. "How did you manage it?" After Merreck told him of their conversation with Tor, Urik scratched his head and took a seat. "Very strange. The extra coins will certainly serve us, but I'm not sure that was wise."

"We had the same concern, but are we really doing anything disloyal?" Telleck asked.

Urik pondered the question for awhile. "No, I suppose not. If some fool from Cishor wants to compensate us for doing nothing, then so be it."

"Exactly," Merreck agreed as he pulled his wet boots from his feet. "Any kills while we were away?"

"Oh yes, the hunting's been wonderful. This long winter has caused the deer to move in closer to the castle than normal." Tales of his exploits was the only thing that would improve Urik's mood more than the news his sons had brought home. "I scored three. It's been good eating for me, and the hides were in excellent shape. You two aren't the only ones who can provide for this home!"

"Well done, father," Merreck said as he placed his boots by the fire, "but do you have any of that meat for your sons?"

Chapter 3

The thick trees of the forest blocked much of the cold wind, but wet ground increased the misery of the three men who crawled to the edge of the tree line. The clothes of the trio remained soaked after having crossed the nearby river, which added to their discomfort. Snow pushed its way into every opening and began to melt against already cold skin.

The trip across the open ground had been difficult, but the night sky provided them plenty of opportunity to avoid the patrols. With dawn approaching, they had reached the protection of the trees on the small hill, which provided them a vantage point to look down upon the community stretched out across the Armen Plains.

As the light continued to grow, more of the inhabitants emerged from their tents. Men began to tend to the large, muscular horses while the women started preparations for the morning meal. The prince of Karren felt a rumbling in his own stomach as he pulled some nuts from one of his pockets while trying to fight off the exhaustion from a night of no sleep.

While the Armen Tribesmen continued about their morning routine, Remen watched with a lack of interest until he nudged the companion on his left. The man glanced at him while Remen mouthed the word 'sleep'. The man nodded and Remen closed his eyes. With nothing of seeming importance occurring below them, Remen had decided he would get some much-needed rest while the other two continued with their observation, and shortly after closing his eyes the prince was asleep.

The sun blazed high in the sky when Remen felt himself being shaken awake. He was annoyed that his friends had let him sleep so long when they were obviously tired as well, but any thoughts of anger were quickly dispelled when he saw a small contingent of warriors meeting with what appeared to be a group of leaders of the Armen Tribesmen. The meeting did not last too long before the group dispersed amongst the tribesmen. Remen was not sure what to think of the matter; the foreign soldiers were a small group, but it was clearly something to report back to his father.

Since he now felt refreshed, and there was no further activity of significance, he ordered his companions to get some sleep themselves. There was nothing for them to do until after dusk, when they would be able to leave their hiding place and return to Karren.

***

They reached their horses, which remained secured in the trees where they had been left, late the following night. After feeding and watering the animals, the three men made their way to the hidden trail in the forest.

"You'd think Regen would have better tasks for the prince than a simple spying mission," one of the men said.

"I guess he believes such tasks will help me earn the crown," replied Remen.

"If you had to earn it, we'd never have a new king," the other man quipped.

"And how exactly should I earn it, Fallad? I'd think putting up with you all these years would have been service enough!" Remen laughed.

"Seems to me that Zhomin here and I have been the ones suffering."

"Leave me out of this," Zhomin said with an exhale that demonstrated his weariness.

"Well, if you don't appreciate your position at the court, I'm sure I could find a suitable job for you in the stables. There's always dung to clean up."

"And how would that be any different than what you put me through?" asked Fallad.

"You could let me know after a few weeks."

"Ha! Your mother would never let me in the castle after working in the stables. And everyone knows that the prince would never find himself in the stables. So how could I report to you?"

Remen wanted to offer a response, but he knew that he would never get the final quip in with Fallad. So, once again, he let his long-time friend come out on top of their banter and turned the conservation to a serious topic. "What did you make of those soldiers?"

"They could have been from Lavrs, but it was hard to tell," responded Zhomin.

"Besides, it would not be unheard of for soldiers to visit the tribesmen. They could have been bartering for horses," Fallad said.

"True, but it is something to report to my father." Snow again began to fall and Remen pulled his cloak tighter about his body. "It'll be good to get home."

***

The vision of the castle was a welcome sight to Remen and his companions, and they hurried their horses in the direction of the gate. It was late in the day when they passed under the portal. The prince dismissed his friends before retiring to his quarters for a quick change of clothes prior to meeting with his father.

"I heard that you arrived some time ago," the king said as Remen entered the outer room of his parents' chambers. "What took you so long to report to me?" Regen stood tall over his son, and his dark eyes glared down before he took a sip from the silver goblet he held tightly in his left hand.

Remen sat upon one of the soft chairs and poured himself some wine. He took a drink himself before responding calmly. "I was very wet and cold from the trip, and I needed to change."

The king turned away, which Remen knew was his way of acknowledging his mistake, but the prince also knew that an apology would not be forthcoming. "Of course," was the king's terse reply before he too sat. With his expression softening, Regen continued. "Did you learn anything?"

The bouquet of the fine wine filled Remen's mouth and traveled down his throat, providing him with a warmth he had not felt in days. He took another drink before turning his attention back to his father. "I'm sorry," he said. "It's been a long few days." Regen's face displayed a mixture of understanding and impatience, which the prince had viewed many times before. Remen sat the goblet down on a side table before continuing. "We entered the Armen Plains unseen and witnessed a meeting between some of the tribesmen and a small group of soldiers who appeared to be from Lavrs. We were not certain regarding their identity, but that's what it appeared. The meeting was short and we could not tell what it was about. Perhaps they were bartering for some horses, but it was impossible to tell for sure."

The king pondered his son's words for a few moments as Remen stood and asked to be excused to get himself some food. "Certainly," Regen replied. "You did well my son."

Chapter 4

Urik left the home early for another hunt the following morning, while Telleck and his brother decided to stay home. They were still tired from their trip and wanted to be rested, since they were to begin Remen's and Shyan's lessons the following day. When they finally rose late in the morning, they sat at their table and ate some stale bread, which they washed down with cool water.

"I'm not sure that I feel right about this," Merreck said. "Do you think we should say something to Remen tomorrow?"

"Remen? Who cares about Remen?" his brother replied.

"We already made the trade. Why not?"

The usual annoyance began to build within Telleck, as he had no patience for rehashing decisions already made. Rather than offering Merreck a sharp retort, he took another sip to allow his aggravation to subside. "It's like Father said," he replied as calmly as possible, "if that idiot Tor wants to give us extra for our trade for doing nothing, why not? And don't forget, we'll have other trips to make to Cishor. If we follow his instructions, he might be generous to us again."

Merreck took his last bite of bread as he tried to hide a knowing grin at Telleck's inner turmoil. "I suppose so. Besides, if Tor is right, we might be better off not telling anyone."

"Of course I am. Now you're thinking straight for once. Let's not discuss this matter again."

Merreck gave his a brother a strong push before rising from his chair. "I'm listening to you? Now this is scary."

The last piece of hard bread flew from Telleck's hand and struck Merreck's ear. When Telleck stood, Merreck pounced like a cat that had just spotted a mouse unaware. But unfortunately for him, Telleck anticipated the attack. He spun and let Merreck's force send them to the ground. Telleck spun his body and was quickly sitting on top of his brother's chest, whose arms were pinned against the ground. Merreck fought for a brief moment before relaxing his body under the weight of his brother's. "All right, get off," he managed to say.

"The better hunter and the better fighter," Telleck pointed out as he stood. Merreck offered his hand and Telleck pulled him off the dirty floor. "How about we get this place cleaned up for Father?"

Merreck nodded as he rubbed his chest; he watched his brother picking up a chair with a feeling of envy. Jealousy simmered like a pot about to boil that his brother's skills surpassed him in every area. As Telleck was replacing his mug in the small cupboard, he somehow managed to bang his knee against the corner of the table. With a curse, Telleck hunched over, and the mug flew against the wall with thundering crash. It splintered into a thousand pieces and Merreck restrained a laugh. Even his temper far exceeds mine, Merreck thought; perhaps it's not so bad.

When they were done straightening up the home, and all the pieces of the mug had been collected, they went out on short hunt looking for rabbit. While out in the cold and wet wilderness, Merreck could help but continue think about Tor and whether they made the correct decision. But along with that, he also wondered if there was truth to the man's words about an evil growing to the north of Karren. If so, he did not put it past the tribesmen.

"What's your problem?" Telleck spat when a shot flew premature from Merreck's bow, causing another rabbit to bolt away. "Your head's not in this, so we might as well head home." Merreck agreed and after returning, the brother wagered at dice until Urik returned. He carried a few squirrels, but no deer this time. They made themselves some stew and then went to bed early, to be ready for the following day.

***

The ride from their home to the castle was fairly short, but the mud and snow had splattered their clothes to sufficiently ruin their appearance once they had reached the gate. They were immediately ushered in and, to their surprise, greeted by Queen Yenyn. She laughed when they dismounted and motioned for the brothers to follow her. "You'll need a change of clothes before joining us for a meal." After changing into fresh garments which would be appropriate for the hunt, they were brought into the dining hall. This was not the first time they had been invited to a meal, but they both sensed the feeling of additional significance. If things went well today, the invitations might come more frequently.

Servants were beginning to bring in plates of food to the long oak table. The sunlight streaming in from the huge windows caused the silver of the trays to glisten and reflect off the polished dark wood.

Next came jeweled goblets, and the myriad colors of the precious stones created a rainbow-like effect in the hall. "Yes, you two must never have been here for breakfast," the queen noted. "The morning light is stunning. Now, please have a seat. My children will be here soon, but the king will unfortunately not be able to attend. He left early this morning on a diplomatic mission regarding some trading routes."

The brothers sat at their designated places, and Yenyn offered them to partake of the fresh water while they waited. After a few moments Remen entered, followed shortly thereafter by Shyan. "So I'm told that you two are quite the traders," the queen said. "Nobody has come back with that amount before for two carts of hides."

"We are happy to be of such quality service to her majesty and the king, and we thank you for such generous compensation," Merreck replied.

"I'd like to know how you accomplished it," Remen said in tone that was more challenging than inquisitive.

Telleck placed his mug on the table and turned to the prince. "You see, it is this thing called competence," he said with a smirk.

"Are you sure that was all there was to it?" Remen's glaring eyes appeared almost too knowing for Merreck's tastes.

"When one is familiar with competence, one realizes what may be accomplished with it," Telleck continued mildly.

"That's enough, boys," the queen interrupted as she gave a stern look to her daughter, who was chuckling quietly. "You will need to behave yourselves when you are out together."

"Of course, Mother," Remen said as he offered a bright smile to both brothers which caused Merreck to immediately put his hand on his brother's forearm. He knew Telleck would not be happy with the observation that the prince had been toying with him, and perhaps had been bested at his own game. Fortunately, his brother did not display any hint of annoyance as their food arrived.

They all ate their meals of cooked eggs and Cishor potatoes in relative silence, with just a few comments about what direction they would be taking for their hunt. Telleck noted, with a mixture of both pleasure and discomfort, that Shyan spent most of the meal looking in his direction.

"We'd best be on our way, Majesty," Merreck eventually said, pleased that Remen and his brother had gotten through the meal without continuing their argument. "Morning is the best time to pick up fresh track."

"Certainly," the queen answered. "The horses and your weapons are ready." She placed her thin arms around the brothers' waists as she led them from the hall. "Please instruct my children well."

***

Four horses sped away from the castle toward the forest, and when they reached the outskirts of the trees, the small group began to look for fresh tracks in the snow. After scouting about for a few moments, Merreck called out and kicked his horse. The others followed as Merreck began the pursuit of their quarry.

It was not long before they spotted three deer foraging for grass through the snow. The heads of the animals shot up when they spotted the riders. After a brief hesitation, the trio bolted. Merreck pushed his horse to the left to force the deer away from the trees. If they entered the forest, the hunters would not be able to follow. The maneuver worked, and the deer raced away through the open land. Remen guided his horse straight at their prey as Merreck continued to ride at their flank, between the animals and the tree line.

Telleck came alongside the prince and pointed at the largest deer. As the horse gained ground, Remen pulled a javelin from his back and hurled it at the deer. The weapon fell harmlessly into the snow, but the deer veered left despite the presence of Merreck. He saw their move and swung farther to his left, then turned back to head straight for them, trying to force the animals back toward the open. Remen followed his prey as Telleck called for him to turn back. Whether the prince heard him or not, Telleck did not know, but Remen's vision was clouded by the snow being kicked up from the hooves of the deer. Telleck called again as Remen pulled out another javelin. He aimed as the deer turned right. His head followed them, so he did not see Merreck through the snow-filled sky. Both horses turned in the direction of the deer, but it was too late. In the cloud of snow the horses collided and both men were thrown from their saddles.

When Telleck reached the scene of the collision, he jumped from his horse and rushed to his brother. A crimson stain covered the snow around Merreck's face and his right leg, which was bent at an awkward angle. Telleck lifted his brother's limp body and turned frantic eyes toward Shyan, who now stood next to him. Remen also came to his side. The prince's body was wet and scratched all over, but he seemed otherwise unharmed. Fortunately the horses were also unharmed, and they hefted Merreck up onto his mount before racing back to the castle.

Chapter 5

Urik joined his son in the dining hall while they awaited word regarding Merreck's condition. Merreck had remained unconscious when they returned to the castle, and Remen had ordered that he be immediately brought to the healers. Once Merreck was taken away, Remen had offered his apology to Telleck who pushed the prince away in response. Remen tried to apologize again, and before Telleck could throw a punch, Shyan jumped between the two. The prince stared at Telleck for a moment before exiting the room. Shyan sat quietly with Telleck until the arrival of Urik. She then excused herself to leave the two men alone.

When a messenger finally arrived, Telleck could no longer contain his anger. "It's about time!" he cried. "What can you tell us?"

"Merreck is alive," the man said. "He finally awoke a short time ago. He is in much pain from his broken leg, but there is apparently nothing else wrong with him."

"What about his head?" asked Telleck. "He was bleeding from the mouth and around his ear."

"He must have struck hard against the ground or on a rock, but there is nothing else damaged other than his leg. The break was very severe, but we splinted it as best as possible. It is unknown how well it will heal, and he has been given a numbers of herbs to keep him asleep."

"Well, that is good news," Urik said.

"Good news?" Telleck barked. "Merreck's leg is broken because of that idiot Remen, and you call that good news?"

"At least he's not dead, and there is nothing else wrong with him."

With his word delivered, the messenger left Telleck and his father alone again in the dining hall. When Telleck realized that he had no idea what he should be doing, Yenyn entered and sat at the table with the pair. The beginning traces of wrinkles around her almond eyes were more pronounced than Telleck remembered, and her gray hair—now tied behind her head—indicated that she had left her chambers before taking the time to properly adorn herself. This was the first time that Telleck could recall seeing her without cosmetics. He was surprised at how different she appeared from the morning and figured that the queen must change her appearance regularly depending on the function she would be attending. He had never seen her appear so unadorned before.

"Rest assured that Regen and I will do whatever we can to take care of Merreck and the two of you," she began. "I spent much time with the healers while they were tending to him. I believe you may have already heard from a messenger?" Both men nodded. "Merreck will be fine, but to be truthful, I'm not sure how that leg will heal. And I did speak with my children. Remen is very upset; he realizes that the accident was his fault. He admits he should have been following your directions, but he lost track of himself in the excitement of the hunt. That is not an excuse; it is what happened. The accident was his fault and he understands this." She gazed at Telleck, causing him to shift uncomfortably in his chair. Certainly Remen or Shyan had shared his reaction to the prince, and he waited to be chastised, but the queen maintained her quiet tone. "You probably should not visit with him today. The healers have given him a large amount of elixir. Go home and keep busy. I would suggest that you go on a hunt tomorrow, then come by in the afternoon; however, if you do not want to leave, that is fine. As I said, we will take care of you. I suggest it only so you keep busy."

The empathy on her face dissolved into a serious and commanding look as she continued. "Now, I realize you had a hard time with my son's apology. I certainly understand that. But I'm offering my apology for my entire family and me." She looked at Urik, then quickly turned to Telleck, and he knew that the apology was now not an offer, but a command. "Return home, and I will see you both tomorrow."

***

The ceiling above appeared hazy. Light pouring in from the window seemed to swirl against the wood and form undefined shapes. Merreck blinked, trying to focus his eyes, but that only made matters worse. Now colors seemed to dance around the rafters. He tried to rub his eyes, but with that minimal effort he immediately forgot about his vision. The slight shifting of his muscles reminded him of his leg. How could he have forgotten? The pain exploded from his tibia and knee like a crash of thunder. Why would the healers let him awaken? He tried to ask for more of the elixir, but could not form any words. The only sound that escaped from his lips was a bellow of pain. His body convulsed, causing the agony to increase. He cried out again and now saw some shapes moving about him. Hands grabbed his body to hold him steady, and he felt a cylinder against his lips. The bitter liquid poured from the container into his mouth. He swallowed and waited anxiously for the relief he knew would soon come.

***

As requested, Telleck and his father prepared for a hunt the following morning, but before they rode off, Telleck threw his javelins to the ground. He knew that sitting at home would be of no benefit, but he had no desire to hunt. Instead they decided to take the earnings from the recent trading mission and head to the market. They rarely spent any time shopping, and all three could use fresh bedding, and some of that produce they had returned with from Cishor would be a welcome change for their diet.

It was a short ride from their home on the outskirts of the Karren lands near the king's hunting grounds to the castle. The sky above was clear and the temperature had warmed considerably from the previous day. That was a welcome respite, but resulted in a significant melting of the remaining snow, causing them to ride through slush and mud. When they reached the castle, they were both filthy, but neither man cared. When they finished wiping their faces they were allowed entry. After stabling the horses, they headed to the market.

They visited the weaver first, but after Urik had pointed to their soiled clothing and noted the bedding would be far from new by the time they returned home, they decided to wait. The weaver offered them a sack at a reasonable price if they made the purchase right then, but Telleck refused. After turning away, he spotted Linny at a table heaping with various fruit and vegetables.

She waved when they approached and offered each an apple. "They're not fresh, but it's the best you'll find this time of year. I really would like to know what they do in Cishor to store their goods." After Telleck and his father each took a bite, Linny continued. "I heard about Merreck. It's a real shame. How is he?"

"We haven't seen him yet today," Urik answered. "The queen said we could come by this afternoon. He has a broken leg, but will apparently be fine."

"Yenyn said it might not heal correctly," Telleck said.

Linny shook her head in disgust. "Is it true? Was it Remen's fault?" Telleck nodded. "He's such a fool. Regen should be back in a day or two. I wonder what the king is going to say."

"Who cares! Whatever Regen says won't change a thing," Telleck said.

Linny's mouth opened to offer what was certainly intended to be a retort, but she stopped herself. "You're right, of course." She glanced around the table and offered them a few other items for no charge. Telleck's foul mood softened at the gesture, but he refused. Between trading missions, she worked in the market along with serving the princess, so she deserved her earnings. He thanked Linny for the gesture and purchased a sack of fruit. After completing the transaction, Telleck and his father puttered around the market until the afternoon, then headed to the palace.

***

Their mud-encrusted coats were taken by a servant and they were led to Merreck's room. Telleck apprehensively opened the door, but his brother looked far better than he had anticipated. His body had been washed, leaving no traces of the blood that had covered his face when Telleck last saw him. He lay asleep on a soft bed with the splint on his right leg clearly visible under the blanket.

"He doesn't look bad at all," Urik commented as he grabbed a chair and sat beside the bed. Merreck stirred at the words and slowly opened his eyes. "How are you?"

Merreck blinked a few times as he looked about the room. When he recognized his visitors, he spoke softly. "I don't feel much. The healers have given me a lot of elixir."

"Did they tell you about the injury?" asked Telleck, who still stood next to his father.

Merreck nodded gingerly. "Broken."

"I guess you'll be here for some time, so you won't be getting in my way on the next trip."

"Who's going to keep you out of trouble?" Merreck smiled weakly.

"As long as Volx isn't around, there shouldn't be any problem. Has Remen visited you?"

"He might have, but I don't recall. I don't remember too much with all the drugs they've given me."

"Well, that bastard better have come—"

"Enough, Telleck," Urik interrupted. "Complaining about the prince isn't going to help."

Telleck knew his father was right, but he did not care at the moment. He nurtured a vivid memory of Remen ignoring his call and riding straight toward his brother. "If that fool had been more careful—"

507

"Enough!" Urik snapped. "Your brother doesn't need to hear this, and you have no idea who might be outside the door."

Telleck was taken aback by the force of his father's words. It had been years since he could remember Urik raising his voice. "Fine," Telleck spat as he moved to the corner of the room to sulk. Urik turned back to the bed and talked quietly with Merreck, who seemed to have a hard time following any train of thought. After a while, Telleck noticed that his brother was beginning to wince in pain. He started on the way to the door in search of a healer, but the door opened at that moment. A middle-aged woman entered carrying a vial. She emptied the contents into Merreck's mouth, who was unconscious before she left the room. "I guess we should get going," Telleck said, but before they could move, a soft knock sounded at the door. They both turned as Shyan entered.

"Asleep again?" she asked.

"Just now," Urik responded, "after getting some more of the elixir."

"That's good." She walked to the bed and gently stroked Merreck's forehead. "He's been through much." She pulled at the blanket to situate it closer over his shoulders.

"Where's your brother?" Telleck asked. "He should be here."

Before Urik could respond to chastise his son, Shyan answered. "He stopped by once, but he probably won't come back. He feels very remorseful about what happened and he is uncomfortable seeing Merreck in this condition." Telleck tried to interrupt her, but Shyan continued. "I know you're furious over this, but you're going to have to get over it. I don't mind when you speak this way to me, but my parents will not tolerate it. You will have to forgive him or you will lose their good will. The king will not allow a disloyal subject to continue on trading missions for him. Do you understand?"

"You're right, of course," Telleck responded. He was angry at the logic but he knew the princess was correct. "I will hold my tongue."

"Good. Now that we have this settled, there was another issue I wanted to discuss, but this is probably not the best location."

"Why don't you two leave?" Urik suggested with a slight grin. "He's asleep and there is nothing you can do for him now. I'd like to sit here with Merreck for a while anyway."

"Very good, please follow me," and Shyan led Telleck from the room.

***

It was strange feeling for Telleck to be alone with the princess in the castle. Yes, he had seen much of her since they were children, but he could not recall a similar situation previously. He followed her from Merreck's room down a few hallways, to a large room in which sat an ornate shelf covering the back wall filled with ancient books; a few chairs and a small table surrounded it. Shyan gestured at the chairs as the two sat.

"What can I do for you?" Telleck asked, feeling extremely uncomfortable about his current situation.

"Don't be nervous. You have nothing to worry about." Shyan's smile demonstrated a dichotomy of both reassurance and apparent desire, which caused Telleck to squirm even more in his seat. His obvious discomfort only seemed to cause Shyan's smile to increase. "My father returned from his mission to the north. He has made arrangements for trade with the Armen tribes, which will be your next mission. However, he has some question regarding their sincerity, so I convinced him to send me along this time."

"What? You're going on the trade route?" Telleck's discomfort evaporated into disbelief. The notion was unheard of: a woman of the court embarking on a trading mission? "The tribesmen are a rough lot. Why would you go, especially if Regen has concerns?"

"They won't know who I am, and if you'll pardon the insult, the *king* does not trust anyone else to secure the information needed." Telleck noticed her emphasis when she said 'king' and knew it was her subtle way of correcting his too-familiar speech.

"But what if the king is correct and we're attacked?"

"We will bring along extra guards, but not enough to pose any suspicion. Besides, we will be bringing only a small amount of goods. If they are planning something, they won't waste it on us."

"What do they have in trade?" He knew the answer to his question, but felt he had to say something, as he was still befuddled by what he was hearing.

"They are skilled weapon makers and breed excellent horses."

After a brief pause, Telleck spoke again. "I suppose there is no way that I'll convince you otherwise, and I also suppose that we're leaving tomorrow. I'd better fetch Urik and head home."

Shyan's face brightened as her slender body rose from the chair. Telleck's eyes briefly surveyed her curves but he quickly turned away. He did not know if she noticed, but figured it did not matter. They would be off together and away from the castle for at least four days. He would certainly find out soon if she would move past her flirtations, and he wondered if that was part of her motivation to join this next venture. He paused at the door as the princess moved through the doorway. As she moved past him, her body brushed against his, causing his mind to race with thoughts of desire. As a commoner, he could not seek marriage with the princess—but if she chose to pursue him, he certainly would not mind.

Chapter 6

The nearly full moon hung low in the sky, casting bright reflections off the frozen pond onto the snow-covered trees and bushes circling it. The scent of the dying campfire hung in the air, while the hoot of an owl gave way to the baying of an unseen coyote. Telleck turned over in his bedroll and stared up at the star-filled sky. The first day away from Karren had been uneventful. Since they had only brought one small cart of hides, the group had made excellent time. He had kept his horse close to Shyan's, expecting to catch any complaints about the cold or the length of the ride, but she only grinned whenever he looked at her.

After stopping for the night and finishing a quick dinner, he waited to see what the princess would do, but to his surprise, she pretty much ignored him. She talked with a few of the guards whom she obviously knew before preparing her own bedroll. "Oh well," Telleck muttered to himself as he drifted off while wondering how his brother was managing.

A bright sun roused Telleck early the following morning. The group packed up their supplies and, after a short breakfast, continued their journey northward along the road which bisected the thick forest. As they rode, the travelers had to remove their cloaks as the weather warmed significantly and the snow began to melt quickly. By the time they reached the Unmeth River, the snow had completely disappeared, which caused the river to flow higher than normal. The waterline reached the small bridge but they were able to safely cross with the cart. They followed the main trail through the trees and reached the Armen Plains shortly after midday. A few different sentry groups of tribesmen stopped them, but they were allowed to continue on their way after short inspections. Horses and livestock grazed in most of the area, as the tribesmen were not much for farming.

After making their way through some small, rolling hills, they heard the muffled sounds of hooves smacking the soft ground. A dozen riders quickly surrounded them and forced Telleck and his group to follow them. Telleck was not surprised by their approach, as his brother and he had made a few trips to the tribesmen in the past, even though Karren did not previously have a trading agreement with them. So he knew that strangers were not allowed to travel north of the hills alone. They continued past hide-strewn tents and saw many of the tribesmen milling about. With this break in the weather, the unlucky few who had been selected were beginning with their minimal planting, while the rest of the tribes would be tending to the horses.

When they reached the central compound, they saw a huge, blazing fire surrounded by a number of benches. Two large platforms sat to the left and right of the fire. The escort ordered them to stop, and as all dismounted, a low figure approached on foot. The man's tan face was wrinkled, with no trace of a beard. He limped slightly as he walked and coughed a few times when he reached Telleck. But despite his age, his long, straight hair was still the dark brown of all the other tribesmen.

"Who you here to see, traders?" the man asked. He squinted as he peered about, trying to bring the group into focus.

"Whichever tribe's tents are in the worst repair. We bring hides from Karren," answered Telleck. While the Armen Tribesmen were one people, they did not have one leader. Three distinct tribes were banded together. Each tribe had a leader who assumed that position in combat, and decisions were made in the group by a vote of the three leaders.

"Yes, yes. I know where you are from, and I know what Karren brings in trade." The man coughed again as he pondered Telleck's words. "Vunta tribe probably has the most use for hides. I'll bring you to Gyraund."

* * *

While pain remained, it was not as severe as it had been. With ample use of the elixir, Merreck was pretty much able to manage it. Now the healers were making him get out of bed. He used crutches to keep weight off his leg, but they told him he needed to move about, if only for short periods. He initially refused, but ultimately was glad that they forced him. The crutches allowed him to get about pretty well, and he was tired of his bed and the foul-smelling room. His trips up and down the hallway of the castle certainly were not much to speak of, but any change in the scenery was a welcome respite.

A servant was just leaving with the remnants of breakfast when Urik arrived. It had been a couple days since Telleck left for his trading mission, and Urik had been his only visitor. After a couple of quiet hours with his father, a knock sounded at the door, then Remen entered. Merreck was well aware of how the accident had occurred, so he was surprised that this was the first time Remen had come by. While they were not friends, the two of them always got along fairly well. He had figured that Remen would have come by to apologize before that moment.

"How are you faring?" the prince asked flatly.

"I've been better."

Remen chuckled as he glanced at Urik, then out the window. "The weather is starting to warm. It seems that spring has finally arrived."

"I wouldn't know," Merreck replied, but he instantly regretted his words. Remen was obviously uncomfortable standing before the man he had injured, and it would not bring any benefit to annoy the prince.

"Of course not, but I'm told that you've started moving around a bit. Perhaps you'll be able to get out soon."

"Stairs don't seem to be a good idea," and Telleck felt a twinge of pain growing in his knee.

"That's probably true," the prince responded. He shifted his weight and glanced to the floor. "Well, I just wanted to check on you and offer my apology for what happened."

Apology, like that will help me now, Merreck thought as his pain began to increase. He reached for a vial on the small table next to his bed and quickly swallowed the liquid with a sense of relief. "I know you didn't mean it," he said while forcing a smile to cross his face, "and your family has taken excellent care of me."

"Yes, and I thank you as well," Urik offered.

"Very good," Remen said as a small trace of relief crossed his face. "I must be on my way now. I have some drills to lead and then must inspect the armory. Be well, and I will stop by again, if you don't mind."

"Some company is always welcome," Merreck responded as his eyelids became heavy from the effects of the drug and moments later he was asleep.

***

Telleck and Shyan stood before four men and one woman. One of the men stepped forward—obviously Gyraund, the leader of Vunta tribe. He turned his sun-darkened face toward the pair before eyeing the warriors behind them. Gyraunds's long, dark hair hung low against the yellow-dyed hide covering his leathery body. "Where are they?" he asked without any trace of etiquette.

"Back there," pointed Telleck, "and you'll find them to be quality hides."

The man pushed past Telleck with an air of superiority as the jewels which hung from his nose and ears swirled about. "I will judge their quality." The warriors stepped aside as Gyraund began to dig through the cart. Telleck tried to read the man's face, and it seemed as if he was presenting a show rather than actually examining the skins. Gyraund then turned back in Telleck's direction. "I guess these will do. What do you want in return?"

"Two young horses and a dozen swords," Shyan replied.

The man stared at the princess with disdain before offering a smile to his companions. He raised his head with his chin jutting out. "Women do not barter amongst the tribesmen, girl."

"That may be," she said, "but we do negotiate in Karren."

"You are not in Karren," he pointed out.

"We mean no offense," Telleck interrupted, not oblivious to the irony that he was the one trying to calm Shyan. "Two horses and a dozen swords is what our king asked in return."

"I don't need for you to defend me, Telleck," Shyan hissed.

"Please calm down..." Telleck stopped himself from using her name.

"Don't tell me what to do!"

Gyraund shared a hearty laugh with his companions. "You Karren men are unable to control your women?"

Shyan spat angrily as her face turned a glowing red. "I was put in charge of this trade mission. You will speak to me!"

The amusement on Gyraund's countenance disappeared as his hand found the hilt of his sword. "Enough of this. We do not negotiate with women." He motioned behind him and at least two dozen warriors stepped forward. "Now, I will give you one horse and six swords for your cheap hides." Before Telleck could protest, he continued. "If you are not satisfied with my offer, I will take your hides and your second-rate horses, and make you walk back to Karren."

***

When the group finally left the Armen Plains with the one additional horse carrying the new blades, Shyan erupted in laughter. "What are you laughing about?" Telleck asked.

"That actually went better than expected," she replied.

"What do you mean? We could have gotten the extra horse and swords if you hadn't acted the way you did."

"Yes, but you forget what our mission was. The trade was secondary, I was sent to determine if the tribesmen were being forthright with my father."

Realization began to dawn on Telleck. "So that was all a show." When Shyan nodded, Telleck felt very ignorant. He was able to read the Vunta leader's showmanship easily enough, but he never would have guessed that Shyan was acting as well. "You wanted to get him annoyed; that was a pretty dangerous game."

"Not really. I wouldn't have let it escalate any further."

"Did you learn anything?"

Her horse bucked a little in its trot as she pulled on the reins. "I think so," she said while they emerged from the last of the hills and approached the river. "They didn't take us seriously. Despite the offense of a woman trying to barter with them, a true partner would have at least attempted to correct my error. We were viewed as subordinates the entire time we were in their camp." Her horse bucked again as they passed a large tree. "He never really even examined our hides."

"Yes, I noticed that."

"I do not trust this Gyraund, and I believe they have no intentions of serious trade with Karren."

"So what does that mean?" Telleck asked.

"I don't know, Telleck. I really don't... which worries me."

Before Telleck could speak again, they heard some commotion from behind trees on their left. All heads turned as a dozen warriors galloped   toward   them   with   weapons   drawn.

Chapter 7

Zhomin and Fallad flanked the prince as he watched his troops engaging in their drills. Remen knew this task to be necessary, but he never felt much desire to facilitate the exercises. His two friends were more than capable of supervising the younger warriors, but his father felt it was good for the soldiers to see the heir to the crown lead them. So, despite the tedium, Remen fulfilled his charge without complaint.

The sound of the wooden weapons striking against each other echoed across the courtyard as the three men looked on. One of the prince's charges was smacked pretty hard against his helmet, and he fell to the ground. Remen stood still as a couple of the other soldiers attended to the young man, and the prince was reminded of Merreck lying alone in his room. His mind was again filled with disgust at himself for causing the accident, and what was worse was how inept he had allowed himself to appear before that fool Telleck. "I can't believe she went off with him," he muttered to himself.

"What was that?" Zhomin asked.

"Nothing."

"Nothing, eh?" Fallad remarked. "You're still smarting that Shyan wanted to go on the trading mission with Telleck."

"He's a competent trader," Zhomin pointed out.

"He's an ass!" the prince retorted.

"I have a hard time believing an ass could have caught your sister's eye," Fallad said with a mischievous grin.

Remen shoved his friend hard against the shoulder and turned his attention back to the injured soldier. Blood was trickling from the man's nose, but he otherwise appeared to be in good condition. With the man back in the drills, Remen decided to get an early start on the rest of the day. He left Fallad in charge of the soldiers, as he was not in the mood to banter anymore, and walked to the armory with Zhomin.

"Does it really trouble you, Shyan's interest in Telleck?" Zhomin asked when they were alone with the weapons. "The king certainly would never allow her to marry him."

"I know that, but he is such an irritant…" As his words trailed off, Remen examined the sharpness of the swords nearest him.

"You seem more aggravated by him than usual. Could it be something else?"

"What are you getting at?"

Zhomin dropped the axe that he was inspecting and turned toward his lifelong friend. "Guilt."

"It was an accident, Zhomin," Remen replied, but the emotion in his voice betrayed his words. "We all know that Telleck is the finest hunter in the kingdom. It was confusing out there…" But I should have known better, Remen completed his thought silently.

"Let's finish our task and not talk of the brothers anymore. I would like to get cleaned up before the festival tonight."

"Do you think you'll finally find yourself a woman?"

"Well, it would certainly be an improvement over spending all my time with the two of you," Zhomin remarked.

Remen could not help but laugh. Not that Zhomin's joke was particularly amusing, but any jest was so rare from him that the prince was caught off guard.

***

After returning to the palace, Remen ran into Linny on the way to his chamber. "What are you doing here?" he asked, as he was surprised to see his sister's servant in the castle while Shyan was away.

"Just wanted to make certain that the princess would not find her rooms in disorder upon her return."

"Come now. How would they have gotten messy when she's not around?" Linny's only reply was a shy look back at the prince. "You miss her, don't you?" When Linny nodded, Remen gave her shoulder a slight squeeze and continued on his way. After she was a few steps down the corridor, he turned back to her. She was not a very attractive girl, but she did have a slender body that he found appealing. He thought back to his conversation with Zhomin, and thought that it was probably time he consider finding his princess. The spring festival of that night would be the perfect time to get serious about selecting his wife.

Once he was cleaned and dressed in a pair of dark wool pants and a brown leather jacket, he left to meet up with his parents in the royal hall.

When Remen entered, the king and Yenyn were sitting on their chairs while a number of the nobles milled about. The prince knew his father's distaste for many of the nobles, and he rarely allowed them in the hall, but the spring festival was one of those times. Remen caught his father's eye while a particularly annoying man was accosting the king with some type of story. Regen flashed a brief, annoyed expression toward his son before returning his attention to the man. Remen smiled as he approached his mother, who sat quietly in the background. While the queen was well liked by the subjects, everyone in the kingdom knew all power rested solely upon Regen's shoulders. There was no hope in finding royal favor through the queen.

Yenyn rose from her chair and wrapped her arm around Remen's elbow as they strode about the hall. She nodded to those who offered her polite greetings, but quickly returned her gaze to her son. "Your father has little use for these ceremonies."

"I know."

"I wonder how you will take to them when you are king?"

Remen did not respond immediately as he considered her words. Not that he was anxious for the death of his father, but he did look forward to one day ruling the kingdom. However, he realized that he never spent much time considering the annoying tasks that would come with the role, and he thought again about the time Regen made him spend training the young soldiers. "I've never really thought much about it before," he replied.

"Well, there will be plenty of time for that later." After accepting a kiss on the cheek from one of the ladies of the court, Yenyn turned back to Remen. "Are you looking forward to the festival tonight?"

A chuckle escaped from his mouth. Who in the kingdom wasn't? The king always provided a huge feast with much drink for all of his subjects, and music and dancing would last well into the night. "Of course."

"There will be many beautiful girls seeking your favor."

"That's funny; I was just having this discussion with Zhomin."

Yenyn stopped and turned to face him. "You do realize that most of the nobles here are negotiating with the king to offer you one of their daughters," she said as the playfulness dissolved from her voice. "I would never force you to marry a girl you did not want to, but your father's patience will not last. You know how he dreads these encounters. If you do not make a decision soon, he will."

Remen gently guided his mother to continue their stroll as he gazed about the chamber. Many of the nobles had their daughters with them, and all the girls were dressed exquisitely, with impeccable cosmetics highlighting their faces. Perhaps this festival would be the most memorable of all.

***

The sound of the music swelled into the night sky as the dancers swirled about. Remen stood off to the side with Zhomin—watching the revelers—while Fallad danced with as many pretty girls as he could find. The prince enjoyed dancing, but only in small doses. Mostly he liked listening to the music and watching the others, especially as the wine began to flow more freely. His stoic friend next to him, however, never danced—despite much encouragement.

Remen's eyes surveyed the scene, watching the girls dancing. He noticed that many of them were returning his gaze, and he enjoyed the attention. "Anyone catch your interest?" Zhomin asked.

"I thought we were here for you."

Before Zhomin could offer a response, Fallad bounced in front of them with a goblet of wine in his hand. "Come on, boys!" he bellowed as some of the dark liquid spilled on Remen's shirt and hand. "The girls are out there!" He pointed toward the town center, where the dancers circled around the huge fire, but Fallad headed back to the dance before either of his friends replied.

Remen laughed to himself as he turned his attention to the musicians, who would continue uninterrupted long into the night. They stood next to his parents, who never participated in the dance, as the spring festival had been designed as the king's gift to his subjects. Regen provided all the meat and wine and—by tradition—did not intrude on the festivities. Remen knew this arrangement was fine with his father, as Regen would never dance, but he also knew his mother would love to participate in the festivities.

Beside Regen, the prince saw one of the nobles trying to talk to him over the sound of the music. Remen recognized the man as one of the lesser nobles, but he could not recall his name. What caught his attention, though, was the girl beside him. She was young, perhaps eighteen summers, with a smooth, pale complexion that seemed to reflect the dancers from the light of the bonfire. Long, nearly white hair hung down her emerald dress, which highlighted the curves of her voluptuous body. The girl looked at the man, who was most certainly her father, with disdain; she was obviously annoyed at the discussion. Remen slapped Zhomin on the shoulder and quickly approached his father. The nobleman did not notice the prince until he had already grabbed the girl's hand and led her into the dance.

Chapter 8

Merreck leaned against the wall in his room, looking out the window. He rested on his cane as he enjoyed the scent of the spring air rushing at his face. The music of the festival had already begun, and since he had fallen earlier that day, the healers would not allow him to descend the castle stairs to partake in the festival. The walls of the room felt like a prison as he took in a deep breath, but coughed when the pain in his knee flared. With a wince, he turned to the small table by his bed and the full vial of the elixir awaiting him there. He desired to limp over to it but stopped himself. The pain was intense; however, he was trying to lengthen the time between his doses. The elixir was strong, but he did not like the numbing effects of the drug on his brain.

Returning his attention to the courtyard below, he watched the people of Karren dancing about the last remnants of snow. Sighing, he dropped on his bed and grabbed the vial. His leg seemed to know that the pain-eliminating drug was close to his mouth, and it started to quiver. After a brief hesitation, he swallowed the liquid and stared at the ceiling. He felt like a failure for not being able to hold out longer, but at least the pain would disappear soon.

A book detailing the history of Regen's family also rested on the table. It was not very interesting reading, but it was at least something to pass the time. He figured he would be able to read a few pages before his brain became too cloudy.

The words relating the battle exploits of Regen's grandfather had started to become blurred. Merreck strained unsuccessfully to focus his eyes, and after dropping the book back on the table, a knock sounded at the door. "Come in," he called.

The door opened, and he saw a figure before him. He tried to recognize the face, but for some reason he could not make it out. "How are you doing?" the voice said.

"Oh, it's you, Telleck. Where have you been?" replied Merreck.

"Your brother is out on an expedition."

Merreck heard the words but they did not register in his brain. "How is Father?" he asked.

"I'm not Telleck," the voice answered. "I'm one of the healers. I've come to check on you."

"Good, that's good. When will he marry again?"

"Merreck, I'm not your brother."

The light began to swirl above him and his head felt heavy, like it was sinking into the bed. "How many deer did we get? We should keep one for ourselves before we report to Regen."

"What did you do, Merreck? Did you take too much of the elixir?"

But Merreck did not respond. At that moment, he was riding through the snow with his brother beside him. They were pursuing two deer. His javelin was raised above his head. The horse gained on the prey as his arm shot forward. The weapon flew through the air, with the deadly point gaining on the animal…

"Merreck! Merreck!" His body shook about him as his eyes opened. "Merreck, are you awake?"

As reality seeped through to his mind, he realized three healers were surrounding his bed. His voice barely managed to escape from his throat. "What happened?"

"You were delirious when I came to your room," one of the healers responded. "You lost consciousness and we couldn't wake you till just now."

"When did you come?" Merreck said, still feeling groggy. "My brother was here, then we went on a hunt."

"Your brother was sent on a mission by the king, and you certainly haven't been out on a hunt."

"Of course not," Merreck agreed as the knowledge of his situation crystallized in his mind.

"We are concerned," one of the other healers said as she checked his splint. "It was a bad break, but you should not still be in so much pain. We are afraid there is another injury other than just the fracture."

Merreck's groggy eyes turned toward his table. "Then I guess you'd better bring me more of the elixir."

The healer paused for a moment. "It seems that the elixir is also causing you problems. We have decided that we can't give you any more."

"What?" Merreck stared in disbelief. "That's great," he muttered as he shook his head in disgust and the pain began to reemerge in his leg. "That's just great."

***

The warriors of Karren rushed their own horses in front of the princess and drew their weapons as the enemy closed in. Eight soldiers had been assigned to the mission with the thought that they would be more than enough to protect such a small amount of goods, but the group from Karren was outnumbered. Telleck pulled out his sword uncertainly. He was a hunter and trader, and only had slight knowledge of what to do with a blade. Should he flee with the princess or join the soldiers in her defense?

As he contemplated his actions, the warriors clashed before him. Steel hit steel as horses kicked about and men bellowed in rage. Telleck's free hand absently reached for a javelin on his back, but his fingers found nothing. He heard a cry of pain as one of the attackers fell from his horse with blood streaming from his throat. "I need to get you out of here," he said to Shyan as he and one of the defenders became surrounded. The warrior of Karren swung his sword desperately. He struck one foe on the arm, but his body went limp as a blade crushed down on his head. His skull exploded in a crimson shower, and pieces of brain spurted out from a gapping crevice.

"We can't leave them," Shyan cried.

"Their job is to protect you," Telleck responded. "Let's go!"

Another guard had his sword knocked from his hand. He hesitated for a moment before he leapt from his horse. He grabbed one of the attackers by the neck, and together they fell to the ground. The pair landed with the Karren warrior on top. He drove his fist into the man's face and collapsed his nose. The cry was muffled as the warrior struck again. He raised and lowered the man's head with frightening speed, until his motion stopped in an instant. Blood rushed down onto the limp body below him as he, too, fell with a blade protruding from his chest.

No longer transfixed by the scene about them, Telleck sheathed his blade and grabbed the reins of Shyan's steed . "Now!" he ordered as he forced both horses to gallop away. As they rode, he realized that he no longer heard the sound of the battle behind them. Releasing the princess' reins, he glanced back and saw two of their foes pursuing. The men did well, Telleck thought. Only two of the enemy remained, and Shyan and he had a head start. He kicked his horse to get every ounce of speed, but then saw an arrow fly above his head. Another followed. What was he to do? But then his horse squealed in pain and collapsed. Telleck hit the ground first, and quickly rolled before the horse could pin him. The animal landed and did not move again.

Telleck pulled out his sword and prepared to defend himself, but the horsemen ignored him and continued after Shyan. He raced after, knowing it was a futile endeavor. He would never be able to catch them, but he had to try.

Shyan's pursuers continued to fire their arrows and Telleck watched in horror as Shyan's horse also fell. He lost sight of what happened next as she was hidden by some brush, but he continued to rush toward her as the enemy reached the spot where she fell and dismounted.

Telleck took a moment to collect his thoughts. He moved to the brush as quickly and quietly as he could. When he reached it, he saw the two men standing above her. He knew he had to act fast, but he realized that he would be dead quickly if he tried to engage the men. Perhaps surprise would allow him kill one, but that would be it. The other would certainly overwhelm him. So out of desperation he held his sword above his head. He judged the weight for a moment, then let it fly. As it hurled through the air, he jumped from the bush. Both men turned as the sword struck one in the chest. The man collapsed with the blade piercing his lung. The other raised his own sword, but before he could strike, Telleck tackled him. They rolled about the ground trying to gain an advantage. While Telleck was not skilled with the sword, he had been wrestling his whole life, either with his brother or the other boys in and about the castle, and he rarely lost.

Telleck managed to get the man's arm behind him and rolled his face down into the mucky ground. The man writhed while Telleck pulled on his arm. His foe cried out as Telleck continued to pull with all his strength. The man tried to squirm out but Telleck would not let go. He relaxed a moment, and his opponent thought he had a chance to break free, but the relaxation was only to re-grip his enemy's forearm. With a mighty tug, Telleck pulled the arm up toward the man's neck. The man screamed in pain as Telleck finally heard the crack of bone.

He jumped off the man and quickly kicked his arm. His opponent screamed again and Telleck kicked him in the head. The man's cries turned to whimpers as Telleck continued the assault. As he raised his leg for another kick, Shyan screamed for him to stop.

With a feeling of bewilderment, he realized that he had forgotten about her during the melee. She stood behind him, covered in mud and a few scrapes but otherwise uninjured. He threw his arms about her, then turned back to their enemy, who lay semiconscious on the ground. "Let me finish the bastard off," he said.

"No, he's no longer a threat, and we need to find out where he's from and why they attacked us."

Telleck sucked in a number of labored breaths as wiped sweat from his face. "You're right, of course," he replied as they approached the man.

Chapter 9

With his wife sitting quietly next to him, the king looked down at his son with a disapproving glare. "I agree that Brynn is very pretty, but her father is only a minor noble. Last night was the first time Kalle had even approached me regarding his daughter."

Regen's mood was clearly agitated and Remen knew he needed to consider his response carefully. "That is another reason I find her so appealing. I don't think Kalle ever considered the fact that his request would be honored. All the other nobles have practically thrown their daughters at me. It was refreshing to find a girl who had no expectations."

"There is a reason why the other nobles have expectations," the king responded flatly, which Remen knew was not a good sign.

"I request your indulgence in this matter, Father. While Kalle's wealth is not great, he *is* a nobleman. There certainly is no custom that would forbid marriage to his daughter."

Remen studied his father's face. Lines of anger increased as his skin flushed, and Yenyn rested her hand on his arm. "He does speak truthfully," she interjected gently, "and she is very pretty."

Rage exploded from the king like lava from an erupting volcano. "I do not need your involvement in this matter, woman!" His red face glared at Yenyn, but Remen read the pang of instant regret in the king's expression. The queen turned away from her husband—as she had done so many other times in the past—while she raised a cloth to wipe her eyes. Remen abhorred this treatment of his mother, which he had watched countless times during his young life; however, he realized that this time presented him with an opportunity. The king certainly would not apologize to Yenyn, but Remen could possibly make use of his remorse.

"We have plenty of wealth, Father; I ask that you allow me to pursue this."

The king's face softened somewhat as Yenyn regained her composure. He did not turn to his wife and he refused to speak, but he did nod in his son's direction.

***

The snow had finally all disappeared and the warm breeze was a welcome change. Remen strolled through the royal gardens with Brynn at his side. No flowers were in bloom yet, which meant the pair would find solitude amongst the barren bushes. "It went as expected," he said. "My father was not happy when I told him."

"My father was just the opposite."

Remen smiled at her beautiful face as he guided her to a bench. "We need to proceed carefully," he continued. "While my father has given me permission to court you, he might still change his mind."

Brynn was quiet for a moment. "At least we know my father won't," she said with a chuckle while linking her arm through his.

Remen felt the warmth of her body against his, and he turned to look into her eyes. "We'll just have to make sure that the king doesn't change his mind." The prince felt a newfound joy as Brynn's eyes twinkled in the light of the sun while she gazed up at him. While Remen was no stranger to women, as many of the young women of the court had made themselves available to him in the past, he had never felt this way around any of them. He was not quite sure what it was about Brynn that he found so appealing. Yes, she was beautiful, but there were plenty of other beautiful girls. Whatever it was, he did not care. He relished the contentment he felt with her beside him, and wondered what his sister would say when she returned.

Chapter 10

The days following the spring festival had brought dire news to the castle: Shyan and Telleck were overdue from the Armen Plains. The fact that his brother was missing was bad enough for Merreck, but the upheaval meant his only visitor had been his father. Matters became more devastating when the scouts who had been sent out just returned and reported that the soldiers were found dead across the Unmeth River along with the attackers, but there was no sign of the princess or Telleck. With the confusion over the loss of Shyan, Yenyn and the prince had stopped visiting. Merreck realized they were busy with other matters, but that did not help alleviate the boredom of his room. And the fact that the healers no longer allowed him to have the pain-killing elixir did not help. Fortunately, the pain in his leg had lessened considerably, but that only seemed to make his knee hurt more. He was starting to move around more using crutches; however, there were not too many destinations he could venture to. Stairs posed too much of a risk, so he tried to visit a few of the other patients in the convalescence rooms. Only a handful of other people were present, and they all suffered from a similar fever. So the healers told him that he was not allowed in their rooms.

He sat on his bed after a short walk, trying to rub the pain out of his leg when Remen finally entered. He was unshaven and appeared exhausted. The prince dropped onto the chair and looked at Merreck with haggard eyes. "You haven't found them yet, I take it," Merreck said.

"We continue the search, and at least we haven't found their bodies. We hold out hope that they are still alive."

For some reason it gave Merreck reassurance that the prince and he were experiencing the same anxiousness over a missing sibling. "Telleck is resourceful. Shyan couldn't be in better hands."

Remen appeared to be aggravated by those words, but the prince let it pass. "I'm sorry I've not been in to visit you, but I was out leading some searches. How are you doing?"

"The pain from the break isn't as bad, but my knee seems worse. The healers have been giving me a salve instead of the elixir. It doesn't help much."

The prince didn't seem to hear his words as he stood. "I'm heading back out tomorrow, but I'll stop in before I leave."

Merreck resisted the urge to offer a sarcastic thank you. "I'm sure they're all right," he muttered as Remen left. A healer entered shortly after to readjust his splint, which increased his agony, and his mind turned from his brother to the persistent pain.

***

Telleck and Shyan had crossed the river through the water instead of over the bridge, to thwart anyone who might be tracking them. They had begun the long trip southward by foot, trying to stay within the cover of trees or shrubs whenever possible. The surviving attacker had told them that they were mercenaries hired to attack anyone trading with the Armen Tribesmen. When questioned who hired them, the man had claimed not to know. All he had been told was that the tribesmen were marshalling themselves for war, and any friend of the tribesmen was an enemy. Shyan wanted to bring the man back to Karren, but he was in pretty bad shape with his broken arm and the beating that Telleck had administered. They had tried to locate any of the horses but the beasts that had survived the battle were gone. So, with little choice, Telleck killed the man and they left the scene.

It took the pair six days of moving slowly through the forest to finally reach Karren. They had heard some patrols, but they hid from view in case the riders were additional mercenaries. Telleck had managed to trap a few rabbits and squirrels, but the pair did not eat well. They were both very haggard when finally reaching the castle, where they were welcomed with much fanfare.

***

The midmorning sun cast a warm glow over the newly-blooming flowers as Telleck sat with his brother in Regen's garden. The air was warm and insects flew amidst the plants. It had been a week since Telleck had returned with Shyan. The king had heaped much honor upon his daughter's protector, to the point where Telleck began to feel uncomfortable with all the attention. He had not been sent out on any new missions, and that was fine for now. It did not hurt that Shyan was spending more time with him. But he had needed to get away and spend some time alone with Merreck.

"So, did they carry you all the way down here?" asked Telleck.

"Yes. It was kind of humiliating, but it's nice to get out of that room and into some fresh air," Merreck answered with a wince as he tried to adjust his splint.

"It's still that bad?"

"Not the break, that doesn't hurt any more. My knee is the problem."

"And no more elixir?"

"No, the healers are afraid what it might do to me, but they think the knee will improve over time."

"It seems the royal family is causing us nothing but trouble," Telleck pointed out.

"Let's not start on that. Remen made the mistake, and you saved the princess. I'm sure Regen will take care of us if I'm not able to trade or hunt any more."

"It's the least he can do."

Merreck turned on the bench to face his brother and immediately regretted the action as a new wave of pain shot up his leg. "Damn it," he mumbled as he sucked his breath in through his teeth. After holding it for a moment, he continued. "I was thinking about Cishor. That nobleman was concerned about problems brewing in the north. I'd think this qualifies."

"Yes, but Regen knows all about it. I couldn't have kept this from him."

"True, but you should probably get back to Cishor and talk to him about it."

"The princess was attacked. I'm sure Tor already knows something that important."

"Of course he does," Merreck responded, knowing that a kingdom the size of Cishor had spies amongst all their neighbors, regardless of friendly relations. "But maybe you can learn something from him."

Telleck considered his brother's words for a moment. It had been nice not having to travel lately, but he was starting to feel restless. "Very well, I'll tell Shyan that I want to go on the next expedition there."

Merreck offered a smile at those words. "So, you've been with her often, huh?"

"What business is it of yours?" Telleck snapped.

"I'm just wondering if I'll be able to attend the wedding," Merreck teased.

"You're lucky you're injured, otherwise I'd give you a good thrashing."

"Remen as a brother, now that will be a sight."

"Enough!" Telleck bellowed, louder than Merreck had expected. They had teased each other all their lives but never over something as pleasant as his relationship with the princess, so Merreck was taken aback by his brother's strong reaction.

Telleck stood, wandered over to a small tree and leaned against it. Though his back was turned, Merreck was shocked to see his brother lift his hand to wipe at his eyes. When Telleck turned back, Merreck saw traces of moisture still on Telleck's cheek. "What is it?" Merreck eventually asked, not knowing what else to say.

"It's just…" Telleck stammered for a moment before continuing. "I know there was nothing else I could have done, but I killed them. I killed two men."

"They were trying to kill you and Shyan."

Telleck's look of anguish immediately turned to anger. "I know that. I'm not a fool. There's nothing I'd do differently, but..." Telleck hesitated for a moment with a pleading look in his eyes, "I killed them."

Merreck looked perplexed at his brother. They had killed countless animals over their years, but never a man. Certainly nobody would fault Telleck for his actions—he was in fact being praised—but it had never occurred to Merreck that his brother would be haunted by his actions. "I guess I never really thought about it."

"I'm just being childish," Telleck continued softly as he struggled to compose himself while returning to the bench. "They got what they deserved." Merreck could tell the assertion was not directed at him; Telleck was trying to convince himself.

"So, what are you going to do about Shyan?" Merreck asked, attempting to change the subject.

"I don't know," Telleck answered as the normal tone of his voice returned. "It was strange, on our way north, I thought I'd finally find out how she felt. But then she barely looked at me. Now that we're back, I can hardly get away from her."

"It's understandable. You did save her life."

"Of course," Telleck responded with his all-too-familiar irritation, "but you know how she was to me before all this. It doesn't make sense."

"Why don't you ask her?"

Telleck wanted to shout at his brother. Ask her? What a stupid suggestion. But then he figured, why not?

***

It was still a strange feeling being allowed to move freely about the castle, and even having servants ask if he needed anything. Telleck was led into a sitting area, where he had to wait for Shyan. The room was fairly large and the portraits which hung on the stone walls did little to soften the imposing feeling. The king and queen stared coldly back at Telleck, as did, he assumed, the king's parents and grandparents. He sat in one of the chairs and grabbed a book which rested on a table. He opened it but struggled with the words: he had never been much for schooling. Merreck had been the one more willing to study, while Telleck had preferred wrestling with the other boys or getting in on a few extra hunts. He dejectedly returned the book to the table and closed his eyes, avoiding the silent inquisition of Karren's royalty.

To his relief, the princess strolled in a few moments later. Her soft hair was tied neatly behind her neck, which displayed a sparkling ruby against her smooth skin. The illumination in the room seemed to increase when she smiled at Telleck. She sat in the chair next to his, and her expression brightened even more. "I heard you asked to see me?"

"I need to ask for your help."

"Anything."

A few stray thoughts crossed Telleck's mind but he focused on his task. "We've been back for a week now, and I'm anxious to get back on the road. It's time for me to get out on a trade."

Shyan face dimmed somewhat when he finished. "If that is what you want."

"I'd like to get back to Cishor, as I had good success there the last time."

She looked at him, then stood abruptly. "I'll see to it," she responded and turned to leave.

Telleck was a bit bewildered by her reaction but he thought quickly and continued. "There is one other thing."

"What is that?" she asked without turning around.

"Please have a seat," he said nervously. After she returned to the chair he continued. "It's just... when we were... in the past I thought..."

Her hand reached out to his arm and gentle fingers stroked his skin. "What are you trying to say?"

Telleck looked up helplessly at the ceiling and the flickering candles hanging from the silver chandelier while the portraits seemed to be mocking him. He took a deep breath, then looked into her inviting eyes. "I'm not oblivious to how you treated me in the past. When we were heading out on our mission, I planned to talk to you about it, but you pretty much ignored me. Now that we've returned, we've barely been apart. I don't understand."

Shyan's hand slipped down to his and their fingers intertwined. "My father always knew that I loved you but he forbade me from telling you. He has no qualms with you and Merreck, but you are commoners. Before we left, he reminded me of that. I thought you might finally approach me, so I did not want to give you the chance. That is why I ignored you. When we returned, and you had saved my life, he had no choice but to relent."

The words hit Telleck like a large rock being dropped into a small pond; ripples flowed all through his body. It took him a moment to comprehend what she was saying. Unless he was mistaken, the princess had just advised him that they could marry. He tried to formulate words, but all he could say was, "Why me?" How could such a caring and beautiful young woman as the princess desire an ill-tempered and not very attractive commoner?

"I love you, Telleck. I have since we were children."

"Me?"

Telleck felt his pulse quicken as Shyan continued. "Yes, you. My friends all laughed at me, but you are the most honest person I've ever met. I desire nothing else."

Telleck gazed into her eyes as comprehension crystallized in his mind. The inclining and suppressed desires of his past years were becoming realized at that very moment. As if to solidify that knowledge, Shyan leaned in close and pressed her lips against his. As Telleck relished in the joy of the moment, the vision of the two men he had killed hung like a storm cloud, blotting out the sun.

Chapter 10

Horse hooves thundered over the ground. Dirt and mud flew in all directions as a light spring rain began to fall. After a call, all the riders kicked their steeds into a full gallop. Their quarry was visible and they needed to be caught before reaching the bridge. The fleeing party would have to slow down to cross, and that would give them their opportunity.

The first horse approached the bridge as the riders from Karren reached their prey. With swords drawn, Remen and his soldiers blocked the bridge from the trailing horses. The lone rider who had crossed gave one look over his shoulder as he galloped his horse out of sight. "Lay down your arms. You are outnumbered," the prince ordered.

Rather than obeying, the mercenaries turned their horses to the west and raced along the river bank. But Remen's men were prepared. With the twang of a bow, an arrow shot from Fallad's hand into the shoulder of the lead rider. The man desperately tried to maintain control of his mount while grasping for the arrow, but the horse bucked and he fell to the ground. With their comrade down and their escape path blocked by the fallen horse and the soldiers of Karren, the horses of the remaining men spun as the mercenaries drew their blades. "Don't be fools," called Remen. "There are eight of you and fifteen of us. Surrender."

"Let us pass," one of the men called. "You have already wounded one of us for no reason."

"You were trespassing on Karren land and did not stop to be questioned," the prince responded as Fallad led the Karren soldiers around to surround the mercenaries against the riverbank. "We had every right to pursue you."

"Since when is Karren so distrustful of strangers?"

Since my soldiers were slain and my sister attacked, the prince thought, but he figured there was no reason to give these men any information. Instead, Remen signaled to his men and four more bows were raised. "I will ask the questions, after you drop your weapons."

"To be left defenseless? We shall never *blue*..." At the word 'blue,' the mercenaries charged.

Arrows flew, but they were too late. The horses crashed into the Karren soldiers with the rain beginning to fall harder. Swords clashed as a crack of thunder sounded. Remen felt a blade glance off his armored shoulder. He blocked another blow while his foe attempted to spin his horse about, but the animal skidded on the mud. Seizing his opportunity, Remen attacked the man's unprotected back. His sword struck thick leather. The man cried out, but the blade slid down and did not pierce. After regaining control of his steed, the man turned about. He swung, but there was not much force behind the strike. Remen easily parried the blow and with a twist of his wrist, sent the man's sword flying to the ground. The mercenary looked at the prince briefly, seemingly astonished that he had been bested. But he did not have much time to be surprised as Remen drove his blade into the man's skull.

With his adversary dispatched, Remen turned toward his men. Four of them were on the ground, and five of the mercenaries remained. He spotted Fallad, who was engaged with one of the enemy, and Remen's friend—who was considered to be the finest swordsman in the kingdom—was barely able to defend himself. Clearly the swordplay of this enemy far surpassed that of the Karren warriors, and Remen realized that he was most likely fortunate to still be alive. If his foe's horse had not skidded, he might very well be the one dead on the wet ground.

"Surrender!" Remen called as he charged forward with his blood-stained weapon out before him. "You don't all have to die!" But the enemy did not heed his words. The prince approached the nearest adversary, who had fought through the defense of one of the Karren soldiers. The mercenary's blade struck his opponent's chin. Bone exploded against the blow, and blood began to flow down his chest. As hands went up to the chin, one more strike against the side of the head ended his suffering. But before the attacker could turn, Remen aimed a mighty blow to the back of the man's neck. The blade cut through skin, bone and nerves, leaving the head hanging useless against the shoulder.

Despite their superior skills, the mercenaries could not overcome the numbers—but they refused to surrender. The battle quickly ended with only Remen, Fallad and five of the Karren warriors surviving. The prince then turned back to the river and the man who had been shot from the horse. He was trying to stumble away as Remen rode over and jumped from his horse. He knocked the man down, placed a foot on his chest and the point of his sword against his neck. "Now you are going to tell me who you are and why mercenaries would be willing to fight to the death."

"We are not mercenaries," the man said between whimpers of pain.

"A convoy from Karren was attacked a couple weeks ago by mercenaries, and now we find you on our land without insignia, and you don't stop to be questioned."

"We are not mercenaries," the man repeated.

"Then who are you?"

"Let me up, please. My shoulder hurts too much."

Remen sheathed his sword and offered his hand to the man. After being pulled from the ground, the man pounced as he pulled a blade from his belt. He tried to bury the blade in Remen's stomach, but the prince blocked him as their arms intertwined. While they wrestled on the ground, the prince threw his head against the wounded shoulder. The man howled but he did not loosen his grip. Remen struck again as Fallad launched his body onto the pair. After Fallad secured the man's arms, Remen stood while his remaining warriors bound their prisoner and bandaged his wound. With that task complete, Remen ordered graves to be dug for his fallen men.

"What about them?" Fallad asked as he pointed to the corpses of their foes.

"We'll leave them where they lie: food for carrion. That is all they deserve."

Fallad looked like he wanted to protest, but he stopped himself, which relieved the prince. He was in no mood to argue over graves for those who killed so many of their comrades, and most likely were responsible for the attack against Shyan. When the graves were completed, they gathered up a few of the horses of the enemy and started back to the castle with their prisoner.

***

"I still find it hard to believe that Regen is allowing you to court Kalle's daughter," Fallad commented when they had stopped for a brief rest and a short meal.

"It took some convincing."

"Of course." Fallad finished a chunk of bread then gave their prisoner a hard stare before taking a drink of water. "I'm surprised you had never met Brynn before the festival."

"I'm not allowed the opportunity to socialize with whomever I'd like."

"I guess not being royalty has some advantages," Fallad replied, and Remen was taken aback that he had not made any jokes about the matter. But he figured his friend was not in the mood for joviality after witnessing so much death.

"Have you talked to her much?" the prince asked.

"Just a few times," replied Fallad as he stood. "I always thought she was beautiful, but I've kept my sights higher," he finished with the familiar twinkle in his eye as he walked behind a tree.

"You'd be so lucky," Remen commented when Fallad returned. He waited for Fallad's comeback, but none came. After the pause, the prince continued. "They were all blond; they look like they're from the southern coast. I've heard of the coastal men being hired out as mercenaries, and I still can't understand why they fought to the death."

"Perhaps he was being truthful when they said they're not. I've never known a mercenary who'd face death for honor, which means they were fighting for something more important than coin."

"That's what scares me," Remen responded before ordering his men to gather up and finish their journey home.

Chapter 12

Telleck sat next to Tor in the small hall in which they'd had their previous discussion. Linny and Bront had again accompanied him on the trip, but they were preparing for the trade while Tor had led Telleck away. "It is a pleasure to see you again, my friend," Tor commented after a sip of wine. "Where is your brother?"

"He had an accident and broke his leg."

Tor's dark face displayed a sympathetic expression that appeared sincere. "I'm sorry to hear that. I hope he is recovering well enough."

"He is managing," Telleck said, then took a drink of the cool water that was next to him.

"Since you asked to speak to me, may I assume that you have something to report?"

Telleck hesitated for a moment. He certainly had no reason to trust Tor, but if he told the story of the attack, perhaps he would secure another large exchange for the hides they had brought. However, that was the reason he had come to Cishor, and besides, Tor probably already knew about the attack anyway. So since he saw no downside, he proceeded with the story.

"Yes, we knew that," Tor said as expected when Telleck had completed his tale.

"You have spies in Karren?" Telleck asked sharply, even though he knew the answer. He began to wonder what the point of Tor's offer was if he knew what was happening in Telleck's homeland.

"Of course!"

Tor's jovial admission only increased Telleck's annoyance. "Then what do you want from me?"

"Please calm yourself," Tor said flatly. "I'm quite sure Regen has spies here. It does not mean that we are enemies. Both sides are just gathering information, and both kingdoms know it."

"Fine, we spy on each other. That's great. But you still haven't answered my question."

"Our spies gather information, but they can only provide so much. Besides, they stay close to the castle. You, my friend, move freely around the land. It is your insight that I desire."

"If you think so, but there is not much else I can tell you."

"You said your attackers claimed to be mercenaries. Do you think they were lying?"

Telleck's mind drifted back to the wounded man he had killed, and his remorse returned. He took another drink before continuing. "I don't know. It all happened so quickly and I wanted to get Shyan safely home."

"What I find interesting is that they attacked you thinking you were friends of the Armen Tribesmen. From what you said, Regen is concerned about the tribesmen. We of Cishor are concerned as well. They are north, and that is where the evil is supposed to rise."

"I don't know about evil, but Shyan and I nearly died because of something happening there."

"If the tribesmen are marshalling for war, that is bad enough. If they have additional assistance it will be even worse."

"What are you talking about?"

"The men of Armen are formidable warriors in their own right. But if they have dark forces on their side… Well, I shudder to think of it."

What is Tor talking about now, Telleck wondered. Dark forces fighting with them? He had no interest in these mystical ramblings. "Believe what you want. I brought you what news I could, per our agreement. Now I'd appreciate a generous trade to honor your end of our bargain, and then we'll be on our way."

Tor offered Telleck a knowing look. "I see you are skeptical, my friend," he said as he rose. "Please accompany me."

Telleck wanted no part of this, but he decided to follow the nobleman of Cishor, if for no other reason than to receive another large cartful of produce to bring home.

***

With the news that Shyan and Telleck were to be married, Urik had been invited to move into the castle, much to his supreme pleasure. Merreck was getting around better on his crutches, and they were given a large room to share on the ground floor. It was nice to be out of the convalescence room, but the boredom was wearing upon Merreck. In the past, if his brother and he were not on a trading expedition, they would be out on a hunt. It was rare when he would spend two days in row without leaving his home. It had been several weeks since the accident, and he had not ventured any further than Regen's courtyard.

If the boredom was not bad enough, the constant pain in his knee made matters nearly unbearable. The salves received from the healers did nothing to quench the constant agony, so they had experimented with a different mixture of the elixir. That only helped dull the pain slightly, so he had asked if he could get on a horse, but was told to wait another week.

Late in the morning he hobbled into the dining hall for lunch. It was still early, so the hall was fairly empty. He was not too hungry, but he was anxious to leave his room. He looked about, but when he did not recognize any of the soldiers, he sat at an empty table. After he started picking at some of the bland meat that had been placed before him, Queen Yenyn and Shyan joined him.

"I don't know," the queen said. "I still have a hard time telling them apart."

"Telleck can walk straight," Merreck quipped with no trace of humor in his voice.

Yenyn let out a nervous laugh as she kissed him on the cheek. "I'm sure that will change soon," said Shyan. "Then you'll need to come up with a different strategy, mother."

"How is the deer, my boy?" Yenyn asked.

"It's kind of dry."

"Soon you'll be out there and getting us some fresh meat."

I'd be out there now if it wasn't for your idiot son, he thought. He mustered up a smile for the queen while trying to ignore his pain. "Yes, I look forward to that." He then turned his attention to Shyan. "How are the wedding preparations coming?"

"It'll take some time, but the ceremony should happen in late summer. There are many people to invite from neighboring lands."

"And I hear we might have a second wedding as well," noted Merreck.

"Let's not be premature," the queen responded. But Merreck saw the look of approval in her face. The news of Remen's courtship had spread quickly through the castle, as did Regen's tepid agreement to the relationship. While the rest of the king's subjects found joy in the news, Merreck was unable to mirror any enthusiasm. "It should be quite an occasion here in Karren," Yenyn continued. "But I'm certain many of the nobles from our neighbors are none too happy that my lovely daughter is marrying someone within the kingdom," Yenyn continued, deftly changing the subject. "She's already had many suitors."

"That's nice," Merreck said.

"Come, Mother, we don't want to bore poor Merreck with talk of weddings."

"You are right, my girl," the queen agreed as her food arrived. Yenyn picked up her fork as Shyan launched into some happy stories from their childhood. Merreck was grateful for the distraction, and that the conversation had turned away from his brother and the wedding.

Chapter 13

Prince Remen stood before his father with the prisoner bound at his side. The man's wound was cleansed upon their return and he had been given a fresh bandage. The king raised his large body from the throne and approached his son. With piercing blue eyes, he surveyed the prisoner. His thick, muscular arms crossed over his chest as he tilted his head of braided gray hair that hung far down his back. "Is this man connected to those who attacked my daughter?" the king asked while not releasing his gaze into the prisoner's eyes.

"He claims not to be, father," Remen answered. "He said he is not a mercenary, but he would not tell us anything else."

"What was he doing on my land?"

"Again, he would not say."

Regen adjusted his crown then pulled his rapier from its scabbard. He placed the tip of the blade atop the man's head and ran the point along the front of his face, across his chin and stopped at the neck. "You are no use to me if you do not talk. If you remain silent, you will die."

"I have nothing to say to you," the man said defiantly.

"Are you certain?"

"Death is preferable to betrayal."

"I can gladly arrange that." The king smiled at the prisoner as he sheathed the rapier. "But we have to find out if you will, in fact, remain silent." He looked over his shoulder to his personal guards. "Take him away and we shall see if we are able to loosen his tongue." The prisoner was dragged from the throne room and Regen turned his attention to the prince. "You did well my son, bringing a prisoner back."

"Father, he may be telling the truth. They also fought with a skill that far surpassed that of common mercenaries."

Regen returned to his throne and offered the seat beside him to his son. "Those who attacked Shyan could certainly have been hired by these men. Your prisoner could have been searching for the mercenaries when they did not return." The king paused as he stood again and punched the wall behind his throne. "Too many of my warriors have died, and nearly my daughter!" After regaining his composure, Regen returned to his seat. "I don't trust the tribesmen, and Shyan said they were attacked because the mercenaries thought they were friends of Armen. This man clearly is not a tribesman. So who is he?"

"He has the look of a man from the southern coast, but I don't know for certain."

"That is disconcerting." Regen leaned back and looked up at the candles decorating the high ceiling. "But if these men are truly enemies of the tribesmen..." The king sighed as his large, scarred hands rubbed his weary face. "We will know soon enough if he is going to talk. Speculation will not help us at this time."

Remen turned in his chair toward the king and hesitated a moment before speaking. "If I may broach another subject while we wait; you could still call off the wedding."

"You dare question my judgment on this, knowing how I feel about your own courtship?" The king then let out a heavy sigh and his agitation melted into resignation. "Your sister has loved Telleck since you were children."

Those words did not sit well with Remen, who had always known of Shyan's affection for the hunter. The fact that his lovely twin sister felt so deeply for an ordinary commoner was bad enough. But for that commoner to be the ill-tempered Telleck was even worse. "He does not deserve to marry her."

"I will not argue this with you any more. Custom dictates that she may choose him. He saved her life, and that makes him worthy, whether we like it or not."

"But you are the king."

"Enough!" Regen bellowed. "His deed has made him worthy and it is her choice. Now, unless you want me to further examine yours, you will be silent on this matter!"

Remen was familiar with the king's tone, and he knew that he needed to end the discussion. "Of course, Father. If I may be excused, I would like to rest for a time before attending to my duties."

"Certainly, I will summon you if we secure any information from the prisoner."

Remen rose from his chair and his heavy, clipped steps were his only display of anger as he strode from the hall. As he reached the stairway, he noticed the door to Merreck's room. He stopped for a moment and considered knocking, but instead continued up the stairs. He did not appreciate the guilt Merreck and his family directed at him. After all, it had been an accident. If Merreck and his brother had been better teachers, it never would have happened. Besides, his family had given him the best care. Rather than blaming him, Merreck should be thankful for all that had been provided.

First the accident and now the engagement, Remen was sick of Urik's family and just wanted them to be gone.

***

After a few hours in his room, Remen went down to the dining hall for a quick meal before heading to the soldiers' barracks. The news of the death of their friends had already been heard, but any grief would have to be ignored. With the possibility of conflict from the north, it was the prince's responsibility to make certain that all his warriors were prepared for battle. He brought the men out for drills with Zhomin and Fallad beside him.

When the men had finished with their customary drills, they started in the direction of their barracks—until Remen ordered them to turn around and resume. After a few moments, Fallad moved the prince away and asked quietly. "Aren't you working them a little hard?"

The prince's countenance hung wearily as he regarded his warriors. "Perhaps, but you saw how those men fought. They made us made us look like children. We need to be better prepared if we run into any of their comrades."

"If you say so, Remen." Fallad turned his attention back to the men and chastised them for not giving a full effort.

"You'd better be more careful out there, Remen," Zhomin said. "We've lost enough good men already. You should probably stay near the castle."

"And what good will that do us?" the prince asked.

"The king's heir must be careful." After a pause, Zhomin continued. "You could send Telleck out when he returns."

"I would like that," laughed Remen.

Fallad called out to the men again to increase their intensity, then turned back to Remen. "Your sister better not hear you talking that way."

"Why not? Is there anything more foolish she can do?"

"Regardless how you feel about him, he did save her life."

"Yes, then give him some gold, but marriage?" Remen spat as his cheeks began to flush.

"He's not that bad." Fallad smiled at the prince and Remen knew his friend was just trying to get him aggravated. Unfortunately, it always seemed to work.

"You don't even know him."

"But it's what Shyan wants," Fallad continued.

"And I want my ass to be covered with gold."

Fallad's all-too-familiar grin flashed across his face. "I'll let your father know that next time I see him."

Remen's bright red face turned to Fallad, and seeing his friend's amusement only caused his anger to increase. "All right, you two," Zhomin said as he stepped between them. "Nothing ever changes, does it?"

The prince began to calm down, as he knew his anger was actually directed at Telleck and Shyan, and not Fallad. If Fallad was entertained by irritating him, that was fine. He trusted both of these men with his life, and he would need strong allies when he became king. Allowing these little annoyances would serve him well in the future. "My father has decided, so we need to drop this matter," Remen ordered, and he knew that once Regen made a decision, he could not be swayed. *Unless you're his daughter,* he thought.

"We certainly don't want to anger the king," Zhomin noted, and all three men knew the truth of that statement. While Regen's subjects regarded him as a fair monarch, he was known to be ruthless whenever he felt wronged. "But that doesn't mean we have to like it."

"It also doesn't mean that it will be bad though," Fallad pointed out.

Remen ignored the comment and said that the soldiers could finally be dismissed; however, training would resume in earnest the following day for all warriors in the kingdom. If nothing else, his men would be prepared for whatever may be awaiting them.

***

The warmth of evening was a wonderful distraction as Brynn and the prince sat under the clear night sky enjoying a refreshing breeze. The fire in the center of the yard grew as servants continued to toss scraps of wood into it. Once the fire had reached its customary height, a priest walked from the outskirts of the audience to present himself to his liege. The man bowed to Regen and gently kissed Yenyn's hand before bowing again to the king. Regen lowered his head and the priest approached the fire. The murmuring of the crowd ceased as the priest turned his back to the flames and raised his arms. When all was quiet, he offered a prayer to the Creator for the bounty of their newly planted crops, along with success in all their hunts. When the prayer was over, the priest expressed his thankfulness to those around and then the music started, as did the dancing.

The flickering of the fire reflected off Brynn's soft skin as she said to Remen, "I know you're not much for this, are you?"

"Maybe later, when the music slows."

"Is this what I have to look forward to? Years of watching everyone else have fun?" she asked with an expression of mock sadness.

"You're wonderful, Brynn," Remen said as he kissed her cheek.

"The prince is making you sit here like one of the old folks, eh?" Fallad interjected as he stuck his head between the pair. "I don't know about the prince, but I'd be honored to dance with such a pretty girl." He turned to Remen, who could see the disappointment in Fallad's face that he was not annoyed by the comment. Fallad then offered his hand to Brynn. "If I may?"

Brynn grabbed Fallad's hand as she stuck her tongue out at Remen, then the two dashed off to join the revelers. Remen watched the pair with a smile as they danced within the group. Brynn's beautiful body swayed with the music, and she continued to look toward him as he watched. He was grateful that she was enjoying herself, and after a couple songs he prepared to join in, but Zhomin came and sat next to him.

"She's lovely."

"Yes, she is," Remen replied as he soaked in the vision of her flowing hair and smooth skin.

"Do you think Fallad is doing you a favor or trying to annoy you?"

"Does it really matter?"

"I suppose not," Zhomin answered. "But this all feels a bit strange: a celebration after the death of so many warriors and a man being tortured in our dungeon."

Remen's joy was suddenly sapped by the words of his friend. He knew Zhomin was correct, but he also knew how much the king's subjects looked forward to the festival. Besides, did he really need to think of those matters all the time? "If you will excuse me," he said as he rose from his seat and jogged into the crowd. After pulling Brynn's arm away from Fallad, he danced with the woman he loved for the rest of the night.

Chapter 14

Tor led Telleck through the courtyard, out the castle gate and into the surrounding city. He was taking Telleck to meet the *wise brother* which he had previously mentioned. Telleck had little interest in this delay, but hoped it would prove beneficial when he received his goods. They walked down a few streets then entered a pub. There were only a few patrons in the establishment and they all offered suspicious looks in Telleck's direction. He did not feel comfortable in this land with his light skin and inability to understand their language, but he followed Tor up the staircase into a small hallway. Tor knocked on one of the four rickety doors, and after a few moments it opened slowly.

The room before him was tiny, just a bed and few books scattered across the dirty floor, and an unbearable stink bore into his unsuspecting nose, but what was truly remarkable was the man who stood before them. He was no taller than an adolescent boy, and the wrinkled, light skin that was visible through his tattered clothes was completely hairless. His head turned slightly to gaze upon Telleck and it appeared that every movement caused the man intense pain. An emaciated arm was raised and nail-less fingers bid them entry. Following a deep breath, Tor entered; however, Telleck hesitated at the doorway. The stench of the room was overpowering, but he forced himself in. With all three men in the room, the door closed behind them, and the slight man slowly lowered himself onto the bed. Tor remained standing as there was no other area to sit, while Telleck covered his nose with his arm. This is the man he wants me to meet? Telleck thought; he's got to be joking.

"Tor, ya come to see me," the man began in Telleck's language. "Why ya come?"

"This is one of the men from Karren," Tor responded.

"Ah, Karrin, gud. Karrin umportant."

"He is the one who was attacked with the princess."

"Ya, ya, I know, attacked. Not gud, very troubling."

"Can we got on with this," Telleck interrupted, "or can we at least go downstairs?"

"No, nut downstairs. Too many ears. We stay 'ere."

Telleck began to wonder if the extra goods were worth the olfactory torture as he said, "Then tell me what you want me to hear so I can leave."

Tor's amiable composure seemed to be waning as well from the foul odor. "Yes, Orth, please continue."

Orth tried to rise from his bed, but the look of pain increased on his countenance and he decided to remain where he was. After a few labored breaths, he began. "I've lived a long time 'n seen many t'ings. Forces marshal north of Karrin. Yar 'ome's threat'n'd. Prinsus and ya attacked. Nut the last time. Karrin fall? Clouded t' me." Orth stopped, and when he remained silent, Telleck turned to Tor with a questioning look, but Tor did not look back. With exasperation, Telleck returned his attention to the ancient man who had not moved. Orth's head tilted slightly, then he finally managed to stand up, gazing at Telleck. "Yer brother wounded. Return t' 'im; keep 'im safe. Turmoil threat'ns."

Orth then returned to his bed and immediately fell asleep. "We can leave," Tor said. "He is finished for now."

"Good," responded Telleck as he immediately exited the room. When the door was closed he spun around to face Tor. "What was that about?"

"Calm yourself, my friend. I am well aware that visiting Orth is far from pleasant, but it is extremely important. He knows many things."

"Like about Merreck's injury?" Telleck interrupted skeptically.

"Yes."

"He could have been told that before we arrived."

Tor led Telleck down the stairs and to one of the tables in the pub. "You may not believe me, my friend, but I can tell you that Orth was told nothing about your brother. We of Cishor have come to realize that Orth learns important facts from somewhere unknown. I suggest you heed his words regarding your brother."

"What, keeping him safe?" laughed Telleck. "That's wise counsel! I never would have considered it before."

"Enough!" Tor barked as the few eyes within the room turned toward the pair. He then lowered his voice, and the first trace of agitation on the man that Telleck had seen disappeared. "This is not only about your brother and yourself, but your homeland, and possibly Cishor as well."

"Fine, what exactly do you suggest I do?" Telleck asked as his annoyance disappeared at the harsh rebuke from him companion.

"Stay close to Merreck. Change your normal activities. Wait until he is able to travel, at which time the two of you should return to Cishor. Perhaps Orth will have more information then."

Telleck wanted to dismiss Tor's words, but the fact that Shyan and he had been attacked gave him pause. And what if it was true that Orth had not been told about Merreck? Telleck decided that with the wedding forthcoming, he could manage to remain in the castle. "Very well. I will return with Merreck when he's able."

Chapter 15

The fresh, late-spring air felt refreshing against his pale face. Being back atop a horse gave Merreck some semblance of freedom for the first time since the accident. The pain from his fracture was completely resolved; however, the motion of his mount caused periodic waves of discomfort to flow from his knee. He tried to ignore them for as long as possible but he eventually had to signal Linny to stop. Merreck climbed carefully from his saddle and pulled out his cane. After limping slowly to a tree, he sat down against it and Linny joined him.

"Still painful, huh?" she asked.

Merreck nodded as he looked across the field and spotted a large buck grazing amongst the lavender wild flowers. It was a beautiful animal who still sported its huge rack. That would be a nice trophy, Merreck thought as he felt a pang of remorse. He wondered if he would ever recover enough to allow his return to the beloved hunt. As he fought off feelings of despair, he said to Linny, "Thanks for coming with me."

Her eyes brightened at his words as she replied, "I'm sure you're tired of being stuck within the castle."

"Yes, and now that Urik has been invited in, he never wants to leave."

"I hear from the other servants that he's making quite a pest of himself," she said with a laugh.

His amusement at his father making a pest of himself lasted only a moment. "That's not surprising."

"And you have to be sick of seeing Remen and the rest of his family."

"I can do without him," Merreck said, "but it's always pleasant when Shyan visits."

"I hear that all she talks about is the wedding," noted Linny, and Merreck sensed a trace of hostility in her tone.

Merreck had to admit to himself that she was correct; he was tired of hearing about the wedding. He turned to Linny and looked into her eyes. "I am happy for my brother, but I'll admit that it is nice to get away from all of that, if just for a time."

"Has the *prince* even apologized to you?" Linny asked as she gently rested her hand on his arm.

"In his own way, I suppose."

"What a bastard." Her fingers began to slowly stroke his skin as she refused to release him from her gaze. Merreck certainly agreed with that assessment, but he felt confused by her gestures. The two had known each other many years, but he had never noticed any indication of desire toward him. He turned to her, which set off agony from his knee. "Now you may never hunt again because of him," she continued.

He looked back in the field. The deer remained there feeding, keeping a wary eye on the pair. The hunt: it was the one true joy for Telleck and himself. Turning back to Linny, he felt a pang of regret; Telleck and he were past the years where most men their age had married. They just spent too much time on the road or in the wilderness to find wives, until now. Telleck was going to be a prince, and what did he have left? The only future he saw for himself was constant pain and seclusion in the castle. "I don't know what I have left," he whispered as he turned away from the deer. "All I have is pain."

"Maybe I can take your mind off that for a time," she said as she leaned over and pressed her lips against his.

***

"How did the ride go?" Telleck asked when Merreck limped back into their room.

"Not well. I couldn't go very far. The knee still hurts."

"Not far? You two were gone for a pretty long time."

"We talked for a while, if you must know."

Telleck laughed at the irritation his brother was displaying. "Talking, eh?" he said as he examined the grass stains on his brother's clothes. "Is that all?"

Merreck limped over to his bed and threw his cane against the wall. "What business is it of yours?"

"Relax," Telleck said as he realized his brother was not displaying his normal, playful aggravation. "Urik is out in the castle, probably annoying more of the nobles, and Remen has requested that I attend an audience with the king. Will you be fine here by yourself?"

"That certainly will not be anything out of the ordinary."

"Do you think you'll be able to ride farther soon? Tor still wants us both to get back to Cishor when we can."

"I don't know. My knee is not getting any better. Unless it starts to improve, I will never be able to make that ride again."

Telleck looked at his brother with an expression of both sympathy and disapproval. While he had no idea how much pain Merreck was in, he did not like the thought of his brother surrendering to it. He opened his mouth to comment, but realized now was not the time to start such a conversation. "I'll be back later for lunch. Perhaps Father will return by then as well."

Merreck stretched out on his bed and covered his eyes, refusing to offer Telleck a response.

Chapter 16

The king sat on his ornate throne with the queen next to him. Remen stood before him, with Zhomin and Fallad at each side. Telleck was behind the prince amidst a number of warriors. "The prisoner is now dead," Regen began. "We tortured him for many weeks. He survived much, but he was extremely disciplined. He provided us with no information. So we are left with very little other than there is an apparent threat from the north. It may very well be the Armen Tribesmen, but I'm not certain. A tribesman would not have been able to sustain what our prisoner did. Our spies tell us that the tribesmen are building their forces, but we do not know their plans. However, we have to make preparations. Telleck, step forward." Telleck looked about in confusion when he heard his name before slowly moving in front of Remen. "You will be a prince of this land soon. We all know that you are unsurpassed in your hunting skills, but Karren is a land of warrior kings. My son will be leading a party north to search for enemies and you will accompany him. You will begin your training now."

Telleck knew King Regen; he knew that when Regen made a pronouncement, he would not be swayed. But he had no desire to leave the castle now, especially with Remen. Merreck's leg was improving, and he hoped his brother's pain would begin to diminish to the point where they could travel again to Cishor. But now any thought of that would have to be delayed. The idea of engaging in battle again was also disconcerting. Unlike Remen and his warriors, Telleck had not been trained in the art of war. The visions of the men he had killed still haunted him, and he did not think he could repeat that act. He knew he needed to discuss this with the prince, but he felt apprehensive. He did not want to be marked as a coward; that was not the case. The thought of battle did not scare him, and he would freely risk his life to protect his family and his home. But to kill another man? He did not think he could do it again.

***

Remen laughed as Fallad knocked Telleck's sword from his hand for the twelfth time. "You'll need to do better than that," the prince said as he stepped forward and pushed Fallad to the side. He grabbed the sword off the ground and put it in Telleck's hand. With a grip that felt too tight for what he was doing, Remen pulled Telleck's arm forward and brought his hand a little lower than Telleck had been holding it. "You've been keeping the sword too high, and that made you have to move it farther than necessary to defend. Now, try it again."

"How is this going to help?" Telleck asked. "We leave in two days. I'll never learn what I need to by then."

"My life and those of my men might depend on you, so you will learn what you can, regardless of how inept you are."

"Listen, Remen, I did not ask for this," Telleck said, not attempting to hide the contempt in his voice. "You've trained all your life for battle. I'm a hunter and a trader."

Remen turned his head away in disgust. "You also weren't born a prince, but you will be one soon. If you want to cancel that, then you will be excused from my party."

"Is that what this is about, hoping I will not marry Shyan?"

"Everyone knows I do not want my sister to marry you, but I have no say in the matter. If you are to be my brother, you will learn to fight."

Telleck sheathed his weapon and looked into Remen's eyes, not sure if he should believe the prince. Perhaps this was the king's plan— to scare him away—but he was not going to back down. "Fine," he replied, "but I need to speak to you alone for a moment."

"Draw your sword and prepare yourself," Remen said, ignoring Telleck's words.

"I will, but I need to discuss a private matter with you first."

Remen's exasperation mirrored Telleck's when he ordered Fallad away. "What is it?"

Telleck paused to summon some patience before he began. "Look, I know you are a superior warrior to me, just as you will never match me as a hunter. You trained for combat; I did not. I will try to learn what you teach me, but..." He hesitated as he sought for the right words. "When Shyan and I were attacked, I killed two men."

"I know that. So you killed two men, and you think you don't need to train?"

"It's not that," Telleck responded angrily. "I've killed countless animals without thought but I never killed a man before." He hesitated as his apprehension grew. "I don't think I can do it again."

The prince looked as Telleck with a blank expression. He then broke out in a laugh as he waved Fallad over. "Fallad, I never would have believed it. My future brother, the mighty hunter, is a coward."

"I'm not a coward, you bastard," spat Telleck. "You two have been trained in combat and to kill since you were children. I wasn't. I wasn't prepared for killing."

Remen's mock humor dissolved and his eyes narrowed. "Are you saying you regret saving my sister?" he hissed.

"Of course not, but just because it was necessary does not mean I'm not haunted by it."

"Well, *brother*, you have two choices. All Karren princes are warriors. You will train and come on the expedition, or you will not marry my sister."

Telleck yanked his sword out and held his hand where Remen had indicated. "Get on with it."

***

Merreck approached Urik with his now-familiar limp, noting the obvious pride on his father's face as Telleck approached on horseback. When Telleck spotted them, he jumped down and approached his family. "Nice cape," Merreck stated. "I always said that you look good in blue."

"I'm told it's royal," replied Telleck as he brushed it behind his shining breast plate. "Regen wants me to look the part."

"You'll be spotted first by an enemy with all that."

Telleck looked down at the shining armor that covered his chest, arms and upper legs. He felt silly wearing the outfit, but if that was what was required of him to marry Shyan, he would make do. The armor, at least, would be of use if they found any trouble, but the flowing cape? That certainly served no purpose. He was accustomed to traveling through the wilderness in soft leather, so he was not used to the extra weight which now covered his body. And what if they did find combat? He glanced at his weapon and wondered if he would be able to draw it.

Merreck followed his brother's eyes to the hilt of the sword then said, "You certainly aren't smart enough to have learned how to use that already."

"Leave your brother alone," Urik ordered. "He is doing much to improve all our lives."

"And I'm not? It's not my fault that Remen—"

"Stop it," Telleck interrupted. "We're both doing what we can, father."

"Of course. I did not mean that."

After a deep breath, Merreck continued. "So what exactly does Remen think you'll accomplish out there?"

"Learning the ways of the warrior, I suppose."

Merreck chuckled, but he knew that between the two, Telleck was certainly the one who could learn the ways of combat, even before his accident. And the thought of his knee brought a reminder of his pain. "Just make sure that you are a better student than he was."

Telleck smiled at the comment. "I need to leave. Be well, and we will return soon," and without another word Telleck returned to his horse. Merreck saw that Remen was prepared to depart as well and he looked with disgust at Telleck, who was mounting his animal.

"What a fine boy," Merreck heard Urik mumble as he left. As the group rode from the castle, Merreck's hard gaze followed Remen away.

***

The courtyard was a bustle of activity. Linny had returned the previous day with a new load of fish from the southern coast. After their previous encounter, she and Merreck spent a considerable amount of time together when she was not away from Karren. He decided to help her out in the market as it would at least get him out of the castle and take his mind off his pain. Selling merchandise was never what he envisioned for himself, as he was used to being out and moving in the wilderness, but it was preferable to the alternative.

After selling a number of apples and a few salted fish for twice their value, Merreck settled triumphantly back in his chair. He then felt arms wrap around his neck and shoulders, and light blond hair cascaded down in front of his face. He looked up into the brown eyes of Linny as she softly kissed his cheek before joining him. "A nice day's worth of wages," she remarked when she noticed the size of his coin sack.

"It seems I have a natural talent for this."

She displayed a sly smile. "Among other things."

"Are we done here?"

Linny sorted through the remaining fish and produce before responding. "You sold a good portion, and I suppose the rest will be fine until tomorrow. Let's gather up."

Merreck helped her crate up the rest of her goods, took what he could and limped after her into the castle. After they stored the crates, they headed to her room. When the door was closed, he rested his cane against the wall and sat down. "So, why were you gone so long?" he asked.

"Shyan sent me on an errand that took longer than I expected. Why, did you miss me?"

"What errand?"

"I'm really getting sick of performing her menial tasks." Linny removed her dusty cloak and stretched out on her bed. "So let's not talk about that."

Merreck was surprised at her words. "Is she really that bad? She's always been nice to me."

"We know why, don't we?"

"I don't know about that. Even when we were all children, she was very pleasant. Maybe not her brother, though."

"And now he's taking Telleck off to war."

"We're not at war," Merreck pointed out.

"But he's being trained for battle."

That was a true statement, but despite Merreck's current annoyance at the prince, the order had come from Regen. Marrying Shyan was Telleck's decision. If becoming a soldier was what was required, who were they to question it? "If that is what Telleck wants, he'll have to deal with it." Merreck stood gingerly and hobbled over to the bed. "And what about us?"

Linny rolled over and began to stroke his hair. "So you think we should get married too?"

"I don't think we can continue on this way very long."

"Are you sure you're not just jealous of your brother?"

"Everyone knows that Shyan is a beautiful woman." Merreck turned over and gazed at Linny. It had been a surprise when she had initiated their new relationship, as he had always viewed her more as a comrade than anything else, but these new thoughts had nothing to do with Telleck. If Linny and he were going to continue on, a scandal would brew within the castle. "But that is Telleck's life now. I have no desire to be part of that family."

"Why, you don't want Remen to be your brother?" Linny said as she playfully tousled his hair.

"I'll never be a warrior now," he replied as he pulled her to him. "However, there are other things I can still do."

Chapter 17

The horses galloped down the path, and Remen was both amused and annoyed that Telleck was leading the way. While his soon-to-be brother was fairly inept with a blade, there was no doubting his expertise on horseback. However, that did not mean that he should be out front. Remen figured that he would let it go for now. If Telleck wanted to act like their leader, that was fine. If the party was ambushed, Telleck might be the first one to die. Then Remen would not have to worry about him any longer.

As midday approached, the prince ordered a stop. After tying up his horse, Remen relieved himself, then had Zhomin bring Telleck over. When the two were alone, they sat down to have their lunch. "You should not be leading the party," Remen said after biting into an apple.

"I was just trying to do my part."

"We are not traders. You are not the leader of this expedition."

"I never claimed to be."

"You should not be leading the group unless ordered."

Telleck spit the shell of a seed onto the ground. "Perhaps my instructor should have told me that."

Remen looked at Telleck with a stern expression. "You are correct. It is my fault; I should have noted your complete ignorance."

Instead of the outburst Remen expected, Telleck only chuckled. "The question seems to be who the ignorant one is—the one who doesn't know the ways of the warrior, or the instructor who doesn't know what to teach."

The prince felt the rage building within him. It was bad enough that Telleck was going to be part of his family, but to question his leadership? "Look Telleck," the prince said angrily, "we may not like each other, but we are unfortunately going to have to coexist. I suggest you learn to temper your comments."

Telleck calmly finished the seeds that were in his hand before he replied. "Listen, you may find this hard to believe, but I don't hate you. However, I do think you are a fool. If you had any sense, you would not have injured Merreck. Why do you worry about me so much?

You've always treated me with contempt. You never cared for your parents' interest in Merreck and me, and you think your sister is marrying beneath her. Rather than worrying about me, you should look into a mirror when we return home."

With that, Telleck stood and walked away from the prince. Remen wanted to order him to return but he restrained himself. It had never occurred to him that Telleck did not hate him. The two never got along well, but for the first time, he wondered if he was the one at fault. And he knew that he would need to learn how to deal with many different personalities when he was king. He had watched his father for years, and ruthlessness could only take a monarch so far. Regen also knew when to hold back and use diplomacy. Remen did not care for being called a fool, and he would deal with that, but he thought it might be a good idea to consider Telleck's words before responding.

Remen quietly contemplated the exchange, eating the rest of his food while his mind drifted to thoughts of Brynn. When his men finished their lunches, Remen ordered everyone to saddle up and they continued scouting the land north of Karren, searching for any potential enemies.

***

Later in the day, Remen's group ran into some riders from the Armen Tribes near the Unmeth River. The tribesmen were on a hunt, and the prince cautioned them that they were venturing onto Karren lands. With a shrug, the tribesmen road off to the north and Remen led his group back in the direction of the castle. On the second day, they came across a group of grubby migrants traveling west from the port city of Lavrs. A quick search revealed the grimy group to be of no threat, so Remen sent them on their way.

Throughout the rest of the journey, Remen had avoided Telleck. It was not that the prince was afraid to talk to him; he just was not sure what he wanted to say. Remen still did not appreciate being called a fool, especially by a subordinate, but he was unsure of the proper response. During their rest periods, he spent his time with Zhomin talking about Brynn. The prince saw that his friend was growing tired of hearing about the girl, but he did not care. When Remen did try to change the subject to Telleck's insult, he did not feel comfortable with the discussion, so he decided to let the matter rest for the moment.

Once they returned to the castle and he had reported to the king, Remen sought out his mother. While he certainly respected his father,

Yenyn seemed to be the more appropriate person with whom to discuss this sensitive matter.

"Please have a seat, my son," Yenyn said as Remen entered her sitting room. She put down the garment she had been sewing, and he kissed her cheek before joining her on the small couch. "What did you want to see me about?"

Remen looked at the queen and hesitated for a moment. "Tell me Mother, how do you feel about Shyan marrying Telleck?"

"If that is what she wants, I am happy for her."

"No Mother, tell me truthfully. I need to know."

Yenyn tilted her head toward the high ceiling a moment before responding. "I would not have chosen him. I've always been fond of Telleck and his brother, but they are not royalty, or even of noble birth. Regen and I were against it, but the decision has been made."

"Then why did you say you are happy for her?"

"Listen Remen, as a mother, I am happy for her. She is marrying the man she loves; not all women have that opportunity." Remen immediately wondered at that comment whether she was referring to herself, but she continued on. "However, as the queen, he is not what I had envisioned. But after he saved her, your father had no choice but to approve. Telleck now has a place of honor in the castle, which makes him suitable to be a prince. You know all this, Remen, so what are you asking me?"

"While I still do not want him to marry Shyan, Telleck and I had a conversation while out on our mission. I now wonder if I've been wrong about him."

The queen's face softened. "You boys have been at odds since you were small. I think you do not understand how similar you two are. Perhaps that is why you've never gotten along well. Telleck is short-tempered, but he is a fine man. You need not worry about your sister."

Remen mulled over his mother's words. Perhaps he had been wrong regarding Telleck all these years. He did not think that he would ever call the other a friend, but was friendship necessary? "Still, I do not like the way Telleck and his brother seem to fault me for the accident. The weather was bad and they had not cautioned me about—"

"But was it your fault?"

"I don't think so."

Yenyn softly placed her hand on top of her son's. "Blame serves no purpose. You are the heir to the throne of Karren. If they cannot move past the accident, that is their problem."

"Thank you, Mother," Remen said as he stood to leave, "but there is one more thing. When I was alone with Telleck, he called me a fool.

I did not punish him at the time, as nobody else heard, but I do not think that the slight should pass unaddressed."

"You are not a fool, my son, and nobody should call the prince such. Deal with it, but deal with it quietly. Do not make a spectacle, but let Telleck know that he cannot speak to the king's son in such a way."

After returning to his room, Remen cleaned off from his journey and gazed into his mirror. He thought back to Telleck's words and made a decision. He would not speak out against the marriage again and he would do his best to train Telleck without animosity. That training would begin the following day, after Telleck cleaned all of the warriors' barracks by himself.

Chapter 18

Despite the use of his cane, the pain from Merreck's knee grew with each step. As the brothers walked away from the throne room, Merreck was happy to be done discussing the wedding arrangements with Shyan and her parents. It was a welcome relief when they finally reached their room. As usual, Urik was gone when they opened the door. Merreck gratefully sat down and stretched out his leg.

"Not any better, huh?" Telleck asked.

Merreck offered his brother an aggravated look for an answer. "So, how is your training progressing?"

"As good as can be expected, I guess, and Remen has been displaying more patience with me now."

"Have you cleaned out any more barracks?" Merreck chuckled.

"Don't remind me. I guess he could have done worse." Telleck went to the window and looked out at the courtyard. He saw Linny at her table, and she glanced at the window before quickly turning away. "It's funny, he's actually been treating me better since I called him a fool."

"Well, he is a fool."

Telleck turned back to his brother display a large smirk. "Ironic, isn't it?"

"What?"

"You are the one angry with him, while he and I are starting to get along."

"You're not the one using a cane."

Telleck wanted to respond, but he did not know what to say. Instead he looked back out the window and said, "How is Linny? I haven't talked to her in a while."

"She's fine," Merreck answered, annoyed at the implication that his brother was checking up on him.

"There is a lot of gossip in the castle about you two."

"So?"

"I'm not sure that the king will tolerate your *activities* much longer if there is no talk of marriage soon."

"Why don't you worry about yourself?"

Telleck knew that his brother had been agitated since the accident, but this animosity directed at him was startling. "Watch your tongue. I'm not opposed to giving a cripple a thrashing."

Merreck's hand reached for his a cane. He prepared to hurl it at Telleck, but his arm dropped and the cane rattled against the hard floor. It was not his brother he was angry with. When he thought about it for a moment, he did not know where this rage was coming from. "I apologize, Telleck. It seems the pain is getting to me more than I realized."

"I guess you won't be able to travel to Cishor anytime soon," Telleck responded, trying to change the subject.

"Not unless you pull me in a wagon. My leg could not take that kind of ride."

"Well, I'd better make one more trip before the wedding. Tor and that strange Orth wanted to see you, but unless they come here, that won't be possible."

"No, but don't worry about me. Linny has been fine company."

Telleck laughed. It was still a strange thought: Merreck and Linny together. But if it made his brother happy, at least it was something after losing his entire life. "Consider my words, brother. Regen does not like that kind of cavorting in his castle. You will need to marry her if you expect it to continue."

"I'll think on it."

***

"Marriage, is that right?" Linny asked as they watched the sun set over the king's pond.

"He thinks Regen is not happy with our relationship not being formalized," Merreck explained.

"Why should it be any business of his?"

"He is the king."

"True, but we fulfill our duties. At least I do. You would be able to, too, if it were not for his idiot son."

Merreck looked back uncomfortably over his shoulder. "Please watch what you say. If you were overheard… well, I'm not sure what would happen."

Linny moved in closer to Merreck. "I'm really getting sick of all of them. You would not believe what Shyan had me do today."

"What?"

"Oh, it doesn't matter now," and Linny kissed him on the cheek. "I wish we could just leave Karren."

Leave Karren? Despite all he had been through, Merreck had never considered the thought. "Where could we go? I would be of no use to anyone in another land."

"All the more reason to despise Regen's family."

"Please, don't talk that way," Merreck pleaded. "We might think it, but Regen would not be pleased if he found out what you are saying."

"So I guess we're stuck here."

"And that brings me back to my initial question. Do you think we should consider marriage?"

"We won't be able to now. Yenyn would never allow that while she's planning the princess' wedding, and Shyan would not be pleased, either."

"I guess that's understandable."

"Then we'd better stop our trysts for now. We don't want to tempt the king's anger any further," Linny said.

Linny's statement struck Merreck hard, but he knew it was true. First Remen took away his life, and now he was losing Linny. What could   be   next?

Chapter 19

The horses left Karren for what would likely be Telleck's last trading expedition. The news of warriors moving near the Unmeth River had reached the castle, along with word that the Armen Tribesmen were marshalling their forces as well. Nobody knew where these additional soldiers were from, and whether Karren would be attacked was unclear, but Regen was taking every precaution in preparing to defend his land. When Telleck had asked to head to Cishor one last time, the king had initially hesitated. After some thought, he granted the request, but only if Shyan went with. Regen wanted her out of the castle if Karren was indeed a target.

Telleck had left Karren with Shyan, Volx, Bront and four soldiers. When they reached the Gorthon Ruins, Telleck ordered a stop. Bront pulled out their provisions and Telleck grabbed some of the food before leading Shyan to a large rock, which they rested against. He handed her an apple and she gazed about the land. "I've never been here before," she said. "It's quite a sight."

"Always seemed so bleak to me," Telleck answered while unwrapping a piece of hard cheese.

The princess moved closer to him as she took another bite of her apple. "Do you suppose it's true, that this land used to be a mountain range?"

"Perhaps, all this rubble had to come from somewhere."

"But mountains? Wouldn't you expect to see more rock?"

That's a good question, Telleck thought. "I never really considered it. But the land does rise from the Karren valley, and we climb down to get to Cishor. Maybe these boulders were the top, and besides, there is a mountain range north of the ruins."

Shyan finished the apple before turning her attention to a small loaf of bread. "But what could cause an entire mountain range to collapse?"

"Who knows? But that is really the least of our worries. Karren may be attacked and you are worrying about a myth?" Telleck felt his pulse quicken as looked at her lovely face, and was once again amazed a woman such as she wanted to marry him.

"We've all heard the stories of Iridan and Jolef but I never really considered them before." She stood up to get a better view of the land. "What if they are true?"

"Does it really matter?"

"I don't know. Perhaps not." Shyan sat back down and pulled his arm around her waist. "It does take my mind off of what may happen at home." After finishing her bread, she took a drink of water. "So tell me, why did you insist on this mission?"

"With the wedding soon, I wanted to go out one last time."

Shyan looked at him with a knowing expression. "There are rumors around the castle that you are a coward."

Telleck's eyes narrowed; he turned away with his jaw clenched. "Is that what you think?"

Shyan's free hand gently turned his face back to her, and the beautiful smile immediately extinguished his anger. "I know better than that. I saw what you are capable of."

Telleck looked at his betrothed. If he was going to marry her, than he needed to trust her. He started to tell her about his previous trips to Cishor and his conversations with Tor when Volx interrupted, "Time t' go."

"Not yet, Volx."

"Need t' go."

"Listen Volx, you are not in charge here," Telleck responded, relishing the opportunity of giving Volx orders. "I am. Now go away."

Volx was clearly upset, but after he looked at Shyan, he left and Telleck continued with the story. "Why didn't you mention this before?" Shyan asked when he had finished.

"I'm not really sure. Tor seemed concerned that not too many people hear it." And by her expression, Telleck knew that Shyan was hurt by his words. "It's not that," he continued. "I never put much stock in it. By appeasing him, I got a good return on the trades. But now, with the tribesmen marshalling and what happened to us, it seemed that I should get back to Cishor. I didn't really mean to keep it from you; I guess it never crossed my mind to discuss it."

"If you say so," the princess responded, but he could tell she was still hurt. "Volx is right, we need to get moving."

Telleck stood and offered Shyan his hand. She grabbed it and he helped pull her up. "You're not upset with me, are you?"

"I suppose not," she answered as they walked to their horses. "I guess I need to remember that you still have much to learn."

***

Streams of late-summer sunlight poured into the castle hall like glistening water rushing down a rocky waterfall. The candelabra along the walls were all polished and flickered with a silvery hue as the warm breeze caused a slight rustling of the candles. The sound of the cane striking the marble floor echoed through the empty chamber as Merreck entered. He limped to the center of the room while trying to ignore the discomfort from his leg. A number of benches had already been pulled in to serve as seats for the upcoming wedding. He sat on the nearest one and rubbed his hand across the newly polished wood. After pulling a vial from his pouch, he raised his tunic and applied some of the salve to his knee. As the cooling effect began to eliminate a small amount of the pain, he rose. He hobbled over to the wall and examined the large wooden containers that would soon hold the flowers to be picked the day of the wedding. The containers were immaculately cleaned and his reflection was plainly visible in the wood. He looked at his face and ran his hand across his chin, noting that he needed to shave. With a sigh, Merreck turned around, but his motion was not as deliberate as it should have been and the pain in his knee increased. Merreck cursed, limped back to a bench and sat down, but after a few moments, the pain had not slackened. He looked at his pouch but figured the salve would do little good anyway, so he would not waste any more of it now.

With no tasks by which he could occupy his time, and since Linny had refused to see him until after the wedding, he decided to head back to his room. As he positioned his cane and prepared to stand, the door to the castle hall opened and Yenyn came rushing in. She started counting the containers along the wall, and was startled when she saw Merreck sitting alone. "Oh, Merreck, my boy, I did not know you were in here."

"I just felt like getting out of my room and wanted to see how the preparations were coming."

"Very well, I think. But we still have much to do, and the wedding is only one week away!" Merreck could tell that the queen felt rushed but she came over and sat by him anyway. "And how are you doing? I haven't had much time to visit you, with all the work that needs to be completed."

"I'm managing," he said, but he figured that if she really had been interested, she could have spared a few moments to come by and check on him.

The queen glanced about the room before returning her attention to Merreck. "And where is Linny?" she asked playfully.

"How should I know?"

"Oh, come now, the two of you are not much of a secret in the castle."

Merreck considered Yenyn for a moment. While she had always liked the brothers, she was still the queen. He had always thought Shyan was a sweet girl, but the princess was not treating Linny very well; therefore, he chose his words carefully. "Those rumors are exaggerated."

Yenyn's playful smile dissolved somewhat. He knew that she was aware he was lying, but he felt it prudent not to mention that they were concerned over how Regen might react regarding their frequent trysts. "If you say so, my boy," she replied stiffly, "but do I hope the rumors return. Shyan thinks very highly of her."

"Really!" Merreck blurted out before he could stop himself.

The remnants of the queen's smile completely disappeared. "What do you mean by that?"

Merreck hesitated for a moment, unsure what to say next. He knew he had gone too far with the queen, but what was he to do now? He considered telling her all that he had heard from Linny. Yenyn was a fair woman, after all, and she had always been pleasant to him, but he could not risk the queen turning any anger to Linny. His life had become difficult without Linny's company. It was only their time together when it seemed that the misery in his knee lessened. Without her around, the pain was all that he thought about. Soon the wedding would be over, and they would be able to move forward with their own engagement. That was a future he certainly did not want to jeopardize. "It's just… I've heard differently since we've been in the castle."

"Come now, Merreck, I've never heard that. Besides, you know my daughter."

"No offense, Highness, but servants speak differently when royalty is not around."

Yenyn remained silent for a moment and he could tell that she was not convinced. After a moment her smile returned. Perhaps she did believe that some of the servants spread rumors when she was not around, but she obviously did not care. That was meaningless to her, especially with the upcoming wedding. "If that is what is being said, I can tell you that they are wrong."

"It's not—"

"Do not worry yourself, Merreck. I'll not pester you any further on this matter. A castle cannot exist without rumors. If this is the worst of it, then I assume Regen does not have to concern himself over a revolt."

"I suppose so, especially with what the king has to worry about now," Merreck agreed. "Do you think it's wise to move forward with the wedding when Karren might be attacked?" Merreck immediately regretted the question. While it was true, he knew that he needed Shyan to be married soon.

"It is troubling, but we can't stop all the business of the castle. Besides, the news Regen is hearing is the tribesmen aren't marshalling as many warriors as initially thought." The queen stood and offered him her hand. "Come, please escort me to my chambers. I have all the information I needed from here. Perhaps you wouldn't mind helping me decided which flowers should go where."

Flower arrangements? Merreck thought. What had become of him? However, he decided he would go with Yenyn. At least he would have something to occupy his time. The queen was a pleasant enough person, even if she was oblivious to how her daughter treated Linny.

Chapter 20

Horses burst through low brush under the heat of the afternoon sun. Sweat flowed down Remen's face as he drove his steed hard toward the fleeing party. The riders clearly wore the gear of the Armen Tribesmen, and when Remen had ordered his group to approach and find out why they were so far south on Karren land, the riders had fled. While Karren spies had noted that the movement of the tribesmen's army had turned to the east, Remen was still concerned, and finding this party on their land magnified that concern. They needed to be captured and questioned.

Fallad and Zhomin raced after the prince, as did a dozen Karren warriors, pushing their mounts to their brink. But the small group from Armen pulled away, as the horses of the tribesmen were far superior to those of Karren. When it finally became clear that their quarry would not be caught, Remen raised his hand to call for a halt.

"We can't stop now," Fallad said as he came alongside.

"Their horses are too fast. We'll never catch them," responded Remen.

"What do you suppose they were doing?" asked Zhomin.

"That's what I wanted to find out," the prince answered sharply.

After his men had a drink of water and the horses were rested, Remen ordered them to turn around and head back home. He despised that thought and wanted to follow the tracks of the tribesmen, but he knew it would accomplish nothing. They would not be caught, and once they had crossed the Unmeth River, Remen would never be able to find them.

The heat of the day wore on the group and the animals as they continued south, and the wearing effect of the weather only worsened Remen's mood. His father had sent him out with explicit orders to capture anyone of suspicion on their land, and the king despised failure even more than Remen. But what else could he have done?

As the shadows lengthened, Remen decided to order a stop to camp for the night. While they were not far from the castle, he wanted to give himself another day before he had to face Regen. Perhaps the men of Armen would return and the extra day could present another opportunity, or if they did not, there was always the possibility of running into some other travelers.

After the group of soldiers had settled down for the night and watches had been assigned, Remen stretched out on the ground near his horse and stared up at the star-filled sky. The night had brought welcomed relief from the heat of the day and Remen's attitude began to improve. He had ordered the chase as soon as the tribesmen were spotted, but they could not have been caught. Their mounts were the fastest in the land. While the tribesmen did trade some of their horses, it was well known that they never parted with their finest.

With his mind drifting away from the failed pursuit, the prince's thoughts turned to Brynn. The courtship had progressed better than he could have desired, even though he had been out on more missions than normal with the threat from the north. He thought of Kalle and the delight the nobleman displayed with Remen's interest in his daughter. It had taken Remen only a few conversations to realize why Kalle was such a minor noble. The man was completely ignorant. Kalle had received a fine inheritance but had squandered much of the wealth in foolhardy endeavors, so it was a significant coup for him that the prince had fallen in love with his daughter. Remen's thoughts brightened his mood and he realized that his sister's upcoming marriage had not even entered his mind.

Fallad and Zhomin joined him after finishing their duties establishing the camp, and they talked long into the night about his future bride, as well as what the land would be like when he was king and they were his two most trusted advisors. The worries regarding the tribesmen drifted away as Remen enjoyed the company of his closest friends, with the anticipation that he would be back with Brynn the following day. Even Fallad's mood was more pleasant than normal. No quips or chiding remarks were expressed, and the prince felt closer to his two lifelong friends than ever before.

It was with much regret that he finally ordered them to sleep as his mind remained focused on the pleasure of seeing Brynn again soon.

***

After eating the following morning, Remen rode his men to the northwest, but they found no trace of any travelers other than themselves. Satisfied that the party they had chased the previous day had not returned, he turned the men to the east. Remen figured they would follow that direction until lunch before looping back southwestward in the direction of the castle. When midday arrived, the men stopped to eat.

The heat of the previous day had returned, and all the soldiers were in a foul mood, even Fallad. So they did not linger long in the clearing where they had stopped before they were back on their horses and riding fast for their homes. While the prince was still concerned over how his father would react to his failure, he would at least be with Brynn.

They had been riding a short while when one of the soldiers advised Remen that he heard some sound off to the left. Remen's stomach tightened as he ordered the men to turn and head into the forest; perhaps they would bring something back to Karren after all. It was not long before Remen heard the commotion himself. As they continued on, the noise increased and the prince realized they were not hearing a small party. Remen's group slowed to a walk as they made out the sound of hooves pounding the road, along with the rattling of armor and accompaniments. The noise was coming from the east and moving away. The forest line would be ending soon and they were nearing the road that lead from Lavrs to Karren. He guided his horse forward a few steps while still shrouded in the forest. To his horror, he saw scores of soldiers on horseback thundering down the road. Hundreds of men rushed by as their armor and weapons reflected the rays of the sun with an eerie brilliance. His stomach dropped, as he knew they could only have one destination in mind.

Zhomin and Fallad were now beside him, also gazing silently upon the scene. War was upon them. It was clear now that the change in movements of the Armen Tribesmen had been a rouse. While Remen did not recognize the men rushing before him, only the tribesmen would have been able to supply the number of horses he saw. Rather than attacking from the north, it appeared that for some reason, the people of Lavrs had allied with Armen to attack Karren.

And what of Karren? Clearly Remen and his fourteen soldiers could do nothing to stop or even slow this horde. And as the attackers raced down the road, Remen had no route to use to reach Karren ahead of them and offer a warning. He looked first at Zhomin, then at Fallad. He had absolutely no idea what to do.

Chapter 21

Patrols from Karren had returned to the castle with reports of the approaching horde. At the speed with which the army was traveling, they would arrive in a short time, and the king had precious little opportunity by which to prepare his defense. As the warriors of Karren rushed into battle, since he could do nothing else, Merreck limped up the stairs to the top of the castle to watch the conflict, with Urik trailing after.

By the time he reached the parapets, the attacking riders had already reached the castle. He gasped at the sight. It seemed inconceivable to him that the Armen Tribesmen could have mustered such an immense force. As the attackers began to circle the walls, the warriors who flanked Merreck loosed arrows into the crowd. The tribesmen were the most skilled horsemen in all the land, and they returned fire without slowing down. Arrows streamed toward Merreck, and the soldier to his left was hit in the chest. The man shrieked and collapsed to the floor. Merreck stooped down to see if he could offer any assistance, but the arrow protruded from the middle of the soldier's chest and blood poured out, covering his tunic and neck. The soldier's left hand clutched at his wound while the other reached up. Merreck clasped the man's hand while pleading eyes gazed back at him. At least he won't die alone, Merreck thought.

Amidst the sobs of his father, Merreck stood back up and saw that most of the attackers continued to circle the castle with bows drawn. Arrows flew from the walls, but most missed their mark of the fast-moving tribesmen, who continued to loose their own arrows at any targets they spotted on the ramparts or in windows. With the defenders pinned down against the deadly onslaught, groups of assailants veered away from the castle into the surrounding village. The villagers had already started to flee, but they were on foot. Merreck watched as the tribesmen chased after. They knocked the women and children to the ground and sword points buried into the flesh of men.

A few Karren warriors who were in the village tried to mount a defense. They gathered in the market square and attempted to form a line, but the horses barreled through. Some arrows flew from buildings in the village, bringing a few of the attackers and a handful of horses to the ground, and then the remaining soldiers sprung. Blades leapt in the air, bringing a crimson shower where they fell. Merreck marveled at their bravery of his countrymen, but he knew they could not last long. The Karren warriors were vastly outnumbered. He watched javelins fly and defenders fall. More horses stormed by and he lost sight of the remaining defenders.

Flames started to erupt from one of the buildings, and Merreck realized that the invaders were throwing torches into the buildings. From one small house he watched a soldier race out carrying a bow. But once he was in the open, a blade struck his shoulder. The man stumbled, then a battle axe crashed down against his skull. From another building he saw a child dashing out with her hair and tunic ablaze; thankfully, the noise of the battle drowned out the girl's cries.

He turned away, back toward the riders still circling the castle, and he realized their strategy had worked to perfection. With Regen's attention focused to the north, an attack from the east was completely unexpected. The speed of the tribesmen's assault gave Regen no time to prepare, and upon their arrival, the invaders had pinned the majority of Karren's warriors in the castle. Once that was completed, they turned their attention to the surrounding village. With the village secure, they need only worry about the remaining forces behind the walls.

What they would do next was a mystery to Merreck. Arrows continued to fly to and from the castle; however, despite being on horseback and in the open, the men of Armen were far more accurate. But they would need to enter the castle in order to secure it. He had very little skill with a bow, as Telleck and he had preferred to hunt with spears. But, he could not stand idly by and simply watch the carnage, so he grabbed the bow of the dead warrior and notched an arrow. He leaned over the wall, seeking a target. As he drew the bowstring back, two arrows came hurtling his way. He tried to duck, but he was not the target. Both arrows struck the other soldier next to him. The man instantly collapsed, but he fell against Merreck. Merreck's knee buckled, and he too landed on the ground with the weight of the corpse pinning his injured leg. Merreck screamed as the pain in his knee intensified to a degree he had not thought possible. Urik immediately dropped down and pushed the body off his son, but the pain did not diminish. His father unsuccessfully tried to stand him up. Despite his anguished cries, Urik managed to drag Merreck to the door and somehow carry him down the stairs.

When they reached the bottom, Urik stopped. He dropped to the floor and attempted to suck as much air into his lungs as possible. Merreck lay on the floor clutching at his knee. "There's no one around,"

Urik said, and Merreck knew that his father meant nobody would be able to assist them.

"Help me up," Merreck said after sucking in a deep, trembling breath. Urik slowly rose and grasped his son's arm. "Get me to the king's chamber," he told his father when he was up. With his weight leaning against Urik, they managed to hobble down the corridor.

***

Yenyn sat ashen-faced in the hall with a few of her servants trying to soothe her trembling nerves when Urik and Merreck arrived. Her eyes gained focus when she saw Merreck and she asked, "What happened?"

"He injured his leg again," Urik replied as Merreck was led to a chair by the servants. Merreck clutched at his knee, trying unsuccessfully, to control the pain as Urik continued. "What's the news?"

"I'm not certain. The last I heard, the attacking archers had ours pinned down. Regen has no idea how they could have mustered such a large army." The queen shook her head in dismay as a large bang echoed through the chamber. Her mouth opened, but no sound came out as another bang sounded. She then began to cry uncontrollably as she covered her face. After a third crash, Yenyn collapsed. Her servants surrounded the queen, and Merreck watched them through his own tears as they again tried to comfort her. He knew the attackers were attempting to break through the castle door when he heard the fourth thunderous crash. If the warriors in the castle could not defend against the battering, it would only be moments before the tribesmen broke through.

He then heard commotion outside and the door slammed open. Regen burst in with a half dozen guards. The king saw his wife, but he had no time to worry over her. "They'll be through soon," he said to one of his warriors.

"You can't, Majesty. Not that," the man responded.

"What else would you have me do—watch everyone die?" Regen bellowed.

The man stood silent for moment. "Very well," he said, bowing, and the warrior left along with the other men.

When they were gone, Regen turned his attention back to Yenyn. He pushed the servants away and sat beside her. "It'll be over soon," he said softly. Regen continued to speak, but Merreck could not make out the words; his pain was too great. He saw his father above him, but his

574

senses became a jumble. His vision clouded as hearing deserted him. All he sensed was agony.

After an undetermined time, the royal guards returned and Merreck began to regain his senses. More soldiers entered the hall and Merreck recognized many of them as Armen Tribesmen. Regen took a deep breath as he turned away from his inconsolable wife and faced his adversaries. One of the tribesmen stepped forth as Regen pulled out his sword. "My castle is yours," the king stated with as much pride as he could gather before placing his blade in his adversary's hand.

Chapter 22

Guards stopped Telleck at the gate to Cishor and he ordered Volx to step forward. It was unsettling to once again have to rely on Volx, and the fact that the conversation between the guard and Volx was taking longer than expected did not help. Telleck sensed agitation in Volx's voice when the gate did not rise. "What's going on?" he asked Volx.

"They say they have no need for trade now," replied Volx.

"Did you tell them we're here to see Tor?"

"Ya, I say it. Tor not able now."

"Tell him that my name is Telleck and Tor is expecting me."

Volx turned his attention back to the guard, and after further discussion, the gate finally opened for Telleck and his group. They were led into the walled city and through the courtyard, where a number of people showed mild interest in the light-skinned travelers, but the sight of traders was a common occurrence. Telleck saw no level of agitation among the people, so he wondered at the unusual reception they had received. When they reached the area where the previous exchanges had been made, Telleck had Volx again ask for Tor. They were advised that the Cishor noble would be unable to negotiate the trade, and they would have to meet with a group of merchants. Telleck reluctantly agreed and bartered for a much smaller amount of produce than what they had received previously. Once the skins were unloaded and their cart filled, the Cishor merchants prepared to send them on their way. After numerous protests by Telleck that he needed to see Tor, the group from Karren was led to a small building outside the castle and ordered to wait.

After the door was closed behind them, Telleck took a moment to look around the one-room stone building. A few small windows dotted the walls, and Telleck figured that the building had been a sentry post prior to the expansion of the city around the castle. They were not made to wait long before the door opened again. Four large men with silvery breast plates and jewel-encrusted scabbards at their sides entered. Telleck pushed Shyan behind him, but relaxed when he realized that the soldier's swords remained sheathed. The warriors moved aside and another figure entered. He was slimmer than most of the Cishor men that Telleck had seen, and his skin was much darker, almost black. He wore a deep maroon leather coat with gold studs lining the center. A small golden circlet with a large ruby glistening in the center covered his short gray hair. His bright eyes fell upon Telleck before shifting to Shyan to take a confrontational step forward.

"You are certainly Telleck," the man said jovially in Telleck's language without a trace of an accent. "Do not worry. I just wanted to get a look at the princess of Karren. And I see that the tales of her beauty are not exaggerated." The man bowed his head slightly in her direction.

"How do you know who she is?" Telleck asked.

"It was not hard to determine. We are aware of your engagement. Who else would she be?"

"And you must be King Zur," replied Telleck.

The king of Cishor bowed again. "I offer my apologies for the accommodations to such honored guests." He turned to Volx, and as he said something in their own language, Volx nodded. "Now, a proper reception is being prepared in the castle for our guests. If you will follow me, your party will be offered some refreshments."

"I do not want to be impolite, but I have come to Cishor to meet with Tor, and—"

Zur raised his hand to interrupt Telleck. "It was I who ordered your conversations with Tor on previous visits, so I am fully aware of what has been discussed. Now come, I do not want to earn the reputation of being a poor host to visiting royalty." With nothing further to say, Telleck and his group followed Zur from the crowded building.

They entered the castle, and each was given a private room in which to clean themselves. Telleck found fresh clothes waiting for him. After he was cleaned and rested, a servant knocked at his door. Telleck asked the man where Shyan was, but the servant did not understand him. So Telleck followed him into the king's dining hall. The empty chamber was much larger than Regen's, and the walls were adorned with maroon tapestries encrusted with all forms of precious metals and jewels. The sight stunned Telleck. It was certainly not out of the ordinary for a king and his personal guards to display jewels, but what he saw hanging on the walls would be a fortune to a dozen kings.

"Impressive, is it not?" Telleck heard from over his shoulder. He turned and saw Zur approaching.

"Yes, but…"

"But why waste so much wealth for decoration?" Zur finished Telleck's unspoken thought.

"Not to be presumptuous, but yes."

"Do you not know the story of Cishor?" the king asked. When Telleck shook his head, Zur continued. "In ages past, Cishor was nothing more than a small village, and the inhabitants were light-skinned, like yourself. The people of my race lived in a different land."

"Where is that?" Telleck asked, feigning interest.

"You traveled through it. My ancestors were from Gorthon."

"What?"

"It is true. As I'm sure you know, Gorthon was once a mighty mountain realm, and my people lived there. Vast caches of precious metals were buried under the mountains, and they dug the mountains for those riches. After the destruction of our mountainous home, the few survivors migrated here, and the Cishor people welcomed them due to the role they had played in stopping the great evil. During that time, all the peoples of this land spoke one language, though there were subtle differences, and my ancestors easily integrated within the town. After they were safely situated, they began to return to the ruins of their land. They began to search through the rubble, and some of the old passageways to the mines were discovered. This brought much wealth to Cishor and my people grew in power. When Cishor became a kingdom, my ancestors dominated. The light-skinned men began to move away which is why Cishor exists as it does now, and our languages evolved to such a difference that they are now distinct."

"Is all that true?"

"It is what I have been told," Zur answered with a shrug. "I have no reason to doubt it and I have been to the mines myself. Many riches still remain under the ruins. So what you see before you is miniscule."

Telleck had a hard time believing that the wealth he saw in the room was miniscule, but he was not about to question the king of Cishor. Besides, he figured, why would Zur want to lie to him? "When are the others coming?" he asked.

"They should be along shortly. You need not worry; your lovely betrothed is being well taken care of."

"Will Tor be joining us?"

"He is seeing to other duties at this time."

Telleck felt disappointed at Zur's response. While the king had made it clear that he was fully aware of what had been discussed with the Cishor nobleman, he did not feel entirely comfortable opening up to a foreign sovereign, regardless of how friendly he appeared. But he became instantly distracted when Shyan entered the hall. Her hair had been washed and was tied neatly behind her neck. She wore a bright blue dress with white ruffles circling her neck. Her face instantly brightened when she spotted Telleck, and her escort led her beside her betrothed.

"The rest should be on their way," the king of Cishor commented as he offered them a seat at his exquisite table.

The trio had just reached for their goblets when the door to the chamber burst open. Telleck jumped to his feet and Zur followed after. To his shock, he saw Remen, Zhomin and Fallad enter the room, escorted by Cishor guards.

"Karren has been conquered," Remen announced, and Telleck collapsed back into his chair.

Chapter 23

Warriors from Armen and Lavrs, and a large crowd milled loudly through the king's hall as a gruff-looking man sat on the throne. As Merreck was pulled into the hall, he wondered why he would be brought before the conquerors. The agony in his knee still burgeoned, but he had somehow managed to survive the trip. Rough hands dragged him forward and he fell to the ground with a whimper. The man stood from the throne and ordered Merreck to do likewise. Merreck forced himself up, and was given a cane to lean on.

"There, as you see, we are not without our sympathies," the man said.

Merreck forced his head up, then gazed about the hall. "Where are Regen and the queen?"

"They are not harmed, if that is what concerns you"

Not really, Merreck thought, and then to his surprise Linny entered. Why had she been brought here as well? What could the tribesmen want with two such commoners? His surprise increased when he realized there were no guards around her, and her movements were free and untroubled.

She came beside and helped steady him by putting her arm around his waist. "I see you found him," she said.

"Yes, we had no idea that it was he who was with the king," the man replied.

Linny nodded, then kissed Merreck on the cheek. "Do not worry," she said softly to him. "Everything will be fine now. With Regen gone, we are free, free to be together. Nobody will tell us what we can't do."

Merreck's confusion grew. "What are you talking about?"

"The Armen Tribesmen have liberated Karren, and us."

Realization began to dawn on Merreck as he looked at her. "You are one of them, aren't you? You're from Armen."

"Does that matter? Armen or Karren? What matters is that now we can be together. Do you hold any allegiance towards Regen or Remen?" At hearing Remen's name his mind returned to the pain, and his knee buckled. He started to fall, but Linny held him up. "Yes your knee, do you want the pain to be gone?"

"What?"

"I can take away your pain, all of it. With your pain gone, nothing will stand between us."

"How can that be?"

The man before him waved to the side, and he saw some movement from his right. Three figures emerged from the shadows, but they were unlike any men he had ever seen before. The first was covered in armor over his entire body; no flesh was visible anywhere. A large sword hung at his side, which his gauntleted hand rested upon. But what was most striking was that every bit of metal was shining crimson. The figure next to him was slender with a gaunt, expressionless face. Thin black hair hung below his shoulders and his black eyes stared back at Merreck. His thin body was covered by a black leather coat and black pants. The two figures parted and a third stepped forward. He was smaller than the man in black and appeared to be emaciated. Thin, translucent skin gave his face a skull-like appearance. A few wisps of hair hung like cobwebs from his fragile head. He wore a tattered and filthy tunic, but nothing else. The man proceeded forward to stand beside Linny.

Merreck turned in revulsion and tried to back away, but the pain was too great, and Linny held him tight. "What is this?" he asked.

"Do not worry," Linny replied. "All is as it should be."

His mind was racing as he looked back at the disgusting creature before him, and his eyes were met with a sick smile.

The man who was obviously the leader of the tribesmen spoke up. "Karren is conquered, but we have use for you, Merreck."

"That's right Merreck," Linny continued softly. Her fingers stroked his hair and face, then traveled down his arm. "If you say the word, I'll take away your pain and we can be together again." She pushed her body against his, and he felt the warmth of her breath on his neck. "Do you want that?"

"Of course I do."

"Then you're ready?"

"For what?"

Linny swayed against him and he felt his desire growing, despite the pain and confusion. She motioned to the tattered man before them. "Tell him you want release."

Merreck stammered as he tried to comprehend what was happening.

"Yes," Linny purred into his ear, "tell him."

"But... I..."

"Don't you feel the pain?"

Suddenly Merreck wondered if someone had struck his leg; his misery exploded like waves of fresh lava flowing from an erupting volcano. He cried out as Linny continued, "It's worse isn't it?"

Merreck nodded as tears poured down his checks.

"Apart from me, it will never go away. Is that what you want?"

Merreck shook his head feebly as he tried to control his heavy sobs.

"Remen is not here," the tribesman said. "Do you desire vengeance against him?"

Linny's fingers wiped the tears away, and then gently massaged his lips. "Yes, we can remove your pain and deliver Remen to you. And you will have me. Do you want all this?"

"Yes."

Linny's hands dropped from his face, and she guided his knees to the ground. "Are you ready?"

"Yes, what do I need to do?"

The shabby man came forward and looked down at Merreck. "Tell him you're ready," Linny commanded.

"I'm ready."

"Tell him you want what he offers."

Merreck's mind stopped for a moment. What was he doing? Linny was a traitor and these people had conquered his home. They obviously needed him for something, but what? Certainly he could not hope to assist Karren and the king if he followed their plan. But it was because of Regen that Linny had been pulled away from him, and it was because of the king's son that his life had been destroyed, and he was imprisoned by his pain. Why should he worry about Regen? Why not be rid of his pain and have his revenge on the prince? And why not have Linny back to satisfy his desires? He turned away from Linny and back toward the creature that stood before him. He then thought of his father and brother. Urik was not in the room and Merreck wondered what he would think of this. But the thoughts of his family were swept aside like debris strewn across a beach from fresh waves of agony flowing from his knee. Linny's hand continued to stroke his skin, granting a small respite from his torture.

"I want what you offer."

The man's sick smile broadened as he stooped down.

"Tell him: now," Linny said.

"Now."

With that, the man brought his face down and pressed his lips against Merreck's. Merreck tried to pull away in disgust, but claw-like fingers kept him from moving. An object began to press its way from the man's mouth into Merreck's. "Don't fight it," he heard Linny say.

He tried to relax, but he was too repulsed by what was occurring. Eventually the object had left the other man and was in his mouth, but the grip was not loosened. "Swallow," Linny commanded, but he hesitated. "Swallow," she repeated, "and your pain will be gone."

Merreck tried to swallow the object but he started to gag.

"Once more, calmly."

He swallowed again, and this time the object slid down his throat.

The creature's foul fingers released Merreck and it was done. He lay on the stone floor, and a strange sensation began to tickle in his chest, then grew into a burning. It flowed from his chest into his arms and down his legs. He cried in pain as his body burned. A trembling strength was building within him, and it needed to escape. He felt its overwhelming power as he cried out. His body rose from the ground and his clothing fell away. He lifted his head to the sky, and a black light poured from his mouth, engulfing the room. While the aura rushed from his body, the burning pain diminished—but as it did, so did he. His thoughts, his consciousness, shrank. He could feel himself getting smaller and smaller as another presence entered his body, rushing to the surface. When they passed each other, Merreck sensed unabashed evil. He continued to shrink, and it was as if he was trapped in a dungeon, looking up at this new person. Merreck still lived, but he was a prisoner in his own body. He felt himself step forward, and all his pain was gone. "It has been too long," he heard himself say.

"We welcome you, Ut," Linny replied. "All is ready."

Chapter 24

The low sun cast its warm rays of orange, purple and maroon across the castle, resting on Remen's troubled face as he gazed out his window. The marvelous beauty of the west juxtaposed the horror the prince of Karren knew was taking root in the east. Cishor had sent out numerous spies into Karren land; however, none returned. It was of no matter, as what could the spies report that he did not already know? His homeland had fallen. He knew not if his parents had been killed, but even if they still lived, he would not be able to find comfort. He could not be with Brynn, and the kingdom, along with his birthright, was gone. Now he was heir to nothing. He was no longer a prince, but a stranger in a foreign land.

He decided to leave his room, but with no particular destination in mind he roamed aimlessly about the castle, attempting to acknowledge the presence of those he passed. It was one of the few times when he was glad that he did not speak the language of Cishor. Remen had no desire to talk to any of them. He just needed to leave his room, to move.

Soon even the castle walls became too encompassing, and he passed under the gate into the city street. He felt conspicuous among all the dark-skinned men and women but they mostly ignored him. They were too busy bringing in produce and preparing the goods for storage to worry about him. Remen did notice some soldiers, but not enough. Even if Zur could be convinced to attack Karren, did they have the strength?

As he walked, Remen saw a few people of light skin, and one was a warrior. He approached the man and said hello, but the soldier did not understand him. The man offered Remen a smile before continuing on his way, and Remen wondered if it was possible to feel more foreign than he did at that moment. With the day quickly fading, he returned to the castle and went to his sister's room. "Where's Telleck?" he asked after she opened the door.

"He left with Tor after lunch. He said they needed to see someone."

"Not Zur, I assume."

Shyan shook her head.

"He doesn't appear to be willing to attack Karren."

Shyan ran her hands down her sides to smooth out the crimson dress she had been given, and took a deep breath. "Can you blame him?"

Remen wanted to chastise her for the comment, but he knew she was right. Cishor's king had no reason to attack the Armen Tribesmen. Certainly Karren and Cishor had been friendly kingdoms; however, engaging in a war would be a huge step to liberate a minor trading partner. "I suppose not," he replied with a heavy sigh.

"And where are Fallad and Zhomin?"

"Zur asked them to assist in integrating our warriors with theirs. It will be difficult."

"What do you suppose will happen to us?" Shyan asked. The sorrow in her voice and tear in the corner of her eye gave him pause. He wondered briefly if she was as concerned about their parents and people as she was about losing her status, but he quickly dismissed the notion. The same thought had crossed his mind; however, he had not resigned himself to their circumstances yet.

"I still plan to convince Zur to attack Karren and reclaim our homes," Remen replied. "I can't just let Father and Mother stay in the hands of the tribesmen." Or Brynn, he thought. "Until then, we'll have to do what is asked of us."

"But what will they have me do?" Shyan paused when she saw the annoyance on her brother's face. "It's not that," she continued. "I'm not complaining. I'm grateful that we are safe and I'm with Telleck, but I can't speak their language. What can I possibly do? I don't want to just sit in my room."

Remen's frustration grew, as the mention of her fiancé only highlighted his separation from Brynn. They had all lost much, but while Telleck was at least with her in Cishor, Brynn remained a prisoner in Karren. What had become of her? Certainly the men of Armen would not care regarding his courtship of her, and if they knew, it might only make matters worse. Everything he valued was in the hands of the tribesmen, but some of his anger melted away when he looked in Shyan's face. At least she's safe, he thought, and Fallad, Zhomin and I are still alive. "Let's not worry about tasks right now. We need to convince Zur to launch an attack," he said. "That's our only concern at the moment."

Shyan's expression brightened slightly at her brother's words, and Remen began to feel guilty for his thoughts. She was actually handling the loss of their home better than he could have expected. "What now?"

"We go see the king again. He might be getting tired of hearing my pleas, but I don't care. I will continue until I change his mind."

Chapter 25

"We're not going back to his room are we?" asked Telleck as he and Tor headed down the streets of the city. "I don't know if I can stand that again."

"I've been there far more times than you, my friend, so I suggest that you don't complain." Telleck was taken aback by the sharp words from the normally even-keeled man. "My apologies," Tor continued, as if he could read Telleck's thoughts. "Much has occurred and Zur is ignoring my counsel. I agree with your prince that we cannot allow Armen to control your home."

"Those of us from Karren appreciate your support, but why are we going to see Orth? Shouldn't Remen and you be talking to your king?"

"There is nothing else I can say to Zur. Our only hope is Orth. Once he knows what has happened, he will be the only one who can convince Zur to change his mind."

Orth? What a strange thought. How that decrepit, ancient man could convince Zur to attack Karren was a mystery. "Do we have to go to his room? Can't we at least meet in the pub?"

Tor thought for a moment. "I suppose that will be fine, my friend," he said, and they continued on in silence.

When the pair reached the inn, they found only a few patrons within, whom Tor politely ordered to leave. The drunken men ignored him until he raised his voice with a commanding tone, after which they stood and staggered out. Tor then said something to the innkeeper, who promptly disappeared through a back door. "Wait here," he said to Telleck, then went up the stairs. Telleck sat at a table and waited only a few minutes before Tor returned with Orth trailing slowly behind. Tor waved his arm at Telleck and said, "There he is."

Orth looked up, squinting until his ancient eyes focused upon Telleck. "Telleck, from Karren," Orth stated as he sat down. "I r'member ya."

"Hello," Telleck responded as the familiar aroma of the man assailed his nose. Fortunately, it was not nearly as appalling in the open room.

"Why ya here?"

"You've heard what happened to Karren?" asked Tor.

"Ya, ya, Armen attack Karren, conquered. I knew would happen. Threat from t' north. I say so."

"You never said Karren would be overthrown," Telleck shouted as his fist struck the rickety table.

"Evil fr'm north. I told, evil fr'm north."

"But—"

Tor raised his hand to interrupt Telleck. "Don't," the Cishor nobleman said softly, and Telleck's only response was a strong glare. "What about Telleck here?" he asked Orth. "Why do you think he's so important?"

"I see many t'ings. Very old. Older t'en all you. Seen many t'ings. See many t'ings."

"What's he babbling about now?" Telleck asked sharply.

"Quiet!" snapped Tor. He took a steadying breath before asking Orth to continue.

"Many t'ings," the old man repeated as he tilted his wrinkled face toward the ceiling. Then his head lowered, and he stared into Telleck's eyes with an attentiveness Telleck had not seen before. "Do you know who I um?"

"Orth," Telleck answered, confused by the question.

"Thut's my name, but it not ulways. I've lived long, far too long, huv been known by muny names during all m' travuls."

Telleck's confusion was only increasing by Orth's ramblings. "Yes, I can tell that you're old. What does that have to do with anything?"

"Do ya know the story of Jaleph and Iridan?"

Telleck nodded his head. "You mean Jolef. Merreck and I used to be told that fable when we were children."

"It's no fable!" Orth bellowed as his head shook, and flakes of skin seemed to fly from his scalp.

"If you say so."

"D' not patronize me, boy," Orth responded quietly.

"Who cares if it's true?" Telleck said as he glared back across the table, his patience nearly gone.

"Perhaps our friend is correct, Orth," interjected Tor as he tried to soothe the tension. "History or myth, what difference does it make to us?"

"It makes ull t' difference!" Orth shouted as vigorously as his diminutive body would allow. "Ull t' difference. I wus t'ere. I lived in Su'Meeryn. I saw it ull."

"I've had enough of this," Telleck said as he stood. "I'll find my way back," and he started to exit the pub.

"Da ya wunt t' save yar 'ome?"

Telleck stopped and turned back around. It was not so much Orth's words, which he did not believe, but the man's tone that gave him pause. When he saw the pleading look in Tor's eyes, he returned to the table and said, "Go on."

"Many names I've 'ad, but's the furst 'ats umportunt. In t'ose duys mu name wus Veake. I was stablemun of Jaleph, king of Su'Meeryn. I wus also a prophet." Orth shook his head and mumbled something with an air of regret. "I knew little then. 'Ave ya 'eard of Naar?" When Telleck remained silent, Orth continued. "'E wus the grutest prophet of all.'E ascended long bufore my burth. "I lurned t'ings from 'im, but I wus confused back then. Wun my eyes were op'ned, my life wus chunged. Sunce I wus the only prophet to huv lived through the last time of t' evil, I would huv to live until t' next time to atone fur my mistuks. It wus my burden—muny, muny years, but now I've seen t' return of evil to our lund. Thut evil seduced our king, turned 'im ugunst our people. Iridan stopped him in the great battle, but much was lost. Costly beyond musure." Orth stopped, and Telleck saw tears running down the man's cheeks. "Muny good people died to stop Jaleph und the evil. But stop it t'ey did. T'ey sacrificed t'emsulves fer ull of ya. Wit'out Iridan und t' ot'ers, t'ere'd be no Cishor, no Karren. Just t' evil of Su'Meeryn would rule ull t'is lund. Ya all've unjoyed t' peace Iridan provided; now's back. T' evil resurfaced in Karren. I see it. I see clearly now. Cishor must uttack Karren, or t' 'orror of Su'Meeryn will return. Un ya t' key, Telleck. Ya must stop t'em."

"Me? How am I supposed to stop them?"

"Ya will be able t'. I know nut'en else yet." Orth then turned his head in Tor's direction. "Now, take me t' Zur."

***

Flanked by Tor and Orth, Telleck stood before Zur. He saw Remen and Shyan off to the side, but could not go to them. Orth had just finished his remarks and Zur appeared exasperated. "We've already discussed this. While I sympathize with the people of Karren, I will not sacrifice my soldiers for them," the king responded in Telleck's language.

"But we risk all our lives if we do nothing," said Tor.

"Do not try me further, Tor," Zur hissed.

"You forget, Majesty, that when the monarchy was established, it was decided that the king would have to listen to Orth when he spoke. Otherwise it would have remained as it did in the days of Gorthon,"

589

Tor said forcefully—but despite the strength of Tor's words, Telleck sensed an anxiousness at the challenging of his king.

Zur said something which Telleck could not understand, and the murmuring in the hall completely disappeared. Despite the clear malice from the king, Tor's posture remained stiff as he replied. The two spoke further as Telleck anxiously awaited the outcome.

"Very well," Zur finally said with a mixture of anger and resignation. He then looked to the side of the hall. "Come here, prince of Karren." Remen expectantly approached the throne. "It seems that you will have your wish. The forces of Cishor shall be marshaled, and we will attack Karren." He then turned back to Tor and said, "Creator help us."

Chapter 26

The image reflecting in the mirror did not please him. While he had possessed many faces through the ages, the last few times he managed to transform himself to keep the same appearance. But this time was different. He had remained dormant for far too long, and the power necessary to alter his appearance was great. While he could not be killed, the beating he had received from Iridan left his essence weak. It took him generations to recover, but he could have returned long ago—but for his master's anger. Failure was not easily tolerated, and Iridan had thwarted him twice. But how could he be blamed, he thought. The first time was seeking out that stupid ring when it possessed no value or power. But that was minor. His body had been killed, but finding a replacement proved easy. The last time, however, now that was different. His plan had worked perfectly. The entire land was poised to be conquered and handed to his master. How could he have stopped Iridan from striking down the dragons? Why should he be blamed? His master failed to provide any mercy, and he had been housed in limbo until now. With his master ready to move again, he was needed.

So there he stood, looking at the unsatisfying reflection. He would have to maintain it for now until the land was conquered. Only then might his master allow him to use his power to transform into his old appearance. Until that time, he would not use his rightful name. The name of Ut would be set aside, and he would use Merreck: the name of the soft voice which he could still hear, buried deep within his consciousness.

He turned from the mirror and had to limp to the door. While the pain from the knee was gone, the damaged leg still did not function properly. That did not bother him; however, following the ages of banishment, a limp barely even registered in his mind. After he opened the door, he looked back at the naked body of Linny, asleep on his bed. If there was anything for which his foul heart could be thankful for, it was that the former Merreck was promised Linny's body for his cooperation. It had been far too long since he had partaken in fleshly pleasures. He would not make that same mistake again.

His three companions were awaiting him as he left his room. They followed him through the corridor until they reached the king's hall. There he found the leaders of Armen, along with Regen and Yenyn in chains.

"There you are, Ut. You've kept us waiting," the leader of the Armen Tribesmen said as he and his three companions entered.

"Do not use that name, Gyraund. The name of Ut will not be associated with this body. Refer to me as Merreck."

The Armen leader appeared somewhat surprised, but he shrugged his shoulders in acquiescence, hoping to atone for any unintended insult. The entity previously called Ut relished in that power. He felt relief at not having to associate with the fool he had to during his last inhabitation. "As you wish," Gyraund replied hesitantly. "We have the king and queen secured. What would you like for us to do with them?"

Merreck's black-clad companion strode forward and examined Regen and Yenyn with a twisted smile. The queen tried to pull herself away while Regen stood firm, but despite the king's expression, fear and confusion shone through his eyes. "What is this, Merreck?" Regen asked. "What are you doing with the tribesmen?"

"At least you used the correct name, but do not worry. The one you knew as Merreck is still here. He is with me, within this body."

"What... do you... mean?" Yenyn stammered to the face which she still recognized; however, her fear clearly displayed that she recognized the difference within him.

"I do not what to deal with this now," Merreck answered. "Throw the king and queen into the dungeon, Gyraund, but do not have them killed. They might be useful in the future. Am I understood?"

"Of course."

After Regen and Yenyn were dragged from the hall, he walked up the dais and sat in the king's chair. His three companions followed and stood behind him as he surveyed the crowd. Ut felt the thoughts of Merreck pleading for his release and laughed to himself. That will never happen, he thought. You agreed to the bargain and this is where you will stay. "Now, Gyraund, we need to discuss our next steps."

Chapter 27

Telleck sat in his room, wondering about the welfare of Merreck and their father. He was pleased that Cishor would be mounting an attack, but would that help his family? Were they still alive? And what could he do about it? Remen would be joining the Cishor soldiers, but he was not a warrior. As angry as he was at the invaders from Armen, he still did not think he could kill another man. Was he a coward? He honestly felt he would do whatever he could to free his homeland, except for killing. It was not that he had any qualms toward the deaths of their enemy, but he could not inflict it himself. The visions of the two men he had killed still haunted him, and he did not want to be a nuisance during an attack. However, he also did not want to just sit back and do nothing.

With these thoughts running through his mind, Telleck left his room to seek out Shyan. After searching for some time, he found her in the kitchens. He almost managed a laugh seeing her working at a table kneading a loaf of bread. When she saw him, she dropped the dough and walked over.

"This is where they have the princess of Karren working," he said indignantly, once the initial shock of seeing Shyan disappeared.

"Do not be angry," she responded as she wrapped her arm around his elbow and led him away. "I volunteered to come here. With the men preparing to leave, I wanted to help with the food for their journey." She looked up at him as they strolled down the hallway. "Of course, I don't know if I'm more of a help or a hindrance. You might not believe this, but I've never worked in a kitchen before."

Telleck smiled down at her as they entered the courtyard outside the castle and sat on a bench. "So you are helping out where you can?" Shyan nodded. "Actually, I've been pondering the same concerns."

"What do you mean?"

"Remen is preparing to go off to war. What am I going to do?"

"You are not a warrior, Telleck."

"I know that," he said sharply, and immediately regretted his tone. "I know," he repeated, more softly. "But people believe I'm a coward and should go anyway."

"That is not true. We both know you are not."

"But I would go, if not for…" he stopped, not knowing what more to say to Shyan about his tortured visions. "I just can't do it."

Shyan gently stroked his face. "Nobody is asking you to."

"They might not be, but I can tell by their looks."

"Do not worry about it. Other needs are required for war, not just soldiering."

"What is there for me?"

Shyan placed her hand in his and guided him up from the bench, back into the castle. "That is what we will have to find out," she said as they headed to the kitchens. "I need to return to my tasks; the bread will not bake itself. Go find Tor, or ask to speak to Zur. Certainly they can find other tasks for you."

Chapter 28

Under a warm morning sun, the soldiers left Cishor—many on horseback, but the majority were required to march. While Remen knew that Cishor was a large kingdom, he marveled at the size of the army Zur mustered. All would be needed due to the disadvantages they would face when they reached his home. The Armen Tribesmen were not only fierce warriors, but every soldier had his own mount. Speed and skill would both be with the enemy, so their size and tactics would be crucial to achieve victory.

The army made its way through the lush farmland of Cishor, and Remen looked about in amazement at the diversity of produce growing about. This was his first time east of the Gorthon ruins, and he had been unconcerned about the scenery when his small group had raced to the castle with the news of the fall of Karren. To his right he saw fruit growing on small trees, and fields of grains on his left. At their passing, field workers stopped their tasks to gaze in awe at the stream of warriors. As there had been no war in the land of Cishor for many years, none had ever seen such a sight.

Volx was riding beside Remen, while Zhomin and Fallad were relegated to marching. The prince missed having his friends close, but he knew Volx was necessary for him to communicate with his allies. At their first stop, Remen checked on Bront, who was part of the contingent carrying the massive amounts of supplies. After Volx had advised him there was nothing to report, the prince tracked down his friends. The light skin of the Karren warriors was not hard to find, and the three men drank some water as they sat down together.

"It's impressive, isn't it?" Zhomin noted as he they gazed at the sea of Cishor warriors. Their jeweled armor glistened in sharp contrast to their skin. It seemed that every soldier boasted a silvery breast plate over a maroon cloak, but a plethora of differing arm bands, ear rings, necklaces and rings also greeted their eyes.

"That's a lot of white teeth," Fallad quipped, but he was the only one who laughed at his inappropriate joke.

Zhomin offered his companion a sour look. "Many of those men will die attempting to recapture our homes."

"At least they'll look good, and we will certainly be able to tell the difference between friend and foe!"

"You're sick," Zhomin barked.

Fallad's usually jovial expression disappeared. "Perhaps you want to tell me how to heal."

Remen saw Zhomin searching for a retort, but he remained silent. The prince was not pleased that they were beginning this journey in a foul mood. What did that mean for the rest of campaign? If the three friends were already bickering, what would they be like when the fighting began? "Enough," he ordered. "We are not the enemy. You will not make offensive comments against our friends here, Fallad. Each of them will be risking his life soon enough. If you have any malice, direct that toward the cowards who remained behind."

"I thought you were not going to bring that up any more," noted Fallad.

"You're right," Remen replied, as he realized that the stress was weighing heavily on each of them. Although Telleck was not a trained warrior, he was still annoyed that his future brother refused to join the army. One man, especially an unskilled fighter, would not make the difference in the upcoming battle—but he could not fathom Telleck's refusal to help liberate his family and home. If he wanted to sit back and help bring the army fresh supplies and treat the wounded, that was his choice. "Let's concern ourselves with our forthcoming task. We will have plenty to fight soon enough."

Fallad looked at Zhomin with an apologetic expression, but remained silent. Zhomin frowned and turned away as he took another drink. After a moment, his normal, stoic face turned back and asked, "Do you suppose she's safe?"

"I hope so, but I try not to think about," answered the prince.

"I'm sure they wouldn't harm such a lovely young girl."

"No, but it's what else they might do that really worries me."

After a long pause, Fallad said, "Pretty nice horse you got there."

"It beats walking," replied Remen. "Your feet hurt yet?"

"I'm fine."

"I'll check back with you on that at dinner time."

"Don't worry about us. We commoners are from a heartier stock than pampered royalty."

"But if not, let me know and I'll order Bront to rub them for you."

The sound of the three friends laughing together was a welcome relief to Remen. Unfortunately, he knew it could not last.

***

A steady rain began to fall as the warriors began to climb into the rocky ruins. The temperature also turned with the arrival of the moisture and a stiff wind blowing from the north. With no vegetation to act as a shield, the cool air whipped around the soldiers and the rain penetrated to their skin. The rain was not heavy enough to stop the march, but that really did not matter. Even if they did stop, there was nowhere to get shelter. Remen pulled a cloak from his bag and wrapped it around his body—which did not help much, as it too was soon drenched.

The path on which they traveled became treacherous as mud flowed down while they continued to rise among the ruins. The pace of the army slowed considerably as men began to slip and fall on the slick rock. The cloud-filled sky brought a premature darkness, and they were forced to stop sooner than had been planned. Remen returned to Bront to search through their saturated supplies for his food. All the bread had been turned into mush, and even the vegetables were soggy. It was an unpleasant meal, but Remen forced as much of the food down as he could manage. After everyone had eaten, watches were set and the men settled down into the mud to attempt to get some sleep.

Remen tried to cover himself as best he could, but the rain continued all night. He may have dozed off a few times, but he really did not know. The terrible conditions, coupled with troubled thoughts of Brynn and his home, did not allow him to relax. He welcomed the arrival of morning with a mixture of trepidation and relief. He knew he had not slept enough, but at least he would be off the muddy ground and not fighting himself to fall asleep in his misery.

Everyone in the camp was up early and they continued on at dawn. When the sun broke through the clouds, the rain finally stopped. As the morning progressed, the wind turned and the heat of the previous morning returned. It was a welcome relief, allowing the warriors to finally begin to dry out. When they stopped for lunch, the food was still wet; the bread and vegetables were mixed like some kind of disgusting pudding. Maybe it's good that Telleck remained back, the prince thought. We'll definitely need fresh supplies after this.

Chapter 29

The feeling of loneliness was strong as Telleck sat in the market watching traders from the southern coast milling about. His thoughts drifted from Urik and his brother to Remen, who was out on the campaign. The merchants of Cishor passed by and offered him differing looks. Obviously they all knew who he was, and some of the expressions were welcoming—but others clearly saw him as having brought war upon their land. Those looks were anything but friendly.

Telleck never imagined that he would miss Volx. It was bad enough staying behind, and his inability to communicate just made matters worse. As he watched a pair of traders bickering over produce, his thoughts turned to Linny and he wondered how she was managing the occupation. Then he considered Shyan. If not for the attack of the tribesmen, they would be married by now, and he would be a prince. It was a strange consideration and he felt cheated, but he knew many of his countrymen had certainly lost their lives. His canceled wedding should be the last of his concerns. Still, he could not lie to himself regarding his disappointment. He had considered asking Shyan to have the marriage in Cishor, but he knew that would have been the wrong decision. They would have to wait first to see how Remen's campaign fared before taking such a move.

His mind once again returned to Merreck; he could not imagine what his brother was going through. The accident had been bad enough; now he was a prisoner too, if he even lived. Did anyone of them live: Regen, Yenyn, his father, Linny? What did the Armen Tribesmen want with Karren? While they were not a friendly people, conquest was not their way. The tribesmen were horse breeders who lived on the open plains. They may be a greedy lot, but what did they want with the forests and castle of Karren?

Then the words of Orth—or was it Veake—returned to his mind: all the talk of an evil growing from the north. He thought again of Orth's last words to him. For some reason, that strange man thought Telleck would have something to do with stopping it. What made him so special? He felt anything but while the surviving men of Karren and the warriors of Cishor were headed off to battle, and he was sitting off by himself.

With a growing sense of resolve, Telleck rose from his seat and headed into the castle. He did not know whether he believed the ancient man, but he could not just sit about feeling sorry for himself. He would find Tor and take some action. What that would be, he had no idea, but it was time for something.

***

An unhappy Zur motioned for Telleck to enter his study and offered him a seat. Tor was with the king, as were a couple of other men who Telleck did not recognize. They were studying at map on a large table and discussing something which Telleck could not understand. One of the men was pointing and motioning angrily at the ruins. Another argued back before Zur raised his hand. With a word, he sent the men away, and once they had left, Telleck was left alone with Tor and the king. "What do you want?" Zur asked sharply.

"I was only looking for Tor. I did not mean to interrupt you," answered Telleck.

"Well you have, and here he is."

"I see that," Telleck replied, his familiar ire beginning to grow.

"Please, gentlemen, let us remember that we are not the enemy here." Tor's unruffled demeanor managed to decrease Telleck's tension, but Zur was clearly still agitated. Telleck certainly understood why: Zur wanted no part of this war, and Telleck was a reminder that what was occurring was out of his control.

"What is it you want?" the king repeated loudly.

With a deep breath, Telleck summoned all his control to before responding. "I'm sorry, but I was thinking of what Orth said. He said something about me being the key to stopping this. I think we've forgotten about it with the soldiers leaving for war."

"If that is true, why aren't you with the warriors? Why are you still here?" Zur asked.

"I've forgotten nothing," Tor said calmly. "But he also said he knew nothing else yet."

"I just don't want to sit back here helplessly."

"You could have joined your prince and went off to war," Zur again noted.

"Do not worry," said Tor before Telleck could answer the king. "There will be a mission for you; of that I am certain. We have yet to learn what that will be, but I'm certain it will be vital. It is probably best that you remain safe here in Cishor, for the time being."

Zur huffed at Tor's words, but they gave Telleck some solace. It was not that he sought danger; however, he felt gratified that he would apparently play some part in the conflict, if Orth was to be believed.

Zur's displeasure was obviously growing. Telleck knew the king loathed being forced to abide by the ancient man's directive and commit his land to war, and this unknown mission for Telleck only reinforced his ire. But Telleck did not care. If Zur thought him a coward, that was his choice. The fact that he would, at some point, play a role in this conflict was gratifying. Whether he would succeed in whatever was to come, he did not know, but for now all he had to do was await further word from Orth.

Chapter 30

The army of Cishor continued pushing its way through the forest, heading toward the castle. They had made good time following the hardship of the first day. After leaving the Gorthon ruins, the warriors continued down the road before moving into the forest. They had not spotted any sentries and wanted to keep it that way. Remen figured that the tribesmen were consolidating their hold on the land and did not expect a counterattack so soon. But it was still prudent to be safe, so when they were approximately a half-day's march from the castle, the horses were tied to trees and the soldiers began to move through the forest. When the army stopped for the night, Remen sat down with Fallad and Zhomin, as it would be up to them to plan the attack on their home.

"Most of the tribesmen will be in the village, as they will want to be near their horses," Zhomin began.

Fallad nodded in agreement. "Some will be in the castle, but not many."

"How can we use that to our advantage?" asked the prince.

"We'll need to concentrate on the village first," Fallad replied. "If we can secure it quickly enough, we can trap the remainder of their warriors in the castle."

"But then we'll have to face them while they're on horseback," Zhomin pointed out.

"The attack will have to be at night," Remen said. "We have to surprise them. If we go in daylight, they will certainly spot us when we leave the forest and be on their horses before we ever get to the village. Unfortunately, we don't know where they are, and some of our own people may be hurt, but we have no other recourse." He grew silent and peered up at the moon. Speed would be their best chance. They needed to inflict as much damage on the enemy as possible before they could manage an organized response. Some of the villagers would certainly get in the way, but he could think of no alternative. "We will have to be swift and secure the village before the tribesmen know what's happening. Once the village is ours, we can lay siege to the castle."

"We will be at the forest edge by late morning," Zhomin noted. "Then we will have to wait until dark."

"Yes," said Remen, "now I'll go find Volx, so he can let the rest of the army know our plans."

***

Remen sat amongst the trees at the edge of the forest with the leaders of Cishor army. They looked out across the short plain in the direction of the village of Karren and the castle. The last remnant of light still illuminated the plain as the sun set behind them. Remen watched some of the Armen warriors moving about the village, and was pleased to see they had apparently found their enemy unprepared. While retaking the castle might still prove difficult, the large force from Cishor should manage securing the village with relative ease.

He wondered again how his parents were faring, and if they even still lived. While the tribesmen were certainly the enemy, they were not savages, and the royalty of Karren should have been spared. The death of the king and queen would serve no purpose—but perhaps the tribesmen would change their minds if Remen and his allies were successful in seizing the town and laying siege. And what of Brynn? Was she safe, or had one of the Armen chiefs used her for sport? Those were thoughts he had to put aside as he rejoined his friends and they waited quietly for the last traces of light to fade.

After darkness had completely set in, Remen adjusted the scabbard at his waist. With the lights from windows and the few streets, the army should be able to make their way in undiscovered. Fighting amongst the buildings in the village would pose some problems with limiting the casualties of the villagers, but speed was necessary. The entire town needed to be secured quickly.

When he felt they were ready, the prince raised his hand. He heard chirping next to him, which was echoed behind. When the chirping stopped, he crept from the trees. The noise that followed was louder than he had expected, but it could not be helped—there was nothing that could be done to lessen the sound of so many men emerging from the brush. He readied his sword as he crossed the plain along with his comrades.

Remen passed the halfway point of the plain and still saw no sign of being noticed. "Perfect," he breathed as he approached the village. He took a quick look behind and saw the dark shapes trailing. He smiled to himself as he readied for battle. When they approached the outskirts of the village, he heard a commotion from his right. He turned to the south but he could not tell what was happening. A cry reached his ears, then another. "What's going on?" he asked quietly.

More cries sounded, as did the clash of steel, and Remen knew they were under attack. What a fool I've been, he thought. While the prince thought he would surprise their enemy, it was evident that the tribesmen knew of the coming attack the whole time, and they had waited for this moment to mount their own assault. The Cishor army was spread out across the plain, defenseless.

He heard horses galloping across the open field, then cries of death. No foe was nearby, so the tribesmen were obviously attacking the center. "Retreat!" he called, "back to the forest!" But other than the few Karren warriors around him, nobody would be able to understand. "Where is Volx?"

After managing to grab Fallad and Zhomin he tried to turn back to the west but in doing so they were heading directly into the combat. "Volx!" he cried.

After a few frightful moments, Volx came up to him. "Here."

"We've got to get back into the forest, or we'll be slaughtered. Make sure they all know."

Volx nodded and called out in his language as he moved away from the prince. With his companions following, Remen tried to make his way back to the trees while continuing to call for a retreat. When he noticed a horse barreling down toward him, he realized his mistake: the Cishor warriors could not understand him, but by calling orders, he was making himself a target. As the horse approached, Remen was able to make out the tribesman on its back. The warrior lowered a short spear and Remen prepared to defend himself.

Just as the point of the spear reached the prince, Zhomin sprung at the attacker.

Remen could not see what exactly happened but the spear was knocked sideways. The horse veered around for another pass, and he felt Zhomin push him away. The prince heard a cry from the attacker as the horse raced at Zhomin, but Zhomin darted to the side and leapt at the rider. He saw both men a second longer before losing sight of his friend.

More horses were moving about as he heard the continued calls from the Cishor warriors to the west. Remen knew he needed to enter the forest with them, but he also knew it was impossible. The horses of the tribesmen swarmed across the field as he was left standing alone. He would never be able to get through and rejoin the army.

"Remen!" The prince heard an urgent whisper beside him. "Remen!"

"Fallad?"

"Yes," Fallad said quietly as he rejoined the prince. "Where's Zhomin?"

"I don't know what happened to him."

"We've got to get out of here," said Fallad.

"I know! But we can't get back to the army."

Fallad grabbed his arm and dragged him to the north. "We can't worry about that now. Let's get to safety and we'll look for them later."

Despite his protests, Fallad continued to drag his prince away from the battle and away from their only allies in the land. As the sound of the combat slowly dissolved, the prince wondered about Zhomin. His friend had probably saved his life, and Remen had no idea if he still lived.

Chapter 31

"You were correct. The force from Cishor is pinned down in the forest, but they still have many warriors. We took the castle due to speed and surprise. When the enemy regroups, they will realize that our numbers are smaller than they thought. I provided plenty of men to take the castle, but we can't withstand the army of Cishor. I'm not sure this is developing as planned, Merreck."

"Do not worry, Gyraund. I have only just returned. With the additional forces coming from Lavrs, we will easily defeat them."

The leader of the tribesmen scowled as he walked toward the window of the audience chamber and took a breath of the late summer air. "I'm not pleased with that," Gyraund continued. "The people of Lavrs are fickle. They will desert us if the battle does not go our way."

Ut took a moment to probe Merreck's thoughts. Merreck tried to hide his knowledge but Ut mocked his attempt: *You can hide nothing from me.* Despite his attempts to the contrary, Merreck confirmed Gyraund's words to be true; however, there was a new thought to consider. "But you forget that I have returned. They will know better than to renege on their agreements now."

"They have no idea who you are. They can't be frightened of what they do not know."

"True." Gyraund's statement was disconcerting, but Ut felt relief at finally dealing with a strong leader not requiring manipulation. If the people of Lavrs could not be trusted, he would have to create some new allies. The task would be more difficult now that the dragons were all destroyed, of which the memory caused Ut to inwardly curse Iridan. His plan had been sound, if not for the return of Chaw Den. How Naar had accomplished that was still a mystery to him, even though Ut had spent many ages pondering the question. Ut then sensed a laugh from within his new body. This time it was Merreck mocking him. A premature notion, my friend, Ut thought. If Lavrs fails us, I still have my master's minions I can summon to this land.

"Merreck," Gyraund interrupted the silent exchange, "what do you propose?"

"Fear not, I have an additional option," he said confidently. "Other forces will be summoned and bow to my command, if need be."

"Very good," Gyraund replied, and at that moment the walls of the room began to shake for a brief moment before becoming still again. "What happened?"

"Relax, Gyraund. It was just a small earthquake. We are near what once was an immense mountain range. Certainly you are accustomed to them."

"I've never felt one before."

Ut quickly probed Merreck's mind and discovered his companion also was unfamiliar with the phenomenon, but it was of no matter. The quake had passed, and he had work to do. The leaders of Lavrs would be arriving soon, and Ut needed to make sure that they saw a formidable sign of strength along with a well-fortified castle.

Chapter 32

The night progressed at an alarmingly slow pace. The fact that they were back in their homeland did little to diminish Remen's apprehension. He and Fallad had managed to flee the ambush of their army, but they were alone in the forest and did not know the fate of their comrades. They managed little sleep and the arrival of the morning light also brought hunger. The pair had no supplies, and their only food was a few meager berries they managed to find within the brush. The prince considered hunting down an animal, but their weapons were their swords, so making a kill would be extremely difficult. After sucking some morning dew from leaves, they headed south through the trees.

Not long into their trek, the pair felt a shaking from the ground beneath them, which subsided nearly as quickly as it had started. Remen felt some trepidation until Fallad mentioned that it must have been an earthquake. Remen had never felt one before, but he had heard of them. With its quick passing, he put the matter out of his mind.

They continued through the trees along the edge of the forest line, knowing their path should cross the soldiers from Cishor soon, if any had survived the ambush. Remen was certain they must have; the attack had been a complete surprise, but many of the Cishor soldiers should have been able to make it back to the safety of the trees.

Despite the shade of the trees, the rising sun brought an uncomfortable heat as Remen and Fallad made their way through the forest. Remen's stomach was growling loudly by the time they finally met some of their allies. The warriors of Cishor nearly attacked them before the prince had been recognized. Remen could not communicate with the men, but the pair was escorted to a small clearing in the forest, where they found Volx sitting with the leaders of the army. Food and fresh water were brought to them as they recounted to Volx their experience during the battle. Remen was pleased to learn that Zhomin had survived the attack, though he had suffered a minor wound to his left shoulder.

As they ate a quick meal, Remen was advised that their casualties had not been as bad as they could have been, and with the arrival of daylight, the forces from Cishor had been able to determine that while the tribesmen had their horses, the Cishor army still outnumbered them.

The warriors of Cishor wanted to attack at dusk when the sun would be in the eyes of the defenders, but that plan concerned Remen, and he asked for a moment to confer with Fallad.

"What are you thinking?" Fallad asked.

"Look, when we first spotted the attackers, they were coming from Lavrs, right?"

"Yes, they had to be. They were riding down the road. They must have moved from their homeland to Lavrs before attacking."

"So they would have to be allied with Lavrs." Fallad nodded at the prince's words. "They were a large enough force to conquer the castle by surprise, but with our allies, we now outnumber them."

"What are you getting at, Remen?"

"The tribesmen have enough horses for themselves, but they cannot have supplied horses for the warriors of Lavrs."

Realization began to cross Fallad's face. "You think more troops from Lavrs will be coming to Karren."

"Right, it only makes sense."

"But wouldn't they be here by now?" asked Fallad. "We were delayed in Cishor for quite a while before Zur made his decision to attack."

"You know the men of Lavrs. They are reticent to commit to anything. They probably wanted to wait to see the results of the attack before sending their own warriors."

"Send their warriors for what? The castle has been conquered."

Remen paused as the apparently strategy of the enemy formulated in his mind. "Armen must have bigger plans if they are involving Lavrs. We may have enough men to retake the castle now, but it would be a long siege. The tribesmen must have considered the possibility of a counterattack from Cishor. They will need additional forces to hold the castle. They must have further plans; it doesn't seem likely they would have engaged in such a campaign to just conquer our land."

"But would they be strong enough to hold Karren and mount another attack?"

"I don't know, but I'm confident reinforcements are on their way to our castle."

"So you're suggesting we move our army to the east."

"Yes, if we are able to defend the road, we can keep the Lavrs reinforcements from joining up with the tribesmen," Remen noted.

"You may be right, but what would it give us? The castle would still remain in the tribesmen's hands."

The prince thought a moment before responding. "If we can stop their reinforcements from arriving, we will thwart whatever the rest of their plans are. The tribesmen certainly will not want to make a permanent home in Karren. Eventually they'll tire of the castle and long to return to their plains." He looked at Fallad with dread darkening his voice. "The only way we can retake our home is to move away from it, and stop those additional soldiers from arriving."

"Well, I don't really like it either, but it is a sound plan. Let's tell the others, and we'll have to get a messenger back to Cishor to let them know where we will be. Hopefully, they will be able to provide us with some more warriors and supplies."

Chapter 33

Orth's ancient eyes peered into Telleck's. "'T messeng'r 'as returned; s as I said b'fur. Ya'r t' un tat needs t' stup 'im."

"You said that previously" Telleck said as he tried to avoid the gaze. "That's my only solace in this," he whispered to himself. "What do you expect me to do?"

"Tis as I said," responded Orth. "Ya must meet t' army. T'ere is a way now to end it furever."

"Can you speak plainly for once, Orth?" Zur asked from his throne as the lines hardened across his face.

Orth sucked a breath through his decrepit teeth as the popping of his joints echoed through the king's hall while he lowered his bony body into one of the chairs. "Tis how I see t'ings, not always clear. I'm very old, ta visions from Naar, just flashes. But t'is I know, Telleck must face t' army, and I go with. My life finally comin' to t' end."

Telleck looked away from Orth to the king, and then back to the old man. "And then what?"

"Nut sure yet, nut r'vealed," answered Orth as his head began to droop. "'T duvelopmunts, 'n opportunity is…" Orth's voice trailed off as sleep threatened to overwhelm him. With a force of will, Orth opened his eyes to gaze at Telleck one last time. "'Twill be 'ard on ya, but wull be our only chance t' be free of 'im fur gud." With his last word, Orth lost the battle and succumbed to sleep.

The barking laugh from Zur contained no trace of humor. "I guess you will return to your home after all."

***

"I'm going with you; I don't care what you say," Shyan replied in a determined voice.

"You need to stay in the castle," Telleck responded as they left the kitchens. "It will be dangerous going back. You'll be much safer remaining here."

When the two were far enough away from the kitchens, Shyan stopped him. She looked about, to be certain they were alone in the corridor. "You seem to forget that I am your princess and you must follow my orders. I will be accompanying you when you leave Cishor, and we will not discuss this further."

Telleck looked down at Shyan's beautiful face and knew there would be no dissuading her. Her brother was already off to war, and now her betrothed would be leaving on some foolhardy mission due to the ramblings of a senile old man. If Telleck and Remen were to fail, there would be nothing for her in Cishor. Even though he still felt it to be unsafe for her to join him, he acquiesced to her wishes. "If that is what you want. I guess we will be leaving tomorrow.

***

The sight of Orth sitting atop a horse was almost comical. Telleck wanted to laugh, but the thought of what they were about to do sobered him. Shyan, Orth and he were preparing to ride toward Karren for his undefined mission. What was worse was that the strange man directing the plan seemed to be equally as in the dark as he. Orth had mentioned something about stopping some 'messenger' which would be vital to defeating the Armen Tribesmen. Telleck was not sure why he was following Orth—and bringing Shyan with him—but the people of Cishor trusted Orth. Telleck did not. According to Orth, he had once been called Veake and had lived for many ages. Orth had said that he lived during the time of Iridan and the great battle which had freed the land from evil. Those are just stories, Telleck had thought, myths. He had never believed them, and he wondered why now he was mounting his horse to follow Orth through the Gorthon ruins. Desperation, he thought. If there was any chance that he would be able to save Urik, his brother and their home, he would attempt it. At least he would not be sitting around Cishor any longer, listening to the barbs of the king and feeling like a coward.

Zur stood beside them with the queen—whom Telleck had not seen before—displaying a smug expression. Telleck felt like rushing over and punching the king in the face, but he turned away. Instead he smiled as he watched Shyan nimbly mount her horse when he heard Tor call his name.

"I'm aware of your feelings regarding this," Tor began, "but listen to Orth. He has a wisdom and knowledge unlike any other man I've met. You will need to put aside your skepticism to accomplish what is needed."

"And what exactly is that?"

Tor glanced at Orth for a moment. "It has not been revealed yet."

"You don't find that troubling?" Telleck asked

Tor shrugged his shoulders as Zur called out in a mocking tone, "What are you hesitating for now?"

Telleck ignored the king, but the ire of Zur's words only intensified his annoyance. "Doesn't this all sound far-fetched to you, Tor?"

"My thoughts are my own, my friend, but you will need to be resolute. Trust Orth and his words. If you are not able to do that, say so now, as this task will be pointless."

Tor's comment was sound, but Telleck knew he could not offer his full trust to Orth blindly. He would embark on this mission, but any commands by Orth would be evaluated before he followed them. "Of course," was all he said.

By the expression on Tor's face, Telleck was aware that the nobleman did not believe him, but what could Tor do? The people of Cishor followed Orth's words, and this is what Orth wanted. With Telleck's apparent noncommittal, Tor was clearly searching for something else to say when they all heard a commotion at the castle gate. Telleck peered over and watched as a warrior was escorted in their group's direction.

When the man reached Zur, Telleck realized that he was wearing the adornments of the soldiers who left with Remen. The man was clearly exhausted but he spoke hastily to the king. Telleck followed Tor toward Zur's side, but he could not understand what was being said; however, he could discern the news was not positive. When the man had finally finished, Telleck spun Tor around for a translation.

"Our army was ambushed by the tribesmen," Tor said. "Fortunately, many of the men were able to escape the assault by retreating to the forest. It seems that your prince believes an army from Lavrs will be marching on Karren. As your home has already been conquered, that can mean only one thing. Cishor will be the next target."

Telleck shook his head as if to dispel the news. If Cishor was the next target, new plans would need to be made. "What should we do now?"

"What do you mean?" Tor asked with a tone of surprise.

"Certainly we will need to change our strategy."

"I think not. It would seem that your mission is even more important now. Our army is moving to protect the road and stop the Lavrs warriors from joining up with the tribesmen. This should give you more of an opportunity to complete your mission."

"But I don't even know what my mission is!"

"Ya', ya', mur opportunity." Orth, still atop on his steed, moved over to join the two. "'E be dustractud. Now's t' time. We go."

Telleck looked at Tor once more before mounting his horse. There was nothing left to say. He would follow Orth, at least for now.

***

Watching Orth on horseback was a strange sight for Telleck. The prophet was so old that it seemed like a gentle breeze would cause his body to disintegrate, but—while his appearance remained unchanged—it was as if every step of the horse brought new vigor to the old man.

With his bride-to-be next to him, Telleck felt a sense of both relief and apprehension. They were returning home, but to what? And would they be able to accomplish this unknown mission?

Despite Orth's apparent newfound strength, they still needed to stop often to allow him rest. They were approaching the Gorthon ruins when they stopped for another break, and Telleck stood next to his horse as Shyan walked behind a bush. Orth shambled over and they felt a rumbling from the ground. "'Nuther urthquake," Orth said.

"You sound happy about that."

"Ya, ya, urthquake, gud."

"And why is that good? We never had any before, and this is the second one in consecutive days."

Orth lowered his frail body to the ground. "Whut we need."

"For what?" asked Telleck as Shyan returned, "for our mission?"

Orth looked up and Telleck saw a deep sorrow in the man's eyes. "Yes," Orth replied as he nodded his wrinkled head.

"Does that mean you now know what we need to do?" Shyan asked, and Orth nodded again.

"So tell us," Telleck exclaimed.

Orth's gaze returned to Telleck, and his grief seemed to intensify. "Yu'r nut ready."

"What do you mean by that?" Telleck spat.

With a loud creaking of bones, Orth rose from the ground, and for once Telleck did not doubt that the man had lived all the years he claimed. Telleck saw ages of wisdom in those anguished eyes. "Ya must trust me. Only one way t' end t'is, but I can't tull ya yut." Telleck wanted to lash out at the old man, but Orth's expression stopped him. Shyan grabbed his arm and gently stroked his back with her free hand.

"Could jeopurdize all."

"How so?" the princess asked.

"Ya dun't know whut must be dun. I do. Can't tell ya yut. Nut t' time." Orth's head dropped as he shambled back to his horse.

Telleck turned to Shyan and asked, "What do you make of that?"

"I'm not sure, but Tor said that we'd need to trust him."

"I know," Telleck said angrily, but he immediately regretted his tone, as Shyan was only trying to help. "But does that mean he should be hiding his plans from us?" he continued in a softer voice, and he once again wondered why this beautiful, kind princess would be in love with such an ill-tempered man.

"What's the alternative?"

And that was the problem. Shyan had portrayed his situation so simply with just a few words. With a sigh of resignation, he mounted his horse and they continued on their way into the ruins.

Chapter 34

Advancing the large army through the forest had been a difficult process, but necessary. Remen was frustrated by their slow progress but there was no alternative. The speed of the tribesmen on horseback, along with their accuracy with their bows, would have caused much damage if they had retrieved their own mounts and moved through the open land.

They had reached the road east of the castle relatively unmolested by Armen arrows, but they would need to be in the open land to stop the Lavrs' soldiers—who they had not yet spotted. Remen peered from the forest and could see a number of mounted tribesmen patrolling the land, looking back through the trees. In discussion with the Cishor leaders, it was decided that they would cut down trees and begin constructing bulwarks in order to defend the road and protect themselves from the deadly harassment of the Armen riders.

The task of felling trees went slowly, as only a few of the warriors carried axes. When night finally arrived, they barely had enough material to drag onto the road and start the process, but they would have to manage. If the Lavrs army arrived before they were finished, they would be overrun, and the entire process would have been in vain.

As the work began, arrows fell amongst the men, but the Armen scouts were shooting blind so not many of the missiles found targets. "I'm not so sure about this plan," Zhomin said as he adjusted the bandage on his shoulder. "We'll be surrounded."

"That's what the fortifications are for," Fallad responded.

"We'll still be surrounded, and how long will our supplies last? They could just wait us out and let us starve."

"The Lavrs army will have limited supplies as well. They won't be expecting us, and will be unprepared for a siege on the road," said Remen. He knew some tribesmen must have ridden ahead to report to the coming army, but there was nothing that could be done about that, and it really did not matter. The large force he was expecting would not be able to increase their speed much. Plus, they would not be able to secure additional supplies.

"Still, it's not good strategy to have enemies on two sides," Zhomin continued.

"That's why we'll be taking the attack to them. The longer it takes for Lavrs to arrive here, the more fortifications we can build."

"So if they come too soon, our defenses will be poor, but if they come too late we will run out of food."

"We've had men hunting in the forest all day," Fallad reassured his friend. "That will continue until the battle starts. I think hunger will be the least of our worries."

"Enough," Remen ordered. "It has already been decided. This is the plan and it is sound. Now, if you're not going to help build the defenses, get some rest."

During the next two days, the men of Cishor and the few Karren warriors spent their time building their fortification. The Armen Tribesmen continued to harass them as much as they could, but with the increasing bulwarks, the damage was minimized. The prince ordered some scouts into the forest in case the enemy decided to travel through the forest, but Remen knew that was unlikely, as the tribesmen's skill on horseback would be neutralized. The lake south of the road provided a barrier to the south, so the attack would come from the road. The only question was when.

***

A light rain began to fall through the dusky sky as a fresh wave of arrows flew through the air. The aerial assault was more pronounced than what the defenders previously experienced, and patrols had returned saying that the army from Lavrs was indeed approaching. With the increased ferocity, the attack would be coming shortly. But the Cishor warriors were prepared for this. They launched their own arrows back in the direction of the tribesmen to keep them at bay as the bulk of their force sprung from their position to surprise the advancing enemy, who would not be expecting to be attacked themselves.

The surprise and speed of their strategy succeeded. They met a few vanguards completely unprepared, and they were all quickly dispatched before any could retreat to warn the Lavrs army of the attack. The rain continued to fall, making the road slippery as Remen dashed forward with his sword ready. The first foe he reached was astonished as Remen's blade sliced through his neck. Without waiting to watch his opponent fall, Remen struck out at the next man. His sword again met flesh as his companions also inflicted considerable damage before the Lavrs warriors formed into a defensive line. That had been expected, and the men from Cishor swiftly formed a wedge designed to push through the line.

The patrols that had tracked the movement of the army had reported that the Lavrs men outnumbered the men of Cishor and their few allies from Karren. With a good amount of defenders remaining behind the fortifications to thwart an advance by the Armen Tribesmen, they were even more outnumbered. Remen could only hope that the surprise of the attack and a sound plan would turn the tide of the battle in their favor.

The Cishor wedge had indeed pushed through the Lavrs line. With Zhomin and Fallad next to him, Remen's sword danced in every direction. The cries of the wounded filled the sky along with the steady rain. Remen parried a strike at his left as he felt a blow against his right shoulder. His knee dropped into the mud as he saw Zhomin's weapon cut through the arm of the man who had struck him. The prince took a quick moment to glance at his shoulder. The man's weapon had not pierced, as he saw no blood flowing. With his friends protecting him, he quickly sprung up and drove his blade into the chin of another foe. Blood erupted from the man's neck and showered Remen with its crimson hue.

The battle continued as a warrior from Cishor pushed next to Remen, but a hammer came down and crushed the man's skull. The body collapsed in a heap without a sound as Remen pounced. His sword struck his opponent's wrist and the hammer fell from his grasp. The man looked up, ready to tackle Remen, but the prince spun quickly and steel entered his rival's heart before he could make his attempt.

The assault had been successful; Cishor had inflicted much damage, but the numbers were beginning to be too much. The defensive lines of Lavrs had reformed and would push forward at any moment. As the sky continued to darken, a call rang forth from behind Remen. He could not see, but the prince knew that a small force was rushing from the forest to strike Lavrs' flank. Fresh cries came from his left as the enemy before them wavered. With a renewed impetus, Remen led a fresh assault. The blades of Karren and Cishor continued to slice through flesh as the men of Lavrs responded in confusion to this new attack. In the gloom, the enemy had no concept of the size of this second force. Retreat was sounded, and Lavrs began to pull away.

Everything was working as planned as the defenders of Karren pushed their attack and continued to inflict casualties. Remen struck at one enemy and the blade struck hip bone. The man stumbled as Fallad's weapon smashed against his face. His nose exploded as Remen finished him off.

While the Lavrs retreat continued, another call came from Cishor. They could not get too far from their own defenses and they broke off their attack. The Cishor warriors rushed behind their bulwarks, knowing that they had dealt a serious blow to their enemy, but they were also aware the conflict was far from over.

Chapter 35

Telleck glanced uneasily about as another tremor shook their campsite. Shyan lay next to him undisturbed, as she had already fallen into an exhausted sleep. Telleck considered his other companion and was thankful Orth was not next to him, and in the open air, Telleck hardly noticed the foul stench escaping through his withered pores. "Do you really believe you have lived all these ages?" Telleck asked the old man.

"Heh, 'as nuthen t' do wuth bulief. I know whut I've seen."

"But how is it possible?"

Orth struggled to rip off a piece of hard bread with his few remaining teeth before surveying the darkening ruins. "Nevur saw the mountuns when they wur stull 'ere," he said with regret. "Nevur saw much tull I left Su'Meeryn. 'Ow wus ut possuble? I don't know. All I know us I 'ad to live untul now. I 'ave t' guide ya. No one ulse knows whut's t' be done."

"And you're still not going to tell me what that is?"

"I can't; ya nut ready." Despite the gloom, Telleck again saw a look of sorrow cross the Orth's countenance.

"If our mission is so important, should we have some soldiers with us?"

"Sulders? Naw, no sulders. Sulders wun't 'elp us fir t'is."

"Just the three of us?"

"No sulders," Orth answered as he returned to fighting with his hunk of bread.

Telleck wanted to argue, but he knew it would be futile, so he just tried to make himself comfortable against the rubble. He gazed up toward the sky as the light continued to fade. His thoughts turned to Merreck and his father while the weather started to chill. He turned to Shyan, who had pulled herself into a ball in her sleep. With a smile, he pulled a covering from his pack and placed it atop her, then closed his eyes. He finally drifted asleep while trying to ignore Orth's annoying munching of his dry meal.

With the arrival of morning, Telleck slowly stood and tried to rub the aches from his body. Shyan was already up, as was Orth, to his surprise. After retrieving a small pouch of nuts and seeds from his pack, he approached Orth. "What now, old man?"

"Ha, ya up," Orth responded, his decrepit body displaying more energy than should have been possible.

"Yeah, that's obvious. What now?"

Orth stood still for a moment. After scratching a piece of filth from his cheek, he slowly pulled himself into his saddle. "Cuntinue on, into Karren."

"I'd still like to know what we're going to do when we arrive."

"Into Karren," was Orth's only reply as his horse trotted away down the path which bisected the tall, rocky ruins.

"He does make it hard, doesn't he?" Shyan said as she came beside Telleck.

"It's not so much that he's keeping his plan a secret. If he has reason to do so, I understand. But how am I supposed to trust someone who claims to have lived as long as he has?"

"The world can be a strange place at times. Dragons once fought a great battle at this spot and the mountain country of Gorthon was destroyed. If that could happen, why not Orth?"

"If you believe in that myth," Telleck answered, unconvinced by Shyan's words.

Shyan turned away to watch Orth trotting down the path. He was not sure, but Telleck wondered if he saw hurt in the corner of her eye as she said, "We'd better not let him get too far ahead."

With Shyan in front, Telleck trailed after, while doubts about the sanity of following the old man swirled through his brain.

Chapter 36

The warriors from Lavrs had finally reached the bulwarks and rushed forward with swords held high. Blades struck downward, seeking skin to cleave. The battle cries of the men—mixed with shrieks of agony and death—climbed through the air to reach the rising sun. Mud kicked up from the ground and flew into Remen's mouth, leaving a foul taste as he rushed to his right where the attackers threatened to breach their defenses. His sword shot out and he heard the crunching sound of steel striking bone; his foe's arm went limp, and an axe fell from the man's grasp.

More warriors streamed over the bulwarks like a waterfall running over boulders in a swift stream. Steel glittered in the morning sun like salmon rushing through water. The sick, sweet smell of sweat and fresh blood penetrated Remen's nose as the swords of the defenders worked in unison like a dam stopping a breach.

Arrows began to land amongst the Cishor warriors from behind. Remen heard a call, and their own arrows shot out to harass the Armen archers. The fighting at the bulwarks was fierce; Remen's blade inflected relentless damage until the attackers finally withdrew. The prince of Karren dropped to the ground, exhausted. He was thankful for the break, but all knew another attack would be launched soon.

As some of the men of Cishor went to work repair the damaged barrier, Remen trudged over to the dwindling supplies and got himself some water. He looked through the food, but was not hungry despite not having eaten since the previous day. He sat down and watched men dragging away a few bodies. Most of the casualties were from Cishor but he spotted a few light-skinned corpses as well. With a start, he realized he had not seen Fallad or Zhomin lately, but was too exhausted to get up and look around. When his body started to relax, the ache returned to his shoulder. His attempts to stretch it out were unproductive; the pain would not diminish.

After a second drink, another of the defenders sat beside him, offering the prince a haggard smile. Remen returned the expression before continuing his scan of the defenders, searching for his friends. The man said something to Remen, but the prince just shrugged his shoulders in response. Following a few awkward moments, his fellow soldier stood and departed. Remen was thankful for the relative solitude as he closed his eyes, and sleep came much more easily than expected.

***

The prince was awakened sometime later and saw a couple men bringing in the skinned body of a deer. As the meat was being prepared, Remen wondered how they had found the animal so close to the battle, but just was thankful for their good fortune. Despite his persistent lack of hunger, he decided that he should probably eat. With some effort he managed to force down a soggy apple, then began to massage his shoulder. After a few moments, he pulled out his sword and did a few practice thrusts. The pain remained but it was more of an inconvenience than anything, and it would not slow him as he fought the enemy.

He sheathed his weapon and began circling the camp, looking for his comrades from Karren. He spotted Fallad, but before he could reach his friend, an alarm sounded signaling another attack. Remen quickly turned and rushed to the bulwarks. As he pulled out his blade, he noticed that he was standing beside Volx. Before he could acknowledge his countryman, the first Lavrs warrior had jumped atop the makeshift wall. Remen's sword struck the man at the same time as Volx's. Their foe fell backwards, but two other warriors took his place. Volx struck again, but his blow was blocked. The attacker swung and knocked the sword from Volx's hand. One of the soldiers from Cishor jumped to his defense, only to be met by an arrow to his neck. Hands grasped the shaft as blood streamed down from the wound. With a quick thrust, a sword punctured the other side of his neck, and the man collapsed. As the attacker turned, Remen's blade dug deep into his stomach. The man screamed in pain while the prince yanked his weapon back out.

Before he could strike again, Remen was set upon by two more attackers. He tried to fight them off but they were too strong and skilled with their weapons. Just before they overpowered him, Volx sprang forward and knocked one of the enemies off balance. Volx then grabbed his enemy's arm and thrust his sword upward, under the man's chin and into his brain. Remen remained at a disadvantage with the other man, but with Volx joining him they were able to disarm their foe, and Remen's sword quickly pierced his heart.

The battle continued for a bit longer before the Lavrs troops again withdrew. Once the combat was over, Remen again dropped to the ground. His body was exhausted and he felt a more intense ache from his shoulder. Volx collapsed next to him, and the prince offered him a hushed thanks. Volx either did not hear the comment or simply ignored Remen, which annoyed the prince, but only for a moment. Volx's attitude was meaningless to him. All that concerned him was that they still lived, and the army of Lavrs remained at bay.

He rested a bit longer before forcing his aching body up, then walked in the direction where he had previously saw Fallad. When he reached the spot, he was thankful to find his friend there, still alive.

Fallad smiled when he saw Remen and said, "Good to see you." It was strange for Remen to hear Fallad speak so stoically, but it was certainly understandable.

"Zhomin?" the prince asked.

"Still alive, last time I saw him."

"When was that?"

"We got separated during the attack, and I haven't seen him since."

"Here I am," Zhomin said as he approached the pair.

"Do you know how many of our countrymen still live?" asked the prince.

"Just a few, I think," Zhomin answered. "Almost all the remaining warriors are from Cishor.

"I was just with Volx. He fights better than I would expect for being a trader."

"I wonder how much longer we can hold this position," Fallad said.

"We've lost a lot of good men, but they've lost even more," responded Remen.

"Come on, let's get something to eat," Zhomin said. "We'll need to be ready when they come again. It might be their final attempt. I don't think they can continue like this."

Remen nodded and was relieved when he noticed that he was beginning to feel hungry. As the three men walked to the supplies, they watched as more bodies were being pulled away from the defenses. Again, most of the bodies were dark-skinned, but he did see a few more from Karren. Remen stopped for a moment and looked out at the Lavrs army that was visible down the road. The anger built up in him over the reality of being forced from his home and being separated from Brynn. He withstood the insane urge to jump over the bulwarks and rush the enemy by himself. Still the rage grew, and with no outlet, the fury turned to tears. He waved for Fallad and Zhomin to continue without him as he stretched out in the mud with his arm across his face. The tears flowed freely, and he did not want any of the other warriors to see him, concerned regarding their reactions if they saw the prince of Karren out of control. The mud and other grime seeped into his clothes, but he did not care. What did filth matter after all the death he had seen?

Chapter 37

"Why can't you dislodge them, Gyraund?" Merreck screamed at the leader from Armen.

"We're doing all we can," Gyraund replied, recoiling slightly away. "They built solid defenses before we realized what they were doing. My men harass them as best we can, but we are too few, and they have their own archers keeping us at bay."

Merreck sneered at Gyraund as he felt his evil power growing within him. His eyes clouded over slightly, and he knew that they had turned completely black. Despite his anger, he smiled as the huge warrior shriveled from him in terror. He raised his hand and felt the black fire forming in his palm. With a slight flick of his wrist, he could strike Gyraund dead. The thought provided intense pleasure, but now was not the time. Despite his incompetence, Gyraund was still useful, so he would save the pleasure of killing for more deserving souls.

"It appears I will have to handle the situation myself," Merreck said calmly as his eyes returned to normal. "You and I will leave immediately to join the attack."

"I don't think that is wise."

"I don't care what you think!" Merreck screamed again. He stared at Gyraund, whose bulk seemed to shrink at the high-pitched tone. "But prior to leaving, bring the king and queen before me; I need something to satiate my desires." Merreck settled himself onto the king's throne, and the Ut entity felt a pleading from deep within him. A grin crossed his face as the soul of Merreck knew what was coming, which brought Ut even more pleasure.

The wait seemed longer than acceptable, but when Regen and Yenyn were brought finally before Merreck, he let his frustration pass. Yes, he controlled all the power in the kingdom; however, it would not be good being too capricious. After all, he still needed these puny men to accomplish his conquest.

"Merreck, what is going on?" Regen asked when he saw the face which stared back at him. "What are you doing on my throne?"

"It is my throne now," he responded, his voice low but sinister.

"What do you mean by that?"

Merreck's body rose and glared down at the stately figure of Regen, then his head tilted in the queen's direction. She was still a handsome woman despite her years, he thought. What a pity.

"What would you have us do with them, Merreck?" Gyraund asked.

With his eyes still fixated on Yenyn, Merreck replied, "You are an incompetent man, Gyraund, but I still need you. Perhaps this demonstration will motivate you to perform better." Merreck's eyes drifted back to the king. "Now, Regen, it is time for judgment to be served. You are a conquered people, and Gyraund here needs an example. Also, it has been too long since I provided myself the pleasure of killing." Merreck paused as he summoned the vile power from within. His eyes clouded over again and the light of the room began to dim. He felt the corners of his mouth raise with glee while he reached forward. With his palm to the ceiling he pointed a finger at Regen. Terror crossed the king's face, but he took a brave step forward, bracing himself for the inevitable. With a moan of ecstasy, black fire built from within Merreck's body and formed into a ball in his hand. "I think not," he whispered.

With his gaze still fixated on Regen, he flicked his hand at the queen.

A squeal of delight escaped his mouth as the black fire leapt from his palm. It blazed forward in an ebony stream, striking Yenyn in the chest. She cried out as a sharp explosion ripped through the hall. Her body collapsed, with streams of a foul-smelling smoke billowing to the ceiling from where her heart used to be.

"No!" Regen bellowed as he dropped to the floor, holding the dead form of his wife.

"Take him back to his dungeon," Merreck ordered with a giggle. As the king of Karren was dragged away from Yenyn's still-smoldering body, Merreck turned to Gyraund. The leader of Armen had heard of the power of Ut, but this was the first time he had actually seen it on display, and Gyraund was clearly distraught by what he had seen. "Now, prepare to leave," Merreck commanded. As Gyraund quickly slithered away, Merreck lingered for a moment. He looked down at the queen with a smile, but the smile quickly faded. While the act of killing her had been pleasurable, that delight quickly evaporated, as killing only brought a temporary satisfaction. He would need to see far more deaths to fulfill himself.

"I have not forgotten our bargain, Merreck; Linny awaits us," he said quietly. "Gyraund will be some time in preparation, but there is one other matter. The woman, Brynn, will be brought to our chambers."

Yes my friend, Ut thought, I shall give you an extra level of vengeance against the prince. My gift to you, but Merreck's thoughts were still pleading for release.

Merreck's body limped from the now-empty room while Ut laughed inwardly at Merreck's continued pleas. Linny was in the room and she came to him when the door opened. Merreck's hands caressed her body as he guided her to the bed.

"I've been waiting for you," she purred into his ear.

"As soon as they are ready, I leave with Gyraund to end the annoyance of Remen and his band," Merreck said while removing her clothes.

"May I join you?"

"I don't see why not." The door opened as he lay atop her. Two guards dragged in a chained and trembling Brynn. "Oh," he continued. "I see our new toy has arrived."

Chapter 38

The day wore on with little activity. Hunger dug into Remen's stomach like the shovel of a miner searching for precious metals. He leaned back on the ground, staring up blankly at the dark clouds which shielded the sun from view. Exhaustion threatened to overtake him as he tried to determine the time of day, but then he thought, why bother? They remained trapped behind their defenses, and Remen began to wonder if they had made the correct decision of setting up their makeshift camp in this spot. Spies had reported that the army of Lavrs remained on the road, but they could not free his homeland while remaining behind the bulwarks.

Remen forced his body up from the ground, feeling the ache emanate from his shoulder. It seemed the pain had lessened, but he wondered if the relief was only due to his fatigue. He walked out into the woods to relieve himself before returning to the supplies to get some food. The army was rationing what little they had left and the prince was given only a small sack of seeds. He grudgingly snatched the bag, even though he knew the recent hunts had concluded with no fresh meat brought back.

With the seeds quickly disposed of, Remen threw the sack away and walked about the camp. Everywhere he looked he saw tired and wounded warriors of Cishor. Some of the men eyed him suspiciously as he walked by, and the Karren prince suppressed his anger at the unspoken insinuation. His allies clearly found him to be the source of their misery, but Karren had not been the land that started this war. He was pleased when he came upon Fallad and Zhomin, but they were both on the ground trying to get some sleep, so Remen decided to not disturb them. He sat next to Zhomin who opened his eyes briefly and nodded to his prince. Remen patted Zhomin's thigh, then closed his eyes too, but despite his exhaustion, sleep did not come.

The sound of men moving about the camp seemed amplified for some reason, and he heard the calls from the lookouts, but he could not understand what they were saying. He tried to shut the noise out, but then he noticed the stench of death and wondered how the smell was just now registering in his brain. He moved his arm to cover his face but then the pain returned to his shoulder causing him to curse loudly. Zhomin stirring next to him was the only response and Remen turned away as a few tears formed in his eyes. The misery of his situation threatened to overwhelm him when sleep finally arrived, bringing a much needed respite.

***

Remen awoke facedown on the ground to a foul taste in his mouth, which he hoped was only dirt as he spit the filth out. His body was stiff and he had a difficult time loosening his shoulder. The sun was low over the western horizon as he stood, looking for his friends. Fallad was gone but Zhomin was still asleep. After a quick glance across the bulwarks, Remen decided to head back to the supplies for a little more food when he spotted a flickering to his right. He looked over and noticed a few more. A call sounded from the camp as Remen recognized the flickering as flaming arrows hurtling toward them. He unsheathed his blade and nudged Zhomin with his foot. "They're coming," Remen said as Zhomin stirred.

The arrows began to land in the camp while the archers of Cishor let loose their own volley. Next Remen heard the sound of the Lavrs warriors rushing the camp. Men and weapons reached the barricade as steel clashed amongst the angry cries of the soldiers.

With Zhomin beside him, Remen fought furiously to repel the attack. He forced away his pain as his sword rose and fell at a frightful pace. His blade struck shields and weapons, but also bone and flesh. Blood began to flow down the wooden bulwarks like a vile sap from what used to be trees.

The defense was holding, and Remen hoped that—due to the dwindling forces of their adversaries—this might be the final assault. He severed the arm of a foe at the elbow, and blood exploded in his face. Then Remen heard a hissing noise, and the Cishor warrior who was fighting alongside him fell to the ground. The prince turned in that direction as a Lavrs warrior jumped atop the now undefended section of the bulwark. Remen swept his sword at the man's ankles. The blade hit and the man fell forward; Remen pounced and drove his weapon into his opponent's back. As he looked up, he heard the hissing noise again. He watched in horror as a narrow stream of blackness impacted another man of Cishor. The warrior instantly collapsed as smoke rose from his chest where the beam of black light had struck him. While Remen tried to figure out what was happening, another ray of blackness came hurling in their direction.

***

Merreck sat atop the largest horse of the tribesmen with his hand pointed in the direction of the Cishor camp. His eyes were shrouded, and his lids closed across the now-black orbs as the power continued to grow deep within his captured body. The power tingled from his chest and rushed through every pore of his flesh. He wanted to hold the power captive and revel in the ecstasy, but he had a task to complete. His eyes slowly opened and he saw the dark skin of another Cishor warrior. After fixating on the man for a brief moment, he opened his hand and another ray leapt from his palm. The beam raced through the sky, and before Merreck could blink, the man from Cishor fell dead. A gleeful laugh escaped his mouth as Merreck let loose another beam of death.

"You see, my dear," he said to Linny without stopping his own personal onslaught, "this is what I am meant to do. This is where I get my most joy: killing." His radiant face turned and saw a look of shock on Linny, and perhaps disgust—he was not sure. But he did not care; her emotions were meaningless to him—obedience was Ut's only concern.

As Merreck's attack continued, he could sense Gyraund's confidence growing beside him. The leader of the Armen Tribesmen raised his hand as the riders behind readied themselves. When his arm dropped, the tribesmen kicked their horses and rushed forward.

***

Defenders continued to drop around Remen as the rest fought desperately to stop the breach. Everywhere the prince looked, he saw arms and blades whirling about. The crimson tides of flowing blood turned to black in the setting sun while the deadly black beams continued to inflict havoc. Remen had never seen anything like it before, but he could not take the time to ponder where those rays were coming from. His sole worry was keeping the warriors of Lavrs out of the camp.

He felt a shiver travel up his arm to his wounded shoulder as he · blocked a furious blow from an attacker. Remen stumbled momentarily from the pain as his enemy leapt the fortification and stood in the camp with his battle axe ready to strike again. The axe fell against Remen's blade and his agony increased. A third blow drove Remen down to one knee; when the prince tried to stand, he slipped on some mud and fell on his back. His foe sprung and, as the man raised his arm, Remen prepared himself for death. The axe hung precariously in the air—but it did not fall. The soldier of Lavrs shook for a moment as blood spewed from his neck and a metal point emerged from his skin. The axe teetered before dropping to his side. As his enemy collapsed, Remen saw Zhomin's hand reaching down.

After being pulled from the ground, the prince had no time to offer his thanks; he quickly turned, seeking his next foe. But before Remen could move further, another black beam came rushing in their direction. This ray was larger than the others, and it was aimed at the bulwark. The beam struck the wood with a thunderous crash, and wood exploded in all directions. Splinters flew at Remen, piercing his skin like a myriad of tiny needles. He fell back while his ears rang from the concussion and blood from the multiple lacerations flowed down his flesh. He tried to force himself to jump back up, but his dazed body did not respond immediately. After lying on the ground for a few more moments, he pushed himself to his hands and knees and looked up. To his alarm, he saw a gaping hole in the fortification where the beam had been struck. Remen got to his feet as the first attacker rushed through the opening.

The rest of the defenders had also recovered, and swords swung in all directions. Remen was pushed back by the fresh assault as he hacked furiously at the enemy. Men cried in pain and fury as the battle grew in ferocity. Body was pushed against body, and in the failing light, it became difficult to distinguish the enemy. The blood continued to trickle down his face and arms as Remen felt a blade slice his left arm. He swung to the left, trying to strike his opponent. His weapon found its target and crushed the man's skull.

As Remen turned back, he felt a bump to his right; he spun and swung again. Steel sliced through the flesh of a neck.

When the man fell, Remen saw with horror the empty eyes of Zhomin staring back at him.

The prince stood unmoving, staring down at the still form of his friend, oblivious to the battle around him. Part of him realized that he was an open target to the Lavrs attackers; he did not care. But before he could be struck, arms pushed him away from the opening. Remen then realized that he heard the call to retreat, and the remaining defenders were rushing toward the woods. With their defense breached, and the mysterious black beams, the men of Cishor could no longer hold their position. They had been defeated. Their mission to free his home had failed.

Chapter 39

The rocky terrain remained monotonous as Telleck and his companions traveled through the Gorthon ruins. They had felt a few more minor earthquakes, each one causing Orth to stop and peer up to the heavens. The old man had not said much, and Telleck thought he saw a look of distress on the wrinkled and withered face.

Telleck's frustration at the old man grew with every silent step through the unchanging landscape, and Shyan took to telling stories to calm his nerves. The presence of the princess was a great comfort to him but the tales of their childhood were a reminder of the family and home he had lost. And would they ever be able to marry? That thought seemed unlikely with what was occurring and this unknown mission of his.

Shyan tried to reassure him with the story of the great battle that had been fought at this spot, and how Orth had lived through those times, but Telleck remained unmoved. He had never believed those old fables, and certainly did not believe that Orth had lived for many ages. So what was he doing here? The trail widened unexpectedly and Telleck glanced over at Shyan, who had sidled her horse next to his. The love of a beautiful and caring woman apparently could create a number of illogical choices.

As the day wore on, Orth reined in his horse and gazed off to the north. Telleck followed the old man's stare, which seemed to rest on a large mound in the ruins. "There," Orth said, pointing at the mound as he slid uncomfortably from his mount. "That's where ut'll be."

"What do you mean?" Telleck asked as.

"We wait 'ere."

"On that mound? I thought we were going into Karren. What can we possibly do here?"

"No, nut up there. We wait 'ere, in ta ruins."

"You want us to wait here in the ruins, Orth?" Shyan asked calmly. "Forgive me, but this does seem pretty strange."

Orth turned away from Shyan back to Telleck and remained silent for a few moments. His eyes traveled around Telleck's face, down his body, then back up. While Orth's body appeared that it might disintegrate at any moment, his eyes remained vibrant and alive. The dark orbs fixed on Telleck's eyes, and Telleck saw an immeasurable sadness staring back at him. "This's whur your task must be completed."

The tone of utter despair from Orth put Telleck aback, and it took him a moment to gather himself. "And what task is that?" he asked softly. "I still need to know."

"It'll be ta 'ardest task ya ever do, but's necessary. Now, no more talk." To Telleck's relief, Orth's eyes turned away, releasing their grip on him. "I need t' rust. No longer need the 'orses. Send thum awuy."

The ramblings of the strange old man were becoming too much for Telleck to take. Here they were, standing in these ruins, alone. Now they were to get rid of their horses? "Send them away, are you crazy?"

"They wun't be of ussistunce unymore. They may give us away." Orth looked back toward the mound and Telleck wondering if was trying to hide his eyes.

Telleck tried to understand his rationale for sliding off his horse as he continued to try to get another glimpse at Orth's face. I guess we've gone this far; we can't stop now, he thought while Shyan took the reins from his hand. After removing all their supplies, she turned the horses around and sent them back down the trail from where they had just come.

"Are we going to have enough food and water?" Telleck asked Orth as the ancient prophet sat amongst the rubble with his back still to the pair.

"Ya," was Orth's only reply as he stretched out and drifted off to sleep.

"I can't believe we're doing this," he said to Shyan.

"I   know."

Chapter 40

Merreck watched, giddy with merriment, the remaining forces of Cishor flee into the forest. He felt pleased that this inconvenience had been dealt with—and had provided the victory—but a part of him was sad. Some of the enemy were still visible but he was no longer able to strike them down. He had used the last bit of his energy to blow the hole into the wooden bulwark, and it would take him some time to recoup his strength. A few more could have been killed, but there would be time enough for that in the near future.

"We were victorious, but we lost many good men," Gyraund said, interrupting Merreck's musings.

"Unfortunate, but not too terribly concerning; Cishor is greatly weakened. We will overrun their land when you release the remainder of your forces for the attack."

"I can't do that; it will leave our home unprotected!"

Merreck turned slowly and offered the leader of the tribesmen a steely glare. "You will do as you are instructed, or I will find someone to take your place," he said slowly and quietly. What did he care of Gyraund's home? Once Cishor was conquered, they could easily retake Armen, if need be. If some women and children were killed before then, well, that bothered him not at all. His plans of conquest of this land had been thwarted before; he would not let it happen again. "Send your messenger to your homeland. Advise the remaining clans to leave at once. We will meet them in the Gorthon ruins." This time it will be different, he thought. "Take your surviving warriors and pursue the enemy. They will be heading to the ruins as well. Slaughter every last one of them. I want no prisoners. I shall return with Linny to the castle, and will lead the rest of our soldiers to Cishor. You will await me in the ruins, and once we are all together, we shall take Cishor." The last order had frustrated Merreck. He would have preferred to lead their troops against the fleeing cowards, but he needed rest. And he could not let Gyraund know of that; nobody could know the limits of his strength, that such a display of his power left him vulnerable.

He turned to Linny and commanded her to follow him home. What a fool you are, he thought to that small voice inside him: manipulated so easily, and she is not even very attractive. But she would serve his purposes for now, and he did need to abide by the bargain.

***

The vision of Zhomin's lifeless body chased Remen's mind as he ran through the forest. All was lost. The Cishor army had been routed, and he had killed one of his closest friends. Karren remained under the control of the Armen Tribesmen. He could not reach Brynn, and there was nothing more he could do about any of it. He thought of turning back and surrendering himself to the enemy. What was left for him now? He stumbled in the dark and the branch of tree cut his arm and cheek; the pain barely registered in his numb brain. After his foot caught in some brush, Remen stopped and turned around. Where was he running to? There was nowhere left for him to go, as he could not imagine returning to Cishor defeated. The despair that filled his soul threatened to drown his heart and he began to walk back in the direction he had come.

With the first few pitiful steps, he welcomed the sound of movement coming toward him. He hoped the noise came from pursuing warriors of Lavrs; they would certainly take him back to the castle and his parents to meet his fate. The commotion grew, and the prince stopped altogether, his eyes closed as he awaited his fate. Remen did not care if he died, but not here. He wanted to return and see his home—and hopefully Brynn—one last time, and then he would resign himself to the punishment of the tribesmen.

He waited for only a brief moment until rough hands grabbed his arms and he was pulled away. When he realized that he was being pulled further into the forest, he started to struggle. He wanted to break free, but the hands held him tight. When he heard the familiar language of the Cishor men, tears began to flow from his eyes.

***

Surviving soldiers were beginning to trickle into the makeshift camp that had been formed within a small clearing. Remen sat among his allies, and nowhere did he see any of his light-skinned comrades. Volx was not present either, so he had no way to communicate with the men around him. All the soldiers were wounded and exhausted, and no one had been able to grab any supplies in the hasty retreat. "What does it matter? We might as well die here," Remen said aloud to a few confused looks.

They rested in the clearing for a couple hours as a few of the men went into the forest in search of some form of sustenance. When they returned with a small number of roots and nuts, Remen was forced to eat something, and the small band began to move west through the trees, back in the direction of Cishor.

As they continued on, several more soldiers joined them, and Remen was somewhat relieved to see Volx. While Remen never particularly cared for the man, at least he would now be able to communicate with his companions. When Volx spotted his prince, he hurried over as he glanced about at the other warriors. "No one else?" he asked in his normal, flat tone, which irritated Remen. It seemed as if Volx was unfeeling to the death of his countrymen.

"No, they're all dead, Volx!" Remen shouted as the memory of his blade slashing through the throat of Zhomin returned. Volx's face remained unfathomable, which only increased Remen's aggravation, and he wondered if Volx cared about his home and his comrades.

"What we do now?" Volx asked flatly. The simple question was more than Remen could take. Without warning, the prince pounced, driving his fist into Volx's face. Remen felt the pain from his knuckles as they cracked against his countryman's cheek, and the agony in his shoulder exploded. Volx stumbled as Remen continued his onslaught. The prince swung again, but this time Volx grabbed his wrist and threw him to the ground with surprising strength. Remen's head struck hard and he was stunned briefly as Volx jumped on top of him. Volx raised his hand, and Remen felt the impact against his nose and his blood immediately began to flow. Volx struck again before a few of the Cishor warriors knocked him away. The prince remained on the ground for a moment, allowing his head to clear while ignoring the hands that were offered to assist him. He slowly stood with narrow eyes, glaring at Volx while wiping the blood from his face. Volx was breathing heavily while glaring back at Remen—two men of Cishor kept hold of his arms in case he decided to strike again.

If they had been back at Karren, Remen would have found an interesting punishment for any subject who had dared strike royalty—even though he had instigated the fight—but they were not home. He wiped more blood away and felt his face beginning to swell, but that was fine with him. He deserved the pain for his failure to free his land. In fact, he deserved worse. "I guess we're even," he said to Volx while he motioned for the men holding his arms to let go. Without another word, Remen sat back down in the clearing, rubbing his shoulder and pushing away those who offered to tend to his wounds.

***

The small group continued their trek through the forest back toward Cishor. After his altercation with Volx, Remen felt even more alone than before. While he could now at least converse with his companions, he felt little desire to speak. On a few occasions he thought of turning away and heading back to his castle, and presenting himself to the tribesmen. He might have, but it would have taken effort to break away and make the journey on his own, and he was too mentally and physically exhausted to embark on such a route. So if for no other reason than a lack of motivation, Remen followed his allies back toward their home.

The march through the trees brought a new series of miseries. Remen's muscles grew tight from the lack of proper rest and lack of sustenance. His nose remained swollen and painful, but thankfully his shoulder did not bother him much, as he barely had to use the arm to fend off the constant assault of twigs and branches, which left numerous cuts and scrapes. To make matters worse, they were constantly assailed by a thick army of biting flies. The unending swiping at the bugs was becoming unbearable when the group stopped and pulled out their weapons. Remen turned to his left, where the other men had heard a noise, but his sword remained sheathed. The sound of movement was now distinct and took his mind away from the bugs when he saw a lone shape emerge from the brush. With a sense of relief, he watched Fallad approach.

Fallad's face brightened when he spotted the prince, but an air of despair remained when he recognized that Volx was the only other Karren warrior in the group. The men of Cishor sheathed their swords and restarted their march as Fallad joined Remen and gave him a tight hug. "Good to see you," he said. Remen's only response was a nod. "Nobody else? Zhomin?"

"All dead," Remen said as he once again tried to push the vision of Zhomin's slain body from his mind.

"Bastards." The two continued to follow the group in silence for a few moments before Fallad spoke further. "So what do we do now?"

"What can we do? They won."

"We might have lost the battle, but we dealt them a hefty blow. They should be vulnerable."

"Vulnerable?" Remen laughed. "Did you see what happened? How can we fight an army possessing such power?" The thought of those black beams inflicting death wherever they struck sent a shudder down Remen's spine.

"Yes, I saw," Fallad responded angrily, "but does that mean we just give up?"

"What exactly do you recommend?" Remen spat.

"We're still alive, Remen. We can't quit on our people. What about your parents and Brynn?"

The voices of both men had increased in volume as they spoke and, even though they could not understand, the men of Cishor watched the pair. Rage was growing in him at the thought of his parents and Brynn in the hands of the Armen Tribesmen, along with the land and his inheritance. He had done everything he could to free Karren, but the attempt had been futile. Now his subordinate was questioning him? Remen's body tensed as he prepared to strike out at his longtime friend, but then he saw Volx's still-emotionless face. His thoughts returned again to Zhomin, causing his ire to dissolve, and all he was left with was his despair. "I don't know," he said as he motioned for the warriors to   continue.

Chapter 41

His strength having fully returned, Merreck led the remaining soldiers of Armen and Lavrs away from Karren. The numbers were not what he would have liked, but the forces of Cishor had also been weakened by the battle. The small voice within laughed at his aggravation and he took a moment to compose himself. Do not worry my friend, he thought, I have other allies to call on if needed. But with the remaining warriors that Gyraund was leading, along with the rest of the tribesmen who should now be heading southwest, there should be no reason to summon those forces.

Regen rode next to him with his arms bound, secured to the horse. The former monarch of Karren bore a stark look of defeat and depression. "The king does not appear excited to witness the coming battle," Merreck said to Linny, whose horse trotted on his other side.

Linny glanced over tentatively, her former playfulness and joviality long gone. While she had been complicit in the Armen Tribesman's victory over her homeland, along with manipulating Merreck to become the willing recipient of Ut, it was clear that she had not grasped the magnitude of his power—or his evil. He could sense her revulsion whenever their bodies joined, but she had not refused him. She remained trapped by her own choices, and there was no escape now. Merreck chuckled at the thought. Linny was too smart to try to break free, and her willingness was irrelevant. Obedience was his only concern. "No, he doesn't," she replied with no trace of emotion.

"I'm certain we will give him a magnificent display."

"Who are you?" Regen asked. "You are certainly not Merreck."

Merreck chuckled. "But I am."

"And much more," Linny whispered.

The king straightened his sagging back as his face took on the regal appearance of old while glaring at Merreck. "I will kill you for what you did to my wife."

Merreck let out another laugh. "You will be joining her in the grave soon enough; I just thought you would like to witness the culmination of my triumph before I slay you as well." Regen's eyes reflected his evil companion's disdain, but Merreck knew the look only masked the king's fear. The memories of Merreck were filled with visions of a strong and merciless sovereign, and a giggle escaped his lips. Merreck moved his horse closer to Regen's and continued quietly, "You may act the part of the defiant, noble monarch, but I know better. At this moment, you are nothing more than a scared, grief-stricken boy. You miss your dead wife and are fearful for your own life." Merreck came even closer and whispered into Regen's ear. "And I revel in your fear and despair." A vile laugh burst from his mouth as he guided his mount away.

***

With the sun setting, Merreck spotted the Gorthon ruins and gazed at them angrily. Soon the spot of his humiliating defeat would bring him to his ultimate victory. In its weakened state, Cishor would be easily conquered. Then, with Cishor, Karren, Lavrs and the Armen Tribesmen under his command, he would conquer the entire land and finally hand it over to his master. Victory—at long last—was at hand.

As the day came to its end, Merreck ordered his army to stop for the night. The following day they would be meeting up with Gyraund's company, as well as the rest of the warriors from Armen. Once in possession of his full force, they would storm the gates of Cishor. With child-like joy he envisioned the blood that would soon be spilled, and he pulled Linny closer to him as they stretched out on the ground. She squirmed uncomfortably as he began to remove her clothes. Her modesty was meaningless, but as he did not want anything to detract from his pleasure on the threshold of this conquest, he motioned for his three companions to stand between them and his soldiers. With the red armor and black leather acting as a barrier, he finished removing her garments while a servant dragged Brynn over. She was naked and her hands were bound. Merreck had her also placed on the ground, next to Linny, and the eyes of both women stared blankly upward as he moved on top of them.

Chapter 42

The light snow which had begun to fall emphasized the crisp morning air. As the men began to move out, the prince of Karren stirred and slowly sat up. Remen looked at Fallad, who was next to him but still asleep. He was happy they had been reunited, but Fallad's presence just made him miss Zhomin even more. He pulled his sword from its sheath and thought of throwing it into the woods. He hated the fact that he continued to carry the weapon that had ended Zhomin's life. Dried blood still covered the steel, as he had refused to clean it—the ebony hue was all that was left of his friend. He re-sheathed the sword; the weapon would remain with him and he would never clean the blade again.

As the rest of the camp rose, the men ate what little food they had scrounged. Remen knew that he must be hungry but he could find no appetite. After forcing his aching body to stand, Volx walked past; Remen spotted a slight sneer from his countryman. He did not deserve the respect of his subject. If Volx hated him, so be it.

"Kind of early for snow, isn't it?" Remen heard from behind him. He turned as Fallad emerged from the trees.

"I suppose so."

"We'll be starting soon. We need to get back to Cishor and plan our next move."

"Right," Remen said.

"This isn't over yet, Remen. We will strike them again."

"Right," the prince repeated as he walked away, but Fallad's hand reached out and held him back. Normally any such insolence would have infuriated Remen, but he merely stopped moving and just looked down at the light dusting of fresh snow on the dirt.

"Enough of this," Fallad bellowed as he spun Remen around. "We've both lost much, but we do them no honor by surrendering." Remen looked in his eyes, and when he did not respond, Fallad's ire grew. "Do you hear me?"

Remen knew that his friend was right, but that knowledge did nothing to heal his despair. He simply nodded and followed the Cishor warriors as they began to exit the clearing.

***

The earth rumbled as Merreck rose from beside Linny's body. He looked about quizzically from the women, then toward his three companions, who still stood motionless between him and the rest of his company. While earthquakes were not unheard of near the former mountain range, he was concerned by the frequency with which they had been coming. It was certainly strange, as was the snow so early in the fall. However, there was nothing he could do about the weather or the movement of the ground… at least, not yet. Following his victory—well, he would see then.

After pulling his clothes on, he pushed past his companions and found Regen already bound and on his horse. "Who are your silent friends, Merreck?" the king asked.

"Servants of mine, not that you need to know."

"They don't seem very useful."

"Perhaps not yet."

"Was this all worthwhile?" Regen asked Linny, who now stood next to Merreck.

"I did what I needed to do." Linny's tone belied her words. Merreck turned to her and sneered at the regret clearly visible on her face.

It's all because of you, Merreck said to Ut. *She was always a traitor, but she despises you. She only does what you order because she's trapped.*

Ut chuckled silently at Merreck. *You cannot taunt me, my friend. I care not why she follows my commands. Control is all that matters.*

"And now you are nothing more than a lap dog to this evil creature," the king continued.

"But she will be a living dog, whereas you will be a corpse shortly," Merreck pointed out.

"Death is preferable to serving you," Regen stated with a tone of unfabricated dignity, which intrigued Merreck. Death was preferable to serving him? Ut searched Merreck's thoughts, and was stunned by the realization that the king was not lying.

"Then I may just have to spare you," Merreck said while mounting his steed.

***

"Another earthquake," Telleck noted after finishing his breakfast. "This doesn't concern you?"

Orth looked at the ground then studied the sky. "No, no," he answered as he wiped a filthy sleeve against his mouth. "No concern."

"So what is it we're supposed to do here?" Shyan asked, and for the first time Telleck noted a trace of annoyance in her voice.

Orth sat motionless for a moment as he returned Shyan's gaze. "They come 'ere," he said. "Battle wul be 'ere, in Gorthon. Is where ya wul 'ave to complete yur task," Orth continued as he turned toward Telleck. Orth slowly rose, reached into his tattered tunic, and as he pulled out his grimy hands, gold sparkled in the rising sun.

"What is that?" Telleck asked.

"For ya," said Orth as he reached to his companion.

Telleck gingerly took the gold from Orth and noticed it was heavier than he had expected. "What are these for?" he asked while inspecting a sparkling pair of shackles.

"Ya wul see," Orth answered as he turned his face away, but Telleck once again saw the distraught expression the old man was attempting to hide.

As Orth shambled away, Shyan approached and examined the restraints. "Pretty costly for a pair of shackles," she noted.

Telleck twisted them in his hands as he looked at the metal. "This isn't gold; it's too heavy."

"What else can it be?"

"I'm not sure. Gold is too costly—and too soft—for shackles." Telleck banged them against each other, causing a loud ringing noise. "Probably some kind of alloy mixture."

"But why?"

Telleck turned in the direction from which Orth left and spotted the strange man looking out in the opposite direction. "Well, obviously we are going to need to bind someone."

"I wonder why he won't tell us who?" Shyan said.

"I don't know, but I get the sense we're going to find out soon."

"It can't be good, if he's keeping it from us."

"You're probably right about that," Telleck agreed, and a sense of dread colder than the crisp air settled over him like a morning fog .

***

The earth rumbled once more beneath the hooves of his horse as Merreck led the soldiers into the Gorthon ruins. He remained troubled by this unforeseen development, but he took solace in the fact that an earthquake could provide him with a benefit, if need be. Regen remained behind him with the red-armored and black-clad warriors flanking him. "It will happen soon, woman," Merreck said to Linny, who was riding next to Merreck's other companion: the frail, shambled figure who resembled death. "Cishor will fall. I will rule this entire land, and you will be the consort of the most powerful emperor ever seen."

"It will be a marvelous day," Linny replied, and Merreck sensed a warming in her tone. The thought of standing beside him as he ruled clearly provided a strong appeal to her.

"You've not won yet, Merreck," the king pointed out.

Merreck found amusement at Regen's feeble attempt to unnerve him. The plans had been prepared too well this time. Throughout his exile, he had seen all that was occurring. Now, with his return, nothing remained to stand in his way. *It will be different this time. Iridan is long gone and I am unstoppable,* Ut thought. But then he heard a reply: *That is what you thought last time.*

"Soon all those who oppose me will join your lovely wife in the grave." Merreck turned to Regen and offered him a vile sneer to emphasis his words. The king stared blankly back at him, which just brought Merreck further merriment. "You will be witness to my final victory, Regen, but I grow tired of your words." Merreck abruptly ordered a stop, then motioned for one of the nearby tribesman to approach. With a flick of his hand, the red-armored warrior removed the shackled king from his horse. "The king talks too much. Take out your knife, tribesman, and remove his tongue. I need his eyes and ears intact to experience my victory, but his words grow tiresome." The warrior hesitated for a brief moment before approaching Regen. Merreck and his slight companion giggled as blood gurgled and poured from Regen's mouth.

***

The trees gave way and Remen saw the rocky terrain of the Gorthon ruins before him. The fact that his small band was approaching Cishor gave him no satisfaction. Soon he would return to that foreign land, but what awaited him? He would be a prince without a land and without his bride, and each day of his wretched life would only remind him of his failure.

The men left the security of the forest with some trepidation, but they saw no sign of the enemy. Even so, the Cishor warriors moved quickly through the open space and into the relative safety of the ruins. The quickened pace was less than desirable for the prince, as each step seemed to inflame the aches which covered his body, but he knew the hardship he suffered was no comparison to what those who remained in Karren where enduring.

"I never thought I'd be so happy to see that bleak landscape," Fallad said.

"Why should you be?"

"Because it means we should be safe the rest of the way to Cishor."

"But we're going away from our home."

"Let's not argue this again," replied Fallad. "We're still alive, which means we still might be of service to Karren."

Remen wanted to refute his friend's words, but he chose to remain quiet, as to further the same disagreement was pointless. So, since Fallad would not allow him to return to the castle, he simply followed the dark-skinned men before him. He had no other alternative. He continued each tortured step out of reflex rather than any determination to reach their destination as they finally entered the Gorthon ruins.

***

"You've done well," Merreck commented as Gyraund approached with a large contingent of warriors trailing behind. Despite the sickening sensation of offering kind words to any mortal man, he knew the importance of providing them occasional praise. He then looked down at his silent companions and probed himself. His strength had fully returned and he looked forward to once again unleashing his power.

Traversing the ruins with so many warriors was slow going. The Armen Tribesmen appeared ill at ease without their horses, but only Merreck and a few others were permitted to ride along the treacherous trail. Their pace was a minor inconvenience, but soon he would witness another glorious battle with its resulting agony and death. The thought made him smile.

As the march was taking longer than he had anticipated, it was with regret that he ordered a stop. The ruins were certainly not the most hospitable place for an army to camp, but they could not risk traveling any further in the gloom. The soldiers were forced to spread out amidst the rock, and their discomfort provided Merreck with some amusement, as did the fact that they would be out of the ruins the following day and on the doorstep of Cishor.

***

The greenish-yellow nail of the skeletal finger pointed down at the soldiers who milled about their camp as the sun dipped toward the horizon. "There, all's 'n place," stated Orth.

"Tribesmen?" Shyan asked.

"Ya, tribesmun and warriors of Lavrs. The enemy. T'ose t'at conquered yar 'ome."

"And what can the three of us do about them?" the princess continued.

"Not us. Telleck's task. 'E wull rid t'is land of the enemy fur gud."

Shyan stepped away from the rocky crag and looked at Orth with a stern gaze. "What do you think he will be able to do against that?"

"Ya 'wull see. T'murrow. I tull ya t'murrow." Orth also backed away from the outcropping and rested his body atop a large rock. "T'murrow I finally get my rest." And with those words, Orth drifted off to sleep.

Telleck pulled the shackles from his cloak and ran his fingers over the smooth alloy. He still loathed being kept in the dark, but at least he would finally have his answer. Shyan moved next to him and he wrapped his arm around her shoulder as they joined Orth on the uncomfortable ground.

Chapter 43

The night was anything but restful; sleep had not come easy lying on the rocky ground, but Telleck enjoyed the presence of Shyan next to him. He stood carefully, trying not to rouse her as he looked back over the rock outcropping. The sun was just beginning to rise in the crisp air, and he saw stirring in the camp of the enemy. With trepidation he wondered what was in store for him. The annoyance of being kept in the dark by the ancient man was gone. Now he would finally learn what Orth's plan for him was, and looking down at the camp, the thought did not put him at ease. What role could he possibly play in this?

He felt a hand stroke his back, and Shyan's gaze followed his to the army below. "I guess this is the day," she said. He nodded but did not look away, as he thought he saw some movement off to the west. "Orth's still asleep," she continued. "I wonder how that man ever wakes up." She paused, waiting for Telleck to respond, but he remained silent. "What's wrong?"

There was no mistaking it now. Warriors were moving from the west toward the camp, and Telleck pointed at them. "There," he whispered. "From the looks of them, they are the remaining army from Cishor, and they're moving in the direction of the enemy."

Shyan peered in the direction he indicated. "Scouts must have reported regarding the coming attack, and they've emptied the castle, but they are far outnumbered. They'll be slaughtered!"

Telleck looked at Shyan, then back at the soldiers of Cishor. She was correct—they did not stand a chance.

"Ah," he heard from over his shoulder. "'T's begun."

***

"Fools!" Merreck laughed. "Cishor comes to attack us? In the ruins?"

"You will annihilate them," Linny replied.

"Yes, if they think they are better off here than behind their walls, we will leave their corpses strewn amidst the rubble." He waved his hand at the leader of the tribesmen. "Take your men forward, Gyraund. Squash them like insects; then we shall stroll into their castle."

At Gyraund's order, his men drew their weapons and rushed forward. "You see, Regen, nothing can stop me now," Merreck continued. "This whole land will bend its knee to me, and you will remain my lap dog to witness it all." The king's silent scowl caused him to second-guess the decision to cut out Regen's tongue. He took consolation that, although he could no longer find amusement at Regen's feeble words, at least the despair was clearly visible in the king's eyes. Merreck did need to find pleasure in any possible circumstance, after all.

Linny's face brightened at their coming victory. "It will be a glorious day."

"You see, my dear Brynn, learn from your friend here. She seizes the moment. Do not let the opportunity pass."

***

With a gesture, Remen signaled for silence from the trailing soldiers as he and Fallad crouched behind a large rock. The enemy was rushing forward toward the army of Cishor, and he knew now why he had survived. This would be his moment. Despite the reinforcements Zur had obviously ordered to meet the attack, they were vastly outnumbered and could not prevail, but at least he would die in combat against those who had taken so much from him.

As he began to spring from his spot, Fallad's hand stopped him. "Where do you think you're going?"

"We have to help them!"

"And what do you think our small band will be able to do?"

Remen turned to his old friend with a stern look. "Listen, you will not talk to me that way. I'm still your prince. If we lose this battle, there will be nothing left."

Volx approached the two men, who were glaring at each other. "Men of Cishor agree. Time to attack."

***

With a triumphant call, the combined forces of Lavrs and the Armen Tribesmen rushed toward the advancing army of Cishor. Telleck watched from his perch as the enemy unsheathed their blades. The men of Cishor braced themselves as the vanguard crashed against their front line. The ringing of steel reached Telleck's ears, along with the first cries of agony as swords found their marks.

"What can we do?" He heard Shyan's voice from over his shoulder. "They will be overrun."

"And Orth thinks I'll be able to stop it?" Telleck shook his head at the absurdity of that statement. How could he be expected to help in this battle? He was just one man, and not even a soldier.; yet Orth called him the key?

"Ya, you the one. I see all clearly now. Naar speaks t' me; I see it all."

"And what is it that you see? Are you going to tell me now?" Telleck asked.

"Ya, now I tell, but ya not gunna like what I 'ave t' say."

***

With the back of his heel, Merreck delightedly nudged his horse forward. His army was forcing the defenders back down the trail from which they had come. The stony brown earth before him began to take on a crimson hue as broken bodies fell amongst the rubble. The smell of death drove Merreck into a frenzy, and he could not resist joining the melee. A black ray sent from his hand struck a Cishor warrior in the face and a shower of skin and blood exploded from his skull. Merreck laughed from the sheer joy of destruction, but here he stopped, allowing himself no further indulgence. While he did not expect any difficulty prevailing in this battle, prudence told him that he should save his power for any possible unforeseen development.

"You see it, do you not, Regen? The men of Cishor may be brave but they are stupid," he said to the mute king. "They fall before us, and we easily push them away." Regen's glare only increased Merreck's amusement. "We will push them all the way back to their castle—if they survive—and it too will be added to my kingdom. Soon this entire land will bow to my will!" Regen's face hardened and flushed, which brought a new wave of giddiness. "And you will witness it all!"

"It will be glorious," Linny intoned from beside him.

***

Crouched behind several large rocks, Remen watched as the tribesmen and their allies continued their successful assault against the soldiers of Cishor. He clutched his sword motionless, ready to spring, but the small band waited. They had decided to strike the back of the enemy column from the side. The hope was that by the surprise—along with striking at both ends—that the confusion would be enough to disrupt their foes, but he did not truly expect that to happen. Their attack would certainly cause damage; however, they were too few to pose much of a threat. At least we'll take more of them with us, he thought.

He took a quick glance at Fallad and easily detected the nervousness on his friend's face. Fallad did not agree with the plan, but he remained beside Remen nonetheless. Fallad would never desert his prince. "I guess this is it," Fallad commented when he noticed Remen's glance.

"I never expected we would end this way," Remen replied.

"At least we're together. If only Zhomin was with us."

The words stung the prince; if not for him, Zhomin could very well be there. He wanted to confess his causing Zhomin's death to Fallad, but he could not bring himself to utter the words. Instead he peered back out, noticing the rear of the enemy's column was passing. "Are you ready?" he asked. Fallad nodded and wrapped his arm around Remen's back. Fallad's lips opened slightly as if to say something, but then closed. Remen knew what Fallad wanted to say, as he felt it himself. The love between the men was only diminished by the absence of Zhomin. The prince paused a moment to give his friend a brief hug and then looked back at the rest of the men. They were all ready. Remen took a deep breath and noticed his despair had all but disappeared. Death was at hand, and he would bring as many of his enemy as possible with him into the bowels of the earth. He turned back and leapt from his rocky lair with a cry.

***

Orth stared at Telleck for a moment before speaking. "You will now understand why I refused to tell you before this moment." Telleck listened, stunned as all traces of the old man's accent disappeared. "And you will know why only you can accomplish this task.

"An evil force is leading that army. I saw it before. It came and corrupted my king and my land. Its name is Ut, and I'm sorry to tell you that it has inhabited your brother."

"What do you mean?" Telleck interrupted.

"Silence!" Orth ordered with such force that Telleck was taken aback. "Merreck lives, but his body is at the command of Ut."

"How do we get this Ut out of him?"

The distraught look on Orth's withered face telegraphed his next words. "We can't. The only way Ut can inhabit someone is by agreement. At some point, Merreck would have had to agree to the joining. The only way to purge Ut from the body is to kill it."

"You're asking Telleck to kill his brother?" Shyan's trembling voice asked.

Orth did not immediately respond. "No, that would only allow Ut to return another time."

"What is it then?" Telleck shouted. The talk was becoming too much for him. He could not believe Merreck would have invited this Ut to inhabit him, but then he thought of Merreck's knee and all the pain he had experienced. Could that have been it? Could it have been too much for him to handle?

"The shackles I gave you," Orth continued calmly in the face of Telleck's anger and frustration. "They are made of an alloy which Ut cannot manipulate. He will soon have to use his power, and will then be vulnerable. Once he is weakened, you will seize him. You should be able to approach without being harassed; when his men see you, they will think you are him. Once you bind him in the shackles, the ground will open before you. Then you will have to carefully lower him into the crevice. His body must not be damaged. Ut will remain within the body so long as it lives, and since he requires no sustenance, he will stay trapped as long as he is within the earth."

Orth fell silent, allowing his words, as well as their implications, to take form in Telleck's mind. "So Merreck is still alive and will be as long as his body is not killed? And you want me to imprison my brother with this Ut for what could be eternity?"

"It is the only way. This is our one opportunity to stop Ut forever."

***

Remen's shoulder ached as he swung his sword again. Their attack had come as an utter surprise, and many of the enemy fell before managing to form a defensive posture. His weapon bounced off a shield, causing a shock of pain through his arm, and he nearly dropped to his knees. The prince took a step back to gather himself before lunging again.

The tip of a blade caught his cheek and he felt the blood begin to flow. The misery grew in his shoulder from his relentless onslaught, but he pushed that aside. He knew his death would come soon and his only consideration was how many foes would join him.

Sweat streamed down his face and the salt stung his cut, but he did not slow his assault. His sword struck out again, and he felt and heard the crunching of bone as he crushed the forearm of a tribesman. The man's cry of pain was quickly silenced as steel pierced his heart.

Fallad fought valiantly beside him, doing his best to protect his prince from his own recklessness. Fallad's blade let loose a river a blood like the breaking of a dam. Everywhere around, bodies fell to the ground, and most were the tribesmen or the men of Lavrs.

The Cishor warriors also swirled their weapons around in a dizzying frenzy. It seemed that all of Remen's allies had resigned themselves to their own deaths, and as a result they fought with an intensity the prince had never before witnessed.

And so, somehow, despite their small numbers, they began to break through the enemy's line. As death blows continued to rain down amidst the enemy, confusion ensued as their line collapsed. Remen yelled a call and pushed his attack even harder.

***

"Fools!" They think their feeble ambush anything more than an inconvenience? They will all die at my hands." Merreck turned his bemused head in Brynn's direction. "I see your beloved is with them. He will die as well, and you will witness it." Ut sensed his inner companion laughing at this development, which only increased the anger hidden by his stoic facade.

Merreck considered letting loose his power at Remen and his small band, but withheld. He did not expect this attack to be anything more than an annoyance, but he still wanted to save his strength, should the battle turn against him. Before he could speak further, he heard Linny barking orders to their troops to rally themselves and repel the fresh attack.

As Merreck's men began to hold the breach, he returned his attention to the front of his army, where the men of Cishor continued to fall before the combined forces of Lavrs and Armen. Their advance continued into a more rocky part of the ruins as blood flowed down the path like a sickening river, causing Merreck to stifle a laugh. *The battle will be over soon, my friend,* Ut thought as he relished the death he would be witnessing. He turned to his three companions. The crimson-armored warrior stood still, while the black-clad man remained unruffled. Only the pale man offered an expression, and his grin mirrored Merreck's glee.

The tribesmen in the vanguard continued to push into the rocky terrain when Merreck noticed one of his men fall. He peered toward the rubble as another collapsed, then a third. "What is this?" he said while watching more continue to drop. His joy at death quickly turned to concern as he saw streams of both dark and light-skinned warriors

651

streaming from what seemed to be out of the ground. It was then that he noticed gaps in the rubble that were openings to what appeared to be tunnels. The warriors of Cishor were far more numerous than he had anticipated, and they apparently had allies he had not foreseen. As defenders continued to emerge from the ground, Merreck knew that his army would soon be outnumbered, and was thankful that he had saved his strength. He would not suffer the same fate as had occurred in this place so long ago.

***

"I can't do it," Telleck said to his ancient companion. "I can't condemn my brother to that fate. I'd rather kill him."

"But killing him would accomplish nothing. We'll be in this same position again in the future."

"Perhaps, but I may be long dead by then."

"We can't be certain; we don't know the times Ut will resurface. Yes, there was a long delay this time—nobody knows that better than me—but the time before, Ut returned after only a year. Our chance is now."

Telleck just shook his head. It did not matter what Orth said; he knew there was no way he could imprison his brother with this creature. He looked back down at the warriors and watched as an attacking force near the rear of the army was being contained, but then he saw the hidden forces of Cishor bursting from their tunnels. They were slaughtering the enemy as they continued to pour forth. "It might not be necessary," Telleck said, as the tide of the battle quickly turned toward his allies. The advance of the army had been stopped, and the forces in the rear were now facing some disorganization as the small ambush force regained momentum. Telleck could now see that the enemy was outnumbered. "We've stopped them," he continued. "They will be defeated!"

"I don't think so," Orth responded as he pointed down. Telleck followed the direction of Orth's finger and saw a shape sitting on a horse. After a few moments, he realized he was staring at the figure of his brother. "Ut is not done." And Telleck saw a black aura beginning to emanate from Merreck's body.

***

Just as the prince and his small band were about to be overwhelmed, the enemy before Remen began to falter. He saw confusion in the eyes of his foes and he increased the ferocity of his attack. The steel in his hand spun about in a blur as the prince's resolve was emboldened. Death was delivered with what seemed to be every stroke. His blade crashed against bone and Remen did not even feel the pain in his shoulder. Where he had once sought to bring about his own demise as a relief from his misery, Remen now envisioned defeating this army and returning triumphantly home.

A call sounded, and their opponents retreated from Remen, Fallad and the others and rushed to the head of the long column. With a brief respite in the battle, Remen peered after the escaping enemy. He realized then that they were not fleeing, but rushing to assist their comrades. Troops of Cishor with light-skinned allies streamed from what had to be tunnels for the mines. The reinforcements were far more numerous than he could have ever imagined, and Remen wondered who the men were fighting beside them. They wore dark red and green adornments, and all had the light yellow or white hair of the men of the southern coast. At that moment, the attack on his sister suddenly made sense—the coastal people had been aware of the troubling brewing from Armen all along. The princess had only unwittingly been a target. They had killed some of his men previously, but now they fought together.

"Follow them!" Remen called as he sprinted after the retreating soldiers. "Keep on them and they will be crushed!"

Fallad dashed after his prince, as did Volx and the remaining soldiers. Their blades would strike the enemy from behind, and surely it would not be long before the battle was won. However, as Remen neared his quarry, he felt a sharp shaking from the ground. He stumbled as he looked about, but nothing unusual caught his eye. Next he heard a loud crack and the earth shook again. Remen fell to his knees and saw the familiar stream of black light striking the ground; rocks and debris flew into the air from the point of the impact as the ground continued to shake. The prince slowly got to his feet and followed the black ray back to its source. There he saw Merreck on horseback, along with Linny and Brynn behind him. The beam of the jet-black light actually emanated from Merreck's outstretched hands, and his eyes. The cracking of the ground continued to rip through Remen's ears as he began to notice an eerie hissing from the black light. He fell again from the shaking of the rocky terrain as he saw a crack beginning to form where the ray continued to assault the ground. The crack widened, and Remen watched with horror as a putrid green hand with elongated, deformed fingers reached up and clutched the top of the earth.

***

The release of power was both exhilarating and draining at the same time. This was why Merreck had saved himself. He had not expected the battle to turn against him, but he would not be caught unprepared again. The dragons might be gone, but there were other allies. If he had his choice, Merreck would not be summoning these now, but he could not let this battle be lost. Merreck had known that the men of the coast may come to the aid of Cishor, but he had had no idea as to the true size of the Cishor army. *Could they have restarted the Gorthon mines?* he thought. It must be. The inhabitants of ancient Gorthon had returned to their ancestral homes—and were far more numerous than he had estimated—but this time, he was more prepared.

"What's happening?" he heard Linny mutter from behind, but Merreck ignored her words. His concentration was vital. Merreck needed to continue opening the crack and summoning his master's minions from the bowels of the earth.

***

Bile threatened to spew from Remen's mouth as the hideous head emerged. It was hairless and bits of flesh flaked away as it climbed from the chasm. Four soulless eyes, situated randomly on its vile face, searched the land. To the side of its head where Remen supposed an ear should be, a square mouth snarled, displaying mangled, black teeth. Skin continued to blow off it like dust on a windy day, but the flesh somehow remained. The naked creature rose to its misshapen feet, and its green head swiveled about. Though the yellowish-brown body resembled a man, its proportions were misshapen. Two long arms of differing lengths sprouted from its right side, while on the left was what appeared to be a small foot. The beast seemed to spot Remen, but he could not be certain, as he had no idea if it could look out from all four of its eyes at once. If it had seen the prince, it ignored him and continued to search. The creature then loped toward the forces of Cishor as Remen's nose caught a strong stink from it. But it was not alone. More hands and arms continued to appear while the crack widened; all the creatures looked different, but were equally hideous. As creatures continued to emerge from the earth, the smell became too much. Vomit spewed from the prince's mouth as he collapsed.

When he managed to look up, the soldiers stood frozen in horror by the vision of these creatures shambling toward them. But the eerie silence was broken by the screams of the Cishor warriors and their allies as cruel fingers clutched and dragged them into the slow-moving mass. Foul teeth bore into flesh; claws and nails tore anything they could grasp. It was not long after witnessing the horrible deaths of many of their companions that the soldiers began to rally themselves. Blades began to cut through what appeared to be a dreadful rainbow of colors of the flesh. The beasts fell easily, but more continued to crawl from the widening crack. Remen's despair immediately returned when he realized that these creatures would soon overwhelm the Cishor forces. Now, with Brynn a mere few feet from him, defeat was only moments away.

***

"You see!" Orth cackled. "Ut still strong. Ya must do as I say. Ya 'r only chance."

As the scene unfolded before him, Telleck looked on in disbelief. What he was witnessing was beyond anything he could have imagined in his worst nightmare. Once they had regained their wits, the men of Cishor easily cut the creatures down, but there seemed to be an endless supply rising from the ground, like a floodwater threatening to destroy every in its path. Soon their sheer numbers would be too much, and the battle would be lost. He had to do something, and he looked down at the shackles. "I can't," he sobbed, turning desperate eyes to Shyan. "What am I supposed to do?"

She looked at him with resignation and sorrow covering her face. What could she say? How could she tell him to imprison his brother? "It must be done," she finally managed to utter in a deep, almost inaudible voice as more of the grotesque creatures clawed their way from the splintered earth.

Telleck turned a weary head to Orth and nodded. Orth sucked in a labored breath through his withered lips and spoke. "This is what must be done…"

***

The ground shook again at Remen's feet as the endless stream of creatures shambled toward him. His mind was frozen, unable to comprehend the image before him. He had heard of supernatural beasts, such as dragons and the like, but he had never really believed the stories. Unfortunately, there was no denying the shapes moving in his direction. He stared into the single, giant black eye of one of the vile creatures while the small hand protruding from its head reached out. A chill swept through Remen's scalp where the scaly fingers clutched his hair. The prince looked down at his sword, but his arm did not move. No fight remained in him. He would die on that spot to this abomination. The fingers pulled harder and another hand extending from the hip of the monstrosity grasped Remen's belt. The prince remained paralyzed as he was pulled closer; his nose was like a funnel as the stench of death and disease filled his entire body, but he did not struggle to break away and flee the horror. As the vile mouth inched closer, the prince knew his misery would soon be over.

The mouth opened welcomingly to Remen's flesh, and he felt disjointed teeth against his cheek when the creature stopped abruptly. He heard a soft squeal as he was showered with a russet-colored liquid and a slime that had once been the skin of the beast. Rough hands dragged the prince away. Remen looked up into the face of Volx, who was panting above him with muck dripping from him blade. "Fight!" Volx shouted as he spun around and reentered the fray.

Remen wiped the grime from his face and watched Volx swing his sword in all directions, dropping creatures in a wide arc around him. The prince had no idea that the trader was such a strong warrior, but skill was certainly not needed to kill these minions from the earth. The men of Cishor continued to repel the creatures, but one of the soldiers was eventually overwhelmed. He screamed in agony as disgusting teeth and misshapen claws ripped skin from his body, but Remen remained motionless. It was not until he spotted one of the tribesmen that he finally raised his weapon and rushed forward with a cry.

His target never saw the charge of the prince, and his head flew from his neck and bounced toward the crack in the earth. Remen now swung his blade with no concern for his own safety. The creatures approached unendingly, but he cut them down with a ferociousness he had never experienced before.

The area around the prince was filled with the muck of the dispatched beasts, but he noticed that more of his allies were being pulled to the ground as the numbers of their foes continued to grow. Fallad was beside him now, and they formed a wall of steel, but it would surely be only a matter of time before they joined their fallen comrades.

***

Telleck climbed down from his rocky perch and approached his brother, who still sat on horseback, alone and transfixed as the black aura continued to flow from his body toward the crack in the earth. He gripped the shackles in his hand, ignoring the battle playing out all around him. A few of the Armen Tribesmen rushed past him and stopped when they saw him. They gave him a confused look, but Telleck pointed in the direction of the battle and ordered them to proceed. They obeyed immediately, grateful to escape his presence. Telleck had wondered if Orth's plan would work, but it was clear that when the warriors saw him, they would not realize that his clothing was different from his brother's. His face and voice was all that was needed.

It was at that moment that Telleck looked up and saw Linny on her horse next to Regen. He quickly hid behind a rock to peer out. Linny represented the one contingent that could disrupt the plan—meeting someone who knew Merreck and him. The dried, blackened blood down the front of the king, along with his haggard appearance, clearly signified Regen was a prisoner; however, he had no idea what to make of Linny. Four warriors from Lavrs guarded the king of Karren. He noticed that Linny smiled while watching the warriors of Cishor and their allies being pushed back by the grotesque beasts, and he realized at that moment that she was a traitor.

Linny and her group were directly between Telleck and his brother, and he had no idea how to get past them. Another moment passed until he decided he had only one option, and he emerged from his spot with a feigned confidence. Striding forward, he pointed at Linny and cried, "Seize her!" The soldiers looked at him quizzically for a moment before he screamed, "Now!"

"What're you doing?" Linny squealed as she was dragged from her horse.

"Bind and gag her immediately," ordered Telleck.

A cloth was stuffed in her mouth as the men searched frantically for some rope, but Telleck was no longer concerned, as she had been silenced. He then turned his attention to Regen, and he saw the spark of recognition in the king's eyes. Telleck could only hope that the king would be smart enough to remain quiet. When the king said nothing, Telleck moved through the rubble toward Merreck.

***

His focus must remain absolute. It had been difficult enough to open the earth, but controlling his master's minions was draining. Without his focus, the creatures would turn on anything they saw, even each other. Summoning the dragons to his bidding was not easy, but they had been willing and intelligent participants in the war. Once they were summoned, Ut had been able to turn his attention to other matters. This was very different. He realized he was starting to weaken, but he would not require much more time. Soon the enemy would be overwhelmed, and he would be able to release the beasts back to their subterranean lair.

He sensed the malevolence of the creatures as they focused on the Cishor warriors and the men of the coast. The beasts continued to fall, but—as their numbers grew—so too did their adversaries. It was glorious. Death surrounded Merreck, and they were horrifying and sickening deaths. He indulged himself a brief moment to let a laugh escape his vicious sneer while continuing to focus his power—but then he felt a sharp impact against his back and he was thrown from his horse.

***

Fallad swung a mighty blow, which dispatched two of the creatures at the same time as another of the Cishor warriors fell. Volx remained beside Remen, as did a few other men, and they were all covered in the filth of battle. The prince tried to ignore the foul, permeating odor, but it was becoming too much. He had already vomited twice and the ache in his shoulder was nearly unbearable. His left arm jerked forward, and he felt teeth pierce the leather covering and his skin. He spun about and his sword sliced down, imploding the head of another beast.

The creatures continued to push forward and Remen saw Volx slip on their remains. The prince pounced and repelled the greedy limbs. He pulled Volx from the filth and the fight continued, but they all knew it would be only moments before they would be overwhelmed. "Goodbye, my friend," he said to Fallad, who had barely a second to look over in response before a deafening thunderclap ripped the sky with a flash of white light.

The creatures stopped momentarily before continuing their assault, but now it was different. Some continued in Remen's direction and his friends, but many of them turned on each other. They also attacked the men of Lavrs and Armen. Remen stood dumbfounded. He had no idea what had happened, but for the second time the battle took a complete turn in their favor. With this change in the beasts, they might be able to prevail after all.

***

Telleck emerged from behind a large rock and saw Merreck sitting on a horse with the black aura pouring from his body. But he also saw the three figures which Orth had advised him about. Telleck pulled out the blade Orth had given him that was made of the same material as the shackles hanging from his belt. The red-armored warrior was the first figure to approach. It lifted a large red sword, but Telleck struck the blade first, and it flew from the red gauntlet. Then, as instructed, he drove the blade into the crimson breastplate, and the armor collapsed to the ground.

Next the black-clad warrior stepped forward. His dark face remained expressionless as he pulled out his black blade. The golden sword of Telleck swung again and struck the black leather, and the warrior immediately fell.

The third figure gazed at Telleck, but did not move. His withered face grinned as Telleck approached Merreck's horse. Despite Orth's reassurance, Telleck remained wary of the frail, foul being, but—as promised—he did not move as Telleck raised the sword. Merreck, still locked in focus on the black aura, was oblivious to Telleck's presence. After a deep breath, Telleck turned the blade sideways and struck his brother across the back with one mighty blow. Merreck's body straightened as he fell from the horse. The black aura fluctuated as Telleck pounced. Careful to not injure his brother's body, he struck twice more with the flat of the sword. With a loud crack and a flash of light, the blackness disappeared.

Trying not to think of what he was doing, Telleck muttered, "You're too weak now to start again." He spun Merreck onto his stomach and pulled out the shackles. Merreck babbled something Telleck could not understand as he placed Merreck's wrists in the shackles. "You won't be able to do it again."

The earth started to shake again as the third figure finally approached, and Telleck thought he saw a look of dismay on the death-like face. The ground shook again, and a crack began to open beneath Merreck's body.

Tears rolled from Telleck's eyes as the crack widened. "No!" Merreck screamed. Telleck fell to his knees, and Merreck turned to him. "Brother, don't do this to me!"

Telleck's body heaved with each sob while Merreck's body slid a few inches into the ground. "Telleck!" his twin pleaded as the crack in the earth opened wider, and Merreck's body slipped further and further, until Telleck could no longer see it. He could only hear the pleas as they became weaker and weaker, until there was only silence.

Pushing himself up, Telleck's tears flowed unabated as he looked into the eyes of Merreck's companion. Telleck grabbed the golden sword while carefully regarding the man. He was short, with a few wisps of hair and a pale, skull-like face. Tattered rags hung from his skeletal limbs. The ugly head tilted to the side as Telleck drove the blade into his chest. The man made no sound, and no blood poured from the wound. The body slowly collapsed and Telleck again fell to the ground as his tears returned.

***

Chaos surrounded Remen. The creatures no longer emerged from the chasm, but they now fought anything that moved. With the dwindling numbers, and the fact that the creatures now had additional targets, Remen, Volx and Fallad dispatched them easily. They did face some of the tribesmen along with the remaining men of Lavrs, but most who were not engaged with the creatures had already surrendered.

The sight and smell before the prince was sickening. Disjointed remains of the creatures were interspersed with the corpses of men. Remen was forced to cover his nose and mouth with his left arm as he continued to swing his blade. The battle was nearly over; they just needed to finish off the remaining beasts. They had actually prevailed and he would be able to return home.

Another beast fell at the prince's feet when he glanced up and saw Brynn and his father just a few feet away, but more creatures—that had not already turned on each other—loped toward the pair. Remen immediately sprung. Blood and filth dropped from his blade as he held it high. Three of the vile monsters fell unknowingly, while more pushed forward. Remen's sword kept up its deadly assault as one reached out an elongated mouth at the paralyzed face of Brynn. Remen leapt between them, knocking the creature and himself to the ground, but the beast was on top of him. He heard Brynn scream as he tried to free his arms, but it was no use. They were trapped under him, and his wounded shoulder went numb. He was defenseless. From the corner of his eye, Remen watched Brynn unsuccessfully try to knock the creature off as teeth ripped into his neck. Pain seared through his body as he felt warm blood escaping from the gapping wound. The mouth of the creature chewed his flesh for a moment before reaching out again, but it stopped abruptly as Fallad's sword collapsed its deformed skull, engulfing Remen in a disgusting shower.

The pain disappeared as Remen felt his life essence flow from his body. Brynn stooped down with a look of horror, while Fallad remained motionless. Sorrow engulfed the prince as he realized that that only a few more moments remained for him, despite the fact that he had finally been reunited with his love. "It's over," he managed to say as blood followed the words from his mouth.

Brynn's mouth moved, but she could form no words. The king was now beside her and reached out to grasp his son's hand. "Yes," Fallad said while clasping the other hand of his prince. "We stopped them, and now we can return home."

"I wish I could see it one more time."

"You will," Brynn managed to say before kissing him on his cheek.

Remen just shook his head. He knew that in a few moments, he would never see anything again.

"We'll bury you there," Fallad stated.

At least I'll have that, Remen thought as life escaped his tattered body.

Chapter 44

Shyan approached and placed her hand on Telleck's back; he peered up and forced himself to stand. He stepped over the motionless figure with the sword protruding from his chest and wiped away the tears that continued to flow from his eyes. Telleck led her to the hole in the ground and they looked down. He saw nothing but blackness, and heard only silence.

"Orth?" he asked after turning away.

"He died right after that loud crash," she replied as they turned their attention to carnage. The stink was drifting toward them and they both covered their faces. None of the creatures remained moving. The surviving warriors of Cishor and the coastal lands were leading the last of the surrendering tribesmen and Lavrs warriors away. They watched two figures approach. Telleck recognized Fallad and Volx. Fallad looked at Shyan and shook his head to her unspoken question.

"We the only left from Karren," Volx said as he continued on away from the battle scene.

Shyan wrapped her arms around Telleck and sobbed silently into his chest. It was then that Regen approached, dragging a still-bound Linny behind him. Shyan spun away from Telleck and rushed to her father with open arms. "Mother?" she asked, but Regen pointed to his mouth, and Telleck realized what had happened to his king. Regen stooped down to remove the gag from Linny, then he kicked her and pointed at Shyan. Linny gazed up in confusion until Regen kicked her again. Understanding crossed her face, and she said, "Yenyn is dead." The words were too much for Shyan and she collapsed into a heap on the ground.

When the king spotted Fallad, he beckoned for the warrior to approach, then pulled a dagger from Fallad's belt. With the blade in his hand, he grabbed Linny by the hair and dragged her up. She remained transfixed as the blade slit her throat. The king shoved her dying body to the side and waved for Fallad to lead him away from the scene.

Telleck sat silently beside Shyan with his arm around her shoulder. When he finally coaxed her to stand, he prepared to follow the king away, then heard a call from behind. He turned to see Tor and Zur. "I'm pleased to note that the two of you survived," Tor said.

"So it was the men of the coast who we saw in our land, and who attacked us?" the princess asked.

"Yes," Zur answered. "They knew of the evil as well, and were suspicious of your trading with the tribesmen. But we could not let anyone know we had allied. If Ut had been made aware, we could not have surprised him as we did."

"That matters not now," Telleck said. The voice of Zur was the last thing Telleck wanted to hear. It was just a reminder of all that had been lost. "Now leave us."

"We've all lost much, Telleck," Tor replied in an understanding tone.

"Not like me," Telleck said as he looked in the direction of the hole in the ground.

"Yes, I know; I saw it all. You did what you had to."

"I thank you for what you've done for us and for Karren, but I do not want to see either of you, or this place, again." He led Shyan away and ignored the further calls from Tor.

They passed by the chasm and Telleck averted his eyes. The land may now be safe from Ut—but it came at such an unimaginable price, Telleck was not sure whether he would be able to live with the thought. He turned to his betrothed for comfort. He then heard the last words from Tor: "The land is finally free."

Following are two short stories that were written a number of years ago. Other than some minor editing, I am including them as they were written. While some of the names noted in the stories are the same as characters in my past novels, no relationship is intended. These stories should be viewed as completely independent.

The Warrior

The battlefield engulfed me like the waves of a crimson sea emptying tons of unwanted debris at its shore. I stood like an island amongst twisted corpses and strewn limbs. I lifted my foot and felt the sucking sensation of mud sticking to my boot, but the only moisture present was blood: my blood, and the blood of the dead. I heard the dull pop as my foot broke the seal of the clinging sludge.

A sword dangled from my right hand like a useless limb. The weapon was black—not red from the blood of my victims, but black. Grime and dirt intermingled with blood to create the dark hue. I twisted it in my hand, trying to examine the blade. Its edge had dulled, leaving the weapon as little more than a filthy stick.

My eyes scanned the horizon; the corpses constructed an eerie landscape of hills and valleys. Hoping to find any sign of movement, I turned to look behind myself and felt a dull pain in my left arm. Blood flowed from a gash that reached from my shoulder to elbow. As I tried to raise the arm, I noticed muscles contorting through the laceration. I searched around for something to use as a bandage, but had no success. With the blood continuing to flow, I dropped my sword, stooped down and ripped a shirt off a corpse. The garment did not approach cleanliness—and sported a foul odor—but I clumsily tied it around the wound anyway.

A rustle sounded from behind me. Hoping to spot a companion, I turned, but only carrion birds greeted my vision, flying toward their feast. They screeched and squawked to each other; the calls sounded like aviary glee. They knew they need not fight over scraps today.

The pain from my arm increased, and I began to notice other wounds across my body; I ignored them. I tried to count the dead. Hundreds lay in every direction. The sun began to set, and I decided to cease my task. But I knew there had to be thousands—thousands dead, except me. I was the only survivor.

I thought back to the battle. How many men had I killed? I could not recall; I did not remember killing anybody. Then I realized I did not remember the battle at all. I did not remember anything, and I also did not remember my name.

I was completely alone.

Stepping over the broken corpses, I departed the scene. The direction did not matter. Where would I go? All I knew was I needed to distance myself from the carnage. Minutes passed. Birds squealed at me as I disrupted their meals. I kicked at one and it flew up, pecking at my leg. I kept walking.

After long minutes, I finally reached fresh ground. I kept moving for hours, until I could no longer discern the terrain, as the sun had set long ago. I searched about until I came to a tree. Sleep overwhelmed me before I hit the ground.

***

It was light when I awoke. As my vision cleared, I saw a young woman standing over me. She looked frightened as she asked, "Are you okay?" After a moment I realized her expression was not fear, but concern regarding my condition. I tried to nod my head, but I do not know if I succeeded.

"Who are you?"

"I don't know," I said. "I don't know."

Her dirty yellow dress flapped in the light breeze as she stooped over me. Shining green eyes trailed up my right arm to the haphazard bandage. "Come with me," she ordered softly. "We need to get you cleaned up."

I took the soft hand she offered me and stood. My entire body felt stiff from a dull pain. "You don't remember your name?" she asked.

"No."

"Well, from your appearance, I take it you were in a battle. But I don't see a head wound."

My hand raised and fingers probed through my hair, and they found no apparent injury. Her hand grasped my elbow as she led me down a small path. I saw her look up at me as if to speak, but we continued on in silence. Following a few moments, we came down into a small ravine which displayed a lush valley. Large trees circled around the ravine walls, with a thick blanket of leaves providing a huge layer of shade. A small creek meandered with rich, blue water sparkling in the sun. Soft grass carpeted the ground except for a rainbow of flowers bordering the creek. And in the center of this exquisite picture, a house sat—with gaping holes in the walls, a collapsing roof and rotten wood rubble for a fence.

"The creek runs behind the house," the woman said. "Let's get you cleaned up."

She brought me into her decrepit home and sat me on a rickety chair. After grabbing a bucket, she exited and quickly returned with water. I slowly pulled the foul shirt from my arm; I felt it peel off dried skin, and the wound reopened. The woman gasped when she saw the huge gash. She soaked a clean cloth and started to wash the arm. I winced a few times, but the treatment did not cause as much pain as I had anticipated. When she finished with the arm, she turned her attention to my other injuries.

As she bent over me—with her attention centered on her task—I examined her face. Long, red hair hung down her back in loose curls. Soft, caring eyes search about my body for any dried blood or missed cuts, and finally, her full lips slightly smiled under high cheekbones, announcing she had completed the chore.

"Why are you doing this?" I questioned her.

"I couldn't just leave you out there, could I?" she replied.

I stood slowly and flexed my arm. It still felt sore, but I managed to move it. Somehow I knew that I had experienced worse pain than this throughout my life. "What were you doing up there anyway?"

"Looking for mushrooms. They grow sweeter around the trees above the ravine—for some reason." She stood, perplexed for a moment, before continuing. "That reminds me; I left my basket where I found you."

"Do you want me to retrieve it?"

She sat cross-legged on the floor before me. "That's okay. I can get it later." She briefly soaked her hands in the remaining water and washed my blood from her fingers. "So, you still can't remember your name?"

I tried to concentrate for a moment, but to no avail. "No, I'm sorry."

The woman laughed slightly. "Don't worry about it."

"Well, you haven't told me your name," I pointed out.

"Dobrah."

That's a pretty name, I thought. "I'd better be on my way," I said.

"Where are you going to go?"

I stood and realized that I knew of no place to venture to. "I don't know," I answered, "but I have already been a burden to you."

"If you like, you can stay here for a while, maybe until your memory returns. My husband died a few months ago and, as you can see, I could use some help around here."

She placed her left hand lightly on my good arm, and her beautiful smile left me no alternative. "I'd be happy to do what I can."

***

Days passed in that lovely ravine, with the presence of Dobrah enhancing the lush landscape. Whether she had me repairing her roof or fixing the fence, she was always nearby with her infectious smile. She would inquire over my health or offer a cold drink. Regardless of the level of my thirst, I found her hard to refuse.

While working, I tried to recall visions of my past, but I constantly failed. When nights arrived, I slept on the ground next to the door. Dobrah had a number of extra blankets, so I managed to make myself quite comfortable. I had the impression that she would not have refused if I requested to lay with her, but I rejected that notion. Despite my growing desire for Dobrah, I felt a friendship for her which I did not wish to abuse. I wanted to wait for my memory to return—or resign myself to permanent amnesia—and then I would be able to give myself over fully to her.

On one of those long nights, while listening to Dobrah breathe peacefully in her sleep, I thought of her husband. Dobrah had never mentioned him since we had first met, and I wondered what his name was and how he had died. I then thought that he might be buried near the house—perhaps I had even walked over his grave. But the unknown man quickly left my mind, as my thoughts always returned to Dobrah, until sleep finally arrived.

After waking early from a less-than-restful sleep, I dressed quietly and left the house. I walked to the tree where Dobrah had first found me. I told myself that I would try to gather some mushrooms for her, but I really just needed to walk. Despite my efforts, my memory was not returning, and I thought—for some reason—the walk might help. When I reached the tree, I searched for the fungus for a few minutes, but I quickly gave up and sat against the trunk. I desperately tried to recall any past memories, trying to picture my mother's face, my father's, but no images surfaced.

Eventually I rose and headed back to the house. When I reached the creek, I spotted Dobrah bathing. She saw me and slowly submerged herself into the water. "I was wondering where you went," she said.

"To get you some mushrooms," I replied.

She looked at my empty basket and smiled. "Not a very large assortment."

"To be honest, I didn't look very hard. I was trying to recall some memories."

Her smile softened. "And you were unsuccessful?"

I nodded my head.

Dobrah began to climb from the water, until she saw me turn my head. She clearly possessed a beautiful body, and I did want to gaze upon her. But I needed to refuse that desire; what if I gave in to my urges? Might I break a vow to a wife I could not remember?

"I'm sorry," I said and sprinted to the house. I reached the door, but could not bring myself to enter. Sliding down the wall, I sat on the ground. After a few minutes, Dobrah approached—fully clothed.

She looked sympathetically at me. "I'm the one who should apologize," she said. "I can't imagine what you're going through."

"It's not... that... I don't want you," I stammered, "but what if I have a wife? What if we lay together and then I remember her? I can't risk that—not yet."

"You know," said Dobrah after a long pause, "I was so lonely, and then I found you. I can't explain what attracted me so much to you. Maybe it was your vulnerability; I normally would not act this way." She sighed heavily. "I just cannot explain it. I'm sorry."

Her expression displayed remorse. I stood before her. I wanted to grasp her to me—not in a sexual way—but to simply comfort her. Her body quivered as we gazed at each other. I stopped myself from hugging her. It seemed too great a risk to feel her body against mine. Would I be able to resist my impulses?

Eventually her bright smile returned. "Are you hungry?" she asked as she walked into the house.

I followed her, and we sat at the table. She brought over a bowl of vegetables. "It's too bad we don't have any mushrooms," she smirked.

We conversed peacefully as we ate. Our previous discussion obviously lightened her mood, as well as mine. It seemed that finally confirming our emotions lifted the tension. Though she did not say it, I knew Dobrah was offering to give me time to come to terms with my amnesia. Perhaps I was selfish by allowing her to wait for me, but I wanted her, too. We would both need to wait.

***

With my help, the house and surrounding area improved over the following weeks, but our relationship remained the same. Unfortunately my memory failed to return. I could remember nothing before overlooking that bleak battlefield.

Dobrah was obviously becoming even happier with my company every day, but I could tell she wanted more, as did I.

I began to tell myself that I would accept my amnesia and give myself to her. *A couple more days,* I would think. *If no memories return in a couple of days I will commit to remain here.*

And then the day arrived; I awoke still possessing no memory. *Today is the day,* I told myself. I felt nervous. Finally, we would have each other. I asked her to take a walk with me, as I wanted to return to the tree where we had first met to tell her. We strolled out of the ravine and up the path. It seemed Dobrah discerned something. She sensed that I planned to change our relationship.

When we reached the tree, Dobrah asked that we walk a little further. She wanted to delay my anticipated announcement, not knowing its outcome. So we continued forward until we started to hear some noise.

"What do you think it is?" I asked Dobrah.

"We're nearing a road. It must be a large group of travelers," she replied. "Why don't we go see?"

We reached the road and saw scores of soldiers; they marched to war. Polished armor glistened in the sun. Spears flickered and colored banners whipped about in the wind. Dobrah absently grasped my arm in nervous excitement as we watched the warriors pass. A few looked at us with mild curiosity. One seemed surprised and approached. He looked quizzically at me, and after a few awkward seconds, recognition dawned in his face.

"Teraken!" he blurted. "It is you! We were wondering what happened."

"Do you know me?" I questioned the man.

He chuckled. "What are you talking about?" He looked at Dobrah with confusion. "Are you going to join us?"

I noticed some of the other soldiers stop and join the man. They began to murmur the name: Teraken.

"You know him?" Dobrah asked.

"Know him?" The man laughed. "Everybody knows Teraken, though he looks a little different without his armor and sword. He is the greatest warrior in the king's army. We thought he died at the Battle of Blue Valley, but his body was never found. Now I know why."

My head started to spin at his words. Then suddenly all my memories returned like a flood, finally breaking through a stubborn damn:

I am Teraken. I am a warrior. I have fought and killed hundreds, perhaps thousands, of men. Of all the soldiers in the king's army, I stand alone. None match my skill. The art of killing is my sixth sense.

Decades ago I lived with my parents. When I reached my early teens, I left home. I had known my calling, and it could not be accomplished on my father's farm. He had pleaded with me to stay. I was their only child. My father dreaded the thought of me dying alone on a battlefield. I laughed. I knew my destiny led down a different path. I would live on the battlefield, not die.

Battle constituted my life. Due to my prowess, many of the noble's daughters became infatuated with me, but I brushed them all aside. I had no time for a wife or family. Love would only distract me from my vocation.

I remembered scores of battles and a myriad of injuries. Swords, axes, spears, hammers: I am a master of them all. I kill with all weapons. I serve the king. I lead his troops. It is my calling, my destiny. I remember it all. All except the last battle. My memory of that combat begins when I surveyed the dead.

I felt Dobrah pulling at my arm. I looked down into her beautiful eyes; they were pleading with me. "Let's go home," she said.

"What are you talking about?" the man asked—who I now knew as Kedin. "The campaign has just started. We're at war!"

I had heard that word countless times: war. Despite all the battles I had fought, I was still young. What more should be expected of me? Had I not fulfilled my obligation? Had I earned the right to quit? I considered the prospect. I could retire my horde of weapons and marry Dobrah. Her small farm could be my home, instead of the battlefield.

Dobrah's hands continued to tug at me while Kedin and his companions chanted my name. I felt the urge to stay with Dobrah, but the yearning for further slaughter began to overwhelm me.

For the first time I felt conflict over my desires. Nothing had ever distracted me from my calling before, but the lure of life with Dobrah threatened to usurp that destiny.

I looked at her again, then back at Kedin. With closed eyes I recalled the vision of the dead on the battlefield, remembering the smell of the freshly slain. The foul odor somehow attracted me—along with the camaraderie of my troops.

I turned back to Dobrah and gently kissed her full lips. "I'm sorry," I whispered. She tried to call to me, but I refused to listen. I could not allow myself to hear her words. Mustering as much dignity as possible, I followed Kedin back to the marching soldiers and ignored the few tears rolling down my cheeks.

Kedin immediately led me to the front of the progression. There he introduced me to the commander, someone whom I had never met before. The man, Pothar, displayed relief at seeing me, but he appeared disappointed as well. Obviously, I posed a threat to his leadership. I tried to give him a reassuring pat on the shoulder, but Pothar smiled blankly and marched slightly further ahead.

"We need to get you some armor and a weapon," pointed out Kedin, and he asked some men to find a novice who equaled my size. They returned with a man and ordered him to strip from his gear. I donned the armor, and when I felt satisfied it fit adequately, the man was excused from the forthcoming battle.

"So what happened at Blue Valley?" asked Kedin.

"I don't remember," I replied. "The only thing I know is that I was the only survivor."

Kedin appeared startled. "We were outnumbered three-to-one. You were just to skirmish, then retreat. When nobody returned, we figured your retreat was cut off. When the enemy failed to advance, we thought they suffered too many casualties and withdrew. You killed them all?"

"Every one of them, but I don't remember the battle. It seemed like I awoke when it was finished, but I had no memory. I wandered until I found Dobrah, and then…" I stopped at that moment. I could not bring myself to discuss Dobrah with him. Kedin was a comrade, not a friend; I could not open myself to him, probably not to anyone.

"Then what?" he asked.

"You talk too much," I spat. I continued the remainder of the march in silence, amidst the protests of my fellow soldiers. They all wanted to know what had happened to me, to hear of my exploits, but their requests garnered only silence.

We marched until nightfall, then set up camp. I was told we would enter combat the next day, and I felt relieved. The sooner I killed somebody, perhaps the sooner Dobrah would escape my mind. Many still tried to talk with me, but I sat quietly, sharpening my new sword. After finishing, I attempted to sleep but found little rest. I eventually managed to doze a few fitful hours before dawn. When the camp began to rustle at daybreak, I quickly rose and climbed into my armor. Within minutes, I led the score of soldiers toward the battle.

Our renewed trek lasted nearly an hour before arriving at the battlegrounds. Most everyone else mimicked my silence; the anticipation weighed heavily on all. Men's nerves saw images of their own deaths, or that of a friend's. My anticipation was different, as death posed no threat to me. My fate would not allow it. I anticipated relief, relief from the visions of Dobrah. My anticipation was that of a man who had been away from home for too long and was finally returning. I smiled for the first time since my amnesia had lifted.

We approached a ravine—similar to the one where Dobrah's house stood—when we spotted the enemy. The ravine marked the site of the imminent battle. Raising my sword, I howled with joy, then bolted from my companions to ignite the fray.

I ran down the sloped ground, and the first enemy I reached died in the twinkling of an eye. Two more deaths followed shortly after. My sword swung as fast as lightening. Blood splattered over me, and I laughed. I felt a stab in my left hip, turned and sliced the hand that still held its blade in my body. The man looked astonished. I giggled as I cracked his skull open.

More came toward me. I waved them on—to hurry their approach. My sword punctured one heart, severed a head and sliced scores of stomachs. Laughter peeled from my lips. "Yes!" I screamed. "Yes!"

A hammer smashed against my breastplate, but it hardly budged me. I kicked sideways and crushed my assailant's groin; he collapsed in pain. I grinned as he raised his hands—pleading for mercy. My sword bisected his quivering hands and split his scalp.

Bodies piled up all around me. I had to climb over them in order to find new opponents. I skidded on the blood, which saturated the ground and speared a man through the throat. After spinning the blade out, my sword continued to swing. Limbs dropped all about me as if I was pruning trees. I slashed and cut, no longer even knowing whom I attacked. It did not matter. I just wanted to kill. And kill I did—better than anybody. Amidst my hypnosis of death, I began to recognize my name being called.

"Teraken!" It was Kedin's voice. "Teraken, what are you doing?"

He turned me around, but my sword spun first. It severed his arm at the elbow with a bellow of glee as he cried in pain. I threw my head forward and we cracked skulls. He collapsed, and I stepped on his throat, then drove my sword through his face.

I continued to slaughter. Anything that moved became my target. As I attacked, I began to wonder if this was all that was left for me: to kill indiscriminately. Another wound quickly pulled me from my short self-examination; a man's flail had struck my right shin. My armor deflected the bulk of the blow, but I could feel the blood trailing down to my foot to intermingle with that of my victims'. My left hand shot forward and yanked the weapon from his fingers. My body spun in a circle, and the spikes of the iron ball pierced his eyes and imbedded into his brain.

I saw friends and companions, but I butchered them all. Pothar died without even seeing me; my sword plunged through his back and reemerged from his chest. When I could not free my blade quickly enough, the weapons of the dead found a new home in my hands. Death followed me throughout the ravine. Eventually I needed to search for men to slay. I had to resort to killing the maimed and wounded. Then finally, mercifully, it was over; I was the only man standing. Only corpses accompanied me. I wondered how many I had killed. It did not matter. I smiled. I had returned home, but then I thought of Dobrah and started to cry. I sank to my knees and wept for what seemed like hours before I eventually managed to stand.

The battlefield engulfed me like the waves of a crimson sea emptying tons of unwanted debris at its shore. I stood like an island amongst twisted corpses and strewn limbs. I lifted my foot and felt the sucking sensation of mud sticking to my boot, but the only moisture present was blood: my blood, and the blood of the dead. I heard the dull pop as my foot broke the seal of the clinging sludge.

A sword dangled from my right hand like a useless limb. The weapon was black—not red from the blood of my victims, but black …

The Eternal Musician

"Remind me again why we're seeking this musician," Rodin sneered while he watched Tybon plunge to his death.

Markis' hand reached forward to grab hold of rock. His fingers ached as he inched his body farther up the mountain. "I've already told you three times." The words sputtered from Markis' mouth as he tried to gulp breaths of air. "Just concentrate on what you're doing."

The mountain loomed above their heads like a straight road disappearing at the horizon. Markis pushed his foot into a small crevice and managed a short rest. He thought he heard a crash and a muffled scream, but he knew the sound of Tybon's impact could not have reached his ears.

That was the third man I've lost on this venture, he thought. It had better be worth it.

Sathen nearly lost his grip, and Markis saw his body swivel against the mountain. "You're certain there's not a path?" Sathen asked.

"If there was, wouldn't we be using it?" replied Markis in a sarcastic tone.

"Yeah, well, when you told us we'd be climbing a mountain, this is not what I had in mind," Sathen said.

Markis pulled himself higher, and he wondered what else Sathen could have thought.

The three men continued their slow trek up the rocky surface. Markis felt the tightness in his muscles increase with each pull. As the mountain grew steeper, the skin started to rip off his fingers. Blood trickled down his hands, causing a less sturdy grip. Still he pulled on. Suddenly a cramp formed in his right calf, and he nearly fell as the pain started a chain reaction of misery throughout his body. He hugged himself against the rocks as he straightened his foot. After a few moments, the suffering subsided, and Markis continued upward.

"You okay?" asked Rodin.

"I guess," Markis answered, and the climb resumed.

It'll all be worth it if we reach the top, Markis thought. We need to find Kee.

Following one of the battles between Markis' army and the southern wild men, his troops had scavenged through the ruins of a ravaged town, uncovered a long-forgotten holy book and brought it to Markis. He had immediately recognized it as the Retten Codex—an ancient, mystical text many believed to be only a fable. Markis took the book to his tent to study that night. The codex spoke of the musician who lived at the pinnacle of this mountain. Kee's music was described as unlike anything ever heard on the planet before. The book called the musician eternal, and said Kee's music would calm even the wildest of men. Markis had figured that if Kee would lead his army against the wild men, perhaps the music could be used as an advantage. If the stories within the book proved true, this music could be a powerful weapon.

Markis' sheath struck a rock, and the sound stirred him from his musings. Lucky I didn't make a mistake as my attention wandered, he thought.

"I think I see a cave!" Sathen called.

"Good," Markis replied, "we could use a rest."

After a few more tortured minutes, the trio finally reached the cave. Markis collapsed to the ground and greedily sucked air into his exhausted lungs, while Rodin sat next to his leader and took off his backpack. Markis opened the pack and pulled out a skin of water. After gulping a long drink, he passed the bag to Sathen.

"How much further do we have to go?" Rodin asked as he accepted the liquid from Sathen.

"I've no idea," Markis replied. He unstrapped his sword, and the weapon clattered against the stone floor. The rattling echoed for many minutes, and the sound distressed Markis. The expanse and darkness made him uncomfortable in this unfamiliar cave.

"Why did we have to bring our weapons?" Sathen questioned. "I don't think we're going to run into any of our enemies up here. They're just getting in the way."

"Haven't I always taught you to prepare for any possible occurrence? This is unknown territory. Don't assume every situation to be safe because you expect it to be," replied Markis. "Safe from enemies, I mean," he added after remembering the image of Tybon hurling to his death.

Rodin reached into the pack, and his hand emerged with a large hunk of dried cheese. He broke off a portion and handed the rest to his leader. Markis split the remainder in half and tossed one of the pieces to Sathen. The three men crunched on their unappetizing meal as the light from the cave opening began to fade.

"I guess we're going to have to spend the night here," pointed out Rodin.

Markis sighed in disappointment. He'd had no idea how long the climb would take when they embarked, but he had never figured on the trek lasting longer than one day. So, no sleeping gear had been brought. "Looks like you're right," he said.

Sathen sprawled on the ground near the cave opening, his body flapping about for a few moments, trying to find a comfortable position.

"Remind me not to volunteer for any more of your missions, will you?" Rodin stated, while he too sought to relax.

"Shut up!" snapped Markis. "Besides, if we're successful, the war will run much smoother. Now, let's try to get some sleep." His head hit a sharp rock as he collapsed to the ground, and Markis smothered a cry of pain. The last thing he wanted to hear was his companions' reaction regarding his unwelcome pillow.

Sleep eluded Markis for what seemed hours. His mind swirled with the possibilities after securing the musician's assistance. If Kee's music came close to matching the description in the recently discovered book, no army could stand against his troops. After conquering the southern wild men, he just might turn his attention to the hill country of the north. A confederation of tribes sprawled throughout that region—an easy target, he thought.

Plans for world dominance continued to swarm through his head until Markis reluctantly fell asleep.

He woke just before dawn. A strange sound reached his ears, and he heard Sathen and Rodin stirring.

"What is it?" asked Rodin.

"I don't know," Markis answered.

The sound grew and became more distinguishable. It sounded like a rattling. No, Markis thought, not a rattling, a scratching.

He fumbled about the ground looking for his sword. When he located the sheath, he drew the weapon and stood.

The noise continued to build. It felt as if a rush of water was filling the entire cave.

"There must be a passage it's coming from," Sathen remarked.

The sound seemed to be scratching directly against Markis' spinal cord. Bumps emerged across his skin, and the small hairs all over his body shot up. With each heartbeat, the volume of the noise increased. Then Markis noticed a change in the sound. At first he failed to comprehend what constituted the difference. Speed, he thought. It's moving faster.

Next, a pounding joined the scratching. Markis braced himself, but he knew not for what. Each thump sent a wave of agony through his head. How could anything make such an intense noise? Trembling hands reached to his ears as he tried to put a barrier between his brain and the sound. He fell to one knee, but just before he thought his head would explode, the noise stopped.

Markis turned in the direction of his men when he felt a strong breeze rush past. Following a loud crash, Sathen screamed. Markis and Rodin rushed toward the sound of crushing bones while a warm liquid splattered Markis' face.

Against the predawn sky, Markis saw the outline of a huge shape on top of his comrade. He sprung forward, and two swords plunged wildly at the creature. A sick cry emerged from the beast, and more blood splattered Markis while the weapons continued to stab and cut. The creature tried to turn and face its adversaries, but the narrow cave opening—in comparison to the beast—did not allow it room to maneuver. The pair continued to strike ferociously. Markis' arm started to tire from the assault, and the creature failed to mount a fresh attack.

Eventually the beast let out a pathetic gurgling and fell out the cave opening. Markis heard the dead bulk strike against the mountainside a few times, then silence resumed. He reached down, searching for his companion, but apparently Sathen had been pulled out with the monster.

"Have you ever seen anything like that?" Rodin panted.

"Well, I didn't actually see it," answered Markis.

"What do you think it was? It was so loud."

"I've never heard of anything living this high up. But it must have been some sort of flying creature. It wouldn't have found enough food up here."

The two men sat quietly at the cave entrance. Neither spoke of Sathen—or the others. Markis peered back into the depths of the cave, but he heard nothing. They waited. They waited for daylight to arrive so that they might continue their climb. Both felt eager to leave the cave quickly. The smell of the spilled blood mixed with stale cheese began to make Markis feel nauseated.

Finally, mercifully, the sun lit enough of the mountainside for their trek to continue. After wrapping supplies around Rodin's body, Markis ventured out of the entrance. His fingers grasped rock, and he pulled his tired body upward toward the mountain peak.

The inches passed by with increasing pain. Muscles felt brittle within Markis' body. Still he climbed. *I must reach the top*, he thought. *After four deaths, the mission must end in success.* He unknowingly grabbed a sharp stone, and it cut fingers down to bone. Markis cried in pain but refused to stop; he refused the desire to let himself drop and end the suffering. Sweat pooled around his forehead and the base of his neck. The heat of the sun bore down on the climbers, much hotter than the previous day.

His shirt stuck to a jagged branch on some long-dead shrub. Markis lost his grip and nearly fell, but Rodin, having seen the problem, grabbed a foot and balanced Markis enough so that his leader managed to regain his hold.

"This is insane!" Rodin yelled. "We're never going to get there!"

"We can't turn around now. We should be near the top soon; our only hope is to reach Kee."

With his shirt in tatters, each movement seemed to invite a new cut, and Markis wondered how much blood he had lost. His stomach growled in hunger, but Markis feared that if they stopped, they would not be able to start again. Besides, he saw no place to rest.

The sun baked the dirt and grime to whatever skin still remained. "Can you get out the water?" Markis called down to Rodin.

"I'll try."

Markis heard Rodin fumbling with the supplies. "Damn!" Rodin exclaimed, "I dropped the pack!"

"We'll have to keep moving," Markis said. "Don't worry about anything but reaching the top."

"What else would I worry about?"

The minutes dragged by like a slow-moving stream. They seemed immeasurable, lacking a beginning and without end. Markis' shirt had long past ripped from his body. The skin on his back remained free from cuts, but it felt tighter and tighter as they climbed higher. With his glowing pink skin, he would have appeared to any passing birds as a salmon fighting its way upstream.

The agony began to overcome his senses. He could not hear Rodin any longer. "Are you still with me?" Markis called; he heard a faint muttering of acknowledgment.

The light began to fade overhead and Markis looked up to see dark clouds rolling in their direction. *Oh great*, he thought, *just what we need*. He wondered how he could have miscalculated the climb so badly. If not for finding the cave, he and Rodin would also be dead now. What had seemed like a simple mission had turned into disaster. The light started to fade. They needed to reach the peak; they needed to reach it soon.

A white flash highlighted the scene, and Markis' heart soared. He saw the top. Thunder crashed and a few stones rolled down the mountain. A couple struck him on the head, but he held firm. "We're almost there," he tried to yell to his companion. He did not know if his weak voice could be heard over the sound of the storm.

Markis climbed on, and a chunk of flesh ripped from his left thigh, sticking to an unseen barb. A few drops of water fell; they felt rejuvenating against his scorched skin. Unfortunately, the brief refreshment quickly turned into danger. The rain fell harder and caused each movement to increase in hazard.

A ledge was now only a few feet away. Another blast of thunder almost shook him from the mountain. The pain had disappeared, replaced by a dull numbness. Markis supposed his senses had been overcome by the agony, no longer able to process pain. His brain had just shut down his ability to feel. The last foot became the most difficult of all; he could not feel the rock against his fingers. He needed to examine each finger visually to make sure his grip was secure.

His face finally emerged over the ledge. His legs dangled uselessly from his body; he could not move them. His arms slipped against the drenched ledge, but he somehow managed to roll his exhausted body to safety. He turned onto his burned back just as the rain stopped.

Rodin also pulled himself onto the ledge. The younger man seemed to have fared the climb better. He stood up, but his foot slipped on a small puddle, and Rodin hurled backward down the mountain. Markis rolled over and peered down as Rodin's scream disappeared into the oblivion of the dusk air.

Markis pushed himself away from the edge. He started to laugh—a laugh of despair and tragedy, of agony and loss, but also a laugh of triumph. Despite all the tribulation, he had reached the top. Now, all he needed to do was locate Kee. But before he could move, Markis fell asleep.

When Markis finally woke, he had no idea how long he had slept. The sun shone softly over his head; blue sky and silvery clouds met his gaze. A moderate temperature and slight breeze soothed his burnt skin. He stood, but his body swayed. He had lost a good deal of blood and had not eaten in a long while.

It seemed every muscle in his body ached. The skin on his back felt like leather; it shot agony to his brain as he moved. Deep cuts covered his palms and each finger. His stomach growled, pleading for food, but no supplies remained.

The terrain around Markis surprised him, as the peak of the mountain appeared much larger than expected. The ground under his feet continued on a flat course for an unknown distance. Markis gathered his will and forced himself onward.

Walking had never seemed such a chore previously. Only his single-minded desire kept his feet moving. He walked in a daze. The numbness he had felt before had returned, but he kept moving. He did not think. He moved strictly on instinct now. His instinct had been forged by the pain and loss of the climb. It had been forged like a deadly arrowhead by a master smith. The desire pushed him forward, as if he were a wounded rabbit struck by the arrow, seeking its burrow.

Markis eventually stumbled into a small mound of rock. His mind shook awake, and he looked around. He saw the side of the mountain plummeting down beyond the mound. Upon closer inspection, he found a crack within the rock, barely large enough for him to squeeze past.

This must be it, he thought with anticipation. He shoved himself into the seam, and the jagged edges poked and ripped his tattered skin. He yelped in pain and fell through. Markis landed on soft ground, but quickly realized it sloped downward. He rolled a short distance, and dirt seemed to find its way into every cut, as if he were a jigsaw puzzle needing a few more pieces to finish the picture.

He stopped abruptly, raising a cloud of dirt. When the brown mist settled, Markis saw a room lit by four circular white globes embedded in the walls. A current of heat reached him from an unknown source. The walls, though made of rock, exhibited a strange blue hue. In the center of the room he saw one chair and a strange table. On the chair sat the most bizarre individual Markis had ever seen, and he knew he had at last reached his destination.

Markis only saw the back of the musician. The being wore a cloak of a multitude of colors. Markis instantly noticed that the colors were not stagnant; they traveled about the garment with each movement its bearer made. It seemed as if a prism rotated some distance away and focused the white light onto the cloak, but Markis saw colors he could not identify. He gazed at the cloak and started to realize that the colors flowed in some sort of pattern. It seemed as if the cloak lived and that it was trying to communicate, but he failed to decipher its message.

When Markis eventually managed to pull his eyes away from the cloak, his mind perceived the music emerging from the creature. He noticed that the reason the table appeared strange was because it was actually an instrument of which he had never seen the like before. Strings and keys covered the base, and pipes rose from the edges. At the floor he saw a score of pedals, and a long tube rose to the being's face.

The music embraced Markis like the arms of a lover. The notes cascaded in a tumult of chords and scales; a mathematical precision embodied the composition. Rhythm, harmony, melody and percussion all emanated from the one instrument. Markis watched the musician's fingers travel over the instrument with lightening speed, yet the music did not sound rushed. Each sound complemented those which came before, like an algebraic equation—any missing note would ruin the piece.

Markis did not move; he could not move. He stood transfixed by the beauty of the music, and it took a moment for him to realize that the musician had stopped playing. The head of long, straight white hair turned, and the face Markis saw defied his conception of humanity. A wide forehead tapered down to a pointed chin, forming a triangle of smooth skin. Small ears barely pushed past the hair, and a tiny, round mouth sat under an almost nonexistent nose. However, the most re-markable feature was the huge eyes. They seemed to cover a quarter of the face. Markis saw no pupils, no irises. He only saw a myriad of col-ors swirling about, as if a rainbow had collapsed into a pool of flowing water. But again, like the cloak, Markis spotted colors he had never seen before—only this time, he thought he saw more shades than the cloak displayed. Markis, knowing he stared at Kee, realized he had expected the musician to be male. However, Kee demonstrated little semblance of gender, but Markis thought he saw a feminine trace ema-nating from the being.

"What may I do for you?" Kee's voice sounded rough and halting, but Markis could not tell if that was merely in comparison to the music.

"Are you Kee?" the warrior asked.

"Who else would I be?"

"Nobody I know, that's for sure."

"How stimulating," the musician remarked. "Now, back to my original question: what may I do for you?"

"I've come to seek your assistance—"

"My assistance?" interrupted Kee. "I do not grant assistance." The being turned back to the instrument.

"Please hear me out," Markis pleaded. "I'm trying to save many of my people's lives. That is important to you, isn't it?"

Kee looked back at her visitor and responded, "I value life."

Markis waited for the musician to elaborate, but the only further re-sponse he received was a change in the patterns within Kee's eyes. Markis saw a splattering about the globes like raindrops in a puddle, but each splash displayed a previously undiscovered color.

"Well, will you help me?" asked Markis.

"I value life; however, my music is of utmost importance."

"That's great." Markis smiled. "Your music is what I'm seeking."

"As it should be."

"Will you help me, then?" Markis again asked.

"State your proposal."

Markis tried to straighten his posture and smooth his hair, but the movement caused a new wave of pain to course through his body. He fell to one knee and let out a cry. When he managed to look up, he saw that Kee had not moved, but her eyes now appeared like a treasure chest of rare and sparkling jewels.

After a few moments of trying to stand, Markis decided to just sit. When he sufficiently situated himself, he began:

"My people are at war. We fight the southern wild men, and I am our war leader. We continue to defeat our enemy in every battle, but I lose many good men. It's quite a waste. After our last battle, I discovered the Retten Codex. It spoke of this mountain, and your existence here. It spoke of your music and the power it possesses. It said that your music can soothe even the most violent person." Markis stopped for a moment to carefully consider his next words. "I want you to lead my army. We could end the conflict with a minimal amount of further deaths. It might seem presumptuous, but I am asking you to help me end this war."

"A noble gesture," Kee said. Markis could not tell if he sensed a tone of sarcasm in her voice.

"I think so."

"And what would you gain from this?"

"I would gain nothing, but many of our families would not lose a husband or brother. With the combination of my warriors and your music, I could be invincible."

Kee's head cocked to one side. "A noble gesture," the musician repeated.

"Will you help me?"

Kee gazed at Markis, then turned back to the instrument. Long, thin fingers moved toward the keys and strings. The small mouth bent towards the raised tube, and the musician's feet arched over the pedals. Then the music started. Markis swayed to the song, symphony, orchestration; his brain failed to form an appropriate description. The war leader found strength to stand, and he felt no pain. The music bore Markis' thoughts away from his war, away from the climb up the mountain and away from the deaths of Rodin and the others. Markis remembered his parents and his marriage; he remembered the births of his children.

As Markis watched, he noticed Kee's cloak. The colors of the garment pulsed to the rhythm of the music. The colors seemed to form a pattern, as if they corresponded to the music, but Markis could not fathom the connection. He eventually closed his eyes to omit any distraction to the beauty of the music. Tears rolled from his eyes, but he hardly noticed. Markis lost track of time; he just listened. When Kee finally stopped her musical creation, Markis opened his eyes. He looked down at his hands. All the cuts and scrapes remained, but he no longer felt any pain. He also realized that all the pangs of hunger had disappeared.

Kee turned back to face Markis. The musician's eyes glittered, a golden hue with lines of purples and dots of emerald. "I have created music unlike any you have ever heard before," Kee said. "I have traveled the many roads of existence." Markis did not understand that statement. "I have determined that my music is eternal; all others are just a shadow of mine: Uthwyn, Mylaan, Rojez, Lynott, Par'thew, Mozart, Deethex, the list is endless. Every great composer has been inspired by my music, whether they realized it or not. But composition is only one portion of music; music must be performed. Inflection, mood and improvisation are all necessary elements. Repetition ruins great music. I have influenced all the virtuosos throughout time and existence. My combination of composition and performance transcends the mortal worlds. I am the eternal musician. True music is the groom, and I am its bride. The music you have heard is the marriage between the eternal and mortality.

"My purpose is to continue my calling. If I cease my creation, all my reflections suffer. My music cannot be used by humans. It transforms humans."

Markis found that the pain was returning to his limbs as he began to realize that his mission had been a failure. "You don't have to give up creating your music to help me," he begged.

"My music will always continue; I may never stop. But my music cannot be used."

As his strength dissipated, Markis again fell to his knees. "But so many more will die. You said you value life."

"I value all life, but I am not the one causing deaths. Look into your own heart." Kee spun back to the instrument, and her soft hands struck the keys. Deep tones echoed throughout the chamber. The music pulsed and thudded directly into Markis' body and he collapsed, facedown. Low notes and heavy chords pierced his soul. He saw himself sitting on a huge throne, ruling over the entire world. He saw corpses piled before him. Blood surrounded his throne like a vile moat while young, beautiful women danced and swayed around the dais. Emissaries and ambassadors from all lands pleaded with him for simple favors. Markis smiled at the scene.

Kee turned back to face Markis. "What does your heart tell you?"

Markis stared at the musician. He contemplated the images Kee's music sparked within him, and knew he needed to respond to her, but what could he say?

"All I want is to save my people's lives," Markis replied.

Kee's eyes turned to a criss-cross of red and black, and all color drained from the cloak until it appeared like a normal, pale garment. "I am unable to help you," she stated.

Markis began to grow angry. After all his turmoil, he did not appreciate this aloof being dismissing his pleas so easily. "So that's it? You're just going to allow so many unnecessary deaths?"

Kee's eyes now lost their red lines; they glared jet black at Markis. "The deaths are not on my hands."

"All my pain, and the deaths of my companions, that was all for nothing. Is that what you're telling me?"

"It is a shame that is all you see."

"That is the only thing of importance," Markis stated.

Kee's head shook, and her eyes glowed a deep blue with silver swirls. "I am sorry you feel that you wasted your visit."

Markis struggled to his feet and prepared himself to exit Kee's home. "Your decision is final?"

"Yes," Kee answered. "Now, how did you plan to get back down?

"I hadn't thought of that."